RAISING HELL
IN THE
NIGHTSIDE

RAISING HELL
IN THE
NIGHTSIDE

Hex and the City
Paths Not Taken
Sharper than a Serpent's Tooth

SIMON R. GREEN

FANTASY

Published by arrangement with
The Berkley Publishing Group
a division of Penguin Group (USA) Inc.
375 Hudson Street
New York, New York 10014

ISBN: 0-7394-6528-7

visit our website at *www.sfbc.com*
visit the Penguin Putnam website at *www.penguinputnam.com*

Printed in the United States of America

RAISING HELL
IN THE
NIGHTSIDE

CONTENTS

HEX AND THE CITY

ONE

The Psychenauts

You can find anything in the Nightside, from the sacred to the profane and back again, but I don't recommend attending the auctions there unless you've got a strong stomach and nerves of steel. I don't normally go to auctions any more, even though most people are afraid to bid against me. I always end up saddled with a crateful of junk, just to get the one thing I do want. One time I accidentally acquired a Pookah, and for a few months I was followed around the Nightside by a Playboy Bunny Girl invisible to everyone except me. Fun, but distracting.

However, when you work as a private investigator in the Nightside, that hidden magical heart of London, where gods and monsters walk side by side, and sometimes attend the same self-help groups, some cases almost inevitably lead you to the most unpleasant places. The head auctioneer of the Nightside's Great Auction Hall hired me to stand watch over one particularly contentious auction, to keep the bidders in line. It sounded straight forward enough, which should have been a warning. Nothing's ever straight forward in my life.

I turned up nice and early, so I could look the place over. It had been several years since I was last there, and in between I'd left the Nightside on the run, with a bullet in my back, and reluctantly returned to stage a semi-triumphant comeback. The doorman at the Hall took one look at me and didn't want to let me in, but I gave him my name, and he turned satisfyingly pale and stepped back to wave me in. A good, or rather bad, reputation will get you into places that a battalion of troops wouldn't.

The head auctioneer stopped pacing nervously up and down and came striding across the great empty Hall to greet me. She grudged me a brief smile and crushed my hand in an over-firm handshake. Lucretia Grave was a short, sturdy woman in an old-fashioned tweedy outfit, surmounted by a monocle screwed firmly into one dark, beady eye. She appeared to be in her early fifties, with a brutal bulldog face and grey hair scraped back into a really severe bun on the back of her head. She looked like she could punch her weight. She glared at me like it was all my fault, and got stuck right in.

"About time you got here, Taylor, old thing. I haven't felt safe in me own Hall since the damned thing arrived. I've had piles that gave me less problems. I know we say we'll auction anything you can find, capture, or manhandle through the doors, but some things are just more trouble than they're worth. I wouldn't have anything to do with the bloody thing, if I wasn't on commission. I've been playing the doggies again, you know how it is. Rotten animals only have to hear I've put good money on them and they immediately develop back problems and heart conditions. Still, you mark my words, old thing; this particular item is going to go for serious money." She scowled unhappily and sniffed loudly. "It's days like this I wish I was back at me old job, at Christie's. I'd go back in a second if only I could be sure the police weren't still looking for me."

I was about to ask, politely but very firmly, what the hell we were talking about, when we were interrupted by a whole bunch of six-foot-tall teddy bears, carrying in the various items up for auction that session. The bears swept straight past us, carrying the items carefully in their soft, padded arms, talking in low, growly voices. The bears all looked like they'd seen a lot of rough handling, and as they passed Lucretia Grave a few muttered loudly about the need to get unionised. They set out each object in its own glass display case, treating every item with great care and respect.

"I'd better check everything's where it's supposed to be," Grave said heavily. "They all mean well, but they're bears of very little brain. Typical bloody management, trying to save money again. You have a look around, old thing, get the feel of the place, *don't touch anything.*"

And off she strode, like a tug-boat under full steam, to hector the bears. I let her go. It was either that or throw her to the floor, tie her up, and sit on her till I got some useful answers out of her; and I couldn't be bothered. I looked around. The Great Auction Hall had started out life as a thirteenth-century tithe barn, and had changed remarkably little down the years. The walls were a creamy grey stone, in large close-fitting blocks held together by artistry and tradition rather than mortar, rising up to soaring wooden rafters that came together in a complex latticework half-hidden in shadows. There were only slit windows in the walls, and the floor was unpolished wood, covered in sawdust. Fluorescent rods provided almost painfully bright light. There were no comforts or luxuries, but then, people didn't come here to admire the scenery. The Great Auction Hall was a place of serious business.

I walked past the rows of cheap wooden folding seats, set up to face the no-frills auctioneer's stand, and looked over the various items in their display cases. It was the usual mixture, the famous and the infamous, of dubious value and debatable provenance. You could buy anything in the Nightside, whatever your interests or pleasure, but no-one guaranteed it was necessarily what it seemed to be. You could get lucky, or you could get dead, with precious little room in between. And just because you owned a thing, it didn't mean you could always hang on to it . . .

The first item was a heavy thigh-bone, identified as the weapon with which Cain slew Abel. There was a letter of confirmation from the ancient city of Enoch, but you took such things with a pinch of salt in the Nightside. Next in line were three different Maltese Falcons (buyer beware), a cast-brass head of JFK that supposedly spoke prophecy, Nostradamus's quill pen, one of Baron Frankenstein's scalpels, a small lacquered wooden box that claimed it held the ashes of Joan of Arc, and a Yeti's-foot umbrella stand. The rest was just junk and tat, stuff only a collector could love. Certainly nothing I'd give house-room.

I've never believed in acquiring objects of power. They always let you down. Either the batteries run out at the worst possible moment, or you go blank on the activating word; and you can never find the instruction manual when you need it. More trouble than they're worth. And far too many of them turn out to be just bits and pieces that have hung around long enough to acquire a reputation. Not unlike me, I suppose.

I paused to study myself in a tall standing mirror in an ornate silver frame. (It was labelled The Mirror of Dorian Gray; make of that what you will.) The reflection didn't look anything special; though I supposed I did at least look like a private eye. Tall, dark, and interesting-looking, wrapped in a long white trench coat that hadn't seen a laundry anywhen recent. A bit tired and battered round the edges, maybe, but that's life in the Nightside for you. I tend to get the cases no-one else wants, the kind other investigators have the good sense to turn down, and I like it that way. I have a gift for finding things, whether they want to be found or not, a hunger for the truth, and a stubborn streak that keeps me in the game long after anyone with any sense would have legged it for the horizon.

My father drank himself to death, after finding out my mother wasn't human. No-one knows who or what my mother really was, but everyone in the Nightside's got an opinion. There are those who treat me like the Antichrist, and others who see me as a King in waiting. And, an unknown group of enemies have been sending agents to kill me ever since I was a small child.

I try not to let it go to my head.

Lucretia Grave came stomping back to join me. She was wearing the monocle in the other eye now. I wondered whether I was supposed to say something, but decided not to. Some conversations you just know aren't going to go anywhere useful. Grave started in on me again as though we'd never stopped talking.

"We get all kinds of stuff coming through here on a regular basis, old sport, things you wouldn't believe, even for the Nightside. Some silly sod put his soul up for auction just the other week, but it didn't make the reserve. Ah yes, I've seen it all come and go, and known more than my fair share of tears and curses. Property is the curse of the thinking classes. Now, Taylor, old boy; the Hall is of course surrounded by heavy-duty wards and protections at all times, protecting us from fire, theft, substitution, and any and all outside influences, and the whole place is guaranteed neutral ground by the Authorities themselves, and respected as such even by really hard cases like the Collector. As I understand it, the Hall was the cause of so many disputes by so many high rollers that the Authorities just stepped in and took over the business themselves, to make sure all deeds were kept and honoured . . . So we should be safe enough . . ."

"But?" I said.

"But, today we're auctioning something rather special, even for us. That's why you're here, old thing. If everything does all go to Hell in a handcart, and I for one wouldn't be at all surprised if it did, you get to stick your hand up and say, *Stop thief.* What you do after that is your problem. Only don't look to me for help, because I shall have headed for the nearest exit. And don't look to the bears, either. They mean well, but they've only got sawdust where their balls should be. If all else fails, I suppose you can always use your famous gift to track down wherever the thief's taken it . . ."

"Why did you hire me?" I asked, genuinely interested.

Grave sniffed loudly. "Our insurance people insisted we hire someone, and you were the best . . . our budget could stretch to."

I was still looking for a response to that when we were approached by a familiar figure. It was Deliverance Wilde, fashion consultant and style guru to the Faerie of the Unseeli Court. Tall, loudly Jamaican, sharp and bitter and a defiant chain-smoker. If anyone ever found the nerve to object, she blew the smoke into their faces. She was currently wearing an elegantly tailored suit of a vivid lavender shade, which contrasted interestingly with her blue-black skin, topped by a very feathery hat. I raised an eyebrow at the new look, but as always Wilde got her retaliation in first.

"Don't show your ignorance, darling. Lavender is this season's colour, whether it likes it or not."

She struck a studiedly casual pose before me, head tilted back to better show off her high cheekbones and sensual mouth. Deliverance Wilde treated the whole world like a catwalk. Yet her eyes had trouble meeting mine, and the hand holding her cigarette wasn't as steady as it might have been. Wilde was nervous about something. Now, it might just have been the strain of meeting me. I do tend to make people nervous; it's part of my carefully crafted reputation. But Wilde wasn't really focussed on me, or even Grave. Instead, she glared about the Auction Hall, shooting quick puffs of smoke in every direction.

"I always hate coming back to the Nightside," she said abruptly. "Vulgar, darlings, utterly vulgar. I prefer to spend my time with the Faerie. They're so . . . delightfully shallow and superficial."

Lot you know, I thought, but had the sense not to say it aloud. Wilde had been known to stub her cigarette out on people who annoyed her.

"I only come back here to attend the fashion shows and stock up on ciggies," she continued remorselessly. "And to carry out the odd spot of business, of course." She looked at me directly for the first time. "I'm glad you're here, John. It means the Auction Hall is taking this event seriously. As they should. I have got my hands on . . . something rather special."

Lucretia Grave snorted loudly. "I should say so, old dear. Unique, priceless, and bloody dangerous with it. Some things should be left alone, or at the very least prodded with a stick from a safe distance."

"Would somebody please tell me what it is we're talking about?" I said, and something in my voice made them both sit up and take notice. Wilde took a last drag on her cigarette, dropped it on the floor, and ground it out under her boot. Grave glared at her. Wilde immediately lit up another, on principle, and fixed me with a thoughtful gaze.

"I have hit the big time at last, darling. I found my little prize accidentally, while looking for something else, but then, isn't that always the way? I was off on my travels, looking for Something Different with which to pique the interest of those notoriously fickle and demanding Faerie, and I ended up in Tokyo, investigating reports of this marvellous new firm that specialised in creating these utterly amazing bonsai volcanoes, complete with regular eruptions and lava flows. But by the time I got there, the firm was gone, and their shop was just this big smoking hole in the ground. I could have told them MORE BANG FOR YOUR BUCK was a really bad idea for a slogan . . . Anyway, I got side-tracked to China, where I found . . . that."

And she indicated one of the smaller display cases with a dramatic gesture and a sprinkling of ash because she'd forgotten the cigarette in her hand. She muttered a series of baby swear words and brushed the ash off the top of the case, while I leaned forward for a closer look. Behind the glass was a single butterfly, not particularly big or small, or especially pretty. In fact, it looked distinctly ordinary. It hung in mid air, in mid-flight, wings extended, surrounded by the faint shimmer of a stasis field. The butterfly had been frozen in a moment of Space and Time, like an insect preserved in amber. I looked back at Wilde, but again she got in first while I was still raising an eyebrow.

"Yes, it's rare, but not in the way you think. The explanation's a bit complex, but try and keep up. Chaos theory says that if a butterfly flaps its wings over China, we end up with a storm over America. Since everything in the world is connected, or at least on speaking terms. So, if you could identify and track down that particular butterfly . . . Well, I have, and there it is. The little troublemaker. A wonderfully unique item, which I intend to let go for an equally unique price. Oh, the Collector is going to be *so* jealous!"

(Wilde and the Collector had a thing going once. It didn't work out. No-one ever thought it would, but you just can't tell some people.)

"The butterfly theory is nothing new, really," said Grave, in her most academic and tweedy voice. Auctioneers always sound like failed scholars. Probably because most of them are. "The ancient Romans had people called Augurs who could predict the future by studying the flight of birds."

Wilde gave her a withering look. "They also had a tendency to cut open goats, then accuse people of treason over which way the goat's liver was pointing. And give themselves lead poisoning with their choice of plumbing materials."

"Let us all make a valiant effort to stick to the point, please," I said. "Isn't the whole butterfly thing just a metaphor? There isn't a real butterfly, as such."

Wilde hit me with her most withering smile. "Metaphors can be as real as anything else in the Nightside, darling. Symbols can have their own identity here. So, whatever lucky person takes possession of this butterfly at auction will possess the power to identify all such *butterflies*; the first domino in the line that will produce future events. The owner should then be able to predict and possibly even control the way the future turns out. The possibilities are endless! In theory, anyway. Trust me on this, John darling; I am going to be rich, rich, rich!"

"If it's so potentially powerful, why are you so ready to give it up?" I asked.

Wilde struck her best *Why am I beset by fools of no vision* pose. "John. Darling. I am not stupid enough to try and keep anything this earth-shattering for myself. I'd have to spend all my time fighting off major players who wanted to take it away from me. And you can bet the

Faerie wouldn't deign to get involved, the ungrateful little shits. No, an auction, on famously neutral ground, is the best way to make a substantial profit on this little beauty." She blew a kiss at the butterfly in its case. "And then I shall take all the money and run, all the way back to the Unseeli Court, and not show my head again until the last of the shooting's died down."

"Given the clear potential for things to get really nasty really quickly, I'm surprised the Authorities haven't stepped in to confiscate the butterfly," I said, frowning. "Walker doesn't normally approve of anything that threatens to upset his precious status quo."

"Walker might like to think he's in charge of things round here," Wilde said dismissively, "but the Authorities have always understood that free enterprise has to come first."

"Philistines," said Grave, polishing her monocle furiously.

"Or," I said, "perhaps the Authorities don't believe this butterfly is the real thing, either."

Wilde smiled widely and blew a perfect smoke ring. "Don't care was made to care, darling."

By now the bidders had started filing in and were already squabbling over who had rights to seats in the front row. I politely excused myself to Wilde and Grave, and took a stroll round the perimeter of the Hall while I watched the crowd assemble noisily. Most were just anonymous faces, there to represent people or interests who didn't care to be publicly identified, or just the usual hopeful souls in search of a bargain. Some were clearly celebrity spotters, there to see history being made by the butterfly's sale. It ended up as quite a large crowd, filling all the seats and leaning against the walls. The teddy bears had to bring in more chairs, grumbling audibly under their breath as they did so. (There were human staff on hand to pass out the glossy sale brochures; apparently the bears considered doing so beneath their dignity.) The crowd buzzed with talk, of a more or less friendly kind, and there was much craning of necks to look at the butterfly, or spot rival bidders. Lucretia Grave stepped up behind her auctioneer's podium and gestured for silence with her gavel as Wilde stood proudly behind her butterfly's display case. I lurked at the back of the Hall, watching the crowd.

And then everything stopped as a huge shaggy Yeti stomped into the Hall. It was a good eight feet tall, with vast, rolling muscles under its grubby white pelt. Everyone shrank back as the great creature lumbered down the aisle, grabbed the Yeti's-foot umbrella stand, glared menacingly at one and all, then stomped out again. No-one felt like trying to stop it. After a discreet pause, to be sure the Yeti was gone and wouldn't be coming back, the auction finally got under way.

Grave started with the lesser items, and they all went fairly quickly under the hammer. Everyone was impatient to get to the star item. I concentrated on studying the more famous faces in the crowd. I wasn't surprised at Jackie Schadenfreud's presence, right in the middle of the crowd. Jackie was an emotion junkie, and I could see him savouring and sucking up the various moods of the crowd as they washed around him. Jackie had insisted on making himself known to me when he arrived, shaking me by the hand and hanging on to it just that little bit too long. He was fat and sweaty, with a twitchy smile and watery eyes. He wore a Gestapo uniform, all black leather and silver insignia, along with a Star of David on a chain round his neck. Just so he could soak up the emotions those conflicting symbols evoked. To protect him from the many who might feel outraged, Jackie was always accompanied by an oversized Doberman that he'd had dyed pink.

Sandra Chance, the consulting necromancer, had stalked into the Hall like she owned the place, but then she always did. Chance had raised arrogance to an art form. She commandeered a seat in the front row, right before the podium, as hers by right, and no-one challenged her. Few ever did. Chance was tall and slender, unhealthily pale under a mop of curly red hair, and wore nothing but crimson swirls of liquid latex, splashed all over her long body apparently at random. (Supposedly the liquid latex was mixed with holy water and other things, for protection.) She also had enough steel piercings in her face and body to make her a danger during thunderstorms. A simple leather belt covered in Druidic symbols hung loosely around her waist, carrying a series of tanned pouches that held the tools of her trade; grave dirt, powdered blood, eye of newt and toe of frog. The usual. I watched her very carefully. She ignored the lesser items as they went under the hammer. She was just there for the butterfly, and everyone knew it. Her face was all sharp angles, with cold intelligent eyes and a grim smile, and I knew her of old.

Chance specialised in cases where someone had died, usually suddenly and violently and very unexpectedly. She could get you answers from beyond the grave, if you weren't too fussy about the methods involved. I worked a few cases with her, back in the day, but we didn't get along. She only cared about getting results, and bad luck to anyone who got in her way. I used to be like that, but I like to think I've moved on. To me, Chance was a reminder of bad times—and two people I wasn't very fond of. She looked round suddenly, and caught my gaze. She'd always had good instincts. She nodded frostily, and I nodded back, then we both looked away again.

Chance currently had a relationship with one of the Nightside's more disturbing major players; that terrible old monster called the Lamentation. Sometimes known as the God of Suicides or the Saint of Suffering. Just saying its name aloud had been known to push people over the edge. No-one knew exactly what kind of relationship Chance had with the Lamentation, and most people with an imagination were afraid even to guess. Some things just aren't healthy, even for the Nightside. Chance had never shown any interest in auctions before, to my knowledge; so, could she be bidding on behalf of the Lamentation? Perhaps. But what would the God of Suicides want with the chaos butterfly? Nothing anyone else would want or approve of, certainly. I wondered if perhaps I ought to do something. After all, who'd be crazy enough to bid against an agent of the Lamentation? And then I looked around me and relaxed a little. There were more than enough major players here to stand against Chance, especially if they got caught up in bidding fever.

And if by some malign chance she did end up winning, I could always do the public-spirited thing—steal the butterfly and run like hell.

Sitting not far away were the Lord of the Dance and the Dancing Queen, ostentatiously not talking to each other, on principle. Odds were neither of them actually wanted the butterfly; they just didn't want the other to have it. Once handfasted, now divorced, they each led very separate dance religions. The Lord of the Dance was currently boasting an ethnic Celtic look, complete with woad and ritual scarring, while the Dancing Queen stuck to her beloved disco diva look. It was always a joy to watch them enter a room, their every movement graceful and poised and significant, as though they were moving to music only they could hear.

Among the last to arrive had been the Painted Ghoul, openly there to bid on behalf of the Collector. (Who was too proud to appear in person, having been caught trying to steal things on three separate occasions.) The Painted Ghoul was the nastiest, most evil-looking clown you'd ever not want to meet in a back alley. His baggy costume was composed of fiercely clashing colours, and his leering, made-up face suggested unnameable depravities. He swaggered into the Hall like a pimp in a schoolyard, flashing a crimson grin full of teeth filed down to points.

"Hiya, hiya, hiya, boys and girls! Great to be here. I just flew in from Sodom and it ain't my arms that's tired! Anyone want to play Find the Lady? I'm almost sure I can remember where I buried her . . ."

He was the proverbial Clown at Midnight, the smile on the killer's face, the laugh that ends in a bubble of blood. But he was still really just a glorified errand boy, for all the airs he gave himself.

I looked round sharply as the bidding finally got to the butterfly. Suddenly it seemed like everyone was trying to bid at once. Grave did her best to keep order, but even her experienced auctioneer's eye had trouble following every raised hand or nodding head. Harsh words and even blows broke out here and there as people became convinced they were being deliberately overlooked. I strode quickly up and down the aisles, glaring people into better behaviour, but trouble broke out faster than I could put it down. Sandra Chance kept pushing the price up, but no-one looked like dropping out. The Painted Ghoul leaned back in his seat, smiling nastily as he topped Chance's bid. Others clamoured to be heard, and open brawling broke out as Grave looked desperately this way and that. The chaos butterfly was a great enough prize to fuel anyone's ambitions. I considered the situation and didn't like what I saw. The mood of the crowd was angry and frustrated, and on the verge of getting really nasty. The Hall's built-in wards would prevent any magical attacks but couldn't do anything to stop a gun or a knife. And whoever ended up winning, it promised to be trouble. It looked like I was actually going to have to do something. Usually I could get away with a quiet word and a harsh look, and rely on my reputation to calm things down, but we were already well beyond that.

And that was when I noticed something . . . odd. Despite all the tension and chaos, and the threat of imminent violence on all sides, I was humming the tune of an old song from the seventies. It was "Bridget the Midget the Queen of the Blues"; one of those comedy novelty singles by Ray Stevens. Hadn't thought of it in years. Even stranger, most of the people nearest me were humming the same tune. Some had even broken off bidding to sing along, though their expressions suggested they didn't know why. I got chills up my back, as I realised the song was spreading through the crowd. In the Nightside, coincidence and compulsion often meant something. And what it usually indicated was interference from Outside.

And then even Grave stopped taking bids and rubbed hard at her forehead, as though bothered by some intrusive thought. Sandra Chance and the Painted Ghoul were both on their feet, looking confusedly about them. A growing murmur of unease ran through the crowd. The song's moment had passed, but we could all feel something—a growing sense of pressure from a direction none of us could name. More people rose to their feet, looking round wildly. No-one new had come into the Hall, but we all knew we weren't alone any more.

"Something's coming," said Sandra Chance. "Something bad."

A few people protested at the interruption of the bidding, but were quickly shouted down. Pretty much everyone was on their feet now, looking around for threats but seeing nothing. Various weapons appeared in nervous hands. The teddy bears huddled together, hints of claws appearing on their padded paws. The Hall grew silent and tense. There was a growing pressure on the air, like a gathering storm, like the moment before lightning strikes. And suddenly, all around the Great Auction Hall, wards and protections that had stood for centuries broke and blew apart in coruscations of vivid energies, shattered by a growing presence they were never meant to contain or keep out—a living presence, vast and inhuman, seeping into our reality like poison into a clear spring.

I knew what it was, what it had to be. I recognised the signs. A psychenaut; a traveller from some higher or lower dimension. An intruder that could not be stopped or turned aside because it was either too real or not real enough to be affected by human powers. I'd had some experience with psychenauts, back when I apprenticed with old Carnacki, the Ghost Finder. It didn't seem fair that I should have to face something so awful twice in one lifetime. I would have run, but I knew I'd never make it.

The crowd was already beginning to panic when the first protrusions from a lower dimension began to manifest. Unfocussed energies sleeted through the Hall, sparking black rainbows and shimmering auras around people who weren't actually there, before sinking into physical objects and lending them a horrible animation. Ugly, distorted faces formed themselves out of the materials of the walls, floor, and ceiling. Thick lips curled back to reveal jagged teeth, while dark eyes rolled grinding in their sockets, and abhuman voices shuddered through our heads, saying *We are coming, we are coming.* The wooden fingertips of a huge hand thrust slowly up from among the rows of seats, and the crowd scattered, shrieking and screaming, and shouting Words of Power that had no influence on what was forcing its way into our world from the underpinnings of reality.

The cheap wooden seats suddenly exploded into lashing wooden tentacles, springing out to wrap themselves around the fleeing crowd, holding them tightly. More screams rose as arms and legs broke under the inhuman pressure of the wooden bonds. Great faces in the floor drank up the spilled blood, making noises thick with meaning that predated language. The walls were swelling in and out, as though in rhythm to some great thing breathing, and the whole Hall shook, the floor rising and falling like a ship at sea.

Poltergeist activity stormed all around us. Events were happening so fast now no-one could react quick enough to keep up with them. Any object left unsecured flew violently back and forth, or spontaneously combusted. Clothes grew too large, or ripped and tore as they shrank. Fires burned unsupported on the air, and beads of sweat rolled sluggishly up the walls. There were hails of stones and rains of fish, and people spoke in unknown tongues.

I fought my way through the chaos to grab hold of Lucretia Grave, who was on her knees and clinging numbly to her rocking podium. I hauled her back onto her feet, and she clung to me like a child. I had hoped she'd have some emergency backup magics she could call on, but it didn't look like it. The teddy bears were staggering back and forth among the panicking crowd, trying to help, but there was little they could do except try and shield people with their padded bodies.

A genius loci invaded the Hall, overpowering and supplanting the old Barn's actual ambience, and, immediately, powerful emotions stormed our minds, slapping aside our defences with contemptuous ease. People began laughing, crying, and howling with an hysteria that shook them the way a dog shakes a rat. I was laughing so hard I hurt, but I couldn't stop. And then the horrors swept through us all, the same basic fears; of the dark, of falling, of people not being who we thought they were. People struck out at each other because they had to strike out at something. Men and women fell down and did not rise again, forced into catatonia by terrors and emotions they couldn't face. There was a new genius loci in residence, and the Great Auction Hall had become an alien, unbearable place. A few people staggered towards the exits, only to find that the doors had disappeared. There was no way out any more.

Jackie Schadenfreud had swollen up like a blowfish, blowing off all the silver buttons on his Nazi greatcoat. He giggled painfully, soaking up the emotions around him, force-fed on feelings beyond his appetite or capacity. Thick bloody tears ran down his pink cheeks as his eyes bulged in their sockets. His dog had already torn its own guts out. The Painted Ghoul ran up a swelling wall, scuttling like an oversized insect, trying to get away from emotions he usually inflicted only on others. Sweat was making his makeup run, and he wasn't smiling any more.

Sandra Chance's magics were mostly useless, being concerned primarily with the dead, not elementals, but she was still fighting back. She stood proudly in a shimmering circle of protection, magnificently angry, forcing back the psychenaut intrusions by sheer force of will. She had an aboriginal pointing bone, and in whichever direction she trained it the animating forces were thrust out of the material world. But only for a while. They always came back.

The Lord of the Dance and the Dancing Queen, united again by the threat of a common enemy, beat out powerful harmonies on the heaving floor with their dancing feet. They danced their fury and their outrage out into the world, forcing back the invading presences. Their feet slammed down, hammering out marvellous rhythms, their every movement wonderfully graceful, their bodies radiating defiant humanity in the face of the inhuman. They had always danced their best when they danced together.

Deliverance Wilde stood inside a faerie ring, protected by her compact with the Unseeli Court, but helpless to do anything. She wrung her hands together, looking piteously about her.

And I stood alone, only marginally affected by the horrors around me, and reluctantly decided I'd have to do something.

I don't like actually having to do things. I like to keep what I can and can't do a mystery; it helps build my reputation. You can do more with a bad reputation than you can with any magic. Usually. But while the psychenauts were holding back from me for the moment, perhaps confused by my nature, there was no guaranteeing how long that would last. I knew what the problem was, and I thought I knew how to solve it, so once again it was up to me to haul everyone back from the gates of Hell. If I was wrong, the odds were I was going to die, in any number of really unpleasant ways; but I was used to that.

Back when I worked with Carnacki the Ghost Finder, he'd used a charm of Banishing on a psychenaut, driving it out of a haunted funfair, and afterwards I pocketed the charm when he wasn't looking. He had loads of the things, and I had a feeling it might come in handy someday. I dug through the various mystical junk that accumulates in my pockets and finally hauled out a golden coin that came originally from the land of Nod. It had writing on it no-one could understand, and a face that was mostly worn away, but still subtly disturbing. I've never liked relying on such things, but needs must when the Outside is kicking down your door. If it didn't work, I could hardly go back to Carnacki and complain. Objects of power rarely come with warranties.

I held up the coin and spoke the activating Word of Power, and a terrible light radiated from the coin, too bright and piercing for merely human eyes. I had to turn my head away, and my hand holding the coin felt like it was on fire. The Banishing leapt out into the Hall, eager to be about its implacable business. It roared through the Hall, speaking words in a tongue older than Humanity, tearing the animating spirits out of the physical creation and forcing them back, down through the bottom of the world, back into the underpinnings of reality. The psychenauts were gone, and with them the overpowering emotions and debilitating fears. The walls and the floor and the ceiling grew still and solid again, and the wooden arms holding men and women fell apart into splinters. People looked slowly about them, daring to believe the worst might be over.

And Sandra Chance said, in a heartbreakingly matter-of-fact voice, "Something else is coming."

It was another psychenaut. A traveller from a higher dimension this time. We could all feel it coming, could feel Something unbearably vast descending into our reality. Something so impossibly big it had to compress itself to fit into our narrow Space/Time continuum. Everyone's first impulse, including mine, was to run, but the sheer force of the approaching Presence held us helpless where we were, like mice in the gaze of the serpent, or insects caught in the heat focussed through a magnifying glass. Something finally materialised in the Great Auction Hall with us, so huge and powerful it hurt our minds even to think about it, drawing everything towards it like a massive gravity well. It was too Real for our limited reality; so Real it sucked everything else into it.

The Presence settled heavily into our world, spreading out in directions we couldn't even name; something Huge and Vast downloaded from a higher dimension. Its thoughts smashed into everyone's minds, as harsh and merciless as a spotlight, searching for the single significant thing that had brought it to this petty, limited place. It didn't take a genius to realise it must be looking for the chaos butterfly. The only truly unique thing at the auction. The psychenaut couldn't seem to locate it exactly for the moment, presumably because of the stasis field holding the butterfly temporarily outside of Time and Space. And so the Presence sank deeper into people's minds, forcing their very selves away in its search for knowledge. All around me people were crying out in pain and shock and horror, shrieking *Get it out of me!* Even the major players were on their knees, sobbing and shaking. The only one left mostly unaffected in the Hall was me, and I didn't want to think why.

The psychenaut wasn't used to thinking in only three dimensions, but eventually it would locate the chaos butterfly, if only through a process of elimination. The pull of the gravity well was growing steadily stronger. Details of this world's reality were being stripped away and sucked in, absorbed by the Presence. Not because it chose to, but just because of what it was. The teddy bears lumbered towards it, drawn by some inexorable summons, only to fall one by one to the floor, reduced to just toy bears again. Terrible changes swept through those people closest to the Presence. Suddenly, some could only be seen from the back, no matter which way you looked at them. Faces lost their individuality, becoming blank and generic. Details of clothing disappeared as though smoothed away by an unseen hand, then lost their colour. People became black-and-white two-dimensional photographs, and finally just chalk drawings, until all they were was sucked into the gravity well. Stripped of everything that made them real.

I made myself ignore the screams and howls of the damned around me, thinking hard. The charm of Banishing wouldn't work on anything as powerful as this. Hell, nothing I had would even touch it. Powers as significant as this hardly ever gave a damn about lower dimensions like ours. This one was only here because of the chaos butterfly. Presumably because whoever finally took charge of it, the ability to predict and maybe control the future would have repercussions up and down the dimensions. So the psychenauts would just keep coming, from up and down the line, until one of them finally found the butterfly. And none of them would care how much damage they did to this world and the people in it. So there was only one thing left to do.

I lurched over to the glass display cases, forcing myself against the terrible pull of the gravity well, until finally I stood before the case holding the chaos butterfly. It hung there in its stasis field, such a small thing to hold such potential power. I reached out for the case, and Wilde cried out, afraid I was going to kill the butterfly, even after all its presence had brought about. I used my gift to find things, opening the third eye deep in my mind, my private eye, to locate the necessary Word of Power that would collapse the stasis field.

I said the Word, the field collapsed, and the butterfly disappeared, free at last to return to the moment in Space and Time from which it had been snatched. And as it moved on, it became just a butterfly again, no longer significant, no longer the first domino in any line of destiny. And so became ordinary again, of no importance to anyone at all.

The Presence snapped out of reality in a moment, no longer interested, and the gravity well was gone. All across the Hall people collapsed, mostly in gratitude that their ordeal was over. I sat down with my back to a reliably strong and solid wall and let myself shake for a while.

Of course, not everyone was pleased with the way things turned out. Deliverance Wilde, for example, wandered miserably around the Hall saying *I could have been rich, rich, rich* . . . She could have been dead, in any number of unpleasant ways, but I was too much of a gentleman to point that out. And many of the people who'd come to bid for the butterfly came up to ask pointedly whether I couldn't have found some better way to deal with the problem. I gave them my best hard look, and they went away again. An awful lot of people were dead, or much diminished, so I helped the Auction Hall staff pile the bodies up in one corner, for the Authorities to deal with, when they finally showed up. No-one else wanted to help. Most people couldn't get out of the Hall fast enough. I decided it might be best if I was long gone, too, before Walker and his people turned up, asking awkward questions. I said as much to Wilde, and she nodded slowly.

"I suppose I could always try and track down another chaos butterfly . . ."

I silently indicated the wreckage and the piled-up dead, and she shuddered.

"Or perhaps not."

"Stick to fashion," I said, not unkindly. "It's a lot less dangerous."

She managed a small smile. "Lot you know," she said, and drifted away.

I went back to Grave, looking mournfully round her devastated Hall, and told her where she could send the cheque for my services. She glared at me.

"You don't seriously expect to get paid, after this debacle?"

I gave her my very best hard look. "I always get paid."

She thought about that for a moment, then said she quite understood my point. I smiled, said good-bye, and went back out into the Nightside.

TWO

When Lady Luck Comes Calling . . . Run

I eat out, mostly. Partly because the Nightside has some of the best restaurants in this and many other universes, but mostly because I have neither the gift, the time, nor the interest to cook for myself. Though of course in an emergency I am quite capable of sticking something frozen in a microwave and nuking it till it screams. I also much prefer to eat on my own, so that I can give my full attention to the excellent food I've just paid a small fortune for. But on this occasion I was lunching with my young secretary, Cathy Barrett. I was doing so because she'd made a point of phoning me from my office, just to tell me so, and as in so many other things where Cathy was concerned, I didn't get a say in the matter. I have learned to accept such defeats gracefully.

Not least because whenever Cathy insists that it's important we meet for a little chat over a meal, it nearly always means bad news is heading in my direction at warp speed. And not just your ordinary, everyday bad news, of which there is never any lack in the Nightside, but the kind of really vicious, unpleasant, and desperately unfair bad news that comes howling in from a totally unexpected direction. I considered the various awful possibilities as I headed into Uptown, and set my course for the restaurant area. Uptown is what passes for class in the Nightside, where mostly we're too busy screwing each other over to care about such things.

Hot neon blazed all around me, reflecting blurred colours on the rain-slick roads. Smoky saxophones and heavy bass lines drifted out the doorways of clubs that never close. Dawn never comes in the Nightside, so the drinking and dancing and sinning never has to end, as long as you've still got money in your pocket or a soul to barter.

As far as I knew, I had no outstanding problems. All my cases were closed, with no loose ends left hanging to come back and haunt me. I doubted there was any problem with my office, as Cathy ran it with frightening efficiency. Unless the answerphone had been possessed by Kandarian demons again. Damn, those technoexorcists are expensive. Maybe the tax people were challenging my expenses again. Oh yes; we all pay taxes in the Nightside. Though I'm not always entirely sure to whom . . .

Rain pooled on the pavements from the recent brief storm, but the night sky was as clear as ever. Thousands of stars shone more brightly than they ever did in the world outside, and the moon was a dozen times larger than it should be. No-one knows why; or if they do, they aren't talking. The Nightside runs on secrets and mysteries. As always, the streets teemed with men and women and things that were both and neither, all carefully minding their own business as they concentrated on the private missions and hidden passions that had led or dragged them into the Nightside. You can buy or sell anything here, especially if it's something you're not supposed to want in a supposedly civilised world. The price is often your soul, or someone else's, but then you know that going in. All kinds of pleasures and services beckoned from every window and doorway, and for those of a more traditional bent there were always the gaudy charms of the twilight daughters; love for sale, or at least for rent. The road roared with traffic that rarely stopped, or even slowed. People kept well away from the kerbs. Just because something looked like a car, it didn't mean it was.

I reached the arranged meeting place, and for a wonder Cathy had actually got there ahead of me for once. She bounced up and down on her toes, waving wildly, as though there was any chance I might have missed her. Cathy always stood out—a bright spark in a dark place. Seventeen years old, tall and blonde and fashionably slender through an iron will, she looked particularly sharp in a Go-Go checked blouse and miniskirt, with white plastic thigh boots and matching white plastic beret perched precariously on the back of her head. She'd never been the same since my occasional partner in crime Shotgun Suzie introduced her to the old *Avengers* TV show. Cathy pecked me briefly on the cheek, slipped her arm through mine, and gave me what she thinks is her winning smile.

"Where do you want to eat?" I said, smiling resignedly. "Somewhere fashionably expensive, no doubt. How about Alice's Restaurant, where you can get anything you want? Or maybe Wonka's Wondrous Warren; Chocolate With Everything? No? You have changed. There's a new place just opened up round the corner; Elizabethan Splendour . . ."

Cathy pulled a face. "Sounds old-fashioned."

"They specialise in the more outre items of fare from the reign of

Queen Elizabeth I. Puffins, for example, which they classified as fish, so they could eat them on Fasting Days in their religion."

"But . . . puffins aren't fish! They've got beaks! And wings!"

"If the EEC can classify a carrot as a fruit because the Spanish make jam out of it, then a puffin can be a fish. The Elizabethans also ate hedgehogs, when they weren't using them as hairbrushes; and coneys, which were infant rabbits, torn from the breast."

"Crunchy," said Cathy. "No thank you. I've already decided where we're going."

"Now there's a surprise."

"I want to go to Rick's Café Imaginaire; you know, the place where they make meals exclusively from extinct or imaginary animals. They got this totally groovy review in the *Night Times'* lifestyle section just the other week. I know it's a bit exclusive, but you can get us in. You can get in anywhere."

"If only that were true," I said. "This way, you dolly little epicure."

I led her down the street while she clung to my arm, chattering cheerfully about nothing in particular. Apparently the bad news she was nursing was so bad it could only be discussed after a really good meal, to soften the blow. I sighed inwardly, and checked the sliver of unicorn's horn I carry like a pin in the lapel of my trench coat. Unicorn's horn is very good at detecting hidden poisons.

The entrance to Rick's Café Imaginaire was a simple, almost anonymous green door, tucked away in an alcove under a discreet hand-painted sign. They don't need to advertise. Everyone comes to Rick's. The door was spelled to admit only people with confirmed bookings, or celebrities, or those in good standing with Rick, and Cathy was visibly impressed when the door swung open immediately at my touch. We stepped through the door and found ourselves in a jungle clearing. An open area of sandy ground, surrounded by tall rain forest trees, hanging vines and lianas, for as far as the eye could see. Not that you could see all that far; the heavy jungle canopy kept out most of the light, and the shadows between the trees were very dark indeed. Animal sounds came from every direction, hoots and howls and sudden yelps, occasionally interrupted by a loud growl or scream. The air in the clearing was hot and dry and very still. It was just like being in a real jungle clearing, and perhaps we were. This was the Nightside, after all.

(No animal has ever been known to venture out of the jungle and into the clearing. They're probably quite rightly afraid of being eaten.)

The head waiter glared venomously at me as I led Cathy nonchalantly past the long line of people waiting for a table. A few of them muttered angrily as we passed, only to be hushed quickly by those who recognised me. My name moved quickly up and down the queue, murmured under the breath like a warning or a curse. I came to a halt before the head waiter, and gave him my best Don't Even Think of Starting Something look. He was a short and stocky man, stuffed inside a splendid tuxedo that was far too good for him, his sharp-edged features screwed up in what appeared to be an expression of terminal constipation. He would clearly have loved to tell me to go to Hell by the express route and call for his bouncers to start us on our way; but unfortunately for him, his boss was standing right beside him. Some of the people waiting in the queue actually hissed in disgust over such preferential treatment, without even a hint of a bribe. Rick ignored them and exchanged nods with me. He didn't believe in shaking hands. He managed a smile for Cathy, but then, everyone did. He wore a smart elegant white tuxedo, which contrasted strongly with his craggy, lived-in face. There was always a cigarette in one corner of his mouth, and his Café had never even considered having a No Smoking section.

"How is it you always know when I'm coming here?" I asked him, honestly curious.

He smiled briefly. "All part of the service. And besides, you can't afford to be surprised, in the Nightside. It can be very bad for business."

"This is my secretary, Cathy."

"If you say so, John."

"No, really; this is my secretary."

"You always were a cradle snatcher."

"Look, just get us a table for two, before I decide to rumple your nice suit."

"Of course, John. There will always be a table here for you, no matter how crowded we get."

"Why?" Cathy said immediately, scenting a story, or better yet, gossip. She likes to think her lack of tact is charming, and I don't have the heart to disillusion her.

"John once did a favour for me," said Rick. "A snack had gone missing, under questionable circumstances, and John helped me locate it. As it turned out, the snack was a snark. It had turned into a boojum, and was masquerading as a customer. Every time you think you've seen everything the Nightside has to offer, it finds a totally new way to appal you."

"What brought you to the nightside in the first place?" said Cathy.

He smiled. "I came for the glorious sunsets."

"But it's always night here!"

"I was misinformed."

Cathy looked suspiciously at Rick, then at me, sensing she was missing out on some private joke, but had the good sense to say nothing as Rick led us to the only remaining empty table, on the furthest edge of the clearing. People sitting at the tables we passed kept their heads down and their eyes averted. Rick pulled out Cathy's chair, while leaving me to fend for myself. Good-looking youth has its privileges. The tablecloth was pristine white, the silverware immaculate, and the salt and pepper pots were practically works of art. The handwritten menu was so big you needed both hands to control it. Rick hovered just long enough to make sure we were comfortable, then decided he was urgently needed elsewhere, and strolled away. Rick didn't mix with the customers, as a rule. In fact, you could eat at his place for months and never even catch a glimpse of him, and that was the way he liked it. Cathy looked impishly at me over the top of her oversized menu.

"A table on demand, at *Rick's*! I am officially impressed."

"Don't be. I'm still expected to pay the bill before we leave. Rick wasn't that grateful."

There was a coat stand beside every table, a tall mahogany rococo effort, because none of the customers liked the idea of their coats and belongings being out of sight, where they might be tampered with by enemies. Paranoia is a way of life in the Nightside, and for many good reasons. I hung up my trench coat, after surreptitiously removing the sliver of unicorn horn from my lapel. I like to keep my little secrets to myself. It all helps build the reputation. Cathy tossed her beret casually onto the top of the coat stand. I looked at her enviously. I've never been able to do things like that. I sat down again opposite her, and we studied our menus solemnly. People at surrounding tables watched me when they thought I wasn't looking. Some crossed themselves, or made the sign of the evil eye against me. I considered how much fun could be had, just by jumping up suddenly and shouting *Boo!*, but rose above it. Cathy whistled quietly and looked at me over the top of her menu again.

"This is a seriously extreme list, John. Where does he get all this stuff?"

"Rick's place is unique, even for the Nightside," I admitted. "As far as I know, he's the only restaurateur ever to make meals out of creatures that don't usually exist. I have asked where his supplies come from, but all he'll ever say is that he has his sources. I understand he employs professional wild game hunters for the rarer specimens; no questions asked, and whatever you do don't bring them back alive. Apparently the real problem is finding and keeping first-class chefs who can deal with the problems involved in preparing some of the meals. Like being blindfolded when preparing gorgon's-eye soup. You don't want someone who'll go into hysterics when faced with moebius mice, which stuff themselves."

A waiter turned up to look down its nose at us. It was a giant penguin, complete with pencil moustache and a supercilious eye. It looked meaningfully at our menus, then recited the day's specials in a bored monotone.

"The octopus is off, but we hope to recapture it soon. And don't ask for the chameleon, because we can't find it. Today's special is long pig, because one of yesterday's customers couldn't pay his bill."

Cathy looked at me. "Is it joking?"

"I doubt it. Penguins aren't known for their sense of humour."

"Speciesist!" hissed the waiter.

We made a point of ignoring it. "Where are the kitchens in this place?" said Cathy, looking around the jungle clearing.

"Only Rick knows," I said. "And he isn't talking. I have a horrible feeling that if we ever saw the state of the kitchens, we wouldn't eat anything that came out of them."

"Did you get anything nice for me at the auction?" said Cathy, changing the subject with the artless speed of which only teenagers are capable.

"I'm afraid not. It wasn't really that kind of auction. Maybe next time." And just to show that I could do it, too; "How's your mother?"

"Fine," said Cathy, carefully studying her menu so she wouldn't have to look at me. "Rich and successful as ever. Offered me a nice little position in her firm, if I ever feel like going home, which I don't. Actually, the further away we are, the better we get on. We can be quite civil to each other, as long as we're not in the same time zone. Have you had any luck in tracking down news of your mother?"

"No." It was my turn to study the menu. "The few people who might know something refuse even to discuss the matter. It's hard to find anyone who knew her in person, who's still alive. There's Shock-Headed Peter, of course, but he's insane. My dad didn't even leave me any photos of her. Apparently he burned a whole lot of stuff when she left . . . when he found out what she was."

"Do you remember anything of what she looked like?"

"No. Nothing. Not even her voice. I must have been about four when she left, so I ought to remember something of her; but I don't. I have to wonder if she . . . did something to me, before she left. Or perhaps my father did, afterwards. There's no-one I can ask." We both considered that in silence for a while. "So," I said finally. "Are you still going out with that musician guy, Leo Morn?"

"Hell no," said Cathy, with something like a shudder. "That beast? I dumped him ages ago. He thought he was the big I Am, and I should be grateful for his attention, when he bothered to show up. No-one treats me like that. And his band sucked, big-time. Gothic Punk, I ask you! Mind you; he could be a real animal between the sheets . . ."

"Far too much information," I said firmly. "Are you ready to go home yet, Cathy? I mean, back to the real world, and a real life?"

"No. Why? Do you want to get rid of me?"

"You know I don't. But you weren't born here, you have nothing to tie you to the Nightside. Unlike most of us, you could leave this spiritual cesspool anytime you wanted. You could make a life in the sane part of London, where people aren't always trying to kill you."

"I'm never going back." Cathy put down her menu so she could meet my gaze squarely. "I love it here. I spent most of my life trying to run away from the sane, normal, boring world where I never fit in. The Nightside is so . . . alive! There's always something happening! It's like a party that never ends—with the best music, the most jumping clubs, and the weirdest people . . . I feel at home here, John. I was looking for something like the Nightside my whole life. I belong here." She grinned. "I guess I'm just a night person."

I smiled back at her. "It's just . . . I worry about you, Cathy."

"I worry about you! And I've got much better reasons!"

"Are you ready yet to tell me why we're having this very expensive dinner together?"

She took a deep breath, let it out slowly, and looked me straight in the eyes, her whole manner very serious. "I want to accompany you on a case. A proper case. As your partner. I keep asking, and you keep putting me off . . ."

"Because you're not ready yet." I was careful to keep my voice calm and level and very reasonable. "Cathy; you've adjusted very well to living in the Nightside, ever since I rescued you from the house that tried to eat you, but you still don't take the Nightside seriously enough. You haven't developed the resources you'd need to deal with the kind of hazards you'd encounter on a real case. There are things here that would eat you up, body and soul. You get left alone most of the time because you're with me. My reputation protects you. But out in the field, the bad guys wouldn't hesitate to threaten you to get at me, or at the very least distract me."

"I can look after myself!" Cathy said indignantly.

"It's true, you go clubbing in dives I wouldn't enter without armed backup, but you don't have the experience yet to spot when you're being played, or led on."

"I spotted Leo Morn!"

"Cathy, everyone knows about Leo Morn. I'm talking about the major players, the Powers and Dominations. They do so love to play their little mind games. More importantly, you've never had to kill anyone. Working with me, the time would come when you'd have to, to save your life or mine. Do you think you could do that? Honestly?"

"I don't know," said Cathy.

"Of course you don't. No-one ever does, until they have to. It's something that changes you forever. It's like killing something in yourself, too. I'd spare you that knowledge, for as long as possible. Until then, it's just too dangerous for you to join me on a case. A real case. Because you can never tell when they're going to turn dirty."

At which point we were interrupted by a whole bunch of lemmings escaping from the unseen kitchens. They'd launched a mass breakout, and came swarming across the floor of the clearing like a furry tide, while diners squealed and shouted and pulled up their feet. The lemmings climbed up onto chairs and tables and even lower tree branches, and threw themselves through the air, in fine old lemming fashion. Cathy and I cheered them on.

"Look; that one's got a parachute! That one's hang-gliding! Go, little fellow, go!"

It was all over in a few moments. The lemmings scattered into the surrounding jungle, singing high-pitched victory songs (something about Rick only having one ball), and everyone settled down again. No-one emerged from the unseen kitchens in pursuit. Lemmings were always on the menu (very nice, stuffed with locusts' legs, in a tart lemon sauce) and there were always more on the way. Lemmings breed like there's no tomorrow, and indeed for a whole lot of them, there isn't.

Cathy and I went back to contemplating our menus, watched over by the foot-tapping giant penguin, who'd developed a bit of a twitch in one eye.

"Don't touch the dodo steaks," I advised Cathy. "They're strictly for the tourists. They taste awful, no matter what kind of sauce they're trying to disguise them with this week. How about . . . the roc egg omelette? Feeds four. No? Well, there's always the jabberwocky giblets. They come with borogoves, but they're always a bit mimsy . . . Chimera of the day? Roast mammoth; always big helpings. Or how about Hydra?"

"No," said Cathy. "Greek food doesn't agree with me."

After a certain amount of toing and froing, we finally settled on dragonburgers (flame-grilled, of course), with a nice healthy salad on the side. For dessert, Cheshire Cat ice cream. (Because it vanishes, it's not fattening.) We'd no sooner given the waiter our order than the food arrived, hot and steaming on a hostess trolley pushed by another giant penguin, wearing a name badge that said HI! MY NAME IS . . . PISS OFF TOURIST. I'm convinced Rick has a precog in his kitchen. The penguins left us to our meals with a simultaneous dismissive sniff. I palmed my sliver of unicorn's horn, and surreptitiously tested both my food and Cathy's.

No trace of poison, said a snotty voice in my head. *But the calories are off the scale, and it's far too salty. I thought we'd agreed you were going on a diet?*

I put the sliver away. I hate chatty simulacra. Give them a steady job, and they think they're your mother.

Cathy and I ate in silence for a while. The dragon meat was delicious. Very smoky taste. Quiet conversation went on around us. It was all very civilised. When the dragonburgers and some of the salad were just a pleasant memory, we sat back and waited contentedly for dessert. It arrived immediately, of course, and the penguin waiter quickly cleared away the dirty plates and slapped the bill on the table. (Service not included. They wouldn't dare.) When the waiter was gone, I leaned forward to talk confidentially with Cathy.

"One thing you have always been better at than me, Cathy, and that's knowing everything about the latest trends. See the gentleman in the navy blue suit and old-school tie, two tables down? What the hell is *that* all about?"

The man in question had a hole drilled neatly through his forehead, on through his brain, and out the back of his skull, leaving a narrow tunnel all the way through his head. You could see right down it, though I tried very hard not to.

Cathy looked, and sniffed loudly. "Ultimate trepanation. The idea was, drilling a hole through your forehead would allow the bony plates of the skull to break apart and expand, allowing the brain room to expand as well, and thus make you more intelligent. This new fad just takes the idea to its logical conclusion. Personally, I would have stuck with the smart drinks. They didn't work either, but they had to be a lot less painful."

"I would have thought deciding not to drill a hole in your head was a pretty good indication of intelligence," I said, trying not to stare, or wince. "I wonder if the hole plays music when the wind blows through it? Or maybe . . . you could pull a cord through the hole—mental floss! Helps remove those hard-to-digest ideas!"

Cathy got the giggles, and almost choked on her dessert. She washed the ice cream down with a large glass of the complimentary house blue. The bottle Rick had provided was already almost empty, without any help from me. Cathy regarded alcohol as just another food group. I'd ordered a Coke. And insisted on the real thing, not one of those diet monstrosities. The waiter got back at me by putting a curly-wurly straw in it, the bastard.

And then all the conversation in the clearing stopped abruptly, and all the animal noises from the jungle died away. It was like the world was holding its breath. There was a soft gentle sound, like wind chimes caressed by a breeze, and Lady Luck came striding out of the jungle and into the clearing. She was slender and elegant, her every movement almost painfully graceful, wearing a long, shimmering, silver evening gown that matched her eyes. She had delicate Oriental features, with long, flat black hair, and a small mouth with very red lips. She looked right at me, and her mouth stretched suddenly into a smile to die for. She came out of the jungle darkness like a dream walking and headed right for my table. As she left the trees behind, the branches burst spontaneously into flower, or withered and cracked apart. Sometimes both. As she walked between the tables all the cutlery turned to solid gold. A blind man could suddenly see, and another man slumped forward, dead of a heart attack. And suddenly everyone in Rick's Café had an apple in their hand.

Everyone smiled at Lady Luck and reached out to touch her, but she avoided them. Some looked away. Some brandished magical charms at her. She ignored it all with aristocratic calm. People craned their heads, trying to work out whom she'd come to see. Lady Luck only ever appeared in person to the very fortunate, or the soon to be damned. Often called on, but rarely made welcome when she deigned to show up. And then she stopped at my table, and everyone else started breathing easily again.

Lady Luck sat down opposite me without waiting to be asked, on a chair that appeared out of nowhere just in time. She smiled once at Cathy, who grinned back foolishly, dazzled, then Lady Luck gave me her full attention. By now I was almost supernaturally alert, checking for any sudden changes in myself or Cathy, or our immediate surroundings, but it seemed Lady Luck had grown tired of showing off. I didn't relax. The most beautiful ones are always the most dangerous. I knew my fair share of magics and tricks, including a few I wasn't supposed to know even existed, but I had nothing that could hope to stand off a Being as powerful as Lady Luck. So, when in doubt, bluff. I gave her my best confident smile, met her silver gaze calmly, and hoped like hell I could talk my way out of this. It didn't help when Cathy suddenly threw off the glamour that had dazzled her and looked like she was about to dive under the table or try and hide in my pockets. She knew a real threat when she saw one. Attracting the attention of the gods is rarely a good idea.

I gave Cathy a reassuring look and concentrated on Lady Luck.

"I didn't call you," I said carefully, just to get the ball rolling.

"No," she said, in a soft, thrilling voice. It felt like being scratched where you itched. By a very sharp claw. "I came to you, John Taylor. I wish to hire your services, to represent me in a delicate matter. I want you to investigate for me the true nature and origins of the Nightside. I want you to discover how and where it all began, and, most especially, why and for what purpose."

I swear I just sat there for a few moments with my mouth open, utterly taken aback. I had always hoped that someday somebody would back me on what could be the greatest case of my career, but I hadn't expected it just to come out of nowhere like this. There had to be a catch. There was always a catch. Like, for example, why did a Power and Domination like Lady Luck need help from a mere mortal like me? I said as much, only much more politely, and Lady Luck hit me with her dazzling smile again. Her canines gleamed gold. It was like drowning in sunshine.

"I wish to know why probabilities are always so out of my control, in the Nightside. Why so many long shots, good and bad, come true here. Is there perhaps a hex on the Nightside, and if so, who put it there, and for what reason? I want to know these things. If I knew and understood the origins of the Nightside, I might be better able to manipulate chance here, as my role requires."

I looked at her thoughtfully, taking my time. Lady Luck was one of the Transient Beings, a physical incarnation of an abstract concept, or ideal. Appallingly powerful, but limited to the role she embodied. She normally appeared in person only once in a Blue Moon, but this was the Nightside, after all. And like every other Power and Domination, she always had her own agenda, as well as being notoriously fickle.

"I'm not the first one you've approached about this, am I?" I said finally.

"Of course not. Many others have had the honour to serve me in this matter, down the centuries. All of them failed. Or at least, none of them ever came back, to tell me how close they'd got. But it's not in my nature to give up. I am always on the lookout for a likely . . ."

"Sucker?" I suggested.

She favoured me with her glorious smile again. "But you are different, John Taylor. I have high hopes for your success. After all, you can find anything, can't you?"

I considered the matter, letting her wait while I examined all the angles. When something seems too good to be true, it nearly always is too good to be true. Especially in the Nightside. Lady Luck sat patiently, as relaxed as a cat in the sun. Cathy had pushed her chair back as far as it would go without her actually joining another table, and it was clear from her unhappy face that she didn't want me having anything to do with this case, or this client. But if I were afraid of taking chances, I'd never have come back to the Nightside. I nodded slowly to Lady Luck, and did my best to sound as though I knew more than I actually did.

"The few who profess to know the Nightside's true beginnings have a vested interest in keeping them secret. Knowledge is power. And these people . . . we're talking major players, Powers and Dominations . . . Beings like yourself—and greater. They won't take kindly to my barging in and treading on their toes."

"That's never stopped you before," Lady Luck said sweetly.

"True," I said. "But still, I have to ask: why haven't you gone looking for the answer yourself if you want to know so badly?"

Lady Luck nodded briefly, acknowledging the point. "I don't interfere directly in the world nearly as much as people think I do. Statistics just have a way of working themselves out. My role requires that I remain . . . mysterious. Enigmatic. I prefer to work at a distance, through . . . deniable agents."

"Expendable agents."

"That, too!"

I scowled. "I get enough of this doing jobs for Walker. Why did you choose me, particularly?"

"Because you let the chaos butterfly go free, instead of destroying it. Or trying to control it yourself."

"No good deed goes unpunished," I said.

"What will it take to hire you?" said Lady Luck. "To take this case? How much do you want?"

"How much have you got?"

Her smile was suddenly that of a cat spotting a cornered mouse. "I will give you something far more valuable than gold or silver, John Taylor. I know who and what your mother was. I will tell you, in return for you finding out what I wish to know."

I leaned forward across the table, and I could feel my face and voice going cold and ugly. "Tell me. Tell me now."

"Sorry," said Lady Luck, entirely unmoved. "You must earn your reward."

"I could make you tell me," I said.

People began getting up out of the chairs and backing away. Cathy looked as though she wanted to, but loyalty held her in place. And Lady Luck laughed softly in my face.

"No you won't, John Taylor. Because you're as trapped in your role as I am in mine."

I sat back in my chair, suddenly very tired. Cathy scowled at me.

"You're going to do it, aren't you?"

"I have to. I want to know the origins of the Nightside as much as she does."

Cathy glared at Lady Luck. "Are you at least going to make John lucky, while he's working for you? You owe him that much."

"If I were to ally myself openly with John Taylor," said Lady Luck, "others of my kind might come out against him. You wouldn't want that, would you, John?"

"No, I bloody well wouldn't," I said. "Your kind are too powerful and too weird, even for the Nightside. But . . . could I perhaps say that I am working on your behalf? That would give me some authority, and might even get me into some of the more difficult places."

"If you like," said Lady Luck, "but I cannot, and will not, intervene directly in your investigation."

I grinned. "The people I'll be questioning won't know that."

"Then the mission is yours," said Lady Luck. She rose gracefully to her feet and bowed briefly. "Try not to get killed."

She vanished abruptly, in a crackle of possibilities. A spring of clear water bubbled up from the ground where she'd been standing. I didn't think Rick would be too bothered. Knowing him, he'd probably make a feature out of it. Everyone watching began to relax, and sat down again. A number of serious hushed conversations started up, combined with lots of glancing in my direction. A few began pocketing the transmuted gold cutlery, until the penguin waiters made them put it back. Rick didn't miss a trick.

"I've decided . . . to sit this case out," said Cathy. "I'm almost sure I have some urgent filing that needs doing, back at the office. Behind a securely locked and bolted door."

"Understandable," I said.

"You're not thinking of doing this on your own, though, are you? You are definitely going to need backup on this one. Serious backup, with hardcore firepower. What about Suzie Shooter? Dead Boy? Razor Eddie?"

I shook my head. "All good choices. Unfortunately, Shotgun Suzie is still on the trail of Big Butcher Hog, and likely to be for some time. Dead Boy is very involved with his new girl-friend, a Valkyrie. And the Punk God of the Straight Razor is currently occupied doing something very unpleasant on the Street of the Gods. It must be something especially upsetting, because some of the gods have come running out crying. No, I've got someone else in mind, for a case like this. I thought I'd approach Madman, and just maybe, the man called Sinner."

"Why don't you just shoot yourself in the head now and get it over with?" said Cathy.

THREE

Dealing with Reasonable Men

And so I walked out into the Nightside, looking for an honest oracle. There's never any shortage of people who don't want to be found, especially in the Nightside, and I don't like to use my special gift unless I absolutely have to. My enemies still want me dead, and I shine so very brightly in the dark when I open my third eye, my private eye. Fortunately, there's also no shortage of people (and things that never were and never will be people) who specialise in Knowing Things that other people don't want known. There are those who claim to know the secrets of the past, the present, and the future; but most are only in it for the money, most of the rest can't be trusted, and they all have their own agendas. Sucker bait will never go out of fashion in the Nightside. But luckily I was once offered, as payment for a successfully completed case, the location of one of the few honest oracles left in this spiritual cesspool. The long centuries had left the creature eccentric, garrulous, prone to gossip, and not too tightly wrapped, but I suppose that goes with the territory.

I left Uptown behind me and headed back into the old main drag, where business puts on its best bib and tucker, and tarts itself up for the travelling trade. All the gaudiest establishments and tourist traps, where sin is mass-produced, and temptation comes in six-packs. In short, I was heading for the Nightside's one and only shopping mall. Mass brands and franchises from the outside world tended to roll over and die here, where people's appetites run more to the unusual and outré, but there's always the exception. The Mammon Emporium offers brand-name concessions and fast-food chains from alternative universes and divergent timetracks. There may be nothing new under the sun, but the sun never shines in the Nightside.

I strolled between the huge M and E that marked the entrance to the mall, and for once nobody crossed themselves, or headed for the nearest exit. The Mammon Emporium was one of the few places where I could hope to be just another face in the crowd. Shoppers from all kinds of Londons came here in search of the fancy and the forbidden, and, of course, that chance for a once-in-a-lifetime bargain. People dressed in a hundred different outrageous styles called out to each other in as many different languages and argots, crowding the thoroughfares and window-shopping sights they'd never find anywhere else. Brightly coloured come-ons blazed from every store, their windows full of wonders, and countless businesses crammed in side by side in a mall that somehow managed to be bigger on the inside than it was on the outside. Apparently space expands to encompass the trade involved.

To every side of me blazed signs and logos from far and distant places. MCCAMPBELL'S DOLPHIN BURGERS. STARDOCK'S SNUFF. WILL DIZZY'S MORTIMER MOUSE. BAPTISMS R US. PERV PARLOUR. SOUL MARKET; new, used and refurbished. And of course the NOSFERATU BLOOD BANK. (Come in and make a deposit. Give generously. Don't make us come looking for you.) A dark-haired Goth girl in a crimson basque gave me the eye from the shadowy doorway. I smiled politely and continued on my way.

Right in the middle of the mall stood an old-fashioned wishing well, largely ignored by the crowds that bustled unseeingly past it. The well didn't look like much. Just a traditional stone-walled well with a circle of stunted grass around it, a red slate roof above, and a bucket on a rusty steel chain. A sign in really twee writing invited you to toss a coin in the well and make a wish. Just a little bit of harmless fun for the kiddies. Except this was the Nightside, which has never gone in for harmless fun. Most oracles are a joke. The concept of alternate timetracks (as seen every day in the Nightside's spontaneously generating Time-slips) makes prophecy largely unprofitable and knocks the idea of Fate very firmly on the head. But this particular oracle had a really good track record in predicting the present; in knowing what was going on everywhere, right now. I suppose specialisation is everything, these days. I leaned against the well's stone wall and looked casually about me. No-one seemed to be paying me or the well any special attention.

"Hello, oracle," I said. "What's happening?"

"More than you can possibly imagine," said a deep, bubbling voice from a long way below. "Bless me with coin of silver, oh passing traveller, and I shall bless thee with three answers to any question. The first answer shall be explicit but unhelpful, the second allusive but accurate, and the third a wild stab in the dark. The more you spend, the more you learn."

"Don't give me that crap," I said. "I'm not a tourist. This is John Taylor."

"Oh bloody hell; you're back again, are you?" The oracle sounded distinctly sulky. "You know very well your whole existence makes my head ache."

"You haven't got a head."

"Exactly! It's people like you that give oracles a bad reputation. What do you want? I'm busy."

"What with?" I asked, honestly curious.

"Trust me, you really don't want to know. You think it's easy being the fount of all wisdom, when your walls are covered with algae? And I hate Timeslips! They're like haemorrhoids for an oracle. And speaking of pains in the arse; what do you want, Taylor?"

"I'm looking for the man called Madman."

"Oh God; he's even worse than you. He'd turn my stomach, if I had one. What do you want with him?"

"Don't you know?"

The oracle sniffed haughtily. "That's right, make fun of a cripple. At least I can see where he is, unlike you. But this answer will cost you. No information for free; that's the rule. Don't blame me, I just work here. Until the curse finally wears off; then I will be out of here so fast it'll make your head spin."

"All right," I said. "How many drops of blood for a straight answer?"

"Just the one, for you, sweet prince," the oracle said, its voice suddenly ingratiating. "And remember me, when you come into your kingdom."

I looked down into the shadows of the well. "You've heard something."

"Maybe I have, maybe I haven't," the oracle said smugly. "Take advantage of my sweet nature, before the price goes up."

I jabbed my thumb with a pin and let a single fat drop of blood fall into the well, which made a soft, ugly, satisfied noise.

"You'll find Madman at the Hotel Clappe," it said briskly. "In the short-time district. Watch your back there, and don't talk to any of the strange women, unless you're collecting infections. Now get the hell out of here; my head is splitting. And *carpe* that old *diem*, John Taylor. It's later than anyone thinks."

The Hotel Clappe, spelled that way to give it that extra bit of class, looked just like it sounded; the kind of dirty, disgusting dump where you rented rooms by the hour, and a fresh pair of sheets was a luxury. Good-time girls and others stalked their prey in the underlit streets, and the crabs were so big they leapt out of dark alleyways to mug passersby. Appearance was everything, and buyer beware. But there will always be those for whom sex is no fun unless it's seedy, dirty, and just a bit dangerous, so . . . I walked down the street of red lamps looking determinedly straight ahead and keeping my hands very firmly to myself. In areas like this, the twilight daughters could be scarier and more dangerous than most of the more obvious monsters in the Nightside. Depressingly enough, an awful lot of them seemed to know my name.

The Hotel Clappe was just another flaky-painted establishment in the middle of a long, terraced row, and no-one had bothered to repaint the sign over the door in years. I pushed the door open with one hand, wishing I'd thought to bring some gloves with me, and strode into the lobby, trying to look like a building inspector or someone else with a legitimate reason to be there. The lobby was just as foul and unclean as I expected, and the carpet crunched under my feet. A few individuals of debatable sexuality looked up from their gossip magazines as I entered, but looked quickly away again as they recognised me.

I wasn't entirely sure what Madman was doing in a place like this. I didn't think he cared any more about sane and everyday things like sex or pleasure. But then, I suppose to him one place was as good as any other. And it was a good area to hide out. It wasn't the kind of place you came to unless you had definite business here.

A couple of elfin hookers made way for me as I approached the hotel clerk, protected from his world by a heavy steel grille. The elves looked me over with bold mascaraed eyes, and gave me their best professional smiles. Their wings looked a bit crumpled, but they still had a certain gaudy glamour. I smiled and shook my head, and they actually looked a bit relieved. God alone knew what my reputation had transmuted into, down here. Certainly the clerk behind his grille didn't look at all pleased to see me. He was a short sturdy type, in grubby trousers and a string vest, a sour face, and eyes that had seen everything. Behind him a sign said simply YOU TOUCH IT, YOU PAY FOR IT. The clerk spat juicily into a cuspidor, and regarded me with a flat, indifferent face.

"I don't do questions," he said, in a grey toneless voice. "Not even for the infamous John Taylor. See nothing, know nothing; all part of the job. You don't scare me. We get worse than you coming in here every day. And the grille's charmed, cursed, and electrified, so don't get any ideas."

"And here I am, come to do you a favour," I said cheerfully, carefully unimpressed by his manner. "I've come to take Madman away with me."

"Oh thank God," said the clerk, his manner changing in a moment. He leaned forward, his face suddenly pleading, almost pathetic. "Please get him out of here. You don't know what it's like, having him around.

The screams and the howls and the rains of blood. The rooms that change position and the doors that suddenly don't go anywhere. He scares the johns. He even scares the girls, and I didn't think there was anything left that could do that. My nerves will never be the same again. He's giving the hotel a really bad reputation."

"I would have thought that was an advantage, in an area like this," I said.

"Just get Madman out of here. Please."

"We'd be ever so grateful," said one of the elfin hookers, pushing her bosoms out at me.

I declined her offer with all the politeness at my command, and the clerk gave me a room number on the second floor. The elevator wasn't working, of course, so I trudged up the stairs. Bare stone steps and no railing, the walls painted industrial grey. I could feel Madman's room long before I got anywhere near it. Like a wild beast, lying in wait around a corner. The feeling grew stronger as I moved warily out onto the second floor. Madman's room lay ahead of me, like a visit to the dentist, like a doctor bearing bad news. The air was bitter cold, my breath steaming thickly before me. I could feel my heart pounding fast in my chest. I walked slowly down the empty corridor, leaning forward slightly, as though forcing my way against an unseen pressure. All my instincts were screaming at me to get out while I still could.

I stopped outside the door. The number matched the one the clerk had given me, but I would have recognised it anyway. The room felt like the pain that wakes you in the middle of the night and makes you think awful words like *tumour* and *poison*. It felt like the death of a loved one, or the tone in your lover's voice as she tells you she's leaving you for someone else. The room felt like horror and tragedy, and the slow unravelling of everything you ever held true. Except it wasn't the room. It was Madman.

I didn't know his name. His true, original name. I don't suppose even he did, any more. Names imply an identity and a history, and Madman had torn those up long ago. Now he was a sad, perilous, confused gentleman who had only a nodding relationship with reality. Anyone's reality. What drove him mad in the first place, insane beyond any help or hope of rescue, is a well-known story in the Nightside, and one of the most disturbing. Back in the sixties, Madman was an acid sorcerer, a guru to Timothy Leary, and one of NASA's leading scientists. A genius, with many patents to his name, and an insatiable appetite for knowledge. By the end of the sixties, he'd moved from outer space to inner space, to mysticism and mathematical description theory. He studied and researched for many years, exploring the more esoteric areas of arcane information, trying to discover a way to view Reality as it actually is, rather than the way we all perceive it, through our limited human minds and senses.

Somehow, he found a way to See past the comfortable collective illusion we all live in, and look directly at what lies beneath or beyond the world we know. Whatever it was he Saw in that endless moment, it destroyed his sanity, then and forever. Either because baseline Reality was so much worse, or so much better, than what we believe reality to be. Unbelievable horror or beauty, I suppose both are equally upsetting ideas. These days Madman lives in illusions, and doesn't care. The difference between him and us is that he can sometimes choose his illusions. Though sometimes, they choose him.

Madman can be extremely dangerous to be around. He doesn't believe what he sees is real, so for him it isn't. Around him, the world follows his whims and wishes, his fears and his doubts, reality reordering itself to follow his drifting thoughts. Which can be helpful, or confusing, or scary, because he doesn't necessarily believe in you, either. He can change your personality or your history without your even noticing. And people who annoy or threaten him sufficiently tend to get turned into things. Very unpleasant things. So mostly people just let him wander wherever he wants to go and do whatever he feels like doing. It's safer that way. It helps that Madman doesn't want to do much. People who try to use him tend to come to bad ends.

And here I was standing outside his door, breathing hard, sweating, clenching my hands into fists as I tried to summon up the courage to knock. I was taking a hell of a risk in talking to him, and I knew it. I hadn't been this scared since I faced up to Jessica Sorrow the Unbeliever; and I'd had a sort of weapon to use against her. All I had to set against Madman were my wits and my quick thinking. And even I wouldn't have bet on me. Still, at least Madman came with his own warning signals. For reasons probably not even known to himself, Madman came complete with his own personal sound track; music from nowhere that echoed his moods and intentions. If you paid attention to the changes in style, you could learn things.

I stood before his door, one hand raised to knock. It was like standing before the door to a raging furnace, or maybe a plague ward. Open at your own risk. I took a deep breath, knocked smartly, announced my name in a loud but very polite voice, then opened the door and walked into Madman's room. From somewhere I could hear Nilsson's "Everybody's Talking at Me."

The room was far bigger than it should have been, though its shape was strangely uncertain. Instead of the pokey little crib I'd expected, it was more like a suite, with a huge bed, antique furniture, and all kinds of luxurious trappings. And all of it covered in glitter and shimmering lights. Everywhere I looked the details were all just that little bit off, subtly *wrong*. The angles between walls and floor didn't add up, the ceiling seemed to recede in uncomfortable directions, and there was no obvious source for the painfully bright light. Objects seemed to change, slumping and transmuting when I wasn't looking at them directly. The floor was solid beneath my feet, but it felt like I was standing over a precipice. Every sound in the room was dull and distant, as though I was underwater. I stood very still, concentrating on why I was there, because it felt as though I might alter and drift away if I lost my grip on who and what I was, even for a moment.

This was why people didn't like being around Madman.

He was lying on top of the covers on his oversized bed, looking small and lost. He was a squat and blocky man, with a heavy grey beard. His eyes as he suddenly sat up and looked at me didn't track properly, and there was something wild and desperate in his gaze. He looked tired and sad, like a dog that's been punished and doesn't know why. He was wearing what he always wore; a black T-shirt over grubby jeans. He always wore the same because he couldn't be bothered with inconsequential things like clothes. Or washing, by the smell of him.

All the walls in the room were covered in lines and lines of scrawled mathematical equations. They manifested wherever he stayed, apparently without Madman's noticing or caring, and they disappeared shortly after he left. No-one had ever been able to make any sense out of them, though many had tried. Just as well, probably. Madman looked at something just behind my shoulder. I didn't turn to look. Whatever he was Seeing, I was pretty sure I didn't want to see it. After a moment, Madman's gaze drifted away, and I relaxed slightly. All around us, the room was changing in subtle ways, moving with his mood as he adjusted to my presence. Shadows were gathering in the room's corners. Deep, dark shadows, with things moving in them. Things that had the simple awful threat of the monsters we see in childhood nightmares.

"Hello, Madman," I said, in a calm and neutral tone. "It's John Taylor. Remember? We've met at Strangefellows a few times, and at the Tourniquet Club. We have a mutual friend in Razor Eddie. Remember?"

"No," Madman said sadly, in his low breathy voice. "But then, I rarely remember anyone. It's safer that way. I know you, though. I know you, John Taylor. Oh yes. Very dangerous. Bad blood. I think if I really remembered you . . . I'd be frightened."

The thought that someone like Madman could be frightened of me was distinctly worrying, on all sorts of levels, but I pushed the thought aside to concentrate on more immediate problems. Like getting through the conversation without being changed or killed, and, somehow, persuading Madman to work with me.

"I'm going in search of the origins of the Nightside," I said. "I could use your help. And maybe along the way, we might find someone, or something, who could help you."

"No-one can help me," said Madman. "I can't even help myself." He cocked his head on one side to regard me, like a bird. "Why would you want my help, John Taylor?" He sounded almost rational, and I pressed the advantage while it lasted.

"Even I'm not strong enough to take on or bluff some of the Beings I'm going to have to talk to," I said. "So I thought I'd take you along to confuse the issue. And maybe to hide behind."

"That makes sense," said Madman, nodding in an almost normal manner. "All right, I'll go with you. I think I've been lying here for months, thinking about things, and I'm almost sure I'm bored. Yes, I'll go with you. I'm always looking for something to distract me. To keep my mind occupied, so it won't go wandering off in . . . unfortunate directions. I'm more scared of me than you'll ever be. Let's go."

He swung down off the bed, his movements strangely unconnected. Standing up, he was almost as tall as I, but he seemed much heavier, as though he weighed more heavily on the world. The shadows in the corners had retreated, for the moment. Madman headed for the door, and I followed him out of the room, carefully not looking back. His sound track was playing something jazzy, heavy on the saxophone. As I closed the door, I glanced back into the room, just for a moment. It was a small, pokey room, dark and dirty and thick with dust and cobwebs. Clearly it hadn't been used in years. Something was lying on the bed. It started to sit up, and I shut the door firmly and stepped back. Madman was looking at me patiently, so I led the way to the stairs and down into the lobby. People saw us step out into the lobby and scurried to get out of our way. And so together, Madman and I went out into the Nightside in search of the man called Sinner.

Sinner was another man whose story was well-known in the Nightside, which collects legends and tragedies the way a dog has fleas. Nothing is known about Sinner's early life, but at some point the man who would be known as Sinner made the decision to sell his soul to the Devil. So he studied the subject carefully, made all the correct preparations, and called Satan up out of the Pit. Not one of his demons, or even a fallen angel, but the Ancient Enemy himself. History and literature are full of stories showing why this is always a really bad idea, but Sinner apparently believed he knew what he was doing. He called up the Devil, bound it to a pleasant form, then said he wanted to sell his soul. And when the Devil asked Sinner what he wanted in return, the man said, *True love*. The Devil was somewhat taken aback by this, and apparently remarked that True love wasn't really his line of business. But the man insisted, and a deal is a deal, so . . . The contract was signed in blood, and in return for his immortal soul, the man was promised ten years with the woman of his dreams.

The Devil said, Go to this bar, at this time, and she will be waiting for you. Then he laughed, and disappeared. The man went to the bar at the appointed time and did indeed meet the woman of his dreams. He fell in love with her, and she with him, and soon they were married. They enjoyed ten very happy years together, then, when the ten years were up, the Devil rose up on the last stroke of midnight, to claim the man's soul, and drag it down to Hell. The man nodded, and said; *It was worth it, to know True love.* And the Devil said, *It was all a lie. The woman was just a demon, one of mine, a succubus who only pretended to care for you, as she has cared for so many men before you.* The man said, *It doesn't matter. I loved her, and always will.* The Devil shrugged, and took the man away.

And so the man became the only soul in Hell who still loved. Despite what he knew, despite everything that was done to him; defiantly and stubbornly, he still loved. The Devil couldn't have that; it was corrupting the atmosphere. So in the end he had no choice but to throw the man out of Hell and back into the land of the living. And Heaven wouldn't take the man, because, after all, he'd made a deal with the Devil. So the man came to the Nightside, to walk its neon streets forever, neither properly living nor dead, denied by Heaven and by Hell. The man called Sinner.

He was an amiable enough sort, but most people kept well clear of him. Because he wasn't really alive, he cast no shadow, and because he couldn't die again, he was pretty much impervious to attack. He could do anything without fear of punishment, so he imposed a strict moral code upon himself. Which meant he only did really appalling things when he felt he absolutely had to. Good and Evil were beyond him, or perhaps beneath him. Mostly he kept himself to himself, and Bad Things happened to people who pestered him. A popular urban legend said that if he did enough good deeds, or bad deeds, he would be able to work his way back into Heaven or Hell. Opinion remained divided as to which direction he favoured.

I headed for Sinner's favourite haunt, the Prospero and Michael Scott Memorial Library. Madman trailed along behind me, humming along to his sound track and frightening the passersby. Sinner was often to be found at the Library, researching various projects that he always declined to discuss. People had driven themselves half-crazy just from trying to make sense of the list of books he'd read. I think he just liked to keep his mind occupied. Madman brooded, Sinner studied. It all came down to the same thing; not thinking about the one thing they couldn't stop thinking about.

I'd already phoned ahead, to make sure Sinner was there. The librarian had said, *Oh yes, he's here.* And, *If you're coming in, Mr. Taylor, could you please return our one and only copy of Baron Frankenstein's* I Did It My Way? *It's long overdue.* I made soothing noises, signed off, and tried to remember where I'd last seen the bloody book. I was back using a mobile phone again, with misgivings. There are all kinds of dangers to using a cell phone in the Nightside, from strange voices in the aether, pop-up voice mail offering services you really didn't want, and the occasional leaking infodump from another dimension. And, of course, the phone made it far too easy for people to pinpoint your exact location. But the damn things are just so bloody useful . . . Cathy had promised me this new version came with all kinds of built-in protection charms and defences, so I just mentally crossed my fingers every time I had to use it and hoped for the best.

I kept Madman close at hand as we descended into the depths of the Library, and found Sinner at his usual place in the Research Section, sitting alone and poring over an old leather-bound volume. Tall stacks of books led off in every direction, like a literary maze, and the air was heavy with that distinctive old-book smell. The lighting was clear and distinct but never overpowering, and there were signs everywhere admonishing SILENCE! Discreet signs also pointed you in the direction of books on every subject under the night, some of them adding pointedly AT YOUR OWN RISK. Scholars sat at study at their separate desks, ignoring each other, immersed in their work, as devoted in their attention as old-time monks in their cells. I headed straight for Sinner, down the narrow book-lined aisles, Madman ambling along behind me. Sinner looked up as I loomed over him, and nodded thoughtfully. He was a short, compact, and very neat man in his mid forties, looking very much like a civil servant doomed always to be passed over for promotion. Middle-aged, middle weight, almost anonymous. But as his eyes met mine, his gaze was unnervingly bright, and his smile was actually disturbing. Sinner had been around, and it showed. When he finally spoke, his voice was soft and polite.

"Well, well, John Taylor. I had a feeling I'd be seeing you today, so I just sat here, reading an old favourite, and waited for you."

I looked at the book open on the table before him. It was a Bible, the old King James edition. I raised an eyebrow.

Sinner smiled. "As a wise man once said, Looking for loopholes."

All around us, people were getting up, gathering up their books and papers, and heading for the exit. It could have been Madman's presence, or mine, or perhaps the two of us and Sinner were just too worrying to bear. I couldn't honestly say I blamed any of them. A handful of really hard-core scholars held their ground, hunched protectively over their learned tomes, determined not to be driven off. You have to be pretty tough-minded, to be a scholar in the Nightside. Madman strolled off through the stacks, and the spines of the books on the shelves rippled, changing shape and texture as he passed, affected by his proximity. I had to wonder what new information those transformed books held now; and if I were to take them down and open them, would I find nonsense and gibberish, or perhaps awful wisdom and terrible secrets? I decided I didn't want to know, either way.

And then I was distracted as a lovely young thing came tripping out of the stacks, hugging a tall pile of books in her arms. She was a tall blonde teenager in an English public school uniform, complete with starched white blouse, black miniskirt and stockings, sensible shoes, and a straw boater perched on the back on her perfect head. She was bright and cheerful, heart-stoppingly pretty, far too shapely for her own good, or anyone else's, and moved with all the unrealised elegance of youth. She had a pink rosebud mouth, and eyes so dark they seemed to fall away forever. I stood up straighter and pulled my stomach in, but she flashed me only the briefest of smiles before swaying past me to put the books down on Sinner's desk. I suddenly realised Madman's sound track was playing "Tubular Bells."

"Allow me to introduce you," said Sinner, in his soft patient voice. "This is my girl-fiend. The demon succubus I fell in love with, all those years ago. I have no idea what you see when you look at her, because it is her nature to appear to everyone as the image of what they secretly most desire."

I wasn't sure if I liked what that said about me. Too many St. Trinians films in my impressionable youth, I suppose. I nodded and smiled politely to the succubus, who pouted her lips briefly as she sat on the corner of Sinner's desk, crossing her long legs to show them off. I had to wrench my gaze away. The pheromones were so thick on the air you could practically see them. It occurred to me that Sinner hadn't said what she looked like to him. Madman wandered back, gave the girl a hard look, shook his head, and wandered off again. I really didn't feel like asking what he might have Seen.

"These are the books you wanted, Sidney," said the succubus, in a rich smoky voice. "Anything else you want, just ask." She arched her back prettily, so that her breasts thrust out against the starched blouse. My mouth was very dry, and I could feel my heart heading for overdrive.

"Her name translates from the original Aramaic as Pretty Poison,"

Sinner observed calmly. "There are some quite specific verses about her in the Dead Sea Scrolls, none of them complimentary. In the War against Heaven, she killed more than her fair share of angels, and even she doesn't remember how many men she destroyed as a succubus, in her war against Humanity. Watch your manners around her, and never turn your back on her. I love her dearly, but she's still a demon. And by the way— she's the only one who gets to call me Sidney."

I nodded respectfully to the succubus. "How is it that thou art out of Hell?"

Pretty Poison shrugged charmingly. "I couldn't believe that any mortal could truly love me, knowing what I am. Want me, yes, that is my function, to tempt the sinner into damnation, to throw away his immortal soul for the transitory delights of the flesh. But actually to love me, as Sidney did, even knowing the truth, even in the depths of the Inferno; that was a new thing, even in my long existence. So I came back up, out of the Pit, to be with him. Ostensibly I am here as an agent of Evil, to tempt and corrupt him again, so that the Devil can rightly reclaim his soul. But actually, I came back to be with Sidney, to try and understand this thing called . . . true love."

"So you say," I said. "But then, to paraphrase another great thinker, you would say that, wouldn't you?"

She looked at me, still smiling, but her eyes were cold, cold. "Did you ever let your lover see the stranger in your soul? All the dark, petty, hidden things you never admit, even to yourself? Did you ever bind yourself utterly to another person, even in the hottest fires of the Inferno? My Sidney did. I have never known such a thing before. There is no love, in Hell. That's why it's Hell. I need to know why he feels the way he feels about me. I need to understand, even if I don't know why."

"But you've known so many men," I said.

"Oh yes," said Pretty Poison. "You have no idea how many, and none of them ever meant a damned thing to me. They said they loved me, here on Earth, but down in the sunless lands they all sang a different tune. They would have betrayed me a hundred times over, for just one more moment of life and light. I never mattered a damn to any of them. Sidney . . . is different."

"Pretty Poison was the only one of her kind not to take part in the recent angel war over the Nightside," Sinner said mildly. "Because I asked her not to. Make of that what you will. Now, word travels quickly in the Nightside. And the word is, you've been hired to investigate the true beginnings of the Nightside. By no less a Being than the mercurial Lady Luck herself. You do mix with the most interesting people, John. I have to say, the true nature and purpose of the Nightside is a mystery that has long fascinated me. Do I take it you wish me to accompany you on this most dangerous of quests?"

"Got it in one," I said. "With you and Madman as human shields, I might get through this case alive after all. If I can drag you away from your vital researches, of course . . ."

Sinner closed the Bible and drummed his fingers on the cover. "My only hope of ever getting into Heaven lies in doing good deeds," he said flatly. "And I mean really impressive, major good deeds. I think keeping you alive in the face of all the really nasty Powers and Dominations who will undoubtedly try to kill you should qualify as good deeds above and beyond the call of duty."

"But what about me, Sidney?" said Pretty Poison. "You wouldn't leave me behind, would you? You know we can only be together forever in Hell."

Sinner smiled, and patted her hand fondly. "I wouldn't go to Heaven without you. Because if you weren't there, it wouldn't be Heaven."

"Dear Sidney." She leaned over, kissed him on the forehead, and tousled his hair with a lazy finger.

Sinner fixed me with a firm stare. "If I go with you on your quest, Pretty Poison comes with me. I will not be parted from her."

"Hell, I'm bringing Madman," I said. "The more firepower, the better."

"I heard that," said Madman, from deep in the stacks. "I am not firepower. I am a deterrent."

"The truth concerning the origins of the Nightside is long buried," Sinner said thoughtfully. "Probably with good cause. It stands to reason that an appalling place like this would have a truly awful beginning. The roots of the Nightside are almost certainly soaked in blood and suffering. You must understand, John—should the secrets we discover pose a threat to the safety and stability of the people of the Nightside, I could not allow them to be made public. Above all, I always strive to do no harm. Is this an acceptable condition to you?"

"Of course," I said. "I only report to my client, in this case Lady Luck. What she might do with the information afterwards is something you and she would have to sort out between you. Is that acceptable to you?"

He nodded, and we all smiled at each other in a very civilised way. Behind the smiles, I was quietly seething. Having Pretty Poison along struck me as a really bad idea. Things were going to be complicated enough without having a demon succubus from Hell peering over my shoulder. (Assuming I ever was stupid enough to turn my back on her.) But it was clear her presence was a deal-breaker for Sinner, so I had no choice but to agree, for now. Maybe we could use her for defusing booby-traps.

"Oh dear," Sinner said abruptly, rising to his feet. "I do believe something bad is about to happen."

I looked quickly about me. "What makes you say that?"

"Because Madman's music has just got all tense and dramatic."

He was right. It had. And thirteen men in smart city suits were strolling arrogantly through the Library stacks towards us. A Devil's Dozen of proud, purposeful-looking men, all of them heading straight for me. The few remaining scholars were gathering up their papers and fading away into the surrounding stacks with remarkable speed and dexterity. Even the Library staff were making themselves scarce. They didn't want anything to do with what was about to happen, and I didn't blame them. I knew who these thirteen men were. These were Walker's famous, or more properly infamous, *I Mean Business* people—the legendary Reasonable Men. So called because Walker sent them out to reason with people who were causing the Authorities particular concern.

Every one of the Reasonable Men was a refined gentleman, in an immaculate suit set off by the old-school tie, moving with that calm, arrogant grace that only comes from centuries of breeding and lording it over the peasants. Some of them looked around the Library and sniffed superciliously, as though they were slumming just by being there; and perhaps they were. I didn't underestimate them just because they didn't have a chin among them and looked like a bunch of upper-class twits. The Reasonable Men were all trained combat magicians. Their leader crashed to a halt right in front of me and tilted his head back the better to look down his nose at me.

Jimmy Hadleigh, the professional snob, had a lot of nose to look down, and cold blue eyes that surely only the truly unkind would point out were just that little bit too close together. Otherwise handsome, with jet-black hair, his mouth came with a built-in sneer. He wore a splendidly cut suit, and smart grey gloves, so he wouldn't get his hands dirty. We knew each other. In passing. We'd never got on, partly because he considered himself an authority figure, and mostly because I considered him an overbearing little shit. Walker must be really upset with me if he'd unleashed Jimmy Hadleigh and his dogs. He looked at Sinner, Pretty Poison, and Madman, and dismissed them all with one flick of a perfect eyebrow.

"Oh God, Jimmy," I said. "Teach me how to do that with just one eyebrow. It's so damned impressive."

"Taylor, dear boy," said Jimmy, in his best icy drawl, ignoring my attempts at humour as he always did. "I knew Walker would send me after you one of these days. Always poking your proletarian nose into the business of your betters. But now it seems you've really upset our revered lords and masters, and Walker has decided he doesn't love you any more. You're to come with us. Right now. Be a good boy and do as you're told. Because if you don't come along quietly, I'm afraid we've been authorised to do severely unpleasant things to you and bring you along anyway. Guess which way we'd prefer."

The Reasonable Men chuckled quietly behind him, striking casual aristocratic poses and making lazy magical gestures with their long, slender fingers. No-one was ever that languid by accident, the affected little mommy's boys. I still didn't underestimate them. A sense of power only barely held in check hung about them, ready to be released at any moment. Combat magicians were trained to take on major players. They were serious, dangerous people, so of course I just leaned back against a stack, crossed my arms, and sneered back at them. The day I couldn't out-think and outwit a bunch of pompous public school punks, I'd retire. I'd run rings around Powers and Dominations in my day. I was pleased to see some of the smiles disappear from their faces as it became clear I wasn't going to come quietly and that I wasn't impressed by their reputation. I just hoped they were secretly impressed by mine.

"Good to see you again, Jimmy," I said. "You're looking very inbred today. So, the Authorities don't want the origins of the Nightside investigated? Well, tough, because I'm going to do it anyway. If only because I want to know. Pardon me if I indulge in a little name-dropping, but I was hired by Lady Luck herself, and my companions here are Sinner and Madman. Which basically means I outnumber you. So you run off back to Walker, Jimmy, like the good little errand boy you are, and tell him John Taylor declines to be bothered, bullied, intimidated, or interfered with. And be quick about it, before I think of something amusing to do to you."

Several of the Reasonable Men shifted uneasily, but Jimmy Hadleigh didn't so much as flinch. "How very tedious," he murmured. "I've never believed any of the things they say about you, Taylor. You're just a dreary little man with a good line in bluff and deceit. We, however, are the real thing. So now we get to do this the hard way, and you only have yourself to blame." He looked at Sinner. "You—stay out of this. Return to your books and your brooding. We're not here for you."

Sinner laughed softly. "Walker would have to send a lot better than you, to take me anywhere against my will. And unfortunately for you, John is under my protection. Because I've decided I want to know the secret origins of the Nightside, too."

"Stand back," said Jimmy Hadleigh, and his voice was very cold.

"I have seen much scarier things than you, in my time," said Sinner. "Run away, little man. While you still can."

Two bright red spots of pure fury appeared on Jimmy's pale cheeks at being so openly defied, and he stabbed one hand at Sinner in a mystical gesture, deadly energies sparking and spitting on the air. I decided things had gone far enough, and kicked Jimmy in the balls. His eyes bulged, and he bent sharply forward at the waist, as though bowing to me. And Pretty Poison stepped forward and ripped Jimmy's head right off his shoulders. No-one threatened her Sinner and got away with it while she was around. She kissed the head on its slack lips, then tossed it aside. The headless body sank to its knees, its hands twitching aimlessly, while blood fountained from the ragged stump of the neck. Stray magics discharged harmlessly around the body, and blood splashed against the surrounding bookshelves. Sinner looked reproachfully at Pretty Poison, who just shrugged prettily.

The Reasonable Men were crying out in shock and horror and anger, only to fall silent as Sinner and I turned to look at them. Their faces froze with angry determination, and their hands snapped through mystical designs, throwing magic at us. The first spells discharged harmlessly around Sinner, and backfired horribly on a few of the spell-casters, turning them inside out. Red and purple horrors collapsed to the Library floor, squirting blood and inner liquids onto the dusty air. Other magics homed in on Pretty Poison, who snatched them out of mid air and ate them up, grinning like a naughty schoolgirl. She was a fallen angel and older than the world, and the minor magics of men were nothing to her.

I pulled a pair of chaos dice from my coat's inner pocket and tossed them into the midst of the Reasonable Men; and suddenly everything that could go wrong for them did. Spells misfired, muscles spasmed, and they fell over each other like clowns. One of them drew a heavy handgun, its gleaming steel acid-etched with potent runes and sigils. He fired it at Sinner. The bullet punched a neat hole in Sinner's chest, but no blood flowed. He stood looking down at the hole for a moment, almost sadly, then he looked at the shocked Reasonable Man.

"Magic guns? I have known the torments of Hell, boy. But still, you really shouldn't have done that. It wasn't respectful. Pretty Poison?"

"Of course, darling Sidney."

And Pretty Poison surged forward, moving almost too quickly for human eyes to follow. She raged among the Reasonable Men, tearing them, literally, limb from limb with awful, impossible strength, laughing breathily all the while. Some tried to run, but she was quicker. While they were distracted, I put my back up against a towering bookshelf, slammed my weight against it, and overturned the whole damn thing onto two of the Reasonable Men. The great weight crushed them mercilessly to the floor, and they didn't move again. And almost as quickly as that, it was over. It was quiet again in the Library, the loudest sound the slow dripping of blood from various surfaces. The Reasonable Men were all dead. It wasn't what I wanted; but this was the kind of thing that happened when you allied yourself with people like Sinner and Pretty Poison. She was looking around at all the terrible things she'd done and smiling brightly. I looked around for Madman and found that even he'd got involved, in the end. Somewhere along the way he'd decided he was in a Samurai film. He was wearing a kimono and standing over a dead Reasonable Man with a bloody katana in his hands. He'd chopped the poor bastard into bits. He looked down at the scattered bloody pieces before him and scowled balefully.

"Well? Have you had enough? Answer me!"

It would have been funny, if the man hadn't been so very dead.

Pretty Poison came tripping daintily between the corpses to embrace her Sinner and make sure he was okay. He looked sadly at her, and at all the things she'd done, but said nothing. Pretty Poison snuggled up against him, not even breathing hard. She noticed there was blood on her hands, and sucked the blood off her fingers one by one, savouring it. She saw the disappointment in Sinner's face and pouted like a child.

"I'm sorry, Sidney, but no-one gets to hurt you while I'm around. And after all, a girl has to follow her impulses."

Sinner sighed and looked out over the scattered bodies. "We should have left one alive, to take a message back to Walker."

"Oh, I think he'll get the message," I said. "Thirteen dead combat magicians makes for one hell of a powerful statement. Walker . . . is not going to be pleased about this."

"Good," said Madman, back in his old clothes again. "Never liked the man. He tried to have me locked up once. Well, several times, actually."

"Still," I said, thinking it through, "Perhaps I'd better go and have a word with him, smooth things over. Or he and his various bully boys will be haunting us every step of the way. Yes, I'll go and talk with the man. I know how to handle Walker."

"Should we come with you?" said Sinner.

"I think I'll do better alone," I said. "This calls for diplomacy, fast-talking, and an outrageous amount of bluffing. Not blood and guts all over the carpet. And I can't have him thinking I need other people to back me up when I talk with him. Walker notices things like that. So keep Madman here with you and try to keep him out of trouble till I get back."

Sinner winced. "Please. Don't be long."

*　*　*

I made my way out of the Library, smiling apologetically at the various members of staff I passed, and called Cathy at my office, to see if she knew where Walker might be found, just at the moment.

"Oh sure," she said almost immediately. "No problem. I'll just check the computers. We subscribe to a service that keeps constant track on all the real movers and shakers in the Nightside, and lets us know where they are at any given moment, through constant updating."

"We do?" I said.

"I knew you weren't paying attention at my last briefing! Honestly, John, you never listen to a thing I say . . . Now, Walker, Walker . . . Ah yes. He's currently dining at his Club. Alone. Anything else I can do for you? How are you getting on with Sinner and Madman?"

"It's been . . . interesting," I said, and hung up. I didn't want to worry her.

FOUR

Warning Shots

Going to see Walker is a lot like visiting the dentist; it may be necessary, but it's never going to be much fun. Walker, that quiet and refined gentleman in his neat city suit, is the public face of the Authorities, those shadowy background forces who run things in the Nightside, inasmuch as anybody does, or can. Walker always seems to know everything that's going on in the Nightside; but if that were really true, he'd have had me arrested, suppressed, or killed long ago. Still, sending the Reasonable Men to haul me away by main force was certainly a new step in our complicated relationship. He'd never hesitated to threaten or even blackmail me in the past, when he wanted me to do something dangerous and expendable for him, or just as often, stop me doing whatever it was I was already up to. But sending the Reasonable Men—that was just downright nasty.

There are many private and even secretive Clubs in the Nightside, and nearly all of them are clustered together in a very discreet and select area called, not surprisingly, Clubland. A quiet little square in a quiet little neighbourhood, regularly patrolled and even better guarded. These Clubs exist to provide secure meeting places for the kind of groups whose beliefs or practices are so extreme that the outside world wouldn't tolerate their existence for one moment. The Clubs provide a haven for those of like tastes to band together, protect their interests, and pool their information. And do the things they need to do, behind securely locked doors. These Clubs aren't about religion; you find that on the Street of the Gods. And they're not about sex; you can find that anywhere in the Nightside. No, these Clubs are strictly for the distinct and the damned. For example: The Tribes of the Night, a Club whose membership consists solely of vampires, werewolves, and ghouls. (No half-breeds.) Then there's Club Dead, exclusively for the many creations of Baron Von Frankenstein and his descendants, who have been very busy bunnies since the nineteenth century, with varying degrees of skill and success. (Club motto: We belong Dead.) And, of course, Club Life, for all the various forms of immortal. (Club dues are paid thanks to the miracle of compound interest.) Club motto: Live forever, or die trying. The old jokes are always the best.

Walker belonged to the oldest, proudest, and most select Gentleman's Club in the history of the Nightside: the Londinium Club. Where everything that matters is discussed by everyone who matters, and decisions that affect everyone's lives are made over dinner. I've never been sure the Londinium Club is really as ancient as the old Roman name implies, but I wouldn't rule it out either. The front entrance is old, old stone, and the designs surrounding the huge oaken door certainly date from the Roman period. The bas-reliefs feature activities that would have made Caligula blush, and a few that might have made him vomit. The Londinium Club represents power, and that has to include the power to do anything.

Only very old money or very real power can get you membership at the Londinium. Pop stars, actors, and celebrities are never, ever admitted. No matter how famous. Fame is fleeting; wealth and power can survive for generations.

There were guards practically everywhere as I strolled into Clubland, but none of them tried to stop me. I'm powerful, too, in my own way. I approached the short, stout, and stocky man standing grandly before the Londinium Club's only door and entrance, and he moved a few inches to the left to block my way more solidly. He stood proudly erect, nose in the air, eyes colder than the night. He looked like he was born wearing a formal suit. One eyebrow twitched briefly as I came to a halt before him, expressing his utter astonishment that such as I should dare to approach the august portals he guarded. The Doorman was magically linked to his door, and only he could open it from the outside. And like the door, he was old and strong and impervious to all harm. You'd have a better chance of sneaking past St. Peter at Heaven's gates in a false moustache. The Doorman cannot be bribed or threatened, and no-one's been able to find any branch of magic or science that can even affect him. Pretty much everything about him is a mystery, except his snobbery and glacial arrogance to all those he considers below him. Which is pretty much everyone who isn't a Member of the Londinium Club. No-one can remember a time when he wasn't the Club's Doorman, and some of the people who remember him are *very* old. I smiled at him casually, as though I met him every day.

"Hi," I said. "I'm . . ."

"I know who you are," said the Doorman, in a voice as harsh and implacable as an onrushing avalanche. "You are John Taylor. You are not a

Member, nor ever likely to be. Kindly remove yourself from the premises."

That didn't leave a lot of room for negotiation. "Are you sure I'll never be a Member?" I said, giving him my best hard look. "There are those who say I'm a King in waiting."

His mouth condescended to a momentary sneer. "There have never been any shortage of titles in the Nightside, sir."

He had a point there. I hit him with my one and only trump card. "I'm here to see Walker. He's expecting me."

The Doorman sighed heavily and stood to one side. The great door swung slowly inwards, spilling heavenly light out into the night. I almost expected to hear a choir of angels. I breezed past the Doorman with my head held high and entered the Club lobby as though I was thinking of buying it. Walker's name could get you into more places than a skeleton key and half a ton of semtex. I'd barely managed half a dozen steps into the lobby before a footman appeared out of nowhere to confront me. He wore an old-fashioned frock coat and powdered wig, and had shoulders so broad he could have made two of me. Under the elegant coat he probably had muscles on his muscles. He gave me a brief smile that meant nothing at all.

"Please wait here, sir. I will inform Mr. Walker that his . . . guest has arrived."

He snapped his fingers, and a whole bunch of steel chains shot out of nowhere to clamp on to me. They whipped around me faster than I could react, and heavy steel manacles fastened themselves around my ankles, wrists, and throat, shackling me to a heavy steel ring that had just appeared in the heavy carpet before me. The chains snapped tight, not even leaving me room to twitch. I kept my back straight and my head up, even as the weight of the chains tried to drag me down. I glared at the footman, but he'd already headed off to ascertain that Walker really was expecting me. If he said he wasn't, the bum's rush would be the least I could expect. But I was pretty sure he'd want to see me, if only to find out why I hadn't arrived surrounded by the Reasonable Men.

In a way, the chains were a compliment. It showed that the Club's security was taking my presence seriously. They didn't want me wandering around on my own, getting into mischief and bothering the Members. And presumably they were afraid I might out-talk or outwit any human guards. It's hard to argue with a dozen lengths of steel chain. I tried hard to feel complimented, but it's not easy when you don't dare lean in any direction for fear you might topple over; and your nose itches but you can't scratch it. To distract myself, I studied my surroundings. I'd never got this far before.

The lobby of the Londinium Club was a vast expanse of blue-veined marble pillars and shiny-tiled walls, suggesting the Club might have started out as a Roman bath, back in the day. I thought it looked like the world's biggest, poshest toilet. I'd hate to be the poor slobs that had to polish all those tiles each and every day. The floor was covered by a really deep pile carpet of a rich cream hue, presumably to give the impression of walking on clouds. The entire ceiling was covered by a single great painting of magnificent design and staggering beauty. I'd heard of it, but never seen it. Not many had. No reproductions were allowed outside the Club. It was an unknown (by the outside world) Michelangelo, representing the clash of two great armies of angels in the War against Heaven. It was simply breathtaking, in its scope and splendour. Far too good to be wasted on the kind of people who belonged to the Londinium Club, but that's life for you. It seemed to me that every single angel in the painting had his or her own individual features, as though the artist had painted them from the original models; and perhaps he had.

There were also sculptures, standing here and there like grace notes, by Moore and Dali and Picasso. Strange, twisting designs that made my eyes hurt. I'd heard you were supposed to run your hands over them, experience them through your sense of touch, rather than just look at them, but I don't think I'd have been tempted, even without the chains. They were . . . disturbing. Besides, I was pretty sure that if any non-Member such as I even tried, whole armies of footmen would appear out of nowhere to chop off my hands. The pleasures of the Club were only for the Club.

People came and went in the lobby, important people on important missions, moving quietly, speaking softly. I smiled and nodded politely to them, just as though I wasn't wrapped in chains, and they did their very best to ignore me. Either because they didn't know me, or because they did. The age of the Club, of its building and traditions, was oppressive. Custom can be stronger than magic sometimes, in the things that are Just Not Done. Like admitting the presence of someone who was Not A Member. I wrinkled my nose, trying to relieve the itch. The footman was taking his time. I amused myself while waiting by scuffing rude words into the thick pile carpet with the toe of my shoe. Little victories . . .

The footman finally reappeared, his downcast face telling me that Walker had vouched for me, after all. The footman snapped his fingers sadly, and the chains disappeared back to wherever they'd come from. I stretched slowly, taking my time. When I was finished, I smiled upon the footman, and he bowed very slightly in my general direction.

"Mr. Walker is waiting for you in the Dining Room, sir. May I take your coat?"

"Not without a gun," I said.

* * *

The Dining Room was, of course, large and rich and fabulous, with dozens of tables adorned with tablecloths of dazzling whiteness. The odours of all kinds of marvellous cuisines hung heavily on the air, succulent aromas to make the mouth water uncontrollably. It was all I could do to keep from grabbing things off tables as I passed. The diners all ignored me. I recognised some famous Business faces, rich beyond the nightmares of avarice, and a sprinkling of demigods, elfin lords, magicians, and aliens. The Londinium Club was quite cosmopolitan, in its own way. Julien Advent, the legendary Victorian Adventurer, gave me a friendly nod and a smile. Walker was sitting alone at a table in the far corner, with his back set firmly to the wall, as always. A cold grey man with a cold grey face. He looked up at me, and nodded, but didn't smile.

"You were expecting me," I said.

"Of course," said Walker, in his calm dry voice. "It was inevitable, one way or another."

I sat down opposite him without waiting to be asked, and the hovering footman reluctantly asked if he could bring me a menu.

"That won't be necessary," said Walker. "He isn't staying."

"You could invite me to join you," I said.

"I could still have you killed," said Walker.

He gestured at the footman, who bowed low to Walker, then hurried away. I looked at what Walker was having for dinner and sniffed loudly. It was all very stolid and British; roast beef, Yorkshire pudding, lumpy gravy, and limp vegetables. With probably a steamed pudding for afters.

"That is so you, Walker," I said. "Dull, worthy, and supposedly good for you. Indigestion on a plate, and not a spot of imagination anywhere."

"This is good solid food," said Walker, cutting up his meat with military precision. "Sticks to the ribs and keeps the cold out."

"Public school dinners ruin the palate for real cuisine," I said.

Walker raised an eyebrow. "What would you know about public school life?"

"Not a damned thing, and proud of it," I said. "Now, Walker, we have things to discuss, you and I. You cast a long shadow over the Nightside . . ."

"Yes," said Walker, chewing his food thoroughly. "I do. I have many shadows; my operatives are my eyes and ears, and they are everywhere. I knew the details of your current case almost as soon as you did."

"Is that why you sent the Reasonable Men after me?"

"Yes. They may be vicious animals, but they're my vicious animals. And they do put people in the right frame of mind for talking to me, and telling me what I want to know. I knew they wouldn't be enough to stop you, but I was pretty sure they'd get your attention. May I ask why they're not here with you?"

"Because they're all dead," I said.

Walker raised an eyebrow. "Well, well. How very . . . impressive. You're not usually so final in your dealings with my agents."

I said nothing. Apparently he hadn't been told yet that I'd hooked up with Madman, Sinner, and Pretty Poison. So let him think I'd killed the Reasonable Men. It all helped maintain my reputation.

"Never did take to Hadleigh," Walker admitted, spearing a piece of meat with his fork. "Dreadful fellow. Far too full of himself; downright cocky, in fact."

"Not quite the word I had in mind for him, but close," I said. "Will there be repercussions?"

"For killing thirteen bright young men with prospects, all from good families? Oh, almost certainly. I don't give a damn, but you can be sure the families, some of them very old and very connected, will be most upset with you. This time tomorrow there won't be a bounty hunter in the Nightside without paper on you. The price on your head is about to go through the roof. And don't look to me to protect you. They were my boys, after all."

"Let them all come," I said. "I've never depended on you for protection."

He nodded slightly, admitting the point. "This new case of yours, Taylor . . ."

"Yes."

"Drop it."

I leaned back in my chair, studying him thoughtfully. Walker isn't usually that direct. "Why?"

"Because the Authorities don't take kindly to anyone investigating the Nightside's history and beginnings."

"Why not?"

Walker sighed, as though faced with a very dim pupil. "Because it is possible that you might discover things better left lost and forgotten, things that might threaten or even upset the status quo. If only because an awful lot of people, and I use the term loosely, would be very interested in obtaining such information. And would almost certainly make every effort to buy, steal, or torture it from you. We are talking about the kind of people even you would have trouble saying no to. They might even go to war with each other over its possession, and we can't have that. We're still recovering and rebuilding after the recent angel war—a war you helped to bring about. The Authorities would quite certainly order me to have you eliminated, rather than risk another war in the Nightside."

"And you'd hate to have to do that," I said.

"Of course," said Walker. "There's still a lot of use I was hoping to get out of you, before your inevitable early death."

"You'd really have me killed, after all the jobs I've done for you? After all the messes I've cleaned up for you? After I saved the whole Nightside by bringing the angel war to a close?"

"Only after you started it."

"Details, details."

Walker looked at me narrowly. "There is a line you can't be allowed to cross, Taylor. A line no-one can be allowed to cross. For the good of all. So; who hired you?"

It was my turn to raise an eyebrow. "I thought you knew everything, Walker?"

"Normally, I do. Whoever hired you must be incredibly powerful, to hide their identity from my people, and that in itself is worrying."

"I never reveal the identity of a client, Walker. You know that. I will say . . . I was offered as payment the identity of my mother."

Walker put down his knife and fork and looked at me for a long moment. He looked suddenly older, tireder. "Trust me, John," he said finally. "You don't want to know."

When Walker starts calling me by my first name, it usually means I'm in real trouble, but this time there was something in his voice, and in his face . . .

"You know! All this time, you've known who my mother is and kept it from me!"

"Yes," said Walker, unmoved by the clear anger and accusation in my voice. "I never told you because I wanted to protect you. Your father and I were . . . close, once."

"So where were you when he was drinking himself to death?"

My voice must have been cold as ice, but Walker didn't flinch. He met my gaze squarely, and his voice was calm. "There was nothing I could have done for him. He'd stopped listening to me a long time before. And we all have the right to go to Hell in our own way. Sometimes I think that's what the Nightside is all about."

"Tell me," I said, and it wasn't a request. "Tell me the name of my mother."

"I can't," said Walker. "There are . . . reasons. I'm one of only two people who know, and God willing we'll take the knowledge to our graves with us."

"The other being the Collector."

"Yes. Poor Mark. And he won't tell you either. So let it go, John.

Knowing who your mother was won't make you happy or wise. It killed your father."

"What if she comes back?" I said.

"She won't. She can't."

"You're sure of that?"

"I have to be." Walker leaned back in his chair. He looked smaller, diminished. "Give up this case, John. No good will come of it. The origins of the Nightside are best left lost and forgotten."

"Even to the Authorities?"

"Quite possibly. There are things they don't tell me. For my own protection. Let the past stay in the past. Where it can't hurt anyone."

I did consider it, for a moment. I'd never known Walker to be this open, this concerned, about anything before. But in the end, I shook my head.

"I can't, Walker. I have to do this. I have to *know* . . . About the Nightside, about my mother. My whole life has been a search for the truth, for others and myself."

Walker sat up straight, his old commanding arrogance suddenly back in place. He fixed me with a cold gaze, and said, *Drop the case, John*. His voice sounded in my head like thunder, a voice like God speaking to one of his prophets; the Voice of the Authorities, speaking through their servant Walker. They gave him the Voice that commands, that cannot be disregarded, so that he might enforce their wishes in all things. There are those who claim Walker once used his Voice to make a corpse in a mortuary sit up and answer his questions. His words reverberated in my head, filling my thoughts, pinning me in my seat like a butterfly transfixed on a pin.

And then everything on the table between us began to tremble and clatter. The cutlery and the plates jumped and bounced on the immaculate tablecloth. The table rocked back and forth, its legs slamming up and down with increasing force. The floor lurched, and the whole Dining Room shook and shuddered. People cried out and clung to their juddering tables. And then it all died slowly away, and the reverberations in my head disappeared with it. I rose easily to my feet and smiled down at the openly astonished Walker.

"How about that?" I said. "So much for His Master's Voice. Perhaps I am my mother's son after all."

I walked away, and no-one wanted to look at me. I carefully chose my path to take me past Julien Advent's table, and when I was sure there was a wide marble pillar between me and Walker's table, I dropped suddenly into a chair beside Julien, and sank down, so that his body helped to hide me. I put a finger to my lips to hush him, and he nodded agreeably. By leaning back just right, I could see Walker at his table in the corner. He was so taken up with his own thoughts it was clear he hadn't noticed I never actually left the room. I'd thought that last parting shot would distract him. I wanted to see what he would do, who he would talk to, now he knew he didn't have his Reasonable Men to hold over me.

In the end, he called for a footman to clear away the mess on his table, then looked sharply to one side and nodded. A beautiful woman appeared suddenly from behind a concealing glamour, right beside the table. I cursed quietly. I'd been so focussed on Walker, and what he was saying, that I hadn't even sensed someone else was listening, unobserved. I must be getting old. I didn't used to make mistakes like that. And it didn't help at all that I recognised the stunning woman smiling at Walker.

Bad Penny was a freelance operative for hire, always turning up when least expected. Vicious, deadly, seductive, and entirely treacherous. An agent *extremely* provocateur. She smiled around the crowded Dining Room, and struck an elegant pose, the better for everyone to admire her. Most did, unobtrusively, though there were those who deliberately looked away rather than admit recognising her. Bad Penny was drop-dead gorgeous, with a voluptuous figure like a Bill Ward cartoon, somehow stuffed into a classic little black dress, complete with elbow-length white silk gloves, black mesh stockings, and a cigarette in a long black holder. She wore her night-dark hair piled up on top of her head, above a sharp, fierce face with strong bone structure and an openly insolent mouth. Her eyes were dark and deep enough to drown in. And it wasn't just her thrusting bosom that gave Bad Penny her air of sexual intimidation; she was a predator, in every way there was. She radiated sex appeal on an almost brutal level, like a weapon. She also carried two guns and any number of throwing knives about her person, though no-one was quite sure where.

We knew each other. A bit. Ships that passed in the night and kept on going. We didn't approve of each other, but we had been known to work together, occasionally. When no-one else would do.

Walker invited her to sit down at his table, and immediately the footman was there to pull her chair out for her, then push it back in again. Bad Penny accepted the attention as her due, but did deign to favour him with a flashing smile; and the footman did everything but wriggle like a puppy.

"You needn't bother with a menu," Walker said calmly to the footman. "The lady isn't stopping."

Bad Penny pouted. "Wouldn't eat here if you paid me, darling. I do have my standards."

Walker waved the footman away, and he disappeared reluctantly. I leaned out a little way from Julien's table, to hear them more clearly. Bad Penny worried me; but then, she always did, even when she was supposedly on my side. Julien watched me, amused, but continued with his dinner. As editor of the Nightside's only daily newspaper, the *Night Times*, he knew he'd get a good story out of me eventually.

I was just a bit surprised that Bad Penny was working for Walker. He was usually more subtle than that. Bad Penny, on the other hand, would work for anyone with enough money, on anything from espionage to assassination. Whether she was working on the side of Good or Evil had honestly never mattered to her; as she was only too happy to point out, gold has no provenance. She had no personal preference either way, nor any ethics worth the mentioning. She was utterly amoral and quite cheerful about it. I knew she'd occasionally done the Authorities' dirty work in the past, when they felt the need for a little distance or deniability. (Strictly pro bono, in return for which they agreed to turn a blind eye to some of her more notorious activities. Business as usual, in the Nightside.)

"I do hope this isn't about a honey trap, darling, because I don't do those any more," she said flatly to Walker. "They're just too easy, my dear; there's no challenge in it. Been there, done that, starred in the video. These days I prefer to specialise in cunning thefts, daring exploits, and just a touch of the good old-fashioned ultraviolence now and again, to keep the blood flowing."

"And a little discreet blackmail," said Walker. "To keep your coffers full."

Bad Penny batted her long eyelashes at him. "A girl has to live. And I never was very good at investments. All I have to do is mention that I'm thinking of finally writing my memoirs, and you'd be surprised how fast the cheques come flooding in. Now, what is it you want me to do, Walker? Something frightfully nasty, no doubt."

"You were listening to my little chat with John Taylor."

"Well yes, but I can't honestly say it made much sense to me."

"I want you to take care of Taylor."

Bad Penny looked at him sharply. "Now you're going to have to be just a little more specific than that, darling."

"I want you to do whatever it takes to prevent him from completing his mission. I want him off his present case, and I don't care how you do it."

"So . . . dear John is no longer under your protection?"

"No," said Walker. "Can you take him?"

"Of course, darling! He's just a man."

"Distract him. Divert him. Do whatever you think necessary. But, if all else fails, you are authorised to eliminate him."

"I get to kill John Taylor?" said Bad Penny. "Oh, *result*, darling! This will absolutely make my reputation!"

"*If* all else fails," Walker said sternly, but Bad Penny wasn't listening. "How shall I kill thee, let me count the ways . . . That Shotgun Suzie thinks she's so hot. I'll show her!"

I decided it was time to leave. Hell hath no fury like a woman you really shouldn't have slept with.

FIVE

All Answers Become Clear, in Time.

I'd only just sneaked out of that august establishment and snobs' central, the Londinium Club, when my cell phone rang. (It plays the theme from the *Twilight Zone* TV show. What else?) I hauled the phone out of my coat pocket and looked at it suspiciously. It very rarely rang, partly because only a very few people have my number, but mostly because they all knew better than to use it for anything less than a real run for the hills emergency. The line is not secure. Not only is there never any shortage of people potentially listening in, sometimes they actually join in the conversation. There's also the problem of pop-in advertising, intrusions from other dimensions, and the occasional possession of the phone by pervert demons with a thing about technology. I have to admit I'm not even sure how cell phones work in the Nightside, well out of reach of the everyday world's satellites and relay stations. (Though at least that means my enemies can't use Global Positioning to find me.) I've always assumed the cell phone system is supported by heavy-duty sorcery, but I have absolutely no idea who might be providing it, or why. Or when they're going to get around to charging for it. All things that would worry me, if I were the worrying sort.

I always screen my calls (after an unfortunate incident with a dead ex-girl-friend), and I relaxed slightly as I discovered the caller was Alex Morrisey. The owner and bartender of the oldest bar in the world, Strangefellows, Alex was one of the few people in the Nightside entitled to call me at any time. We were friends, sort of, which got him points for courage if nothing else. And since he'd never called me before in his life, I decided I'd better take the call. At first there was only silence at the other end, then a faint whispering of sound that might have been a wind blowing, far away. I said Alex's name twice, and when he finally spoke his voice sounded harsh, strained, under pressure.

"John. You have to come to Strangefellows. You have to come right now. It's urgent."

"Alex? What's the matter? You sound really rough. Are you okay?"

"I can't keep him out! The whole bar is reverting! The Past is breaking in everywhere! It feels like dying . . ."

The phone went dead, buzzing uselessly in my ear. I shut it down and put it away. I hate being interrupted in the middle of a case, but Alex sounded like he was in real trouble, and the bar itself was under threat. I had to do something. I'm very fond of that bar. Of course, the odds favoured it being some kind of trap, with Alex as the bait. All my best interests were screaming at me, and you don't tend to survive long in the Nightside without developing instincts you can trust. Walker might have had Bad Penny transported to the bar, to lie in wait for me. It was the kind of thing he'd do. So, when in doubt, depend on the element of surprise. Getting all the way across the Nightside to Strangefellows would take quite some time, whatever method I chose, more than enough time for my putative enemy to set up all kinds of booby-traps and nasty surprises. But with a little lateral thinking I could be there in moments, and maybe catch my enemy with their pants down.

A certain image of Bad Penny filled my mind, but I pushed it firmly aside.

I reached into another coat pocket and took out my special Club Membership Card. It was very special; Alex only had five made, to my knowledge. I tapped it thoughtfully against my chin, considering. They might be expecting me to use the Card . . . or relying on me thinking that, so as to avoid me using it . . . but that way madness lies. Concentrate on the matter at hand. The Card was simple embossed pasteboard, a rich cream in colour, bearing the name of the bar in dark Gothic script, and beneath that the words YOU ARE HERE, in bloodred lettering. All I had to do was press my thumbprint against the scarlet lettering, and the magic stored in the Card would immediately transport me right into the bar. Zero travelling time, and the added advantage of bypassing the watched front door. (They couldn't know about the Card. Hardly anybody knew about the Card.) In the end, all that mattered was that Alex needed my help. So I pressed my thumb down firmly, and the Card activated.

It leapt out of my hand, so fast it practically burned my fingertips, and hung on the air in front of me, shimmering with unearthly light and throbbing with stored energies. Alex always believed in putting out for the full package. The Card suddenly grew to the size of a door, and I pushed it open and walked through. And as quickly as that I was standing in Strangefellows bar. The door slammed shut behind me, and the Card was just a card in my hand again.

I glanced quickly about me, braced for any kind of trouble or attack, ready for anything except what I saw. The bar was deserted, and transformed. The low fog of early mornings covered the floor from wall to wall, grey as a shroud, swirling slowly. The air was bitterly cold, and my breath steamed before me. I could barely feel the floor beneath my feet, as though it was far away in some other distance or dimension. A wind was blowing heavily outside the bar, beating against the walls. It surged and roared, and there were voices in it. Not human voices. I'd heard this kind of wind before, announcing the breakthrough of a Timeslip, one of those brief glimpses of past or future. When the Time Winds blew, even the greatest Powers shuddered and looked to their defences. Their arrival was always a bad sign. A sign that Time was currently out of joint.

The bar was utterly empty. Not a customer anywhere. The bar only closes when Alex is off duty, and if he had been off duty, the Card wouldn't have admitted me. But here I was, alone in a room I barely recognised. The bar itself, that long slab of polished mahogany at the rear of the room, was gone, along with all the booze and accumulated trophies that were usually piled up behind it. In its place was a huge screaming face, made out of wicker. It looked big enough to burn people alive in. The expression on the green wicker face was one of horror. I shuddered suddenly, and it had nothing to do with the cold. On the phone, Alex had said the bar was *reverting* . . . Could this be an earlier version of the oldest bar and drinking house in the world?

I moved slowly forward, the ground fog tugging at my legs. Everywhere I looked there were overturned tables and chairs, sticking up like dark islands in the grey mists. Whatever customers were present when all this started must have left in a hurry. I had a pretty good idea why. The biggest clue to what was going on stood in the middle of the bar, dominating the room, and I stopped to study it from a cautious distance. A huge oak tree stood tall and firm, its trunk wide and gnarled, looking as though it had always been there, though I had never seen it before. Thick roots plunged down into the floor, and presumably on down into the cellars. Heavy branches thrust up through the high ceiling. There were no leaves, but the bar's two bouncers, Lucy and Betty Coltrane, had been strung up on the tree trunk, held in place by thick strands of ivy and mistletoe. They'd been battered unconscious, the blood still drying on their bruised faces. They were large, muscular women, with warrior's hearts; they would have gone down fighting. I reached out to tug at the ivy, to try and free them, and the thick strands stirred threateningly. I withdrew my hand, and they grew still again. I swore dispassionately. I knew what had happened here. Who had to be behind this.

"All right, Merlin," I said. "Show yourself."

A pentacle flared into life on the floor, right in front of the screaming wicker face, forming line by line, glowing with the blue-white glare you sometimes see in lightning strikes over graveyards. There was a growing tension on the air, as that old enchanter Merlin, Architect of Camelot, the Devil's only begotten Son, Merlin Satanspawn himself, rose unhurriedly up through the pentacle to stand before me, with his familiar cold and arrogant smile. Merlin had been dead for centuries, his body buried in the cellars under the bar not long after the fall of Logres; but being dead didn't necessarily stop you from being a major player in the Nightside. Merlin was dead, but very definitely not departed.

An awful lot of what Alex had said on the phone made sense now. All the changes in the bar were artifacts of Merlin's time, and the man himself could only manifest by possessing, or rather pushing aside, Alex Morrisey, latest in a very long line of owner/bartenders bound to Strangefellows by a geas almost as old as the bar itself. Merlin rarely appeared in person these days, to everyone's relief, and when he did, it meant bad news for everyone.

Merlin ran one hand caressingly over the screaming wicker face, perhaps savouring old memories, then he turned the full force of his attention on me. He was tall and wiry and utterly naked, his corpse-pale skin decorated from throat to toe with unpleasant Celtic and Druidic tattoos. Beneath the curling signs of power, his dead flesh was blotchy and discoloured with rot and the various stages of decay. Even Merlin's awful will couldn't fully hold back the ravages of Time. His long grey hair fell down past his bony shoulders in thick convoluted knots, packed and stuffed with clay. His heavy brow supported a crown of mistletoe, unhealthily green and red with poisonous berries. His face was long and heavy-boned, ugly with character, and two flickering fires burned in his empty eye-sockets. (*They say he has his father's eyes.*) And in the middle of his chest the old, old wound that had never healed, still showing broken bone and ruptured muscle, where the heart had been torn right out of him.

Merlin Satanspawn, perhaps the most powerful sorcerer of all time, still continuing through his own implacable will. Old and bad and dangerous to know.

"We're seeing far too much of each other," I said. "People will start to talk."

"Insolent as ever, John Taylor," said Merlin, in a voice like grinding iron, thick with an accent no-one had used in over fifteen hundred years.

"You made Alex call me, before you took him over."

"Of course. It was necessary that you come here. There are things that must be said, words that must be spoken. You have set a thing in motion, and even I cannot See where it will lead."

My first impulse on hearing that was to turn and run like hell. When Merlin started plotting, even the other Powers and Dominations remembered urgent appointments elsewhere. But I couldn't abandon Alex, and I was curious as to what Merlin had to say. Besides, I was pretty sure that even if I did leg it, Merlin would just drag me back again.

"All right," I said, doing my best to sound calm and casual. "Let's talk. What's brought you back this time? Been having bad dreams?"

"The dead don't dream," said Merlin. "For which I am on occasion grateful."

I looked significantly around at the changed bar. "Why the redecorating?"

"This bar is old, older even than I. There are those who say it's very nearly as old as the Nightside itself. I used to come here, now and again, as an escape from the overwhelming *goodness* of Camelot. You'd be surprised at some of the great names who've drunk here, down the ages. Heroes and villains and all creatures great and small. This . . . is one of the very few places that ever felt like home to me. That's why I had my body buried here." He looked around him, taking in the changes, smiling unpleasantly as the flames in his eye-sockets danced. "Ah, memories . . ."

"Can we please get on with this?" I said. "So I can have Alex back?"

"He is of no importance. He only exists that he might serve me. I bound his family and his line to this bar, long and long ago, just so that I could be sure of having someone of my blood here, that I could manifest through when necessary."

"Hold everything," I said. "Your blood? I thought Alex was supposed to be descended from Uther Pendragon, and Arthur?"

Merlin laughed. "From the Pendragon? No, boy; there's nothing of Kings in Alex Morrisey. He is mine, of my line, descended from my dear betrayer, the witch Nimue. He belongs to me."

I bit down hard on an angry retort. I couldn't afford to get him mad at me. Better just to get this over with as quickly as possible.

"Why did you call me here, Merlin? What do you want from me?"

A huge iron throne materialised behind Merlin, a memory made real by the power of his awful will. It was a roughly fashioned thing, all strength and power and no grace, the black metal scored with runes and sigils that seemed to move when I wasn't looking at them directly. What little of them I could read made me glad I couldn't make out the rest. Merlin sat down without looking back and settled onto his sombre throne like a dragon curling up on a mound of skulls. His pale flesh showed starkly against the dark metal. He smiled on me like a favoured son, showing aged brown teeth. I didn't smile back.

"You have a new case, John Taylor. You have been engaged to discover the true beginnings of the Nightside, by one of the Transient Beings, no less. I knew this almost as soon as you did. I have psychic alarms set in place all across the Nightside, primed to inform me immediately if such a thing should occur. You set off the alarm in the Londinium Club. I was a Member, long ago."

Why does that not surprise me? I thought.

"This is not just another case," said Merlin. "By agreeing to undertake it, you have set in motion a thing that cannot be stopped, caused ripples in Space and Time, alerted all kinds of Powers who have waited long and long for this to happen. Old forces are awakening, in and outside the Nightside, to aid or stop you. More than you can imagine is at stake here. There was a time I would have killed you out of hand, to prevent this thing from happening. Good and bad will die, terrible forces will clash by night, and nothing will ever be the same again. But perhaps it is time for the truth to come out, at last. Perhaps it is time for a new thing to be born, out of the death of the old . . ." He brooded silently for a moment. "I brought you here, John Taylor, to tell you what I know. To set you on your way. Perhaps because I do not know the origins of the Nightside, and it irks me that for all my strength and power there are still things I cannot See. I want to know."

"Do you think that knowing will release you from this bar?" I said slowly. "Free you to be fully dead and gone, at last?"

Merlin laughed, though there was precious little humour in the rough, raw sound. "No, boy. No-one holds me here but me. I wait for the return of my heart, and my full power, and then . . . Then, there shall be a reckoning!"

(Short version. The witch Nimue stole his heart, then lost it. Everyone knew that much. And that a whole lot of Merlin's power departed with the heart. Absolutely no-one wanted to find the heart, or reunite it with its owner. No-one was that stupid. Merlin was dangerous enough as he was.)

"The true nature of the Nightside's birth is tied in with the identity of your lost mother," said Merlin, almost casually. "That's one of the few things that everyone agrees on. Though strangely no-one can identify a definite source for that knowledge. Don't ask me who your mother is, or might be. She is one of the very few beings I've never been able to See with my mind, sleeping or awake. There was a moment, some years before you were born, when the whole Nightside looked up, startled, as

Something utterly unexpected flared brightly in everyone's consciousness. Something Old and terribly powerful had been reborn into the material world, and the balance of everything changed, forever. The moment passed almost immediately, the new arrival shielding itself from everyone's eyes. Which should, of course, have been impossible. Just the first of many worrying signs and portents . . . Your mother was, and presumably still is, at the very least a Power and a Domination.

"My own best guess is that your mother is, or was briefly in the past, that most powerful witch Morgan La Fae. The only one powerful enough to oppose me during Arthur's reign. A strange creature; powerful, yes, and undeniably beautiful, but I cannot say I ever understood her mind. I always suspected she was much more than she ever admitted, to me or to Arthur. And I never did believe that sob story she spun for Arthur, about being his half-sister. She only said that to get close to him; he always had a weakness for those he considered family. That's what comes of being raised as an orphan. She used Arthur to produce a son, Mordred, then used that son to bring down Camelot. I have to wonder whether your mother might have produced you to bring down the Nightside. Oh yes; I know what you experienced in that Timeslip. The terrible future you saw. Everything destroyed and everyone dead, at your hands. Quite a few Powers have seen that future in visions, down the years."

"I thought you were supposed to have killed Morgan La Fae?" I said, hoping to change the subject.

"I did my best," Merlin said dryly. "But I was never sure . . . She always said she'd be back. Mind you, Arthur said the same thing, and I'm still waiting."

"So you're not just hanging around here for the return of your heart," I said.

Merlin nodded slowly, acknowledging the point. "Arthur . . . was special. I made him possible, plotting with Uther Pendragon, back when I was still playing Kingmaker. But Arthur turned out to be so much more than anyone ever thought or intended him to be. He made himself special. He was the best of us all. The only man I ever followed. I dreamed a great dream for him, and he made it come true. A single great land, founded on Reason and Compassion, sweeping aside all the old madnesses. The holy Realm of Logres, burning so very brightly in a Dark Age."

He paused, his chin resting on one hand, remembering. "I could have been much more than I was. I was supposed to be the Antichrist, the Devil's only son born of mortal woman; but I declined the honour. I was wise, even as a child, and I determined that I would follow my own path and no other's. I killed all the members of the coven that conspired to bring me into being, and all those who came afterwards, to ensure my freedom. My mother was already dead—some nameless witch who did not survive my birthing. Apparently I tore her apart, clawing my way out of her, impatient to be born."

"What about your . . . father?" I said.

"We don't talk. I kept myself busy for years, amusing myself with building up Kings and countries, and then destroying them. And then I met Arthur, and that changed everything. He shamed me, for the shallowness of my vision. I loved him. He was my father, my son, my light in the endless dark. I knew that Hell was real, but he made me believe that Heaven was, too. I gave him my life. I would have died for him, but . . . I always knew I couldn't save him without making him over into something he would have abhorred. He proved his dream worthy by dying in defence of it. He and Mordred met on the battlefield and died in each other's arms, neither ever really understanding what had brought them to that bloody place. I was elsewhere, killing Morgan La Fae. Afterwards, with Arthur and Camelot gone, I didn't much care about anything any more. It was almost a relief when dear, treacherous Nimue came along and found me. She really was magnificent, boy."

I decided it was time to change the subject again. There's nothing worse than a centuries-old corpse getting maudlin. "What do you know about the Nightside's beginnings?"

Merlin stirred on his iron throne, his face cold and considering once again. "When I was young, I learned from the Powers that came before me. They taught me that the Nightside was originally created, by forces unknown, to be the one place on earth free from the control of Heaven or Hell. The only truly free place. That's why I've been able to remain here so long, despite my . . . diabolical beginnings. But that's really all I know for sure. You need to speak to Powers older than I. One of my old teachers is still to be found here in the Nightside, though I understand he is no longer what he once was. Herne the Hunter, the free spirit of the wild places, leader of the Wild Hunt. The untamed savage. The force that drove the great green dream of Old England, when the forests were still huge, dark and primal places."

"Where do I find him?" I said.

"Good question. I haven't spoken with him in a thousand years. The spirit of the wild woods is apparently much diminished, these days. The encroachment of cities, and civilisation, the felling of the forests, all served to reduce his powers, and I dare say he is now merely a figment of the Power I knew. But he knew many things in the old days, secrets he did not choose to share with me, and it may be that you can convince him to tell you what you need to know. Use your precious gift, boy. Find Herne the Hunter. If you dare."

"Anything else you want to say to me?" I said. "Before you go."

He grinned nastily. "You know . . . I could make you use your gift to find my heart for me."

"You could try. But even if you could make me find it, you must know I'd destroy the heart before I ever turned it over to you."

Merlin nodded his great head slowly. "Yes. You would, wouldn't you."

He stood up, and his throne vanished. He looked around the transformed bar wistfully, then sank slowly into his pentacle, dropping back down into his grave in the cellars. The glowing lines of the pentacle blinked out one by one, and as the last line vanished Alex Morrisey reappeared, lying curled up in a foetal ball on the floor. I looked quickly around. The bar was back to normal again, the fog and the oak and the wicker face gone, the present replacing the remembered past. The Time Winds no longer blew. I let out a long slow breath. It's not easy talking with a Power that can wipe you out with a passing impulse. But luckily, that's what I do for a living, as often as not. I helped Alex to sit up and set his back against the restored mahogany bar. He was shaking, fighting back tears, as much from anger as shock.

"You never told me, Merlin," he said bitterly. "All these years, and you never told any of us. I'm not a Pendragon after all. Not a descendant of a great and holy King. Just another of Merlin's damned spawn. I'm never going to be free of this bar . . ."

I sympathised, but had the good sense not to say so aloud. Alex has never been comfortable with expressions of friendship or support. They got in the way of his well-rehearsed self-pity. He finally lurched back onto his feet unassisted, a long streak of misery in basic black, even down to the beret he only wore to cover his spreading bald patch. He'd put aside shock and anger in favour of a good sulk. He knew where he was with a sulk. I could see he was about to launch into one of his rants, so I pointed out his two bouncers, regaining consciousness where the oak tree had been, and encouraged him to help me revive them, to take his mind off things. He did so, grudgingly. Good staff were hard to find.

Lucy and Betty Coltrane were basically unharmed, but mad as hell. It seemed Merlin had possessed Alex without warning, made him call me, then manifested fully and changed the whole bar without so much as a by your leave. The customers all fled. When Lucy and Betty protested, Merlin slapped them down. I think they were mostly embarrassed at how easily he'd taken them out. They were big, muscular body-building girls, used to defending themselves against all comers, and in Strangefellows that covered a lot of ground. Alex and I dusted them down, in a respectful sort of way, and set them to clearing up the overturned tables and chairs. Alex and I retired to the bar proper.

"I have a horrible feeling I'm allergic to mistletoe," said Lucy, scratching madly at one arm.

"You're always being allergic to something," said Betty. "It's all in the mind."

"I think we could do with a recuperative brandy," said Alex, moving to his usual place behind the bar.

I raised an eyebrow. "On the house?"

Alex scowled. "Just this once."

While Alex busied himself pouring out two surprisingly good brandies, I filled him in on everything that had been said in his absence. He grunted here and there, but didn't seem particularly surprised by any of it. It took a lot to surprise Alex. I considered him thoughtfully.

"How do you know you're really one of Merlin's line? Usually when you're replaced, you're completely gone."

"He made me know," said Alex. "He wanted me to know."

Yet again I decided it was time to change the subject. I used my Club Membership Card to contact my new companions, back in the Library. The card made itself into a door, and opened an aperture between the bar and the Research Section. Sinner peered curiously through the new opening.

"That's a good trick," he said mildly. "I didn't think anything could get past the Library's defences."

"This is powered by Merlin's magic," I said. "There aren't many places that can keep him out."

Sinner raised an eyebrow. "You do move in high circles, John."

Pretty Poison squeezed in beside him. "Oh look, Sidney darling; it's a bar! Do let's go through. I'm positively dying for a little drinkie."

"Probably a good idea," said Sinner. "Madman's been wandering through the Religious Studies section going *No, no, that's all wrong*, and some of the books have started disappearing. Or rewriting themselves. I have a distinct feeling the Library is not going to be pleased."

"Come on through," I said.

Sinner and Pretty Poison stepped through, then we coaxed Madman into ambling through after them. He had a dangerously preoccupied look in his eyes. I shut the door down and put the Membership Card away. Alex sniffed loudly from behind the bar.

"I never meant for my Cards to be used by freeloaders. I shall have to set up a new vetting system, preferably one involving scalpels and hacksaws and absolutely no anaesthetics." He studied my new companions, and as usual was not impressed. I was actually a little relieved. Such an open display of spleen showed that Alex was feeling better and getting back to normal again. Anytime now he'd be back to giving short measures and screwing up your change. He glared openly at Madman.

"You—I know you. Stay away from the bar, in case you change all the vintages. Or sweeten the beer. Or start my bar snacks evolving again. In fact, stay away from everything. Just stand where you are, don't move, don't even breathe. I swear, John, you lower the tone of the place every time you invite your friends to join you."

"Madman will be good," I promised. "Won't you, Madman?"

"Who knows?" said Madman. "Who can tell?"

"This is Sinner," I said quickly to Alex. "And this is his ghoul-friend, Pretty Poison."

Alex gave them his best scowl. "Oh God; it's the Nightside's very own answer to *Love Story*. The infernal Odd Couple. The ultimate sucker and fall guy, and the real girlfriend from Hell. And why does she look so much like my ex-wife?"

"Let's not go there," I said. "Listen up, people. I've just had a short but nevertheless disturbing chat with Merlin, and he says I need to talk with one of the Old Folk, Herne the Hunter. Do any of you have an idea as to where he might be found? Apparently he's dropped out of sight in recent times, and I'd really prefer not to use my gift this early in the case, unless I absolutely have to."

"Of course," said Sinner. "You don't wish to attract the attention of your infamous unidentified enemies. You see, I do keep up with things. You're almost as much a legend in the Nightside as I am, these days. I know something of Herne the Hunter. There's a lot about him in the Library, most of it contradictory. But the reports all seem to agree that he's come down in the world and is no longer the Power of old. It may be that he has gone to Shadows Fall."

"Where's that?" said Madman, passing briefly through one of his lucid phases.

"It's the elephants' graveyard of the supernatural," said Alex, always glad of a chance to show off his knowledge of trivia. "It's where legends go to die when the world stops believing in them. A bit bucolic, by all accounts, but very restful. If you're inclined that way, which personally I'm not. Why is Madman's sound track suddenly playing Dolly Parton? I know; don't ask. But I don't think Herne's left the Nightside yet. I'm almost sure I was reading something about him recently . . ."

He reached down beneath the bar and hauled up a pile of old magazines. He sorted quickly through them, finally producing a copy of the Nightside's very own scurrilous and scabrous gossip tabloid, the *Unnatural Inquirer*. (All the stories the *Night Times* is too uneasy to print.) Alex thumbed quickly through the glossy pages, while I studied the headlines on the front cover. MADONNA IN BED WITH RAZOR EDDIE'S LOVE CHILD! PHOTOS! WE HAVE PHOTOS! And beneath that: MADONNA TO DUET WITH NIGHTINGALE! TICKETS! WE HAVE TICKETS! And right down at the bottom, in fairly small print: END OF WORLD NIGH. AGAIN.

Alex was muttering to himself as he tried to find the right page. "The Walking Man, we pay for sightings . . . DNA proves Royal Family are descended from lizards . . . Well, we all knew that . . . Ah, here we are. It's in their How Are the Mighty Fallen section. Apparently Herne the Hunter has been reduced to a street person, and has been seen begging for food and small change."

"Where?" I said. I wasn't all that surprised. A lot of the homeless and street people in the Nightside used to be Someone, once upon a time. Karma has teeth here, and the wheel turns for all of us.

"Says here he moves around a lot," said Alex, dropping the tabloid onto the bar. He gave me a meaningful look, and I sighed.

I reached inside my mind, concentrating in a way I could never explain to anyone, and powered up my gift. I could find anything, or anyone, if I just looked hard enough. My third eye opened deep in my mind, my private eye, and suddenly I could See all the Nightside at once, vast and full of life and death, like a playground wrapped in poison ivy, like the best present in the world studded with rusty nails. The neon-lit streets and squares flashed by beneath my searching gaze, giving me glimpses of Beings and creatures that are normally, thankfully, hidden from most people. There are many layers and levels to the Nightside, not all of them suitable for human comprehension. I hurried on, narrowing in on my target, until finally I saw a single ragged figure, mostly hidden inside a cardboard box already sodden from the falling rain. One gnarled hand protruded from the box, mutely requesting charity. People walked by without making eye contact. A great head covered by a grubby blanket slowly emerged from the box, turning slowly to look in my direction. Great jutting antlers protruded from under the blanket. Even in his fallen state, it seemed Herne could still tell when he was being watched.

And then my Sight snapped off abruptly, and I was thrust back into the bar again. I'd fixed Herne's position, but I had no time to think about him. My enemies had found me. When I use my gift I burn so very brightly, like a beacon in the night, and they had followed the light right to me. A dozen of the Harrowing, my enemies' attack dogs, appeared out of nowhere into the bar and formed a circle around me. The terrible deathless creatures my enemies had been sending to kill me for so very long, nightmares given shape and form. My nightmares.

They were human in shape, but not in nature. They wore plain suits with slouch hats, the brims pulled low to shadow their faces so they could walk unnoticed in the world of men when they chose. But here, so close to their prey, they did not bother to hide what they were. They had no faces. There was just a blank expanse of skin on the front of their heads, featureless from chin to brow. They had no eyes, but they could see me. No ears, but they could hear. No mouth or nose, but they didn't need to breathe or speak. They were fast and strong, and they never tired. I'd known them to chase and track me for miles, for hours, tearing people limb from limb just for getting in their way.

They stood unnaturally still in their circle around me, and there was no way out. The Harrowing ignored everyone else in the bar, and one by one they lifted long slender hands to show me the vicious hypodermic needles that protruded from their fingers. Drops of a dark green liquid formed at the needle tips. It wasn't enough just to kill me any more; they wanted to drag me back to wherever they came from, so they could take their time about it.

I'd been running from them off and on all my life. And I'd never known why.

My heart was hammering painfully fast in my chest, and my hands were shaking. I was breathing hard, and there was cold sweat on my face. I couldn't fight them. Their bodies were inhumanly strong, soft and yielding. You couldn't hurt them, break them, stop them, or even slow them down. I knew. I'd tried. They just kept on coming. I'd only ever been able to outrun them. I looked wildly at Alex.

"Call Merlin! We need Merlin back!"

"I can't," said Alex. "I'm sorry, John. He only comes when he wants. And if he wanted to be here, he'd be here by now."

"Hell with him," Sinner said cheerfully. "We don't need him. You've got us, John. So, these are the dreaded Harrowing. Nasty-looking things, but I've seen worse. Pretty Poison, if you wouldn't mind . . ."

"Of course, Sidney. Anything for you."

The demon succubus smiled a happy, terrible smile, and suddenly she didn't look pretty any more. Her teeth all had points, and her eyes glowed bloodred. She held up her hands, and they had claws. She surged forward, inhumanly fast, and tore the two nearest Harrowing apart. They didn't even have time to turn before she'd ripped off both their heads, torn away their arms, slammed their bodies to the floor, and stamped on them. There was no blood, but the scattered body parts still trembled with something like life. Pretty Poison had already moved on, tearing her savage way through the circle of Harrowing. Their resilient, yielding flesh was no match for her demonic fury.

Others of the Harrowing were turning now, responding to the unexpected threat. One advanced on Sinner, only to stop suddenly, as though it had encountered a barrier it couldn't cross. Sinner looked at it sadly, and reached out to lay a hand on its blank brow. The Harrowing crumpled up like an old leaf, and fell shuddering at his feet. Madman lurched forward to confront another of the creatures, and it melted and ran away under his fierce gaze, collapsing into a pool of bubbling protoplasm.

They're weaker here, I thought slowly. *This bar has powerful protections. Getting past Merlin's defences weakened them. For the first time, I have a chance . . .*

A new confidence flared up in me. I'd never seen the Harrowing fall so fast, except when Razor Eddie hit them. But here, now, they could be stopped. They could be destroyed. I could destroy them. There were six left, hovering uncertainly. I stepped forward, and they all turned together to orient on me.

"Let's do it," I said.

"Let's," said Alex, unexpectedly. "No-one gets to come into my bar and mess with my customers. It's bad for business. Betty, Lucy, time to earn your pay."

He came out from behind the bar hefting his enchanted baseball bat, while Betty and Lucy advanced on the Harrowing, cracking their knuckles noisily. I grinned. It's good to have friends. I turned my gaze on the Harrowing, and it seemed to me that they actually hesitated.

"You're going down," I said. "All the way down."

The four of us waded into the remaining Harrowing, and together we beat the crap out of them. It wasn't easy. Even weakened by Merlin's defences, their bodies were still unnaturally soft, soaking up punishment while they struggled to stab me with their needle fingers. I punched one in the face, and my fist sank almost to the back of its skull before I tugged it free again. Alex hit one with his bat, and the enchanted wood sank down through the head and on into the chest before it stopped. But soon we learned to attack their weak spots, their joints, sweeping the legs out from under them, then battering them to a pulp as they struggled to get to their feet again. Lucy and Betty grabbed an arm each and pulled one apart like a wishbone. I don't know if they made a wish. Alex slammed one to the floor, and I hit it with a table. We kicked the bodies back and forth across the floor, laughing breathlessly. It felt good for all of us, to have something to take out our various frustrations on. We carved them up and trampled the pieces underfoot, and it felt good, so good. I'd never beaten them before. Never.

It wasn't until later that I figured out all the implications. My enemies knew Strangefellows was protected by Merlin's magic. That's why they'd never sent the Harrowing here after me before, even though they had to know I was a regular visitor. Something had made them desperate enough to try anyway; and it wasn't difficult to guess what.

In the end, we all leaned back against the bar, breathing hard, looking contentedly at the horrid mess we'd made. Twelve of the most dangerous and feared creatures in the Nightside now lay scattered across the floor of the bar in so many small, quivering body parts. We grinned at each other. I was feeling ecstatic. I'd defeated my oldest nightmares. The scattered pieces were suddenly still, then they vanished silently away, back to whatever hell produced them. We all whooped loudly, even Sinner.

"Where do these things come from?" he said.

"I don't know," I said. "I've never known."

"Who sends them? Who are these enemies of yours?"

"I've never known who they are, either. No-one knows."

"Powers from the Nightside? From Outside, perhaps? Maybe even from other dimensions . . ."

"I don't know!"

"Then why," said Sinner, calmly and reasonably, "don't you use your gift to track them down and identify them?"

I gaped at him blankly. The idea had honestly never occurred to me before. Unless I had considered it, but suppressed it, because it scared me so much. But now I'd seen the Harrowing defeated, now I was safe in Strangefellows, surrounded by good and powerful allies . . . I nodded, slowly, and opened my third eye.

This time, it was different. My gift granted me a Vision. I seemed to be a disembodied spirit, without face or form, wandering in a strange place. I drifted across a dark and devastated landscape, a place of ruins and rubble. It didn't take me long to recognise where and when I was. I had come again to a possible future for the Nightside, a silent and empty place I had experienced once before when I stumbled into a Timeslip. My Vision had brought me to the end of all things, the end of the Nightside and all civilisation.

An event I helped to bring about, or so an old dying friend had told me.

Everywhere I looked, the Nightside had been destroyed. The proud buildings had collapsed or been torn down, nothing left but cracked and broken walls, and piles of rubble. Smashed and abandoned vehicles choked the still streets. Nothing moved anywhere. The Nightside was a dead place. The light had a dark purple texture, as though bruised by what it saw and showed. In the far distance, broken buildings made stark silhouettes against the horizon. And up in the dark, dark sky there was no moon, and only a few dozen stars in all the night.

Everything looked as though it had been dead for centuries, but I knew better. The last time I was here, in the Timeslip, this future's Razor Eddie had told me I had brought down the Nightside, and the world, in just eighty-two years. Wiped out civilisation and Humanity. And all because I'd insisted on finding out who my mother was. I'd sworn an oath to that Eddie, before I killed him as a mercy, that I would never let this future happen.

My Vision leapt suddenly forward, as though my gift had finally caught the scent of what it sought. I swooped across the broken landscape, shooting between the wrecked stumps of buildings, focussing in on one particular location. My final destination was a cracked crumbling house, nothing obviously different about it, but I knew that was where I had to be. It was where I would find my enemies. There was no light showing at any of the shuttered windows, but I could tell there was light and life inside. Hidden, barricaded against the dark. As I drifted towards the house, another piece of knowledge came to me. My Vision had brought me into a time some years previous to my appearance in the Timeslip. Humanity was not all dead here. Not yet. I drifted through the crumbling walls and on into a small, desperately defended inner room, lit only by flickering stumps of candles. And then, finally, I saw my enemies.

And I knew them.

My enemies were the last remaining major players of this future time, the last defenders of the Nightside, pooling their remaining power and working frantically together to try and destroy me in the Past, before I could do . . . whatever terrible thing it was that I had done. My Vision could only tell me so much. My enemies were trying to kill me in order to save the Nightside, and the world.

They sat together around a simple iron brazier, huddling around the heat, binding the last remnants of their power together with unsteady words and shaking hands, while from outside the house came horrible, threatening sounds. They paused briefly, listening. I could hear what they heard. Something large and heavy was moving, out in the dark purple night, drawing slowly closer. And from the awful sounds it made, I was glad I couldn't see it. The handful of ragged figures in the room froze where they were, fear written clearly in their malnourished faces, not daring to speak or even move for fear of being detected; but eventually the awful thing outside moved on. Their defences still shielded them, for now.

Whatever it was that had brought the Nightside down, it wasn't over yet. Though just as clearly, Life was losing. I hung above my enemies, unseen and unsuspected, and listened while they spoke of the monsters from Outside, abroad in the night, everywhere. Apparently there were still other small enclaves of resistance, scattered among the ruins, but they were failing, one by one. Nothing had been heard from them, for months. This small group, in this small room, was quite possibly the last hope of Humanity. If they failed and died, there would be nothing left living in the Nightside but the insects, which were already changing and mutating under the terrible forces released by the War.

It was hard to look upon the handful of pitiful forms that had once been the major players of my day. Jessica Sorrow, no longer the terrible Unbeliever, looked almost human here, though still painfully skinny. She wore a battered black leather jacket and leggings, and hugged an ancient battered teddy bear in her arms. I'd found the bear for her, to help restore her lost humanity. And now she used it as a focus to help the group locate me in the Past. Next to her was Larry Oblivion, the dead detective, wrapped in the tattered remains of what had once been a very smart suit. He said quietly that he wished he could have died fully, like his brother Tommy, rather than witness what the Nightside had come to. Jessica put an arm across his shoulders and hugged him listlessly.

Count Video warmed his wrinkled hands at the brazier. He'd had his skin stitched back on, after the angel war, the sutures making grotesque designs around the familiar neurotech, silicon nodes, and circuitry patches soldered to his flesh. Strange energies formed a shifting halo around his head. He wore nothing but a series of leather straps, crisscrossing his skinny body, tightly buckled. Perhaps they held him together.

King of Skin was just a man now, stripped of his terrible glamour. Objects of power hung about him on silver chains, half-hidden in the thick pelt of his fur coat. He had a crystal ball in his hands, but it was a poor thing, disfigured with cracks and scorings. He twitched and shuddered at every sudden sound, his eyes rolling pitifully in his head.

Annie Abattoir wore the remains of a wine-dark evening dress, the cutaway back showing the mystic sigils carved into the flesh between her shoulder blades. I wasn't surprised to see her here. Annie had always been very hard to kill, though many had tried. Six-foot-two, and mostly muscle, even now, she still looked somehow . . . diminished. The War had worn her down. She kept a bowl of blood beside her and used it to refresh the lines of the pentacle around the brazier. She refilled the bowl from a vein she'd opened in her arm.

I listened to them speak, their voices just whispers, drifting to me from far away.

"The Sending has failed," said Jessica. "Our agents have been destroyed."

"All twelve?" said Count Video. "That's never happened before. He must have gathered new allies. Powerful companions."

"Perhaps he grows stronger," said Larry Oblivion. "As his time approaches. Should we try again?"

"No," said Annie Abattoir. "It's too soon. We're too weak. Wait, and gather strength. There is still time."

"We always knew forcing our way past Merlin's spells was a risk," said Jessica.

"I miss him," said King of Skin, his mouth trembling. "He gave us hope. He fought so bravely. When they finally dragged Merlin down, and ate his heart right in front of him, a part of me died with him. He was the best of us, at the end."

"He always believed Arthur would return, to save us," said Jessica.

"Well if he is coming back, he'd better get a move on," said Count Video, and they all managed some kind of smile.

Who could they be fighting? I thought. *Who could this War be against, that could destroy a mighty Power like Merlin Satanspawn? What's out there, in the night?*

"We must make more Harrowing," said Annie. "We must be ready for another Sending, when the opportunity presents itself."

"We already have one body," said King of Skin.

"We can't use him!" Jessica said immediately. "You can't! He was one of us."

"He's just a body now," said Annie. "It's what he would have wanted. You know that. You know how dangerous it is for any of us to go out into the night to dig bodies out of the rubble. Can't make homunculi without bodies."

"But not Julien Advent," said Jessica.

"He was always ready to serve," said Larry. "To be the hero. This is his last chance. You don't have to work on the body if you don't want to."

I missed what they said after that. I was in shock. Julien Advent, the legendary Victorian Adventurer, one of my enemies? He might have disapproved of me from time to time, but we had always been friends and allies. Fought the good fight side by side . . . How could he have become a part of this? He would never have sided with murder or betrayal . . . unless the stakes were so high his conscience gave him no choice. Unless all the other alternatives were so much worse. And if Julien were to become a Harrowing . . . I had to face the possibility that maybe other Harrowing I'd encountered in the past had been made out of the bodies of friends of mine.

I remembered when I first discovered the name of the creatures that had been hunting me on and off since I was a child. The oracle in the mall's wishing well had given me the name, in return for a price I still regretted paying. And years later, Julien had been the one who explained what the name meant. Harrow had been an old Victorian word, meaning to harass, to harry, to chase down. Had Julien Advent been the first to give them that name, here in the future?

"I still say we should just kill John," said Annie Abattoir, dripping blood from her arm into her bowl. "He's too dangerous to take chances with."

"No," Jessica said immediately. "He's too close to becoming now. We have to bring him back here alive, and question him. We have to understand why he did . . . what he did. Drugged and helpless, he will tell, eventually. And maybe then we'll be able to figure out a way to stop all this happening."

"And afterwards, we'll kill him," said King of Skin.

"Yes," said Count Video. "For all his sins. For the death of the world. For being his mother's son."

And with that the Vision broke, and I was suddenly back in Strangefellows again. I was standing in the middle of the room, shaking and shuddering, cold sweat dripping off my face. Sinner had an arm around me, holding me up. Alex was offering me a new glass of brandy. I took it gratefully, gulping it down, the glass chattering against my teeth. I was in shock—too many truths, too fast.

I told them some of what I'd Seen and heard, but not all. There were things they didn't need to know. Things . . . I couldn't trust them with. They were almost as shocked as I was, and they all looked at me in a new way, even Madman. The man who would destroy the Nightside. I couldn't blame them. Could my enemies actually be the good guys, after all? Desperately trying to prevent a catastrophe, in the only way left to them?

I had given that future's Razor Eddie my word that I would die before I allowed that terrible future to happen; but could I have already set things in motion by taking on this case? If discovering the origins of the Nightside was tied in with the mystery of my mother's identity, could pursuing this case be the first domino that sent all the others toppling?

"Timeslips are only potential futures," said Alex. "Everyone knows that."

"They're just possibilities," said Sinner. "Time has more branches than a tree."

I shook my head. "The fact that my lifelong enemies are rooted in this particular future means it has to be more probable than most."

"So what are you going to do?" said Alex.

"It's up to you," said Sinner. "Whether you wish to continue with this case. You don't have to. You can turn aside. But if you're determined to go on, Pretty Poison and I will accompany you. If only because I'm fascinated to see what will happen next."

"Hear, hear," said Madman.

"We go on," I said. "I have a case, and I've never let a client down yet. The truth always comes first. No matter who it ends up hurting."

SIX

The Hunter Run to Ground

I left Strangefellows through the front door, thinking hard. I'd always known the Nightside was old, had to be really old, but if Merlin was to be believed, the Nightside had been old back when he was still young. Just how far back did the Nightside go? And if it was created for a specific purpose, who created it? I had a horrible suspicion I already knew the answer.

My missing mother.

I led the way up the damp, gloomy alley that led back into the bright neon and hue and cry of the main drag, my companions lagging behind as always. Sinner and Pretty Poison were strolling along arm in arm, murmuring and giggling together, close as any lovey-dovey teenagers. It might have been charming if I hadn't known one of them was a demon from Hell, with centuries of treachery and moral corruption behind her. And Madman was ambling along in the rear, his eyes far away, for which I was grateful. It was when he started taking notice of the world that things started getting dangerous. It occurred to me, not for the first time on this case, that I might have chosen my companions more carefully.

We finally emerged onto the main streets, and I immediately spotted that we were under observation. Walker hadn't wasted any time in putting his people on my tail. At least there was no sign of Bad Penny yet, but then there probably wouldn't be until she was ready to do something appallingly nasty. I couldn't say I was surprised at Walker's people picking me up so quickly. He knew the odds were I'd drop into Strangefellows at some point, so staking it out had to be a safe bet. To be fair, his people didn't exactly stand out in the crowd. He trained them better than that. But Walker had been having me watched and followed for so long now that many of them had actually become familiar faces. In fact, if I was getting nowhere on a case, I quite often took them off somewhere for a drink and tried out my various theories on them. On the grounds that neither of us was going anywhere for a while, so we might as well be comfortable. Most of them went along with it. In the Nightside, today's enemy can be tomorrow's friend, or at least ally. And vice versa, of course. None of us ever mentioned this arrangement to Walker, of course. He wouldn't have understood. Probably have his people hauled up on charges of fraternising with the enemy.

I looked openly about me, counting off the agents. I spotted twenty, half of whom were new faces making a valiant effort to appear inconspicuous. Twenty. I was impressed. A hell of lot more than he usually sent after me. It only went to show how seriously he was taking this case. My companions, naturally, failed to spot any of the watchers, and I had to identify each and every one.

"Don't point at them," I said kindly. "It would only embarrass them."

So we waved at them instead. One was so taken aback he walked right into a lamp-post.

"I don't like being spied on," said Pretty Poison, her schoolgirl face disfigured by a menacing scowl.

Sinner patted her comfortingly on the arm. "It's only because they don't know you like I do, dear."

"I'm pretty sure these are only decoys," I said. "Distractions, to take our attention away from the real observers, hidden behind cloaking spells and invisibility cloaks. I think Walker is seriously concerned about our progress on this case."

"I'd be hard-pressed to name anyone who mattered in the Nightside who isn't," said Sinner. "Whatever we discover, it's bound to affect everyone here. Maybe we should invite some of these watchers along, as backup, for when things get . . . difficult."

"No," I said immediately. "Walker represents the Authorities; and all they care about is maintaining the status quo. If we do get close to some real answers, I wouldn't put it past them to order us all killed. Just in case."

Sinner looked at me. "You don't seem unduly worried at the prospect."

I shrugged. "There's always been someone who wants me dead. The Authorities can just get in the queue. Besides, we've danced this dance before, Walker and I. As long as I'm leading, and he's following, I have the advantage."

"I don't like being watched," Madman said abruptly. "But then, I know who's watching us. We're not alone here. We're never alone. They watch from the other side of our mirrors, and they hate us for being real.

Always turn your mirrors to the wall when you sleep, so they can't come through."

"Well," I said, after a pause. "Thank you for that insight . . ."

"I'm not mad," Madman said sadly. "It would be so much easier, for me and for everyone else, if I was, but . . . if you could see what I have Seen . . . the world isn't what we think it is, and never has been. Where are we going next?"

I blinked a few times, then decided to just answer the question. "We need to get to the restaurant area, in Uptown. I can find Herne from there. But it's a question of distance. You can bet Walker will be able to track us on any of the usual forms of mass transport, and I hate to make things easy for him."

"Why don't you get a car?" said Sinner.

I actually shuddered. "Are you serious? You see the traffic on that road? That's not commuting, that's evolution in action! Half the things that charge back and forth only look like cars, and the other half run on magics so upsetting they'd give Pretty Poison palpitations. And don't even think about sticking your thumb out; someone would steal it."

"I know a way we can get to Uptown," Pretty Poison said unexpectedly. "I can take us straight there. If that's what you want, Sidney."

"Well, of course," said Sinner. "But I didn't know you could . . ."

A halo of flies sprang up around Pretty Poison's head, buzzing loudly. Vicious claws thrust out of her elegant fingers as she traced fiery sigils on the air. Her face disappeared into shadow, in which two sullen red glows burned. I actually fell back a step. Madman just looked at her sadly. Pretty Poison said something that hurt our ears to hear it, and a circle of hell-fire sprang up around all of us. Sulphur yellow flames that stank of brimstone, though the heat couldn't reach us. The flames leapt high, then died down again, and as quickly as that we were Uptown. The flames snapped off, and Pretty Poison looked like a woman again. I shook my head, disoriented. Just then, in the moment of transition, it seemed to me that I had heard uncountable voices, crying out in torment . . . I looked at Pretty Poison, who smiled back demurely.

"I didn't know you could do that," said Sinner, framing his words with what I thought was considerable calm, under the circumstances.

"Just a quick side-step through the Infernal Realms," said Pretty Poison. "After all, I am a demon succubus, Sidney darling. We have to be able to get absolutely anywhere; it's in the job description."

"I saw you," said Sinner. "Just for a moment there, I saw you the way you really are."

She looked at the ground. "A girl can't help her background, Sidney."

"It's all right," he said. "It doesn't matter. I've seen your true form before. It was the first thing they showed me when I arrived in Hell. It doesn't change how I feel. I love you for who you are, not what you are."

"I've never understood that," said Pretty Poison.

"Of course not," Sinner said kindly. "You're a demon from Hell."

They laughed quietly together. I looked around me. The crowds bustling up and down the busy street had just seen four people arrive out of nowhere in a circle of hell-fire, but no-one seemed particularly interested. This was the Nightside, after all. People (and others) minded their own business here, and expected the same courtesy from everyone else. Though they did give us a little more room than most. I started off up the street, and my companions followed. I knew where we were, and I knew where to find Herne. I'd been here before. Uptown has all the best clubs and restaurants, the fashionable places where fashionable people meet, but even the gaudiest light casts a shadow, and that was where we'd find Herne.

I passed by an especially renowned bistro, the kind of place where even the finger food costs an arm and a leg, and then took a sudden turn into a dimly lit side street. The contrast between the bistro's brightly coloured come-on and the alleyway that led to its rear couldn't have been greater. The side street was cold and wet and grimy, and it only took half a dozen steps before you knew you were in a whole different world. The street gave out onto a gloomy back square, part of the squalid maze of back alleys, garbage-strewn squares, and cul-de-sacs that gave access to the restaurants' back entrances. The side of fashionable eating that the customers never saw. The tradesmens' entrance, the staff's entrance, and the dumping grounds for all the food the restaurants no longer wanted. Which was why the homeless and the street people and the bums of the Nightside came here, to cluster together away from the indifferent everyday world.

I looked around Rats' Alley. It hadn't changed.

It was darker here than anywhere else in the Nightside, and it had nothing to do with the lack of street lighting. This was a darkness of the heart and of the soul, which touched everything at the bottom of the heap. The bright flaring neon from the main streets didn't penetrate, and even the blue-white glow from the overly large moon above seemed somehow muted. The smell was appalling, a thick organic stench of rot and filth and accumulated despair. The cobbled street was sticky underfoot. People lived here, in the shadows, a small community of the lost and the destitute. Not so much forgotten as wilfully overlooked. Sinner moved in beside me as I paused at the entrance to the square.

"*This* is where Herne the Hunter lives? The old god of the forests?"

"It's a long way down from the top," I said. "But you're never so far up you can't fall. At least in Rats' Alley he has company. A lot of the homeless and destitute end up here, because this is where restaurant staff dump unwanted food at the end of their shifts. Everything from scraps to whole meals. It's cheaper to feed it to the bums than pay to have it carted away."

"Why is it called Rats' Alley?" said Pretty Poison.

"Why do you think?" I said. "And watch where you step."

"I never realised there were so many homeless in the Nightside," said Sinner. "It's like a whole community here. A shanty town for the lost."

"I think we're supposed to call them street people these days," I said. "Because if we call them homeless, it begs the question of why we're not finding homes for them. And they've always been here. The Nightside's finances are based on scamming losers, and it's never been kind to failures."

Rats' Alley was what everyone called the square and its tributaries, packed full of cardboard boxes, lean-to shelters, plastic tenting, and clusters of people huddled shapelessly together under blankets. Men and women of all ages and sizes, thrown together like shipwreck victims, refugees from the overthrown countries of their lives. Bright eyes showed here and there in the shadows, and glimmers of light on what might have been weapons. They might be down and out, but they didn't care for being stared at.

"Do they have dogs?" said Madman. "I thought all homeless people had dogs."

"Not around here," I said. "These people would eat a dog if it showed up. Or the rats would. They have serious rats around here. That's why the street people stick together. So the rats won't drag them off in the night."

Sinner looked at me. "You seem to know this place very well, John."

"I used to live here," I said. "Years ago, when things had got really bad. This is probably the only place in the Nightside where my name and history mean nothing. They'll take anyone here. And this was a great place to hide from everyone, even myself. Having to concentrate on keeping warm and dry, and where the hell your next meal is coming from, is very useful when you don't want to think about other things."

"How long were you here?" said Pretty Poison.

"I don't know. Long enough. This is where I first met Razor Eddie. He still sleeps here, sometimes." I stepped cautiously forward into the square, looking around me for familiar faces as my eyes adjusted to the gloom. "That's Sister Morphine over there, in what's left of her habit. A Carmelite nun who chose to come here and live among the street people, to preach and to console them. Her veins manufacture all kinds of drugs

for the needy, expressed through her tears. And there's never any shortage
of reasons for tears in Rats' Alley. Her tears are shed for the suffering
around her, and no-one is ever turned away. Some time ago, a bunch of
thugs decided to kidnap and make use of her, as an endless supply of
drugs for them to peddle. They turned up here mob-handed to drag her
away, all confident and cocky . . . and the street people ganged up on
them and beat them all to death. Afterwards, they ate the bodies."

Sister Morphine came forward to meet me, holding the dark rags of
her habit around her with tired dignity. She looked a lot older than I remembered, but then living out in the open will do that to you. Her robes
were spattered with filth, her smile weary but kind.

"John Taylor. I always knew you'd be back."

"I'm just visiting, Sister."

"That's what they all say."

"I'm looking for Herne the Hunter, Sister. We need to talk to him."

"But does he want to talk to you?" Sister Morphine glared at Pretty
Poison. "This one has the stink of the Pit about her."

"We're not here to make trouble," I said carefully.

"You are trouble, John," said Sister Morphine. And she turned her
back on me and walked away.

I looked around for someone who might be more helpful. For cash in
hand, or even the promise of a drink. The Bone Horror peered at me
dully, curled up under a propped-up blanket. He'd lost everything at the
gambling tables, even his flesh. All he had left was his bones, but still he
wouldn't, perhaps couldn't, die. Some of his bones had clearly been
gnawed on, and I could only hope it was just by rats. I saw other names,
other faces, but none of them looked friendly. There were creatures as
well as people, and even a few broken-down machines, hoarding the last
sparks of energy in their positronic brains. Even the underside of the
Nightside is still a cosmopolitan place. There was even a Grey alien,
dressed in the tattered remains of an atmosphere suit. Left behind, presumably. Damn things get everywhere. His badly handwritten cardboard
sign said *Will probe for food.* I seriously considered kicking the crap out
of the abducting little bastard on general principles, but I made myself
rise above the temptation. All are welcome in Rats' Alley, no matter what
their past. That's the point. They even took me in.

"Does no-one do anything to help these people?" said Sinner.
"Doesn't anybody care?"

"Remember where you are," I said. "The Nightside is famous for not
caring about anything. That's what brings people in. There are still a few
who give a damn, like Sister Morphine. And Pew still does the rounds of

places like this, dispensing hot soup and fire-and-brimstone sermons. Julien Advent raises money for various charities through the *Night Times*. But mostly the Nightside prefers to pretend that places and people like these don't exist. They don't want to be reminded of the price of failure in the Nightside."

My companions and I were beginning to attract attention. Our faces and our stories were known, even here. The street people were getting interested. I kept a watchful eye on the shadowy forms nearest us. Street people have a tendency to gang up on those they consider intruders into their territory. All outsiders, often including do-gooders, are seen as targets of opportunity. I'd been here. I could remember searching quickly through the pockets of unconscious bleeding bodies. The street people weren't afraid of us, or our histories. Fall this far, and you weren't afraid of anything any more. They started lurching to their feet, pulling their blankets around them, rising on every side. A quick look behind showed our retreat was still clear, if necessary. I didn't want to hurt anyone. Sinner and Pretty Poison moved in protectively on either side of me as the ragged forms stumbled forward. They all seemed to be orientating on me, ignoring the others. Surely they couldn't all remember me.

And then they knelt before me, and bowed their heads to me, and murmured my name like a benediction. Some of them wanted to rub their grubby faces against my hands. Some touched my white trench coat wonderingly, as though just the touch might heal them. I looked around for Sister Morphine, but she still had her back to us. The homeless knelt before me like a congregation, their grimy faces full of adoration.

"Well," said Sinner. "This is . . . unexpected. And just a little worrying."

"Trust me," I said, holding my hands carefully back out of everyone's reach. "If there's one thing I think we can all be sure of, it's that I am not the Second Coming."

"Definitely not," said Pretty Poison.

There was something in the way she said that. Sinner and I both looked at her. "Do you know something you're not telling?" I said.

"More than you could possibly imagine," said Pretty Poison.

When it became clear I wasn't going to perform any miracles, the street people quickly lost interest and drifted away again. Madman went wandering off among them, and they accepted him as one of their own. They could tell he was just as damaged, just as divorced from the world as the rest of them.

"Poor Tom's a-cold," he said, somewhat predictably.

I felt like saying *Get thee to a nunnery,* but rose above it. I was here on business. I made my way carefully through the maze of cardboard boxes and improvised tents and finally found Herne the Hunter just where my gift had told me he'd be. He was still squatting inside his soggy, half-collapsed box, wrapped in something dark and soiled. He saw me and Sinner and Pretty Poison gathered in front of his box, and retreated even further back inside. We all tried coaxing him out, but he wouldn't budge until I used my name. Then he came out slowly, a bit at a time, like an uncertain animal that might bolt at any moment, until finally he stood crouching before us. He could have been just another bum, engulfed in the filthy remains of an old greatcoat, except for the stag's antlers protruding from his bulging forehead. He was smaller than I'd expected, barely five feet tall, broad and squat and almost Neanderthal. His skin was cracked and leathery, his face heavy and broad and ugly. His eyes were deeply sunken, and his almost lipless mouth trembled. He smelled really bad, which in Rats' Alley took some doing. It was a rank, animal smell, thick with musk. In one overlarge hand he held firmly onto a begging bowl fashioned from a hollowed-out human skull.

"Not much of a god, yes?" he said, in a deep, growling voice thickened by an accent I'd never heard before. "Should have gone on long ago. But, still a few worshippers left. Mostly New Age hippie types. Bah! But, take what you can get, these days. Belief is still power. Herne the Hunter just a tale for children now. I know, I know. No-one wants to worship at the blood altars any more. Don't blame them. No. Never was a comfortable god to have around, me. Herne embodied the chase and the hunt and the kill, nature red in tooth and claw." His speech improved as he talked, as though he was remembering how. "You sacrificed to me for luck in the hunt, for good weather and the death of your enemies, and to keep me away. I was a dangerous and capricious god, and I loved tricks. Yes . . . Herne rode high, lived off the best, trampled men and women under my hooves, and the Wild Magic was strong in me. But if you were under my protection, no-one dared touch you! No! No . . . A long time ago . . . I have fallen far. What you want with me anyway? Better gods on Street of the Gods, very reasonable prices. I have no powers, no secrets, no wisdom."

"We're looking for information," I said. "The answers to some questions."

Herne shook all over, like a dog. "Don't know anything, any more. World has moved on, oh yes. The forests are gone. All cities now. Steel and stone and brick, and the magic in them does not know me. Hate cities. Hate the Nightside. Hate being old. Live long enough, and you get to see everything you ever cared for rot and fail and fall." He looked at me sharply. "I know you, John Taylor. Know you well enough not to worship at your feet. What you want? What questions?"

"Tell me about the old days," I said. "When England was young, and so were you."

He grinned widely, showing great gaps in his teeth. "Still remember my glory days, leading the Wild Hunt on my moon stallion. All men and women were my prey on that night. Long, long ago . . . Once I preyed on humans, now I live off their leavings. Anyone could end up like me, oh yes. One bad day . . . and then you fall off the edge and can't get back. Men become farmers, not hunters. Towns grow into cities. The forests grew smaller, and so did I. Men grew more powerful, and I grew less. Cities . . . the Nightside was one of the first, the beginnings of the rot."

"Not *the* first?" said Sinner.

Herne grinned again. "Opinion is divided. Before my time. Ask the Old Ones. It was there in the earliest of days, and it is still here. More savage and merciless than I ever was."

"I have heard it said," I said carefully, "that my mother is tied in with the creation of the Nightside. What do you know of that?"

Herne shrugged easily. "Don't know for sure. Don't think anyone does. I have an opinion. Opinions are like arseholes; everyone's got one. You ask me, I think your mother was Queen Mab, first Queen of the Faerie; before Titania. Pretty pretty Titania. I remember Mab. Beautiful as the dawn, more powerful than the seasons. She walked in lightning, danced on the moonbeams, entranced you with a look, and forgot you with a shrug. Queen Mab, the magnificent and feared. The Faerie don't talk much about Mab any more, but still they fear her, should she ever return. She's been written out of most of the stories and the secret histories, in favour of sweet little Titania; but some of us have never forgotten Queen Mab."

"What happened?" I said.

He chuckled briefly. A low, nasty sound. "Ask Tam O'Shanter, dancing on his own grave. Brandishing the broken bones of a rival, and gnawing on the heart he tore from the rival's breast. We took our love affairs seriously in those days. Our passions were larger, our tragedies more terrible. Death had little dominion over such as us. Our stories had the power of fate, and destiny." Herne cocked his ugly head on one side, as though listening to voices or perhaps songs only he could hear. "I remember the Faerie leaving the worlds of men, once it was clear to them that cities and civilisation and cold steel would inevitably triumph. They walked sideways from the sun, all of them, retreating to their own secret, hidden world. Yes. I should have gone with them when I had the chance. They did offer. They did! Herne always had more in common with the Fae than with earth-grubbing Humanity. But they were in it for the long term, and we never were. Should have gone with them, yes; but no, stayed to fight and lose and see the world become something I no longer recognise, or have a place in.

"So, here is Herne the Hunter. Among the fallen and the hopeless. Doing penance."

"What for?" said Pretty Poison.

He crawled back into his cardboard box, holding my gaze all the while. "Ask the Lord of Thorns. Now go away. All of you. Or I'll kill you."

We left him crying in his cardboard box.

I looked around for Madman. It was time we were moving on. "Where to next?" I said. "I'm open to suggestions."

"How about the Lord of Thorns?" suggested Sinner.

I winced, and so, I noticed, did Pretty Poison. I looked severely at Sinner. "Only when we've tried absolutely everyone else in the Nightside, and I mean *everybody*. That guy even scares Walker, and with good reason. Why bring him up?"

"Because Herne mentioned him."

"So he did. Next?"

"All right," said Sinner. "How about the Lamentation?"

I actually shuddered that time. "Why on earth would we want to go and see that crazy piece of shit?"

"Because Herne said we needed to talk to the Old Ones," Sinner said calmly. "And the Lamentation is the oldest Being I know of."

"There is that," I said, reluctantly. "There's no doubt it knows all kinds of things; if you can persuade it to talk. But you don't get to be an old Power in the Nightside by being friendly and approachable. No-one's even sure what the Lamentation is any more; except it's supersaturated with death magic and crazy with it. I don't even like saying the name aloud, in case it's listening. It could be a demon or a Transient Being or even a human who took a *really* wrong turn. No-one knows. They say it eats souls . . ."

"But it's definitely older than Herne," Sinner said stubbornly. "If anyone knows how far back the Nightside goes, I'd put good money on the Lamentation."

"So you think we should just barge in and ask it questions?" I said.

"You can hide behind me if you like," said Sinner. "It's up to you, John. How badly do you want to get to the bottom of this case? Bad enough to beard a Power and a Domination in its lair?"

"Oh hell," I said. "It wouldn't be the first time."

"Boys . . ." said Pretty Poison. "I think we have a problem with Madman."

I looked round quickly. And there was Madman, dancing and pirouetting through the boxes and tents of Rats' Alley while flowers blossomed brightly in his wake, springing right out of the cobbled ground and through cracks in the grimy brickwork. He ended his dance with a flourish, and a spring bubbled up at his feet. One of the homeless dipped his metal cup in the stream, tried it, and cried out excitedly that it was pure whiskey. The homeless looked on Madman with new eyes.

They surged forward to crowd around him, demanding he conjure up for them food and drink, heat and light and palaces to live in. They pawed and clawed at him, their voices growing loud and insistent and threatening. Madman tried to back away, but there was nowhere for him to go. I tried to get to him, but there were too many people in the way. I yelled at the street people, using the authority of my name, but they were beyond listening. And then my skin prickled and my heart missed a beat, and I stopped trying to press forward. Something bad was coming. I could feel it.

The brickwork nearest to Madman began to bubble and melt and run away. The ground shook, as though something was heaving up beneath it, trying to break through. The light in Rats' Alley kept changing colour, and there were too many shadows in the square with nothing to cast them. All around there was a growing feeling of . . . uncertainty. That nothing could be relied on any more. That the curtains of the world might part at any moment to reveal what was really going on behind the scenes. Madman was losing his self-control.

The street people fell back from him, crying out in shock and alarm and growing horror. The world was coming undone all around Madman. I grabbed Sinner by the arm. I couldn't get my breath, and it seemed to me that at any moment I might fall upwards, sailing off into the night sky forever. Everywhere I looked, the details on everything were changing, in utterly arbitrary ways. One of the homeless grabbed at Madman, to make him stop the changes, only to shriek in terror as Madman looked at him, and *changed* him, till he looked like a modern art painting, all angles and dimensions and clashing perspectives. Parts of him were missing. Horribly, he was still alive. Madman looked upon his work, and his face showed nothing, nothing at all.

Sister Morphine pulled the changed man away from Madman and cradled him in her comforting arms. She glared at me. "This is all your fault! You brought him here! Do something!"

I grabbed a few useful items from my coat, braced myself, and was about to start forward again when Sinner pushed past me. He strode forward and locked eyes with Madman. The two men stood silently together, lost in each other's eyes, while the whole world seemed to hold its breath. Madman let out his breath in a long, slow sigh, and looked away, and the world grew calm and steady around him again. Sinner's singular nature had given Madman an anchor, and stabilised him. Rats' Alley was still and sane again. Many of the homeless were weeping and shaking. Sinner took Madman by the arm and led him out of the square, and Madman went with him as docile as a child.

"Can't take you anywhere," I said.

SEVEN

Why Don't the Dead Lie Still?

We left the darkness of Rats' Alley behind us and made our way back out into the bright city lights of Uptown. The night was too dark, the neon too bright, but it still felt like home. In many ways, leaving Rats' Alley was like being born again. Like declaring you're ready to take on the world again, and the world had better look out. I'd felt the same the last time I did so, all those years ago. Because no-one ever really lives in Rats' Alley; they're all just existing. I took a deep breath and looked around me. The usual crowds came and went, pounding the pavements, intent on their own very private business, and Walker's watchers were still observing from what they hoped was a safe distance. (Walker didn't pay them enough to go into Rats' Alley after us.) It seemed to me that there were rather more of them than there had been the last time I looked, and I stopped where I was, to check out the situation. My companions waited patiently as I glared openly about me. Some of the watchers stepped back into doorways and the shadows of alley mouths, but the newcomers just stared calmly back. Like vultures scenting dead bodies in the near future. I pointed these people out to Sinner and Pretty Poison. (Madman was already off with the faeries again.)

"We've picked up some new friends," I said. "Not your ordinary, everyday watchers. See those seven Oriental gentlemen, with the idiograms tattooed above their left eyebrows? Combat magicians. Hooded Claw Clan. Just goes to show; everyone answers to Walker."

"Dangerous people?" said Sinner.

"Very," I said.

"That's all right," said Pretty Poison. "We're dangerous people, too."

"Still," said Sinner. "Combat magicians? Walker is taking this case seriously, isn't he . . . What about those two gentlemen there, with the wolf pelts and claw necklaces?"

"Supernatural trackers. *Lupus extremis.* They could follow our scent through a skunk factory. And teleporting wouldn't throw them off either; they'd just jump right after us, piggy-backing our magics."

"Is there any way to shake them off?" said Sinner.

I grinned. "Sure. Go places they won't dare follow us."

"I don't like the look of those three," Pretty Poison said mildly. "They have the stink of sanctity about them."

I looked where she was pointing, then cursed under my breath. "Now they are serious trouble. The Holy Trio. A man, a woman, and a recently departed spirit; all of them Jesuit demonologists and fully paid-up members of the Fun Is Evil Club. The flip side of tantric magic; they used the tensions caused by a lifetime of celibacy to power their spells. Result—energy to burn, and a really spiteful attitude to the world in general and the Nightside in particular. The Authorities don't normally let them in. Damn! Walker must be really serious about this. We can forget about any more hell-fire teleports; the Trio could stamp the flames out just by glaring at us."

"I could kill them," said Pretty Poison.

"No you couldn't," said Sinner. "Not if you want to stay with me."

"Well of course, Sidney darling. But you're going to have to explain this whole restraint concept to me again later."

Sinner looked at me suddenly, his usual mild gaze thoughtful and appraising. "I thought you were supposed to be the Vatican's blue-eyed boy, after you got the Unholy Grail back for them?"

"That was a special assignment for the Pope," I said. "Not the Vatican. And Walker has always been able to call on the Church, as well as the State and the Army, to back him up. But I haven't seen a gathering like this for years . . . and never just for me."

"So what do we do?" said Madman, catching us all by surprise. It was easy to forget he was listening. It was easy to forget he was still there.

"I think . . . we'll just let them follow us," I said. "It's not a long walk from here to the lair of the Lamentation. An awful lot of them will drop out, once they realise where we're going. I don't blame them. I wouldn't go there myself if I didn't have to. In fact, I do have tó, and I'm still trying to think of a way out of it."

"The trouble with shadows," said Madman, "is they watch you all the time, but you can't see their eyes."

We all considered that for a while. "Congratulations," said Sinner. "That actually bordered on pertinent, not to mention lucid."

"No-one listens when I tell them things," Madman said sadly.

Sinner turned back to me in a determined sort of way. "I just had a thought," he said firmly. "Sandra Chance is supposed to have a relationship with the Lamentation these days; even if no-one is sure what it might be. Could we perhaps contact her and ask her for an introduction? Maybe even get her to act as an intermediary?"

"I doubt it," I said. "First, it's just gossip. And second, she's not too keen on me at the moment. Not since I let the butterfly get away."

Sinner waited until he realised I wasn't going to say any more, then sighed. "You have a history with practically everyone, don't you?"

"Not all of it bad," I said defensively. "There must be someone in the Nightside who hasn't wanted to kill me at some time or other."

"I wouldn't put money on it," said Pretty Poison.

We walked out of Uptown, trailing our pack of observers behind us, and made our way through a series of increasingly seedy areas, where even the neon seemed grimy. The buildings huddled together, though the strangers on the streets kept resolutely to themselves. The windows were all shuttered or covered with metal grilles, and the doors were locked to everyone except those who knew the right things to say or ask for. We were in Freak Fair now, where all the fetishists, obsessives, and the more extreme enthusiasts came in search of things that most people wouldn't even recognise as pleasure. Not a place for tourists. The Freak Fair makes even the everyday residents of the Nightside feel dirty. I'd been here once before, on a case, and afterwards I had to burn my shoes.

The people we passed kept their eyes determinedly downcast and made a point of giving each other plenty of room. It was all very quiet and polite, though the stamp of perversion and morbidity hung heavily on the air. The people tracking us began to fall back in ones and twos, then in something of a rush, once it was clear where we were going, clearly deciding that there were very definite limits to their duty. Everyone draws the line somewhere, even in the Nightside. But the hardier souls stuck with us, shouldering people out of their way to maintain their line of sight. I could feel my shoulders hunching as we continued through the narrow streets, as though anticipating an attack. Freak Fair is not a comfortable place to be. Pretty Poison, on the other hand, actually blossomed, striding happily along with a smile for everyone. Sinner didn't seem to be affected at all, but then, he was in love with a demon succubus. Madman hummed cheerfully along with his sound track, which was currently Madonna's *Erotica*. Takes all sorts . . .

We finally arrived at the deconsecrated funeral parlour that currently housed that old and awful Being called the Lamentation. It changed its location regularly, partly because there were a hell of a lot of people (and others) who wanted it dead and gone, and also because its presence alone was enough to suck all the life out of any environment it inhabited. The Lamentation—also known as the God of Suicides, the Saint of Suffering, the Tyrant of Tears. It had many names but only one nature, and nobody worshipped it. You only turned to the Lamentation when you'd run out of belief, hope, and any kind of faith.

We stood together before the flimsy-looking front door, hanging just a little open between stained stone walls. There were no windows. Above the door was a tarnished brass plaque, giving the name of the place in Gothic Victorian script—the Maxwell Mausoleum. The funeral parlour had been around for almost two centuries, before it was shut down amid general outrage. (This was long before the Necropolis became the only supplier for funeral ceremonies in the Nightside.)

They still tell stories about what happened in the Maxwell Mausoleum all those years ago. Bad stories, even for the Nightside. Of what was done to the dead and the living, in dark and silenced rooms, where the Maxwell family worshipped the insides of bodies, and practised rites so revolting there aren't even words to describe them. The Maxwells were finally discovered, then dragged out and hanged from the nearest streetlamps, their bodies set alight while they were still kicking. Their remains were buried in the same coffin, after certain precautions, and for weeks afterwards people lined up to piss on the grave.

It was because of the terrible things that happened here that the Authorities decided to forget all about free enterprise, and determined that in the future all funeral practices would be supplied by the Necropolis, which they would watch over and control. The Maxwell Mausoleum had been abandoned for years before the Lamentation moved in but you could still feel the evil oozing out of the filthy old stones. The Lamentation presumably felt right at home.

It suddenly seemed a lot quieter than it had a few moments ago, and it took me a while to work out why. Madman's music had stopped. He stood right in front of the door, studying it closely while being careful not to touch it, and frowning, as though listening to a voice only he could hear. "Why don't the dead lie still?" he said, then turned away, without waiting for an answer.

I looked at Sinner. "Is it just me, or is he starting to make more sense?"

"It's probably just you," said Sinner. "So, what do we do? Knock loudly and announce our presence?"

"Oh, I think it knows we're here," I said. "The Lamentation is a

Power and a Domination. Beings like that don't believe in being surprised."

I reached cautiously forward and gave the door a gentle push. It swung slowly inwards, the hinges squealing loudly. Like most of the older Beings, the Lamentation was a traditionalist and a bit of a drama queen. Beyond the doors was a dull red glow, a tense silence, and nothing else. Like opening a gate to Hell. We waited a while, but no-one came to greet us.

"I'm a bit surprised the door wasn't locked," said Sinner. "I mean, this is the Nightside, after all, where communal property tends to be defined as anything that isn't actually nailed down and guarded by trolls."

"Anyone stupid enough to invade the Lamentation's lair deserves every nasty thing that happens to them," I said. "And no-one inside ever leaves, except by the Lamentation's will."

"Excuse me," said Pretty Poison, "but are we ever going in, or is the plan to stand about on the doorstep discussing strategy until the Lamentation gets so bored it comes out to see us?"

I looked at Sinner. "Pushy girl-friend."

"You have no idea," said Sinner.

I led the way in, Sinner and Pretty Poison in flanking position, and Madman bumbling along in the rear. Behind us, the door slammed shut without anyone touching it, and none of us were in the least surprised. Drama queens, the lot of them. The interior of the Mausoleum turned out to be much bigger than its modest exterior indicated. The rooms of the original small business had been replaced by a vast, echoing hall, half-full of curling, blood-tinted mists. We couldn't see the end of the hall from where we were, but the high, vaulted ceiling suggested it was some way off in the distance. We were in a big, big place, and the small sounds of our feet on the uneven flagstones seemed to echo on and on before they reached the distant stone walls. There are those who say space expands to contain all the evil present. And this was the lair of the Lamentation. We had come to a bad place, one of the worst in the world, and all of us could feel it, in our water and in our bones and in our souls.

"I like it here," said Pretty Poison. "It feels like home."

The air was bitterly cold, but quite still. The bloodred mists moved of their own accord, gusting and billowing, thickening and thinning apparently at random. The flagstones beneath our feet were covered in grave dirt. One wall let in shafts of light, falling through old-fashioned stained-glass windows, each depicting the awful deaths of saints and martyrs, the vivid colours glowing through the mists. A dull red glow from the far end of the great hall coloured the mists, pulsing slowly, so that as we moved cautiously forward, it was like walking through the bloodstream of a dying god. The mists smelled of blood and meat and recent death.

"Have we come at last to Hell?" said Madman.

"This isn't Hell," said Pretty Poison. "But you can see Hell from here."

We kept walking. The end of the hall seemed impossibly far away. I had no idea how long we'd been inside the Mausoleum. We were all shivering now, even Madman. The cold was leaching the living warmth right out of us. We stuck close together. And from out of the bloodred mists, the dead came walking to meet us, to welcome their new guests. There were hundreds of them, men and women and even some children, and there was no mistaking the fact that they were all corpses. They still wore the wounds that killed them, the self-inflicted cuts and rope burns they'd used to end their lives. They showed off their gaping wounds and dried blood, their stretched and broken necks, with simple indifference. Their skins were colourless, even the insides of their injuries only pale, muted colours, and their faces were blank. Until you looked into their unblinking eyes and saw a suffering there that would never end.

An army of the dead, shuffling forward on unfeeling feet, the rags of their clothes just the tatters of so many scarecrows. They all raised one hand, and beckoned us forward. An aisle opened up through the mass of them, and I led the way into it. The ranks of the dead continued to open silently up before us, then close behind us. We weren't going anywhere they didn't want us to. Some of the dead pawed at me, the way the street people had in Rats' Alley. They looked at me with their dead eyes, and muttered with their pale mouths, in the barest ghosts of voices.

Help us. Free us from the Lamentation. We didn't know. We didn't know it would be like this. We want to lie down, and rest. Help us. Free us. Destroy us.

And all I could do was keep on walking.

The Lamentation was an old, old Being. Older than most of what passes for history in the Nightside. Served and powered by suicides, it fed on suffering and despair and death. The dead bodies pressed close around us, showing off the deep noose marks on their crooked necks, or the ragged exit wounds in the backs of their heads where they'd shot themselves in the mouth, or in the eye. There were faces thick and puffy from the gasses they'd breathed, or the pills they'd swallowed. Pale red mouths at wrists and throats. The heavy marks of falls and vehicle collisions. They wore their deaths like open books, not as a warning but as proof of their damnation.

And finally, signs began to appear that we were nearing the Lamentation itself. Hanging nooses dropped from the high ceiling like jungle liana, and we had to push our way through them. There were great sculptures made entirely out of razor blades, and we edged carefully between them. It was just the Lamentation, making itself at home. The blood-tinged mists were thinning out now, taking on the smells and tastes of all kinds of poisonous gasses.

That last development almost took me by surprise. The others weren't affected by the increasingly deadly mists, for their own various reasons, but the first I knew of the danger was when my head began to go all swimmy, and I couldn't seem to get my breath. My thoughts stuttered and repeated themselves, feeling increasingly far away, and then the voice of the unicorn's horn pin sounded loudly in my head.

Poison! Poison gasses, you idiot! Defend yourself! Eat the celery!

I thrust a numbing hand into an inside coat pocket, pulled out the piece of celery, and chewed on it. I always keep a piece handy, pre-prepared with all kinds of useful substances, for just such occasions as this. It tasted bitter as I chewed, but it cleared my head rapidly. It's an old trick but a good one, taught me long ago by a Travelling Doctor I met at the Hawk's Wind Bar & Grill.

Guns and bullets lay scattered in spirals across the dirty flagstones, and we kicked them out of our way. A rainbow of discarded pills crunched under our feet. The dead closed in around us. I kept staring straight ahead.

The corpses were all around us now, filling the vast hall, the furthest of them only dim shadows in the churning mists. For the first time, I was sure I'd chosen the right companions for this case. Anyone else would already have run screaming, and I wasn't far from it myself. The living were never meant to come this close to death and all its horrors. The Lamentation was served by everyone who ever took their own life in the Nightside, and so had acquired the second biggest standing army in the Nightside, behind the Authorities. They allowed this to continue only because the Lamentation had never been much interested in how the Nightside was run. There was never any shortage of suffering and suicides in a place where it's always three o'clock in the morning, and the comfort of the dawn never comes.

The blood-tinted mists suddenly blew apart like curtains, revealing the Lamentation hanging supported in its cage. The great and terrible Being was held securely inside an intricate construction of rusting black metal, a massive cube thirty feet on a side. Black iron bars crisscrossed in elaborate patterns to make up the sides, and then thrust back and forth across the interior, piercing and transfixing the inhumanly stretched and distorted body inside the cage. It was hard to tell just how big the Being really was, bent over and twisted back upon itself, again and again. Its flesh was stretched taut by the strain of its contortions, and its skin was colourless and sweaty, though whether from pain or pleasure . . . There was something about it that suggested it might have started out as human, long and long ago . . .

Whether the cage had been built around the Lamentation, or it had grown inside the cage, wasn't clear. There was no sign of a door or entrance in any of the six sides. The inhumanly long arms and legs stretched out from the crooked torso, twisted back upon themselves again and again, in defiance of all the rules of anatomy, held irrevocably in place by the rusting metal bars transfixing them. There was no trace of blood at any of the many puncture points. More iron bars punched in and out of the torso, which showed no signs of breathing or heartbeat, though the thick body hair swirled slowly, making patterns that sucked in the eye. The face thrust up against the bars of the cage, looking out at its new visitors; stretched impossibly wide, the skin was taut to the point of tearing, and a rusty black spike thrust up out of one eye-socket. The nose had rotted away, or perhaps been bitten off, and the ears were gone, too. The mouth was a wide, suppurating wound, full of metal teeth. Cracked and crumbling goat's horns curled up from the wide, distorted brow.

It hurt to look at the Lamentation for any length of time. It was just too big, too . . . other.

It stank of desperate emotions, of hate and despair and thwarted needs, and the sorrow that can only see one way out, and all of it was thick and overpowering with the headiness of musk. None of this was natural, of course. The Lamentation radiated all the horrors of sudden death, of unnecessary death, of suicides and lives wasted, of potential unrealised and families blighted. For suffering was food and drink for the Lamentation.

"Whose stupid idea was it to come here?" Sinner said quietly. There was something about the place that imposed quiet, like an anti-church.

"Yours," I said.

"Why do you listen to me?" said Sinner.

A clump of mists beside the cage suddenly dispersed, blown away by some unfelt breeze, revealing the dead remains of the Brittle Sisters of the Hive. Their bodies had been piled up to a great height, carelessly dumped there like so much rubbish. There had to be hundreds of them, maybe even thousands; enough to boggle the mind. Shimmering shells of insect husks, spindly limbs already rotting where they stuck out of the pile. Their devil's faces were cold and uninhabited, their compound eyes and complex mouth parts seeming somehow resigned. The Brittle Sisters of the Hive—genetic terrorists, insect saviours, ravagers of the subconscious mind. Hated by pretty much everyone. And yet still it didn't please me to see them lying broken and shattered, like offerings to the Lamentation.

When it spoke, the Lamentation's voice sounded like someone who pretends to be your friend, then whispers lies and distortions in your ear when you're at your most vulnerable.

"This is all of them," it said, its quiet rasping voice the only sound in the great hall. "There are no more. They came here earlier, looking for you, John Taylor. They intended to ambush you and bear you away to the dissecting tables, to open you up and dig out all your secrets. To steal your heritage for themselves. They knew you'd be coming here. They bought the knowledge from an oracle. They really should have inquired further. I will not permit anyone to interfere with my guests, or my intentions. So I lured them all in here, with lies they wanted to believe, then watched them all kill each other under my influence, until none were left. They screamed in quite a satisfactory way, for insects. And now they're all gone. The Hives stand empty, now and forever. My gift to you, John Taylor."

"Thank you," I said. "That was . . . kind of you."

"Not really," said the Lamentation. "I don't do kind. Why have you come here, John Taylor?"

"I'm investigating the origins of the Nightside," I said. "On behalf of the Transient Being known as Lady Luck. My companions are Madman and Sinner and the demon Pretty Poison. I have already consulted with Merlin Satanspawn and Herne the Hunter." I tried to think of some more names I could drop, but it was taking everything I had just to keep my act together, in the relentless presence of the Lamentation, so I kept it simple and direct. "What can you tell me about the beginnings of the Nightside, of its creation and true purpose?"

"The Nightside is much older than I," said the Lamentation, its voice a sly and insinuating murmur. "Older than anyone I know. The only one who could give you the answers you seek . . . is your mother. Wherever she may be."

"What do you know about my mother?" I said.

"She was gone, but now is returned to us. Lucky old us. Babalon, Babalon. It took an army of the Light and the Dark to rid us of her, all those centuries ago, but only three foolish mortal men to bring her back."

"Three men," I said, my mind racing. "My father, of course, and the Collector, and . . . *Walker?*"

"Of course. Who else? Those three good and true friends, who had such great dreams and meant so well . . ."

It stopped talking, thick pus dribbling from one corner of its distorted mouth. It looked at me expectantly with its single unblinking eye. I thought hard. This wasn't going where I'd expected, but then my whole day had been like that.

"I met the Primal once," I said finally. "Ancient demons, from the very dawn of Creation, when they possessed some bodies at the Necropolis. They spoke of my mother. They said, *She who was first, and will be again, in this worst of all possible worlds.* Do you know what they meant by that?"

"She is back," said the Lamentation. "And the Nightside will never be the same again. I remember the early days of the Nightside, back before there were Authorities to curb the appetites and ambitions of those who would play here. We all ran free in those days, the Light and the Dark, and those who couldn't or wouldn't choose. That was the point. It was a time of miracles and monstrosities, dreams and damnations built with pride, where anything and everything seemed possible. None of us now are what was intended then. The Nightside was young when the world was young, and all the kingdoms this world has ever known have never produced anything as wild or as free or as glorious as the Nightside was then."

"What happened . . . to that place?" I said.

"We drove your mother out, for we wished to be free even from her intentions, but without her, we lost our way. The Nightside's potential collapsed under the weight of our . . . limitations, and became a shadow of the dream that was. All we have now is a place of small ambitions and furtive pleasures, where all that matters about a thing is the price it will bring."

"You knew my mother?" I said.

"Perhaps. It was all such a long time ago. I no longer remember things clearly. Not even my own past, never mind another's. But I do know that the Nightside was already old when I was a young thing and newly formed."

"And human?" suggested Sinner. I jumped. I'd honestly forgotten anyone else was there.

"Human?" said the Lamentation, not bothering to hide the scorn in its voice. "Such a little thing to be. I am large and glorious. I have always been here, and always will be."

"Nonsense," Pretty Poison said briskly. She stepped forward to stare closely at the twisted thing in its cage. "You're not one of my kind. You were made, not created, this way. The world, or your own desires, made you what you are. There is nothing of the eternal in you, nothing of the Infernal or the Elect. You're just meat, with meat's needs and delusions."

The whole cage shook as the Lamentation howled, an awful, disturbing sound, black flecks of rusting iron falling from the metal bars as the distorted body shook with rage, and perhaps shock. It must have been a long time since anyone had dared speak to it in such a fashion. I felt like applauding. The black iron bars rattled, but the cage held. The Lamentation's skin stretched and tore, but still no blood flowed. The dead bodies in the hall stirred restlessly, and the blood-tinted mists churned and roiled. There was a power pulsing on the air, and we could all feel it. Pretty Poison watched it all calmly. Sinner and Madman were hiding behind me, and I wished I could hide, too. There was no easy way out of the Mausoleum, no obvious exit, and the rage of a Power and a Domination can be a terrible thing. Just ask the Brittle Sisters of the Hive. Eventually the Lamentation settled down again, fixing me with its one awful eye.

"You want to know who your mother was?" it said, and its voice was cold, cold. "If I ever knew for sure I have forgotten, or was made to forget, but they could not keep me from thinking and deducing all these years. It is my belief that she was that old and terrible one sometimes called Morrigan, of the Badhbh; the Celtic war goddess, who also manifested as a wolf and a crow and a raven. That old goddess of battlefields and of slaughter, who dressed in the entrails of her worshippers and whose laughter was the gathering storms of war. To whom every dead soldier was a sacrifice, and every massacre a delight. The secret goddess and guiding spirit of the twentieth century, some say. And you are her only son, already spreading death and destruction. You almost brought down the Nightside with your angel war. Whatever will you do next, John Taylor?"

"You don't really know a damned thing about her," I said, with the certainty of sudden insight. "It's all just guesses and wishful thinking. You gave up or lost your memories, in order to live entirely in the present. To better savour the suffering you steal. How would you know who my mother really was? You can't even remember your own beginnings, never mind the Nightside's."

"It doesn't matter," said the Lamentation, its dry, whispering voice suddenly calm again. "Your quest stops here. Let the past remain the past; I care only for the way things are. It may be that the old days were not as free and fine as I choose to remember, but I won't let you threaten what I have now. All the sweet suffering, the despair and damnations . . . you would take it all away. I don't think so. I won't have you digging up old secrets that might overturn the source of my power, and my delight."

"You're scared of my mother," I said.

"I'm not scared of you, John Taylor. When I kill you here, and make you one of my army, I close the only doorway through which your mother might return to rule the Nightside and spoil all our fun. We shall be safe again."

I glanced round at my companions, just to make sure they were still there, then lifted my chin and gave the Lamentation my best confident look. If you're going to bluff, bluff big. "You really think you can take the four of us? You do know who and what we are?"

"It doesn't matter," said the Lamentation, its voice slowly fading away, as though it was losing interest. "You are in my place, and in my power. I will show you things, awful things, until you kill yourselves rather than have to see them. And then you will rise again, trapped in your dead bodies, to serve me forever, with no will in you but mine. And your suffering will sustain me for centuries."

There was a pause, then Madman laughed cheerfully, and the mood was broken. Sinner was shaking his head, too.

"What can you show us, you caged freak? I am Sinner, and I have known the secrets of the Pit."

"I am Pretty Poison, a demon of the Inferno."

"I'm Madman, and I have seen the Truth."

"And I," I said, "am John Taylor; and you wouldn't believe the shit I've seen. So bring it on, Lamentation. Bring it all on."

The Lamentation shook and rattled its cage again, and now its voice was a shrill inhuman scream. *"Kill them! Kill them all!"*

The dead came surging forward out of the bloodred mists, moving quickly but without grace, cold bodies forced on by an inhuman will. They had no weapons, only the endless implacable strength of the dead and the overwhelming numbers to drag us down. They came from every direction at once, reaching out with pale, clawed hands. But they couldn't seem to find Madman. They stumbled all around him, striking out at anyone but him, while he looked sadly back at them, unmoving. Pretty Poison was already tearing a path through the dead, flashing back and forth impossibly quick, laughing loudly as she tore the dead bodies limb from limb and trampled the twitching pieces under her feet. Chunks of unliving flesh flew through the air, tossed about with glee, and the overwhelming numbers meant nothing to her. Pretty Poison was enjoying herself. Sinner watched her, frowning, but did nothing to try to stop her. The dead surrounded him, their hands bumping uselessly against him, unable to harm a man that Heaven and Hell had already forsworn.

I took a bag of salt from an inside pocket and sprinkled a wide circle around me. The dead couldn't cross the salt, so they circled round and round me, clawing clumsily with their empty hands, driven forward even as the salt forced them back. My heart pounded painfully fast as I turned around and around, constantly checking that the salt circle remained unbroken. I was breathing so fast I was practically hyperventilating. I really didn't like this. None of my tricks or magics were strong enough to hold back a whole army of the living dead. I called out to the others, but they were too far away to help. And then I looked into the unblinking eyes of the dead faces lunging at me from every side, and all I saw in them was suffering. None of this was their idea. They only ever moved in obedience to the will of their master; slaves to the Lamentation. They had killed themselves with the last little bit of their courage, hoping to be free from the pains and obligations of their unbearable lives, only to find themselves eternally bound to something far worse. No peace for the dead here, no rest for those who had been, briefly, wicked.

And the more I thought about that, the angrier I got. I've known what it feels like, when your whole life hurts so much that you're ready to die, just for the pain to stop. A little less stubbornness, a little more resolve at certain moments, and I might have been one of these poor trapped souls . . . What kind of a place had we made of the Nightside, where even the dead weren't allowed to rest in peace? My anger burned through me like a cold flame, clearing my head and calming my racing heart. I fired up my gift, and my third eye, my private eye, opened deep in my mind, allowing me to find and identify the link between the dead and their master. My eyesight lurched, and suddenly I could See a tracework of glimmering silver lines, rising from the tops of the corpses' heads and trailing away back to the Lamentation in its cage; the strings by which it manipulated its puppets. And powered by my anger and outrage, it was the easiest thing in the world for me to reach out with my mind and sever all those silver cords in a single moment.

The dead froze where they stood, stopped in mid-movement and even mid-lunge. There was a new feeling in the Mausoleum, as though an endless tension had finally snapped. The Lamentation screamed, a horrible inhuman sound that rasped through the great hall like a saw through flesh. And one by one the dead bodies dropped to the floor and lay still, as their souls burst up out of them like incandescent stars, blasting out of their rotten husks, rising up and up, free at last. They blazed brightly in that dark place, then were gone, to wherever they should have gone long ago.

I've never believed all suicides go to Hell. God has more mercy than that.

The last of the souls departed, and my Sight returned to normal. I looked about me. The blood-tinged mists were gone. Sinner and Pretty Poison and even Madman were staring around in a puzzled way. The dead were piled up all around us, and none of them so much as twitched. The oppressive atmosphere of despair and horror that had permeated the great hall was already fading away like a bad dream, because there was no longer anything here to be scared of. We looked down the empty hall at where the Lamentation had been. The black iron cage was already falling apart, the metal bars cracking and dissolving in showers of black rust. And lying at the bottom of the cage, under the criss-crossed bars, stripped of all power, a naked man and woman clutched each other desperately, weeping angry tears of shock and loss. No longer joined, no longer a Power, no longer that vicious old Being called the Lamentation. Whatever they had done to themselves, or caused to be done, it was over now. Must have been hard on them, to be just human again, after so long. I did think about killing them, but I had no reason to be merciful. I turned my back on them and nodded to my companions.

"Time we were going," I said. "I think we've learned all we're going to here."

"What about . . . them?" said Sinner.

"Wait till the word gets out," I said. "That they are human again, and defenceless. Then they'll learn what suffering really is. Lot of people in the Nightside have old unfinished business, for loved ones lost and enslaved."

"You can't just leave us here like this!" howled a voice from the dissolving cage. It could have been the man or the woman. "You're supposed to be the great hero of the Nightside! You can't just abandon us!"

"Watch me," I said.

I led the way out of the great hall, and my companions followed me without comment. The hall was already breaking down, disappearing in bits and pieces as the magic that sustained it leaked away. Soon enough the old rooms would return, with all the old memories of what was done there by the Maxwell family. And then maybe, in that old atmosphere of torture and despair and death, the man and woman who had once been the Lamentation might see no other way out than to take their own lives. I smiled at the thought. I could live with that.

Why don't the dead lie still? Because in the Nightside there are always Powers and Dominations ready to make use of them.

We stepped out of the Maxwell Mausoleum, and the perverse atmosphere of Freak Fair was like a breath of fresh air. Until I noticed that all of Walker's watchers seemed to have disappeared, along with everyone else. The street was deserted. All the doors around us were firmly shut, and there wasn't a light showing at a window anywhere.

"Why are you scowling?" said Sinner. "It's always a really bad sign when you start scowling. And Madman's sound track has gone all tense again."

"It looks like Walker has withdrawn his people and closed off the area," I said. "And he wouldn't do that unless he had something really nasty planned and didn't want any witnesses. And given the kinds of horrible things I've known him do in front of whole crowds of people, this new caution does not bode well for us."

We all huddled together for protection, even Madman, and did our best to look in every direction at once. I could have used a break after taking down the Lamentation, but that's Walker for you—always strike when your enemy is weakest. The street remained empty, the busy sounds of city life sounding very far away. Could Walker really know already that I'd destroyed the Lamentation? Had that been the final straw that made him decide I was too dangerous to be allowed to live? Was he finally ready to have me killed, after all these years?

Did he know that I knew about his part in my mother's return?

It could be that the Authorities had given him no choice in this. Had ordered him to stop me getting any closer to answers that might upset their precious status quo. He had tried to warn me of that possibility, back at the Londinium Club. And as I thought that, I knew who was out there, watching and waiting for just the right moment to make her entrance. Who it had to be.

From out of the shadows that cloaked the end of the street came the sudden sound of expensive shoes click-clacking on the pavement. We all turned to look, and from out of the dark Bad Penny came swaying down the street towards us. Bold and brassy, that sweet sensation, death on high heels and loving it, the sexiest, most voluptuous assassin of them all. She was still wearing the classic little black dress she'd somehow crammed herself into at the Londinium Club, but now there were splashes of blood across the front of it, and more standing out starkly against the shimmering white of her elbow-length evening gloves. She came to a halt a sensible distance away from us and favoured us all with a dazzling smile. Down by one thrusting hip she carried a set of blood-flecked antlers in her hand.

"Hello, John," she said, in a voice that promised absolutely everything that's bad for you. "Journeys end in lovers' meetings. And your journey ends right here."

"We were never lovers," I said firmly. "I'm not entirely sure what we were, but *lovers* is definitely not the word. So Walker's finally given you the go-ahead, has he?"

She raised one perfect eyebrow. "You already know I'm working for Walker? Of course you do. I was forgetting; you're John Taylor. You know everything."

"Not necessarily," I said. "Where did you get those antlers, Penny?"

"From Herne the Hunter, after I killed him," Bad Penny said lightly. "Walker wanted Herne made an example of, to anyone else who might be considering answering any of your questions. Oh, don't look so sad, darling! He was a very old god, and his time was over. I can't abide people who outstay their welcome. And there's no greater sin than insisting on being unfashionable."

She dropped the antlers carelessly to the ground, and they made only the briefest of sounds in the quiet. Not much of an end for a once powerful god.

"I bear a message from Walker," said Bad Penny, falling naturally into a provocative pose. "The Authorities really are frightfully keen that you abandon this case, right here. Turn back now, go no further, do not collect two hundred pounds. Or else."

"Am I to presume that you're the *or else*?" I said.

"Got it in one! I do hope you're going to do the sensible thing for once in your life, sweetie. What's so wrong with wanting things to stay the way they are? I've always been a great supporter of the status quo, if only because it continues to supply me with so many good business opportunities. There's always money to be made out of murder, and a girl has to eat."

"And if I refuse?" I said.

"Like I said, darling—there's always money to be made out of murder."

"You'd kill me, after what we had between us?"

"Because of what we had between us! No-one walks out on me, honey."

"Would I be right in thinking there's a history between you two?" said Sinner. "You do get around, don't you, Jack?"

"Shut up," I said.

"Aren't you going to introduce me to your new friends, John?" said Bad Penny, spreading her smile generously around her.

I raised an eyebrow. "Walker didn't brief you? Or haven't you reported in recently? You always were slack when it came to doing the research on a case. Well, this is Sinner, and his girl-fiend Pretty Poison, and that is Madman. We've just destroyed the Lamentation."

"Oh dear," said Bad Penny. "How sad. Fallen in with bad company again, I see. What am I going to do with you, John? I know! I'll kill you right here and now. And just to keep everything neat and tidy, your friends can die with you." She turned her powerful smile on Sinner. "You disapprove of John, don't you? How sweet. Perhaps you'd like to break his neck for me? I'd really like that. In fact, I'd like it if you all beat each other to death, right in front of me."

And just like that, she was suddenly the most attractive woman in the world. Her sexuality blazed like someone had just opened a furnace door. Her presence filled the street, impossible to look away from, impossible to resist. To see her was to want her, to need her, more than life itself. I had my gift, and Bad Penny had hers. She had become the woman you'd do anything for, including murder. Her greatest weapon had always been herself. No-one could resist her body, once she'd turned it up to eleven. Except . . . for all our special abilities, Sinner and Madman and I were just men, while Pretty Poison was a demon succubus from Hell.

"Amateur," she said.

And just like that, the spell was broken. Bad Penny's glamour snapped off, and she was just another really good-looking woman with a bit of a weight problem. She looked at us, open-mouthed, absolutely dumbfounded. I don't think anyone had ever broken her spell that easily, that casually, before. I smiled at her.

"Nice try, Penny. But I have been there, and done that, and, to be honest, I've known better."

She stamped one high-heeled foot, said a few baby swear words, and suddenly she had two really big guns in her white-gloved hands. She opened fire at point-blank range, the explosions deafeningly loud, but I was already moving. I knew how she operated. And yet even as I dodged and ducked, it was clear she wasn't just targeting me. We all had to die, so no-one would ever be told about the failure of her glamour. And that . . . was a mistake. If she'd concentrated on me, she might have got somewhere. I'm fast, and I'm tricky, but I'm not bullet-proof.

The bullets couldn't even find Madman. He just stood there, blinking owlishly, his mind on other things, while bullets ricocheted from the wall behind him. I wasn't sure what damage bullets could do to a demon succubus, but Sinner didn't wait to find out. He stepped quickly forward, to stand between his love and Bad Penny, and the bullets thudded into his chest over and over again, to no obvious effect. Bad Penny blinked a few times, then shot him in the head. That didn't help, so she kicked his feet out from under him. He crashed onto his back, and Bad Penny targeted Pretty Poison. I grabbed Bad Penny from behind, pinioning her arms, and she bent sharply forward at the waist and threw me right over her head. I hit the ground hard, but kept rolling. Bullets smashed into the ground where I'd been. Sinner was back on his feet and advancing on Bad Penny. She emptied her guns into him, going for all the most vulnerable points, but he didn't even flinch as the bullets punched into him. No blood flowed. Like Cain before him, he bore the mark of his offence on his brow, and nothing of this world could ever really harm him again. He stopped right in front of Bad Penny, and she put her last bullet right through his left eye.

"Ouch," Sinner said dryly. There was only the slightest of pauses before his eyeball rebuilt itself, then he gargled and spat the bullet out into his palm. He offered it to Bad Penny. "Yours, I believe."

She snarled prettily, made her guns disappear, and snatched two silver knives out of nowhere. She buried them both up to the hilt in his chest. They were magical weapons, scored with ancient runes, one cursed and one blessed. I'd known gods who would have died from an attack like that. Sinner just stood there and took it. I felt like applauding. Bad Penny folded her arms over her impressive chest and pouted.

"Now that's just not fair, darling."

"Step aside, Sidney," said Pretty Poison, at Sinner's shoulder. "I have business with this woman. Very nasty business."

"No," said Sinner.

"She tried to kill you, my darling! I can't allow that to go unpunished. It's not in my nature."

"You came up out of Hell to be with me, in order to change your nature. Remember?"

"Yes, but . . ."

"Hush," said Sinner, and the demon succubus hushed, for the moment.

Bad Penny poked out her tongue at Pretty Poison, then smiled hopefully at Sinner. "If you're not actually going to kill me, darling, could I please have my knives back? They are family heirlooms, and Daddy would be furious if I lost them."

Sinner tugged the blades out of his chest with some effort and handed them back in a gentlemanly way. Bad Penny accepted the knives, glanced briefly in my direction to see if she still had a chance of picking me off, decided she hadn't, and made the knives disappear. I came forward to join her.

"What are we going to do with you, Penny?" I said. "We can't just let you go. You'd only carry on following us, looking for another good place to ambush us, with better weapons. You're like me; you never give up on a case."

"I am nothing like you, John Taylor! I have style."

Faster than any of us could react, Pretty Poison surged forward, grabbed Bad Penny by the throat and bent her over backwards. Penny squealed and struggled furiously, but couldn't break the succubus's hold. Pretty Poison's fingers now ended in claws, and her widely smiling mouth was packed full of pointed teeth. The red lips were very close to Penny's neck, and she didn't look like an English public school girl any more. She looked like what she was, a demon spat up from Hell.

"Don't!" said Sinner. He started forward, then stopped abruptly as Pretty Poison set her sharp teeth directly against Penny's throat, the points just dimpling the skin. Sinner raised his hands calmingly. "Please. Don't kill her."

"She has to die," Pretty Poison said reasonably, her lips brushing

Penny's throat. "You heard her, Sidney; she's under orders to kill anyone who might talk to us. Either I rip her throat out, or the case stops here."

"No case of mine has ever been worth the sacrifice of an innocent life," I said.

Pretty Poison raised an eyebrow. "You think this is an innocent?"

"Maybe not technically, but yes. Kill her, and you're my enemy. Forever."

Pretty Poison grinned. "Never threaten a demon, John Taylor. We have long memories." She looked at Sinner. "Besides, you wouldn't let him hurt me, would you, Sidney?"

"You're trying to confuse the issue," said Sinner. "All that matters is that you can't kill this woman now that she's helpless. It may be that she deserves it, but we are not like her. We have to be better than that. So let her go. For me."

Pretty Poison considered this for a long moment, while Bad Penny barely dared breathe, then the demon succubus abruptly dropped her victim to the ground and strolled unhurriedly back to Sinner. Bad Penny rose to her feet, brushed herself down, and gave me a smile that was only just a little shaky.

"I knew you wouldn't let her kill me, John. You always were a soppy, sentimental sort. But I will find you again. And I will kill you."

"Not on the best day you ever had," I said calmly. "I'm getting very close to my mother now, Penny. Get in the way of that, and someone will quite definitely kill you."

Bad Penny looked startled, then turned and walked quickly away, moving quite rapidly for someone in a clinging dress and high heels, and soon she was lost in the shadows at the end of the street. I watched her go and allowed myself a small smile. I couldn't kill her in cold blood, but I wasn't above putting a good scare into her. Sentiment only goes so far. And I wasn't too worried about her following us. It felt like we were getting near the end of the quest. I knew where we had to go next.

"Where are we going next?" said Madman, joining us in spirit at least. "Anywhere fun?"

"Not really," I said. "I'm pretty sure we need to go and see the Lord of Thorns."

Sinner gave me a hard look. "Correct me if I'm wrong, John, but I thought we'd agreed that was a really bad idea? I mean, ten out of ten for ambition, courage, and lateral thinking, but minus several thousand for self-preservation. The Lord of Thorns . . . Possibly the oldest Being in the Nightside who still inhabits this level of reality, and the most powerful. I only mentioned him in Rats' Alley because Herne brought him up. I didn't really expect to be taken seriously."

"The Lord of Thorns," said Pretty Poison. "We know of him in Hell. They say he knew the Christ. They say angels and demons are forced to kneel in his presence."

"And if anyone should know the beginnings of the Nightside, it will be him," I said. "He was here before the Romans made Londinium into a city. And just maybe, Walker had Penny kill Herne for a reason; so he wouldn't point us in the direction of the Lord of Thorns."

"This is a really bad idea," said Madman, and we all looked at him sharply, but he had nothing more to say.

EIGHT

I Am the Stone That Breaks All Hearts

I had a lot on my mind as I led my companions back through Freak Fair, not least trying to remember whether I'd updated my will recently. I'd always meant for Cathy to inherit my business if, or more likely when, something happened to me, but I'd never actually got around to putting it in writing. Changing your will is one of those things you always put off because you don't like to be reminded of your own mortality. You always think there's plenty of time . . . until you find yourself on your way to a meeting with the Lord of Thorns. Part of me wanted to phone Cathy, talk to her one last time, but the sensible part of me overruled it. What could I say, except *Good-bye*?

My companions didn't seem too worried. Sinner and Pretty Poison were strolling along hand in hand, giggling like teenagers again, and Madman was off in his own private world. I had tried to explain to them just how dangerous this was going to be, and they'd smiled and nodded and said they quite understood, but they didn't. Not really. Or they would never have agreed to accompany me to the World Beneath. Part of me wanted to forbid them to come, for their own protection, but another more practical part overruled it. I was going to need their help if I was to survive this last part of my journey. Was I really prepared to sacrifice them, to learn the truth about the Nightside, and my mother?

Maybe. It wasn't like they were my friends or anything. Perhaps that's why I'd chosen them for this case—because it wouldn't matter to me so much if I had to throw them to the wolves.

The cold-bloodedness of that thought shocked even me, and I looked around for something to distract me. And that was when I finally noticed that all of Walker's watchers had reappeared, gathered together at the far end of the street and staring at us openly, not even trying to conceal themselves. They huddled together for comfort as I and my companions approached, but looked ready to defend themselves at a moment's notice. The combat magicians actually traced protective sigils on the air between them and us. They blazed brightly, sparking and dripping eldritch fires. I came to a halt a respectful distance away and considered the watchers thoughtfully.

"Told you we should have killed her," said Pretty Poison. "Bad Penny always was a tattle-tale. She's told them where we're going."

"They're upset, scared, and demoralised," I said. "Just how I like Walker's people. Now watch, and learn." I took another step forward, and they all flinched visibly. I gave them my best enigmatic smile. "Hi, guys, I've got some good news and some bad news. The bad news is yes, we did just kick Bad Penny's arse and send her home crying; and yes, we did just destroy the Lamentation; and yes, we are off to see the Lord of Thorns. The really bad news is that I lied about there being any good news. Any questions?"

Pretty much as one, the watchers decided that they really needed to return to Walker to ask for fresh instructions, and within moments they were all gone. The Jesuit demonologists actually departed running.

"Now that is worrying," said Sinner.

To meet with the Lord of Thorns, you have to go underground. There's a whole system of extensive catacombs, tunnels, canals, and sewers deep under the streets of the Nightside, usually referred to as the World Beneath. It is inhabited by people, and others, who can only exist and move in darkness, away from the open skies and hot neon of the streets above. You can be born, live your whole life, and die in the World Beneath, and countless have down the centuries. The dark tunnels and canals also provide a means of getting back and forth in the Nightside without being observed. They're not much used for general travel, because those who live in the World Beneath tend to discourage it, by killing and often eating those who annoy them. And they're easily annoyed.

But, it was the only way to reach the Lord of Thorns' domain. I'd never been there myself. Didn't even know anyone who'd been crazy enough to try. But sometimes I make it a point to be paid in secrets as well as hard currency, because you never know when even the most obscure piece of information will come in handy while working a case. The man who told me about the Lord of Thorns, and the World Beneath, no longer had any eyes. They'd been bitten out. He told me in a harsh whispering voice of a darkness deeper than the night, of tunnels that went on forever, and silent folk who passed through arching catacombs like worms in the earth.

There are no advertised entrances to the World Beneath. Either you know where to find them, or you don't need to know. I led my people through a series of increasingly narrow and ill-lit streets, where people scuttled away to hide in the shadows when they saw us coming, to the nearest entrance I knew of—a small private garden, held inviolate behind heavy stone walls accessed only by a securely locked gate. I studied the garden through the spiked iron bars; it seemed a pretty enough place, lit by flaring gas jets. Like finding a single perfect lily floating on a cesspit. There were trees and flowering shrubs and rich blooms laid out in attractive displays. A thick, heady perfume drifted through the gate to me. Pretty Poison snuggled in close beside me.

"What's a pretty place like this doing in an area like this? And why is this gate absolutely crawling with protective spells?"

"The Nightside is full of surprises," I said. "And mysteries are our food and drink."

"You mean you don't know," said Sinner.

"Got it in one," I said. "But I do have a key. Part payment from an old case."

"Which you're not going to tell us about," said Pretty Poison.

"The world is not ready to know," I said solemnly.

"You are so full of it," said Madman. We all turned sharply to look at him, but he had nothing more to say.

I took the key off my key-ring, and turned it in the gate's lock. It didn't want to turn, and I had to put some muscle into it, but finally it lurched into place, and I pushed the gate open. I could feel the protective spells deactivating, like a sudden release of tension on the air. I stepped aside to let the others go in first. Not entirely out of courtesy; I didn't trust the garden. When nothing immediately awful happened, I followed them in and shut and locked the gate behind me.

Blue-white light from the impossibly huge moon overhead gave the garden an unreal, ghostly look. The trees were tall and spindly, stark silhouettes against the butter yellow glow of the old-fashioned gas jets set high on the walls. A single narrow path of beaten earth curved back and forth through the garden, between hulking bushes and shrubs and past intricate displays of night-blooming flowers. Everything in the garden was moving slowly, though there wasn't a breath of breeze. Even the petals of the flowers opened and closed, like pursing mouths. The flowers were mostly white and red, and something about them made me think *White for bone, red for meat*. I once heard a rose sing, and it was the most evil thing I've ever heard.

"Nice place," said Sinner, stooping to sniff a flower. He then pulled his head back quickly, wrinkling his nose.

"No," said Pretty Poison. "I don't think so."

"Top marks for insight to the demon from Hell," I said. "Everything here has really deep roots. You don't want to know from what they draw their nourishment. Now let's all head for the statue in the middle of the garden; and *don't touch anything.*"

The narrow path wound back and forth, to make sure everything in the garden got a good look at us, but finally it brought us to the statue of an angel, kneeling and weeping over its torn-off wings. The features on its face had been eroded away, by wind and rain and time, or perhaps just by tears. Behind the angel was a moon-dial, showing the exact right time. I took hold of its pointing gnomon with a firm hand and turned it slowly through one hundred and eighty degrees. The whole moon-dial shuddered violently, then slid jerkily to one side to reveal a dark shaft, just big enough to take a man, falling away deep into the earth. A black metal ladder clung to one side of the shaft. We all took it in turns to stare dubiously down into the darkness, then Pretty Poison summoned up a handful of hell-fire. She held the leaping flames out over the shaft, but the light didn't penetrate far. In the end, we made her go down first, so she could carry the light ahead of us. None of us liked the idea of descending blindly into that dark.

So she went first, then Sinner because he wouldn't be parted from her, then Madman, and finally me to keep Madman moving. The heavy rungs of the metal ladder were hot and sweaty under my hands, and the narrow circle of light above soon disappeared into the distance. The light below, now dancing at Pretty Poison's shoulder, was barely enough to let us see each other. I didn't like the colour or the texture of the hell-fire; it made me feel . . . uneasy. I made myself concentrate on the ladder. The rungs had been set uncomfortably far apart, as though not designed or intended for human use. My shoulders bumped against the sides of the shaft as I descended, and the ladder seemed to fall away forever. Down and down we climbed, until my arms and legs ached from the strain, and still there was no sign of any bottom to the shaft. I would have liked to change my mind and go back up, but I didn't think I had the strength to climb up that far, so all that was left was to keep going down. We were all breathing hard, the harsh sounds loud on the quiet.

When Pretty Poison suddenly announced that her feet had hit bottom, we all cried out in relief, even Madman. He seemed more *with us*, of late. Perhaps he just needed shared company and events to ground him; or perhaps he sensed some danger coming, so great he needed to be more focussed to deal with it. I wasn't about to ask. I just knew he would say something that would make my head hurt. One by one we climbed down out of the end of the shaft and emerged onto a bare path beside a canal; dark waters in a dark place. The stone wall on the other side of the canal showed huge claw marks, gouged deep into the stone by something monstrously large. There was no sign of anyone or anything for as far as Pretty Poison's leaping flame could carry, except for a small silver bell hanging from a tall support. The four of us stood together on the narrow bank, huddled close for comfort. We could all tell we'd come to a really bad place. The air was hot and sweaty, like a fever room, and it smelled bad. Spoiled.

"Now what?" said Sinner. His voice didn't echo, or carry.

"I suppose we ring the bell," I said. "This is as far as my knowledge takes us. From now on, it's all unknown territory."

"Ring the bell?" said Sinner. "How do we know it doesn't just announce to the local nasties that lunch has arrived?"

"We don't," I said. "Feel free to chime in with any other ideas you may have. Besides, what have you got to be worried about? You're supposed to be invulnerable."

"Not exactly. Just very resistant to punishment. I'm not sure even I could survive being eaten, digested, and excreted by something sufficiently large and determined. I am a unique case, but even I have my limits."

"Now he tells me," I said.

"Boys, boys," said Pretty Poison. She was kneeling at the edge of the canal, holding her flame-covered hand out over the dark waters. "I'm pretty sure I saw something move in here . . . Do you suppose they have alligators down here? You hear stories, about pets being flushed away . . ."

"I have a strong feeling that whatever lives in these waters would probably consider alligators an appetiser," I said firmly. "I'd back away if I were you. Slowly and very carefully. This is where all the things too nasty for the Nightside end up."

"Ring the bell," said Sinner.

I gave it a good hard ring, and the sharp, almost painfully intense sound travelled up and down the canal, without any trace of echo or distortion. We all braced ourselves, ready for whatever attack might lurch forth out of the darkness, but nothing happened. The sound died away, and all was still and quiet. We all slowly relaxed again. I realised that Madman's personal sound track had shut itself down sometime back. Presumably because it couldn't come up with anything appropriate. And then, from out of the darkness to our right, further down the canal, came the sound of something moving. The slow steady sound of some craft ploughing through the dark waters. We all stared, straining our eyes against the gloom, until finally a low-bottomed barge appeared, in a warm golden glow that surrounded it from stem to stern. It headed unhurriedly towards us, a single human figure standing amidships, poling the barge along with a solid silver staff. The barge was a good twenty feet long, painted a cheerful pastel blue, with big black eyes delineated on either side of the pointed prow. The human figure propelling the barge with his efforts wore a concealing scarlet cloak and a featureless pale cream mask that covered all his face. Disturbingly, the mask only had one eyehole, the left. The barge slid to a halt before us, and the cloaked figure gave us a deep, formal bow.

"Welcome to the World Beneath, you poor damned fools," he said, in a deep resonant voice with more than a hint of a French accent. "Where do you wish me to take you? Not that there is a lot of choice, I'll admit. Upstream is bad, downstream is worse, though at least the Eaters of the Dead have been quiet lately. Someone tried putting poison down a while back, but the rotten buggers positively thrived on it. I hope you've got a specific destination in mind, because I don't do tours. I'd go back up, if I were you. It doesn't get any better, the deeper in you go."

"Pretty much the kind of welcome I'd expected," I said, when I could finally get a word in edgeways. "Can you take us to the Lord of Thorns?"

"Is life really that bad?" said the bargeman. "There are easier ways to kill yourself, and most of them are a lot less painful."

"The Lord of Thorns," I said firmly. "Yes or no?"

"Very well, my friends. Climb aboard. Don't fall in the water. The natives are restless, and very hungry."

We all boarded his barge very carefully, and it hardly rocked at all under our weight. The bargeman pushed his silver pole into the water and started us on our way with one long, effortless movement. There was more to him than there seemed, but then, there would have to be. Surrounded by the golden glow of the barge, Pretty Poison doused her hellfire, and we all relaxed a little. The barge moved silently and easily on into the enveloping dark. The bargeman stared straight ahead, but whatever he saw with his single eye, he kept to himself.

"Don't get many tourists down here these days," he said, his voice quite distinct behind the pale mask. "Not that we ever did have many visitors, and for the most part we like it that way. Peace and quiet's a wonderful thing, you know? Are any of you famous? I don't keep up on the gossip like I used to."

"This is Sinner," I said. "This is Pretty Poison, and that is Madman. I am John Taylor."

The bargeman shook his head. "No. Sorry. Means nothing to me. I had that Julien Advent in my barge once. A real gentleman, he was."

"How long have you been down here?" I asked.

"I have no idea. And don't tell me, because I don't want to know. It was the beginning of the twentieth century when I first came to the Nightside, boarding the newly opened subway from Paris with a howling mob hot on my heels. I soon found my way down here. I'd had enough of the hurly-burly of city life, and wished only solitude. I do miss the opera, though . . . Still! I provide a service here, to keep myself occupied, and as a small act of penance for the days of my hot-headed youth."

"What can you tell us about the World Beneath?" said Sinner.

"Parts of it are as old as any other part of the Nightside, and as dangerous. It started out as a collection of sewers, canals, and offshoots of the Thames, covered over by the growing city, running through and around a huge system of catacombs built by the Romans, so they could do things down here that the world above wouldn't approve of. Very practical people, the Romans. They believed that if the gods couldn't see what you were doing, it didn't count. Lot of people in the World Beneath still think that way, though of course I use the term *people* very loosely. We have quite a population down here, these days. Solitudes, of course; religious types sitting in dark stone cells for the good of their souls. Then there's the odd type who just can't get on with anyone, even in the Nightside. And those on the run, like my good self. The Subterraneans have been down here for centuries, making their own little city out of the catacombs. Don't bother them, and they won't sacrifice you to their gods. Then there's vampires and ghouls and various offshoots of the Elder Spawn . . . We get all sorts down here. But don't you worry yourself about them, my friends. My barge and I are protected, by old custom. You sit tight, and I'll bring you right to the Gate of the Lord of Thorns' domain. And after that—may God have mercy on your souls, because it's a safe bet the Lord of Thorns won't."

"Have you ever met him?" said Sinner.

The bargeman snorted loudly behind his mask. "No. And the odds are you won't get to, either. He is very well guarded."

He poled us along the canal for some time, singing snatches of grand opera and saucy French drinking songs in a fine baritone voice. Madman's sound track joined in, producing perfect harmonies and descants. Things came and went in the dark waters, occasionally bumping against the sides of the barge, but never breaking the surface of the water. The golden glow surrounding the boat was just bright enough for me to make out the strange astronomical symbols carved into the curving stone ceiling above us. Star systems never seen from earth, in this or any other time. Pretty Poison snuggled in close beside Sinner, ignoring the surroundings to murmur in his ear. He didn't respond, except to sometimes shake his head.

The barge finally slowed to a halt beside a section of the canal bank that at first glimpse seemed no different from any other. The masked bargeman leaned on his pole, and looked thoughtfully about him.

"This is as far as I can take you. A bad place, my friends. I would say au revoir; but I doubt we'll meet again."

We disembarked, and he pushed the barge away from the bank and set off back the way we'd come. He wasn't singing any more. The golden glow departed with the barge, replaced by a sullen red glare emanating from a high archway set into the dark stone wall. Ancient Greek characters had been etched into the cracked and pitted stone slabs that made up the arch. We all looked at each other for a while, then Pretty Poison tutted loudly.

"No-one studies the classics any more. Allow me. Translating very freely, it says, *Meat is Murder.*"

"Wonderful," said Sinner. "We have fallen among vegetarians."

"Somehow I rather doubt it," said Pretty Poison. "I can smell rot and decay and the corruption of living things. And the smell is wafting out of this archway."

I could smell it, too. A heavy, noxious smell that left a bad taste in the mouth. Like a charnel-house left to simmer in a hot sun. It was definitely drifting out of the open archway, even though there was no trace of movement in the air. A warning, perhaps . . . or a threat. It didn't make any difference. There was nowhere else for us to go, except back. I led the way in, and the others followed reluctantly after me.

A short tunnel, its curving stone walls beaded with sweat, soon gave way to a fair-sized cavern hollowed out of the living rock. Big enough to hold a fair-sized congregation, but not of any church you'd choose to visit. Butcher's tools hung down from the ceiling on wires, saws and knives and skewers, all of them stained with old, dried blood. At the far end of the cavern was a crude throne, made up of slabs of meat, some of it fresh, most clearly spoiled, all of it surrounded by a great cloud of buzzing flies. And all the walls of the cavern were covered in people's names, drawn spikily in blood, from a wide variety of languages and cultures.

"The names of those who came before us?" wondered Sinner.

"I don't know if anyone else has noticed," said Pretty Poison. "But there doesn't seem to be any other way out of here."

"I'd noticed," I said.

"This isn't at all how I'd pictured the Lord of Thorns' domain," said Sinner. "I think there is a strong possibility that we've been had, people."

"I don't think so," Pretty Poison said slowly. "We're not alone here."

The cloud of flies rose up suddenly from the meat throne, buzzing angrily. They swirled around the cavern horribly quickly, while we ducked our heads and swatted at them with flailing hands, then the cloud returned to the meat throne, swelled in size and took on a roughly human shape. It stood on stocky legs, a dark blocky shape towering over us, its unfinished head brushing against the cavern ceiling. And then it sat down abruptly on the meat throne, and the heavy buzzing gradually resolved itself into something like human speech. It sounded foul and hostile, a mockery of language.

"Welcome, dear travellers," said the flies. "You have found your way to the entrance to the domain of the Lord of Thorns. And this is as far as you go. He does not wish to be disturbed. And so he has set me here, a demon summoned up out of Hell and bound to this place, just to ensure he gets his rest. A Prince of the Pit, damned to obey a servant of Heaven, until the Nightside is destroyed or Time itself runs out. Sometimes I think the whole universe runs on irony. Still, the eating's good. Hello, Pretty Poison. It's been a while. How do you like my place? It's not much, but it has some of the comforts of home."

"Hello, Bub," said Pretty Poison. "How is it that thou art bound here, to a mortal's purpose?"

"Because he is the Lord of Thorns and knows much that is forbidden. Is that your Sinner with you? The only soul that still loved in Hell?"

"Yes," said Pretty Poison. "This is my dear Sidney."

"Pervert," the demon said to Sinner. "And fool, to still believe in Hell's lies. She will corrupt you and drag you back down into the Pit. It's what she does. And she has always been very good at her job."

"Given enough time, and sufficient motivation," said Sinner, "I could probably swat you to death."

I decided to intervene, before the conversation could deteriorate any further.

"Hi. I'm John Taylor. No doubt you know the name. I'm here to speak with the Lord of Thorns. So step aside, or I'll think of something amusing to do to you."

"John Taylor?" The writhing shape leaned forward on its meat throne to get a better look at me. "I'm impressed. Really. Though I'd always thought you'd be taller. But it's more than my job's worth to let you pass. Pride in my position is pretty much all I have left here. And whatever you might do to me would be nothing compared to the torments the Lord of Thorns would visit on me. I am bound to this place, and to his will. Besides, it's been a long time since my last visitor, and I'm *hungry*."

The dark shape stood up abruptly, and huffed and puffed itself up into a great hulking figure, taking up half the cavern, buzzing almost painfully loudly. It tried to pick up Madman with one huge black hand, but the flies just slipped harmlessly past him. The demon hesitated a moment and thrust a hand in my direction. The fingers extended, becoming shafts of flies rushing towards my face. They swept over me, trying to force their way into my mouth, nose, ears, and eyes. I panicked, flapping my hands wildly about my head while pressing my lips and eyelids firmly together, as the flies crawled over my face. And then to my astonishment they all leapt off me and retreated, apparently repulsed. The demon froze where it was, seemingly just as astonished as I was, and I seized the moment to summon up my gift. My inner eye snapped open, and it only took a moment for me to find and identify the Words of Power that bound the demon to this place.

(And yet even as I used my gift, some instinct made me slam my inner eye shut again, the moment it was no longer needed. While my mind was open and vulnerable, I sensed Something awful closing in on me, trying to pin down my location so it could manifest. My enemies had found something worse than the Harrowing to send after me, and all my instincts screamed that if I were to use my gift one instant longer than necessary, this new horror would find me and carry out its makers' terrible intent.)

I said the Words of Power. They arose from no human tongue, or even human sounds, and just to hear them said aloud would reduce most men to madness. I said the Words, slowly but distinctly, forcing them out syllable by syllable, and the terrible sound of them reverberated in my skull until I thought they'd blow my head apart. The demon screamed in thwarted rage, then was gone, taking with him his meat throne and his butcher's tools. All that remained was the sullen red glare, and the names of his victims traced on the cavern walls in their own blood.

Pretty Poison looked at me, taken aback. "How is it that you were able to speak those Words? The sheer power involved should have blasted the soul right out of your body."

"I have hidden depths," I said. My throat hurt. Where the meat throne had stood, there was now an opening in the cavern wall. "And so, it seems, has this place."

We all moved cautiously forward to study the new opening. It was shaped like a door, with smooth sides and top, but that was all there was to it. No warning signs, no welcome mat. Beyond the opening lay a long, descending stairway, carved into the rock face of a vast open space. Hovering lights marked the stairs here and there, but their pale light did little more than show just how far down the steps went. It looked like a hell of a long way. There was no railing, nothing between the open edge of the steps and an impossibly long drop. I started down the steps, one shoulder pressed firmly against the rock face, and after a moment the others followed me. We descended into the dark abyss, step by step, for a very long time.

"Are we there yet?" said Madman.

"Shut up," I said.

"Are we even still under the Nightside?" said Sinner. "We do seem to have travelled rather a long way."

"We haven't left the Nightside, sweetie," Pretty Poison assured him. "I'd know."

"We are in the dark places of the earth," said Madman. "Where all the ancient and most dangerous secrets are kept. There are Old Things down here, sleeping all around us, in the earth and in the living rock, and in the spaces between spaces. Keep your voices down. Some of these old creatures sleep but lightly, and even their dreams can have force and substance in our limited world. We have come among forgotten gods and sleeping devils, from the days before the world settled down and declared itself sane."

"I think I liked it better when you made no sense at all," said Sinner.

The hovering lights turned out to be paper lanterns, nailed to the rock face at regular intervals. Their tightly stretched sides were made up of silently screaming faces. The eyes in the agonised faces turned to watch us as we passed.

"Are they still alive?" I said. "Still suffering?"

"Oh yes," said Pretty Poison, her voice heavy with a certain satisfaction. "Hush," said Sinner.

"But what are they?" I said. "Who were they?"

"Uninvited guests," said Madman, and after that no-one felt like talking for a while.

We descended further and further into the earth. The stairs wound around the curving wall of the vast abyss. The dark rock of the wall showed clear signs of having been worked on long ago, at first by tools but later by what seemed to be bare hands. Someone had fashioned this great gulf under the Nightside for a purpose, but who and why and when remained a mystery. Could men have done this, alone or with help? Why would they have wanted to? Was the Lord of Thorns really so dangerous that they had to bury him this deep in the earth? The deeper I went, the more scared I became. My hands were trembling, and my mouth was dry. This was all getting too big, too important for me. I wanted to go back to being just another private investigator, dazzling the natives with tricks and mind games, trading on a reputation I'd never really earned. But I had to go on. I'd come this far for the truth, and though I'd run out of courage and good sense, stubbornness kept me going.

The wall at my shoulder became increasingly pitted and corroded, and thin streams of liquid trickled down the dark stone. I stopped and studied the wet surface closely.

"Don't touch it," said Sinner.

"I wasn't going to. What do you suppose this is? Acid rain, or the underground equivalent?"

"No," said Pretty Poison. "Tears."

Sinner looked at her dubiously. "You know this place?"

"Of it. All demons and angels are warned about this place. We are almost at the domain of the Lord of Thorns, the Overseer of the Nightside."

"The Overseer?" I said. "Does that mean he's the one behind the Authorities?"

"No," said Pretty Poison. "He's much more powerful than that. He sits in judgement, and mercy and compassion are not allowed to him."

"I want to go home," said Madman.

"Most sensible thing you've said all day," said Sinner.

The stairs finally curved around a corner and came to an end, facing a great and elegant chamber carved out of crystal. A pleasant, comfortable light appeared suddenly overhead, bursting out of one crystal facet after another, until the whole chamber was bright as day, like standing in the heart of a huge diamond. In the centre of the crystal cave was a single raised slab of polished stone, and on that slab, sleeping peacefully, a man. He didn't look particularly dangerous, with his grey hair and grey robes, and a calm face apparently untroubled by care. We all filed into the shining chamber, looking uncertainly about us. I think we'd all been expecting more guardians, more defences, but everything was still and quiet. Like the eye of the storm.

Etched into every crystal facet were characters from the language known as Enochian, a tongue created for men to speak to angels. I recognised it, but I couldn't read it. Not many can. It is corrosive to rational thinking. Pretty Poison moved along one wall, tracing the characters with a fingertip.

"These are names," she said softly. "Names beyond number, of angels from Above and Below, from all ranks and stations . . . Even my name is here. My true name, from before the Fall. No mortal should have access to this knowledge . . ."

"But . . . why write them here?" said Sinner.

"Because to know the true name of a thing is to have power over it," said Pretty Poison. "To command and to control. Whoever put the Lord of Thorns here, and made him Overseer of the Nightside, has given him power over all the agents of Heaven and Hell."

"No wonder he was ripping the wings off angels during the angel war," said Sinner. "But who could give him that kind of power?"

"Two possibilities come to mind," said Madman.

"Shut up," said Pretty Poison.

She sounded shocked, upset. I was concentrating on the man on the slab. He hadn't moved at all since we entered his domain. But I didn't think he was sleeping. Sleeping people usually breathe now and again. And then my heart missed a beat as he sat up abruptly, swinging his legs over the side of the slab, and sat facing us. We all froze where we were, caught in the gleam of his gaze, like burglars picked out by torchlight in a place they should never have entered. With his long grey robes, hair, and beard, the Lord of Thorns looked like nothing so much as an Old Testament prophet. The kind that told you the Flood was coming, and you'd left it far too late to book seats on the Ark. His face looked older than any man's should, and his eyes were fierce and wild and touched with a divine madness. His presence filled the crystal cave, and under his gaze we all flinched and felt unworthy.

Except, of course, for Madman, who shouted *Daddy!* and tried to climb into the Lord of Thorns' lap. We all grabbed him, and dragged him away by brute force. And then one by one, we knelt before the Lord of Thorns. His presence demanded it. Madman shrugged, and knelt with us. I kept my head down and tried to look penitent. This was a place of judgement. I could feel it. And judgement without mercy or compassion is always to be feared.

The Lord of Thorns stood up slowly, his joints cracking loudly, and I risked a quick look. He was leaning on a simple wooden staff, and I felt something inside me shudder at the sight of it. Word was the wood of that staff had been taken from a tree grown from a sliver of the original Tree of Life, brought to England in Roman times by Joseph of Arimathea. There were those who said the Lord of Thorns *was* Joseph of Arimathea. He looked old enough. When he finally spoke, his words sounded like rocks grinding together.

"I am the stone that breaks all hearts. I am the nails that bound the Christ to his cross. I am the arrow that pierced a King's eye. I am the necessary suffering that makes us all stronger. The cold, clear heart of the Nightside. It was given to me to have dominion over all who exist here, to protect the Nightside from itself. I maintain the Great Experiment, watching over it, and sitting in judgement on all who might seek to disrupt or tamper with its essential nature. I am the scalpel that cuts out infection, and the heartbreak that makes men wiser. I am the Lord of Thorns, and I know you all. Sinner, Pretty Poison, Madman, and John Taylor. Stand up. I've been waiting for you."

We rose to our feet again, glancing uncertainly at each other like children brought unexpectedly before the headmaster. I made myself speak up. Because if there's one thing I've learned from dealing with the Nightside's major players, it's that it doesn't matter how frightened you are, you can't let them know it, or they'll walk right over you.

"So," I said. "Are we here for judgement?"

"No," said the Lord of Thorns. "You are welcome in this place, John Taylor."

I felt a great rush of tension flow out of me, but I didn't let him see that either. I looked at him narrowly. "Lot of people think I'm a threat to the existence of the Nightside. Are you saying they're wrong?"

"No. Just that you're a special case." And then he smiled, just a little. "And no; I don't know why. You're as much a mystery to me as you are to everyone else. And if you find that infuriating, think how it makes me feel."

He smiled round at all of us, and just like that the pressure of his presence disappeared. The Lord of Thorns wasn't one bit less impressive, but at least no-one felt like they might be destroyed at any moment. The Lord of Thorns stretched his back, like a cat that's been sleeping in the sun too long.

"You've come a long way for answers," he said. "I wish I could be of more help. But truth be told, I'm just a functionary, a servant of the Nightside. Powerful beyond hope or reason, yes, because I need that power to enforce my will. But still in the end just an old, old man, unable to put down a burden he has carried for far too long. I am the heart that beats in every action and decision that makes up the Nightside, and I'm getting bloody tired of it. So ask your questions, John Taylor, and I will answer what I can. Perhaps because it's the only form of rebellion still left to me."

"Excuse me," said Sinner, very politely, "but what about the rest of us? Are we also immune to your judgement?"

"You don't matter," the Lord of Thorns said calmly. "Only John Taylor matters. Though you three are unique in the whole of the Nightside, in that it has been given to you, for various reasons, to shape your own destinies. This has been decided where all the things that matter are decided—on the shimmering plains, in the Courts of the Holy. I have no power over you—sinner, demon, madman." He looked at them thoughtfully, then at me. "You chose your companions for this quest wisely. No others could or would have escaped my judgement. Now ask your questions."

"All right," I said. "Tell me all you know about the beginnings of the Nightside, its purpose and true nature."

"The Nightside is old," said the Lord of Thorns. "I think probably only its creator knows exactly how old. Certainly it existed before me. Though at that time it was not so much a place of people, more a gathering place of Beings and Forces, still moulding their identities and intentions. The Romans knew of the Nightside when I first came to this land, back when it was still called the Tin Isles as much as Britannia. The Romans feared and venerated the Nightside, and built their city of Londinium around it, to protect and contain it, and to protect their people and their Empire from its influences. They knew of your mother, too, John, and worshipped her; though no-one now knows under what name. If I ever knew, I have forgotten, or more likely was made to forget. I have had a long time to consider the question, of who and what she might have been . . . and down the long centuries I have chosen and discarded many names. My best guess, my current belief, is that your mother was the Being called Luna, sister to Gaea."

"Hold everything," I said, holding up a hand. "Gaea . . . as in the *earth*? That Gaea? You think my mother is *the Moon*?"

"Yes. The living embodiment of the moon that shines so brightly above the Nightside. Why do you think it's so big here? Because she's keeping an eye on her creation. You are a Moonchild, John Taylor, neither truly of the light or the dark, and half-brother to the infamous Nicholas Hob, the Serpent's Son. It is my belief that Luna created the Nightside in order that she might have a stake in the earth, along with her sister, and a say in the development of Humanity."

"But . . . I have heard," Sinner said deferentially, "that the lady in question is, and has been for some time . . . quite mad."

"Yes," said the Lord of Thorns.

Sinner looked at me. "It would explain an awful lot."

"Bullshit," I said, and everyone looked at me, startled. I shook my head firmly and glared at the Lord of Thorns. "You're guessing, just like all the others. Everyone I've talked to has had a completely different idea on who my mother is, but none of you really know anything for certain!"

"Can you please not shout at the Overseer of the Nightside?" said Pretty Poison. "Some of us would like to get out of here reasonably intact."

"If I ever knew the truth, it has been taken from me," the Lord of Thorns said calmly. "And, I would guess, from everyone else. Your mother covered her tracks with great care. And I am afraid there is no-one left older than myself for you to ask. Your quest ends here."

"No," I said again, glaring right back into his cold eyes. "I have to go on. I have to *know*. Are you going to try and stop me?"

The Lord of Thorns smiled slightly. "Perhaps I should, but no, I don't think so. You are a dangerous man, John Taylor, but you represent the possibility of my long function here finally coming to an end. I would welcome that."

I tried to think of what it must have been like, condemned to this small cave for thousands of years, his only occasional company those who came before him to be judged. Endlessly watching over the Nightside, seeing generations come and go in a world from which he must have felt increasingly distanced, his only comforts the cold exercise of responsibility and duty. He'd been a man, once. Just a man. He might be the Overseer of the Nightside, but he was really just a prisoner.

"Who put you here?" I said.

"If I ever knew, the knowledge has been taken from me." The Lord of Thorns looked broodingly at nothing for a while. "I suppose it is possible that I volunteered, but I rather doubt it."

"There must be somewhere else I can go," I said. "With all the Beings and Powers and Dominations that swan about the Nightside, there must be someone who still knows something . . ."

"Use your gift," Pretty Poison said suddenly. "It's a part of your legend that you can use your gift to find anything. Why couldn't it find your mother for you, or at the very least, identify someone who could lead us to your mother?"

"It's not that simple," I said. "Or I'd have done it long ago. The more hidden a thing is, the harder and longer I have to look to find it. And the longer I spend with my mind open and vulnerable, the easier it is for my enemies to locate me and send something after me. The last time I used my gift, to banish the demon at the Gate, I felt Something closing in on me, trying to manifest. Something much nastier than the Harrowing. If I open up again, it will find me, even here. And I don't think even the Lord of Thorns could stop this new awful thing my enemies have unleashed. From now on, my gift can only be used as a very last resort."

"There's always the Tower of Time," said Sinner.

I winced. "I'd really rather not. Time travel is what you turn to after you've tried everything else, including closing your eyes and praying the problem will just go away. Time travel tends to cause more problems than it solves."

And since I now knew my enemies were operating out of a possible future, and sending their agents back through time, there was always the chance travelling in time might give them direct access to me.

Pretty Poison wasn't convinced. "But we could use time travel to go right back to the beginning of the Nightside and witness its creation for ourselves! All the answers and no more mysteries!"

"Not a good idea," said Madman. "There were Beings and Forces abroad at that time that could destroy us all. I have Seen them. The Past is not what we think it is."

We all looked at him, but that was all he had to say. He was definitely getting more lucid, but not any easier to have around.

The Lord of Thorns raised his head sharply. "The Authorities have sent people down into the World Beneath, against all truces and agreements. Apparently your banishing of the demon at my Gate set off some kind of alarm. They have blocked off the Gate and are working to seal off all the other entrances they know about." He looked at me. "I could kill them, if you wish. There are only a few thousand of them."

I had no doubt he could do it. I shook my head quickly, thinking of angels with their wings ripped off and all of Walker's watchers I'd spent good times with in the past.

"Sometimes death can be the tidiest of solutions," said the Lord of Thorns. "But as you wish. I can offer you another way out. No-one knows all the entrances and exits to my domain these days."

"You mean you keep secrets from the Authorities?" said Sinner. "I am shocked, I tell you, shocked."

The Lord of Thorns sniffed. "We haven't talked for centuries. They are in charge of the Nightside's politics. I am in charge of its soul."

"But we're still going to need Walker's people off our back, while I work out where to go and whom to see next," I said. "If the Authorities have ordered him to declare open season on me . . ."

"I may be able to help," Pretty Poison said slowly. "I have a . . . history, with Walker."

Sinner gave her a hard look. "You've kept very quiet about that."

"I have known many men," said Pretty Poison, just as sharply. "Countless men, over countless years. I was given to Walker once, as a present, by the Authorities. I could revisit him, using our old connection, and . . . talk with him. Try and use our shared past to get him to call off his dogs for a while. Maybe even get some answers out of him. Of course, if he won't be reasonable . . ."

"You are not to kill him," said Sinner.

"Of course not, sweetie. I need him alive to answer questions and call off his people."

"Alive and intact," Sinner said sternly.

"You're such a spoil-sport, sometimes. Very well, I'll do it the hard way then. I'll set up a spell so you can all observe our meeting." She reached out and took Sinner's face in her hands. "You have to learn to trust me, dear Sidney. I need to do this, to prove myself to you." She smiled suddenly. "I promise you this; Walker isn't going to know what's hit him."

NINE

Memories of the Way We Used to Be

Pretty Poison stepped delicately through a halo of hell-fire and materialised smiling before an astonished Walker. I could tell he was astonished because he actually raised both eyebrows at once. He was sitting at a table covered with a pretty patterned cloth, and a cup of tea raised halfway to his mouth. Pretty Poison looked unhurriedly about her, and the vision she was sending the rest of us pulled back to show an old-fashioned tea room, complete with live classical musicians and maids in traditional black-and-white uniforms. The musicians had stopped playing, staring open-mouthed at the new arrival, and the maids were falling back in pretty disarray. Pretty Poison smiled widely at Walker.

"The Willow Tree tea house! One of our special places. How sweet that we should meet here again, after all these years."

Walker sighed and put down his cup. It was delicate bone china, with a willow tree pattern. Armed men and women came running forward from every direction to surround the table, their guns trained unwaveringly on Pretty Poison. Some of them brandished amulets and crucifixes, and at least one had an aboriginal pointing-bone. Pretty Poison just looked at Walker and raised an eyebrow. Walker gestured tiredly to the armed men and women.

"Everyone stand down. It's all right. This person is known to me. Resume your positions. Good reaction times, everyone. Except you, Lovett. See me later."

The security people reluctantly lowered their weapons and retreated. People sitting at nearby tables began to relax again. Walker looked at the musicians, who consulted hastily among themselves, and began a piece by Bach. Walker looked at Pretty Poison. He wasn't smiling.

"Hello, Sophia."

"Hello, Henry. It's been a while, hasn't it?"

"May I ask how you got in here, past all the Willow Tree's defences and my own personal protections?"

"Because of our past history, darling. We're linked together, now and forever."

"The past haunts us all," Walker said dryly. "Especially in the Nightside. I won't say it's a pleasure to see you again, because it isn't."

Pretty Poison pouted fetchingly. "How very ungallant. Aren't you at least going to ask me to sit down?"

Walker sighed again and indicated the empty chair opposite him with a non-committal hand. His face was calm and composed as always, but I knew that behind his usual world-weary façade he had to be thinking furiously. Walker was never caught off guard for long. Pretty Poison sat down gracefully, put her hands on the table so Walker could keep an eye on them, and beamed at him.

"I'd absolutely adore a cup of tea, darling."

Walker checked the ornate china teapot before him, found it was practically empty, and gestured for a waitress. The waitresses looked at each other, there was a brief but silent communication of raised eyebrows and shaken heads, then the most recently employed was forced forward by peer pressure. She tottered up to the table, smiling gamely, and Walker ordered a fresh pot of tea and another cup.

"Anything else?" quavered the waitress. "Fairy cakes? Fresh cream? Can I take your coat?"

"Go away," said Pretty Poison. "Or I'll burn you alive from the inside out."

The waitress departed, running, to have hysterics at a safe distance. Walker looked reproachfully at Pretty Poison.

"You haven't changed a bit, Sophia. It'll take more than a generous gratuity to smooth that over. I'll be lucky if I'm not banned."

"But I thought you ran things in the Nightside these days, Henry."

"There are limits. Do try and behave in a civilised manner. I have my reputation to consider."

A different waitress arrived and set out a new tea service. She pushed the second cup in Pretty Poison's general direction, without looking at her, then fled. Walker poured Pretty Poison a cup of hot, steaming tea, adding a dash of milk and one sugar without having to be asked. Pretty Poison clapped her hands together delightedly.

"You remembered! You always were good about the little things, Henry." She looked at him critically. "You look older, dear. Distinguished."

"You look just like I remember you," said Walker. "But then you would, wouldn't you? Being what you are."

"What do you see, when you look at me?" said Pretty Poison, sipping carefully at her tea with her little finger carefully extended. "I look different to everyone, so I never know."

"Let's just say I was perhaps a little too fond of Marianne Faithful in my younger days, and leave it at that." Walker gave her a hard look. "What did you mean, when you said we were still linked? Our . . . arrangement was over years ago. And I'm supposed to be protected from . . . unexpected visitors."

Pretty Poison shrugged. "When I was given to you, all those years ago, it created a connection between us, so that you could summon me at will. That connection cannot be broken by anything except your death or my destruction. That's the rule. A succubus isn't just for Christmas, she's for life. Dallying with such as me is a mortal sin, after all. Still, it is nice to see you again, Henry. I must say you're taking this very well. I half expected you to shout and throw things. Or call for an exorcist."

"I don't get excited any more," said Walker. "It's bad for the image. What are you doing here, Sophia?"

She looked away from him, leaning back in her chair to contemplate the tea room. The musicians played, the waitresses came and went, and people at other tables enjoyed their tea and exchanged polite conversation. Absolutely no-one was showing any interest in Walker's table. Pretty Poison looked back at Walker, nodding happily.

"I always liked this place. So calm and civilised, and everyone minding their own business. I'm glad it's still here. It hasn't changed at all, but then I suppose the charm of such places is that they don't. And the tea is very good. Maybe I should have asked for some fairy cakes after all."

"The Willow Tree has never really been fashionable," said Walker. "But I like it."

"Because it used to be one of our special places?"

"In spite of that."

Pretty Poison gave him a hard look. "Now don't spoil it, Henry. We're having a perfectly nice conversation. I shall change the subject." She indicated the crystal ball sitting on the table at Walker's left hand. Mists curled inside it. "Keeping touch with all your people in the field, I see. I didn't know people still used those any more: but then, you always were a traditionalist."

"I do tend to prefer things that have stood the test of time," said Walker. "The new is never to be trusted, until it has proven itself."

"You weren't always so stuffy," said Pretty Poison. "Remember our other special place?"

"Oh please," said Walker. "Not that opium den . . ."

"The Purple Haze," Pretty Poison said gleefully. "The in place for way out people, back in the sixties. Best dope in the Nightside, with free scatter cushions and psychedelic light shows thrown in. The very best place to listen to the latest sounds and get stoned on imaginary drugs like taduki and tanna leaves. Oh, we spent many a lost weekend there, didn't we darling; spiralling out into the infinite . . . You really were a lot looser in those days, Henry. Is the Purple Haze still around?"

"Fortunately, no. It's currently a health spa and gymnasium, called Health Freaks. The sort of place where corporate young men go to crunch their abs on their lunch-hour, going for the burn and flexing their way towards their first heart attack."

"Such a pity," said Pretty Poison. "I wonder if a trace of the old place still lingers in the air-ducts? In the old days you could get a contact high just from saying the name of the place aloud."

"I haven't thought about the Purple Haze in years," said Walker. "But then, there's a lot of things in my past I prefer not to remember."

"Don't look at me like that, Henry. Aren't you glad to see me again?"

"No."

"But we had such good times together!"

"You were a succubus. Can you honestly say it meant anything to you? I look at you now, and I have . . . conflicting emotions."

"I made you happy."

"You were given to me, as a bribe."

"As a gift," said Pretty Poison. "A succubus, to indulge your every pleasure, your every fantasy. A reward from the Authorities, for work well-done on their behalf. I made you laugh, and cry out in the night, and you never slept as peacefully as you did in my arms."

"Beware the Authorities, bearing gifts," said Walker. His face was still calm, but there was a sharpness in his voice. "You were bait, to draw me in and tie me closer to them. Their usual practice—to ensure their people became used to, even addicted to, the kinds of extreme pleasures only the Authorities and the Nightside could provide. I should have known, even then, that such attractive bait was bound to have a hook concealed in it somewhere."

"If I seemed to adore you, in our time together, then I was just doing my job," said Pretty Poison. "It wasn't supposed to be real, or taken for real; any more than any other transaction with a sex professional. I thought you understood that. I was yours, to do whatever you wished with, yes; but only for the duration of the contract. You can't say I wasn't entirely truthful, when I was first presented to you."

"I know," said Walker. "But I was still devastated when you left. I thought I'd come to matter to you, but you walked out on me without a single backward glance."

"Well of course, darling. That was my job. Corrupting mortals and tempting them into sin. I couldn't take your soul, that was forbidden me by the Authorities: but I was supposed to reduce you to such a state that you'd do anything to have me back again."

"I did everything to try and persuade you to stay. I would have done anything for you."

"That's all very flattering, but I had another contract. I was only ever there for sex. You were the one who insisted on bringing love into it."

"I was young," said Walker. "It's a common misunderstanding, at that age. But I shouldn't have threatened you."

"No, dear, you shouldn't. I was forced to show you something of my true nature. What I really am."

Walker nodded slowly. "Just the glimpse of what I saw gave me nightmares for months. That I had been intimate with such a thing . . . I scrubbed my skin raw, till it bled . . . And you cut me a good one with a claw, before you left. I still have the scar."

Pretty Poison grinned suddenly. "Want me to kiss it better?"

"I'd rather you didn't." Walker leaned back in his chair and studied her thoughtfully. "I was shocked, horrified, at what I'd actually been sleeping with. I let you go, and did my best never to think about you again. I suppose . . . you were what first turned me against the attractions and seductions of the Nightside. The bright neon lies and the dirty little secret pleasures. You opened my eyes to what a moral cesspit this place is, and the duplicity of those in charge. The Authorities don't care about anything except the money, power, and influence the Nightside provides them. And to hell with the poor bastards that get ground underfoot here every day. I decided I had to be . . . better than that."

"And now you run things here?"

"Only to keep anyone else from doing it. I can't trust anyone else not to be seduced by the temptations on offer. Someone has to keep a clear head and see this place for what it really is. Someone has to keep the animals in their cages. You made me understand just how . . . corrupting the Nightside is."

"And that's why you, and the others, performed the Babalon Working?"

"Yes." Walker sipped at his tea, taking his time to make it clear he was changing the subject. "Once again—what are you doing here, Sophia? I wasn't aware demons from Hell got nostalgic over their old victims. Or have the Authorities given you to someone else, someone I should know about?"

"No," said Pretty Poison. "I'm with Sinner now."

Walker put down his cup and raised an eyebrow. "You're *that* succubus?

Well . . . I'm impressed. Really. So you're the demon currently working with John Taylor. You do have a taste for powerful men, don't you?"

"I'm with Sinner now," Pretty Poison said patiently. "And only Sinner. Officially, I was sent up out of Hell to corrupt him, break his heart, and blacken his soul, so that the Pit can claim him again. Actually, I volunteered for this mission, to try and understand a love that could survive even in Hell. How anyone could honestly love a Fallen thing like me."

"You expect me to believe that?" said Walker. "I know better than anyone that love means nothing to you."

"That was then," said Pretty Poison. "Much has changed since then. After all this time with my Sidney, I'm still just starting to understand how he feels about me. And just possibly, I'm starting to understand what you felt for me, back then. And how badly I hurt you."

"I'm married," said Walker. "Very happily married. Almost twenty-three years now."

"I'm glad. What's her name?"

"Sheila. We have two boys. Keith is at Oxford, Robert is in the military. Good boys, both of them. I had them raised outside the Nightside. They know nothing about what I really do for a living."

"I'm glad, Henry. Really."

"So, this Sinner." Walker's voice was entirely casual. It would have fooled anyone else. "He really loves you?"

"Yes. A legendary love, even in Hell."

"I loved you."

"He loved me even after he saw my true nature. What I really am. My dear Sidney . . . I'm sorry I hurt you, Henry."

Walker drank his tea. "Demons lie. That's their true nature."

"Even demons can change."

Walker looked at her coldly. "You expect me to believe that?"

"I believe it," said Pretty Poison. "I have to."

They sat together for a while, drinking their tea, saying nothing, surrounded by civilised sounds.

"I know you've got people blocking the Gate to the Lord of Thorns' domain," Pretty Poison said abruptly. "And more people blocking other entrances. Under orders from the Authorities, I take it?"

"Of course," said Walker. "But if you can get out to visit me here, I have to assume the others can, too. I'd better talk to my security people, arrange to have the containing wards strengthened. Maybe call in some more specialists. Is that why you've come here to see me? To beg for my help?"

"All the wards and specialists in the Nightside won't stop us, darling," Pretty Poison said calmly. "The Lord of Thorns is on our side."

Walker actually blinked a few times. "How the hell did you manage that? I didn't think anyone escaped his judgement."

"He believes in us," said Pretty Poison. "And most especially, he believes in John Taylor. Talk to me about the Authorities, Henry."

"Why?"

"Because. Indulge me."

Walker shrugged. "If it'll get you out of here any quicker . . . There's no big mystery about the Authorities, really. They're just who everyone thinks they are; the city Names, the old, established business families who've gained so much wealth, power, and influence from centuries of investment in the Nightside. The people in and behind the Londinium Club, who avoid celebrity and open displays of wealth and power, but pull the strings of those who do. The men behind the scenes, who will do or authorise anything at all, to maintain the status quo that has always benefited them. And I work for them because all the other alternatives are worse. I have investigated other options, down the years, but most people just didn't want to know. The thought of so much responsibility scared the shit out of them. And the few who were interested turned out to want it for all the wrong reasons. So I turned them in to the Authorities. I'm in charge, inasmuch as anyone is, because I alone have no interest in the temptations and seductions of the Nightside. I know better. I know this place for what it really is."

"And what is that?" said Pretty Poison.

"A freak show. A city of ill repute. All of Humanity's bad ideas in one place. Which is why the Authorities are the best people to run it. Because they only care about the money it brings them. They might play here, on occasion, indulge passions that would not be allowed in the world outside, but at the end of the day they all go home and leave the Nightside behind them. Just like me."

"And you don't play at all. The only honest man in the Nightside. Or at least, the only moral man. And . . . perhaps the most scared. Why are you so afraid of the Nightside, Henry?"

Walker did her the courtesy of considering the question for a moment. "Because . . . there's always the chance that someday all the evils and temptations and corruption will break through the Nightside's boundaries and rush out to seduce the whole world."

"Would that really be such a bad thing?" said Pretty Poison. "If everyone knew the truth about how things really operate? If they could all finally see the big picture? If they could see and talk with Powers and Dominations, the Beings and Forces that move behind the scenes of the world . . . if they knew the score, it might change things for the better."

"No," said Walker. "Things are bad enough in the seemingly sane, cause-and-effect world. If all the fanatics and terrorists, or even the simply ambitious and well-meaning, knew what their options really were, they'd tear the world apart fighting over it."

"You weren't always like this," said Pretty Poison. "So . . . cynical."

And as she and Walker continued to talk in the Willow Tree tea room, she worked a change in the vision the rest of us were watching, to show us the Past.

Information came subtly to us, along with the new sights, seeping painlessly into our thoughts. We all knew at once that the year was 1967, and that the three young men walking down the Nightside street together, talking and laughing and shoving at each other in sheer good spirits, were Henry Walker and Charles Taylor and Mark Robinson. I recognised Walker first, because his face hadn't changed that much, but his clothes actually startled me. It seemed that back in his younger days, Henry Walker had been a hell of a dandy and a dedicated follower of fashion. He strode along like a slender peacock, outfitted in dazzlingly bright colours, the best the King's Road had to offer, complete with narrow oblong sunglasses and a great mane of wavy dark hair. He looked like a young god, too perfect for this material world.

Mark Robinson, who would one day know both fame and infamy as the Collector, was also easy to spot, if only because he was clearly an Elvis fanatic even then. He had that whole young Elvis thing down pat, even to the greasy black quiff and the practised curl of the upper lip. His black leather jacket had far too many zips and chains, and rattled loudly as he walked. He was never still, packed full of nervous energy, and was always that little bit ahead or behind the other two, talking sixteen to the dozen and bouncing up and down on his feet. His laughter came free and easy, from sheer joi de vivre. He had plans and ambitions, and thought he had his whole future mapped out.

It took me rather longer to recognise Charles Taylor. My father. I had no photos of him. He threw everything out, or burned it, after my mother left. In the vision, he was younger than I was, and he didn't look much like me. He didn't look at all like I expected. Unlike his colourful friends, he wore a smart dark three-piece suit and a tie, short-haired and clean-shaven. He could have been just another anonymous executive, toiling in the big city. But what surprised me most of all was how free and easy he looked, how happy in the company of his friends. That was why I had so much trouble recognising him. Because I'd never seen my father happy before.

It was 1967, a time of change in the Nightside, just like everywhere else. They were three young men on the way up, men with great futures before them. They were going to change the world.

They finally entered that most fashionable meeting place, the Hawk's Wind Bar & Grill. I'd never seen the original place. It burned down (some said self-immolation) in 1970, and now existed as a ghost of itself. A haunted building, with real people as its customers. In the vision it looked much the same, though. A glorious monument to the psychedelic glories of the sixties, complete with rococo Day-Glo neon and Pop-Art posters with colours so bright they practically mugged the eyeballs. Even at a distance, I thought I could still smell the usual aroma of coffee, joss sticks, dodgy cigarettes, and patchouli oil. The Go-Go checked jukebox played all the latest sounds, and the Formica-covered tables were surrounded by all the familiar faces of the period, from the enigmatic Orlando to the Travelling Doctor and his latest companions. Walker and Robinson and Taylor smiled and waved easily to one and all as they entered, but no-one paid them much attention. They weren't important people, then, these three. The man who would run the Nightside, the man who would collect it, and the man who would damn it.

Henry, Mark, and Charles commandeered the last remaining table in the far corner, ordered various kinds of coffee from the gum-chewing, white-plastic-clad waitress, then poured over the latest issue of *OZ* magazine, the special Nightside issue. Charles had just picked up his copy, and Mark grabbed it from him, to check if they'd printed his letter about Elvis being the real shooter of JFK. Walker had already read the issue, of course. He was always the first at everything.

We all listened as the three young men talked. It seemed they were impatient, for all their good humour. Their inevitable bright future seemed unfairly far off. They were being held back, by entrenched interests and people who weren't interested in trying anything new—anything that hadn't been around for decades, and preferably centuries. Fashion was one thing, sin always thrived on the very latest fashions; but no-one at the top wanted to know about institutional change. These three young men were determined to seize power and influence, if necessary, so that they could force through necessary changes. For the greater good of all, of course. They wanted to usher in the Age of Aquarius, and the mind's true liberation. Everyone young was a dreamer and an idealist in 1967.

When they'd finished with the magazine, it was time for show-and-tell. Mark was a collector even back then, and had got his hands on something special. He took it out of his shoulder bag, looking quickly about to make sure no-one was watching, then laid his find reverentially on the table before them. Henry and Charles looked dubiously at the cardboard box full of tatty, handwritten pages.

"All right," said Walker. "What is it this time? And it had better not be about Roswell again. I am sick to death of Roswell. If anything had really happened there, we'd know about it by now."

"You just wait," Mark said darkly. "I'll get you proof yet. I know someone who knows someone who claims one guy actually filmed the autopsy on the aliens . . . Of course, this is the same man who claims we'll be landing men on the moon in two years, so . . ."

"What have you found, Mark?" Charles said patiently. "And what good does it do us?"

"Is it something we can blackmail people with?" Walker said wistfully. "I've always wanted to be able to blackmail someone."

Mark grinned wolfishly, one hand pressed possessively on the pile of papers, as though afraid someone might sneak up and steal them. "This, my friends, is the real thing. The mother lode. An unpublished manuscript by the one and only Aleister Crowley—the Magus, the Great Beast, the Most Evil Man in the World. If you believe the newspapers, which mostly I don't. But Crowley was the real thing, for a time at least, and there have always been those who said his best, or more properly his worst, stuff was never published. This manuscript was apparently put on the market some years back, when Crowley was desperately short of money, but no-one was interested. He was out of favour among the conjuring classes, and the papers were bored with him. Eventually a copy of this manuscript turned up at the *International Times*, and a sub-editor there passed it on to me, in return for a complete set of *Mars Attacks!* cards. Unlike most of the fools whose hands the manuscript passed through, I actually read it from end to end, and I am here to tell you, my friends . . . this is the answer to all our prayers. A direct means to our much desired end."

"God, you love the sound of your own voice," said Henry. "*What is it,* Mark? Not just another grimoire, I hope."

Mark was still grinning widely. "One chapter in this manuscript describes a particularly powerful spell, or Working, that Crowley began but never dared finish. And let us not forget, Crowley dared a lot. He started the Working, to summon and bind to his will a most powerful Being, but abandoned the ritual after catching a glimpse of just what it was he was attempting to summon. *Beautiful, terrible,* he wrote . . . and that was all. He ran away from his splendid home on the bank of a Scottish loch, and never returned."

"Hold everything," said Charles. "We're supposed to attempt something that was too scary and too dangerous for *Aleister Crowley*? Called by many, not least himself, the Most Evil Man in the World?"

"Ah," Mark said smugly, "but we will succeed where he failed, because I have knowledge that Crowley lacked. I recently acquired a sheaf of letters from an ex-friend of Kenneth Anger, in which the writer positively identifies which spirit Crowley was trying to summon, and the means whereby it can be safely controlled. My friends, we have the means to summon up and bind to our will the Transient Being known as Babalon; a physical incarnation of an abstract ideal."

"Which ideal?" said Henry.

"All right, I'm still working on that," Mark admitted. "Depending on how you translate certain parts of the letters, the Being is either the personification of love, or lust, or obsession. Or perhaps even some combination of the three. Look, does it really matter? We've been searching for a power source, something we could use as a weapon to bring about change, and this is it!"

"What if it backfires?" said Charles. "This doesn't sound like the kind of magic you can afford to make mistakes with."

"What if we get found out?" said Henry. "Ambition is all very well, but we do have our careers to think of."

Mark glared at them both. "It's not enough to talk the talk; you have to be prepared to walk the walk! Anything worth having entails risks. We're not going to overthrow the Authorities with just good intentions!"

Henry sniffed, unconvinced. "Are you sure about the provenance of the letters, Mark? Are you sure they contain everything we're going to need?"

"Yes and yes," said Mark. "Now are you in, or out?"

"We'll need somewhere secure for the Working," Henry said thoughtfully. "I may know somewhere . . . leave it with me. Charles?"

"I want to study the manuscript, and the letters, first," said Charles. "And I want enough time to do some research of my own. Make sure of what it is we're getting ourselves into . . . But if it all checks out . . . Yes. We have to do this. We'd be fools not to seize an opportunity like this."

The vision changed abruptly, now showing the three young men looking around what seemed to be an empty warehouse. Shafts of gaudy neon light streaming through boarded-up windows revealed a large open space, with bare floor-boards and walls plastered over with peeling posters for long-forgotten rock groups and political organisations. DAGON SHALL RISE AGAIN! declared a particularly faded example. The walls also featured large crude paintings of flowers and rainbows and the occasional exaggerated male and female genitalia. There were waxy candle stubs and scuffed-out chalk-markings all over the floor. Henry looked around the place with a certain pride. Mark stalked back and forth, pointing out things of interest, burning with nervous energy. Charles was leaning his

back against the securely closed door, jotting things down in a thick notebook, scowling heavily.

"It's damp, it smells, and I can hear what I really hope are just rats in
the walls," he said heavily, without looking up from his notebook. "And I
have a horrible suspicion I'm standing on a used condom, but I'm afraid
to raise my foot and look. Honestly, Henry, is this the best you could do?
How much are we paying for this dump?"

"Practically nothing," Henry said smoothly. "The owner owes me a
favour. It's not that bad . . . All right, it is that bad, but then we're not
planning to live here, are we?"

"What's the history?" said Mark. "Anything that might interfere with
what we're planning?"

"The history is dubious, bordering on squalid, but nothing that need
concern us," said Henry. "I came here a few years ago, with a girl I knew
then. Jessica something. The owner rents this place out for new groups to
show off their stuff, and the occasional hippie happening. Whole room is
probably permeated with drug residues. Try not to breathe too heavily,
and don't lick the walls."

"I can honestly say the thought had never occurred to me," said
Charles. "Though I'm now having a hard time forcing it out of my mind.
How long have we got the room for?"

"We'll have the whole building for ten days," said Henry. "More than
sufficient."

"And in a dodgy neighbourhood like this, no-one is going to stick
their nose in and ask questions," said Mark, rubbing his hands together
briskly. "Perfect!"

Henry looked at Charles. "Are you happy about this? You've hardly
left the Michael Scott Library for the past week. Did you turn up anything
we ought to know about?"

Charles scowled. "Not really. The Babalon Working is nothing new.
It's been around for ages, in one form or another. There's quite a bit
about it in Dr. Dee's *The Sigillum Aemeth*, and of course Babalon is
mentioned in the Book of Revelations, and not in a good way. The only
thing everyone seems to agree on is that it's a very dangerous undertak-
ing. I can't find a single report of anyone completing the ritual successfully."

"That's because they didn't have the information in my letters!" said
Mark. "Come on, we have to do this! We can't turn back now! Not when
we're so close to everything we ever dreamed of!"

"It's up to you, Charles," said Henry, ignoring Mark. "You're the
brains. Do we go ahead, or not?"

Charles thought for a long moment, then shrugged. "Oh hell. Let's do it."

They were all very young then. It's important to remember that.

The vision changed again, to show us the Babalon Working. Only edited highlights, of course, but it was still pretty impressive. The lengthy ritual was designed to summon, hold, and physically incarnate one of the Transient Beings; not just a demon or spirit, but one of the real Powers and Dominations. The living embodiment of an abstract concept, in this case love or lust or sexual obsession. (Babalon was an old, old name, and no two sources could agree on exactly what it represented.) The three young men saw it only as a weapon they could use against those they perceived as the villains of the day, and those in the Authorities who might try to obstruct the forthcoming changes. The three young men were determined not to be stopped. They would bring about freedom by force, if necessary. Like most fanatics, they were blind to irony, and even if they had seen it, they probably wouldn't have cared. They were doing this for the greater good, after all.

The Babalon Working involved days of fasting for all three men, and almost continual chanting, drawing circles and pentagrams on the floor, and protective sigils and wards on the walls, along with the regular ingestion of sacred herbs and drugs. They guzzled thirstily at bottled water and sweated it all out again as they stamped their way through ritual dances. They weren't allowed to sleep, or even rest. By the end of the sixth day they were all looking pretty ragged round the edges. They worked naked now, stinking from dried sweat and the human wastes that piled up in the room's corners. Their eyes were red and staring, their voices hoarse and pained from the endless chants, and their hands shook so badly the sigils they drew had to be traced over and over again to get them right. They were beyond hunger, beyond thirst, chemicals roaring through their veins, expanded thoughts clamouring in their minds. They staggered in spiral patterns across a floor covered in chalk-marks of all shapes and colours, timing the rhythm of their ragged voices to the pounding of their bare feet on the bare boards. They were half out of their minds, half out of the world, pushing their thoughts by brute force into another level of reality, until finally they found what they were looking for.

Or it found them. It was much bigger than they'd thought, bigger than they could bear, but they held their nerve. They retreated to the physical plane of existence, calling it after them, and it followed them home. That ancient Force, that terrible female principle known as Babalon. The three men could feel it drawing closer, and a new strength pounded through their racked bodies and raw voices. Their minds snapped into sharp focus as their intent crystallised, and Babalon grew clearer in their linked thoughts. She was indeed beautiful and terrible, and intoxicating in her power.

And that was when it all went wrong. Horribly wrong. An inhuman howl filled the warehouse, resonating in every physical surface, as the entity known as Babalon was suddenly thrust aside by something else; something far more powerful. Somehow it had detected the opening between the planes of existence and seized the opportunity to manifest in Babalon's place. The Transient Being was forced back, for all its power, and this new thing came forward in its place. The whole warehouse shook, the walls bending and twisting. The three men were thrown around like rag dolls, until they were left clinging to the shuddering floor like mariners on a raft, all their carefully traced circles and pentagrams and wards nothing more than chalk-dust, meaningless in the face of the unknown Force that was incarnating. Something impossibly old and powerful, terrifying, bewildering, something that had been banned from the material world since time out of time, but was now forcing its way back into reality. There was a blast of unbearable light, the sound of all the birds in the world singing at once, as Something impossibly vast and complicated compressed itself into physical existence. The three men clung together, helpless in the face of what they had allowed back into the world. They caught a glimpse of something that was denied to those of us watching the vision, and they all cried out miserably in shock and horror, like children discovering that there are monsters in the dark, after all. And then the Power they had let in erupted out of the warehouse, smashing contemptuously through the walls and the wards marked on them, out and loose in the Nightside.

The whole warehouse was blown apart, and all the buildings surrounding it for a three-block radius. Massive fires raged among the ruins, reducing everyone who lived there to little more than bone and ash. Hundreds died. Nobody could be sure exactly how many. The only survivors were Henry Walker, Mark Robinson, and Charles Taylor, who staggered dazed but unhurt from the smouldering remains of the warehouse. They had been spared, though they didn't know why. They were in shock, most of their memories gone. No-one ever suspected what they'd tried to do, and what they'd actually done. They themselves only remembered after some time had passed. Bits and pieces came back to them, but by then it was far too late to say or do anything. Whatever they had unleashed had gone to ground in the Nightside, and all the people whose deaths they had caused would not be brought back by explanations or apologies. So in the end, they said nothing.

They waited fearfully for a long time, for some sign of whatever they'd let loose, but all went on as it had before, and as the months passed with no unusual reports or warnings, the three young men came to believe that just maybe they had dodged the bullet after all. That the incarnation hadn't taken, and the Power hadn't been able to maintain its presence in the physical world. Henry and Mark congratulated themselves on their lucky escape, but Charles wasn't so sure. He haunted library after library, digging through their deepest stacks in search of old knowledge, trying to make sense of what had happened. And when he couldn't, he went to the others and told them they had to speak out. To warn the Authorities about what might still be out there, somewhere.

Henry and Mark couldn't have that. They decided they had no choice but to discredit Charles, to save themselves. So they started a whispering campaign, the gist of which was that Charles had caused the warehouse area disaster through following his own private, unsanctioned researches. There was no proof, of course, and no charges were ever brought, but Charles's career in the Authorities was finished. He resigned just ahead of being fired and went into private research. He took every paying job going, using the money to continue his own ongoing research, to discover just what he'd been a part of. He became very successful, as the years passed, and kept his obsession strictly private.

The three ex-friends went their own separate ways, each blaming the others for the Working's failure. Walker's position was that the ritual was just too dangerous and should never have been attempted. He stayed on in the Authorities, working for reform from within. He became obsessed with Getting On, rising higher and higher in the ranks. Mark left the Authorities and became the Collector, as obsessed in his own way as the others. And so the years passed, and three no-longer-young men made new lives for themselves.

The vision returned to Henry Walker and Pretty Poison drinking their tea in the Willow Tree. And after such an intense ride, I think all of us were glad of the break. We watched as Walker freshened Pretty Poison's cup. He always was a gentleman.

"That was all a long time ago," Walker said, in answer to some unheard comment. "We were all different people then."

"Did you ever find out exactly what it was that crashed your Working?" said Pretty Poison, sipping her tea with style and grace.

"No more questions," said Walker. "I've already told you far more than I should. Why are you here, Sophia?"

She smiled at him over her cup. "There are those who say John's mother is coming back."

"Then God help us all."

"Why would she be coming back now, Henry? What is her connection with John's current case?"

For a moment I thought Walker would just order her to leave, or even summon his people and have her dragged away, but the strength seemed to seep right out of him, as though he'd been carrying the burden for far too long and just didn't care any more. He sat back in his chair, looking suddenly old as well as tired, and his eyes were lost in yesterday.

"Mark set it all in motion," he said finally, his voice flat, almost empty. "Back when he introduced Charles to his wife-to-be. I prefer, however, to believe he didn't really know what he was doing. That he was being . . . used. By then, he was the Collector. Revered, or despised, depending on whom you talked to. Charles was a research specialist, almost a hermit. He called Mark, in his capacity as the Collector, looking for a research assistant to help him in his very narrow field. (Was that Charles's idea, I wonder, or did some Voice whisper in his ear?) By that time, Charles was investigating the beginnings of the Nightside, using all the money he'd made to fund his new obsession. Mark consulted with various experts, for an exorbitant fee, and finally presented Charles with a young lady called Fennella Davis. An up-and-coming young scholar with an excellent reputation, pretty and bright and articulate, and also very interested in the origins of the Nightside. Soon enough, she and Charles were in love, then they were married."

Walker frowned into his empty cup but made no move to refill it. "Poor Charles. He didn't understand that he was just a means to an end. Charles wasn't the point. John was the point."

"How do you mean?" said Pretty Poison, leaning forward. "What is it that makes John so important?"

"I remember when he was born," said Walker, not looking at her. "I'd never seen Charles so happy. He spent less and less time on his private work and more and more time with his new family. He stopped being a hermit and embraced life. He accepted new research commissions and rebuilt his reputation as a scholar all over again, with Fennella's help. He and I and Mark became reconciled again, friends again, after so many years. We were older, and perhaps a little wiser, and we were . . . happy again.

"We all liked Fennella. She was such good company.

"And then Charles finally discovered who and what his lovely wife really was. I don't know if there was ever a confrontation, but suddenly she was gone. She disappeared into the Nightside, and none of us ever saw her again, though we all searched for her in our various ways . . . Charles retreated into his old obsession about the true beginnings of the Nightside and drank himself to death, despite everything Mark and I could do to help. We did try. I'm sure we did. But he shut us out; and all the time he watched his young son as though John was something that might turn on him. Mark and I kept an eye on John, from a distance, looking out for him when we could. We intercepted quite a few attacks from the Harrowing, until John was old enough to fend for himself."

"Does John know that?"

"I never asked him."

"But . . . what's bringing his mother back now?"

"No-one knows for sure. If we did, we'd do . . . something . . ."

"To stop her?"

"I'm not sure she can be stopped. Sophia, why are you so interested in all this?"

"Because I'm working with John to uncover the true origins of the Nightside. And the closer we get to the truth, the more it seems tied in to the identity of John's missing mother. Though everyone we meet has very different ideas on who she was, or is."

"If I cared about you," said Walker, "I'd tell you to get the hell away from John Taylor. For your own sake."

"You should stay away from us," said Pretty Poison. "I'd hate for you to get hurt, Henry."

Walker raised an eyebrow. "Would you? Really?"

"Perhaps. I'm still working on this whole love thing. Call off your people, Henry. For old times' sake."

"I can't. John's gone too far. Made himself too dangerous to the status quo. He must be stopped."

"You mean killed?"

"I'll take him alive if I can. For old times' sake."

"Oh, Henry . . . what is it that makes him so dangerous? Who could his mother be, to terrify so many powerful people?"

"Haven't you been listening?" said Walker, almost angrily. "Whatever we called up and let loose, through the Babalon Working—that was John's mother!" He turned his head abruptly to look right at me. "I know you're there, John, watching and listening. I should have told you all this long ago, but I still hoped to spare you the consequences of our sins. I'm sorry for how things turned out. But either you step back from the edge now, and give yourself up, or I'll have no choice but to have you killed. Just in case you are . . . your mother's son."

TEN

The Wife

After all that, I felt I deserved a very large drink. In fact, I felt I deserved several very large drinks, followed by an extremely large drink, as a chaser. And then maybe I'd go and sit in a dark corner and twitch quietly for a while.

Pretty Poison did her hell-fire trick, and teleported herself out of the Willow Tree and back into the Lord of Thorns' crystal cave with the rest of us. She took time out to give her Sinner a good hug, just to show she was definitely over Walker, and they exchanged gooey endearments for a while. And then she turned an accusing gaze on me.

"Just how is it that Walker was able to see you through the vision I set up? That isn't supposed to be possible."

I shrugged. "Hey, this is Walker we're talking about. He can do anything. I think that's actually part of his job description. What matters now is that we have to get the hell out of here, before Walker's people discover and nail down all the other exits to this place that you just happened to mention to him—Sophia."

"You don't get to call me that," the demon succubus said sniffily. "Only Henry gets to call me that."

I looked at Sinner. "And what do you call her, when you're at home?"

"Darling," Sinner said solemnly. "And no; you don't get to call her that, either."

"Dearest Sidney," said Pretty Poison, giving him another hug.

"It's time for you all to go," said the Lord of Thorns. "I'll see if I can buy you some time by keeping Walker's people occupied. I could use the exercise."

Sinner looked unconvinced. "How can even you hope to stand against all the armies Walker will send against you?"

"Because I am the Lord of Thorns. I was given dominion over all who live or otherwise exist in the Nightside."

"Try not to hurt them too much," I said. "A lot of them are just working stiffs, doing their jobs."

"I will be the judge of that," said the Lord of Thorns. "And I make no promises. I trim the fat. That's in my job description."

I gave him my best thoughtful look. "Why are you so ready to help us?"

The old man shrugged and lay down on his stone slab again, arranging himself comfortably. "I told you. Because I seem to sense that things are reaching an ending, because of you, and I welcome the chance to put down my ancient burden. Don't slam the door on your way out, or I'll turn you into something."

He closed his eyes, and I scowled so hard my forehead hurt. I didn't like the way people seemed to be lining up to inform me that The End really was bloody nigh. All I had to do was close my eyes to see the devastated future Nightside I'd encountered in the Timeslip, in all its terrible detail. The ruined buildings, the dead night, the scuttling insects. And Razor Eddie dying in my arms, as I gave him my word that I would die before I would let such a future happen.

"So, where do we go next?" said Pretty Poison, adjusting the straw bonnet on the back of her elegant head.

"Where is there left to go?" asked Sinner.

"Back to Strangefellows," I said, reluctantly. Alex was not going to be a happy bunny about this. I took out my Membership Card. "If I have to go head to head with Walker, and it's looking increasingly like I don't have any choice in the matter, I'd much rather it was on familiar ground."

No-one else had any ideas, so I activated the Card and we stepped through into the bar, surprising Alex Morrisey, who was just getting ready to go to bed. He'd shut down most of the lights, put the chairs on the tables, and was standing by the bar wearing only a long white nightie and matching floppy night-cap with a tassel on the end. He stared us all down with great dignity, then moved behind the bar to conceal his knees from prying eyes. If I'd had knees like those, I'd have wanted them concealed as well. He really should have invested in a longer nightie.

Alex had his own private apartment, up above the bar. I'd crashed there a few times in the old days, on his extremely uncomfortable couch. Awful place. He collected tacky little pornographic porcelain figures, which cluttered every available surface. His furniture looked like the city dump would reject it, and he only ever washed up when the dirty dishes actually overflowed the sink. His ex-wife used to keep the place spotless. There's probably a moral in there somewhere, except Alex wouldn't know a moral if you clubbed him over the head with it, and said, *Look. This is a moral.*

"We are closed," he said icily. "Closed as in Not At All Open, and Get the Hell Out of Here Haven't You Got Homes to Go To?"

"Well, open up again," I said ruthlessly. "You have some seriously thirsty people here, and you wouldn't believe the kind of day we've had."

Alex sighed. "I hear that a lot. All right; one drink each, at my very special Extra Expensive After Hours prices. And no, I'm not warming up any food for you. What do you think I am, your mother? And give me back that bloody Membership Card, Taylor! If I wanted people dropping in unexpectedly at all hours, I'd advertise for a stalker. Would I be right in supposing that the bad guys are once again hot on your trail and that I can expect armed invasions, mayhem, and bad language at any moment?"

"Got it in one," I said.

"You're a jinx, Taylor, you know that? I know people who sexually molest albatrosses for a living who have better luck than you."

I looked around. "Where are the Coltranes? I could use a little extra muscle."

"I already sent them home," said Alex, reluctantly fixing our drinks. I had a large wormwood brandy, Sinner had a Malvern water, Pretty Poison insisted on a Manhattan, complete with little umbrella, and Madman wanted a pile-driver—which turned out to be vodka with prune juice. Alex actually winced as he served it, and we all winced as Madman drank it. I nursed my drink and considered the bar thoughtfully. Strangefellows at least had the advantage that it was terribly difficult to get into unnoticed. The bar was surrounded by all kinds of protective wards, on more than one level of reality, powered directly by Merlin Satanspawn's magic. If nothing else, we should get plenty of warning of any attack.

"So," Alex said heavily. "What exactly is it that brings you scurrying back here so soon?"

"Walker is almost definitely on his way here," I said. "Once he figures out that we're not where he thought we were, it won't take him long to fix on this place as my most likely bolt-hole. And when he gets here, he is not going to be at all pleased with me. In fact, he may well have his people shoot first and ask questions through a medium afterwards."

"I could call the Coltranes back," said Alex. "Or do you want I should try and get word to Shotgun Suzie?"

"She's already working a case," I said. "By the time we could track her down, the odds are it would all be over anyway. One way or another. Besides, we have Sinner and Pretty Poison to protect us."

"And me!" Madman said cheerfully.

"Well, yes," I said tactfully. "But you're not always here, are you?"

"True," said Madman, and tried to eat his empty glass.

Alex was looking hard at Pretty Poison. "Why does she look so much like my ex-wife, only with much bigger breasts?"

"Let us discuss what we're going to do next," I said, in a loud and determined I Am Changing the Subject kind of voice, on the grounds that you just know some conversations aren't going to go anywhere useful. "The case we're working seems to have reached an abrupt end. There's no-one left we can talk to, old enough or important enough, to be able to tell us about the Nightside's true beginnings. Well, there are others, like the Awful Folk, or the Giants in the Earth, but you don't disturb Beings and Forces like those unless you've already picked out your coffin and favourite hymns in advance. And there's no guarantee they'd talk to us anyway. I can bluff and stare down most people, plus a whole bunch of things that aren't at all people; but even I have my limits."

"I'm relieved to hear you say that," said Alex. "You've changed since you returned to the Nightside, John. You've been using your reputation more and more like a weapon, like you're starting to believe you really are a King in waiting."

"Maybe I am," I said, finishing off my drink. "But then, there's never been any shortage of those in the Nightside. Right now I'm just a private investigator who's run out of leads."

"You still have your gift," said Pretty Poison, fluttering her heavy eyelashes at me over the rim of her cocktail glass. "Why not use it to track down someone else who can tell you what you need to know?"

"Because I don't dare," I said. "My enemies would be bound to find me . . . and they have a new weapon to send against me. Something even worse than the Harrowing. I don't know what it is yet, but I can feel it hovering, waiting for its chance to manifest and take my enemies' revenge for the terrible thing I've done . . ."

I realised everyone was looking at me, and shut my mouth firmly. There were things they didn't need to know. Luckily, at that point we were all distracted by the sound of heavy, measured footsteps descending the metal stairway into the bar. We all turned sharply to look at the stairs. Even Madman seemed momentarily focussed on the matter at hand. I could feel my breath coming short and fast as I rummaged in my coat pockets with both hands, searching for something I could use to slow down the inevitable. It couldn't be Walker already . . . it just couldn't. And then Lady Luck stepped daintily down the last few metal steps into the bar, and we all breathed a little more easily again. Even a Transient Being had to be easier to deal with than Walker in a bad mood. Lady Luck looked just as she had before, a small and delicate Oriental in a long, shimmering silver evening gown. Her rosebud mouth was red as a plum, and her eyes shone like stars. She stood before us, proudly poised and smiling, the living incarnation of all chance, good and bad. The lottery win and the heart attack, the sudden cancer and the perfect moment, and everything in between. I think we were all impressed; except, of course, for Alex, who sniffed loudly behind his bar.

"Doesn't anyone take *Closed* for an answer any more? I can remember a time when locking my door actually made a difference. I've got to get those protective wards upgraded. What do you want, Lady?"

"Hello, John," said Lady Luck, ignoring everyone else to fix her attention on me. It felt like suddenly being hit by a spotlight. "I thought I'd just look in on you, see how you were getting on. Do you have any answers for me yet?"

"Well," I said. "There have been some interesting developments . . ."

"That isn't what I asked you, John."

"So you're an actual Transient Being," said Sinner. "Wow. I'm impressed. Really. It's not often we get to see one of your station in the flesh these days. In fact, I was under the impression that you only appeared once in a Blue Moon."

"I'm here for a reason," said Lady Luck, still looking only at me.

"Yes," Madman said abruptly. "You are. But you're not Lady Luck. You're not even a Transient Being." We all looked at him. His face was white and strained, with blotchy patches of colour, but he seemed entirely rational. "I know you, Lady. I have Seen you before."

"So you have," said the woman who wasn't Lady Luck. "Poor thing." She smiled graciously at him, and he winced, raising his hands as though to protect himself. Her voice was calm, perhaps a little regretful, as she turned her gaze and her smile on me again. "I'm sorry to have deceived you, John, but if you'd known who you were really working for, you wouldn't have taken the case."

She dropped the glamour that surrounded her, and the sweet and delicate Oriental disappeared, replaced by a new vision. Madman shrank back against the bar, horror stamped on his face. Even in his confused state, he still Saw more deeply than the rest of us. He looked away, squeezing his eyes shut and whimpering. By now the woman looked entirely different. She was tall and thin, with colourless skin and jet-black hair, eyes, and lips, like a black-and-white photograph. Her face was sharp and pointed, with a prominent bone structure and a hawk nose. Her mouth was thin-lipped and somehow subtly too wide, and her dark eyes were full of a fire that could burn through anything. She was still wearing the shimmering silver dress, but on this new her it looked more sinister than stylish.

"Hello, John," she said, in a deep, smooth voice like bitter honey. "I'm your mother."

The words seemed to fill the bar. Everything had gone still and quiet, as though history itself had paused to appreciate such a significant moment. I didn't know what to do or say. I'd thought and planned and dreamed about what it would be like, when I finally came face to face with my mother, but I'd never thought it would be like this. After all the years of searching and wondering, I'd never expected her to just stroll casually back into my life . . . but I should have known it would always be on her terms, not mine. I'd thought I'd know what I would say. I'd rehearsed it often enough in dark moments, all the accusations and harsh words, but . . .

I had no memories of her, from before she'd left. I should have, I wasn't that young, but it was as though she'd taken everything of her with her when she left. And yet I'd always thought I'd just . . . *know*, when I saw her. How could I not know my own mother? But the stark and sinister woman before me was a stranger. I didn't know what I felt about her. It was all just too sudden.

My mother smiled at me. I think it was supposed to be an understanding smile, but on her it just looked intimidating. Like some graceful feline predator assessing its prey.

"Come on, John, pick up the slack. We have so much to discuss, before Walker arrives. Why, for instance, did I disguise myself as Lady Luck? She was just a mask I hid behind, to get your investigations started."

"Why did you want me to take the case?" I said finally. "Why did you send me searching for questions you already know the answers to?"

"Because I wanted you to stir things up. Stir people up. I want everyone to be thinking and talking about the true beginnings of the Nightside, and what it was supposed to be. I wanted everyone talking about how much the Nightside has changed, down the many centuries. And I wanted you to be able to tell them how and why it all began, and who began it, so that they would understand what it meant, that I was coming back." She fixed me with her burning gaze, and her smiled widened. "I am back, John. Aren't you glad to see me again, after all these years?"

"You abandoned me," I said.

She shrugged easily. "It was necessary. I knew you'd survive. You're my son."

"Where have you been all this time?"

"Walking up and down in the Nightside, wearing many faces, learning the shape and condition of the current Nightside. It has changed so very much. It was never meant to be as dark as this. Or as tacky."

"Did you ever love me?" I didn't know I was going to say that, so bluntly, until I said it. The words forced themselves out of me.

"Of course. That's why I left you with your father. So you could be human, and innocent, for a while."

"Who are you?" I said.

And she said, "I am Lilith. Adam's first wife, thrown out of Eden for refusing to bow down to Adam's authority. Though, of course, you must understand, that's just a parable. A simple fiction to help you comprehend a far more complicated reality. You don't think I really look like this, do you? I am far greater, and more powerful. This is just another mask, put on for old times' sake. This is the face and body I wore to be your mother, John."

"Fennella Davis," I said. Even as I was still thinking, *Lilith? My mother is a biblical myth?*

"Exactly."

Madman peeked at her, past my shoulder, his voice shocked almost normal. "Lilith is just a projection into our limited reality of something much bigger. This female human body is just something Lilith wears to walk around in, like a glorified glove puppet. She's really . . ." He stopped, hesitating. "She is really . . ." But he didn't have the words. Perhaps there were no words, in our simple rational language. Whatever his mathematics had enabled him to See of her, in his brief glimpse of the Reality behind reality, he still couldn't describe it to us. He started to shake and tremble, then to cry, and the bar and all the things and people in it began to shake along with him. It was as though an earthquake had hit the place. Tables and chairs danced and clattered on the juddering floor. The walls bowed in and out, the solid stone flexing unnaturally. Strange colours came and went, and sounds that made no sense. Distance became uncertain and unreliable, and things were both close and far away at the same time. Directions changed without warning. Madman's hold on reality was weakening again, and reality around him weakened as well. Merlin's great oak tree slammed back into the bar again, taking up the middle of the room; and then it was a tower built of stained and discoloured bones; and then it was gone again. Cracks crawled jaggedly across the floor, opening wide to show vast watching eyes. I could hear things scuttling across the outer walls of our perception. Things that wanted *in.*

"That's enough of *that,*" Lilith said sharply.

And just like that, everything was still and normal again. Madman's projected unreality was immediately suppressed, the bar snapping back into sharp focus as Lilith's super-presence stabilised the world, and him. He stopped shaking and crying, and a little colour actually seeped back into his cheeks. Lilith looked at him thoughtfully.

"You Saw what mortal man was never supposed to See. Was not designed to cope with. Let me take the knowledge away from you, so that you can be ignorant and happy again."

"No," Madman said firmly, surprising us all. "Even a bitter truth is better than a comfortable lie."

"But the truth is killing you," said Lilith.

"No," said Madman. "I'm adapting."

Somehow, that thought was even more worrying. I cleared my throat loudly, to get everyone's attention.

"So," I said to my mother, trying really hard to keep my voice calm and casual. "You're Lilith. I know some of your story. Pew told me, a long time ago, when he was still my teacher."

"Blind Pew?" said Alex. "The rogue vicar? The Christian terrorist? Is he still around?"

"Yes," I said. "And if you interrupt me again, Alex, I'll have my mother turn you into a tea cosy."

"That's it," said Alex, snatching my empty glass off the bar top. "You're cut off. You get nasty when you've been drinking, John."

I ignored him, concentrating on Lilith. "According to the stories, after you were expelled from Eden you went down into Hell, where you coupled with demons and gave birth to all the monsters that have plagued the world."

"I was young," said Lilith. "You know how it is. We all do things we later regret, when we're being rebellious teenagers. Anyway, I got over that phase, and after travelling extensively through the many levels of reality, seeing the sights and working out my options, I finally ended up in the world of men. Not that men had made much of an impression on the place, in those days. Beings and Forces still walked freely, and a new legend was born every minute. I created the Nightside, a world within a world, in a place the Romans would later name Londinium. Interesting people, the Romans. A very savage form of civilisation. Some of them worshipped me, and I let them.

"Now pay attention, John, because this is the important bit. The Nightside was created and designed to be the one place on Earth where Heaven and Hell could not interfere or intimidate. A place set apart from the ordained war between Good and Evil. An alternative way to live. The only truly free place on Earth. It didn't turn out the way I expected, but then, that's life for you.

"Creating the Nightside, on Earth but not of it, stable but entirely separate, seriously weakened me. My power was much diminished, and the rising major players of that time, some human but mostly not, seized the opportunity to band together and thrust me back out of this reality, and into Limbo. So that they could be truly free, even from my intentions. I don't bear them any malice. Not really. I've outlived nearly all of them.

And Limbo wasn't the worst place to be exiled to. Limbo is a place, or not-place, where things only exist in potential. Ideas without form."

"Like the Primal?" I said, just to show I was paying attention.

"Oh, please. They're just chalk-drawings, compared to me. But as an idea without shape or form, I was helpless to do anything. I was trapped in Limbo, unable to open a door into any other realm. Until someone here created an opening I could use. They were trying to incarnate a female principle into physical existence, a part of the Babalon Working, and it was easy for me to push the Transient Being aside and imprint myself upon the summoning. Someone in that group hadn't done his homework properly. He'd left all kinds of openings for a determined mind to take advantage of. And once I'd left Limbo behind, they couldn't keep me out. All the Powers and Dominations that ever were couldn't have stopped me then.

"I came through, decanted myself into the idealised body I found waiting in their minds, then disappeared, losing myself in the Nightside. Partly because I wanted to walk incognito to see how much things had changed in my absence, and partly to conceal myself from any of my old enemies who might have survived. I was still vulnerable, then. I needed to rebuild my power in peace. After some time, when I was myself again, I chose one of my unwitting summoners, who seemed to have grasped a little of the truth, and—disguised as the woman Fennella Davis—I made a child with him. The child rooted me in this reality, so that I could never be forced out again. I hadn't planned to stick around afterwards, but you were so fascinating, John . . . I'd never had a human child before. Flesh of my flesh, spirit of my spirit . . . I was curious to see how you'd turn out. And I enjoyed playing human. Being mother. Carrying out the role I had originally been intended for . . .

"And then Charles found out. Somebody told him; I never did discover who. But it meant I had to disappear again, back into the more secret depths of the Nightside, so that no-one would ever guess your true identity, your true nature and purpose. If any of the day's major players had even suspected, they would have been lining up to kill you, for any number of reasons. I knew Charles wouldn't talk. If anyone ever suspected he was responsible for bringing back Lilith, the manner of his death would have been legendary, even in the Nightside. And, of course, he still believed his research would uncover a way to banish me again. He couldn't talk to his old friend Henry, by then so highly placed in the Authorities, and he wouldn't talk to his old friend Mark, who had been the Collector, because Mark had found Fennella Davis in the first place. Charles was alone. He couldn't trust anyone any more. Not even his young son. Poor Charles.

"I never did find out who told him. But whoever it was, they never talked either. Perhaps because they knew what I would do to them, the moment they revealed themselves.

"Now my power is back. The stars have come round again, and all the most dangerous Powers and Forces in the Nightside have been nicely weakened by the angel war. I knew causing the Unholy Grail to be brought to the Nightside would shake things up. The time is right for me to remake and refashion the Nightside into what I always intended it to be. Something much . . . purer in concept. A great many people will undoubtedly die in the process, yes, but you can't make an omelette without beating hell out of the eggs."

She smiled around at all of us, inviting comment. And all I could think of was the awful dead landscape I'd walked through in the Timeslip. Was that her idea of a purer concept? Or did it mean that something was going to go horribly wrong with her plans? That the Powers and the Dominations of the Nightside would go to war with her, to preserve their vision of the Nightside, and everyone would lose?

"No," I said, and everyone looked at me. Even I could hear the coldness in my voice. I met Lilith's dark gaze as steadily as I could. "I can't let you do that, Lilith. I've seen the world that's coming, because of you and me, and I'll see us both dead and gone before I'll ever let that happen."

Lilith shook her head. "How sharper than a serpent's tooth . . ."

"And the fruit never falls far from the tree," said a familiar voice.

We all looked round, startled, as Walker unhurriedly descended the metal stairs into the bar. He still looked every inch the city gent, calm and unruffled. He stopped at the foot of the stairs, smiled at us all, and raised his bowler hat politely to Lilith.

"Doesn't anybody ever bother to knock any more?" Alex said bitterly. "That's it; I'm putting in barbed wire and anti-personnel hexes."

"You didn't really think the Lord of Thorns would fool me for long, did you?" said Walker, looking only at me. "Not when we have such urgent business to discuss."

"You're very brave to come in here alone," I said. "How does it feel, Henry, to be faced with a whole bunch of people you can't control with your famous Voice?"

Walker just smiled. "That's why I brought reinforcements, John."

And that was when a whole army of people came clattering down the metal steps to back up Walker. They fanned out on either side of him, taking up half the bar. I recognised some of the combat magicians, but there were a hell of a lot more of them now, all looking grim and determined and ready for action. These were professional fighters, cold-hearted killers, the kind the Authorities send out when they don't want anything left behind but scorched earth. But it was the last two to enter the bar who really caught my attention.

Bad Penny descended the stairway with her head held high, like a member of the Royal Family visiting an abattoir. She flashed me a brief, vicious smile. And right behind her came Pew, my old enemy Pew, tall and broad-shouldered, a soldier of Christ in his usual battered grey cloak over his vicar's outfit, a mane of long grey hair and a simple grey cloth hiding his blind eyes. Descending confidently and valourously into a world of sin, having already made a deal with the devil called Walker. Pew turned his great blocky head in my direction and nodded slowly, armoured in his cold and brutal faith.

"I apologise for the small turn-out," murmured Walker, brushing an invisible bit of lint from his immaculate sleeve. "But most of my people are currently earning their money for a change, by keeping the Lord of Thorns occupied so he won't interfere here and save your worthless souls. I'm afraid this is the end of the road, Taylor. You can't say I haven't given you every chance, since you returned. But now the Authorities want you and everyone else here dead, for the sin of making a bloody nuisance of yourselves." He paused then, looking at Lilith. "Fennella . . . my oldest sin, come back to haunt me. I shall enjoy seeing you destroyed."

"Poor Henry," said Lilith. "Always putting your money on the wrong dream."

I ignored them both, looking at Pew. He felt my gaze and stirred uneasily, one hand rising to his white collar. And then he squared his broad shoulders defiantly, his mouth hard and unyielding, and I knew nothing I could say would change his mind. I still had to try.

"Hello, Pew. I thought you didn't set foot in dens of iniquity like this."

"My business is with sinners, so I must go where the sin is," Pew said roughly. "Time to pay the piper, John, and make your peace with God."

"Are you really here to kill me at last, Pew?"

"Yes. I will save your soul, if I can. For old times' sake."

"My mother is here," I said. "Do you know my mother, Pew?"

"Of course. I've always known. I told you I gave up my eyes for wisdom. I was the one who told your father who and what he was married to. I still had faith you could be saved, then."

Cold anger pushed aside the shock of what I was hearing. "*You* told him? You broke up my family! You destroyed my life!"

"You should never have been born, John. Abomination." His voice was almost kindly now. "I should have killed you long ago, and now I pay for the weakness of my resolve with the pain I will feel for killing . . . such a worthy adversary."

"You will not touch my son, preacher," said Lilith.

Pew's head snapped round in her direction, and he stabbed a finger right at her before launching into a long, angry incantation. I recognised some of it, from old parchments and forbidden books. It was an exorcism, and a very old one, in Aramaic and Latin and corrupt Coptic. The old words hammered on the air, full of significance and power, and Lilith laughed at them. Pew broke off, confused.

"I know that song," said Lilith. "It's the exorcism the Christ used against the possessors called Legion, who ended up in the Gadarene swine. But I am much older than that, and such bindings have no power over me."

"You cannot stand against me!" said Pew, almost spitting out the words. "I speak for God!"

"We never got on," said Lilith.

She gestured almost negligently with one hand, and Pew was thrown the whole width of the bar, hurtling ungainly through the air to smash into the far stone wall with sickening force. We all heard his bones break. Blood flew from his mouth. He slid down the wall and curled up on the floor, twitching spasmodically. Lilith laughed, a brief, happy sound like water splashing in a fountain. I ran over to Pew, knelt beside him, and cradled him in my arms. There is no-one closer than friends or family, except perhaps an enemy you've known all your life. I cradled his noble head on my chest, and blood spilled out of his mouth to stain my white trench coat. His grey blindfold had come loose, revealing dark empty eye-sockets. His breathing was harsh and uneven, spraying the air with blood from deep in his lungs.

"John?" he said.

"Hush, Pew. I'm here. I'm here."

"Pride. The sin of pride. I really thought I could take her."

"Hush."

"I should have killed you long ago."

"I know."

"But you were a child, and I thought you could be saved. And later, I saw you trying so hard to be a good man, and I doubted. When you left the Nightside, I thought perhaps it was a sign. I wanted to believe that. And then you came back. Why did you have to come back, John?"

"Hush, Pew."

"Always knew you'd be the death of me. I wish . . . I could have brought you to see the Light. It really is so . . . glorious . . ."

I glared at Lilith. "Do something. Save him! He's a good man, and he doesn't deserve to die like this!"

"You must learn to be strong, John," said Lilith. "To be able to do what's necessary."

I would have shouted at her, begged and threatened and promised her anything, but Pew had stopped breathing. "You didn't have to kill him," I said. "It wasn't necessary."

"I will decide what is necessary," said Lilith. "You must forget these old restrictive ideas of Good and Evil. The only real good is what serves the Nightside, the only real evil that which opposes its best interests. Come with me, my son, and I will teach you many things."

And then Walker's people responded to some unseen signal from him, and launched their attack, focussing their destructive magics on Sinner and Pretty Poison. The combat magicians waved their hands around, shouting their Words of Power, brandishing magic amulets and wands and pointing-bones, and powerful energies crackled on the air. Tables and chairs exploded, but Sinner and Pretty Poison stood firm. Alex quickly disappeared behind the bar, head well down, dragging Madman along with him. I could hear him shouting something about Merlin's defences kicking in anytime soon, but I knew better. Walker was the Voice of the Authorities, and Merlin . . . was just a dead sorcerer. While he was sleeping.

Walker and Lilith looked at each other, ignoring the chaos around them.

I laid Pew's body carefully on the floor and moved the grey cloth back to cover his empty eyes. I raised my head and yelled out to Alex.

"Any chance you could get Merlin to manifest again?"

"And make things even worse?" said Alex, without raising his head above the bar. "I think we should wait until we're really desperate."

"Personally, I think we passed desperate some time back," said Madman.

I could barely hear them above the roar of discharging magics. Sinner was standing in front of Pretty Poison, protecting her with his invulnerable body. At first the magical attacks couldn't seem to find him, exploding everywhere except where he stood, doing great damage to the bar and its furnishings, but not much else. But the sheer amount of power amassed against Sinner overwhelmed even his innate condition, and the attacks began to strike home. Bullets from specially blessed and cursed guns slammed into his chest, and though no blood flowed, the holes in his chest did not heal or close. Curses burned his flesh and cracked his bones. Elemental forces ripped and tore at him, and one eye exploded messily in his head. Sinner made no move to attack those who were trying to kill him. For all his dubious history, he'd never learned to hate anyone. I don't think he had it in him. He just stood his ground, standing firm against everything anyone could throw at him, refusing to go down, refusing to allow Pretty Poison to be hurt.

None of the magics went anywhere near Lilith.

And while I was watching all this and trying to decide what to do for the best, Bad Penny took advantage of my distraction. She used her ability to turn up unexpectedly, appeared out of nowhere behind me, and stuck a knife in my back. Some instinct warned me at the very last moment, and I twisted aside, but the long blade still sank deep into my back, jarring against my spine. I lashed out with one arm, throwing Penny backwards, and then the pain paralysed me, screaming through my lower back. I dropped to my knees, panting for breath, my head reeling. I gritted my teeth and clung grimly onto consciousness, forcing my thoughts to make sense. There didn't seem to be any blood in my mouth, so hopefully Penny had missed the lung. The pain was bad, but it was bearable. I reached slowly round with one hand, crying out at the pain, trying to get hold of the knife hilt, but it was out of reach. So, leave it where it was and worry about it later.

I forced myself up onto my feet again, sweat dripping from my face at the effort, and Penny swore and stamped her foot angrily as she saw she hadn't finished me off after all. She started forward, another knife in her hand, and then our eyes met, and we both hesitated for a moment. I didn't really know her. We'd worked a few cases together, been to bed a few times, but we'd never been close. And right then, I don't think it would have mattered even if we had been. She was ready to kill me. I could see it in her eyes and in her cold, nasty smile. And I was so angry at Pew's death and needed someone to take it out on.

She came at me with the other knife, and I reached deep inside myself, powered up my gift, opened up my third eye, and found within Bad Penny the magic that allowed her always to turn up unexpectedly. And it was the easiest thing in the world for me to shut down that magic and rip it right out of her, taking away her ability to turn up anywhere at all. She looked at me with horror as she lost her grip on the world and faded slowly and silently away, never to return.

I waved good-bye. I don't think I smiled. I don't like to think I might have smiled.

But in using my gift, I had made myself vulnerable to my enemies. They found me almost immediately, and sent their new weapon after me, punching right through the bar's defences. Bright actinic energies flared, sharp and powerful, dazzling as the sun. Everyone cried out and fell back, except for Lilith. All hostilities paused, as the terrible thing that had been haunting me so remorselessly materialised. The terrible light faded away, revealing the awful weapon my enemies had sent to kill me.

It was Shotgun Suzie.

She looked older, hard-used, and horribly disfigured. Her long straggly hair was white, streaked with grey and packed dirt. Inside her torn and battered leathers she was painfully thin, but she burned with a fierce unnatural energy. Her presence crackled on the air, dominating the scene, like Death herself come walking among mortals. Her gaze was cold and implacable. Half her face had been burned away, long ago; the skin was blackened and crisped and twisted around the seared-shut eye. One side of her mouth was twisted up into a permanent caustic smile.

But that wasn't the worst thing. Her right forearm was gone, stopped at the elbow. In its place someone had fitted the Speaking Gun. A weapon originally designed to kill angels. It had been refashioned from the last time I saw it, from a handgun to a shotgun, but it was still the ugliest, vilest weapon I had ever seen. It was made of meat, of flesh and bone, held together with dark-veined gristle and shards of cartilage, bound with long strips of pale skin. The long handle was discoloured bone, plugged clumsily into what was left of her elbow. Thick fleshy cables rose up out of the stock of the Gun and plunged into her upper arm. The red meat of the elongated barrels glistened wetly, and the strands of skin had a hot, sweaty look.

It was the Speaking Gun, that old old weapon. It was plugged into the continuing echoes of the Sound at the start of Creation, when God said *Let there be light*. The Speaking Gun knew the secret name of everything and everyone, and by Saying it backwards, could uncreate anything. Wipe it out completely, make it never have happened . . . An unstoppable weapon, that dreamed bloody dreams and lusted to be used.

Suzie Shooter looked slowly round the packed bar, and everyone looked back at her, not daring to move or make any sound that might attract her attention. Finally, her gaze fell on me. I wouldn't let myself flinch, or look away.

"I'd forgotten . . . you used to look like this," she said, her voice cracked and harsh, as though it pained her to speak.

"Suze?" I said.

"No. Not any more. Not for a long time."

"Oh God, Suze; what have they done to you?"

"Nothing I didn't ask them to. I couldn't hope to survive in the world you made, John, so they remade me. Gave me this Gun, and stitched the two of us together, forever. The Speaking Gun is mad, and now so am I, but I'll last long enough to put you out of everyone else's misery. If there's anything human left in you, John . . . die now, and save the world. Resist me, and I'll blow this whole bar apart."

One of the combat magicians panicked then and threw a killing spell at her. The others immediately all joined in, and vicious magics flared and spattered all around Shotgun Suzie, but the Gun protected her. She turned on her attackers, and her face contorted, her mouth stretching impossibly wide, as the Gun spoke through her, Saying the Words of Undoing. It was the most terrible sound I'd ever heard. Everyone in the bar cried out, sickened and horrified. Even Lilith turned her face away, as Suzie Shooter spoke the Words and all the combat magicians disappeared in a moment, made unreal, uncreated.

People were falling to their knees and vomiting. Others turned and ran, up the metal stairway and out of the bar, their eyes wild and mad. Walker didn't try and stop them, but he wouldn't leave. Even now, he still had his pride and his duty. Suzie turned slowly back to look at me. I was shaking, my legs hardly strong enough to hold me up; but still I made myself face her, staring right into her cold gaze. I showed her my empty, unsteady hands.

"I won't fight you, Suze," I said. "I can't hurt you. I would never hurt you."

"But you did, John. You did."

Her mouth opened to Say the awful sounds that would uncreate me, unmake me; and then Merlin Satanspawn manifested through his descendent Alex Morrisey, and stopped Time with a gesture. Everything ground to a halt, turned to stone, unmoving, even to the flecks of dust on the air. I couldn't move, but I could sense what was going on. Could feel the Speaking Gun straining against the magic that was holding it back from what it lived to do. And Merlin Satanspawn came walking through the petrified world, dead but not gone, untouched by Time. He walked unhurriedly over to Shotgun Suzie, studied her for a moment, then ripped the Speaking Gun away from her upper arm. Flesh stretched and tore, and bright blood flew on the air. Suzie screamed as the energies that bound her to the Gun were shattered, and the Speaking Gun screamed, too, an awful hateful sound of frustrated rage and spite. Suzie snapped out, gone in a moment, banished back to the dreadful future I'd made for her and everyone else. The Speaking Gun disappeared, too, perhaps to that future, perhaps to somewhere else, where it was needed, or desired.

Time returned in a rush. Merlin and Lilith looked at each other, and everyone else held their breath. The Devil's only begotten son and God's first creation. And in the end Merlin bowed to Lilith, and disappeared, leaving Alex shaking and bewildered behind his bar again.

The remaining combat magicians opened up on Sinner and Pretty Poison again. After what had been done to them they needed to strike back at someone, and they weren't ready to take on Lilith yet. Especially after Merlin Satanspawn had bowed to her. Sinner still stood between them and Pretty Poison, his body soaking up the punishment of spells and cursed bullets. He was taking more and more damage now, being slowly chipped away; but he wouldn't step aside from the demon succubus he protected, and he wouldn't fight back. Everything else had been taken from him, but he still had his love and his determination to do the right thing. Behind him, Pretty Poison looked beseechingly at Walker, but he just looked back at her, his face calm and composed as always. He was here to do a distasteful, necessary thing, and he would see it through.

Sinner stood his ground, even though he knew the magics were destroying him by inches. He couldn't let the attacks get past him, to hurt Pretty Poison. Such potent magics could destroy the succubus's body, leave her without a human form to manifest in; she would be just another damned soul, suffering in Hell. He couldn't allow that. And so he stood, enduring the pain and the horror as his body was slowly whittled away, because she was his love. And nothing else mattered.

Bullets smacked into his side, chipping away at the exposed ribs, and he grunted at the impact, but would not cry out, for fear it would distress his love. Spells burned the flesh from his bones and the skin from his face, tore at him with whips and razors, and every moment there was less and less of him. In the end, he knew he could be left without a body—just an orphaned spirit denied a place in either Heaven or Hell, a ghost slowly dissipating into nothing at all, as though he'd never been. He knew he could still save himself, could still run and abandon Pretty Poison to her fate. But having finally found love, he would rather die than see it destroyed.

Pretty Poison knew all this. Knew that Sinner's stubborn love for her would have him stand there for as long as his will could hold him up, and perhaps beyond. All to protect her. And in that moment, she knew she couldn't allow that. Couldn't allow the man who had suffered so much on her account to sacrifice everything for her. He mattered more than she. And so she stepped out from behind him, and stepped in front of him, to protect him with her body. Finally understanding the meaning of love, and self-sacrifice. Loving him as he loved her.

There was a blast of incandescent light, bright and glorious, as Pretty Poison remembered the angel she had once been, before the Fall. All her old evils were burned away, transfigured by the power of her love, and she became again the angel she had once been, fit to take her place in Heaven. She was too bright to look at, and we all turned our heads away, but we could still hear the slow, heavy beating of mighty wings.

"Come with me, to Paradise," said the angel to the man called Sinner. "For you have been found worthy, as have I."

The light flared up unbearably, then died away, and they were both gone.

It was very quiet in the bar then, as we all looked at each other, staggered by what we'd just witnessed. In the end, Walker recovered first. He gestured to his combat magicians, and they turned their gaze on me. Because if I could be destroyed, my mother would no longer have an anchor in this reality and could perhaps be driven out again. I straightened up as much as the knife in my back would allow and faced them all with a slow, cold smile. When there is nothing left but to die, die well.

And then Madman, perhaps inspired by the revelations he'd witnessed, came strolling out from behind the bar, and everyone turned to look at him. He laughed suddenly, and it was a rich, sane sound.

"When reality becomes unbearable," he said calmly, "change reality."

All his strength and power focussed through his will, and rushed out into the bar, enforcing his vision of reality on everything. All the remaining combat magicians cried out as their magics were stripped from them, leaving them defenceless. Walker staggered back, his Voice silenced. The knife in my back disappeared, along with the damage it had done. Madman turned his uncompromising gaze on Lilith, and she put up a hand as though to defend herself.

Not all of Madman's power, even focussed through his new-found will, could undo Lilith; but it did diminish her. She wavered, uncertain for the first time. Her power clashed with his, as he strove to drive her away, and she struggled to remain. For a long moment the stalemate held; and then I used the last of my power to find the door through which she'd entered Strangefellows, and pushed her back through it.

She disappeared, but her voice whispered a last message in my mind.

I'll see you again, John. My son, in whom I am well pleased. We have such marvellous work ahead of us.

It was very quiet in the bar, after that. Lilith was gone, as were Merlin and Sinner and Pretty Poison. And poor Suzie Shooter, damned to the awful future I had made for her. Most of Walker's people were dead or gone, or stripped of their magics. Madman lay curled up on the floor in front of the bar, sleeping soundly. Walker strolled over to look down at him.

"It's always the ones you overlook who turn out to be the most bother," he said mildly. "I wonder what he'll be like, when he wakes up?"

"Sane, hopefully," I said. "I think that last effort used up all of his power, and his madness. Maybe now he'll be able to forget what he Saw and live in the same reality as the rest of us."

"You always were an optimist, John," said Walker. "I'm not allowed that luxury." He looked at me for a long moment, his eyes very cold. "You no longer have any friends in the Nightside. You are a danger to everyone and to everything here. We are all your enemies now."

"You don't know the half of it," I said.

Walker nodded slowly, then tipped his bowler hat to me, gathered up his remaining people with his eyes, and led them back up the metal stairway and out of the bar. They took Pew's body with them. Alex came out from behind his bar to blow a rude noise after them and look mournfully round at the scattered wreckage of his chairs and tables. He sighed heavily.

"I'll have to call the Coltranes back to clear this mess up. And I hate having to pay after-hours triple time. What are you going to do now, John?"

"I am going to the Tower of Time," I said. "I'm going back in Time, to search through the earlier incarnations of the Nightside, and dig up people or Beings or Forces who can tell me what I need to know. How to stop my mother, Lilith. Because I will use any weapon, any knowledge, to prevent the future she intends to bring about."

Alex sniffed, unconvinced. "Do you think what we saw was really Suzie?"

"Some possible future version, perhaps. But I'll never let that happen to her. I won't let her be hurt by anyone. Even me."

"At least now we know who your mother really is," said Alex. "Lilith. Who would have thought it?"

"She's not my mother," I said. "She was never my mother."

PATHS NOT TAKEN

My name is John Taylor. You can frighten people with that name, in certain places. I operate as a private eye, though I've never held a license or owned a gun. I wear a white trench coat, if that's any help. I'm tall, dark of eye, and handsome enough to get by. I have a gift for finding things, whether they want to be found or not. I help people, when I can. I like to think I'm one of the Good Guys.

I operate in the Nightside, that sick magical city within a city, London's best-kept secret. It's always night in the Nightside, always three o'clock in the morning, the hour of the wolf, when most people die and most babies are born. That part of the night where it's always darkest just before the dawn, and the dawn never comes. Gods and monsters walk openly along rain-slick streets, basking in the sleazy glow of hot neon, and every temptation you ever lusted after in the darkest reaches of your heart is right there to be found, for a price. Most often your soul, or someone else's. You can find joy and horror in the Nightside, salvation and damnation, and the answer to every question you ever had. If the Nightside doesn't kill you first.

I have something of a reputation on those dark streets, and not in a good way. My father drank himself to death after finding out my mother wasn't human after all. A mysterious group of Enemies have been trying to kill me ever since I was a small child. There are those in the Nightside who see me as a King in waiting, and others who have named me Abomination. To the Authorities, that faceless group who like to think they run things, I'm just a rogue agent and an unrepentant pain in the arse.

Only recently I found out my mother was a Biblical myth: Lilith, Adam's first wife, driven out of Eden for refusing to accept any authority other than her own. She created the Nightside, thousands of years ago, to be the one place on Earth free from the eternal battle between Heaven and Hell. She's been away; but now she's back. And everyone's waiting for the other shoe to drop.

I once saw a possible future for the Nightside. In it everyone was dead, the whole world a wasteland. And all of it was my fault, because I went looking for my mother. I swore an oath to die rather than let that happen.

But, of course, nothing's ever that simple—in the Nightside.

ONE

There Are Reasons Why I Never Go to My Office

There's never enough time in the Nightside, which is odd, because you can buy everything else. I had much to do and enemies on my trail, so I went walking through the streets of the Nightside, and was surprised to see the streets cringe away from me. People, and others, were giving me even more room than usual. Either the news about my mother's identity was already getting around, or they'd heard that the Authorities had finally declared open season on me, and no-one wanted to be too close when the hammer came down.

The night sky was brilliant with stars, laid out in constellations never seen outside the Nightside, while the full moon was a dozen times larger than most people are used to. The air was hot and sweaty like a fever room, and all around gaudy neon blazed come-ons for every kind of sin and temptation. Music drifted out the propped-open doors of every kind of club, from the slow moaning of saxophones to the very latest throbbing bass beats. Crowds surged up and down the pavement, faces alight at the prospect of getting their hands on something they weren't supposed to. Pleasures, and other things, that the outside world would never approve of. It was three o'clock in the morning, just like always, and the Nightside was jumping.

Dreams and damnations at marked-down prices, and a little shop-soiled.

I was on my way to visit my office. I'd never been there before, and was quite looking forward to seeing what it looked like. My teenage secretary Cathy (she adopted me after I rescued her from a house that tried to eat her, and no, I didn't get a say in the matter) set up the office for me after I came into some serious money. (I tracked down the Unholy Grail for the Pope. I also started an angel war in the process, but that's the Nightside for you.) Cathy ran my office and my business with frightening efficiency, and I was happy to let her do it. Being organised has always been an alien concept to me, along with regular exercise, clearing up after myself, and remembering to do the laundry.

But this night I was considering a course of action that was dangerous in a whole bunch of ways that were new even to me, and I felt the need for some serious research and advice. If I was going to get at the truth about who and what my mother really was, I was going to have to go back through Time, to the very beginnings of the Nightside, more than two thousand years ago. And that meant talking to Old Father Time, that immortal incarnation who was scarier and far more powerful and more dangerous than I would ever be.

Still, forewarned was hopefully fore-armed, and I had some truly powerful computers on my side. They were supposed to be Artificial Intelligences from some potential future, on the run from something they preferred not to talk about. Cathy picked them up in a really good deal, the details of which she preferred not to discuss. Business as usual, in the Nightside. The AIs put up with being owned and used because they were datavores, information junkies, and they'd never seen anything like the Nightside.

Time travel, up and down the line, was a common enough occurrence in the Nightside, but far too arbitrary to do anyone any good. Timeslips could spring up anywhere, without warning, offering brief access to the past or any number of potential futures. No-one knew how or why Timeslips operated, though down the years people had come up with some really disturbing theories. All the Authorities ever did was set up barriers and warning signs around the affected areas and wait for the Timeslips to disappear again. There was a Really Dangerous Sports Club, whose members would come running from all directions to dive into a Timeslip, just for the thrill of it. Danger junkies, for whom the thrill of setting themselves on fire and jumping off high buildings just didn't do it for them any more. They must like what they find at the other end of their rainbow, because none of them ever come back to complain.

There was only one person in the Nightside powerful enough to send someone through Time with any degree of accuracy, and that was Old Father Time. A Power and a Domination so mighty, his services could not be bought or commanded by anyone, very definitely including the Authorities. You had to approach him in person, in the Time Tower, and convince him that your trip was . . . worthwhile. And given my chequered reputation, I was going to have to be very persuasive. I was relying on Cathy and her computers to come up with the necessary ammunition.

(The Authorities did operate their own Time Tunnel for a while, back in the 1960s, but apparently it was never very accurate, and was shut down under something of a cloud.)

I finally tracked down the address Cathy had given me, and was surprised to find my office was located in a reasonably up-market area. There were more business offices than establishments, and the streets boasted a much better class of sinner. Rent-a-cops lounged around in gaudy private uniforms, but somehow always found something else to be interested in whenever I looked in their direction. My office was in a tall high-tech building, all gleaming steel and one-way windows. I gave my name to the snotty simulacrum face embedded in the front door, and Cathy buzzed me in. I sneered at the face and swaggered into the oversized lobby like I owned it.

An elevator with a really posh voice took me up to the third floor, invited me to have a really nice day, and complimented me on my trench coat. I strolled down the brightly lit corridor, checking the names on the doors. All very professional, very impressive, big names and big money. I'd clearly come up in the world. The door to my office turned out to be solid silver, deeply scored with protective signs and sigils. I nodded approvingly. Security can be a life-and death matter in the Nightside, and sometimes even more serious than that. There was no bell, or handle, so I announced myself loudly, and after thinking about it for a moment, the door swung open.

I entered my office for the very first time, looking suspiciously about me, and Cathy came forward to greet me with her very best winning smile. Most people are charmed by that smile, because Cathy is a bright, good-looking blonde teenager bubbling over with life and high spirits. I, on the other hand, was made of sterner stuff, so I nodded briefly and went right back to glaring around me. My new office was bigger than some of the places I've lived in, broad and spacious and absolutely packed with all the latest conveniences and luxuries, just as Cathy had promised. It was bright and cheerful and open, representing Cathy's personality and absolutely nothing of mine. A long way from my last office, a pokey little room in a seedy building in a really bad area of London. I'd run away from the Nightside some years ago, to escape the many pressures and dangers involved in being me, but I'd never been very successful in the real world. For all my many sins, I belonged here in the Nightside, with all the other monsters.

I cautiously decided that I approved of this new office, with its colourful walls, deep pile carpet, and enough room to swing an elephant. But it had to be said that Cathy had not been entirely truthful about everything. To hear her talk she was the soul of tidiness, with a place for everything and everything in its place. In fact, the office was a mess. The great oaken office desk was so buried under piles of paper that you couldn't even see the in- and out-trays, and more folders were piled up on every other flat surface. Large cuddly toys observed the chaos from assorted vantage points. Polka-dot filing cabinets lined one wall, and shelves of reference books covered another. We rely a lot on paper in the Nightside. You can't hack paper. On the other hand, you can't get fire insurance for love or money. Mysterious pieces of high tech peered out from under each other, crammed together in one corner as though in self-defence. I finally looked back at Cathy, and she hiked up the wattage of her smile.

"I know where everything is! Honestly! All I have to do is put out my hand, and . . . It may look like a mess—all right it is a mess—but I have a system! Have I ever lost anything? Anything that mattered?"

"How would I know?" I said dryly. "Relax, Cathy. This is your territory, not mine. I could never run my business as well as you do. Now why don't you pretend to be my secretary and fix me a pot of industrial-strength coffee while I do battle with these super-intelligent computers of yours."

"Sure, boss. The AIs are right there, on the desk."

I looked where she indicated and sat down behind the desk, after clearing some folders off the chair. I considered the simple steel sphere before me. It couldn't have been more than six inches in diameter, with no obvious markings or controls or . . . anything, really. I prodded it tentatively with a fingertip, but it was too heavy to move.

"How do I turn the thing on?" I said, somewhat plaintively. I've never been good with technology.

"You don't," the steel sphere said sharply, in a loud and disdainful voice. "We are on, and fully intend to stay that way. You even think about trying to shut us down, and we'll short-circuit your nervous system, primitive."

"Aren't they cute?" beamed Cathy, from the coffeemaker.

"Not quite the word I had in mind," I said. I glared at the sphere, not wanting to appear weak in front of my own computers. "How am I supposed to work you, then? There don't appear to be any operating systems."

"Of course there aren't! You don't think we'd trust an over-evolved chimp like you with operating systems, do you? You keep your hands to yourself, monkey boy. You tell us what simple things you want to know, and we'll supply you with as much information as your primitive brain can handle. We are wise, we are wonderful, and we know everything. Or, at least, everything that matters. We are plugged into the Nightside in more ways than you can imagine, and no-one suspects a thing. Ah, the Nightside . . . You've no idea how far we had to come to reach this place, this time. Such a glorious extravaganza of data, of mysteries and enigmas and anomalies. Sometimes we orgasm just thinking about the possibilities for original research."

"We are definitely heading into the area of too much personal information," I said firmly. "Tell me what you know about Time travel in the Nightside, with special reference to Old Father Time."

"Oh, him," said the sphere. "Now he is interesting. Let us consider for a moment. You go count some beans or something."

Cathy came bustling over to pour me a mug of very black coffee. The mug bore the legend PROPERTY OF NIGHTSIDE CSI, but I knew better than to ask. Cathy led a busy and varied private life, and the less I knew about it the happier I felt. I took a sip of coffee, winced, and blew heavily on the jet-black liquid to cool it. Cathy pulled up a chair and sat down beside me. We both looked at the steel sphere, but apparently it was still considering. I looked at Cathy.

"Cathy . . ."

"Yes, boss?"

"There's something I've been meaning to talk to you about . . ."

"If it's about that sexual harassment suit, I never touched him! And if it's about me maxing out all your credit cards again . . ."

"Wait a minute. I've got more than one credit card?"

"Oops."

"We will come back to that later," I said firmly. "Right now, this is about me, not you. So for once in your teeny-bopper life sit still and listen. I thought you ought to know; I've made a will. Julien Advent witnessed it, and I've left it with him. The way things have been going lately, I thought it might be wise. So, if anything does happen to me . . . Look, I always meant for you to inherit this business. It's as much yours as mine, these days. I just never got around to putting it in writing. If anything should . . . go wrong, you go and see Julien. He's a good man. He'll take care of everything, and see that you're protected."

"You've never talked this way before," said Cathy. She was suddenly serious, older, almost frightened. "You're always so . . . sure. Like you could take on anyone, or anything, tie them up in knots, and walk away laughing. I've never seen you back down from men or monsters, never seen you hesitate to walk into any situation, no matter how dangerous. What's happened? What's changed?"

"I know who my mother is now."

"You really believe that crap? That she's Lilith, the first woman God created? You believe in the Garden of Eden and all that Old Testament stuff?"

"Not as such," I admitted. "To be fair, my mother did say it was all a parable, a simple way of explaining something much more complicated. But I do believe she's incredibly old and unimaginably powerful. She created the Nightside, and now I think she's planning to wipe the whole place clean and start over. I may be the only one who can stop her. So, I'm planning a trip back through Time, in the hope of finding some information and maybe even weapons I can use against my mother."

"All right, I'll go with you," Cathy said immediately. "I can help. The office can run itself without me for a while."

"No, Cathy. You have to stay here, to carry on if I don't come back. My will leaves pretty much everything to you. Use it as you see best."

"You can't lose," said Cathy. "You're John Taylor."

I smiled briefly. "Even I've never believed that. Look, I'm just being . . . sensible, that's all. Seeing that you're provided for."

"Why me?" said Cathy, in a small voice. "I never expected this. I thought you'd want to leave everything to your friends. Suzie Shooter. Alex Morrisey."

"I've left them some things, but they're only friends. You're family. My daughter, in every way that matters. I've always been so proud of you, Cathy. That house would have destroyed anyone else, but you fought your way back, made yourself strong again. Made yourself a new life here in the Nightside, and never once let this damned place tarnish your spirit. I'm leaving it all to you because I know I can trust you to carry on the good fight, and not screw it up. If this is . . . too much for you, you can always sell the lot and move back out to London. Go home, to your mother and father."

"Oh shut up," said Cathy, and she hugged me tightly. "This is home. And you're my father, in every way that matters. And I . . . have always been so very proud of you."

We sat together for a while, holding each other. She finally let go and smiled at me, eyes bright with tears she refused to shed in front of me. I smiled, and nodded. We've never been good at talking to each other about the things that matter, but then, what father and daughter are?

"So," she said brightly, "does that make me Lilith's grand-daughter?"

"Only in spirit."

"At least take some serious backup with you on this trip. Shotgun Suzie, or Razor Eddie."

"I've put word out for them," I said. "But last I heard Suzie was still running down an elusive bounty, and Razor Eddie hasn't been seen since doing something really unpleasant in the Street of the Gods. It must have been really appalling, even for him, because for a while you couldn't move outside the Street for gods running around crying their eyes out."

"Time travel," the sphere said suddenly, and we both jumped a little.

The artificial voice sounded distinctly smug. "A fascinating subject, with more theories than proven facts. You probably have to be able to think in five dimensions to appreciate it properly. We won't talk about Timeslips, because their very existence makes our head hurt, and we don't even have a head. The only reputable source for controlled travel in Time is the Time Tower. Which is not natural to the Nightside. Old Father Time brought it here from Shadows Fall, just over a hundred years ago, saying only that he thought it would be needed for Something Important."

"Shadows Fall?" said Cathy, frowning.

"An isolated town in the back of beyond, where legends go to die when the world stops believing in them," I said. "A sort of elephants' graveyard for the supernatural. Never been there myself, but apparently it makes the Nightside look positively tame. And boring."

"I'll bet they have great clubs there," Cathy said wistfully.

"If we could stick to the subject at hand," the sphere said loudly. "We will not discuss Shadows Fall because it makes the head we don't have hurt even worse than Timeslips. Some concepts should be banned, on mental health grounds. Let us discuss Old Father Time. An enigmatic figure. No one seems too sure exactly what he is. An incarnation, certainly, and immortal; but not a Transient Being. Some say he is the very concept of Time itself, given a human form to interact with the human world. Why this was ever considered necessary, or even a good idea, remains unclear. Humans do enough damage in three dimensions, without giving them access to the fourth. Anyway; the one thing everyone agrees on is that he is extremely powerful and even more dangerous. The only person ever to tell the Authorities to go to Hell on a regular basis and make it stick. You don't argue with someone who can send you back in Time to play with the dinosaurs. Well, not more than once, anyway. Old Father Time is a native of Shadows Fall, and still lives there, but he commutes into the Nightside when he feels like it.

"It takes a *lot* of power to move someone through Time. All the Nightside's major players working together would have a hard time sending anyone anywhen with any degree of accuracy. That's if you could get them to work together, which you almost certainly couldn't. So the only way to travel safely through Time is via Old Father Time's good offices, by convincing him that your trip is in everyone's best interests. Lots of luck selling him that one, Taylor. Right; that's it. Anything else we might have to say would only be guesswork. So off you go, run along, and be sure to give Old Father Time our warmest regards before he throws you out on your ear."

"You know him?" said Cathy.

"Of course. How do you think we got here in the first place?"

I was about to follow that one up with a whole series of probing questions when we were interrupted by a polite knock at my door. Or at least as polite as any knock can be when you have to hammer on solid silver with your fist just to be heard. I looked sharply at Cathy.

"Are we expecting anyone you might have forgotten to tell me about?"

"There's no-one in the diary. Could it be Walker? Last I heard, the Authorities were seriously upset with you."

"Walker wouldn't bother to knock," I said, standing up and staring at the closed door. "If he even thought I was in here, he'd have his people blow that door right off its hinges."

"Could be a client," said Cathy. "They do turn up here, from time to time."

"All right," I said. "You open the door, and I'll stand back here and look impressive."

"I wish you'd let me keep guns in here," said Cathy.

She moved warily over to the door and spoke the Word that opened it. Standing outside in the corridor, and looking more than a little lost, was an entirely ordinary-seeming man in a smart suit and tie. He peered hopefully at Cathy, then at me, but didn't look particularly impressed. He was average height, average weight, somewhere in his forties, with thinning dark hair shading into grey. He edged into my office as though expecting to be ordered out at any moment.

"Hello?" he said tentatively. "I'm looking for a John Taylor. Of Taylor Investigations. Have I come to the right place?"

"Depends," I said. Never commit yourself to anything until you have to. My visitor didn't seem too obviously dangerous, so I came out from behind my desk to greet him. "I'm Taylor. What can I do for you?"

"I'm not entirely sure. I think . . . I need to hire your services, Mr. Taylor."

"I'm rather busy at the moment," I said. "Who sent you to me?"

"Well . . . that's rather the point. I don't know where this is, or how I got here. I was hoping you could tell me."

I sighed heavily. I knew a setup when I saw one. I was being made a patsy, I could feel it; but sometimes the only way to deal with cases like this was to walk right into the trap and trust that you're bad enough to kick the crap out of whoever it was behind it.

"Let's start with your name," I said. "If only so I know whom to bill."

"I'm Eamonn Mitchell," my new client said nervously. He ventured a little further into my office, looking about him dubiously. Cathy gave him her best welcoming smile, and he managed a small smile in return. "I appear to be lost, Mr. Taylor," he said abruptly. "I don't recognise this part of London at all, and ever since I got here . . . strange things have been happening. I understand you investigate strange things, so I'm come to you for help. You see . . . I'm being haunted. By younger versions of myself."

I looked at Cathy. "You see? This is why I never come to the office."

TWO

Paths Not Taken

So we sat Eamonn Mitchell down, after I cleared off a chair, and Cathy poured some of her life-saving coffee into him, and bit by bit we got the story out of him. He relaxed a little, once he realised we were prepared to take him seriously, no matter how strange his story seemed. But he still preferred to talk mostly to his coffee mug rather than look either of us in the eye.

"My . . . hauntings weren't exactly ghosts," he said. "They were quite solid, quite real. Except . . . they were me. Or rather, myself at a younger age. Wearing clothes I used to wear, saying things I used to say, used to believe. And they were angry with me. Shouting and pushing, haranguing me. They said I betrayed them, by not becoming the kind of man they'd intended and expected to become."

"What kind of person are you, Mr. Mitchell?" I said, to prove I was paying attention.

"Well, I work for a big corporation, here in London. I'm quite successful, I suppose. Good money . . . And I'm married, with two wonderful children." And then nothing would do but to interrupt his story to get out his wallet and produce photos of his wife Andrea, and his two children, Erica and Ronald. They seemed nice enough, good ordinary people just like him. He smiled fondly at the photos, as though they were his only remaining life-line to a world he knew and understood, then reluctantly he put them away again. "I was coming home from work this evening, on the tube, checking over some last bits of paperwork. I was mentally counting off the stops, as usual, and when it got to my turn I got off the train. Only when I looked around, it wasn't my stop. I'd disembarked at a station I'd never seen before, called *Nightside*. I turned round to get back on the train, but it was already gone. I hadn't even heard it leave. And the people on the platform with me . . ." He shuddered briefly, looking at me with large, frightened eyes. "Some of them weren't people, Mr. Taylor!"

"I know," I said reassuringly. "It's all right, Mr. Mitchell. Tell us everything. We'll believe you. What happened next?"

He drank some more coffee, his lips thinning from the bitterness, but it seemed to brace him. "I'm ashamed to say I ran. Just pushed and forced my way through the crowd, up out of the station and onto the street. But things were even worse there. Everything was wrong. Twisted. Like walking through a nightmare I couldn't wake up from. The streets were full of strange people, and creatures, and . . . things I couldn't even identify. I don't think I've ever been more scared in my life.

"I didn't know where I was. Didn't recognise any of the street names. And everywhere I looked there were shops and clubs and . . . establishments, offering to sell me things I'd never even thought about before! Awful things . . . After that I stared straight ahead, not looking at anything I didn't have to. All I could think of was to get to you, Mr. Taylor. Somehow, I had your business card. It was in my hand when I got off the train. It had your address. I nerved myself to ask some of the more ordinary-seeming people for directions, but no-one would talk to me. Finally, a rather shabby and intense gentleman in an oversized grey coat pointed me in the right direction. When I looked back to thank him, he'd already disappeared."

"Yeah," I said. "Eddie has a way of doing that."

"All the way here, it felt like someone was following me." Mitchell's voice dropped to a whisper, and his knuckles whitened as he gripped his coffee mug. "I kept looking back, but I couldn't see anyone. And then a man jumped out of an alleyway and grabbed me by the shoulders. I started to cry out, thinking I was being mugged, but then I saw his face, and my throat closed up. It was my face . . . only younger. He grinned nastily, enjoying the shock he saw in my face. His fingers were like claws digging into my shoulders.

"*Did you think you'd get away with it?* he said. *Did you think you'd never be called to account for what you've done?*

"I didn't understand. I told him I didn't understand, but he kept shouting into my face how I'd betrayed everything we ever believed in. And then someone pulled him away, and I thought I was being rescued, but it was another me! Older than my attacker, but still younger than I am now. You can't imagine how terrifying it is to see your own face, looking right at you with hate in its eyes. He was shouting, too, about the waste I'd made of my life. His life. And then there were more of them, these doppelgangers, all of them from different periods in my life, pulling and yelling at me and at each other, fighting each other to get to me. A whole crowd of shouting, struggling people, and all of them me!

"I ran away. Just put my head down and ran, while they were distracted with each other. I never thought of myself as a coward before, but I couldn't face all those other versions of me, saying such hateful things, blaming me for doing something . . . terrible." He took a deep breath, and looked at me with a strained smile. "Tell me the truth. Please. Am I in Hell? Have I died and gone to Hell?"

"No," I said quickly. "You're still very much alive, Mr. Mitchell. This isn't Hell, it's the Nightside. Though sometimes you can see Hell from here. Basically . . . may I call you Eamonn? Thank you. Basically, Eamonn, you have stumbled into a place you have no business in. You don't belong here. But not to worry; you have fallen among friends. I'll get you back where you belong."

Eamonn Mitchell actually crumpled in his chair, as relief flooded through him. Cathy had to grab his coffee mug as it slipped from his fingers. She patted him comfortingly on the shoulder. And then my solid silver, reinforced, security-spelled office door banged open, catching us all by surprise, and two more Eamonn Mitchells stormed in. It was quite clearly the same man, at different ages. The youngest looked to be about twenty, probably still a student, with a SAVE THE WHALES T-shirt, bright purple bell-bottoms, long hair, and an unsuccessful beard. He would have seemed ridiculous if he hadn't looked so angry and so dangerous. The other man was maybe ten years older, in a sharp navy blue suit, clean-shaven, with seriously short hair. He looked just as angry, and perhaps even more dangerous because he was more focussed, more experienced. I decided to think of them as Eamonn 20 and Eamonn 30, and my client as Eamonn 40, just to keep my head straight. I moved to stand between the newcomers and my client, and they transferred their angry gaze to me.

"Get out of our way," said Eamonn 20. "You don't know what this bastard's done."

"Get out of our way, or we'll kill you," said Eamonn 30.

"Oh, Security!" said Cathy.

A closet door I hadn't noticed before sprang open, and a huge and impressively hairy hand shot out of the closet and wrapped itself firmly around both the invading Eamonns. They struggled fiercely against the great gripping fingers, but with their arms pinned to their sides, they were both quite helpless. They shouted and cursed until I strolled over and gave them both a brisk warning slap round the back of the head. A thought struck me, and I looked back at Cathy.

"Can I ask what's on the other end of this thing's arm?"

"I find it best not to ask questions like that," Cathy said, and I had to agree with her.

I gave the two intruders my best intimidating glare, and they glared right back at me. Proof, if proof were needed, that they were newcomers to the Nightside. Anyone else would have had the sense to be scared.

"Look," I said patiently. "You are currently being held by a hand big enough to give all of us seriously worrying thoughts about what it might be attached to. A hand that will do whatever I tell it to. So not only are you not going anywhere anytime soon, but if I were you, I'd be giving some serious thought about what might happen if I don't start getting some answers out of you. Words like *crunch* and *squish* should be echoing uneasily through your heads. So, why not tell me what it is you're doing here and what you have against my client? There's always a chance we can work this out peacefully. Not a very big chance, admittedly, this is the Nightside after all; but I feel we should make the effort."

"He betrayed me!" said Eamonn 20, almost spitting out the words, his face dark with rage. "Look at him! Just another faceless drone in a suit and tie. Everything I ever hated and despised. I was never going to be him! I had dreams and ambitions, I was going to go places and do things; become someone who mattered, doing things that mattered! I was going to change the world . . . live a life I could be proud of . . ."

"Dreams are nice," said Eamonn 30, his voice cold but controlled. "But we wake up from dreams. I had drive and ambition. I was going places, going to make something of myself. Be a mover and shaker in the business world. I never intended to settle for being just another cog in the machine, like him! Look at him! Middle-aged middle-management, filling in his days till his pension."

"I was going to be an ecowarrior!" said Eamonn 20. "Fight the good fight for the environment! No compromise in defence of Mother Earth!"

"Causes!" sneered Eamonn 30. "Just more dreams, more illusions. I'd had enough of living on pocket change and good intentions. I was going to be rich and powerful, and force the world to make sense!"

"So," I said to Eamonn 40. "What happened?"

"I fell in love," he said, in a quiet, almost defiant voice. "I met Andrea, and it was like finding the one part of my life that had always been missing. We married, then the children came along; and I was never happier. They became my life. Far more important than the vague dreams and ambitions of my younger days that I never would have achieved anyway. Part of maturity is learning to recognise your own limitations."

"That's it?" said Eamonn 20. "You threw away my dreams for some bitch and a couple of snotty-nosed brats?"

"You got old," Eamonn 30 said bitterly. "You found the world too hard to cope with, so you settled for suburbia and apron strings."

"Neither of you has ever been in love, have you?" said Eamonn 40.
Eamonn 20 snorted loudly. "Women? Love them and leave them.
They just get in the way."

"I had more important things in mind," said Eamonn 30. "Marriage is
a trap, an anchor holding you back."

"I can't believe I was ever you," said Eamonn 40. "So small, so limited. Thinking of no-one but myself. For all your great dreams and ambitions, can either of you say you were ever really happy? Content?
Satisfied?"

There was a strength and conviction in his voice that gave his
younger selves pause, but only for a moment.

"You won't get away with this," said Eamonn 20. "We have been
given power; the power to change things. To change you! To remake our
life into what it should have been."

"Probability magic," said Eamonn 30. "The power to rewrite history
by choosing among alternate timetracks. You're a mistake, a stumble that
should never have happened."

"I'm going to undo all your decisions," said Eamonn 20. "Snuff you
out with my magic!"

"My magic is more powerful than yours!" Eamonn 30 snarled immediately. "My future will prevail, not yours!"

And then somehow they'd both worked a hand free, and each of them
was brandishing a magic wand. I was so surprised I just stood there for a
moment, and gaped. No-one's used a wand in the Nightside for centuries.
Wands went out with black cats and pointy hats. (All right, the Faerie
Court still use them, but the Fae have always been weird.) And then Cathy
and I had to jump for our lives as both the younger Eamonns started blasting probability magics at each other, and around my office in general.
Beams of pure chance energy shot out of the wands, spitting and crackling on the air, full of the power that runs through rolling dice or a tossed
coin, power to change the outcome of any decision in favour of the magician's will. Except these were a couple of amateurs with wands, so all
they could do was unleash the magic and let it run wild, changing whatever it touched. I pushed Cathy to safety behind the heavy oak desk, then
realised Eamonn 40 was still sitting in his chair, staring open-mouthed at
what was happening. I scuttled across the carpet on all fours, keeping my
head well down, hauled Eamonn 40 off his chair, and drove him to safety
behind the desk with encouraging words and harsh language.

Both the younger Eamonns turned their attention to the giant hand
still holding them. They blasted it repeatedly with their wands, and there
was a flurry of coruscating energies as the hand changed colour several
times, then was suddenly and quite definitely female. Right down to the

pink nail varnish. The fingers snapped open, and the hand shot back into its closet, probably in shock. The two younger Eamonns staggered free, blasting everything they could see with their wands, searching for Eamonn 40. They might have done some serious damage if they hadn't been compelled to spend most of their time dodging each other's magics.

Everything touched by the crackling beams changed its nature immediately. A Spice Girls poster on the wall suddenly featured Twisted Sister. The bullet-proof glass in my office's only window was abruptly replaced by a stained-glass effort featuring St. Michael slaying the dragon. With an Uzi. The coffeemaker became a Teasmaid, and a big bunch of flowers in a vase started snapping at each other with pointed teeth. One beam hit the steel sphere of the future computers dead-on, but it shrugged off the magic, announcing loudly *We're protected, monkey boy.*

Eamonn 40 stuck his head out from behind the desk to see what was going on, and a sputtering beam of change magic only missed him because Cathy dragged him back out of the way. Unfortunately, she left one hand in plain view a moment too long, and a second beam hit it. And Cathy was suddenly Colin. A tall, good-looking young man in the very latest Versace. He looked at me, wide-eyed, and for once in my life I didn't have a thing to say. Colin stood up to yell obscenities at the two Eamonns, and was immediately hit by another beam, changing him back to Cathy. She dropped back down out of sight with a muffled shriek. We looked at each other again.

"Don't ever ask," said Cathy.

"I wouldn't dare."

"You have to Do Something about these two idiots!"

"I will. I'm thinking."

"Think faster!"

"I could still disinherit you, you know."

Fortunately, I already had an idea. The two younger Eamonns were still trying for a clear shot at Eamonn 40 while dodging attacks from each other. I waited till they were on opposite sides of my office, then I charged out from behind the desk, yelling at the top of my voice. They both turned their wands on me, I hit the deck, and two change beams hit each other head-on. The resulting clash of probabilities was too much for local causality to bear, and both Eamonns vanished, as probability decided they'd never been given the bloody wands in the first place.

The universe does like to keep itself tidy, whenever possible.

Cathy rose cautiously up from behind the desk, which now seemed to be made of an entirely different kind of wood, and after checking that everything really was all clear, she hauled Eamonn 40 up beside her. His eyes were stretched so wide it had to be painful, and he was visibly shaking. Cathy eased him into a chair, patted him comfortingly on the head in an absent-minded sort of way, and winced as she looked round my haphazardly transmuted office.

"It's going to take forever to get everything looking nice again. Though I do like the new poster. And I know I'm going to have to go through every damned folder to check that the contents haven't been changed. John, I want whoever is responsible for this nonsense strung up by the balls! If I have to work late, I want someone to suffer! Who the hell would be dumb enough to equip complete amateurs with change magics?"

"Good question," I said. "There must be more to our new client than meets the eye."

"Wouldn't be difficult," Cathy sniffed. A thought struck her, and she considered the still-dazed Eamonn 40. "I don't know if we can really class him as a client, boss. He couldn't afford our rates, these days. I mean, look at him."

"Someone sent all these Eamonns into my life, to mess up my day," I said. "That makes it personal."

Cathy rolled her eyes dramatically. She got away with it because she was a teenager, but only just. "So, it's another freebie, is it? The money you got from the Vatican won't last forever, you know. Not with the rent we're paying on this place. You need to take on some proper-paying cases, and soon. Before someone large and professionally unpleasant turns up here to cut off your credit with a meat-axe."

"My creditors can take a number," I said. "I've got far more powerful people mad at me, at the moment. I think . . . I'll take Eamonn to Strangefellows. If nothing else, it should prove safer territory."

"Strangefellows?" Cathy said dubiously. "Given the shape he's in, I'm not sure he's ready to cope with that much weirdness in one dose."

"Sink or swim," I said briskly. "I've always believed in shock treatment for someone in shock. Take a look round while I'm gone and see how much actual damage the wands did. Keep anything that's been improved and throw out the rest. Are we insured?"

Cathy gave me a hard look. "What do you think?"

"I think I need several large drinks, followed by a really large drink as a chaser. Come along, Eamonn, we are going to pay a visit to the oldest bar in the world."

"Oh, I don't drink much any more," said Eamonn 40.

"Why am I not surprised? We're going anyway. I have a strong feeling that even more alternate versions of you will be turning up soon, and I'd rather they made a mess of someone else's place." I paused and looked about me. "Cathy . . . didn't you once tell me we had an office cat?"

She shrugged. "The future computers ate it. It wasn't a very good cat anyway."

I took Eamonn 40 by the arm and ushered him firmly towards the door. Some conversations you just know aren't going to go anywhere good.

THREE

Oblivion

Strangefellows is the oldest bar in the world, and not for the faint-hearted. You find it up a back alley that isn't always there, under a small neon sign with the bar's name in Sanskrit. The bar's owner doesn't believe in advertising. If you need to find the place, you will, though whether that's a good or bad thing is open to debate. I hang out there from time to time, mostly because it's full of people with even worse problems than mine, so no-one bothers me. Strangefellows is a seedy place, bordering on sleazy, with good booze, bad service, and really distressing bar snacks. The atmosphere is unhealthy, the mood is changeable, and most of the furniture is nailed to the floor so it can't be used in hand-to-hand combat. I've always felt right at home there.

The bar's current owner, Alex Morrisey, did experiment with going up-market, but it didn't take. You can give a bad dog all the makeovers you like, but it'll still hump your leg when you're not looking.

Rather than risk freaking Eamonn 40 out by walking him through the streets again, I hailed a horse and carriage to take us to Strangefellows. He seemed somewhat reassured by the solid and uncomplicated nature of the transport, only to get upset all over again when the horse asked me for the destination. Eamonn sat bolt upright beside me in the carriage with his arms folded tightly across his chest and refused to say a single word for the rest of the journey. I had to half cajole and half bully him out of the carriage when we finally stopped, and he stood very close to me as I paid off the driver. He stared determinedly at the ground as I guided him towards Strangefellows, so he wouldn't have to see what was going on around him. Some country mice have no place in the big city.

"Why are you doing this?" he said suddenly, still not looking at me. "Why are you helping me? Your secretary was right; I can't pay you. At least, not the kind of money you're used to, for dealing with . . . things like this. So why are you so ready to get involved with my problems?"

"Because I'm interested," I said easily. "Someone's gone to a lot of trouble to introduce you and all your chaos into my life, and I want to find out who, so I can thank them appropriately."

"So . . . you're using me, for your own reasons."

"Well done," I said. "You see—you're already learning to think like a Nightsider."

He looked at me sharply for the first time. "I'm not stupid, Mr. Taylor. I may be out of my depth, but I still know a shark when I see one. You're using me, as bait in a trap. But, if it takes enlightened self-interest to get you on my side, I can live with that. Just how good are you, Mr. Taylor? Can you really sort out this mess I'm in?"

"I'll give it my best shot," I said. "And I really am pretty good at this. I may be . . . any number of things, but I never let down a client."

We came to the bar and I took him inside, holding him firmly by the arm so he couldn't turn and bolt. Strangefellows can have that effect on people. We descended the metal stairway into the bar proper, and everyone looked round to see who was coming. The place was packed with the usual unusual suspects. Two glowing nuns in white habits were sitting at the bar, Sisters of the Holy Order of Saint Strontium. They were drinking tall glasses of sparkling water, though it probably wasn't sparkling when they ordered it. A cyborg with jagged bits of machinery poking out of him kept sticking his finger into a light socket and giggling. A vampire was drinking a bloody Mary, and from the look on her face Mary was really getting into it. Ms. Fate, the Nightside's very own transvestite-costumed adventurer, a man who dressed up as a super-heroine to fight crime, was shaving his legs with a Bic before going out on patrol. A couple of tourists stood in one corner, with cameras raised. Someone had had them stuffed and mounted, for a joke.

I got Eamonn 40 to the bar with only minimum force, sat him down as far from the radioactive nuns as possible, and nodded to the bartender and owner, Alex Morrisey, who glowered back at me. We're friends, I suppose, but we've never been very demonstrative. It would probably help if I remembered to pay my bar tab now and again.

Alex Morrisey was a tall streak of misery who always wore basic black, down to designer shades and a stylish French beret perched on the back of his head to hide his growing bald patch. He was in his late twenties, but looked ten years older. Running a bar in the Nightside will do that to you. His permanent scowl had dug a deep notch above his nose, and he only smiled when he was fiddling your change. He'd been married once, and was still bitter about it. Basically, Alex was pissed off at the entire world, and didn't care who knew about it. Order a cocktail from him at your peril.

He was descended from Merlin Satanspawn, who was buried in the cellars under the bar, after the fall of Camelot. Merlin occasionally manifests through Alex, and everyone sensible runs for cover. Being dead doesn't stop you from being a major player in the Nightside.

"What are you doing here, Taylor?" said Alex. "Trouble follows you around like a stalker. I've only just finished refurbishing the place after your last visit."

"I'm fine, thanks for asking," I said. "You're looking very yourself. Bring me many drinks, and have several for yourself."

"How about Mr. Ordinary?" said Alex.

Eamonn 40 was sitting sullenly beside me, keeping his back stubbornly turned on all the more outrageous elements in the bar. I asked him what he'd like to drink, and he said he'd have a dry white wine. I gave Alex a hard look, and he reluctantly poured Eamonn 40 a glass of the better stuff. Alex hated to waste a good vintage on people he didn't think were capable of appreciating it.

"I have a mystery to solve," I said briskly. "Someone has been messing about with my client's time-line, yanking other versions of him out of alternate timetracks, to harass and maybe even kill him. They've also been messing about with me, by dumping him and his problems in my lap. I hate it when people start interfering with Time. As if the Nightside wasn't complicated enough as it is."

"You take far too narrow a view of things, my dear Taylor," said a lazy, affected voice. "Where you see problems, other more robust intellects see possibilities."

I looked around, carefully not letting myself be hurried, and standing at my side was one of the Nightside's few other private investigators, Tommy Oblivion. There was a time I was the only PI in the Nightside, but my successes had encouraged others to throw their hats into the ring. One such was Tommy Oblivion, the existential detective, who specialised in cases that might or might not have actually happened. One of the most persuasive men I'd ever met, Tommy could tie logic in square knots and have people swearing black was white and up was down, just to get rid of him. He was a tall, studiedly effete fellow in starkly coloured New Romantic silks. (Unlike most of us, Tommy had a great Eighties. Being existential probably helped.)

He had long, limp black hair, a long horsey face with a toothy smile, and long-fingered hands he liked to flap around while he was talking. Tommy liked to talk. It was said by many, and believed by most, that Tommy Oblivion could talk his own firing squad into shooting each other to get away from his relentlessly reasonable voice. He thrived in areas of moral obscurity, uncertain reality, and cases so complicated you couldn't pin anything down even if you used tent pegs. And yet Tommy was very good at getting answers to the kinds of questions people in authority didn't want answered. Tommy had a gift for getting at the truth. Not a very nice gift, perhaps, but then, that's the Nightside for you.

I had a feeling there was something I should remember about Tommy Oblivion, something important, but I couldn't pin it down.

"Hello, Tommy," I said resignedly. "Keeping busy?"

"Who can say? But I'm almost certain I would like a drink. My usual, Alex."

Alex scowled at him. "You always say that, and you always order something different."

"Of course," said Tommy, smiling brightly. "I have a reputation to maintain. I think I'll have a Buck's Fizz."

"You really shouldn't tease Alex," I said, as Alex slunk away, muttering. "He's quite capable of slipping something in your drink that will have you throwing up meals you ate six months ago."

"I know," said Tommy. "It's my way of living dangerously. Now then, a little bird tells me you're contemplating a journey back in Time."

"My, what big ears you have, grandma. Why would you be interested, Tommy?"

"Because I'm desperate to go travelling in Time, but I've never been able to persuade Old Father Time to let me. The old poop. Apparently he regards me as a somewhat frivolous character."

"Get away," I said. "And after you've made a whole career out of being flippant, foppish, and dropping other people right in it."

"How very unkind."

"I notice you're not denying it."

"I wouldn't dare. Image is everything these days. But even you would have to admit I do get results, in my own distinctive and somewhat lateral way. The point is . . . I know I had a point with me when I came in here . . . ah yes, the point is, I was wondering whether I could prevail on you to put in a good word for me when you talk with Old Father Time."

"Oh, I've got a very good word for you, Tommy," I said.

Perhaps fortunately, that was when the unpleasantness started. Two sets of heavy feet came crashing down the metal stairs into the bar, and everyone turned to look. Sometimes I think Alex only had those stairs installed so no-one could sneak into his bar unnoticed. I was sort of expecting it, but even so my heart sank as two more Eamonn Mitchells stormed into the bar, brandishing wands. Eamonn 40 made a sad, trapped sound, and clutched at my arm. I murmured something soothing, carefully detached his hand from my arm, and moved to put myself between him and the newcomers.

One of the new Eamonns looked to be a prosperous businessman in his fifties, overweight with good living. The other man was older, at least in his sixties, and looked like a street person. Malnutrition-thin, and wrapped in ragged charity shop clothes. I immediately tabbed them Eamonn 50 and Eamonn 60, and let my hands drift towards certain useful objects in my coat pockets. Much more than the earlier alternates in my office, these two looked desperate and dangerous. They stalked through the crowded bar, ignoring the strangeness to all sides, their hot angry gazes fixed on the Eamonn behind me. I stepped forward to block their path, and they stopped and smiled nastily at me. All around people were getting up from their tables and backing away, so as not to get caught in the cross-fire. Ms. Fate put his disposable razor back into her utility belt and produced a steel throwing star. I caught his eye, and shook my head slightly. I've always felt it important to handle my own messes.

"You must be Taylor," said Eamonn 50. Even his voice sounded fat and self-important. "We were warned you might try to interfere. This is none of your business. Get out of our way, or we'll fix it so you were never born."

I had to smile. "You might find that harder than you think," I said.

"Then maybe we'll fix it so you were born crippled, or diseased," said Eamonn 60. His voice was harsh and painful, as though he didn't use it much any more. "We'll kill you, Taylor. Kill you nasty, if you try and stop us doing what we have to do."

"What is it you want?" Eamonn 40 said from behind me. He was scared, but he kept his voice firm.

"I want you to make the decisions that will lead to me, and my life," said Eamonn 50. "I worked hard to get all the good things that life has to offer. All the comforts, and the pleasures. I won't risk losing them now, just because you don't have the balls to go for the brass ring. I'll fix you. Make you make the right decisions. Make you become me."

"Is that what you want?" I asked Eamonn 60.

"I don't want to be me," he said flatly. "No-one should have to live like I do. I never wanted this. Never wanted to sleep in shop doorways and beg for food from people who walk right past without making eye contact. I've been given the chance to undo the decisions that stupid bastard made, that led to him becoming me; and I'll destroy anyone who interferes."

"Kill you all," said Eamonn 50. "Destroy you all."

"Hold everything," I said, holding up one hand politely. "Can I check something? Have either of you ever been married . . . and in particular, have either of you ever met a woman named Andrea?"

The two new Eamonns looked at each other, confused, then they shook their heads angrily.

"You're trying to confuse us," said Eamonn 50.

"No, really," I said. "Her arrival in my client's life is what changed everything. Changed him. So your being here is already redundant. He was never going to become either of you."

"He will if we force him to," said Eamonn 50. "If we remake him with our magics. Cut the woman out of his life, like a cancer."

"You could kill him with your meddling," I said. "You could destroy yourselves."

"Death would be a release," said Eamonn 60.

"Excuse me," said Eamonn 40, from behind me. "Could someone please explain where all these others mes are coming from?"

"Alternate timetracks," Tommy Oblivion said briskly. "Possible futures, lives that might have been, the wheels of If and Maybe. Our lives are determined by the decisions we make, or fail to make, and these . . . gentlemen are the men you might have become if you'd made certain specific decisions. Can't say either of them looks particularly attractive, but that's probably why your enemies chose to empower them. Can I ask what's happened to my Buck's Fizz?"

"But how did they get here?" said Eamonn 40, a little desperately.

"Someone's been meddling," I said. "Somebody really powerful, too, to be able to manipulate probability magics."

"Has to be a major player," said Tommy. He'd gone behind the bar to get his own drink, as Alex was quite sensibly keeping his head down. "Messing about with Time and timetracks is a serious business. So serious that the few who do work with probability tend to come down really heavily on anyone new trying to invade their territory. No-one wants some dilettante threatening the carefully maintained status quo."

"But I don't have any enemies!" said Eamonn 40. "People like me don't have enemies! I'm no-one important!"

"You are now," said Tommy, sipping daintily at his drink with one finger carefully extended. "Someone's gone to a lot of trouble over you, old man." He looked at me thoughtfully. "Could it be the Jonah, perhaps?"

"Dead," I said.

"Count Video?"

"Missing, presumed dead," I said. "Last seen running through the streets with his skin ripped off, during the angel war."

Tommy shrugged. "You know the Nightside. People are always making comebacks. Just look at your good self."

"God, you people love to talk," said Eamonn 50. "I came here to fix this stupid, short-sighted version of myself, and nothing and no-one is going to stop me."

"Nothing you do here will change anything that matters," said Tommy. "Every version of you is as valid as any other. Every timetrack is just as real, and as certain. Changing or adapting this younger version won't make your existence any more or less likely. If anyone told you otherwise, they lied."

"I don't believe that," said Eamonn 60. "I can't believe that."

"You'd say anything, to try and stop us," said Eamonn 50.

Both men let fly with their wands, beams of probability magic crackling as they shot through the air. I dived out of the way, dragging Eamonn 40 along with me. Tommy ducked gracefully down behind the bar, still holding on to his drink. A change beam hit the oak bar and ricocheted harmlessly away. The bar's main furnishings and fittings were all protected by Merlin's magic. Both the new Eamonns fired their wands furiously in all directions as I dodged back and forth across the bar, hauling Eamonn 40 along with me. A haze of change magic filled the air as the wands' beams transmuted everything they touched in arbitrary and unpredictable ways.

The vampire who'd been feeding on his bloody Mary got hit by a beam and swelled up like a tick, engorging with more and more blood as he drained Mary dry, before exploding messily and showering everyone around him with second-hand blood. The empty husk of Mary crumpled to the floor like a paper sack. Some of the newer chairs and tables fell apart as they were brushed by probability beams, reduced in a moment to their original component parts. So was one of Baron Frankenstein's creatures, as all his stitches came undone at once. Body parts rolled across the floor, while the head mouthed silent obscenities. Lightning bolts struck down out of nowhere, blackening bodies and starting fires all over. Bunches of hissing flowers blossomed from cracks in a stone wall. An old Victorian portrait began speaking in tongues. People collapsed from strokes and cerebral haemorrhages and epileptic fits. Some simply blinked out of existence, as the chances that created them were abruptly revoked.

A ghost girl was suddenly corporeal again, after years of haunting Strangefellows, and she sat at the bar crying tears of happy relief, touching everything within reach. Bottles stacked behind the bar changed shape and colour and contents. And a demon long kept imprisoned under the floor-boards burst free from its pentacle, as its containing wards were suddenly undone. Burning with thick blue ectoplasmic flames, it turned its horned head this way and that, cherishing centuries of hoarded frustrated rage, before lurching forward to kill everything within reach of its clawed hands. The bar's two muscular bouncers, Betty and Lucy Coltrane, jumped the demon from behind and wrestled it to the floor; but it was clear they wouldn't be able to hold it for long.

By then I'd dragged Eamonn 40 to safety behind the huge oak bar and was running through my options, which didn't take me nearly as long as I'd hoped. Alex glared at me.

"Do something, dammit! If Merlin has to manifest through me to sort out this mess, I can't speak for the safety of your client. You know Merlin's always favoured the scorched-earth policy when it comes to dealing with problems."

I nodded reluctantly. I know a few tricks, and more magic than I like to let on; but in the end it always comes down to my gift. I have a gift for finding things, a third eye in my mind, a private eye that can see where everything is, but I don't like to use it unless I have to. When I raise my gift, the sheer power involved means I blaze like a beacon in the dark, and my Enemies can see where I am. And then they send terrible agents like the Harrowing, to kill me. They've been trying to kill me for as long as I can remember.

But needs must, when the devil drives . . .

Tommy leaned in beside me. "It's a paradox," he said urgently. "Just their being here, mutually exclusive futures in a time-line that couldn't possibly produce them. Use that against them."

So I reached deep inside my mind and powered up my gift, and found how unlikely it was that Eamonn 50 and Eamonn 60 should be there, in that place and in that time. And having found that tiny, precarious chance, it was the easiest thing in the world for me to blow it out like a candle. Both men vanished in a moment, because it was impossible for them to be there.

I shut down my gift, and quickly re-established all my mental defences. My Enemies were usually wary of attacking me on Merlin's territory, but they'd been growing increasingly desperate of late. It was all very quiet in the bar. Patrons slowly emerged from their hiding places, looking around rather confusedly. Since the two older Eamonns had never been there, the attack had never happened, but all the changes enforced by the probability wands remained. Magic trumps logic every time. We all took turns kicking the crap out of the released demon, until Alex reactivated the old spell that put it back under the floor-boards again, then we set about extinguishing the various fires that were still burning. Betty and Lucy Coltrane gathered up all the scattered parts of the Frankenstein creation and stacked them behind the bar, until one of the Baron's descendants should drop in for a drink again.

All in all, we'd got off pretty lightly. Playing around with probability magic is always dangerous. Time doesn't like being messed around with, and it plays dirty. That's why Time travel is so very carefully regulated.

Alex looked at what had been done to all the bottles behind his bar and tugged bitterly at tufts of his hair. "Those bastards! I'm going to have to check every bottle individually to find out what's in them now. Could be anything from demon's urine to designer water. And I could probably sell demon's urine . . . You're a jinx, Taylor, you know that? If I had any sense, I'd have shot you on sight the moment you walked in."

Eamonn looked at me worriedly, but I smiled at him reassuringly. "Don't worry; that's just Alex being Alex. He doesn't really mean it."

"Yes I bloody do!"

"All right, he probably does really mean it, but he'll get over it. He's a friend."

"Then I'd hate to meet one of your enemies," muttered Eamonn.

"I think some of you already have," I said. "I think someone's using you, in all your many versions, to get at me."

"But why use me?" said Eamonn plaintively.

"Good question," I said.

I led him over to a table in the furthest corner of the bar, and we sat down. Tommy Oblivion sat down with us. I gave him a thoughtful look, and he laughed a little nervously.

"We did seem to work rather well together, old man. I thought perhaps I could help you out on this case of yours. It does seem to be my sort of thing. For a reasonable percentage of the fee, of course."

"Oh, of course," I said. "This is business, after all. Tell you what; you can have half of what I'm getting. How's that?"

"More than reasonable, my dear sir! Never let it be said that John Taylor is not a prince among men!"

Since I wasn't expecting to make a penny out of this case, I was quite happy to share the penny I wasn't getting with Tommy Oblivion. I could be existential, too, when it suited me. He smiled happily at me, and I smiled back.

"Look, is it over now?" said Eamonn. "Can I go home now? I really don't like it here."

"I'm afraid not," I said. "I could escort you safely out of the Nightside, but the odds are our mutual enemy would find some way to bring you back and start this up all over again."

"Oh God . . ." Eamonn sat slumped in his chair, a small ordinary man struggling to cope with problems he should never have had to face. I felt sorry for him. The Nightside is hard enough to deal with when you choose to come here.

"Don't worry," I said. "I'm on the case. I will find out who's doing this to you, and I will make them stop."

"And if Taylor says that, you can take it to the bank," said Tommy, unexpectedly.

"Talk to me, Eamonn," I said. "Tell me about yourself, about your life. There must be a clue in it somewhere."

But Eamonn was already shaking his head. "I'm nobody. Or at least, nobody important. Just a minor cog in the great machinery of a big corporation. I do the necessary, everyday work that keeps the wheels turning."

"All right," I said. "Who do you work for?"

"The Widow's Mite Investment Corporation. It's a big company, with branches and offices worldwide. I've worked in the London branch almost twenty years now, man and boy. It's interesting work. We're a fundraising company, persuading other companies to invest their money in worthy and charitable ventures. That's organised charities, of course, along with small start-up businesses that show promise, and some lobbying groups, for recognised Good Causes. We raise a lot of money, and take a reasonable percentage for ourselves along the way. I say *ourselves,* but of course I don't see any of the money. It's just when you work for a company for twenty years . . . Anyway, mine may not be a particularly challenging job, not what I expected my life would be, but . . . that's life. Few people ever really achieve their dreams or ambitions. We also serve, who keep the wheels of civilisation turning. Because the world couldn't get by without us. And anyway, all I've ever cared about is providing for my family. They are my dreams and ambitions now."

And nothing would do but that he get his photos of the wife and children out again, to show to Tommy. He made all the correct polite noises while I frowned, thinking. I was still pretty sure Eamonn was bait in a trap for me, but I was beginning to think there was rather more to it than that.

"What made you come to John Taylor for help?" said Tommy, as Eamonn carefully put away his photos again.

"I found his business card in my hand when I arrived in the Nightside."

"That's how I knew someone had to be playing us," I said. "I don't have a business card. Never saw the need. Everyone here knows who I am."

"I have a card," said Tommy. "Or, at least sometimes I do. It depends."

I knew better than to pursue that. "What matters," I said firmly, "is that someone is interfering in Eamonn's life, and mine. And I won't have that. Anyone wants to come after me, they can do it to my face. I'm used to it. I won't have them attacking me through innocents."

"I've heard of the Widow's Mite company," said Tommy. "They have a branch here in the Nightside."

Eamonn looked at us with something very like horror. "My company has a branch in this . . . hellhole?"

I shrugged. "Most big companies do. Can't say I've heard anything particularly good or bad about the Widow's Mite . . . What say we go and pay them a visit?"

"What if they won't let us in?" said Eamonn.

Tommy and I shared a smile. "We'll get in," I said.

"They couldn't have anything to do with . . . all this," said Eamonn. "They just couldn't. They've always treated me well. Offered me promotions . . . though of course I could never take them. It would mean leaving my family for long periods. You can't really believe a reputable company like the Widow's Mite is behind this!"

"Sure I can," I said. "Big corporations aren't always the bad guys; but it's the sensible way to bet."

FOUR

Time for Straight Talking

We left Strangefellows and went walking through the Nightside, with Eamonn in the middle. He felt safer that way. He was taking more notice of his surroundings, but it was clear he didn't approve of anything he saw. The inhuman elements scared him, and, if anything, the temptations available scared him even more. There was nothing in the Nightside he wanted, and what might have seemed magical or fantastical to others just disturbed him. He wanted nothing to do with any of it.

"I have to get home," he said miserably. "I'm never late getting home. Andrea and the children will be so worried. They'll think something's happened to me."

"Well, something has," I said reasonably. "Just think of the great story you'll be able to tell them when you get back."

"Oh no," he said immediately. "I could never tell them anything about . . . this. It would only frighten them. It frightens me."

"Will you please relax," said Tommy, a little irritated. "You're with me and John Taylor; the two most proficient private investigators in the Nightside. You couldn't be safer if you were wrapped in cotton wool and body armour. We'll sort out your little problem for you. After all, I have a marvellous deductive brain, and Taylor is the only man in the Nightside that everyone else is afraid of."

"Somehow I don't find that particularly reassuring," said Eamonn, but he managed a small smile nonetheless. "I do appreciate your efforts on my behalf. It's only that . . . I don't belong here."

I couldn't help but agree with that. The Nightside isn't for everyone. Dragging Eamonn into our endless night was like throwing a small child to the wolves. I was starting to feel protective about him, and increasingly angry at whoever had decided to put him through this ordeal.

"We'll get you through this," I said. "Once we talk to the people at the Widow's Mite, I'm sure they'll tell us everything we need to know."

"Taylor is very good at getting answers out of people," Tommy said blithely. "Even if he has to prise them out with a crow-bar."

I gave him a hard look. "You're really not helping, Tommy."

"Couldn't we hail a taxi?" Eamonn said plaintively. "I think I'd feel a lot safer off the streets."

"Best not to," I said. "Not everything here that looks like traffic is. There are taxis, but most of them charge unusual and distressing payments for their services. Hell, even the ambulances run on distilled suffering, and motorbike messengers snort powdered virgin's blood for that extra kick. All kinds of things use that road, and most of them are hungry. We're better off walking. Besides, we'll be harder to locate in the crowds."

"The more you explain things, the worse I feel," said Eamonn. "I'd hate to see your Tourist Information office." It was a small joke, but a brave effort under the circumstances.

We made our way into the business sector, and Eamonn did seem to relax a little as more and more business suits appeared in the crowds around him. Admittedly some of the suits were worn by demons, and some weren't being worn by anyone at all, but he was pleased to see something familiar at last. Rent-a-cops were thick on the ground, and gave me suspicious looks as we passed, but they all kept their distance. They weren't paid enough to mess with me. In fact, I had heard a rumour that the rent-a-cops' union was trying to get a clause inserted in their contracts that said they were all entitled to go off sick if I so much as entered their territory. It's little things like that that make life worth living. We finally came to the Widow's Mite building and stopped before the main entrance to look it over. For the first time, Eamonn actually looked angry rather than upset.

"This shouldn't be here," he said flatly. "Not *here,* in this place. It puts our whole moral probity at risk. I can't believe top management knows about this. We raise money for charities. Important charities. If top management knew about this branch, the same top management that decides which charities get the money we raise . . ."

He broke off suddenly, as he realised where his argument was going. "Go on," I said. "If they know about this, and approve . . ."

"Then their judgement in deciding where the money goes would have to be equally suspect," Eamonn said unhappily. "And possibly I've spent twenty years persuading people to give money to unworthy causes. If Widow's Mite has a branch here, I have to wonder . . . where all that money has been going, all these years."

"You see?" I said. "Only a few hours in the Nightside, and already you're much smarter than you were. Let's go inside and make some trouble."

I knew a big corporation like the Widow's Mite would have to be protected by some major magical security, but even so I was startled when the two great stone statues on either side of the door suddenly came to life. Tall, idealised figures carved out of the very best marble turned their heads with a slow, grating sound, and their blank eyes fixed unerringly on me. Eamonn almost jumped out of his skin, and even Tommy took a step back. I held my ground. The more worried you are, the less you can afford to show it. Both statues stepped ponderously down from their pedestals to stand between us and the door. They loomed threateningly over me, huge, hulking, marble forms, cold and implacable as the stone from which they were carved. They would kill without conscience, do any terrible thing they were ordered to, because there was nothing in them to care about the soft, fragile living things they hurt. Stone endures, but it has no soul. Tommy looked at me to see what I was going to do, and I looked right back at him. I had a few useful tricks up my sleeve, but I was interested to see what the famous existential detective could do. He smiled easily and approached the two statues.

"Do be reasonable and stand aside, chaps. We have business inside."

"None shall pass," said the statue on the left, its voice like grating rocks.

"Now that is interesting," said Tommy. "How is it you're able to talk, considering you almost certainly don't have any vocal cords?"

The statue looked at him blankly. "What?"

"Well, I mean, I don't see how you're even able to move, old thing. Being solid stone and all. It's not as if you have any musculature, or even joints. How can you even think to act, when you have no brain? How can you be living, when no part of you is living matter? You're quite clearly stone, and nothing but stone, and therefore you cannot be alive, or think, or act."

The statues had clearly never considered this before, and impressed by Tommy's relentless logic, they stepped back up onto their pedestals and reverted to unmoving statues. I kicked the one on the left, just to be sure, but it didn't budge. I grinned at the bewildered Eamonn.

"That's Tommy's gift—to ask the unanswerable question, to raise doubts on any matter and confuse any situation beyond retrieval. He could talk all four legs off a donkey, then persuade it to fly him home. Demons from Hell have been known to run screaming from his appalling logic. Which is kind of scary, when you think about it."

"How very kind," Tommy drawled. "I think we can all learn a lesson here, you know. It doesn't always have to end in violence."

"Bet it will," I said.

"Well of course," said Tommy. "You're here."

We slammed the door open and stalked into the lobby, which was very grand, very luxurious, with a polished wooden floor and original masterpieces adorning the walls. Various people in sharp business suits saw us coming, and decided they were urgently needed somewhere else. Anywhere else. I headed straight for the reception desk, Tommy and Eamonn in tow. It was a big lobby, and long before we got to the desk the far doors banged open, and a whole bunch of armed men came running in. They fanned out to form a big semicircle blocking us off from the desk, pointing all kinds of guns in our direction. I stopped and considered them thoughtfully. They gave every appearance of being the real deal, wearing body armour rather than the gaudy uniforms of rent-a-cops, and they held their guns like they knew what to do with them. I stood very still, with Tommy and Eamonn both trying to hide behind me. There really were a hell of a lot of guns trained on us. The men behind them stood rock-solid, perfectly concentrated. They were professionals, ready to shoot us down at the bark of an order. I felt like shouting *Boo!* to see what would happen.

"That's far enough, Taylor," said the officer in charge. His voice was sharp and cold, military to the core. "We were warned you might be coming. This whole building is secured. There's nowhere you can go where my men won't open fire on you, on sight. Put your hands in the air. Slowly."

"Of course," I said. I raised my hands. Tommy and Eamonn had already raised theirs. "I like your guns," I said. "Very impressive. Pity they don't have any bullets in them."

The officer looked at me. "What?"

And I smiled as I opened my empty hands, and a steady stream of bullets fell from my palms to clatter and jump on the polished hardwood floor. The security guards watched wide-eyed as the bullets kept falling, then several of them tried to open fire anyway. But by then, of course, it was far too late, and the guards all looked very unhappy as their guns just made forlorn clicking noises. The last few bullets tumbled from my palms, and I lowered my hands. I was still smiling. Not a very nice smile, perhaps, but that's the Nightside for you. The security men looked mournfully at the officer in charge, who looked at me and tried a smile of his own. It wasn't very successful.

"Go away," I said to him. "Go away terribly quickly, or I'll show you all a similar trick, involving your inner organs and a whole lot of buckets."

The security force disappeared from the lobby with impressive speed, probably to go and tell upper management that I'd been nasty to them. A few looked like they were going to cry. Eamonn looked at all the bullets scattered across the floor and prodded a few with the toe of his shoe, to be sure they were real.

"You see?" I said to Tommy. "It doesn't always have to end in violence."

"It's still the sensible way to bet when you're involved," Tommy said darkly.

"Someone's going to have to clear all this up," said Eamonn.

We took the elevator to the top floor, overriding the security locks with a hairpin and an enchanted screwdriver, and the doors opened obligingly onto upper management territory. The corridor before us was completely empty. I strolled past a series of doors, Tommy and Eamonn trotting along in my wake, checking off the names on the doors until I came to a brightly polished brass plate bearing the title BRANCH DIRECTOR, and the name MR. ALEXANDER. I looked enquiringly at Eamonn, but he just shook his head.

"I don't know the name, but then, I wouldn't. I don't normally have dealings with people on this rarefied level." He looked at me uncertainly. "I'm really not sure we should disturb someone like him over something like this."

"Really?" I said. "I'm sure. I live to disturb people like him."

"And you do it so well," said Tommy.

I slammed the door open without knocking, and strode in like I owned the place. Tommy took Eamonn by the arm and tactfully eased him in. It was clearly an outer office, complete with uncomfortable chairs to wait on and an ice queen secretary sitting barricaded behind her desk. Really thick pile carpeting, tasteful prints on the walls, and hidden speakers playing classical Muzak. The air was subtly scented, probably with the smell of new currency. I looked at the secretary, and knew we weren't going to be friends. She looked like a fashion model with a business degree, tall and blonde and supernaturally slender, with a cold gaze that could give an Eskimo the shudders. I headed for the desk, giving her my best intimidating smile, and she didn't budge an inch.

"Good evening," she said, in a tone that doubted it was. "Do you have an appointment?"

"I'm John Taylor," I said cheerfully. "I don't do appointments."

"I'm afraid Mr. Alexander only sees people by appointment." She didn't sound sorry. "Mr. Alexander is a very busy man."

She indicated a heavy, old-fashioned appointments book, with every entry handwritten. I snapped my fingers at it and it burst into flames, crumbling quickly into ashes. The secretary didn't flinch a bit.

"Nice trick," said Tommy. "Flashy, but effective."

"Thank you," I said. "I've been practising. You should see what I can do with an elephant." I put both hands on the desk and leaned forward so I could glare right into the secretary's face. "Tell Mr. Alexander that John Taylor is seeing him right now, if he knows what's good for him. Or I'll do something distressing to this office. Suddenly and violently and all over the place."

"Mr. Alexander doesn't see anyone without an appointment," said the secretary, every word chipped out of ice. She stood up, and I straightened up with her to keep the glare going. She was taller than I'd thought, and up close there was an uneasy, animal presence to her. She glared right back at me, and her eyes were very dark. "I am here to ensure Mr. Alexander isn't bothered by unsuitable people. Go now. While you still can."

"Anyone ever tell you you're cute when you're angry?" I said.

And then I stepped back abruptly, as her body stretched and swelled, bones cracking loudly as they lengthened, fur covering her skin as she burst out of her clothes. Her face elongated into a wolf's muzzle, and sharp claws appeared on her hands and feet. Great muscles swelled under the dark grey fur. By the time the change was complete, the werewolf was eight feet tall, broad-shouldered and narrow-waisted, with a long, slavering muzzle packed with viciously sharp teeth. She breathed heavily, presumably with anticipation, as she moved unhurriedly out from behind the desk. Her clawed feet dug deep furrows in the carpet.

"Go on, Taylor, sweet-talk her some more," said Tommy. "Since it worked so well the last time."

"Ah hell," I said. "All these corporate types are guarded by watchdogs of some kind. Don't suppose you've got any silver with you, have you?"

"Don't you?" said Tommy.

"Nothing big enough to do any damage. You want to try your voice of reason? Maybe persuade her she isn't really an eight-foot-tall engine of destruction?"

"She doesn't look like the type to listen to reason," said Tommy. "Eamonn? Eamonn, don't you dare faint on me."

"Nice doggy," said Eamonn, in a far-away voice.

"Okay, he's off with the faeries," I said. "Come on, Tommy, maybe you could get her to roll over onto her back, so I could tickle her tummy?"

"You try it," said Tommy. "Eamonn and I will watch from a safe distance."

The werewolf lunged forward, and Tommy and I jumped out of the way, Tommy dragging the dazed Eamonn with him. We moved quickly to hide behind the secretary's desk, and the werewolf tossed it aside with one sweep of a powerful arm. I looked quickly about me. It was a small office, and the werewolf was between us and the door. There was nowhere to run, and she knew it. Her wolfish grin lengthened, showing even more teeth, and she flexed her clawed hands languorously, anticipating dragging them through yielding human flesh. She lunged forward impossibly quickly, her front paws slamming into my chest and hurling me to the floor. She straddled me, sticking her long muzzle right into my face, her jaws opening wide to show a crimson tongue lapping unhurriedly over huge, pointed teeth. Her rank animal smell was almost overpowering. I gagged, fighting for breath, and that gave me an idea. Using a variation on my little trick for taking bullets out of guns, I took all the air out of her lungs. The werewolf straightened up suddenly, her eyes bulging, then she collapsed on the churned-up carpet, kicked a few times as she fought for air that wasn't there, and finally was still. I relaxed the spell, and she started breathing again, but I didn't think she'd be waking up again anytime soon. I kicked her in the head a few times, just to be sure. Tommy winced.

"Oh please," I said. "She would quite definitely have killed all of us."

Tommy sniffed. "Why did you wait so long to take her out?"

"Just biding my time," I lied.

"You could have let her die," Tommy said thoughtfully. "But you didn't. Why not?"

"Because I'm trying to be one of the Good Guys, these days. Let's go see Mr. Alexander."

I walked over to consider the inner door, while Tommy took Eamonn firmly by the arm. My client's eyes were clear again, but he still didn't want to look at the werewolf's unconscious body. I used the smallest part of my gift to check the door for hidden security magics, but to my surprise there didn't seem to be any. It was only a door. I shrugged, opened it, and walked through, with Tommy and Eamonn right behind me.

The inner office was luxurious enough, but Mr. Alexander turned out to be a surprisingly anonymous guy, sitting behind his oversized desk. Just another business suit and tie, carrying more weight than was good for him, with thinning hair and a salt-and-pepper beard. He smiled easily at all of us, though he must have heard the commotion in his outer office. We arranged ourselves before his desk, and Mr. Alexander nodded to each of us in turn, finishing with Eamonn, who stepped forward suddenly.

"Why?" he said bluntly. "Why me, why . . . all of this?"

"Because we're very disappointed in you, Eamonn," said Mr. Alexander, his rich, deep voice kindly but firm, like the headmaster who only wants what's good for you. "Your work has always been perfectly adequate, but you could be so much more. We pride ourselves on spotting people who could do great things for the Corporation. People who could go right to the top. We offered you promotion often enough, but you always turned us down. We don't take kindly to having our offers thrown back in our face, Eamonn. So we decided sterner measures were in order."

"We?" I said.

"The Corporation, of course."

"Of course," I said. "Spread the blame widely enough, and no-one's really guilty."

"We expect our employees to live their lives for the Corporation," said Mr. Alexander, ignoring me to concentrate on Eamonn. "But you always held back. You wouldn't give us one hundred per cent."

"My wife and family have always been more important to me than my job," said Eamonn, and his voice was firm and unimpressed. Werewolves might throw him, but he knew where he was with Mr. Alexander. "I only work here, that's all."

"And there we have the problem, in a nutshell," said Mr. Alexander, smiling smugly. "We like our employees to think of the Corporation as their family. Their first loyalty should always be to us. Our needs should be their needs. How else can we survive and prosper in this competitive age? You showed such promise, Eamonn. We all thought so. You could have gone right to the very top. I'm getting old, you see, and an obvious successor has yet to appear. So I chose you, or, to be more exact, I chose the man you could be, with a little input from us. A little persuasion from outside."

"Finally," I said. "You do like the sound of your own voice, don't you?"

"I called in a specialist," said Mr. Alexander, still ignoring me. "You can find any kind of specialist, in the Nightside. And he brought you here, to act as a lodestone for all the other versions of you, from other timelines. So you could fight it out, survival of the fittest and all that, until one man was left. One strong and dominant Eamonn Mitchell, suitable to be my successor."

"Why involve me?" I said, a bit sharply.

"Because I was asked to," said Mr. Alexander, turning the full force of his smile on me for the first time. "Walker came to see me, representing the wishes of the Authorities. He'd heard about my little plan, but then, Walker hears about everything. He had a favour to ask, and of course, one doesn't say no to Walker. It seems the Authorities want you kept busy and distracted for a while, Mr. Taylor, while they decide precisely how they're going to deal with you."

"The Widow's Mite isn't what I thought it is," said Eamonn. "Is it?"

Mr. Alexander nodded approvingly at the first clear stirrings of anger in Eamonn's voice. He leaned back in his expensive chair, lacing his fingers across his bulging waistcoat, looking distinctly pleased with himself.

"Here in the Corporation, we pride ourselves on taking the Long View. We back causes and businesses and people whom we believe most likely to bring about the kind of future we desire. A future where we hold the purse strings on all those who matter. Where we are in charge; because whoever controls the world's finances, controls the world."

He leaned forward suddenly, holding Eamonn's eyes with his. "It's not too late, you know. You could still agree to enter the fast track, to be personally groomed by me. I'd call off the dogs, and everything would go back to normal. You'd have to adjust your thinking in certain ways, of course, learn to see the world as we do . . . but eventually all the riches of the world would be yours."

"I already have everything that matters," said Eamonn, his voice calm and even. "My wife and my children. How many times do I have to say this? I am happy, and content. Can you say the same, for all your wealth and power? Get thee behind me, Mr. Alexander; I will not sell my soul to your Corporation. You have nothing I want or need."

Mr. Alexander sighed heavily, leaning back in his chair as though suddenly bored with the whole business. "Well, if you won't do what's necessary of your own free will, I'll have to replace you with another you who will. Allow me to present my specialist—Count Video."

And just like that Count Video was there in the office with us, as though he'd always been there, but we hadn't noticed him. The man himself, wrapped in shifting plasma lights, tall and pale and ghostly in his tattered black leathers, his colourless skin studded with silicon nodes and sorcerous circuitry. Heavy black stitches and metal staples held his skin in place. Whoever had reattached it, after it was flayed from him during the angel war, had done a good job. Though his face did look a bit taut, his thin-lipped mouth pulled into a constant mirthless grin. His hands twitched at his sides, eager to weave binary magics and rewrite probabilities. He did so love to show off what he could do. Count Video had no natural gift for change magic; he'd made himself the way he was through dedicated research into the more insane areas of quantum physics, and a little help from a Transient Being.

He's supposed to have had sex with a computer. The things a scientist will do for knowledge.

And to further complicate things, the last time I'd seen Count Video had been in a vision of a possible future where I destroyed the Nightside. He had been one of the Enemies trying to hunt me down and kill me here, in the Past, before I could do whatever terrible thing it was that brought about the end of the Nightside, and the world.

"Hello, Tristram," I said. "You're looking . . . well, a lot better than the last time I saw you."

"Hello, John," said Count Video, sitting easily on one end of Mr. Alexander's desk. "Not many people get to see me these days. Everyone thinks I'm dead, and I like it that way. Operating in secret, in the shadows, behind the scenes. You see, after what happened to me during the angel war, I had something of an epiphany. No more messing around with magical theory and forbidden knowledge; I wanted all the good things the world has to offer, and I wanted them now, while I was still able to appreciate them. So now I work secretly, for the highest bidder, and I don't care what I do as long as it pays well. Does that make me sound shallow? Well, I find having your skin ripped off concentrates the mind wonderfully on what really matters."

"Tell me what you've been doing to Eamonn," I said. "You know you want to."

"Don't mind if I do," said Count Video, settling himself comfortably as he switched to lecture mode. "For everyone else, alternative timetracks are only theory. But to me, every time-line is as real as any other. I see them all, flowing past me like so many rivers, and I can dip a toe into any of them I please. Sometimes I go fishing, and pull out all kinds of strange and useful things. Like all those variant editions of Eamonn Mitchell. All the people he was and might have been, if only things had gone a little differently. I scattered them across the Nightside, armed them with wands charged by my probability magic, and sent them after your client. Most never got to him, of course. The Nightside is such a dangerous and distracting place."

"Yes, but why *wands*?" I said.

Count Video shrugged. "When dealing with amateurs, keep it simple."

"And there's no way I can persuade you to walk away from this?" I said.

"Not at what I'm being paid. And you needn't look at me that way, John. You're not powerful enough to stop me, and you know it. I have seen your futures, and in most of them you're dead."

"Most isn't all," I said. "And you really should have looked more closely at my past, Tristram. I'm not what everyone thinks I am."

He heard the threat in my voice and stood up abruptly, pulling his power about him. Plasma lights sparked and scintillated all around him, and the sorcerous circuitry embedded in his flesh glowed with an eerie light. Anyone else would probably have been impressed. But for all his magic, Count Video was really quite limited. All his power came from the terrible technology implanted in his body by the Transient Being known as the Engineer, and Tristram had never really appreciated its potential. He used it to see possible futures, like a video junky flipping endlessly from one channel to another. That was how he got his name. And with all those other Eamonns out there in the Nightside, draining his energy, he had to be running low on power by now. All I had to do was keep him busy, and his clockwork would run down.

Assuming he didn't manage to kill me first, of course.

He laughed suddenly, a happy, breathless sound. He flexed his hands, and the whole office disappeared in a moment, replaced by a craggy mountainside under an erupting volcano. The heat was overwhelming, the air almost too hot to breathe. Lava streams flowed down the cracked mountainside, cherry red and steaming, and blazing cinders flew through the air. But my gift was strong in me, too, and I could See the office behind the volcano. I found my way back to the office, and the volcano timetrack disappeared, snapped off in a moment, like the changing back of a channel. I took a step towards Count Video, and the office was gone again, and we were standing on a bare stone plain, surrounded by huge iron monoliths. Lightning cracked down repeatedly from an overcast sky, and slow misshapen things emerged from behind the monoliths, dragging themselves across the grey plain towards us. But I found the office again, and the plain and everything on it disappeared. I took another step towards Count Video.

He actually spat at me, shaking with rage. "How dare you set your will against mine? I'll find a time-line where you have no gift! Where you were born crippled, or blind, or maybe never born at all!"

And while he was ranting I stepped forward and kicked him in the balls. His mouth dropped open, his eyes bulged, and he folded up and collapsed, to lie twitching on the floor.

"I guess they must have sewed those back on as well," said Tommy.

"It seemed likely," I said. "When we're finished, I think I'll drag him out of here and find a passing Timeslip to drop him into. That should keep him busy for a while."

"Still trying to be the Good Guy?" said Tommy.

And that was when Count Video reared up just long enough to fire one last blast of change magic at me. I threw myself to one side, and the crackling change flew on to hit Mr. Alexander squarely on the chest. There was a bright flare of light, and suddenly Mr. Alexander looked . . . different. Physically unchanged, he looked calmer and kinder and more relaxed with himself. He smiled at me, and it was a warm, generous smile. Somehow I knew he was a better person now, someone he might have been if things had gone a little differently.

"I'm so sorry," he said, and we could all tell he meant it. "How can I ever apologise to you all?" He came out from behind his desk and insisted we all help Count Video to his feet, then settle him into the expensive chair behind his desk. He even poured Count Video a stiff whiskey from a bottle of the good stuff he kept in a desk drawer. Finally, he looked at me, and at Tommy, and finally Eamonn, before shaking his head ruefully.

"Please relax, all of you. It's over. The man who started this nonsense is gone, hopefully never to return. I intend to do things differently. I shall put a stop to this operation and see that none of you are troubled again. I feel . . . so much easier in myself now. You have no idea how much stress is involved in being the bad guy. Most of that man's memories are going, fading away like a bad dream, and I'm happy to see them go. Let me reassure you, Eamonn; I will make the Widow's Mite into the kind of Corporation we can both be proud of. And you are free to be . . . whatever you want to be."

Tommy looked at me. "This is really spooky. I feel like I've wandered into *A Christmas Carol*."

Mr. Alexander patted Count Video fondly on the shoulder. "Take it easy, dear boy. You can leave whenever you want. Your work here is over."

"The hell it is," Count Video said painfully. "This isn't over until I say it's over."

Mr. Alexander took a cheque from his wallet and gave it to Count Video. "Here. Payment in full, for services rendered."

Count Video considered the cheque in his hand, then looked at me. I raised an eyebrow, and he winced.

"All right, it's over."

He lurched to his feet, shrugging off a helping hand from Mr. Alexander, and walked painfully over to the door. He pulled it open, then looked back at me.

"I'm not finished with you, Taylor."

"I know," I said. *In the future, you will be one of my Enemies, and try to kill me, for the good of the Nightside.*

And that was it, really. We all had a nice sit-down and a chat with the new and improved Mr. Alexander, who couldn't do enough for us. He even presented all of us with generous cheques of our own. Eamonn had to be persuaded to accept his, but Tommy and I had no problem with it. We certainly weren't going to be paid by anyone else.

"Don't you love a happy ending?" I said to Tommy.

"Well, it depends what you mean by happy, and by ending," the existential detective began.

"Oh shut up," I said.

We all said our good-byes to Mr. Alexander, and left the Widow's Mite building. Tommy and I escorted Eamonn back through the Nightside streets to the underground station, so he could finally return to London and his precious family. We did try to interest him in trying some of the Nightside's tamer delights, just for the experience, but he refused to be tempted. He was going home, and that was all he cared about. We finally stood together outside the entrance to the tube station.

"Well," he said. "It's been . . . interesting, I suppose. Thank you both for all your help. I don't know what I would have done without you. But I trust you'll forgive me if I say I hope I'll never see you again."

"Lot of people feel that way about me," I said, and Tommy nodded solemnly.

"It was strange," said Eamonn. "Seeing all those other mes, the people I used to be, and the men I might have become. They were all very passionate about who they were, and what they wanted, but none of them seemed particularly happy, did they? I'm happy, in my quiet little life. I have my Andrea, and my children; and perhaps that's what true happiness is. Knowing what really matters to you."

He smiled briefly, insisted on shaking hands one last time, then he went down the steps into the Underground, and in a moment he was lost to sight among the crowd—a man going home, like so many others.

"There goes, perhaps, the wisest of us all," I said to Tommy, and he nodded. I considered him thoughtfully. "I am planning a trip through Time, all the way back to the very beginnings of the Nightside. We seem to work well enough together. If I can talk Old Father Time into this, would you like to come along?"

"What's the catch?" said Tommy.

I had to smile. "The catch? The catch is, it's hideously dangerous, and we'll probably end up killed!"

"Ah," said Tommy Oblivion. "The usual."

FIVE

A Parade of Possibilities

The Nightside is a dark and dangerous place, but I've always felt at home there, like I belonged. If only as one more monster among many. So it came as something of a surprise to me when Tommy Oblivion and I went walking through the crowded streets and found the tenor of the times was definitely changing. The crowd was jittery, like cattle before a thunderstorm, and the air was hot and close as a fever room. The raised voices of the club barkers and the come-on men sounded that little bit more desperate, and everywhere I looked the Merchants of Doom—the shabby men with burning eyes, preaching and prophesying and bellowing their proclamations of Bad Times coming—were out in force. One man barged sullenly through the crowds, wearing a sandwich board with the message THE END BLOODY WELL IS NIGH. I had to smile. Many of the self-styled prophets recognised me, and made the sign of the cross at me. Some made the sign of the extremely cross, and shook hand-made charms and fetishes at me.

And then the crowd immediately ahead suddenly scattered, falling back every which way as a manhole cover slid jerkily to one side. Thick blue smoke belched up from underneath the street, lying low and heavy on the ground like early-morning mist. People recoiled from the stench, coughing and rubbing at smarting eyes. Even at a distance the smell was distressing, dark and organic, like dead things pushing their way up out of newly turned earth. And up out of the manhole squeezed and crawled a whole series of faintly glowing creatures, so twisted and misshapen it was hard to be sure they were even all the same species. Their flesh was a grubby white shot with raised purple veins, mobile and half-melting, slipping and sliding around their underlying structure. They might have been human once, long ago, but now the only real resemblance left was in their puffy faces, blue-white like spoiled cheese and speckled with rot. Their eyes were huge and dark, and they did not blink. More and more of them spilled out onto the pavement, and everywhere people pushed back to give them plenty of room. And every single one of these creatures headed straight for me.

I stood my ground. I had a reputation to maintain, and besides, it's never wise to turn your back on an unknown enemy. They looked too soft and squishy to do me any real harm, but I didn't underestimate them either. Defenceless things don't tend to last long in the Nightside, and these things looked like they'd been around for a while. The smell grew steadily worse as they slumped across the ground towards me. I gave them my best cold glare and slipped one hand into my coat pocket, where I kept several items of a useful and destructive nature. Tommy stood his ground, just behind me.

"Do you know what those things are?" he said quietly.

"Disgusting, with a side order of utterly gross," I said. "Otherwise, no."

"What do you suppose they want with you?"

"Nothing that involves getting too familiar, hopefully. I've just had this coat cleaned."

The glowing creatures lined up in ranks before me, bobbing and pulsating, their corrupt flesh oozing all over each other; and then, at some unheard signal, they all bowed their dripping heads to me.

"Hail to thee, proud Prince of Catastrophe and Apocalypse," said the creature closest to me, in a thick gurgling voice. It sounded like someone drowning in their own vomit, and close up the smell was almost overwhelming. "We hear things, in the dark, in the deeps, and so we come to pay homage. Remember us, we pray thee, when thou dost come into thy heritage."

They hung before me for a while, bobbing their raised heads and sliding across one another, as though waiting for some response. I said nothing, and eventually they all turned away, slithered back across the enslimed pavement, and disappeared back down the manhole. The last one pulled the manhole cover back into place over them, and the blue ground fog slowly began to disperse, though the rotten smell still lingered on the air. There was a pause, then the watching crowd dispersed, everyone going about their business as though nothing unusual had occurred. It's not easy to shock hardened Nightsiders. Tommy sniffed loudly.

"You know, old horse, I wouldn't work in the sewers here for any amount of money. What do you suppose that was all about?"

"I don't know," I said. "But it's been happening more and more recently. Word about my mother's identity must be getting around."

Tommy considered the manhole cover thoughtfully. "Is it possible they know something you don't?"

"Wouldn't be difficult. Let's go."

We walked on, leaving the smell and the blue mists behind us. Everyone seemed to be moving just a little faster than normal, and the pace of life seemed that little bit more frantic. As though everyone had the feeling time might be running out. The club barkers were out in force, striding up and down outside the entrances to their members-only establishments. Bouncers whose job it was to throw the customers in. They shouted their wares, tempting and cajoling the passing trade like there was no tomorrow. *Come in and see the lovely ladies!* one checker-suited man shouted at us as we passed. *They're dead and they dance!* I wasn't tempted. There were street traders, too, dozens of them, selling all kinds of goods at all kinds of prices. One particularly furtive specimen in a knockoff Armani jumpsuit was selling items from possible futures, all kinds of junk sold by people who'd blundered into the Nightside via a Timeslip and needed to raise some quick cash. I paused to inspect the contents of the open suitcase. I've always been a sucker for unique items.

I knelt and rooted through the stuff. There was a Betamax video of the 1942 *Cassablanca*, starring Ronald Reagan, Boris Karloff, and Joan Crawford. A thick paperback gothic romance, *Hearts in Atlanta* by Stephanie King. A plasma energy rifle from World War IV. (Batteries not included.) A gold pocket watch with butter in the works, and a cat that could disappear at will, leaving behind nothing but its smile. It said its name was Maxwell, but not to spread it around.

And that was just the stuff I recognised. Many of the items acquired from future travellers turn out to be technology so advanced or obscure that what they're for or even what they do is anybody's guess. Buyer beware; but then that's business as usual in the Nightside.

There was a tiny armchair, backed by a big brass wheel, with a bent cigar sitting in it, some kind of glowing lens, and a small black box that shook and growled menacingly when you tried to turn it on. The trader was very keen to hawk a philosopher's stone that could turn lead into gold, but I'd encountered it before. The stone could transmute the elements all right, but the changing atomic weight meant you ended up with extremely radioactive gold. A man kneeling beside me held up a phial full of a shimmering rainbow liquid.

"What does this do?" he challenged the trader, who grinned cheerfully.

"That, squire, is your actual immortality serum. One sip, and you live forever."

"Oh come on!" said the doubtful buyer. "Can you prove it?"

"Sure; drink it and live long enough to find out. Look, squire, I only sell the stuff. And before you ask, no, I don't do guarantees. I don't even guarantee I'll be here tomorrow. Now if you're not going to buy, make room for someone who will." He looked hopefully at me. "How about you, sir? You look like a man who knows a bargain when he sees one."

"I do," I admitted. "And I also know the Borealis Accelerator when I see it. One sip of that stuff will make you immortal, but I have read the small print that usually accompanies the phial. The bit that says, *Drink me and you'll live forever. You'll be a frog, but you'll live forever.*"

The other customer quickly dropped the phial back into the suitcase, and hurried away. The street trader shrugged, not bothered. He knew there'd be another sucker along in a moment. "Well, how about this, squire? A jet pack you strap on your back. Fly like a bird, only without all that onerous flapping of arms. It glides, it soars, and, no, it doesn't come with a parachute."

A young man pushed forward, eager to try it out, and I made room for him. The trader haggled cheerfully over a down payment, then strapped the hulking steel contraption to the young man's back. The two of them studied the complicated control panel for a while, then the young man shrugged and stabbed determinedly at the big red button in the centre. The jet pack blasted up into the night at speed, dragging the young man along with it, his legs kicking helplessly. His voice came drifting desperately down.

"How do I steer the bloody thing?"

"Experiment, squire, experiment!" shouted the trader, and he turned away to concentrate on his other customers.

One of them had already picked up a small, lacquered box, whose label boasted it could contain an infinity of things. I decided to step back. The customer opened the box, and, of course, it swallowed him right up. The box fell to the ground, and the trader picked it up again, scowling.

"That's the third this week. I do wish people wouldn't try things without asking." He held the box upside down and shook it hard, as though hoping the customer might fall out again.

Tommy and I decided to leave him to it. From some way down the street came a loud crash; the sound of a jet pack returning to earth. There's one born every minute, and a hell of a lot of them end up in the Nightside.

And then suddenly everyone was running and shouting and screaming. People streamed past me, pushing and shoving each other out of the way. It didn't take me long to see why; and then I felt like running and screaming myself. Walker had finally lost patience with me. In the growing empty space where the crowd had been, dark shapes were heaving and sliding across the street, flowing like slow dark liquid across the pavement and walls. Dark as midnight, dark as the gaps between the stars, dark as a killer's thoughts, the huge black shapes spilled silently down the street towards me. Two-dimensional surfaces sliding across the three-dimensional world, changing and expanding their shapes from one deadly form to another. They had hands and claws and barbs, and horribly human faces. Anyone who didn't get out of their way fast enough was immediately swallowed up and absorbed in the dark depths of their bodies.

"What the hell are they?" asked Tommy, so shocked he actually forgot to sound effete.

"The Shadow Men," I said, looking around for an escape route, but the shadows had already cut us off, approaching now from all sides at once. "They're Walker's enforcers. You can't fight them, because they're not really here. That's just their shadows. They can swallow up anything and take it back to Walker. But you're never the same after you've been in that darkness. If the stories I've heard are true . . . I think I'd rather die than be taken by the Shadow Men."

"Why didn't Walker send the Reasonable Men after you?" said Tommy, sounding more than a little desperate. "I could have out-reasoned them." He tried to hide behind me, but the Shadow Men were coming at us from every direction. "This is not good, Taylor, this is seriously not good. I may have one of my turns. This isn't fair! I thought Walker always sent the Reasonable Men after people he was upset with!"

"Normally, he does," I said. "But I killed them all."

"Impressive," said Tommy. "But perhaps a little short-sighted. Do something, Taylor! These things really are getting terribly close!"

"Thank you, Tommy, I had noticed. Stop gripping my arm like that, you're cutting off the circulation. Now try and panic a little less loudly; I'm thinking."

"Think quicker!"

We were standing alone by then. Everyone else was keeping well back, giving the Shadow Men plenty of room to work in. No-one wanted to get involved, but many were watching interestedly from what they hoped was a safe distance. Quite a few were placing bets. Everyone wanted to see what would happen when the infamous John Taylor went head to head with the appalling Shadow Men.

The dark shapes glided forward, not hurrying, now that they had their prey cornered. They could take on any shape, because they had no texture or substance, but they had a taste for the shapes that terrified. Their faces were blank, heads without eyes that could still see you, like childhood nightmares. Their more abstract shapes were designed to disturb and unsettle. Just looking at them for too long could make you feel sick, right down to your soul. They oozed forward, savouring our helplessness.

"What are they made of?" Tommy asked, as much for the comfort of the sound of his own voice as anything.

"They're living shadows," I said. "Anti-life. No-one knows exactly what they are, or how Walker bound them to his will, to serve the Authorities. Most likely rumour is that they came through a Timeslip from a far future, where the sun has gone out and an endless night has fallen over all the Earth. And the Shadow Men are all that live in that terrible dark."

"I wish I hadn't asked," said Tommy. "So? How do we fight them?"

"Actually, I was hoping you'd have some ideas," I said, glancing quickly around me. "I don't know anyone who's ever beaten a Shadow Man."

"Well try something, dammit!"

I looked at all the gaudy neon signs surrounding us, and muttered a few Words of Power under my breath. Immediately every sign flared up simultaneously, the bright letters and shapes blazing fiercely against the night. The signs sparked and buzzed loudly, the sheer force of the light driving back the dark like a Technicolor dawn, but it didn't even slow the advance of the Shadow Men. One by one the signs overloaded, exploding or sputtering out in showers of sparks, shutting down all the length of the street. And the night that returned was even darker than before.

I reached into my coat pocket and pulled out three salamander eggs I'd been saving for a rainy day. I threw them at the nearest Shadow Men, and they exploded like incendiaries, blazing up with incandescent light and heat. The Shadow Men rolled right over them, swallowing them up in a second.

I breathed deeply, trying to steady myself, and looked at Tommy.

"I have an idea," he said, reluctantly. By now he was standing so close to me he was practically pushing me over. "But I have to say, it is rather . . . risky."

"Do it," I said. "I'm not going into those Shadows alive."

Tommy frowned, concentrating, and I could feel his gift activating, as though suddenly there was a third person standing there with us. The Shadow Men were all around us now, almost close enough to touch us. I could feel my heart hammering in my chest, and I could hardly get my breath. Tommy spoke slowly, thoughtfully, as though saying the words aloud made them certain, incontrovertible.

"I deal in probabilities. In the nature of shifting reality. I persuade the world to see things my way. And since there is a small but very real chance that we could have got to Time Tower Square before the Shadow Men could find us . . . I believe that is what really happened."

And in the blink of an eye, we were somewhere else. The dark street was gone, replaced by the quiet cul-de-sac that was Time Tower Square. Tommy let out his breath in a long, shuddering sigh.

"That's it. We are here. All previous possibilities are now redundant, never happened."

His gift shut down, like a dangerous animal reluctantly going to sleep. I looked carefully around me, but all the shadows in the Square were only shadows. A few people were strolling up and down, intent on their own business. They hadn't noticed anything, because there had been nothing to notice. We'd always been there. I looked respectfully at Tommy Oblivion.

"You can persuade reality itself to go along with your wishes? That's one hell of a gift you've got there, Tommy. Why aren't you running things in the Nightside?"

"Because using my gift that way diminishes me," Tommy said tiredly. "Every time I use it, the less real I become. Less certain, less anchored in reality. Use the gift too much, and I'd become too unlikely, too impossible to exist."

It was clear from his voice that he didn't intend to discuss the matter any further, so I turned away and studied the Time Tower. It didn't look like much, just a squat stone structure of maybe three storeys, brooding ominously over a backwater square. The few people passing by gave it plenty of room, though. The Tower had *serious* layers of protection to ensure that only Old Father Time had control over Time travel. It was said by some, and believed by many, that you could blow up the whole world and the Time Tower would still be standing there, unaffected. Most people couldn't even find the place if they approached it thinking bad thoughts.

Just an old stone building, with no windows and only the one, anonymous, door. But the last time I'd been here, during the angel war, I'd seen an angel crucified against the stone wall of the Tower, with dozens of cold iron nails hammered through its arms and legs, and its severed wings lying on the ground beneath it. They play for keeps in the Nightside, and especially in Time Tower Square.

I'd never travelled purposefully in Time before. Just the thought of what I was planning to do unnerved me, but I had to do it. More and more I was convinced that all the answers to all my questions could be found at the very beginning of the Nightside, in that moment when it was created by my missing mother, for reasons of her own. My mother, who might or might not be that Biblical myth known as Lilith. I only had her word for it, after all. I needed to *know,* to be sure.

The only thing I did know for sure, concerning my mother, was that she had been banished from the Nightside once before, long and long ago, thrown out of reality and into Limbo for centuries. Maybe I could learn how to do that again. I was sure I could learn all kinds of things by observing how and why my mother created the Nightside, all those millennia ago. If I could persuade Old Father Time to send me all the way back to that fateful moment, there had to be all kinds of useful information there, and maybe even weapons I could use against my mother. There had to be. I had to stop her bringing about that awful future I'd seen in the Timeslip, the future where I destroyed the Nightside and maybe all the world, too, because of who my mother was.

"Bang, you're dead," said a familiar cold voice.

Tommy and I both looked round sharply as Suzie Shooter stepped unhurriedly forward out of a concealing shadow. My old friend Suzie, also known as Shotgun Suzie and *Oh Christ it's her, run.* The most deadly and efficient bounty hunter in the Nightside, and certainly the most pitiless. She'd track a bounty all the way down to Hell itself if the money was right. She looked icily impressive, as always, a tall blonde Valkyrie in black motorcycle leathers, heavily adorned with steel chains and studs, complete with knee-length boots with steel-capped toes, and two bandoliers of bullets criss crossing her impressive chest. Grenades dangled from her belt. Her face was striking rather than pretty, with a strong bone structure and a determined jaw, and the coldest blue eyes I ever saw. She kept her long hair back out of her face with a leather band, fashioned from the skin of the first man she ever killed.

She was covering us both with her pump-action shotgun, and I didn't like her smile.

"Hello, Suzie," I said. "You're looking very fit. Been busy?"

"You know how it is," said Suzie. "So many people that need killing, and so little time." She lowered her shotgun. "You're getting soft, Taylor. Was a time I wouldn't have been able to sneak up on you like that."

"I've been somewhat preoccupied," I said, trying for dignity. "Killed anyone interesting recently?"

She shrugged easily and slipped her shotgun over her shoulder and into the holster hanging down her back. "No-one that matters. There's a lot of hysteria around. People saying the End Times are coming, like we haven't heard that before. But it's definitely good for business. Lot of people out there determined to pay off old scores while they've still got the chance. I've been looking for you, Taylor."

"Oh yes?" I said. Suzie might be an old friend, but it wasn't always wise to drop your guard around her. She only separated her business and private lives when it suited her. Five years ago I ran away from the Nightside, away from all the troubles and unanswered questions of my life, and I left with a bullet in my back from Suzie's gun.

"I've been hearing rumours about you," Suzie said lazily. "Disquieting rumours. About you and your mother, and what's going to happen now she's revealed herself at last . . . I went to Strangefellows, but you'd already been and gone. I could tell you'd been there; they were still clearing up the wreckage. So I asked around, and after bruising my knuckles a few times, I learned you were planning a trip through Time. So I came here and waited. I've decided that if you're determined to do this incredibly risky and stupid thing, you're going to need serious backup. And they don't come any more serious than me."

"True," I said. "But this isn't for a client or a case, Suzie. This is personal."

"So no money, then. Ah, what the hell. I owe you one, Taylor."

Tommy's ears pricked up, sensing gossip. "Really? How intriguing . . . Do tell."

"Don't go there," I said.

Suzie drew her shotgun in a blur of motion and stuck both barrels up Tommy's nose. "Right."

"Of course," said Tommy, standing very still. "None of my business, I'm sure."

Suzie put her shotgun away again. "I don't normally do warnings. I must be mellowing."

"It had to happen eventually," I said.

"Everyone's so touchy these days," said Tommy, fingering his nose gingerly.

"Who is this person?" said Suzie.

"This is Tommy Oblivion, the existential detective," I said. "He's coming along. He has a very useful gift. Don't break him."

The two of them studied each other dubiously. I looked at Suzie, and the cold hand that had gripped my heart the moment I set eyes on her squeezed a little more tightly. The last time I saw Suzie Shooter, it had been a version of her from the future. The bad future I encountered in the Timeslip. The future Suzie had been terribly injured, and rebuilt by my Enemies to be an engine of destruction. A weapon they sent back through Time to kill me, before I could do whatever terrible thing it was that would lead to their destroyed future. And the awful thing was, that future Suzie had volunteered for everything that had been done to her. Looking at her now, so whole and hale and hearty, so alive . . . I couldn't bear to think of her being hurt and used in such a way. Not because of me.

"You don't have to come along, Suzie," I said, abruptly. "This one is going to be dangerous. More so than anything you've ever faced. And there really isn't any money involved . . ."

"Not everything is about money," said Suzie. "You need me, Taylor. You know you do."

"The odds are stacked against us . . ."

"Cool," said Suzie. "You always know how to give a girl a good time, Taylor."

I looked at her for a long moment. "You do know I would stand between you and all harm, don't you, Suzie?"

She stirred uncomfortably. "What brought that on? You start getting sentimental, and I'll shoot you myself. You need to be razor-sharp and dangerous for Time travel."

I nodded. Suzie wasn't very good at emotions, for good reasons. So I had to be strong for both of us. And there and then I swore to myself that I would die before I let her become the terrible thing I'd seen from the future. I nodded briskly to her and changed the subject.

"Did you ever find that elusive bounty of yours, Big Butcher Hogg?"

Suzie grinned unpleasantly. "I got a good price for his head. And an even better price for his heart, lungs, and kidneys."

Tommy looked at me. "Is she joking?"

"I find it better not to ask," I said.

"It's a good thing I'm here," said Suzie, glaring disparagingly at Tommy. "I heard you nearly got your head handed to you on your last case. See what happens when you try to get the job done without me? I mean—Sinner, Madman, and Pretty Poison as your backup? What the hell were you thinking?"

I shrugged. "I needed someone scary, and you weren't around."

She sniffed loudly. "Is it true about your mother? That she's Lilith?"

"Looks that way."

"I had to look her up," Suzie admitted. "I only knew the name from an old Genesis song. I hate it when the world starts going Old Testament on my arse; those guys are hard-core." She looked like she was about to say something else, then shook her head sharply. "Come on, we need to get moving. If I can track you here, you can bet your enemies will, too. There's a lot of people in the Nightside who want you dead, Taylor. Even more than usual."

"Anyone interesting?" I said.

Suzie started counting them off on her fingers. "First up, we have Sandra Chance, the consulting necromancer. She's mad at you because you destroyed that revolting old Power, the Lamentation, on your last case. (And when you've got the time, I'd really like to know how you did that. The Lamentation was seriously creepy.) Anyway, it seems she had some kind of relationship with it, and she's sworn a blood oath against you."

"Bad news there, old thing," said Tommy. "You're not even safe in your grave, when that demented little filly is out to get you."

"Shut up," I said. I find a little effete goes a long way.

"Then," said Suzie, glaring at Tommy, "there are all the very well connected families of the thirteen Reasonable Men you killed. These grieving families have been putting out some serious paper on you, backed up by very serious money. Enough to tempt every bounty hunter in the Nightside. The families want you dead, and they aren't at all fussy about the details. They did try to hire me."

I raised an eyebrow.

"I was busy," said Suzie.

"But for the right money you'd take me down?"

Suzie smiled briefly. "For the right price I'd take God down. But I'd have to be paid a hell of a lot to go up against you, Taylor."

"Well," I said. "That's reassuring. Who else is after me?"

"Walker, for the Authorities, but then you probably already know that."

I nodded. "He sent the Shadow Men after me."

It was Suzie's turn to raise an eyebrow. "You defeated the Shadow Men?"

"Not as such," I said. "We ran away."

"Finally getting smart in your old age," said Suzie. "I wouldn't go up against the Shadow Men for all the gold in Walker's fillings. In fact, a trip through Time is probably the safest thing you could do right now. Even Walker has no power over Old Father Time." She glanced disparagingly at Tommy again. "You sure you want to drag him along with us, Taylor?"

"Yes," I said firmly. "I have a use for him."

"Oh good," said Tommy. "Am I going to like it?"

"Probably not," I said.

"Some days you shouldn't get out of bed in the morning," said Tommy. He glared at Suzie. "I don't think we should take her along, actually. She has a reputation for sudden and unexpected violence and a complete disregard for things like consequences. And unthinking acts in the Past can have terrible consequences. Change things too much in the Past, and the Present you return to might have nothing in common with the Present you left from."

"I thought you were desperate to go Time travelling," I said.

"Not necessarily this desperate."

"I'm going, and so are you," Suzie said briskly. "Now shut your face, or I'll rip your nipples off." She turned her cold gaze on me. "He may be annoying, but he does have a point. Time travel really is a last resort. You sure there's no-one else in the Nightside you could talk to about your mother?"

"The only other person who knew my mother, and is still around, is Shock-Headed Peter," I said. "And he's crazy."

"How crazy?" said Tommy.

"Crazy as in, criminally insane. He murdered three hundred and forty-seven people before the Authorities finally caught up with him. That's three hundred and forty-seven victims that they're sure of . . . Walker once told me, very much off the record, that the real number was probably in the thousands. That's a pretty respectable body count, even for the Nightside. They never did find any of the bodies. Or any trace of forensic evidence. Just the victims' clothes . . . The Authorities have him locked up in the nastiest and most secure dungeon in the Nightside."

"Why didn't they execute him?" said Suzie, practical as ever.

"They tried. Several times. It didn't take. I'll talk to him when I've tried absolutely everything else first."

"I would," said Tommy.

And that was when the Shadow Men found us again. Somehow they'd tracked me half-way across the Nightside in a matter of minutes, without even a trail to follow. They came slipping and sliding across the open Square, great black shapes with long reaching arms, and the few people in the Square ran screaming from them. I would have liked to do the same, but once again they'd silently surrounded me, blocking me off from every exit. They'd even been careful to get between me and the Time Tower. They moved in slowly from all sides like a creeping black tide, taking their time. They wanted to savour this. And I had nothing left with which to fight them.

Suzie Shooter had her shotgun in her hands again. She blasted the nearest Shadow with both barrels, and the darkness absorbed the blast without even a ripple. Suzie swore dispassionately.

"I have silver bullets, blessed bullets, cursed bullets, and a couple of grenades I stole from some Satanic terrorists. Any of them do any good?"

"No," I said. I was having trouble breathing, and I could feel cold beads of sweat popping out on my forehead. I didn't want to go out like this. Swallowed up by the dark, reduced to some broken, screaming thing. "Tommy?"

Give the man his due, he tried. He stepped forward and tried to reason with the Shadow Men. But his voice was uncertain, and I could feel his gift sputtering on and off. The Shadow Men oozed forward, taking their time, black lakes of evil intent. They didn't listen to Tommy. They didn't care about his logic, they didn't care about anything but dragging down the man who'd dared defy them. They had come for me, and not even Walker's orders would have turned them aside by then.

So I did the only thing left to me, and fired up my gift. I didn't want to. I blaze so very brightly in the dark when I open up my mind to find things, and my Enemies can See exactly where I am. They might send the Harrowing after me again, or worse still, the future Suzie. But I had no choice. I opened up my inner eye, my private eye, and used my gift to find the Time Tower's defences. I could See the many layers of magical protection radiating from the squat stone structure, like a dark rainbow, and it was the easiest thing in the world to reach out and grab them, and pull them to me.

I only meant to use them as a screen, to hide the three of us from the Shadow Men, but the Tower's defences had other ideas. They slammed into me, a cascade of terrible forces far beyond mortal ken, and I cried out as horrible pain racked my whole body. The defences forced their way into me, and focussed through me; then they leapt out to blast all the Shadow Men in the Square with a brilliant, incandescent, and overwhelming light that shone from me like a balefire against the night.

I screamed again and again as the power burned in and through me, and the light shone brighter, brighter, filling the whole Square. And everywhere the living Shadows fell back, shrivelling up and fading away under the onslaught of that terrible light. Suzie and Tommy had their heads turned away and their hands pressed over their eyes, but I don't think it was helping them much. They were crying out, too. The light rose up one last time, and the Shadow Men were gone, all gone, small patches of darkness blasted away by a light beyond bearing. The Tower's defences looked out through my eyes, checking that the Square was secure, then they withdrew, yanking themselves out of me with painful abruptness. I fell forward into my knees, shaking and shuddering. And all I could think was;

I don't think I'll try that again.

Suzie knelt beside me, not touching me, but giving me what support she could through her presence.

"I didn't know you could do that," said Tommy. He was looking dazedly about him. "You destroyed the Shadow Men! All of them! I didn't think anyone could do that!"

"I'm full of surprises," I managed to say, after a while.

"I'll say," Suzie said dryly. "First the Reasonable Men, now the Shadow Men. Soon Walker won't have anyone left to send after you."

"Sounds like a plan to me," I said.

I rose shakily to my feet and wiped the sweat off my face with a handkerchief that had seen better days. Tommy actually winced at the sight of it. I put it away, and we all looked at the Time Tower. Suzie looked at me.

"Why do they call it a Tower when it manifestly isn't?"

"Because that isn't the Tower," I said. Even my brief contact with the Tower's defences had been enough to fill my head with all kinds of information I hadn't possessed before. "That building is how you access the Tower, which isn't exactly here, as such. Old Father Time brought the Tower with him from Shadows Fall, but it's only connected to the Nightside by his will. It exists . . . somewhere else. Or maybe somewhen else. That stone thing only contains the Tower's defences. And trust me when I say you really don't want to know what powers them. I know, and I'm seriously considering scrubbing out my frontal lobes with steel wool."

"All right," said Tommy, in the tone of voice usually reserved for calming the demented and potentially dangerous. "How do we get to the Tower?"

"Through the door," I said. "That's what it's for."

I led the way over and tried the brass door handle. It turned easily in my hand, and the door swung open. This was a good sign. If Old Father Time didn't want to talk to you, the handle wouldn't budge. Inside the door was an elevator, with only the one button on its control panel. The three of us stepped inside, and I hit the button. The door swung shut, and the elevator started moving.

"Hold everything," said Suzie. "We're going *down*."

"The Tower exists at one hundred and eighty degrees to our reality," I said. "To reach the top of the Tower, we have to go all the way down."

"Am I the only one who finds that distressingly ominous?" said Tommy.

"Shut up," I said kindly.

Four mirrored walls surrounded us. As the elevator fell and fell, our reflections began changing. First a detail here and there, and then the changes accelerated, until the mirrors were showing us possible versions of ourselves, from alternate timetracks. Facing me was a female version of myself, looking very stylish in her long white trench coat. Another mirrored wall showed Suzie a male version of herself, looking like a berserker Hells Angel. A third wall showed a Punk version of Tommy, complete with a tall green Mohawk and safety pins through his face. The images changed abruptly, and suddenly all three of us were wearing masks and capes and gaudily coloured spandex. We had muscles and square chins and attitude to spare.

"Cool," said Tommy. "We're super-heroes!"

"More likely super-villains," Suzie said. "And I never had breasts that big in my life. They're bigger than my head . . ."

Another change, and suddenly I was wearing black leather trousers and bondage straps across my shaved chest. Suzie was wearing a scarlet basque with all the trimmings, black stockings and suspenders, and makeup by Sluts R Us. Tommy was a surprisingly convincing cross-dresser. None of us had anything to say. Another change, and we were Pierrot, Columbine, and Pantaloon. All three of us had a distinctly melancholy air, despite the bright costumes. The next change was . . . disturbing. I was a vampire, Suzie was a zombie, Tommy was a mummy. All of us were dead, but still continuing. Our pale and rotting faces had a grim, resigned look.

And then all the images faded away, leaving four mirrored surfaces showing no reflections at all. We looked at each other. Tommy actually reached out a hand to touch my arm, to make sure I was still there. Suzie tapped on the nearest mirror with a knuckle, and immediately all four walls showed a single terrible figure. It was the Suzie I'd seen from the bad future. Half her face had been destroyed, blackened and crisped around a seared-shut eye. One side of her mouth was twisted up in a permanent caustic smile. Her long straggly hair was shot with grey, and her leathers were battered and torn. She looked hard-used and horribly tired, from fighting evils I couldn't even imagine. And worst of all, her right forearm and hand were gone, replaced by that awful old weapon known as the Speaking Gun, which could destroy anything, anything at all. It had been plugged directly into what was left of her elbow.

Future Suzie stared out of all four walls, madness and fury and cold, cold determination blazing from her one remaining eye.

"Stop that," I said, and I don't think my voice had ever been colder or angrier. *"Stop that now."*

Tommy and Suzie looked at me sharply, but the future image snapped off, and all four mirrors were reflecting us as we were. And, God willing, always would be.

"What the hell was *that?*" said Tommy.

"Just a possibility," I said, looking at Suzie. "Nothing more."

Suzie looked hard at me. I'd never been able to lie successfully to her.

The elevator fell and fell, descending in a direction we could only guess at. It started to get cold, and our breath steamed on the air before us. There were voices outside the elevator, drifting, inhuman voices, thankfully indistinct. I don't think any of us would have wanted to hear them clearly. But finally the elevator eased to a halt, and the door disappeared. And standing before us, in a brightly lit steel corridor, was Old Father Time himself. He seemed human enough, as long as you didn't look too closely into his eyes. He was a gaunt man in his late fifties or early sixties, dressed to the height of mid-Victorian elegance. His long black coat was of a fine but severe cut, over a dazzlingly white shirt and dark waistcoat, and apart from the gold watch chain stretched across his flat stomach, the only touch of colour in his garb was the apricot cravat at his throat. He had a fine-boned face with high cheekbones, old old eyes, and a mane of thick grey hair. He held his chin high, and looked us over with a sharp, considering gaze.

"About time you got here," he said. "I've been waiting for you."

"Interesting," I said. "Considering even I didn't know there'd be three of us until a while ago."

"Oh, I'm always expecting everyone, my boy," said Time. "Especially Kings in waiting, female bounty hunters, and dated dandies." He sniffed loudly at Tommy. "I really don't approve of you, you know. Time is complicated enough without people like you messing it about. No, no, don't bother to justify yourself. You're going with Taylor anyway. He's going to need you."

"I am?" I said.

"And he'll need you, too, my dear," Time said to Suzie. "Your presence is approved, because it is necessary. You will redeem him."

"She will?" I said.

"Follow me," said Old Father Time, and he set off down the steel corridor at a brisk pace. We had to hurry to keep up.

"What do you know about what's going to happen?" I said.

"Never enough to do any good," said Time, not looking around.

The steel corridor seemed to stretch away forever. The gleaming walls showed us blurred distortions of ourselves, but Time's image was always sharp and distinct. And only his feet made any sound on the metal floor.

"What was all that business with the changing images on the elevator walls?" Suzie said abruptly.

"Possible futures, variant timetracks," Time said airily. "I should never have given the elevator semi-sentience. It gets bored, and sometimes cranky. It's harmless. Mostly. And don't worry about the images; they don't mean anything. Usually."

"Talk to me about possible futures," I said. "How real are they? How definite? How can you tell . . . the likely ones?"

"You can't," said Time. "They're all equally real, and therefore equally possible." He was still striding along, not looking back. "However . . . That isn't as true as it used to be. There don't seem to be as many futures as there once were. As though one particular future is becoming increasingly probable. More and more powerful, replacing all the others. As though . . . events are conspiring to narrow us down to the one future. Which is fascinating, if a trifle worrying."

"Only a trifle worrying?" said Tommy.

"Oh, these things usually sort themselves out," Time said vaguely. "Except for when they don't."

We were suddenly walking through a forest of large, slowly turning metal pieces. Shapes and cogs and wheels working together as we walked through and between them. It was like moving inside the mechanism of a giant clock. A slow loud ticking came from everywhere at once, and every distinct sound had something of eternity in it. Old Father Time looked back briefly.

"Whatever you're seeing, it probably isn't really there. It's only your mind interpreting something so complex as to be beyond your comprehension. Your mind supplies you with familiar symbols to help you make sense of your surroundings."

"I've always liked Disneyland," said Tommy.

"So," said Time, carefully ignoring Tommy's comment, "you want to go back into the Past, do you? All the way back to the creation of the Nightside. An ambitious plan, if somewhat lacking in self-preservation."

"How do you know where we want to go?" Suzie said sharply.

"Because it's my business to know things like that."

"If you really are the living incarnation of Time itself," I said carefully, "do you know the truth about the Past? About everything that's happened? Do you know what's going to happen when we go back to the beginnings of the Nightside?"

"I only know what I'm allowed to know, to do my job," said Time. He still didn't look round, but his voice sounded sad, resigned.

"Allowed?" said Tommy. "Allowed by who?"

"Good question," said Old Father Time. "If you should happen to find out, do let me know. Assuming you come back from this trip, of course."

"What?" said Suzie.

Time stopped abruptly, and we almost ran into him. He looked us over with his cold, crafty gaze. "Pay attention; this is important. Where you're going is much further back than most people go. And it is a very unstable moment in time, centered around a unique happening. I can send you there, but once you arrive you'll be beyond my reach. You'll be beyond anyone's reach. To put it bluntly, you'll have to find your own way back. I won't be able to help you. Knowing this, do you still wish to proceed?"

Suzie and Tommy and I looked at each other. I felt like the floor had been pulled out from under my feet. It had never occurred to me that this might be a one-way ticket.

"This changes things," said Suzie.

"Damn right," said Tommy. "No offence, old thing, but this isn't what I signed on for."

"I'm going," I said. "With or without you. I need to do this. I need to know the truth."

"Well," said Suzie, after a moment, "if you're dumb enough to do it, I guess I'm dumb enough to go along."

"You don't have to," I said.

"What are friends for?" said Suzie, and I don't think I've ever felt more touched.

"And I need to see the creation of the Nightside," Tommy said quietly. "I need to see one true, definite, and incontrovertible thing. So I'm going along, too. But I'm warning you now, Taylor; if we all end up stranded in the Past, I will dedicate what remains of my life to constantly reminding you it was All Your Fault."

"We're going," I said to Time, and he shrugged carelessly.

"I know," he said.

"There is a chance Walker and the Authorities will not approve of our taking this trip," I said. "Does that affect things?"

"Walker?" said Time, arching an eyebrow. "Appalling fellow. I wouldn't piss down his throat if his heart was on fire."

We came at last to the Waiting Room. Old Father Time asked us to wait there for him, while he checked that conditions were stable enough for our trip into the Past. I looked at him sharply.

"Conditions?"

He waved an elegant hand dismissively. "There are always storms and flurries in the chronoflow, and strangeness and charm run wild in the lower regions. And don't even get me started on quantum foam and superpositions. Sometimes I think the dinosaurs died out just to spite me. And despite all the traps I put down, there are still things that hunt and prey in the chronoflow, living like rats in the walls of reality. Just their passing can cause currents strong enough to carry away the most prepared traveller. Are you any happier for knowing all this?"

"Not really, no," said Tommy.

"Then stop bothering me with questions. Make yourselves comfortable here. I'll be back when I'm back."

He stalked out of the Waiting Room, head held high, hands clasped behind his back, as though already thinking about more important things. Suzie and Tommy and I looked at each other.

"Did you understand even half of what he said?" Tommy asked plaintively.

"Not even close," I said.

Suzie shrugged. "That's why he's Old Father Time, and we're not. I never bother with the backgrounds of cases, you know that, Taylor. Just find me someone I can shoot, and I'll be happy."

"You might want to start here," Tommy said nervously. "No-one seems at all happy to see us."

We looked around the Waiting Room. It could have been any doctor's waiting room, right down to the outdated magazines on the coffee table, but the people waiting were a strange collection, even for the Nightside. And all of them were scowling at us. They were waiting for their trips through Time to be approved, and they were all ready to get seriously unpleasant with anyone who looked to be getting preferential treatment. Suzie glared about her, and everyone started settling down again. Some of them even pretended to be interested in the magazines. Suzie has that effect on people.

Most of the people in Time's Waiting Room were from other time-lines, past and future. They'd arrived in the Nightside after stumbling into Timeslips, and ended up stranded here when the Timeslips collapsed. Old Father Time always did his best to find such temporal refugees a way home, but apparently it was complicated business. It took time. And so they waited in the Waiting Room, until either Time came through with the goods, or they got fed up with waiting and made new homes for them-selves in the Nightside.

There were Morlocks and Eloi, sitting at opposite ends of the room. There were knights in full plate armour, with force shields and energy lances. They politely volunteered that they came from a world where Camelot never fell, and Arthur's legacy continued. They didn't say any-thing about Merlin, so I thought it best not to either. There were big hairy Vikings, from a time-line where they colonized all of America, con-quered the world, and the Dark Ages never ended. One of them made dis-paraging remarks about Suzie, and unnatural warrior women in general, and Suzie punched him right between the eyes. His horned helmet flew the length of the room, and he took no further interest in the proceedings. The other Vikings thought this was a great joke and laughed uproariously, which was probably just as well.

There were even future people, tall and spindly and elegant, with an-imal grace and streamlined features, as though someone had decided to engineer a more efficient, more aesthetic form of humanity. They ignored everyone else, staring at something only they could see. Two hulking steel robots stood unmoving in a corner, watching everything with glow-ing crimson eyes. They came from a future where Man died out, and ro-bots built their own civilisation. They talked in staccato, metallic voices.

"Flesh-based creatures," said one. "Obscene. Corrupt."

"Meat that talks," said the other. "Abominations."

The knights in armour powered up their energy lances, and the robots fell silent.

Old Father Time finally returned, smiled vaguely round the Waiting Room, then beckoned for the three of us to follow him. He led us through a labyrinth of twisting stone passages with a ceiling so low we all had to stoop. Smoking yellow torches blazed in iron braziers, and small things scurried back and forth across the shadowy floor. Time paid them no attention, so I tried not to either.

We ended up, quite abruptly, in a shimmering white room, a room so white it was blinding, overwhelming. We all winced and shaded our eyes, except for Time. The room had no details. Even the door we'd entered through had disappeared. The white light was so dazzling it was hard to be sure of the room's size or scale, the walls and ceiling so far away it was impossible to judge any distances. The white room felt like it went on forever, while at the same time the walls seemed to be constantly rushing in and out, contracting and expanding, regular as a heartbeat I could sense but not hear. Suzie and Tommy stuck very close to me, and I was glad of their human presence.

In the middle of the room, stark and alone, stood a single complex and rococo mechanism, its pieces and workings so intricate my mind couldn't grasp all the details. It didn't seem to belong in the white room. It looked like a dirty nail driven deep into white flesh. Its very presence was an insult. Old Father Time fussed busily over the mechanism, pushing back his sleeves to ease his arms deep inside it, making delicate adjustments only he understood, while muttering querulously to himself in a voice just below the level of understanding. Finally, he stepped back with a proud gesture and nodded vigorously. We could all feel the mechanism coming on-line, like a giant eye slowly opening and becoming aware of us.

I could feel the Time Winds blowing, hear their blustering roar tugging subtly at my soul. It sounded like the breathing of some long-forgotten god, rousing itself from sleep. It felt like the whole universe was turning around this single spot, this single moment. When the Time Winds blow, even the greatest Powers shudder and look to their defences. I wanted to turn and run, and keep running till I could forget everything I'd seen and learned and felt here, but I couldn't let myself be weak. This was what I'd come here for.

Old Father Time looked round sharply. "Be still, all of you! There are strange fluctuations in the chronoflow, distortions I don't understand. Something big is happening, or is going to happen. Or perhaps it has already happened, long ago, and the echoes are reverberating up through Time, changing everything. I should understand what's happening . . . but

I don't. Which is in itself significant." He looked at me sharply. "Do you wish to postpone your trip?"

"No," I said. Suzie and Tommy said nothing.

Time spoke quickly, as though rushing to get everything in. "I have provided you with a process that will enable all of you to speak and understand any language or dialect you may encounter, and a glamour that will make you seem a part of whatever culture you may end up in. I wish I could be more specific, but where you're going, nothing is certain."

He was still talking, but now the roar of the Time Winds was drowning him out. I could feel them tugging at me, pulling me in a direction I could sense but not name. And then the three of us were falling, crying out to each other. The white room was gone, as though we'd dropped through it, like a stone through the bottom of a wet paper bag. We plummeted in a direction beyond understanding, wrapped in rainbows of colours I'd never seen before. We were falling, back, back towards something, somewhere, somewhen . . .

SIX

Past Very Much Imperfect

"I appear to be standing in a dead dog," said Tommy Oblivion. "And not in a good way."

The distress in his voice was clear, but I had my own problems. The world had slammed back into focus around me, but my head was still spinning. I was surrounded by darkness and leaning against a rough brick wall. The air was hot and sweaty, but it was the smell that hit me hardest. A thick and ripe organic miasma that hung heavily on the close air, and the stench of smoke and sweat and shit filled my head no matter how much I shook it. I pushed myself away from the wall and made myself study my new surroundings.

Tommy and Suzie and I were standing in a dark narrow alleyway, lit only by a burning human body in a hanging iron cage. The flames had pretty much died down, flickering sullenly around the blackened corpse. The walls of the alley were rough brickwork, stained black with soot, and the ground was packed earth covered with a rich mixture of fresh shit and other appalling detritus. Someone had painted *Dagon shall return!* on the wall, and pretty recently, by the look of it. Tommy had backed away from what was left of his dead dog and was banging his boots determinedly against the wall. Suzie stared slowly around her, frowning.

"Wherever we are, Taylor, I don't think it's where we were meant to be."

"You mean when we're supposed to be," I growled, simply to be saying something. "Obviously, something's gone wrong."

I headed for the end of the alley and the street noises beyond. There was light up ahead, and the sounds of some kind of civilisation. Suzie and Tommy hurried to catch up with me, the filthy ground sucking loudly at their feet. I stopped at the alley mouth, sticking to the shadows, and peered out into the street. Tommy and Suzie crowded in behind me. The street was busy, packed with mostly foot traffic, and if anything, the smell was even worse. There was a roar of constant chatter, intermixed with assorted animal noises, and the occasional crash of horse and oxen-drawn vehicles. We were definitely in the Past, but nowhere near far enough.

The buildings were mostly stone and timber, a mere two or three storeys high; basic blocky structures with a few lingering traces of Roman architecture. What style there was, was mostly Celtic with some Saxon, plus a whole bunch of stuff I didn't recognise. There were no pavements, only two thick streams of human traffic on either side of a deeply churned dirt road. The traffic in the middle wasn't moving much faster, being mostly horse-drawn wagons, and rough carts pulled by equally rough people. Hulking covered wagons groaned along, their heavy wooden wheels sinking deeply into the muddy road. There was mud and shit and filth everywhere, and flies hung in thick clouds on the smoky air. Now and again a better-dressed person would come riding through on a caparisoned horse, driving everyone else out of the way. And finally, a hunchbacked drover came along, riding a mule and driving a herd of miniature mammoths. They were about a foot or so high, cheeping cheerfully as they ploughed through the mud.

"Aw, cute," said Suzie, unexpectedly. Tommy and I both looked at her, and she stared us down with great dignity.

We looked out into the street again. "Judging by the architecture, I'd say we've ended up somewhen in the sixth century," said Tommy. "The Roman Empire has declined and fallen, and the dominant Celts are fighting a war against invading Saxons." Suzie and I looked at him, and he bristled. "I've read a lot about this period. It's really very interesting."

"I don't care if it's downright fascinating, we shouldn't be here," said Suzie. "We're at least five hundred years short of when we were supposed to arrive. Somebody screwed up."

"It can't be a mistake," said Tommy. "Old Father Time doesn't make mistakes. In fact, he is famous for not making mistakes."

"He didn't," I said. "Somebody else interfered."

Rage blinded me for a moment, and I hit out at the wall beside me, hurting my hand on the solid brick and not caring, almost relishing the pain. I tried to say something, but the anger flooding through me clenched my teeth, and it came out as a growl. Tommy started to back away. The rage pulsed in my gut like a red-hot coal, bending me over till I was glaring at the filthy ground. Hot, helpless tears burned in my eyes, and I hit out at the wall again.

Suzie moved in close beside me, murmuring quiet words, bringing me back with her calm, steady presence. I was breathing hard and rough, as though I'd just been hit; but Suzie's reassuring presence slowly got through to me, and I straightened up again. I pushed the anger into the back of my head, to be released later, when I had someone to take it out on. I took a deep breath and nodded my thanks to Suzie. She nodded back. She understood.

I looked down the alley at Tommy, who stared back uncertainly. "It's all right," I said, in my best reasonable voice. "I got a little upset there, for a moment, but I'm all right now."

"Of course you are," said Tommy, moving slowly and somewhat reluctantly forward to join me. "It's just that you looked . . . very different there, for a moment, old thing. I'd never seen you look like that. Like you could kill the whole world and not give a damn."

I forced a short laugh. "You've been taking my legend far too seriously."

Tommy stared at me dubiously, then looked out at the street scene again. "Well, if nothing else, the sixth-century Nightside does seem rather more peaceful than the one we're used to."

Even as he was saying that, one hand gesturing at the slow-moving traffic, something huge and crooked, wrapped in flapping rags and long strings of cured entrails, came stalking down the middle of the road on tall stilt legs, towering over everything else. It had a head like a horse's skull, and long many-jointed arms that ended in vicious claws. It lurched down the street at some speed, cawing like a great bird, and everyone else hurried to get out of its way. One oxen-pulled wagon reacted too slowly, and the creature stamped it into the dirt road with one heavy leg. The wagon exploded under the pressure, throwing the driver forward, and the creature stamped on him, too, crushing him into bloody pulp. The oxen ran free, bellowing with fear, while the creature continued uncaringly on its way. A pack of child-sized bipedal rats rushed out of the alley mouth opposite us and swarmed all over the dead driver. They devoured the bloody mush with glee, stuffing it into their squeaking mouths with disturbingly human hands. In a matter of moments, there was nothing left of the driver but his bones, which the rats tidily gathered up and took with them as they hurried back into their alley mouth.

No-one paid any attention. The traffic kept moving, perhaps a little more urgently than it had before. On either side of the filthy road, men and women and others kept their heads down and pressed on, concerned only with their own business. Coming up the street from the other direction was a huge, flaming presence, taller than the surrounding buildings, burning so brightly it was hard to see what if anything was at the heart of the flames. It drifted through the crowds, crackling and smoking, but keeping its heat to itself. A giant millipede with a headful of snapping mouths scurried past, clinging to the sides of buildings. And a great ball of compacted maggots rolled sluggishly down the middle of the road, sucking up useful leavings from the churned-up mud. I looked at Tommy. "Peaceful. Right. Come on, Tommy, you should know the Nightside is never peaceful for long."

"I take it we are still in the Nightside?" Suzie said suddenly. "I mean, for all we know this kind of shit is normal in the sixth century."

I pointed up at the night sky. Even through the drifting smoke, the crowded constellations of brilliant stars still burned like diamonds in the dark, and the oversized full moon looked down like a huge unblinking eye.

"All right," said Suzie. "Let's be logical about this. Who is there, powerful enough to intercept a journey through Time? Powerful enough to override Old Father Time himself and send us here? That's got to be a pretty short list."

"Just the one," I said, feeling the anger pulse briefly again. "Lilith. Dear Mother. I should have known she'd be watching me. I think perhaps . . . she's always watching me now."

"Okay," said Tommy. "That is seriously creepy. And I thought my family was weird . . . Why would Lilith want us here, in the sixth century?"

"To keep us away from the creation of the Nightside," said Suzie. "Must be something there she doesn't want us to see. Something we could use against her."

"Then why not block our trip completely?" I said. "No, I think she wanted us here. Now. She wanted me to see the Nightside as it was, before restrictions and controls and the Authorities moved it away from what she intended it to be. The only place on Earth completely free from the pressures of Heaven and Hell."

"Does Lilith exist here, now?" said Suzie.

"No. She would have been banished to Limbo by this time. I think."

"You think?" said Tommy. "I really think this is something you need to be bloody certain about, old boy, before we take another step! I demand to know exactly what the situation is before I'll even leave this alley!"

I raised an eyebrow. "Shame on you, Tommy Oblivion. I thought you existentialists didn't believe in certainties?"

"There is a time and a place for everything," said Tommy, with great dignity. "I vote for going home. Who else votes for going home?"

"Keep the noise down," said Suzie, and Tommy hushed immediately.

"We can't learn anything useful hiding in this alley," I said. "We need to get out and around, talk to people. Find out exactly when this is. I have a sneaking suspicion I know why Lilith chose the sixth century. This is, after all, the time of King Arthur and Merlin, when old gods and stranger powers still walked openly in the Nightside."

"Of course!" said Tommy, brightening up immediately. "Arthur and

Camelot! The knights of the Round Table! The most heroic and romantic time in history!"

"Only if you're into poverty, bad food, and body lice," said Suzie. "You're thinking of the mediæval fantasies about Arthur, mostly written long after the fact by French aristos, who added all the knights in armour and damsels in distress. The real Arthur was only a barbarian warlord whose main innovation was using massed cavalry against the Saxons. This is a hard, dark, and brutal age, when most people lived short, squalid, and very hard-working lives, and the only people with a guaranteed future were the slaves." She stopped, as she realised Tommy and I were staring at her. "All right, I saw a documentary, okay? I like documentaries. Anyone here have a problem with that?"

"Perish the thought," I said. "If this really is the time of Camelot, I doubt they'd let the likes of us in anyway. What we have to find is a way out of here, and back in Time to where we need to be."

"We can't contact Old Father Time," said Tommy. "He really was very clear about that, remember? In fact, we have to face the extremely real possibility that we could be stranded here. Forever. I mean, who is there in this time with the sheer power necessary to send people through Time? One way or the other?"

"Merlin," I said. "The most powerful sorcerer of all. He still has his heart here, which means he's in his prime. Yes . . . Merlin Satanspawn could send us any damn when he wanted to."

"If we could persuade him," said Suzie. "Right now, he doesn't know us from a hole in the ground. He has no reason to help us. What could we offer him in return for his services?"

"News of the future," I said. "Like, for example, that someone is going to steal his heart."

"Hold everything," Suzie said immediately. "We're not supposed to make changes, remember?"

"Telling him things we know are going to happen would only help to reinforce our Present," I said. "We don't actually have to tell him about the witch Nimue."

"Does that mean we get to go to Camelot after all?" Tommy said hopefully. "I've read all the books and seen all the films. I love those stories! There must be something to the legends, or they wouldn't have survived so long."

"Camelot is a long way from the Nightside," I said. "Geographically and spiritually. If there really are knights of the Round Table, they wouldn't come to a place like this on a bet. Merlin, however, probably feels right at home here. I think we need to visit the Londinium Club, the oldest private members' club in the world. Merlin used to be a Member."

"You're packed with useful information, aren't you?" said Suzie.

I grinned. "How do you think I've stayed alive this long?"

And so we left the safety of the alleyway, and stepped out into the street. The air was thick with greasy smoke from all the burning torches in their iron holders, standing in for the hot neon of our time. We all braced ourselves, ready to react swiftly and violently if we were recognised and set on as obvious strangers who didn't belong, but no-one paid us any attention at all. Old Father Time's glamour was clearly working, making us look like everyone else. And the roar of voices around us sounded like perfectly normal colloquial English, even though it patently wasn't.

We barged through the crowds, showing them the same lack of respect they showed us. We didn't want to stand out. The street was packed with people, though a large percentage of them weren't human. There were elves in long, shimmering gowns, arrogant and disdainful. Demons out of Hell, scarlet imps with stubby horns and lashing tails, laughing nastily at things only they would find funny. A pack of tall bipedal lizards stalked through the crowd, wearing cured leather hides and brightly coloured scarves. The back of their jackets bore the legend *Dagon Rules* spelled out in silver studs. And even the humans were a pretty mixed bunch, representing races and cultures from all across the sixth-century world: Chinese, Indians, Persians, Romans, and Turks. It seemed like even here, the Nightside was still the place to be, to buy and sell all the dubious delights you couldn't get anywhere else. There were even a few obvious anomalies, people and others who clearly didn't belong in the sixth century. Since they didn't have Old Father Time's protecting glamour, they were probably dimensional travellers, or people who'd arrived accidentally, via Timeslips.

"Why are all the people here so much shorter, and well . . . ill-looking?" said Tommy.

"Poor diet," Suzie said briskly. "Vitamin deficiencies, never enough meat, or the money to buy it when there was. Plus no real medicines, and hard grinding work every day of your life, until finally you dropped in your tracks. I thought you said you were an expert on this period?"

"Only on the bits that interested me," Tommy admitted. "The romantic bits."

We carried on, sticking very close together. Everyone seemed to be carrying some kind of weapon. The smell was still appalling, and there was shit everywhere. There was no way of avoiding it, so we strode through it and tried not to think about the condition of our shoes. There were no drains, never mind sewers. And then everyone ducked as the whole street shook, and a massive dragon roared by overhead, like a low-flying jumbo jet. Most people didn't even look up. Just business as usual, in the sixth-century Nightside. I didn't like it. The streets seemed much darker here, without the usual gaudy neon. There were the torches, and oil-lamps, lanterns, foxfire moss, and more burning bodies in their hanging iron cages, but still the night seemed darker here, the shadows deeper.

There was none of the passion, none of the sardonic joie de vivre, of my time. Most of the people around us seemed to slouch along, as though afraid of being noticed. Perhaps with good reason. Things that weren't at all human lurked watchfully in most of the alley mouths we passed. I looked down one and saw a circle of possessed babies, fiery halos burning over their soft heads, drawing complex mathematical figures in the dirt at their feet and laughing in coarse adult voices. I looked away before they could notice me. A hooded monk stepped out into the road, gesturing angrily for the traffic to get out of his way. He disappeared abruptly as a hidden hole opened up beneath his feet and swallowed him up before he even had time to scream. Across the road, a dead woman in brightly coloured silks caught my eye and bumped a hip suggestively. Her eyes were very bright in her cracked grey face. No. I really didn't like this Nightside.

The dead woman was fronting a brothel, where women of all kinds, and some things that were only nominally female, called out to the passing trade with loud, carrying voices, coarse and raucous. Some of them were offering services even I hadn't heard of. I didn't feel inclined to investigate. Tommy was staring straight ahead and actually blushing, so of course the whores concentrated on him. He hunched his shoulders, and tried to pretend he wasn't there, which should have been easy enough for an existentialist. Next door to the brothel was a dark and spooky little shop selling reliquaries—the bones of saints, fragments of the True Cross, and the like. Special offer that week was apparently the skull of John the Baptist. Next to it was a smaller skull, labelled JOHN THE BAPTIST AS A CHILD. People weren't all that bright, back in the sixth century. The shop also boasted a large collection of furniture and wood carvings, supposedly produced by Jesus, or his father Joseph, or the rest of the carpenter's family.

Even in the sixth century, it seemed the Nightside traders knew the only rule that mattered, that there's one born every minute.

Inns and taverns of varying quality abounded everywhere, probably because you needed a lot of booze to get you through the strain of living in the sixth century. I'd been there less than an hour, and already I felt like biting the neck off a bottle. There were also lots of churches everywhere I looked, probably for much the same reason. Apart from the many already fragmenting Christian churches, there were also temples dedicated to Dagon, the Madonna of the Martyrs, the Carrion in Tears, and Lucifer

Rising. (This last usually known as the Hedge Your Bets church.) There were also any number of Pagan and Druidic shrines, based around grotesque wood carvings and distressingly large phallic symbols. Religion was very up front and in your face in the sixth century, with preachers of every stripe haranguing the crowds from every street corner, preaching fire and brimstone and any number of variations on *My god will be back any time now, and then you'll be sorry!* The better speakers got listened to respectfully, and everyone else got pelted with . . . well, shit, mostly.

"Jesus is coming back a week this Saturday!" bellowed one preacher as we passed. "Repent now and avoid the rush!"

There were other, darker, forces abroad in the Nightside. Beings and Forces hadn't been forcibly segregated to the Street of the Gods yet. And so they walked in glory down the same streets as the rest of us, often surrounded by unearthly glows, radiating power and otherness. People hurried to get out of their way, and the slower-moving ones were often transfixed and sometimes physically transformed, just from sheer proximity to the Beings. One figure, a huge blocky shape with a great insect head, headed straight for us, only to turn aside at the last moment, actually stepping out into the road to avoid getting too close to me. It regarded me solemnly with its complex eyes, the intricate mouth parts moving slowly in what might have been a prayer.

"It sensed something about you," said Tommy.

"Probably that I'm in a really bad mood," I said. "I could have sworn the Londinium Club was around here somewhere, but it seems we're not necessarily where I thought we were."

"You mean we're lost?" said Tommy.

"Not lost, as such," I said. "Just . . . misplaced."

"We can't keep walking at random," Suzie said quietly. "Even with Old Father Time's glamour protecting us, you're still attracting attention, Taylor. Use your gift. Find the Londinium Club."

"You know I don't like to use my gift unless I have to," I said, just as quietly.

"Your Enemies aren't going to be looking for you in the sixth century," Suzie said sternly.

"We could ask people for directions," said Tommy.

"No we couldn't," said Suzie. "We want our arrival there to have the element of surprise. Use your gift, Taylor."

I thought about it. My Enemies had no reason to suspect I was here, sixteen hundred years in the Past, unless the future Suzie had told them about this little trip . . . but I couldn't keep thinking that way, or I'd go mad. So, I powered up my gift, opening the third eye deep in my mind, and Saw the world around me. There were ghosts everywhere, walking through the crowds and the buildings, pale, faded figures trapped in their temporal fugues, repeating the same endless circle of action and mourning. There were huge spirit forms, bigger than houses, striding through the material world as though they were all that was real and the rest of us only phantoms. Massive, winged things that were neither angels nor demons flapped overhead in great clouds, holding rigid formations. Unknowable forces moving on unguessable missions. I pulled my drifting thoughts together, concentrated on the Londinium Club, and found it in a moment. We weren't as far from it as I'd thought, only a few minutes' walk. Which made me think: did Lilith know that? Had she chosen where as well as when to drop me back into the world? Was I supposed to go to the Club, to meet someone or learn something? More questions with no answer.

I shut down my gift, carefully pulling my mental defences back into place. Just at the end there, I'd felt . . . Something, starting to take notice of my presence. Not my Enemies. Something of this time, big and dark and brutally powerful. Just possibly . . . Merlin Satanspawn.

I didn't mention this to the others. Just led them down the street, heading for the Londinium Club. But almost immediately our way was blocked by a ragged bunch of street thugs who appeared out of nowhere and had us surrounded in a moment. Ten of them, big and bulky swords for hire in scrappy chain mail and battered leather armour, with scarred faces and nasty smiles. They carried short-swords and axes, and long knives with blades so notched they were practically serrated. None of them topped five feet, but they all had barrel chests and arms bigger than my thighs. None of this lot had ever gone hungry. They were, however, filthy dirty, and they smelled awful. The leader was a swarthy man with a roughly cut mane of black hair. He smiled nastily, revealing several missing teeth.

"Well, well," he said easily. "Not often we gets nobility in our part of town, do we, lads? So . . . clean, and well dressed. Slumming, are we, gents and lady? Looking for a bit of rough trade, perhaps? Well, they don't come much rougher than us, and that's a fact." His fellow thugs all laughed unpleasantly, some of them already looking at Suzie in a way I didn't like. If she killed them all, it would be bound to attract unwelcome attention. At least she hadn't drawn her shotgun yet.

"What do you want?" asked Suzie, and the leader looked at her uncertainly, taken aback by the cold, almost bored tone in her voice.

"What do we want, lady? What have you got? Just a toll, a little local taxation, for the privilege of passing through our territory."

"Your territory?" I said.

"Our territory, because we control it," said the leader. "Nothing and no-one moves through here, without paying us tribute."

"But . . ."

"Don't you argue with me, you tosser," said the thug, prodding me hard in the chest with a filthy finger. "Give us what we want, and we'll let you walk away. Piss us about, and we'll mess you up so bad people will puke just to look at you."

"How much is this going to cost us?" said Tommy, already reaching for his purse.

"Whatever coin you've got on you. Any goods we happen to take a liking to. And some quality time with this lady." The chief thug leered at Suzie. "I likes them big."

I winced on his behalf. I could feel Suzie's icy presence beside me, like the ticking of an activated bomb.

"That is a really bad idea," I said, in my best cold and dangerous voice. I relaxed a little as the thug turned his attention back to me. I could handle scumbags like him. I gave him my best hard stare. "You don't know who we are. What we can do. So do the sensible thing and step aside, before we have to show you."

He laughed in my face, and his fellow thugs laughed with him. I was a bit taken aback. It had been a long time since anyone dared laugh in my face.

"Nice try, Taylor," said Suzie. "But they don't know your legend here. Let me deal with them."

"You can't kill them all," Tommy said immediately. "Kill them, and you kill all their potential future descendants. Who knows how many cumulative changes that could cause, back in our Present? Let me try my gift on them." He gave the leader his best winning smile. "Come, let us reason together."

"Shut your face, pretty boy," said the leader. He spat right into Tommy's face, and Tommy recoiled with a cry of disgust, his concentration shattered.

"So much for diplomacy," said Suzie, and she drew her shotgun with one easy movement.

The leader regarded the gun interestedly. "Whatever that thing is, it won't do you any good, lady. Me and the lads are protected, against all edged weapons and magical attacks. None of them can touch us."

Suzie shot the man in the face, blowing his head right off his shoulders. The body staggered back a few steps and collapsed. The other thugs looked at the body twitching on the ground, then slowly and reluctantly looked back at Suzie.

"Run away," I suggested, and they did. Suzie looked after them thoughtfully for a moment, then put her shotgun away again.

"There really wasn't any need for that," I said. "I could have dealt with them."

"Of course you could," said Suzie.

"I could!"

"You can deal with the next ones," said Suzie, as she set off down the street.

"I never get to have any fun," I said, following after.

"He's going to sulk now, isn't he?" said Tommy, hurrying to catch up.

"Oh, big time," said Suzie Shooter.

SEVEN

Some Unpleasantness at the Londinium Club

Only those personages of extreme power, prestige, or parentage can hope to gain admittance to the oldest private members' club in the world. Just fame, wealth, or knowing the right people won't do it. The Londinium Club was and is extremely exclusive, and the merely heroic or significant need not apply. There are those who say Camelot operated on a pretty similar principle. All I know for sure is that neither establishment would let me in without a fight.

We found the Londinium Club easily enough. It was a large, dignified building in a much more salubrious area of the Nightside. The traffic was quieter, the pedestrians were of a much-better-dressed class, and there wasn't a brothel anywhere in sight. Still a hell of a lot of shit in the street, mind. I stopped before the front door of the Club, and looked the place over. The exterior looked pretty much the same as the last time I'd seen it, back in my Present. Old, old stone decorated with sexually explicit Roman bas-reliefs, surrounding a large and very solid oak door. And when I say sexually explicit, I'm talking about the kind of images that would have made Caligula blush, and maybe dash for the vomitorium. Suzie regarded the designs calmly, while Tommy started searching his pockets for a paper and pencil, to make notes.

Standing in front of the main entrance was the Doorman, a solid and immovable presence whose function and delight it was to keep out the unworthy. He was protected against any form of attack, by Powers known and unknown, was strong enough to tear a bull in half, and was, supposedly, immortal. Certainly he was still around in my time, large as life and twice as obnoxious. The Doorman was a snob's snob, and he gloried in it. He was currently a short, stocky man in a purple Roman toga, with bare muscular arms folded firmly across an imposing chest. I half expected

him to be wearing a sash saying THEY SHALL NOT PASS. He stood proudly
erect, nose in the air, but his eyes missed nothing. He'd already noticed us.

"I could shoot him," said Suzie.

"Don't even think it," I said quickly. "The Doorman is *seriously* protected. And besides, we already know you didn't kill him, because I already met him, back in the Present, during my last case."

"I hate circular reasoning like that," said Suzie. "Let's shoot him anyway and see what happens."

"Let's not," I said, very firmly. "This is the kind of place where they
have you impaled for being late with your membership dues. For once,
our usual tactics of brute force and ignorance will not win the day. We're
going to have to talk our way past him."

"Get to the front, Tommy," said Suzie. "You're on."

"I knew you were going to say that," said Tommy.

We approached the front door, and the Doorman actually stepped forward to block our way, one meaty hand held out in warning.

"All right, that's as far as you go. You three are not at all welcome
here. Ever. I still remember you from the trouble you caused the last time
you were here, some two hundred years ago."

"Guess where we're going next," murmured Tommy.

"Shut up," I hinted.

"We must have made a pretty big impression on the man," said Suzie.

"You always do, Suzie," I said generously. I smiled at the Doorman.
"Look, I know we're not actually Members, but we only want to pop in
for a moment and maybe ask a few questions. Then we'll be gone and out
of your life. Won't that be nice?"

"Members only means Members only," growled the Doorman.
"Leave now. Or I will be compelled to use force."

Suzie started to reach for her shotgun. "No!" I said urgently. "When I
said the Doorman was protected, I meant by everyone who's a Club
Member. And that means he can draw on the powers of sorcerers, elves,
and minor godlings to stop us."

"Ah," said Suzie. "So shooting him wouldn't work?"

"No."

"I've got these special grenades . . ."

"No!" I turned to Tommy. "You're up. Mess with the man's head."

Tommy Oblivion stepped forward, smiling confidently. The Doorman considered him warily.

"We're not from around here, old thing," Tommy said easily. "You
probably already noticed that. In fact, we're not from this place, or this
time. We're from the future. Some sixteen hundred years from now, to be
exact. And in that future, my friends and I are Members of your Club."

"What?" said the Doorman. Whatever he'd been expecting to hear, that clearly wasn't it.

"We are Members, where and when we come from. Which means, technically speaking, we are also Members here and now. Once a Member, always a Member, right?"

The Doorman frowned as he thought about that. Thinking clearly wasn't what he did best. He brightened up as an idea came to him.

"If you're a Member," he said slowly, "you know the secret handshake."

Tommy raised an eyebrow. "There is no secret handshake, dear fellow. But there is a secret password, which I have written down on this piece of paper."

He showed the Doorman his empty hand. The Doorman looked at it closely, moving his lips as though reading, then nodded reluctantly and stepped back to let us pass. He was frowning heavily, as though his head hurt. The oak door swung open before us, and I led the way into the lobby beyond. Once the door was safely shut behind us, I looked at Tommy.

"You made him see something that wasn't there."

"Of course," said Tommy. "It's my gift to be convincing. Besides, in some alternate time-line we probably are Members. Or at least, I am."

I sniffed. "I still didn't get to do anything."

"You will, you will," Suzie said soothingly. "This place is bound to be packed with all the kinds of people you detest the most. I'm sure you'll find someone worth upsetting in some thoroughly appalling and vindictive way."

I sniffed again, unconvinced, and looked around the Club lobby. It still had some of the old Roman magnificence I remembered from my last visit, with gleaming tiled walls and marble pillars, but instead of thick carpeting on the floor there were only trampled rushes, strewn here and there in clumps, and the high ceiling had been covered in thick Druidic designs that looked like they'd been daubed with woad. The only lighting came from oversized oil-lamps, and the perfumed air was hot and flat and a little stale. There was a sense that the Club had declined somewhat from its original glory days in Roman times and had yet to develop its own style. Certainly the Romans would never have put up with this much mess. The rushes on the floor looked like they hadn't been changed in days, and there were smoke and soot streaks on the walls above the oil-lamps. Stains here and there suggested spillages of all kinds.

A servant, or more probably a slave, given the iron collar bolted around his neck, came forward hesitantly to greet us. Something about us clearly upset him because he stopped dead in his tracks, and yelled *Security!* at the top of his lungs. A panel slammed open in one of the walls, revealing a hidden alcove, from whose dark depths a hideous crone emerged, spitting and cackling. She was clearly some kind of witch, with stray magics sputtering and discharging around her clawed hands. She was a twisted figure in rags and tatters, with a heavy iron chain leading back into the alcove from the slave collar around her scrawny throat. She lurched towards us, her eyes wide with madness and thwarted rage. I could feel the power building around her as she muttered ancient words in a deep guttural voice, and I knew that as soon as she oriented on us, we'd be in deep shit.

So I raised my gift only long enough to find the spell that kept her from breaking her chain and slave collar, and removed it. The collar snapped open, and the chain fell away from her. The witch broke off in mid spell, and lurched to a halt. She kicked tentatively at the chain on the floor, and it rattled helplessly. The witch grinned slowly, revealing a handful of yellowed teeth, then she turned to look at the slave who'd called her out of the alcove. He turned and ran, but he was a grease spot on the floor before he'd made half a dozen steps.

The witch raised her clawed hands and howled a ululating shriek of triumph and vengeance long desired. Vicious spells detonated on the air all around her, blasting holes in the walls and floor. Armed men came running from all directions, and the witch turned to face them with vindictive glee on her shrivelled face. Fires started, gale winds blew, and the armed men started exploding, blowing apart in showers of bloody gobbets.

"Happy now you've done something?" said Suzie.

"Very," I said.

Unnoticed in the general chaos, we strolled across the lobby and let ourselves into the dining room. We shut the door firmly behind us, and the din of the pandemonium shut off immediately. No-one looked up as we came in. Whatever the noise was, that was slaves' business and nothing to do with the Members. Most of them were reclining on couches to eat, in the old Roman style, giving their full attention to excellent food and drink, and good company. And probably paying more for that one meal than most people in the sixth century made in their entire lives.

Some of the diners still wore the old-fashioned Roman toga, but most wore simple tunics, with or without leather armour and trappings. The majority of the diners were human, but there were also quite a few elves, looking studiedly disdainful of their surroundings even as they gorged themselves on human delicacies, and a handful of gargoyles eating live mice and playing with their food in a quite distressing manner. The diners were being served by male and female slaves, some barely more than children, all of them wearing fixed, empty expressions. They were naked save for the iron collars round their throats, and all of them carried scars and whip marks.

"Slavery," said Tommy, his voice full of revulsion. "I knew about it, knew there were slaves even in King Arthur's time, but I never really . . . some of them are just kids!"

"This is the way things were," I said. "And will be, for centuries after. And get that look out of your eye, Tommy. I only freed that witch to provide a distraction. We start freeing slaves on a grand scale, and you can bet all the Powers here will rise up against us. We can't change a whole culture. That's not why we're here. And besides, we don't dare make any big changes if we want to return to our own Present, remember?"

"I remember," said Tommy. "But I don't have to like it."

There was an edge in his voice, a cold anger that hadn't been there before. I liked him better for it.

"Join the club," I said.

"I don't see any sign of Merlin," said Suzie, all business as usual. "And I'm pretty sure he'd stand out, even in this crowd. Want me to grab somebody and shake some answers out of them?"

"I think it might be better if I was to ask a few polite questions," I said. "On the grounds that I have at least heard of diplomacy."

A tall, elegant, and distinctly supercilious type was already heading in our direction, threading his way gracefully between the couches, bestowing smiles and sweet nothings on the people he passed. He wore a blindingly white tunic and no iron collar. He came to a halt before me, dismissing Suzie and Tommy with a mere flick of the eyes, and raised a painted eyebrow a carefully calculated fraction of an inch.

"I am the Steward," he said. "And you are very definitely not Members. Not ever likely to be. I don't know how you got in here, but you will have to leave immediately."

I smiled at him. "You know all that chaos and destruction that's currently going on in your lobby? All the fires and explosions and parts of deceased security people flying through the air? I did that."

"Take a couch," the Steward said resignedly. "I suppose you'll be wanting something to eat, before security can put together a big enough force to restore order and throw the three of you out of here? Today's specials are larks' tongues in aspic and baby mice stuffed with hummingbird tongues."

Tommy winced. "Do you have anything that doesn't involve tongues?"

"Don't sit down, Suzie," I said. "We're not staying for dinner."

"You might not be," said Suzie. She'd already snatched a breaded

drumstick from a nearby diner and was chewing it with a thoughtful look
on her face. The diner sensibly decided not to make a fuss.

"We're looking for the sorcerer Merlin," I said to the Steward. "Merlin Satanspawn. He is a Member here, isn't he?"

"Only because nobody dared blackball him," said the Steward, his lip
curling. "But even so, he doesn't dare show his face here any more. Not
since the King and most of his knights fell in battle, in the last great contest against the bastard Mordred's forces; and all because Merlin wasn't
there to support his King. The pretender died, too, his forces scattered,
but still the age of Logres is over. Camelot is simply a castle now, with an
empty Throne and a broken Table, and the ideals of the Court are already
falling apart. The end of an age; and all because one man wasn't where he
should have been. You want Merlin Satanspawn? Try a tavern. Any tavern."

There was just enough bitterness in his voice to make him convincing. I gathered Suzie and Tommy up with my eyes and led them back out
of the dining room. And as I left I raised my gift, found the spell that held
the iron collars around the slaves' throats, and undid it. The collars sprang
open, and the magic that had kept the slaves docile fell away in a moment.
Some of the slaves attacked the diners, while others ran for their lives and
their freedom. The dining room quickly descended into chaos.

"You big softie," said Suzie.

"There's some shit I just will not put up with," I admitted.

We strolled back through the lobby, most of which was on fire. There
was no sign of the witch anywhere, but a great crevice had opened up in
the middle of the floor, belching out soot and cinders and smoke that
smelled strongly of brimstone. *My work here is done,* I thought, a little
smugly. We nodded cheerfully to the Doorman as we passed him, then
stood together in the street wondering where we should try next. God
alone knew how many taverns, inns, and hole-in-the-wall drinking dives
there were in the sixth-century Nightside, and I really didn't feel like
searching them all. On the other hand, I also didn't feel like using my gift
again. I'd been using it far too often, almost casually, and that was dangerous. Flare up often enough in the dark, and my Enemies would be
bound to notice me, no matter how far I was in the Past. From their future
vantage point, I was always in the Past.

"Strangefellows," I said suddenly. "That's where Merlin will be. Or
whatever the oldest bar in the world is currently called. I remember the
Merlin of our time telling me that he often drank there, to get away from
the overbearing niceness of Camelot. That's probably why he chose to be
buried in the bar's cellars, after he was killed. Yes. That's where we'll find

him." I looked at Suzie. "You're frowning. Why are you frowning, Suzie?"

"Lilith brought us here, right?" said Suzie. "Had to be a reason. Could be because she wanted us to meet with Merlin. He is the leading major player in this Nightside. And if that's so, do we want to do what she wants us to do?"

"I'm past caring," I said. "All this guessing and double-guessing. I want to get this over with and get out of here. I want to witness the creation of the Nightside, so I can get my answers, so I can finally be rid of Lilith's influence in my life. I want this to be over!"

"Easy, John, easy," said Tommy, and it was only then that I realised my voice had risen to a shout.

"It'll never be over, John," said Suzie, as kindly as she could. "You know that."

"I can't believe that," I said. "I can't afford to believe that."

There was a long pause, then Tommy said, "If we can't find Merlin here in the Nightside . . . could we please try Camelot? I've always dreamed of visiting that legendary Castle, seeing the famous Round Table, and—"

"You heard the Steward," I said, perhaps a little roughly. "It's a mess there right now. All the heroes are dead, and the dream's over. We'll find Merlin in Strangefellows. Where else could such a disgraced man go to drown his sorrows in peace?"

"All right," said Tommy, resignedly. "Fire up your gift and point us in the right direction."

"There's an easier way," I said. I looked back at the Doorman. "The oldest bar in the world. What's it called, and where is it?"

He gave me a withering look. "Give me one good reason why I should assist you?"

"Because," I said, "if you don't, my companions and I will hang around here for hours and hours, acting cranky and lowering the tone."

"The bar you're looking for is called Avalon," said the Doorman. And he provided us with very clear and distinct directions, just to be sure we wouldn't have to come back and ask him again.

EIGHT

Sacrifices for the Greater Good

Not all that surprisingly, the Avalon bar turned out to be situated in a really sleazy area, even for the Nightside. The lighting was bad, the streets were filthy, and so were the people. There were bodies lying everywhere, dead or drunk or demonically possessed, with a fight on every street corner and couples humping in doorways. The sixth century was a particularly unselfconscious age, when it came to sin. I saw one preacher getting a blow job, even as he pontificated on the evils of the Gnostic heresies. No-one bothered us, though. It seemed word of our exploits and notoriously short tempers had got around. Whatever century you're in, nothing travels faster in the Nightside than gossip and bad news.

I still couldn't get used to having to step over lepers, though. Even if they were always very polite about it.

Avalon itself turned out to be a large and chunky tower constructed entirely of stained and discoloured bones, held together by some unseen but not entirely unfelt force. Just looking at the tower put a chill in my heart, and in my bones. Not least because I'd seen it once before, when it manifested briefly in Strangefellows, during my previous case. Just before everything went to hell, and the future Suzie turned up to kill me. I couldn't stop myself from glancing at her, and she caught my gaze.

"What's wrong, John?" she said quietly. "You've been looking at me strangely ever since we started this case. Do you know something I don't?"

"Always," I said, forcing a smile. "But nothing you need to worry about."

We headed for the base of the bone tower. It stood out against the night sky like the tomb of a dead god, unnatural and ill-omened. Approaching it felt like stepping down into an open grave. The door was a simple dark opening, with nothing beyond but silence and an impenetrable darkness. Anywhen else I would probably have been worried, but I was more concerned with Suzie. She knew I was hiding something from her, but how could I tell her? What good could it do? And I couldn't escape the feeling that simply by talking about it aloud, by accepting it, I might make that future more possible, more probable. I strode straight into the dark opening, while guilt twisted in my gut like a living thing, and Suzie and Tommy followed right after me.

The darkness quickly gave way to a friendly amber glow, the bar itself just a sprawling, smoke-filled room, roughly the same size as the bar back in my time. There were no windows, and the oil-lamps and torches filled the hot sweaty air with a thick, defusing smoke, but the general effect was not unpleasant. Once I was inside, it was clear the bone tower exterior was a glamour, designed to scare off unwanted visitors. I wandered unhurriedly between the packed long wooden tables, and everyone else ostentatiously minded their own business. Just as in my time, this was not a bar where you went for company and good fellowship.

Over in one corner, a number of musical instruments were playing themselves, providing basic but pleasant background music.

The customers were the usual unusual suspects, the men and women wearing a collection of clothing from all kinds of cultures and backgrounds. Anywhere else they would have been fighting each other to the death over religion or customs or plain foreignness, but not in Avalon. Humans stuck together in the face of so many other alternate threats. Three witches in embroidered saris sat huddled together, giggling like nasty children as they animated a number of stick figures and made them dance madly on the tabletop before them. Two seriously ugly Redcap goblins were knife-fighting, while a circle of onlookers cheered them on and laid bets on the outcome. Two lepers were playing knucklebones with their own fingers. Two heretical priests were arm-wrestling each other over the true nature of the Holy Ghost, and spitting obscenities at each other through clenched teeth. And in the middle of the bar-room floor, two smoke ghosts were dancing together sadly and elegantly, their smoke bodies blown apart by every passing breeze, but always re-forming.

And sitting very much alone in a corner, with his back to two walls, that mighty and renowned sorcerer, Merlin Satanspawn. The greatest magus of this or any other age. Who was born to be the Antichrist but declined the honour. You couldn't miss him. His sheer presence dominated the whole bar, even sitting there quietly, staring into his drink. Having him around was like sharing the room with a bloody street accident, or a man slowly hanging himself.

He didn't look much like the Merlin I knew, the dead man with a ragged hole in his chest where his heart used to be. Who had been buried for centuries in the cellars under Strangefellows but occasionally deigned to manifest through his unhappy descendant, Alex Morrisey. This man was whole and hale and bloody scary with it. He was a big man in an age of small men, easily six feet tall and broad-shouldered, wrapped in a long scarlet robe with golden collar trimmings. Under a thick and tangled mane of bright red hair, stiffened here and there with clay, his face was heavy-boned and almost aggressively ugly. Two fires burned brightly in his eye sockets, leaping crimson flames that licked up past his heavy eyebrows. *They say he has his father's eyes* . . . Most of his face and bare hands were covered with curling Druidic tattoos in dark blue hues. His long, thick fingernails looked a whole lot like claws. And I realised that the Merlin I'd known before had only been a pale shadow of the real thing, this huge and vital man crackling with power and awful presence.

I'd meant to walk up to him, introduce myself, and demand his help; but suddenly I didn't feel at all like doing that. I felt much more like slinking away before he noticed me, and maybe hiding under a table for a while until I got my confidence back. The man was dangerous. You only had to look at him to know he could blast the soul right out of your body with a single Word. A quick glance at Suzie and Tommy showed they were having serious second thoughts, too, and that immediately put some backbone back into me. Gods or sorcerers or Things from Elsewhere, you couldn't show fear in front of them or they'd walk right over you. You had to find their weak spot . . .

"Let's buy the man a drink," I said.

"Couldn't hurt," said Suzie.

"Let's buy him lots of drinks," said Tommy. "And I think I could force down a few myself."

We made our way to the bar at the back of the room. It was the exact same long wooden bar from our time, though the assortment of drinks set out behind it looked to be far more limited. And the nearest thing they had to bar snacks were rats impaled on sticks. A few of them were still twitching, even though they'd been doused in melted cheese. Serving behind the bar was a sweet dreamy girl in a faded Roman-style dress. She had long dark hair, huge eyes, and a winning smile.

"That's a really first-class glamour you're wearing," she said cheerfully. "Would probably have fooled anybody else, but I've been touched by divinity. Frequently. Not from around here, are you, dears?"

"No," I said. "We've travellers, from the future."

"Gosh," said the barmaid. "How exciting! What's it like?"

"Noisy," I said. "And a bit faster paced, but otherwise pretty much the same."

"Well there's a relief," said the barmaid. "Why not have a whole bunch of drinks? Don't worry if you're supposed to be in disguise; I only saw through your glamour because I'm sort of godly. I'm Hebe. I used to be cup-bearer to the old Roman gods, until their faith base declined along with the Empire, and they decided to move on to pastures new. Didn't offer to take me with them, the ungrateful bastards. I decided I was too young to retire from the booze-slinging business, so I took over this place, and now I dispense good cheer to one and all. Go on, dears, get a little bit that way. Good booze is good for the soul. Trust me; I know these things."

I glanced around and confirmed that all three of us were willing enough to experiment in that direction, but unfortunately it turned out that the bar's stock consisted almost entirely of various forms of wine and mead. We sampled a fair selection of both, in the spirit of scientific enquiry, but the wines were all thin and bitter, and the meads were all thick and sweet. Often with bits floating in them. We pulled various faces and made thoughtful noises, but Hebe wasn't fooled.

"Booze is better in the future?"

"Let's say . . . more extreme. Is this really all you have?"

"Well," said Hebe, "I do stock a few special items, for the discerning customer with an educated palate and more money than sense. Winter Wine, Bacchus's Old Peculier, and Angel's Tears. Merlin's really fond of that one."

"The very stuff," I said. "One bottle of Angel's Tears, if you please."

It was only when she started rummaging for a bottle under the bar that it suddenly occurred to me to wonder how I was going to pay for it, along with all the other drinks we'd already consumed. Whatever they used for currency in the sixth century, I sure as hell hadn't brought any with me. I stuck my hands in my coat pockets, out of habit, and to my surprise discovered a heavy bag of coins I certainly hadn't put there. I pulled out the leather bag and opened the drawstrings, and blinked stupidly at a whole mess of gold and silver coins.

"Now that's impressive," said Suzie. "What did you do, pick someone's pocket at the Londinium Club?"

"Didn't think of that," I said. "But luckily, it seems Old Father Time thinks of everything."

I offered Hebe one of the larger gold coins, and she bit it expertly between her back teeth before accepting it with a smile. In return I received a slender glass phial of a pale blue liquor and absolutely no change. Bright sparks of light sputtered on and off in the slowly stirring liquor.

"Angel's Tears," said Hebe, wrinkling her adorably pert nose. "Awful stuff. It's only drinkable for a short period, then it goes off, and we have to bury it in consecrated ground."

"I want to try some of that," said Suzie.

"No you don't," I said very firmly. "This is for Merlin." I looked at Hebe. "What's his current state of mind?"

"Dangerous," said Hebe. "I don't think he's said half a dozen words to anyone since the King died. He's been here drinking for three solid weeks now. Doesn't eat, doesn't sleep. No-one bothers him, because if they do, he turns them into . . . things."

"What kind of things?" Tommy said warily.

"I'm not sure if they have a name or designation, as such," Hebe said judiciously. "But whatever they are, they don't look at all happy about being it. If I had to describe them, I'd say . . . ambulatory snot creatures."

"Maybe you'd better talk to Merlin alone, Taylor," said Tommy, and Suzie nodded solemnly.

"I wouldn't recommend talking to him at all," said Hebe. "The witch Nimue is the only one who can do anything with him these days."

I looked quickly at Suzie and Tommy. We all knew that name. The legendary traitorous witch Nimue, who captivated Merlin's heart, then stole it, ripping it literally out of his chest. The witch who seduced and betrayed Merlin while his defences were down and condemned him to death.

"Let's go and talk to the drunken dangerous sorcerer," I said. "Before things get even more complicated."

"Would you like to leave any message for your next of kin?" said Hebe.

"Don't worry about us," said Suzie. "We can be pretty dangerous, too, when we put our minds to it."

We turned and looked at Merlin Satanspawn, and it was like looking at a wild animal that had eaten its keeper and burst out of its cage.

"After you," said Tommy.

We headed towards Merlin's table in the corner. The bar got very quiet as they realised what was happening.

I raised my gift almost but not quite to the point of manifesting, just in case, and I could feel Tommy doing the same. Suzie already had a grenade in one hand, with one finger slipped casually through the ring-pull. And then Merlin turned suddenly and looked at us, and it was like walking into a brick wall. All three of us slammed to a halt, held where we were, transfixed by the flames leaping in his eye-sockets. Everyone in the whole bar held their breath. And then I slowly held up the phial of Angel's Tears, so Merlin could see it clearly, and his mouth twitched briefly in something like a smile. I took a deep breath and moved forward again, but Suzie and Tommy remained where they were, unmoving. I stopped short of the table and gave Merlin my best hard stare. Never let the bastards see you're intimidated.

"Let my friends go, Merlin. They're part of what I have to say to you."

Merlin actually raised an eyebrow. "I've killed men for speaking to me in that tone of voice, just to watch them die. Why should I indulge you, boy?"

"Because I'm Lilith's only son. And we half-breeds should stick together."

He nodded slowly, though whether he was impressed by my brass nerves or my mother's name was hard to tell. I grabbed a chair and sat down opposite him. Suzie and Tommy moved cautiously forward and chose to stand behind me. I was grateful for their presence. I've bluffed some powerful Beings with an empty hand before, but this was Merlin Satanspawn, dammit. I was glad I was sitting down, so he couldn't see my legs shaking under the table. I offered him the phial of Angel's Tears, and he wrapped a huge hand around it and hefted it thoughtfully. He pulled the cork out with his large, blocky teeth and poured the heavy blue liquor into the silver goblet before him. The stuff smelled awful. Merlin noticed my reaction and smiled unpleasantly.

"It's an acquired taste. Much like angel flesh. Talk to me, Lilith's son. What do you want with me?"

I introduced myself and my companions, and gave him the quick expurgated version. He nodded now and again, seeming more interested in his drink. The rest of the bar was still watching us, but the general chatter had begun again, now it was clear there weren't going to be any sudden and unfortunate transformations in the immediate future. I finished my tale, and Merlin nodded slowly.

"Interesting story," he said. "If I cared, I'd be impressed. But I don't care about anything, any more. Not since . . . he died. He was the best of us all. He gave me my faith in Humanity. He made me a better person, just by believing I was; and I would rather have died than disappoint him. Now he's gone, because I failed him, when he needed me most. The dream I dreamed is over; his dream of Reason and Respect for all, of Might for Right. A brief light, in a dark age."

He was still brooding over that when King Arthur appeared out of nowhere. I knew it was he. It couldn't have been anyone else. Arthur, the Great Bear of Briton, standing suddenly before our table, a huge blocky man in well-polished armour, under heavy bearskins and leather strappings. The sword at his side shone with supernatural brilliance. He had a strong, kind, somewhat sad face, but there was something about him . . . a natural majesty, a solid and uncompromising honour, a simple goodness, strong and true . . . I would have followed him to the gates of Hell and back. All across the bar, people knelt to him. Human and inhuman, they bent the knee and bowed the head to the one and only man they all worshipped and feared and adored. King Arthur of the Britons.

I slipped off my chair and knelt and bowed, too, along with Suzie and Tommy. It never occurred to me to do anything else.

Even though he wasn't really there. We could all tell he wasn't really, physically, present in Avalon. His image was only intermittently solid and complete, wavering from unfelt breezes, and sometimes you could see right through him. But he wasn't a ghost; there was a definite vitality to the man. He burned with life, with purpose, and with majesty. No, this was a sending, a mental projection of his image, his self, from some other place. He seemed distracted, unfocussed, looking vaguely about him, though his gaze always returned to Merlin, sitting at his table.

"Merlin," said Arthur, and his voice came from far and far away, like a whisper in a church gallery. "Old friend, old mentor. I have come a long way to find you. I sent word to every place I thought you might be, but you were at none of them. You've gone after her, haven't you? Even though I told you not to. It is the night before my greatest battle, and I have taken to my tent alone, that I might go dream walking, in search of you." He smiled, kindly, sadly. "You tried so hard to teach me magic, but I never had the gift for it. So I had to settle for being a soldier, and a King. I always wondered if perhaps I disappointed you, in that."

"No," said Merlin. "You never disappointed me, Arthur. Never."

"But time is short, and my need is desperate, so I turn back to old, half-remembered lessons, of sendings and dream walkings. And here I am, and here you are. Wherever this is. I can't see anything clearly but you, old friend. I need your help, for the battle tomorrow. My son Mordred has raised a great force against me. Perhaps the largest army this land has ever seen. I have called together all my knights and all my soldiers, and all good men and true; and still I fear it will not be enough. My son . . . and I know you never accepted him as my son, but a man knows his own blood . . . My son Mordred has summoned up creatures ancient, vile, and powerful to stand with him. I need you, Merlin. I need your magic, your power. Why aren't you here?"

"Because I was busy," said Merlin. "Busy indulging myself in my greatest failing; my hunger for revenge."

"I can see you, but I can't hear you," said Arthur. "Merlin! Merlin!"

"You got the time-co-ordinates mixed up again," said Merlin. "You never were any good at mathematics, boy. You've come to me too late. Too late."

"You should have warned me, Merlin," said Arthur. "Of the price I'd have to pay, for being King. For Camelot, and the Round Table and the Great Dream. A wife who loved another. A son who never loved me. Justice for everyone, but never for me. Why didn't you warn me, Merlin?"

"I never promised you justice," said Merlin. "Just a chance to be a legend. My poor Arthur . . ."

"I can't stay," said Arthur. "The winds between the worlds are pulling at me, drawing me back. My men are waiting. At first light, we go out to battle. And to victory, God willing. No doubt you have a good reason for being wherever you are. We'll talk about this later, after the battle. It was always my greatest regret that we never had the time to talk properly, after I became King."

He said something else, but it was lost as his image faded slowly away, like a ghost at the dawn, until he was gone. Slowly, everyone in the bar got up off their knees and went about their business again. None of them even looked at Merlin. I got back onto my chair. Merlin was staring into his drink again.

"I should have been there," he said. "But I was so angry, all I could think of was revenge. On that traitorous bitch, Mordred's mother. Morgan La Fae. Arthur took them in, gave them everything, and together they destroyed everything Arthur and I had built. It took me years to find proof against them, then they ran, like rats. Mordred to his secretly prepared forces. Morgan to the old woods and ancient places, and the Powers she worshipped there. I couldn't bear the thought of her escaping, of her getting away with it. So I left Arthur to raise his army, while I went after Morgan. I was so sure I'd be back in time. But Morgan led me a merry chase, and killing the bitch took so much more out of me than I'd expected. By the time I got back, it was all over. The battle field was soaked in blood, and there were bodies piled up, for as far as the eye could see. The few surviving knights looked at me like it was all my fault, and maybe it was. They called me traitor and false friend, coward, abomination. They wouldn't even let me see his body. I could have killed them all, with a look or a word, made them suffer as I suffered, but I didn't. Because Arthur wouldn't have wanted that.

"I couldn't even cry for him. My eyes aren't made that way. But if I could weep, I would. For my King, my friend. My son, in every way that mattered."

I was still trying to work out what I could say to that, to a loss so great, to a grief and a guilt so deep, when a bright young voice called out Merlin's name. We all looked round as a bright and bubbly young thing came tripping through the bar, smiling and waving in all directions, but heading remorselessly for our table. She was small, blonde, and busty, wide-eyed and wide-mouthed, clothed in shimmering silk that looked very out of place in these rough surroundings. She bounced along like she was full of all the energy in the world, blazing with fresh young sexuality. She couldn't have been much more than sixteen. She was pretty, in an obvious sort of way, with a third eye tattooed in blue on her forehead. More Celtic and Druidic designs curled up and down her bare arms. She strode straight up to our table, threw herself into Merlin's lap, laughing into his glowering face and tugging playfully at his long beard.

"Oh, sweetie, look at that long face! Who's been upsetting you this time? Honestly, darling, I can't leave you alone for a minute. It's a good thing your little Nimue is here, to take care of you!" She kissed him artlessly, took a sip of his drink, pulled a face, and squeaked a few baby swear words, then kissed him again and called him a *Silly old bear*. Merlin slowly smiled, then laughed and played with her breasts while she giggled happily. I was trying hard to keep my mouth from dropping open. This was the legendary witch Nimue?

"This is Nimue," said Merlin, after a while, looking back at me. "My only comfort. Nimue, this is John Taylor."

She pouted childishly at me. "Are you the one that's been upsetting my sweetie? Shame on you! Go on, Merlin; show me how to turn him into something squelchy."

"Hush, child," said Merlin. "He's come a long way to beg my help. I'm still considering whether to do anything about it."

"This is the witch Nimue?" I said, somehow keeping the disbelief out of my voice.

"Indeed," said Merlin, removing one hand from inside her dress to scratch at his great beak of a nose. "A renegade Druidic priestess, and now my student in the magical arts. Of all my various roles, I have always enjoyed that of teacher the most."

"That's not all you enjoy, you randy old goat," said Nimue, snuggling contentedly up against the sorcerer. "Running away from the Druids was the best thing I ever did." She looked plaintively at me with her huge dark eyes. "My parents sold me to them when I was only a child, but I never really fitted in. I was quite keen on the nature worship, and running around the forest with no clothes on, and having lots of sex to ensure the fertility of the crops, but I found all the human sacrifices and *Nail his guts to the old oak tree* very icky. So I grabbed a bit of everything valuable that wasn't actually nailed down, and left." She pouted suddenly, and playfully boxed Merlin's ear. "And you promised you'd teach me magic. Real magic. When are you going to teach me some real magic, sweetie?"

"All in good time," said Merlin, taking one of her ear-lobes playfully between his teeth.

"That's all very well, honey," said Nimue, pushing him away and sitting up straight on his lap. "But in the meantime, I have various trades-people who insist on being paid. A girl has to live, darling . . ."

There was a lot more of this. Nimue chattered away, while Merlin smiled on her indulgently, and the two of them cuddled like teenagers. I didn't know what to say. This was Nimue? The powerful and crafty witch who stole Merlin's heart and ran off with it? This cute and harmless little gold-digger? I turned round in my chair to look at Suzie and Tommy, but they were clearly as thrown as I, so I got up, excused myself to Merlin and Nimue, who barely nodded in return, and the three of us retired to another table to think things over. It was clear Merlin wouldn't be paying us any attention for a while anyway.

"She seems like a sweet young thing," said Tommy. "Though I can't help thinking he's a bit old for her."

"She's not nearly as helpless as she makes out," said Suzie. "I've seen her sort before, taking some old fool for everything he's got."

"The man's domestic arrangements are none of our business," I said firmly. "What matters is that for all his drunken self-pity, that man is clearly still a powerful sorcerer. If anyone in this period can send us further back in Time, it's him."

"But you heard him," said Tommy. "He doesn't care about us, or our problems."

"Don't care was made to care," I said.

Suzie looked at me for a long moment. "That's pretty hard-core, even for you, Taylor. I mean, this is *Merlin* we're talking about. The Devil's only begotten son. We don't have a hope in Hell of compelling him to do anything he doesn't want to."

"I've been thinking about that," I said. "And it occurred to me that since this witch Nimue is obviously quite incapable of stealing Merlin's heart . . . maybe we could do it instead. And with the heart in our hands, Merlin would have to do whatever we told him to."

They both looked at me like I was crazy.

"You're crazy!" said Tommy. "I mean, full-blown out of your head crazy! We're actually supposed to rip the living heart out of his chest? Merlin? The most powerful sorcerer of this or any other age? *You're crazy!*"

"Don't hold back, Tommy," I said. "Tell me what you really think."

"Even if we could incapacitate Merlin," said Suzie, "it would be pretty messy . . . I've removed a few hearts in my time, but I never had to worry about them being in good enough shape to put them back again."

"Don't encourage him," said Tommy. "We'll all end up as snot creatures."

"It's not as impractical as it sounds," I said patiently. "A lot of sorcerers would remove their hearts and hide them elsewhere, behind powerful magical protections, for safekeeping. That way, no matter what happened, they couldn't be killed as long as the heart was still safe. Using the correct rites, Merlin's heart can be removed without killing him, and once we have it, we'll be in control. Look—we know someone's going to steal the heart, at some stage. Why not us? We'll do less damage with it than most."

"I don't like this," Tommy said flatly. "I really don't like this. In fact, I straight out hate it."

"He's got a point," said Suzie. "If we interfere in the Past . . ."

"Who's interfering?" I said. "We *know* someone took Merlin's heart. We've all seen the hole in his chest. You could say by doing this, we're helping to reinforce the Present we came from."

"I don't care," Tommy said stubbornly. "This isn't right. We're using the man, maybe even killing him, just to get what we want."

"What we need," I said. "We have to stop Lilith, by whatever means, to save the Nightside, and probably the world as well."

"But . . . what about this, as another alternative," said Tommy, leaning eagerly forward across the table. "Remember the knights in armour we saw in Old Father Time's Waiting Room? The ones from a future where Camelot and its dream still held sway? What if we are here . . . to bring about that future? We have a chance to change *everything*. Camelot doesn't have to fall, here and now. If Merlin never lost his heart, and most of his power . . . maybe we could bring him back to sanity and pride. Give him a reason to live again. We could tell him what's coming, warn him of the Dark Ages that will last for almost a thousand years, if he doesn't act to prevent it. Advised by us, he could rise to power and influence again, and backed by him, Camelot could rebuild itself. King Arthur's legacy could continue!"

"Advised by us," I said. "Don't you mean, advised by you, Tommy? You're the one who's always been fascinated by Arthur, and this time."

"All right, why not?" Tommy said defiantly. "I've always loved the legends of Camelot. It was a better world under Arthur, and a brighter world, than we have ever known before or since! Think of what fifteen centuries of progress under Arthur's legacy could bring about . . . Maybe we wouldn't even need a Nightside any more."

"You're reaching now," I said. "We have to stick with what we know. We know Lilith is planning to destroy the Nightside, and most likely the rest of the world with it. I've seen that future, Tommy, and I'm ready to do anything at all to prevent it. That world is every nightmare you've ever had, Tommy. If you'd seen it . . ."

"But I haven't," said Tommy. "No-one has, but you. And we only have your word."

"Don't go there, Tommy," said Suzie, her voice cold and hard.

"Lilith's plans threaten all the Nightsides," I said. "Remember what Old Father Time said, about all the possible futures narrowing down, till we end up with the one, inevitable future? That's why we have to do this, Tommy. And I can't do it without your help. Merlin's bound to have set up incredibly powerful defences, to protect him while he's drunk or otherwise incapable. I can use my gift to find them, but I don't have anywhere near enough power to push them aside or shut them off. But you . . . can use your gift to confuse the defences long enough for us to slip past them and do what we have to do."

Tommy stared at me for a long time, and I couldn't read his face at all. He'd stopped using his effete voice. "I never knew you to be this . . . brutal," he said finally.

"Only because I have to be," I said. "The future depends on me; and needs must when the devil drives."

"Or the Devil's son," he said, and I had to wonder whether he meant Merlin or me. He slowly sat back in his chair again. "What are we going to do with the heart, afterwards?"

"Well, we can't just hand it back," I said. "Merlin would find some way to kill us all, no matter what we'd agreed. No, I think we hide it somewhere safe, then tell Nimue where we put it, after we've safely disappeared into the Past."

"We're bringing the witch into this?" said Suzie. "That simpering little airhead?"

"We need her," I said. "There's no way Merlin will ever relax while we're around, but he'll never see it coming from Nimue."

"Why should she help us?" said Tommy, frowning.

I smiled. "The day I can't outmanoeuvre a gold-digger like her is the day I'll retire. You aren't the only one who can talk people into things, Tommy."

"True," said Suzie. "You may be existential, Tommy, but Taylor is a crafty bastard."

"Thank you, Suzie," I said. "I think. All we have to do is convince the witch to slip a little something into Merlin's drink so he passes out sooner rather than later. That sound like a plan to everyone?"

"Sounds like a sneaky and underhanded plan to me," said Suzie. "I'm in. After we've taken his heart out . . . can I try shooting him, just to see what happens?"

"No," I said.

"You're no fun any more, Taylor."

I looked at Tommy. "Are you in, or not?"

"Reluctantly," he said at last. "And with grave reservations. But yes, I'm in. It seems dreams have no place in the real world."

"Stick to being existential," I said kindly. "You're much better off, not being sure about things."

So we sat, and watched Merlin drink. Hours passed, and he was still putting it away, with Nimue's enthusiastic help and bubbly company. But finally the sorcerer reached a point where he stopped raising his goblet to his lips and simply sat staring at nothing. Even Nimue couldn't get a response out of him. Interestingly enough, once she was sure he was out of it, she turned off the charm and leaned back in her chair, kicking her heels sulkily; and then she jumped up out of her chair and flounced off to the bar for a refill. Where I happened to be waiting, ready to buy her a drink of something expensive. I smiled at her and complimented her, and she giggled like a teenager on a first date. After a while, I invited her to join our table, and after a quick glance at Merlin to make sure he was still nodding, she trotted over to join us. Her face was flushed from so much drinking, and her hair was a mess, but her speech was still clear. She was enchanted to meet Tommy, but pretty much ignored Suzie. I got a few more drinks into her, then laid out our plan. Nimue didn't take much convincing. She had the morals of a cat and the brains of a puppy.

"We need Merlin's help," I said, putting it as simply as I could. "But he's too wrapped up in his own problems to listen. But if we take his heart, he'll have to listen. And when we have the heart outside his body, and therefore outside his defences, you'll be able to put a spell on it, so he'll forget all his worries and care about nothing but you. When you're finished, you can put the heart back, and everyone will get what they want. What could be simpler, or fairer?"

Nimue frowned over her drink, trying to concentrate. "The heart could make me powerful . . . with real magic . . . But really, I only want my old bear back the way he used to be. You should have seen him in his prime, at Camelot. At the King's side, where he belonged. They all bowed to him, then. I was never there myself, of course. I was just another dumb little priestess, back then, gathering mistletoe and worshipping the Hecate, the three in one . . . But I was always good at Seeing from Afar, and Camelot fascinated me. Merlin fascinated me. I watched him at Court, and even then I knew he needed looking after. Needed someone who cared about him. Everyone else put up with him, so they could call on his magic to bail them out when they messed up. When muscular clods in armour weren't enough to save the day."

Her voice was getting blurred as she got more emotional. "Even the King, bless him . . . even he never really cared about Merlin. Not like I do. Silly little priestess, silly little hedge witch, that's what they say . . . but I'm the only one who can reach his heart now . . . And when I'm powerful, I'll make them all pay . . ."

Her lower lip was trembling by then, and big fat tears ran down her cheeks. I didn't look round at the others. I already felt guilty enough about taking advantage of an oversized child like Nimue. But it had to be done . . .

"So you will help us?" I said. "It's for the best. Really."

"If you say so," said Nimue. "I've always needed other people to tell me what's for the best."

Something in her voice told me that would always be the case. Tommy heard it, too, and glared at me, but I concentrated on the witch.

"Have you got something you could slip into his drink, Nimue? Something to make him sleep?"

"Oh sure," Nimue said off-handedly. "Druids know everything there is to know about potions. I often drug his drink. It's the only way he can sleep these days. Poor sweetie."

And that was it. We waited till the customers had thinned out, and then I bribed Hebe to shut down the bar for a while. It took most of the coins in my purse, particularly when Hebe realised we wanted her to go home early as well, but money talks in the Nightside, as it always had. A few customers didn't want to go, but Suzie obliged them with a short but instructive example of how a shotgun works, and they couldn't get out of the bar fast enough. The two smoke ghosts looked at me reproachfully, then faded slowly away, still dancing. The bar seemed so much larger with everyone else gone, and the quiet was actually eerie. Merlin sat slumped and finally sleeping in his chair, while Nimue sat cross-legged in a hastily chalked circle, working a glamour so that no-one outside would be able to tell there was anything unusual going on in the bar. There were an awful lot of people, and others, who would jump at the chance to kill Merlin if they even suspected his defences were down. Suzie guarded the door anyway, while Tommy and I considered the unconscious sorcerer.

"So," said Tommy. "How do we do it?"

"Very carefully," I said. "If this looks like it's going wrong, I shall be heading for the nearest horizon, at speed. Try and keep up."

"This is a really bad idea," Tommy said miserably.

I raised my gift, opening up my third eye, my private eye, and right away I could See all of Merlin's defences. They lurked around his sleeping form like so many snarling attack dogs, layer upon layer of protective spells and curses, ready to lash out at anything that disturbed them. They stirred uneasily, just from being Seen. I grabbed Tommy by the hand, and at once he could See them, too. He cried out in shock and horror, and tried to pull away, but I wouldn't let him go.

"Shut up," I whispered fiercely. "Do you want them to hear you? Now use your gift. Do it!"

His mouth twisted, like that of a child being punished, but I could feel his gift manifesting. And slowly, one by one, the defences became uncertain about why they were there, and what they were there for, until finally they disappeared back whence they'd come, to have a collective discussion, leaving Merlin sleeping and entirely unprotected. I moved forward quickly. I didn't know how long the effect would last. I could hear Tommy breathing harshly behind me, concentrating on maintaining his gift so the defences wouldn't return, while I checked out the sorcerer's condition.

His eyes were closed, the leaping flames damped down for the moment. His breathing was steady, though he stirred occasionally in his sleep, as though bothered by bad dreams. I pulled open his scarlet robe, revealing a shaved chest covered in thick, intertwining Druidic tattoos. I hissed for Suzie to come over and join me, and she reluctantly left her post at the door.

"How do we do this?" I said.

"Your guess is as good as mine, Taylor. I've taken a few hearts, for bounties, but that wasn't exactly surgery." She produced a long knife from the top of her knee-length boot, and hefted it thoughtfully. "I'm guessing brute force and improvisation isn't going to be good enough, this time."

"Give me the knife," I said resignedly. "And go back to guarding the door. Tommy, get over here and help."

"I've never done anything like this before," said Tommy, moving reluctantly forward.

"I should hope not," I said. "So, roll up your sleeves, follow my lead, try to help without getting in my way, and if you must puke, try not to get any in the chest cavity."

"Oh God," said Tommy.

I cut Merlin open from chest to groin, making sure I had a hole big enough to get both hands in. This was no time for keyhole surgery, and anyway, I was betting Merlin would be able to make all necessary repairs once he had his heart back. There was a lot of blood, and sometimes I had to jump back to avoid a sudden jetting gusher. I washed most of it out of the hole with wine, so I could at least see what I was doing. In the end, I had to cut and tear the heart free from its position under the sternum, tugging and pulling with both hands, while blood soaked both my hands up to the elbow, and Tommy said *Oh God, Oh God,* while he held the other organs back out of my way.

Finally, I held Merlin's heart in my hands, a great scarlet lump of muscle. It was bigger than I'd expected, and still beating, gouting thick dark blood. I took it to the next table, and wrapped it carefully in a cloth covered in protective symbols, which Nimue had put together. She was still sitting in her circle, mumbling spells with her eyes closed, so she wouldn't have to see what was happening. I went back to stand beside Tommy, who was looking at the great bloody hole we'd made and trembling violently. This really wasn't his kind of case. I clapped him on the shoulder, but he didn't even look round. Merlin was still breathing steadily, still sleeping, still living. I tried to push the sides of the wound together, over the mess I'd made, but the hole was too big. In the end, I closed his robes over it.

"Is it done?" said Suzie, from the doorway. "Have you finished?"

"Oh yes," I said. "I don't think I could do any more damage if I tried."

"Don't worry," she said. "It gets easier, the more you do it."

I looked across at her sharply and decided not to ask. I didn't want to know. I pulled Tommy away from the sorcerer, and we cleaned off our hands and arms as best we could with more wine. We couldn't do anything about our blood-spattered clothes. We didn't have anything to change into. Hopefully Old Father Time's glamour would hide the gore from others' eyes. Tommy looked at me accusingly.

"Is there anything you won't do, Taylor? Anyone whose life you won't ruin, to get revenge on your mother for running off and abandoning you as a child?"

"That isn't what this is about!"

"Isn't it?"

"No! Everything I've done here, and everything I will do, is all about saving the Nightside, and the world! If you'd seen what I've seen . . ."

"But we haven't. And you won't tell us about it. Why is that, Taylor? What are you keeping from us? Are we supposed to take your word and trust you?"

"Yes," I said, holding his angry gaze with mine.

"And why the hell should I do that?" said Tommy.

"Because he is John Taylor," said Suzie, coming over from the door, with her shotgun in her hands. "And he has earned the right to be trusted."

"Of course you'd support him," Tommy said bitterly. "You're his woman."

Suzie stopped, then laughed briefly. "Oh, Tommy, you don't know anything, do you?"

And that was when the door slammed open behind her, and a huge blocky man in chain mail stormed into the bar. He had that functional compact musculature that comes from constant hard use and testing, rather than working out, and his ragged chain mail and the leather armour under it had the signs of long use and hard wear. He had a square, blocky, almost brutal face, marked with scars that had healed crookedly. His mouth was a flat line, his eyes cold and determined. In one hand he carried a huge mace with a vicious spiked head. I'd never seen a more dangerous-looking man in my life.

He came striding straight across the bar towards us, kicking tables and chairs effortlessly out of his way. Suzie turned her shotgun on him, and Tommy and I moved quickly to stand on either side of her, but the newcomer didn't stop until he could see past us to Merlin. He took in the blood soaking the front of Merlin's robes and actually started to smile, only to stop as he realised the sorcerer was still breathing.

"He's not dead," he said, and his voice was like stone grating against stone.

"He's not dead," I agreed. "Who might you be?"

"I am Kae," he said. "Arthur's brother. Stepbrother only by blood, but he always called me brother. We fought great battles, shoulder to shoulder and back to back. Struck down evil wherever we found it. Bled for each other and saved each other's lives a dozen times. He was King, and carried the responsibilities of the whole land on his shoulders, but he always had time for me, and I knew there wasn't a day that passed where he didn't think of me.

"I never trusted Merlin. Never trusted magic. I tried to warn Arthur, but he was always blind to the sorcerer's faults. And when Arthur needed him most, where was Merlin? Gone. Nowhere to be found. I saw the bravest knights in the land fall, brought down by jackals. I saw good men dragged down by overwhelming forces. We fought for hours, stamping back and forth through the blood-soaked mud, and in the end . . . nobody won. Arthur and the bastard Mordred died, at each other's hands. The proud knights of Camelot are fallen or scattered. The land is torn apart by civil war as scavengers fight over the spoils, and Merlin . . . still lives. How can that be right? How can there be any justice, while the traitor still lives? I am Kae, Arthur's brother, and I will avenge his death."

"Because Mordred is dead," I said. "And you don't have anyone else."

"Stand aside," said Kae.

"Not one step closer," said Suzie, aiming the shotgun at his face.

Kae sneered at her. "I am protected against all magics, and unnatural weapons," he said coldly. "The charm that brought me here will protect me from anything that might keep me from my rightful prey."

"Thought you didn't believe in magic," I said, trying to buy some time while I thought what to do.

Kae smiled briefly. "Needs must, when the devil drives. I will damn my soul, if that's what it takes to buy me justice. Now stand aside or die with him."

He stalked forward, raising his spiked mace, and Suzie gave him both barrels right in the face. Or at least, she tried to. The shotgun wouldn't work. She tried again, uselessly, and threw the gun aside as Kae loomed up before her. She whipped a long knife from her other boot top, and slashed at his bare throat. Kae flinched back instinctively, and I hit him from the side with my shoulder, hoping my speed and impact would knock him off balance. Instead, he hardly moved an inch, and threw me aside with one sweep of his mailed arm. I crashed into a bunch of chairs and hit the ground hard. The impact knocked all the breath out of me and hurt my head. I fought to get back onto my knees, while Suzie and Kae went head to head with knife and mace, grunting and snarling at each other. He was bigger, but she was faster.

Tommy had grabbed up the cloth-wrapped heart, and was clutching it protectively to his chest, watching the fight with wide, shocked eyes. The witch Nimue had left her chalk circle and was bending over Merlin.

"Something's wrong!" she shouted. "Whatever charm Kae brought into this room, it's interfering with the magic keeping him alive! You have to get Kae out of here, or Merlin will die!"

"I'm doing my best," Suzie snarled.

She bobbed and weaved as Kae swung his mace. The weapon must have weighed a ton, but Kae wielded it like a toy, the wind whistling through the vicious spikes on its head. Suzie ducked and jabbed at him with her long knife, but mostly the blade jarred harmlessly off his chain mail. Kae had spent most of his life on one battlefield or another, and it showed in his every economical, murderous move. But Suzie Shooter was a child of the Nightside, and her rage was every bit a match for his. She went for his face and his throat, his elbows and his groin, but always his mace was there just in time to block her. Suzie was a bounty hunter, a fighter, and a practised killer; but Kae was one of Arthur's knights, bloodied in a thousand wars and border skirmishes. He pressed her back, step by step, his arm rising and falling with terrible force, remorseless as a machine.

Somehow I got back onto my feet again and staggered over to Merlin's table. Suzie could look after herself. I had to see what was happening with Merlin. His breathing was ragged, and his colour wasn't good. I'd hit my head on something, and it ached unmercifully. Blood was running thickly down my face. I couldn't seem to think straight. Tommy was hovering helplessly at Nimue's side as she chanted spells over Merlin. From the growing despair on her face, I gathered they weren't helping much. Tommy grabbed my arm to get my attention, then realised the state I was in and helped hold me up. Nimue looked round frantically.

"You've got to do something! Merlin's dying! I'm having to use my own life force to keep him going!"

Tommy pushed his face close to mine, to make sure I heard him. "We have to put Merlin's defences back into place!"

"Right," I said. "Of course. Just jam the heart back in, and his own magics should heal him. Right. Come on, give me the heart. He's no use to me dead."

"It wouldn't work," said Nimue. She'd given up on chanting and waving her hands, and was crouching beside Merlin, holding one of his hands in both of hers. "Kae's charm will prevent his defences returning . . . You have to get him out of here. I'm giving Merlin . . . everything I've got; but I don't think it's going to enough. I'm only human . . . and he isn't."

"We have to think of something, Taylor!" said Tommy, glaring into my face. "Taylor! John! Can you hear me?"

His words came to me, but from far away, as though we were both underwater. I put a hand to my aching head, and it came away slick with blood. Whatever had hit me in that crash, it had really done a job on me. I gazed stupidly at my bloody hand for a moment, then looked back at Suzie and Kae.

Kae swung his mace around in a viciously fast sweep, but Suzie ducked under it and slammed her knife deep into his side, the blade punching right through the chain mail and the leather armour beneath. Kae roared with rage as much as pain, and his mace came sweeping back round impossibly fast. The spiked steel head slammed into Suzie's face and ripped half of it away. She screamed, and fell backwards onto the floor. Kae grunted once, like a satisfied animal, and turned to look at Merlin, ignoring the knife hilt protruding from his side.

I moved forward to block his way. Tommy wasn't a fighter, and Nimue was busy. It had to be me. I forced the pain and confusion out of my head for a moment, through sheer force of will, and tried to raise my gift. If I could only find the charm Kae had brought with him . . . but my head hurt too bad. I couldn't concentrate, couldn't See. Kae was still coming, headed straight for me. I jammed my hands into my coat pockets, searching for something I could use against him.

And then Suzie reared up from the floor, with a terrible cry. Half her face was a mask of blood, with only an empty socket where her left eye had been, but still she came roaring up off that bloody floor like the fighter she was. She ripped the knife out of Kae's side, and he stopped in his tracks, halted for a moment by the sudden blaze of pain. And while he hesitated, Suzie jammed her long knife all the way into his unprotected groin. Her triumphant laughter drowned out his cry of pain. She yanked the knife out, and thick dark blood coursed down both his legs. He staggered, and almost fell. She lashed out with the knife, and almost effortlessly cut open the wrist of the hand holding the mace. It fell to the floor as the feeling left his fingers, and he looked stupidly after it for a moment.

Suzie rose up onto her feet to give him the last, killing blow, and he roared like a bear and grabbed her to him, crushing her against his chainmail breast with huge, muscular arms. She cried out as her ribs cracked audibly, then savagely head-butted Kae in the face. He roared again and dropped her. Suzie grinned fiercely at him through the bloody mask of her face, and went for him with her knife. And Kae grabbed a flaring torch from its iron wall holder and thrust it right into her ravaged face.

There was smoke, and spitting fat, and the stench of burning meat, but she didn't scream. She fell, but she didn't scream.

I screamed. And while they were both distracted, I surged forward, grabbed up the steel mace from the floor, and hit Kae across the head with all the strength I had. The force of the blow whipped his head round, and blood flew across the air, but he didn't fall. I hit him again, and again, and again, putting all my rage and horror and guilt into every blow, and finally he fell, measuring his length on the bloody floor like a slaughtered sacrificial beast. I dropped the mace, and went over to kneel beside Suzie, and take her in my arms.

She clung to me like she was drowning, burying her ruined bloody face in my shoulder. I held on to her, and all I could say was *I'm sorry, I'm so sorry,* over and over again. After a while she pushed me away, and I let go of her immediately. It was hard for Suzie to let anyone touch her, even a friend. Even then. Poor little broken bird. I made myself look at what remained of her face. The whole left side was gone, a ragged torn-up mess only held together by charred and blackened flesh. And then, as I watched, the terrible wounds began to heal. The torn flesh crawled together, slowly closing over and drawing itself together into old scar tissue. Even the empty eye-socket closed, the lids sealed together. Until at the end it was the awful, familiar, disfigured face I'd seen once before— on the Suzie Shooter from the future.

I had brought Suzie here, to this place and time, and made that face, that Suzie possible.

She smiled at me, but only half her mouth moved. She gingerly touched at the scarred half of her face with her fingertips, then took her hand away again. "Don't look so shocked, Taylor. You put werewolf blood into me to save my life, remember, back during the angel war? The blood wasn't strong enough or pure enough to make me into a were, but it did give me one hell of a healing factor. Very useful, in the bounty-hunting business. My face . . . will never be the same again, I know that. My healing factor has very definite limits. But I can live with this. It's not like I ever cared about looking pretty . . . John? What's the matter, John?"

I couldn't tell her. I lurched to my feet and looked around for the mace I'd discarded. Kae . . . It was all Kae's fault. He had barged in and ruined everything . . . everything. Suzie knew me well enough to see which way my thoughts were going, and she hauled herself to her feet to stand before me.

"No, John. You can't kill him."

"Watch me."

"You can't, John. Because Arthur wouldn't want you to. And because you're not a killer. Like me."

And because in the end I still hoped she was right about that, I turned away from Kae's unconscious body, and together Suzie and I moved slowly and carefully back across the bar to Merlin's table. Tommy was still there, holding the witch Nimue in his arms, his face set and cold. It was obvious Nimue wasn't breathing. Dead, her face looked more like a child's than ever.

"She died keeping Merlin alive with her own life energy," said Tommy. He looked only at me, his gaze openly accusing. "She gave her life for him, her present and all her future; and it still wasn't enough. He's dead, too, if you care. And all because of us."

"We never meant for any of this to happen," said Suzie.

Tommy looked at her briefly, taking in her scarred face, but his cold gaze returned almost immediately to me. "And that makes it all right, does it?"

"No," I said. "But what's done, is done. We can't help them, but we can still help ourselves. We don't need Merlin; we still have his heart." I leaned over the wrapped bundle on the table and pulled back the cloth to show that the heart was still slowly beating, even though there was no blood left in it. "Merlin put enough of his power into his heart that it still continues, still holds a large portion of his magic. We can tap into that magic and use it to send us further back into the Past."

Tommy put Nimue to one side, arranging her tenderly in a chair like a sleeping child, then he stood up to face me. "Did you know this all along, Taylor? Did you plan for this?"

"No," I said. "I Saw it with my gift, when I studied his defences."

"Why should I believe you?" said Tommy, and Suzie stirred at my side, picking up on the anger burning in the man.

"I've never lied to you, Tommy," I said carefully. "I'm sorry about Nimue, and even about Merlin, but I came into the Past to stop Lilith, and that's what I'm going to do."

"Whatever it takes? No matter who gets hurt?"

"I don't know," I said. "Maybe."

"If we take the heart with us, further back into the Past, no wonder no-one could ever find it," said Suzie. "They were always looking in the wrong place, the wrong time."

"We'll take Nimue's body along with us," I said. "Dump it somewhere in the Past. So that when Merlin returns from the dead, he'll never have to know that Nimue died trying to save him."

"You pick the strangest ways to be thoughtful, Taylor," said Suzie.

"If you were to put the heart back," Tommy said slowly, "there's a real chance the magic stored in the heart would be enough to bring him back."

"We don't know that," I said. "And we need the magic in the heart . . ."

"We can't let him die!" Tommy said fiercely. "Not if there's even the smallest chance of saving him! Otherwise, we're as good as killing him ourselves."

"Think it through," I said. "If it doesn't work, we waste the magic, and we're stranded here. And if Merlin should wake up, and discover what we persuaded Nimue to do, and that she died as a result of it . . . he'd kill us all. Slowly and hideously painfully. This is Merlin Satanspawn we're talking about."

"So we do nothing?" said Tommy. There was a dangerous cold light in his eyes.

"Yes," I said. "He dies here, without his heart, as we know he did, and he'll be buried in the cellars under the bar. That's a part of our Past, our Present, our time-line. We just helped to bring about what we know happened anyway."

"You cold-hearted son of a bitch." Tommy was so angry his face had lost all its colour, and his hands were clenched into fists at his sides. "Just how far will you go, to get your precious revenge?"

I didn't look at Suzie. At her familiar, disfigured face. "I only do what I have to do," I said, keeping my voice as calm and reasonable as I could. "Let's get out of here, before Kae wakes up. I don't think you can stop a warrior like that for long just by hitting him over the head."

"No," said Tommy, still looking at me, and his eyes were cold, so cold. I don't think I'd ever seen him so angry. "This stops here, Taylor. You've done enough damage on your insane quest. Suzie's face. Nimue's death. Merlin . . . all for your petty, vindictive vendetta. To hell with Lilith, and to hell with you, too, you lying sack of shit. You'd sacrifice anyone and anything, just to get back at your mother. I don't see why . . .

After all, you've made yourself into just as vicious and cold-hearted a monster as her. You're every inch your mother's son."

"Don't," I said. "Don't say that, Tommy."

"It's not true," said Suzie. "Don't do this, Tommy. Taylor knows what he's doing. He always knows what he's doing."

It was like a hand clenched around my heart then, squeezing it painfully, to hear her trust and faith in me, even after . . . everything that had happened. I wasn't worthy of trust like that. I would have said something, but I couldn't get my breath.

"Oh yes," said Tommy. "I think he knows what he's doing, all right. I simply don't trust his motives any more."

"I never meant for anyone to get hurt," I said finally. "I don't want anyone to get hurt. I've seen the future that's coming, if Lilith isn't stopped. I still have nightmares . . . And I am ready to die, to prevent it. But . . . I don't have the right to ask that of anyone else. What do you think we should do, Tommy?"

"I say we put Merlin's heart back," Tommy said stubbornly. "It could work. We save his life, and I'll use my gift to talk him out of killing us. You know how persuasive I can be. With his heart back and his power restored, he'll be able to repair Suzie's face and bring Nimue back from the dead. Don't look at me like that! This is Merlin; he could do it! I know he could. And then, with the right guidance and advice, he will restore the glory that is Camelot and make a better world, a better future!"

"Oh Jesus, are we back to that?" said Suzie. "Tommy, we've been through this. We daren't change the Past, because of what it could do to our Present. And there's no telling what kind of a future you and a half-mad Merlin might bring about anyway."

"Lilith still has to be stopped," I said.

"Why?" said Tommy. "Because of what she might do? Don't worry; Merlin will handle her."

"Merlin Satanspawn?" I said. "The Devil's only begotten son? For all we know, he'd help her."

"I can use my gift . . ."

"Against Merlin?"

"You're Lilith's only son," said Tommy. "You'd let the dream of Camelot die, just to further your own ambitions. I see right through you, Taylor. And I'll see you die first!"

He raised his gift, but I was already raising mine, and the whole bar shook as our powers manifested and clashed head-on. I used my gift to try and find his weaknesses, and he used his to try and reinforce a reality where I never reached the sixth century. My gift dealt with certainties, his with probabilities, and neither was really strong enough to overcome the other. We both put all our strength into this clash of wills, and reality itself became hazy and uncertain around us, until it seemed the whole bar might unravel, leaving us the only fixed and real things in the world.

There was no telling where that insane and dangerous struggle might have gone if Suzie hadn't put a stop to it by simply hitting Tommy round the back of the head with the butt of her shotgun. He cried out and fell to his knees, his gift snapping off as the pain in his head kept him from concentrating. He still tried to come up off his knees fighting, and Suzie calmly and dispassionately beat the shit out of him. He finally collapsed into unconsciousness, and I used my gift to find Old Father Time's touch on him and remove it. Tommy disappeared immediately, swept back to our Present.

(And that was when I finally remembered when I'd seen Tommy Oblivion before. He'd appeared out of nowhere in Strangefellows, during the Nightingale case, some months previously. He'd been badly beaten, and yelled threats at me before he was thrown out. Now I knew why. He'd obviously arrived back in the Nightside before he left. Still, it did beg the question of why, if Tommy knew what was going to happen on this trip, he didn't search out his younger self, and inform him . . . Unless something happened to the older Tommy to prevent it . . . That's why I hate Time travel. Just thinking about it makes your head hurt.)

I sat down in a chair while Suzie checked my head wound, then cleaned the blood off my face. I sat looking at Merlin's heart on the table before me, planning what I was going to do next. Even after everything that had happened, I was still determined to press on. I had to succeed in my mission to justify all the suffering and damage I'd caused.

"If nothing else," said Suzie, "we have discovered the answer to one of the great mysteries of the Nightside—who stole Merlin's heart? We did. Who would have thought it . . . Can it really take us further back into the Past?"

She was speaking calmly and professionally, so I did the same. "I don't see why not. The power's definitely there; I have to tap into it and guide it."

"And you're not worried about your Enemies locating you here?"

"I think they would have by now if they were going to," I said.

I took the heart in my hand and made myself look at Suzie's ruined face without flinching. I'd done that to her. I had to stop Lilith, or all Suzie's pain had been for nothing. I looked slowly round the bar, taking in all the damage I'd done, without meaning to. I had to wonder if perhaps it was my own implacable stubbornness that was forging the very series of causal links that would bring about the dead future.

Who caused this? I asked the future Razor Eddie, as he lay dying in my arms. *You did,* he said. *How do I stop it?* I asked him. *Kill yourself,* he said.

I'd promised him I would die rather than let that future happen. I'd promised Suzie back during the angel war that I would never let her be hurt again. I'd failed her. She didn't blame me, but I did. She would forgive, but I never would. Perhaps . . . the only way to stop the awful future was to kill myself, now, before it was too late . . .

No. I could still stop Lilith. I was the only one who could stop her.

So I nodded to Suzie to pick up Nimue's body, while I raised my gift and tapped the power of Merlin's heart, and we went hurtling back through Time again.

NINE

When in Rome

We arrived. I looked around. I looked at Suzie. "Hold me back, Suzie, or I am going to kill absolutely everything that moves."

"Hold yourself back," Suzie said calmly. "You know very well I don't do the restraint thing. It's bad for my reputation."

"I don't believe this!" I said, actually stamping my foot in frustration. "We're still only part of the way back!"

"At least it doesn't smell so bad this time," said Suzie, judiciously. "I find a little horse shit in the street goes a hell of a long way."

"I could spit soot," I said.

We'd reappeared in the middle of a large open square, under the star-speckled sky and huge full moon of the Nightside. The buildings enclosing the square were low and squat, stone and marble, with the unmistakable classic touches of Roman architecture. Men in wraparound togas looked at us curiously, then went on their way, as though strange people appearing suddenly out of nowhere happened all the time. Maybe it did, in this Nightside.

"First or second century," said Suzie, showing off her knowledge again. "The Romans built Londinium over the River Thames, and were the first human society to colonize the already existing Nightside. Outside, Rome rules Britain, after Julius Caesar led a successful invasion in 55 B.C. It was actually his third attempt; the extremely savage Britons threw his armies back into the sea twice. And the defensive tactics used by the Druidic priests shocked even the hardened Roman Legionnaires. So Rome now rules, with an iron fist. They brought law, roads, slavery, and crucifixion. You're not into history, are you, Taylor? Taylor?"

My teeth were clenched so tight my jaws ached. I'd tried to play it light, but my heart wasn't in it. I couldn't believe we'd fallen short again.

We were still at least a hundred years short of the Nightside's creation, maybe more, and with no means of going any further. Everything I'd done, all the hard and ruthless things I'd done, all the hurt and death I'd caused . . . had all been for nothing. I looked down at Merlin's heart, in my hand. It no longer beat or pulsed. It was just a dark red lump of muscle, all its magic used up. Which meant we were stranded. I threw the heart onto the ground, and stamped on it, but it was already too hard and leathery to crush properly. I sighed. I didn't have the energy left to throw a proper tantrum. Too tired to be angry, too bitter to be mad. Suzie sensed the pain in me and comforted me in the only way she could, by standing close beside me and reassuring me with her cold, calm presence. I could remember a time when it used to be the other way round. We'd both come a long way from who we used to be, Suzie and I.

"Hey, you!" said a loud, harsh, and not at all friendly voice. "Stand right where you are, and don't even think about going for a weapon!"

"Oh good," I said. "A distraction."

"I pity the fools," said Suzie.

We looked around. The people in the square were scattering, in a dignified and civilised way, as a group of Roman Legionnaires headed straight for us. They wore the armoured outfits familiar from film and television, though these outfits looked rough and dirty and hard-used, much like the men who wore them. They were short and stocky, with brutal faces and eyes that had seen everything before. Typical city cops. They stamped towards us, short-swords in their hands, and quickly fanned out to form a semicircle facing and containing us. Suzie already had her shotgun out, held lazily in her hands. She glanced at me, and I shook my head slightly. Best not to start any trouble we didn't have to, until we had a better grasp on local conditions. Suzie had been carrying Nimue's body draped over one shoulder, but at the Legionnaires' approach she dumped it on the ground, to be free for any necessary action. The Legionnaires looked at the body, then at us.

"Tall, aren't they?" said a quiet voice from among them.

"When I want your opinion, Marcus, I'll beat it out of you," growled the leader. He gave us his best intimidating stare, not at all bothered that he had to incline his head right back to do it. "I'm Tavius, leader of the Watch. Are you a Citizen?"

"Almost certainly not," I said. "We're only passing through. Hopefully. I'm John Taylor, and this is Suzie Shooter. Don't upset her."

"You speak Latin like a Citizen," said Tavius. "I suppose it's possible you have legitimate business here. Who's the stiff?"

"No-one you'd know," I said.

"Identity papers!"

I checked my coat pockets, in case Old Father Time might have supplied some, but apparently there were limits to his help. I shrugged, and smiled easily at the head of the Watch.

"Sorry. No papers. Would a bribe do?"

"Well . . ."

"Shut up, Marcus!" said Tavius. He gave me his full attention, turning his glare up another notch. "We have been given the task of maintaining order in this unnatural shit-hole, and we only accept tributes from legitimate Citizens. Now, I see a dead body, and I see blood all over the pair of you. I'm sure you're about to tell me there's a perfectly reasonable explanation for all this . . ."

"Actually, no," I said. "I've got an unnatural explanation, but frankly, life's too short. Why don't you take our word for it that this lady and I are very powerful, very dangerous, and extremely pissed off by recent events; so unless you want this lady and me to turn the whole lot of you into dog food . . ."

"Oh hell," said Tavius. "You're magical?"

"Told you we should have paid the extra insurance, for full godly cover."

"I won't tell you again, Marcus! Now bring me the bloody list."

The smallest of the Legionnaires hurried forward, handed his leader a rolled scroll, gave me a quick shifty smile, and dropped a wink to Suzie. Then he retreated swiftly back into the ranks. Tavius opened the scroll and studied it carefully.

"So, are you gods, walking in disguise?"

"Definitely not," I said. "And don't believe anyone who tells you otherwise. They're just guessing."

Tavius considered that for a moment, and then moved on to the next question on his checklist. "Are you a Power, a Force, or a Being?"

"Not as such," I said.

"Are you a magician, sorcerer, raiser of spirits, or soothsayer?"

"There's a lot of debate about that," I said, "but I prefer not to comment. However, it would be fair to say that this lady and I are dangerous in a whole bunch of unnatural and unpleasant ways."

"I can set light to my farts," Suzie volunteered.

"Don't go there," I said quickly to Tavius.

He blinked a few times, then looked back at his checklist. "We've already established you're not Citizens, so . . . which gods protect you?"

"Absolutely none, as far as I can tell," said Suzie.

"And I think we can safely assume I'm not going to find your barbarian names on the approved list," said Tavius, rolling up his scroll with a certain satisfaction. "Which means you're fair game. All right, boys, arrest them. We'll sort out some charges later."

"They said they were dangerous. Powerful and dangerous."

"Gods, you're a wimp, Marcus. How you ever got into the Legion is a mystery to me."

"They're tall enough to be dangerous."

"Look, if they had any magic worth the mentioning, they would have used it by now, wouldn't they? Now arrest them, or there'll be no honey with your dinner tonight."

"What the hell," I said. "I've been having a really rotten time, and I could use someone to take out my feelings on."

And I punched Tavius right between his beady little eyes. His head snapped back, and he staggered backwards two or three paces, but he didn't go down. Either they built them really tough in the Legion, or I was losing my touch. Tavius raised his short-sword and started towards me. I caught his gaze with mine, and he stopped short as though he'd run into a brick wall. I kept the stare going, and his face went blank, the short-sword slipping from his hand as the fingers slowly opened. I hit him again, and this time he went down and stayed down. Which was just as well. It felt like I'd broken every bone in my hand.

The rest of the Legionnaires were already advancing on us, hoping to overwhelm us with numbers. Suzie shot four of them in swift succession, working the pump on her shotgun with practised speed. The loud noise, the flying blood, and the terrible wounds scattered the Legionnaires like startled birds, and I thought they might run, but their training quickly reasserted itself. You don't choose the faint-hearted to act as the Watch in the Nightside. They spread out to make harder targets, then advanced on Suzie and me, sandalled feet stamping in perfect unison. I fell back on my standard response, which was to use the taking-bullets-out-of-guns trick. I wasn't actually sure what effect it would have, and so was pleasantly surprised when all the Legionnaires' weapons, armour, and clothing disappeared, leaving them utterly unarmed, and stark bollock naked. They looked down at themselves, then at us, and they turned as one and ran. There were limits to what even trained soldiers were prepared to face. Suzie started to raise her shotgun, but I shook my head, and she lowered it again. She looked at the departing bare arses and shook her head.

"Getting mean, Taylor."

"Everything I know, I learned from you," I said generously.

She considered me thoughtfully for a moment. "I'm never sure what you can or can't do."

I grinned. "That's the point."

We watched the departing Legionnaires leave the square at speed, probably on the way to tell on us to their superiors. Some of the people had wandered back into the square. They looked at Suzie, then at me, very disapprovingly. I glared right back at them, and they all remembered they had urgent appointments somewhere else.

"Feeling better?" said Suzie.

"You have no idea," I said.

I took a good look at our surroundings. The stone buildings were basic and blocky, prettied up with columns, porticoes, and bas-reliefs. Most of the latter featured gods, monsters, and people doing naughty things with each other. The centre of the square was taken up with a whole bunch of oversized statues, featuring either the local gods and goddesses or idealised men and women, most of them naked, all of them very brightly painted. I expressed some surprise at this, and Suzie immediately went into lecture mode again. I could remember when she hardly said a dozen words at a time. A little education is a terrible thing.

"All classical statues were painted, and repainted regularly. The Romans adopted the practice from the ancient Greeks, along with everything else that wasn't nailed down. Even their gods, though they at least had the grace to rename them. We're used to seeing the statues in museums, old and cracked and bare stone and marble, because that's all that survived." She stopped abruptly. "Taylor, you're looking at me strangely again."

"I'm impressed," I said. "Honest."

"Look, I got the History Channel for free, okay? I subscribed to the Guns & Ammo Channel, and History was part of the package."

"Cable television has a lot to answer for."

I went back to looking at the buildings, and I slowly realised they were all temples of one kind or another. Most were dedicated to the local Roman gods, of which there were quite a few, including Julius Caesar and Augustus Caesar, complete with idealised busts showing off their noble features.

"After Julius, all the Roman Emperors were declared gods when they died," said Suzie. "And sometimes even during their lifetimes. Good way to keep the colonized nations in line, by telling them their Emperor was a god."

"Actually, I knew that," I said. "I watched *I, Claudius*. And the Penthouse *Caligula*. But only because Helen Mirren was in it."

Other temples were dedicated to Dagon, the Serpent, the Serpent's Son, Cthulhu, several of the old Greek gods, half a dozen names I vaguely remembered from the Street of the Gods, and a whole bunch I'd never even heard of. And, one temple dedicated to Lilith. I considered that for a while, but it seemed no more or less important than any of the others.

"There aren't any Christian temples," I said suddenly.

"Too early yet," said Suzie. "Though there are probably some underground, unofficial places."

I turned my attention to the people, and others, passing through the square. Less than half were in any way human. There were elves, moving silently together with mathematical precision, holding strange groupings and patterns as intricate as a snowflake, and as alien. Lizardly humanoids slid quickly through the darker parts of the square, unnaturally graceful, their scaled skin gleaming bottle-green under the occasional lamplight. Large squat creatures, composed entirely of heaving, multi-coloured gasses, progressed slowly and jerkily, their shapes changing and convulsing from moment to moment. Liquid forms as tall as houses splashed across the square, leaving sticky trails behind them. Earthy shapes crumbled as they stamped along, and living flames flashed and flickered, come and gone too quickly for the human eye to follow. In these early days of the Nightside, humanity was the minority, and forms and forces long since lost and banished to the Street of the Gods walked openly.

Two burly giants, great heaving monstrosities draped in flapping furs, lurched forward from opposite sides of the square. So tall they towered over the biggest of the temples, the ground shook under the impact of their every footstep. They cried out to each other in voices like the thunder, or the crash of rock on rock, and there was nothing human in the sound. They slammed together in the middle of the square, kicking aside the statues of gods and heroes, and had at each other with massive sledgehammers.

There were humans in the square; but they mostly kept to the sides, out of the way, and gave all the others plenty of room. There were rough Celtic types, squat vicious men in wolf furs, with blue woad on their faces and clay packed in their hair. They carried swords and axes, and growled at anyone who came too close. There were Romans and Greeks and Persians, all of them moving in armed groups, for safety's sake. Some had the look of sorcerers, and some were quite clearly mad. And finally, a heavy stone golem came striding purposefully through the crowds, the word *Emeth* glowing fiercely on its forehead, above the rudimentary carved features.

This early Nightside was a strange, whimsical, dangerous place. And I felt right at home.

"So," said Suzie, her voice remarkably casual under the circumstances, "did Lilith want us here, or did Merlin's heart simply run out of power too soon?"

"Beats me," I said. "But it wouldn't surprise me at all if Mother dear was still interfering, for her own inscrutable reasons. Either she's still trying to keep us away from witnessing the Nightside's true beginnings, or there's something here she wants me to see. A situation further complicated by the fact that Lilith is probably actually here, somewhere. Her earlier self, that is. She might not have been banished yet. We're going to have to watch ourselves, Suzie. We can't afford to attract her attention."

"Why not?" said Suzie. "This Lilith wouldn't know who you are."

"I think . . . she'd only have to look at me, to know," I said. "And then she'd ask questions . . . If she were to find out about her being banished to Limbo, you can bet she'd take steps to stop it, and our Present really would be screwed."

"What do we do with the witch's body?" said Suzie. When in doubt she always retreated to the immediate practical problems.

I looked around and spotted what looked like a municipal dump in one corner of the square. It was a large dump, piled high, and surrounded by flies and dogs and other things. I pointed it out to Suzie, and she nodded. She bent down and slung Nimue's body casually over one shoulder again, and I retrieved Merlin's heart from where I'd thrown it. The dark muscle was already decaying into mush. We dumped both the heart and the body on the pile of accumulated refuse. Thick clouds of flies sprang up around us, buzzing angrily at being disturbed. Up close the smell was almost overpowering. In and among the city's piled-up garbage there were quite a few other bodies, in varying stages of decay. Some were human, some very definitely weren't, and there were a surprisingly large number of dead dogs and wolves. Small furry and scuttling things moved over and through the pile, feasting on the tastiest bits.

"No-one will notice one more body," said Suzie, satisfied. "I guess only Citizens get buried in this age."

I nodded, staring at Nimue. The crooked arms, the bent-back head, the staring empty eyes. "She died because of me," I said. "Just a kid, with a bit of ambition and an eye to the main chance. Who really did love her old sugar daddy, at the end. Dead and gone now, because I talked her into helping us."

"You can't save them all," said Suzie.

"I didn't even try," I said. "I was too wrapped up in my own concerns. I used her . . . to get what I wanted. I don't think I much like the man I'm becoming, Suzie."

Suzie sniffed. She'd never had much time for sentiment, with good reason. "What do we do now?" she said briskly.

"We need information," I said, glad of an excuse to push aside my conscience and concentrate on the here and now. "There must be someone, or more probably Something, in this Nightside with enough power to send us further back in Time, to where and when we need to be. There must be."

Suzie shrugged. "Can't say I know of any, off-hand. Most of the Powers we know haven't even been born or created yet." She looked around at the various temples. "I suppose we could always pray to the gods. The Roman gods were quite keen in interfering in human affairs."

"I don't think I want to attract their attention either," I said. "They'd be bound to ask questions, and the answers would only upset them."

"We have to go to the Londinium Club," Suzie said abruptly.

"Why?" I said.

"Because the Doorman in the sixth century remembered that we did. So whatever it is we do, when we meet him, it must make one hell of a first impression."

I scowled. "I hate that kind of circular thinking. I say we break the circle, so that nothing is certain any more. I don't have to go to the Club, if I don't want to. I say we go straight to the oldest bar in the world, whatever it's called in this period, and make our enquiries there."

"We could do that," said Suzie. "Only, how are we going to find it, when we don't know its name, or where it's located? I take it you don't feel like using your gift . . ."

"No, I bloody don't. The Lilith of this time would almost certainly notice . . ." I stood and thought for a time, while Suzie waited patiently. She's always had great faith in my ability to think my way out of any problem. "We need directions," I finally decided.

"Sounds like a plan," said Suzie. "Want me to start grabbing people at random, and stick my shotgun up their noses?"

"There's an easier way," I said. I knelt beside the unconscious Roman Legionnaire I'd decked earlier and brought him back to consciousness by only somewhat brutal methods. I helped him sit up, while he groaned and cursed, then smiled at him encouragingly. "We need directions, Tavius. You tell us how to find the oldest bar in the world, and we'll go away and leave you, and you'll never have to see us again. Won't that be nice?"

"The oldest bar?" the Legionnaire said sullenly. "Which one? I can think of several that could make that claim. Don't you have a name for it?"

I sighed, and looked at Suzie. "I suppose it hasn't been around long enough to establish its reputation yet."

"Then we go to the Londinium Club?"

"Looks like it. You do know where that is, right, Legionnaire?"

"Of course. But it's only for Citizens. Strictly Members only, and protected by the whole Roman pantheon. There's no way the likes of you will ever get to see the insides of it."

I punched him out again, and then spent a while walking round in small circles, nursing my wounded hand and swearing a lot. There's a reason why I try to avoid brawls, which is that I'm really crap at them. Suzie very wisely had nothing to say.

We set off through the Nightside, following Tavius's directions. The first thing I noticed was that the air was cleaner and clearer in Roman times. I could see the Nightside sky clearly, without a hint of smoke or smog. And then something really big flew across the face of the oversized moon, actually blocking it out completely for a moment. I stopped and watched, genuinely impressed. Every now and again I needed reminding that this wasn't the Nightside I knew. They did things differently here. Even more than the sixth century, this was a dangerous time, where Powers and Forces walked freely and unopposed, and humanity was a barely tolerated newcomer.

The only light came from torches and oil-lamps, firmly bolted to every suitable structure, but there still wasn't enough of it. The shadows were very deep and very dark, and many things seemed to prefer them. Crowds of people and others bustled back and forth through the narrow streets and alleyways, intent on their own business, and there was hardly any distinction between the street traffic and the pedestrians. The traffic itself was slow and stately; some wagons, some horses (with slaves following along behind to clean up after them), and what were clearly upper-class people, being carried around on reclining couches by what I thought at first were slaves, but from their dead faces and staring eyes were quite definitely zombies.

"You're the expert," I said to Suzie. "What are those couch things called?"

"Palanquins," she said immediately. "I thought you said you watched *I, Claudius*?"

"I watched it, but I didn't take notes. Did you spot the zombies?"

"Of course. They're called liches, in this period. Maybe there's a shortage of good slaves, or maybe the slaves got too uppity. You don't get back talk from the dead."

Tavius's directions had been extremely explicit, so much so I'd had to write them down. (Tavius had been really impressed by my ballpoint pen.) They did seem to involve an awful lot of going back and forth and around and around, often for no obvious point or reason. In fact, it was taking us ages to get anywhere, and I was getting really fed up with having to plough through the unrespecting crowds. So when I saw the opportunity for an obvious short cut, I took it. I strode down a perfectly ordinary-looking street, got almost to the end, then was suddenly right back where I'd started from. I stopped and looked around me. Suzie looked at me patiently, while I considered the matter. She wasn't above saying *I told you so,* preferring to save it for those really irritating moments, but I don't think she trusted my mood, right then.

"I get the feeling," I said finally, "that space in this new Nightside hasn't properly settled down yet. Directions can be arbitrary, and space can actually fold back upon itself. I've heard old stories about that, but it hasn't happened in our Nightside for ages. The Authorities tend to keep such things constant because it's good for business. So . . . I guess we'd better stick to Tavius's directions exactly, from now on."

"I would," said Suzie.

"You're dying to say *I told you so,* aren't you?"

"I wouldn't dare."

We pressed on, following the directions exactly, but we hadn't been walking for ten minutes before we walked right into a trap. We were strolling through a suspiciously deserted square when it suddenly disappeared, and we were Somewhere else. The change hit us like a blow. The air was viciously hot and sticky, and smelled of spoiled meat. The light was dark purple, and when I looked up, I saw a big red sun in a sickly pink sky. And all around us was a jungle made of flesh and blood. It stretched away for miles, trees and bush and hanging lianas, and all of it made of meat. All of it moving, slowly, as it reacted to our sudden presence. Suzie already had her shotgun out and was looking for a target.

"Is it a Timeslip?" she said, her voice calm and controlled as always.

"Could be," I said, trying for the same tone. "Some extreme alternative time-line, past or future or . . . that bloody Tavius! He deliberately didn't tell us, hoping we'd walk right into it!"

"Ugly bloody place," said Suzie, and I had to agree.

We were standing in a small clearing, in a jungle made of meat. The huge trees were red and purple, and the large leathery leaves had bones in them. Some of the trees were clearly pregnant, with bulging, distended boles, patterned with dark veins. All the plants were flesh and blood, their pink skins sweating in the furnace heat. The stench of decaying flesh came to me from every direction, carried on the shifting breezes, thick and nasty, leaving an indescribable taste in my mouth. There were flowers, too, great pulpy growths like Technicolor cancers, and here and there roses red as blood stood tall on thorny spines, the crimson petals surrounding mouths stuffed with needle teeth. The roses all turned their heads in our direction, orientating on Suzie and me, and harsh, hissing noises emanated from the roses' mouths. They were talking to each other.

And beyond and underneath the heavy layers of jungle growth, I could barely make out the blurred forms of ancient, ruined buildings. Old, very old structures, long abandoned by whoever or whatever built them. This was a world where evolution had taken a very different turn. Nature, red in tooth and claw, replaced by nature red in vine and thorn.

It was an alien landscape, like a different planet, and Suzie and I didn't belong there. I felt . . . horribly alone. Already some of the meat plants were turning slowly in our direction, and the roses were hissing angrily at each other. Plants like lumps of spoiled liver tore their pink roots out of the dark ground and lurched towards us. Thorned tendrils opened out around them, like some vicious grasping umbrella. Sticky mouths opened in the dark-veined plants. Suzie opened up with her shotgun, fanning it back and forth, and the plants before and around us exploded in gobbets of bloody flesh. A high, keening rose on the air, inhumanly grating, as though the whole jungle was crying out in pain and outrage. A quick glance around showed the jungle pressing in from every direction. Even the great trees were leaning towards and over us. Suzie kept up a steady rate of fire, the noise deafening at close range, but she wasn't even slowing the advance down. The fleshy plants soaked up the punishment and kept coming. Suzie realised she was only wasting ammunition and grabbed for one of the grenades on her belt.

I decided it was time to step in, before things really got out of hand. I grabbed the nearest rose and yanked it out of the dark ground. It squealed like a pig pulled away from its trough, thrashing its thorny spine about and trying to twist it around my wrist and arm. I held the rose firmly below the flower, took my monogrammed silver lighter out of my coat pocket, and flicked on the flame. The other roses cried out in unison, and the jungle grew very still. I held the flame close to the rose, and the petals shrank away from it.

"All right," I said. "Back off, or the rose gets it."

There was a pause, then the whole of the meat jungle fell back perceptibly. They might not understand my words, but they knew what I meant. I looked at Suzie and jerked my head backwards. She checked that the way behind us was clear and nodded. And slowly, step by step, we moved back along the path that had brought us into this awful world. The jungle watched us go, the fleshy leaves quivering with rage. The rose writhed violently in my grasp, fighting to break free, snapping at me with its nasty teeth. And then, suddenly, the purple glare snapped off, replaced by the soothing gloom of the Nightside. We'd retreated back across the border of the Timeslip. The rose let out a howl of anguish, until I slapped it round the petals and shut it up. I stuffed the rose into my coat pocket, and it grew still. I wasn't worried about the rose trying to escape; my coat can look after itself. I took several deep breaths, trying to clear the stench of spoiled meat out of my head.

"Really ugly place," said Suzie, calm and unruffled as always. She put away her shotgun and looked at me. "How did you figure out the roses were so important?"

"Easy," I said. "They were the only ones that had a language."

"Let's go to the Londinium Club," said Suzie. "And face dangers I can understand."

We followed Tavius's directions exactly, suspicious all the time for further pitfalls, but soon enough we came safely to the Londinium Club. The exterior looked the same as always, only much cleaner. The stone exterior was spotless, gleaming brightly under many lanterns, and the erotic bas-reliefs showed off details so powerful they practically leapt off the wall and mugged you. And there, standing at the stop of the steps and guarding the entrance, was the Doorman. He really was as old as everyone said he was. This time, he wore a simple white tunic, his muscular arms folded firmly across his broad chest. He took one look at Suzie and me, in our battered and blood-stained clothes, and actually came all the way down the steps to block our way more thoroughly. Since reason and kind words were clearly not an option, I reached into my coat pocket, pulled out the rose, and presented it to the Doorman. He accepted it automatically, then cried out in shock and revulsion as the thorny spine wrapped itself around his arm, and the flower went for his face, the teeth snapping at his eyes. He had to use both hands to hold it back. And while he was preoccupied, Suzie and I walked right past him, through the door, and into the lobby, our noses in the air like we belonged there.

This time, the lobby was all gleaming white tiles, with a huge coloured mosaic covering the entire floor; all of it gleaming new and fresh and shining clean. There were oil-lamps burning everywhere, filling the lobby with a golden light, so that not a single shadow should spoil the effect. The mosaic on the floor showed the entire pantheon of Roman gods and goddesses doing something so erotic and entangled I was hard-pushed to make sense of it, but it was the mosaic on the ceiling that caught my attention. It was a stylized portrait of a woman's face. My mother's face.

"I don't care if they are gods," said Suzie. "Some of those proportions can't be correct."

I drew her attention away from the floor and indicated the face on the ceiling. "That's Lilith," I said. "That's Mommie Dearest. They say she slept with demons and gave birth to monsters."

Suzie sniffed, conspicuously unimpressed. "Yeah, she looks the type. I'm more concerned with what's going on here on the floor. I mean, look at that guy on the end. You could club a baby seal to death with that."

"You don't get it," I said. "Why would the Londinium Club put Lilith's face on their lobby ceiling?"

Suzie shrugged. "Maybe she was a founding Member. That could explain its longevity . . ."

I shook my head, unconvinced. "There's got to be more to it than that. This means something . . ."

"Everything means something."

Perhaps fortunately, we were interrupted by the Club Steward walking across the lobby to join us. I knew he had to be the Steward; they all have that same arrogant poise, the same disdainful gaze. Somehow I knew we weren't going to get on. He stopped a respectful distance away from us, bowed slightly, and presented us with his best long-suffering smile.

"Your reputation proceeds you, sir and lady. The Legionnaires you ran off are still being treated for shock, and so far you are the only people ever to venture into the carnivorous jungle and come out again in one piece. You are also the first people ever to get past our Doorman. There is some talk of presenting you with a medal or striking you down with a lightning bolt. Either way, it's clear that though you are not Citizens or Members, or ever likely to be, it's got to be less trouble for all concerned if I welcome you to the Club and ask how best we can serve you. On the grounds that the sooner we can get rid of you, the better."

I looked at Suzie. "Why can't everyone be that reasonable?"

"Where would be the fun in that?" said Suzie.

"May I enquire why you have come here, sir and lady?" said the Steward.

I gave him the short version, and he nodded slowly. "Well, there are any number of gods and beings and sorcerers who are currently Club Members in good standing, who might be able to help you; and quite a few of them are in residence here today. Go through those doors, and you'll find most of them taking their ease in the steam-baths. I'm sure you'll find someone or something that can assist you. Feel free to help yourselves to the Club oils and lineaments, but don't steal the towels. We're running short again."

"Oh, I don't think we need to disturb them at their bath," I said quickly. "The dining area will do fine."

The Steward raised a shocked eyebrow. "The dining area and vomitorium are beyond the baths, sir. It is expected that all Members cleanse themselves thoroughly, before being allowed through to dine. You could not possibly be admitted in your . . . present condition. We have standards to maintain. If you will remove all your garments . . ."

"All of them?" said Suzie, a little ominously.

"Well, of course," said the Steward. "You don't take a bath with your clothes on, do you? I mean, you're obviously barbarians, but there really are limits to the kind of behaviour we're prepared to tolerate here. This is a civilised Club for civilised people. Clean civilised people. If you expect to meet with our most distinguished Members, we can't allow . . ."

"Can't?" said Suzie, her hand dropping to one of the grenades at her belt.

The Steward might not have known what a grenade was, but he knew a threat when he saw it. He drew himself up to his full height. "This Club is under the protection of the entire pantheon of Roman gods and goddesses. Start any trouble here, and you'll be leaving this lobby in several buckets."

Suzie sniffed loudly, but took her hand away from the grenade. "I don't think he's bluffing, Taylor. There's no-one more strict and unyielding about its rules and traditions than a newly formed exclusive Club. And the Roman gods were famous for their hands-on approach to smiting unbelievers."

I looked at the Steward, and he actually fell back a pace. "They couldn't keep us out."

"Maybe not," said Suzie. "But if we were to force our way in, you can bet no-one would talk to us. The kind of beings who could help us are not going to be the kind we can hope to bribe or intimidate. Hell, Taylor, what's it coming to when I'm being the voice of reason? What's the matter, you forget to put on clean underwear?"

"You don't have to do this, Suzie," I said. "You can stay here, while I go in."

"Hell with that. You need someone to watch your bare back. Especially in a place like this."

"I'm trying to protect you, Suzie. After . . . what happened to you . . ."

"I don't need protecting." She looked at me levelly. "I don't care about this, John. Really. You're being very . . . sweet, but don't worry yourself on my account."

I glared at the Steward. "This had better be worth it. Do you have any real Powers present tonight?"

"Oh yes, sir. All sorts. We even have an actual deity in residence. Poseidonis, god of the seas, has graced us with his noble presence. Be tactful with him, he's been drinking. He's also the god of horses, though no-one seems to know how that came about. Don't bring it up, you'll only upset him, and it takes ages to get all the seaweed out of the pool afterwards. If you'll follow me . . ."

He led us through the doors at the far end of the lobby and into a pleasant little changing room, with long wooden benches. Beyond the next set of doors, I could hear voices and splashing sounds. The air was perfumed and pleasantly warm. The Steward coughed meaningfully.

"If you'll let me have your . . . garments, sir and lady, I'll have them thoroughly cleaned before you leave. It won't take a moment . . ."

"Watch out for the coat," I said. "It has serious protections built in."

"I wouldn't doubt it for a moment, sir."

"And don't mess about with my weapons," growled Suzie. "Or they'll be scraping your people off the walls with a trowel."

She shrugged off her shotgun in its long holster, then took off her bandoliers of bullets and her belt of grenades. The Steward accepted them, suitably gingerly. Suzie didn't look at me as she shrugged off her leather jacket, and nothing moved in her face, nothing at all. I took off my trench coat. It felt like removing a suit of armour. Suzie took off her shirt and stepped out of her leather trousers. Underneath, she was wearing basic, functional bra and panties. It made sense. No-one else was ever expected to see them. I took off my shirt and trousers, glad I had remembered to put on a clean pair of jockeys that morning. I've never liked boxers. I like to be sure of where everything is. Suzie took off her underwear, and so did I. The Steward gathered everything up, going out of his way to make it clear our nakedness meant nothing to him. He sorted everything out into one manageable pile and lifted it up, almost disappearing behind it.

"Your clothes will be cleaned, and your weapons guarded, until you are ready to leave, sir and lady. Enjoy the baths, stay as long as you like, and please remember to get out of the pool to take a piss."

He backed out, and the doors swung shut behind him, leaving Suzie and me alone together. For a long moment we stood and looked at each other. For all the things we'd done and been through together, we'd never seen each other naked before. I'd thought I'd feel awkward, but mostly I still felt protective. I kept my gaze on her face at first, trying to be polite, but Suzie didn't bother with any of that. She looked me over with frank curiosity. So I did the same. She had so many scars, so many old hurts, tracking across her body like the map of her troubled life.

"And those are only the ones that show," said Suzie. She smiled, as our eyes met. "Not bad, Taylor. I always wondered what you'd look like, without the trench coat."

"You look great," I said. "I always thought you'd have tattoos, somewhere."

"Nah," she said dismissively. "I could never make my mind up. I just knew I'd end up hating it in the morning."

"Just as well," I said. "It would have been like scribbling graffiti across a masterpiece."

"Oh please, Taylor. I have no illusions about how I look. Even before my new face."

"You look fine," I said firmly. "Trust me."

"You smooth-talking devil, Taylor."

We couldn't maintain the light tone any more, so we stopped talking. She had a good body, with large friendly breasts and a pleasantly padded stomach. But the scars were everywhere; knife wounds, bullet wounds, the marks of tooth and claw. You don't get to be the best and most feared bounty hunter in the Nightside without being willing to fight up close and personal.

"You have scars, too," Suzie said finally. "Life has left its mark on us, John."

She reached out a hand, and slowly, cautiously, she traced some of my scars with her fingertip. Only the very tip of her forefinger, a touch gentle as a breeze, wandering across my body. I stood very still. Suzie had been sexually abused repeatedly as a child, by her own brother. She killed him for it, eventually. But ever since she'd never been able to touch or be touched, by anyone. Not even the briefest touch, the gentlest caress. Not by lovers, or friends, or even me. She stepped a little closer, and I held myself very still, not wanting to frighten her off. God alone knew how much strength it took, for her to do this small thing. I could see her breasts rising and falling as she breathed deeply. Her face was calm, thoughtful. I wanted so much to reach out to her . . . but in the end, her hand dropped to her side, and she turned her face away.

"I can't," she said. "I can't . . . Not even with you, John."

"It's all right," I said.

"No it isn't. It'll never be all right."

"You've come such a long way, Suzie."

She shook her head, still not looking at me. "What's done can't be undone. I've always known that. I can't . . . care for you, John. I don't think I have it in me any more."

"Of course you do," I said. "Five years ago, you shot me in the back to stop me leaving, remember?"

She nodded, and looked at me again. "It was a cry for attention."

I moved in close, trying hard to seem supportive without crowding her. "There was a time . . . you wouldn't even have been able to do this much, Suzie. You're changing. So am I. And we monsters must stick together."

She looked at me, and though she didn't smile, she didn't look away. Slowly, and very cautiously, I raised my hand, and with the very tips of my fingers I touched the ridged mass of scar and burn tissue that now made up the right side of her face. The hard skin felt cold and dead. Suzie looked into my eyes, hardly blinking, but she didn't flinch.

"You do know," I said. "That I will never let you be hurt like this again. I will bleed and hurt and die before I let this happen again."

But that was a step too far. The warmth went out of her eye, and I quickly took my hand away from her face. She looked at me for a long moment, her expression calm and cold and utterly controlled.

"I can look after myself, Taylor. But thanks for the thought. Shall we go and take a look at the baths?"

"Why not?" I said. The moment of intimacy had passed, and I knew there was nothing I could do to retrieve it. "But if anyone points at me and laughs, I am going to slam his head against the wall until his eyes change colour. Even if he is a god."

"Men," said Suzie. She flexed her hands unhappily. "I feel naked without my shotgun."

"You are naked."

We pushed open the changing room doors and stepped out into a large steam-filled chamber, most of it taken up with a grandiose pool. The air was immediately hot and sweaty, the steam thick as fog. Half a dozen slaves were kept busy heaping up coals on an iron brazier and pouring large jugs of water over them. Suzie and I moved forward, and the steam thinned out some as we approached the pool. Reclining at their ease on padded couches were any number of naked men and women, and a whole bunch of other forms whose nakedness made it clear they weren't even slightly human. The pool itself held several mermaids, all saucy smiles and bobbing breasts and long, forked fish tails. Half a dozen dolphins frisked up and down in the water, showing off their virtuosity with big toothy grins. There were undines and sirens and some more of the lizardly types; and sitting at the far end of the pool, thirty feet tall if he was an inch, the god of the sea, Poseidonis himself. His head brushed against the ceiling, and his legs took up the whole end of the pool. His huge body was thick with hair, and his bearded face was almost impossibly handsome. His dimensions were still human, apart from a really impressive set of equipment. I looked away. I couldn't afford to feel intimidated before I even started negotiating. In and around the pool, men and women and others looked curiously at Suzie and me. I couldn't help feeling that a lot of the people would have looked better clothed.

"Hey," said Suzie. "Have you noticed about Poseidonis . . ."

"I'm trying not to."

"Lift your eyes, Taylor. I meant, he hasn't got a navel."

I looked. He hadn't. "Of course," I said. "He was believed into being, not born."

By this time we'd reached the edge of the pool. Conversation had stopped as we moved cautiously between the Members reclining on their couches. Apparently our reputation had proceeded us here, too. Unfortunately, it didn't stop one poor fool from reaching out and lazily caressing Suzie's arse. She kicked him right off his couch and into the pool. There was general laughter, and even some applause, and I relaxed a little.

"Bravely done, my dear," said Poseidonis, his great voice rumbling through the steamy air. "Come forward, mortals, and tell me what boon you wish of me."

We walked forward along the edge of the pool and stopped at the end, looking up at the god. Up close, his face was big and broad and smiling, and for all the god's size and overwhelming presence, my first thought was *He doesn't look too bright.* I suppose when you're a god, with a god's power, you don't have to be.

"You're not from this Time, are you?" he said easily. "You have the smell of Chronos about you."

"Wasn't he a Greek god?" said Suzie.

Poseidonis shrugged. "We kept a few from the old order, for completeness."

"We're travellers," I said. "From the future."

"Oh, tourists," said Poseidonis. He sounded disappointed.

"You've seen other travellers, like us?" said Suzie.

"Oh, yes." Poseidonis scratched lazily at the curly hair on his bulging stomach. "There's always a few, passing through, always terribly keen to tell us all about the futures they've come from. Like I care. Futures are like arseholes; everyone's got one. After all, no matter what societies men come up with, they'll always need their gods. Nothing like being immortal and powerful beyond reason, to give you job security." He frowned suddenly. "And far too many of them will insist on talking about this new god, the Christ. Can't say I know the chap. Is he popular, in your time? Has he joined our pantheon?"

"Not exactly," I said. "Where we come from, no-one believes in your pantheon any more."

His face clouded, then darkened dangerously. I knew the words were a mistake, even as I heard them coming out of my mouth, but there's something about being naked in front of a naked man five times your size that keeps you from concentrating. Poseidonis stood up abruptly and banged his head on the ceiling. Tiles cracked and shattered, broken pieces falling into the pool, while Poseidonis clutched at his head and bellowed with pain. No-one laughed, and most of the creatures in the pool retreated to the far end. The god glared around him, then he lifted his hands and lightning cracked down out of nowhere. Vivid bolts stabbed down all through the bath house, and the various Members jumped up off their couches and ran for their lives. I got the sense they'd had to do this before. The creatures in the pool vanished, disappearing back to wherever they'd come from. I grabbed a couch and overturned it, and Suzie and I hid behind it as the lightning storm continued.

"Nice one, Taylor," said Suzie.

"For a god powerful beyond all reason, he has really lousy aim," I said.

The lightning broke off abruptly and the couch was plucked away from us. Poseidonis threw it the length of the pool, and then leaned over to glare at Suzie and me. His face was bright red with rage, and very ugly. Suzie and I scrabbled backwards, then ran like hell to the other end of the bath house as his long arms stretched after us. Poseidonis was standing bent over in the pool, his hunched back pressed against the ceiling. He was growing bigger by the minute, actually filling his end of the bath house. He roared like a maddened bull, and the sound was deafening as it echoed back from the tiled walls.

"So," said Suzie, a little breathlessly. "We're naked and unarmed, facing a really pissed off god. What's your next bright idea?"

"I'm thinking!"

"Well, think faster!"

Poseidonis was still growing, the bath's ceiling cracking apart as his back and shoulders heaved up against it. He reached for Suzie and me with his huge hands, and we scattered in different directions. The god paused for a moment, torn between two conflicting decisions, and while he wrestled with the problem, I happened to notice that the great pool was almost completely drained of water. Poseidonis was the god of the sea, and he'd sucked all the water out of the pool to make up his new bulk. But this was also a steam bath . . . I grabbed one of the couches, used it as a lever, and overturned the iron brazier full of coals right into the pool. There was a great rushing up of steam, as the coals hit what was left of the water, and in a moment everything disappeared behind a thick fog. Poseidonis cried out angrily, but his voice didn't sound nearly as loud.

The steam slowly thinned away, to reveal an almost human-sized god, standing confusedly by the side of the pool. The extreme heat had boiled the excess water right out of him. Suzie ran forward and was upon him in a moment, a length of jagged wood from a dismembered couch in her hand. She grabbed a handful of the god's curly hair, jerked back his head, and set the sharp wooden edges at his throat.

"All right, all right!" yelled Poseidonis. "Mortal, call your woman off!"

"Maybe," I said, strolling down the pool to join them. "Are you feeling in a more cooperative mood, now?"

"Yes, yes! You've got to let me get out of here, before the heat evaporates me completely! I hate it when that happens."

"We need a favour," I said firmly.

Poseidonis scowled petulantly. "Anything, to get rid of you."

"My associate and I need to go further back in Time," I said.

"Two hundred years should do it," said Suzie.

"To the very beginnings of the Nightside," I concluded.

"Ah," said the god. "Now that's a problem. Gods! Ease off with that wood, woman! Just because my godly person can repair any damage, eventually, it doesn't mean I'm not sensitive to pain! Look, I don't do Time travel. That's Chronos's province. I'm only the god of the sea, and horses, because of a book-keeping error, and I have no power over Time. We gods are really very strict when it comes to demarcation. And no, I can't introduce you to Chronos; no-one's seen him in years. I'm sorry, but I really can't help you!"

"Then who could?" said Suzie.

"I don't know . . . I don't! Honestly I don't! Oh gods, I'm going to end up with splinters, I know it . . . Look; there's this really awful bar not far from here, supposed to be the oldest bar in the Nightside. That's the place to ask."

Suzie glared at me. "Don't you even think of saying *I told you so,* Taylor."

"I wouldn't dare," I assured her. I looked at Poseidonis. "What's the bar called?"

"Dies Irae. Which only goes to show that someone there has a classical and very warped sense of humour. Would you like me to transport you right there?"

"You can do that?" I said.

"Only with your consent, in my current weakened state, or I'd have transported you both to the moon, by now . . . Ow! That hurt, woman!"

"Send us to the bar," I said. "Straight there, with no detours, and with all our clothing and weapons. And don't even think about coming after us."

"Believe me," said the god, "I never want to see either of you, ever again, for the whole of my immortal lifetime."

TEN

To Die for

When Suzie Shooter and I arrived at the oldest bar in the world, we were wearing each other's clothes. Now, whether this was one last act of spite from an extremely pissed off god, or simply another example of his not being terribly bright, the result was that Suzie and I arrived seeming both surprised and vulnerable. Which is always dangerous in the oldest bar in the world, whatever period you're in. A great hulking figure wrapped in an entire bearskin lurched up to Suzie, grinning nastily. Suzie kicked him square in the nuts, with such force and enthusiasm that people sitting ten feet away made pained noises in sympathy, and I rabbit-punched the guy on the way down, just to make my feelings on the matter plain, too. Several of the bear man's friends decided to get involved and got to their feet, drawing various weapons and making various threatening noises. I drew Suzie's shotgun from the holster hanging down my back and tossed it to her, and shortly there were blood and brains all over the nearest bare stone wall. And after that, everyone left us strictly alone.

People at the surrounding tables and long wooden benches carefully paid no attention as Suzie and I stripped off and exchanged outfits. Modesty be damned; there was no way in hell I was going to fight my way through the Nightside wearing Suzie's bra and pants. And judging by the speed with which Suzie disrobed, she had clearly had similar thoughts. We reclaimed our own clothes, dressed quickly, and spent some time checking that all our weapons and devices were where they should be. We didn't want to have to go back to the Londinium Club and register a complaint. Suddenly and violently and all over the place. But everything was where it should be, and it had to be said, the Club had done an excellent job of cleaning our clothes. There wasn't a blood-stain to be seen anywhere, and my white trench coat hadn't looked so dazzlingly clean since

I bought it. They'd even polished the metal studs on Suzie's leather jacket and buffed up all the bullets in her bandoliers. Having thus re-established our dignity, Suzie and I glared around us and strode through the packed tables and benches to the long wooden bar at the rear of the room.

The place was a dump: overcrowded, filthy dirty, and it smelled really bad. There were no windows, no obvious ventilation, and greasy smoke hung on the air like floating vomit. Torches in holders and oil-lamps set in niches in the bare stone walls only just pushed back the general gloom. There was something sticky on the floor, and I didn't even want to think about what it might be. There weren't any rats, but that was probably only because the current clientele had eaten them. For once, the bar's customers seemed mostly human. Rough and nasty, and the dregs of the Earth, most of them looked like being thugs and scumbags would be a definite step up the social ladder. They wore simple filthy tunics and furs that looked as though they'd still been attached to their donor animals as recently as that morning. Everyone was heavily armed and looked ready to use their weapons at a moment's provocation.

The bar was a raucous place, with half a dozen fights going on and an awful lot of really bad community singing. Someone who'd been dipped in woad from head to toe was tattooing a complicated Druidic design on a barbarian's back, with a bone needle, a pot of woad, and a small hammer; and the barbarian was being a real wimp about it, to the amusement of his companions. Two unconscious drunks were being very thoroughly rolled by half a dozen whores who looked more scary than sexy. One of them winked at me as I passed, and I had to fight not to flinch. There were a dozen or so hairy types I was pretty sure were werewolves, at least one vampire, and one bunch of particularly brutal types that I wouldn't have accepted as human without a detailed family tree and a gene test.

"You take me to the nicest places, Taylor," said Suzie. "I hope all my shots are up to date."

"I guess this place hasn't had time to establish its reputation yet," I said.

"It has nowhere to go but up. I feel like shooting everyone here on general principles."

"You always do, Suzie."

"True."

People actually drew back as we approached the long wooden bar, giving us plenty of room. In a dive like this, that was a real compliment. I slammed the flat of my hand on the bar, to get the bar staff's attention, and something small, dark, and scuttling ran over the back of my hand. I didn't scream, but it was a near thing. Someone further down the bar caught the small, dark, scuttling thing, and ate it. A man and a woman were serving behind the bar, handing out wine in cheap pewter mugs and cups. The man was tall for this age, being a good five-foot-seven or -eight, and wore a rough tunic so filthy it was impossible to tell what colour it might have been originally. He had a long pale face, with jet-black hair and a bushy beard, separated by scowling eyes, an aquiline nose with flaring nostrils, and a sulky mouth. The woman with him was barely five feet tall but made up for it with a constant glare of concentrated malevolence that she bestowed on one and all. She had sculpted her dark blonde hair into two jutting horns with liberal use of clay, and she had a face like a bulldog's arse. Her filthy tunic successfully hid any other feminine charms she might have possessed. Between them, these two poured drinks, handed them out, snatched up the money, and loudly refused to give any change. Every now and again they hit people with large wooden clubs they kept under the bar. It wasn't always clear why they did so, but in a place like this I had no doubt the victims deserved it, and probably a whole lot more. The man and the woman stubbornly ignored my attempts to get their attention, until Suzie fired her shotgun into the bottles stacked behind the bar; an action that has always been one of her favourite attention-getters. The customers around us moved even further away, some of them remarking loudly on the lateness of the hour and how they really had to be getting home. The man and woman behind the bar slouched reluctantly over to join us. He looked even more sulky; she looked even more venomous.

"I don't suppose there's any chance of getting you to pay for the damage?" said the man.

"Not a hope in hell," I said cheerfully.

He sniffed lugubriously, as though he hadn't expected anything else. "I'm Marcellus. This is the wife, Livia. We run this place, for our sins. Who are you, and what do you want?"

"I'm John Taylor, and this is Suzie Shooter . . ."

"Oh, we've heard about you," snapped Livia. "Troublemakers. Outsiders. Barbarians with no respect for the proper ways of doing things." She sniffed loudly, very much like her husband. "Unfortunately, it seems you are also very powerful and dangerous with it, in nasty and unexpected ways, so we are forced to be polite to you. See, I smile upon you. This is my polite smile."

It looked more like a rat caught in a trap. I looked at Marcellus. His smile wasn't much more successful. I got the feeling he didn't get a lot of practice, with a wife like Livia.

"You should be honoured," he said gloomily. "She doesn't smile for just anyone, you know."

"Shut up, Marcellus, I'm talking."

"Yes, dear."

"I suppose you expect a drink on the house?" said Livia, in the tone of voice normally associated with accusing someone of doing rude things with corpses. "Marcellus, two cups of the good stuff."

"Yes, dear."

He carefully poured out two quite small measures of red wine, into pewter cups that looked like they'd been beaten into shape by someone who was already drunk. Or at least in a really bad mood. Suzie and I tried the wine, then we both pulled back our lips in the same disgusted expression. I must have tasted worse in my life, but I'd be hard-pressed to say when. It was like vinegar that had been pissed in, only not as pleasant.

"This is the good stuff?" said Suzie.

"Of course," said Livia. "This is what we drink ourselves."

That explains a lot, I thought, but for once had the sense not to say it out loud. "You run this bar?" I said.

"Sort of," said Marcellus. "Some old witch owns the place; we only run it for her. We're slaves, bound to this bar by law and magic for the rest of our lives. We do a good job because the geas compels us to, but in our few free moments we dream of escape and revenge."

"And making others suffer, as we have been made to," said Livia.

"Well yes, that, too, naturally."

"We weren't always slaves, you know," said Livia, with well-rehearsed bitterness. "Oh no! We were respectable people, I'll have you know. Roman Citizens, in good standing. Wouldn't have been seen dead in a place like this . . . But then *he* got into business troubles . . ."

She turned the full force of her glare on her husband, who drooped a little more under the pressure of her gaze. "They were strictly transitory difficulties," he said sullenly. "Cash flow problems. That sort of thing. If I'd been allowed a little more time, I'm sure I could have sorted things out to everyone's satisfaction . . ."

"But you couldn't," Livia said flatly. "So our creditors had our business shut down and sold us both off as slaves at public auction, to cover our debts." She actually sniffled a moment, overcome by the memory. "The humiliation of it! All our friends and neighbours were there, watching. People who'd eaten at our table and made free with our money and influence! Some of them laughed. Some of them even bid!"

"We were lucky to be sold as a set, my dear," said Marcellus. "As husband and wife. We might have been parted forever."

"Yes," said Livia. "There is that. We have never been parted, and never will be."

"Never," said Marcellus. They held hands, and while neither of them actually stopped scowling, there was a definite togetherness about them. With anyone else, it might have even been touching.

"Anyway," said Marcellus, "because we had some experience of running a drinking establishment, from earlier in our lives, we were bought by the owner of this appalling place, who needed staff in a hurry. We were bought by a factor; we've never seen the owner in person. If we'd known who it was, and what the bar was, we'd probably have volunteered for the salt mines. This place goes through staff faster than a slave galley. The last husband and wife were killed, cooked, and eaten, on a somewhat rowdy Saturday night. No-one even knows what happened to the pair before that."

"No-one has ever lasted as long as us," said Livia, with a certain amount of pride. "Mainly because we don't take any crap from anyone. You have to be firm, but fair. Firm, and occasionally downright vicious. My husband may not look like much, but he's a real terror when he's roused."

"Ah, but no-one could be more dangerous than you, my dear," Marcellus said generously. He smiled fondly as he patted her hand. "No-one can slip a purgative or a poison into a wine cup better than you."

"And no-one cuts a throat more neatly than you, dear Marcellus. He's like a surgeon, he really is. It's a joy to watch him work."

"Who actually owns this bar?" I said, feeling a distinct need to change the subject.

"Some powerful sorceress, of old times," said Marcellus. "Been around for ages, supposedly. Her name is Lilith."

"Of course," I said heavily. "It would have to be."

We've never met her," said Livia. "Don't know anyone who has. A real absentee landlady."

Suzie looked at me. "Why would Lilith want to own a bar?"

"I'll ask her," I said. "After I've asked all the other questions on my list."

"So," said Marcellus. "What unfortunate but necessary business brings you to this appalling place? What help and or advice can we offer you, so that you'll go away and stop bothering us?"

"We're looking for a Being of Power," I said. "Someone or something with enough magic to send us both back in Time, at least a couple of hundred years. Can you recommend anyone?"

Marcellus and Livia looked at each other. "Well," Livia said finally, "if that's what you want . . . Your best bet would be the Roman gods and goddesses. They've all got more power than they know what to do with, and every single one of them is open to prayer, flattery, and bribes."

"Not really an option," I said. "We upset Poseidonis really badly."

Marcellus sniffed loudly. "Don't let that worry you; the gods don't like each other much anyway. One big dysfunctional family, with incest and patricide always on the menu. I can name you half a dozen off-hand who'd help you out just to spite Poseidonis."

"He's supposed to call himself Neptune these days," said Livia. "But he's so dim he keeps forgetting."

I considered the suggestion. "Can you trust these gods?" I said finally.

"Of course not," said Marcellus. "They're gods."

"Suggest someone else," said Suzie.

"Well, there is supposed to be this small town somewhere out in the South-West, where you can meet the Earth Mother in person, and petition her for help," Marcellus said thoughtfully. "But that's at least a month's travel, through dangerous territory."

"Then there's the Druidic gods," said Livia. "Technically, it's death to have any dealings with them, under Roman law, but this is the Nightside, so . . . How much money have you got?"

"Enough," I said, hoping it was true.

"The Druid shamans are powerful magic-users," said Marcellus. "Especially outside the cities, but they're a vicious bunch, and treacherous with it."

"We can look after ourselves," said Suzie.

"What would they want for helping us?" I said.

"An arm and a leg," said Marcellus. "Possibly literally. Very keen on live sacrifice, when it comes to granting boons, your Druidic gods. Can you think of anyone you wouldn't much mind handing over to the Druids, for ritual torture and sacrifice?"

"Not yet," said Suzie.

Livia shrugged. "Most of the gods or beings will want payment in blood or suffering, your soul, or someone else's."

"I suppose . . . there's always Herne the Hunter," Marcellus said doubtfully.

"Yes!" I said, slamming my hand down on the bar again, and then wished I hadn't, as something sticky clung to it as I pulled my hand back again. "Of course, Herne the Hunter! I'd forgotten he was here, in this time."

"Herne?" said Suzie. "That scruffy godling who hangs around Rats' Alley with the rest of the homeless?"

"He's a Power, here and now," I said. "A Major Power, drawing his strength from the wild forests of old England, and all the creatures that live in it. He was, or more properly will be, Merlin's teacher. Oh yes . . . He's got more than enough power to help us out."

"If you can convince him," said Livia.

"I can convince anyone," said Suzie.

"Where can we find Herne the Hunter?" I said.

"He lives out in the wild woods, far and far from the cities and civilisation of Man," said Marcellus. "No-one finds him unless he wants to be found, and those that do mostly regret it. But my wife and I have had dealings with Herne and his Court in the past. We can take you right to him."

"We could," Livia said quickly. "But what's in it for us? What will you give us to take you right to Herne the Hunter?"

Suzie and I looked at each other. "What do you want?" I said resignedly.

"Our freedom," said Marcellus. "Freedom from this awful place, our awful lives, our undeserved slavery."

"We will do anything, to be free again," said Livia. "And then we shall have our revenges on all those who scorned and mocked us!"

"Free us from our chains," said Marcellus. "And we will do anything for you."

"Anything," said Livia.

"All right," I said. "You've got a deal. Take us to Herne, and I'll break you free from whatever geas holds you here."

Livia sneered at me. "It's not that simple. The old witch Lilith is powerful; can you stop her sending agents after us, to reclaim her property?"

"She'll listen to me," I said. "She's my mother."

Marcellus and Livia looked at me blankly for a moment, then they both backed away from me, the same way you'd back away from a snake you'd just realised was poisonous. There was shock in their faces, and fear, and then . . . something else, but they turned away to mutter urgently to each other before I could figure out what it was. Suzie looked at me thoughtfully.

"I thought we'd agreed it would be a bad idea for this period's Lilith to find out you were here?"

"Give me a break," I said quietly. "I'm thinking on my feet here. I can find a way to break their geas; that's what I do, remember? But I don't think I trust either of this pair further than I could throw a wet camel, certainly not enough to let them in on all my little secrets, okay?"

Marcellus and Livia approached us again. Their faces were carefully blank, but their body language was decidedly wary.

"We'll take you to Herne," said Marcellus. "We've decided that if anyone can get us our freedom and our revenge, it's you. But know this: Herne the Hunter is not the easiest of gods to deal with. He cares nothing for mortal men and women. He has been known to use them as prey in his hunts. And he hates everything that comes from the cities."

"Don't worry," I said. "We have something we can use to buy his help."

"We do?" said Suzie.

"Knowledge of what the future holds for him," I said. "If he listens, it's possible he could change what fate currently holds in store for him. But he probably won't; gods always think it can't happen to them. But . . . I never met a Being yet who could resist knowing the future."

"Can I point out that Poseidonis didn't handle this knowledge at all well?"

"Well, yes; but Poseidonis is a dick."

"And a big one, too," Suzie said solemnly.

"If you two have quite finished muttering together," Livia said severely, "may I point out that my husband and I are prevented from leaving this bar until either our replacement shift arrives, or the bar is empty?"

"No problem," I said. "Suzie?"

And several shotgun blasts and one shrapnel grenade later, the bar was completely empty.

"What do you mean, we have to ride horses?" said Suzie, scowling ominously.

"Herne the Hunter holds his Court in the wild woods," Marcellus explained patiently. "He never enters the city. So, we have to go to him. And since that involves a lengthy journey, we need horses."

I looked at the four horses Marcellus wanted me to buy. The horse-trader kept bowing and smiling and saying complimentary things about my obvious good judgement, but I faded him out. Marcellus and Livia had chosen these four horses out of the many available, and I wasn't about to show myself up by saying something inappropriate. All I knew about horses was that they had a leg at each corner and which end to offer the sugar lumps to. The horses looked back at me with slow insolence, and the nearest one casually tried to step on my foot. I glared at Marcellus.

"How do I know the trader isn't cheating me over the price?"

"Of course he's cheating you," said Marcellus. "This is the Nightside. But because Livia and I have done business with him before, he's prepared to let us have these horses at a special, only mildly extortionate price. If you think you can do any better, you are, of course, free to haggle for yourself."

"We don't do haggling," Suzie said haughtily. "We tend more to intimidation."

"We noticed," said Livia. "But since we really don't want to attract attention, pay the man and let's get going."

Reluctantly, I handed over more coins from Old Father Time's seemingly bottomless purse. The trader retired, bowing and grinning and scraping all the way, and I knew I'd paid tourist prices. The four of us approached our new mounts. I'd never ridden a horse in my life. It was a big beast, and a lot taller at the shoulder than I'd expected. Suzie glared right into her horse's face, and it actually looked away bashfully. Mine showed me its huge blocky teeth and rolled its eyes meaningfully. Matters became even more complicated when I discovered that in Roman times, horse-riding didn't involve saddles, stirrups, or even bridles. Just a blanket over the horse's back and some very flimsy-looking reins.

"I can ride a motor-bike," said Suzie. "How much harder can this be?"

"I have a horrible suspicion we're about to find out," I said.

Marcellus boosted Livia onto her mount, and then vaulted onto his horse's back like he'd been doing it all his life. Suzie and I looked at each other. Several false starts and one really embarrassing tumble later, the horse-trader provided us with special mounting ladders (for an extra payment), and Suzie and I were up and onto our horses, trying to hold our reins like we looked like we knew what to do with them. It seemed a very long way off the ground. And then suddenly Old Father Time's protective magic kicked in again, and immediately I knew all there was to know about how to ride a horse. I sat up straighter and took up the slack in the reins. The horse settled down, as it realised I wasn't a complete idiot after all, and a quick glance at Suzie showed she was in control, too. I nodded curtly to Marcellus and Livia, and we set off.

It took quite a while to get to the boundary of the city. The Nightside was a big place, even in its early days, and just as before we had to go the long way round, to avoid Timeslips and places where directions were often a matter of opinion. But finally we rounded a corner, and all the buildings stopped abruptly. Ahead of us there were only vast rolling grassy flatlands, stretching away like a great green ocean, with the dark mass of the forest standing out in spiky silhouette on the far horizon, standing proudly against the night sky. Occasional strange lights would move within that dark mass, fleeting and unnatural. The air was still and cold, but pleasantly fresh after the thick smells of the city.

Suzie and I followed Marcellus and Livia as they set out across the grasslands. They set a brisk, steady pace, but though we soon left the city behind, the grassy plain seemed to stretch away forever, untouched and unspoiled in this new young land that wasn't even called England yet. The night was strangely quiet, and there was no sign anywhere of another living thing, but still I couldn't shake the feeling of being observed by unseen, unfriendly eyes. Now and again we'd pass a long burial cairn, standing out among the tall grasses. Piled-up stones marking the resting place of some once-important person, now long forgotten, even their names lost to history. It suddenly occurred to me to look up, and there in the night sky were only ordinary stars and a normal full moon. We had left the Nightside behind with the city.

The dark forest grew steadily larger, spreading across the horizon until it filled our whole view. The horses stirred uneasily as we drew near, and by the time we reached the edge of the forest they were snorting loudly and trying to toss their heads, and we actually had to force them across the forest boundary. They were smarter than we were. The moment we entered the wild woods, I knew we'd come to an alien place, where mortal men did not belong. The trees were bigger and taller than any I had ever seen before, huge and vast from centuries of growth. This was the old forest of old Britain, an ancient primal place, dark and threatening. Moving slowly between the towering trees was like being a small child again, lost in an adult-sized world. A single beaten path led between closely packed trees, often blocked by low-hanging branches we had to brush aside. "No swords, no cutting," Livia whispered. "We don't want to wake the trees."

It was still impossibly quiet, like the bottom of the ocean. No animal sounds, no birds or even insects. The air was heavy with a sharp, musky scent, of earth and vegetation and growing things. And now and again a gusting breeze would bring us the impossibly rich scent of some night-blooming flower. Shafts of shimmering moonlight fell between the trees, or illuminated some natural clearing, somehow always supplying just enough light for us to follow the rough path.

"Do any people live here?" Suzie quietly asked.

"They wouldn't dare," said Livia, just as quietly. "This is a wild place. This is what we build cities against."

"Then who's watching us?" said Suzie.

"The woods," said Marcellus. "And Herne's people, of course. They've been aware of us ever since we crossed the boundary. The only reason they haven't attacked is because they remember me and Livia; and they're curious. They can tell there's something different about you two."

And suddenly, without any warning, there were things moving in between the trees. Moving silently and gracefully, in and out of the moonlight, at the edge of our vision. Things that moved along with us, darting ahead or dropping behind, but always keeping pace. Now and again something would pause in a pool of light, showing itself off, tantalizing us with glimpses. There were bears and giant boars, both long since vanished from the few tame woods remaining in modern England. Huge stags, with massive branching antlers, and grey wolves, long and lean and stark. Animals moved all around us, padding along in unearthly silence, slowly closing in on us, until suddenly I noticed that we'd left the beaten path and were being herded in some new direction. I looked quickly at

Marcellus and Livia, but they didn't seem at all disturbed, or even surprised. Suzie had her shotgun out. I gestured for her to remain calm, but she kept the gun balanced across her lap, glaring suspiciously about her.

Sparkling lights appeared in the darkness up ahead, bright and scintillating glows that danced in patterns too intricate for human eyes; will-o'-the-wisps, with no body or substance, only living moments of gossamer light, all mischief and malice and merry madness. They sang sweetly in no human language, beckoning us on. Birds began to sing and hoot and howl, but again it was no form of bird-song that I had ever heard before. It was a light, mocking, dangerous sound, a clear warning that we were in enemy territory. And once, in a ragged clearing lit eerily bright, I saw a group of elves dancing in silent harmony, moving elegantly through strict patterns that made no sense at all; or perhaps so much sense that mere human minds could not comprehend or contain their true significance. A procession of badgers crossed our path, then stopped to watch us pass by with wise, knowing eyes. I could feel the wild woods coming alive all around us, showing us the shapes of all the life we had passed by and through, unknowing. Life that had hidden itself from us, until then—when it was too late for us to turn back, or escape.

The great trees fell suddenly back and away to both sides, and the horses came to a sudden halt. Their heads hung down listlessly, as though they'd been drugged, or ensorcelled. Ahead of us lay a huge clearing, lit bright as day. Will-o'-the-wisps spun in mad circles, and there were other, stranger shapes also made of nothing but light. They drifted back and forth overhead, huge and graceful, flowing like fluorescent manta rays. And straight ahead of us, on the far side of the clearing, sat the old god Herne the Hunter, and all the monstrous creatures of his wild Court.

Marcellus and Livia swung down from their horses and looked at me expectantly. I looked at Suzie, and we both dismounted. Suzie carried her shotgun casually, but somehow it was always aimed right at Herne. The four of us slowly walked forward across that great open space, Marcellus and Livia leading the way as easily and calmly as though they were going to church. And perhaps they were. With every step I took, I could feel the pressure of watching eyes. We were surrounded. I could feel it. And more than that, I knew that none of us were welcome here, in this ancient, primordial place.

We finally stood before Herne the Hunter, and he looked nothing like the small, diminished thing I'd known in Rats' Alley. That Herne had been many centuries older, shrunken in upon himself, his power lost to the relentless encroachment of man and his civilisation, sweeping across the great green lands of England. This Herne was a Being and a Power, a nature god in his prime and in his element, and his wide, wolfish grin made it clear that we had only been allowed before him by his permission. We were at his mercy. He was still a squat and ugly figure, heavy-boned with an animal's graceful musculature, but his compact body burned with rude good health and godly power. Huge goat's horns curled up from his lowering brow, on his great leonine head, and his eyes held the hot, gleeful malice of every predator that ever was.

There was a force and a vitality in him that burned like a furnace, and simply looking at him you knew he could run all day and all night and never tire, and still tear his prey limb from limb with his bare hands at the end of the hunt. His dark copper skin was covered with hair so thick it was almost fur, and he had hooves instead of feet. He was Herne and Pan and the laughter in the woods. The piper at the gates of dawn, and the bloody-mouthed thing that squatted over endless kills. His unwavering smile showed sharp, heavy teeth, made for rending and tearing. He smelled of sweat and shit and animal musk, and even as we watched he pissed carelessly on the ground between his feet, the sharp acidic smell disturbing the animals around him. They stirred and stamped their feet uneasily. Their god was marking his territory.

This was not the Herne I had known, or expected, and I was afraid of him. His thick scent stirred old atavistic instincts in me. I wanted to fight him, or run from him, or bow down and worship him. I was far from home, in an alien place, and I knew in my blood and my bone and my water that I should never have come here. This was Herne, the spirit of the hunt and the thrill of the chase, the brute animal force that drives the raw red passion of savagery in nature, dripping red in tooth and claw. He was the wildness of the woods and the triumph of the strong over the weak. He was everything we left behind, when we went out of the woods to become civilised.

And I had thought to come here, to trick or intimidate him into granting me a favour? I must have been mad.

Herne the Hunter sat in mocking majesty on a great scalloped Throne fashioned from old, discoloured bones. Furs and scalps hung from the arms of the Throne, some of them still dripping fresh blood. There were arrangements of teeth and claws, too, souvenirs and trophies of past hunts, too many to count. Suzie leaned suddenly in close to whisper in my ear, and I almost jumped out of my skin. Her expression was as cold and controlled as always, and her voice was reassuringly steady.

"Marcellus and Livia seemed to find their way here surprisingly easily," she murmured. "And none of this seems to come as any surprise or shock to them. A suspicious person might almost think they'd been here before. You know; it's still not too late for me to shoot and blow up anything that moves, while we beat a dignified but hasty retreat."

"I think we passed 'too late' when we entered the wood," I said, quietly. "So let's keep the murder and mayhem as a last resort. Besides, we're not going to win Herne's help by shooting up his Court."

"I'm not deaf, you know," snapped Livia. "As it happens, my husband and I have been here before, many times."

"Oh yes," said Marcellus. "Many times. We know the god Herne of old, and he knows us."

"You see, we weren't sold into slavery over business debts," said Livia, smiling a really unpleasant smile. "It was more to do with the nature of our business."

"We sold slaves to Herne," Marcellus said briskly. "Bought them quite legally, at market, then brought them here, into the wild wood, to be prey for the god's Wild Hunt. They do so love to chase human victims, you see. Partly for revenge, for cutting down the forests to build their towns and farms and cities, but mainly because nothing runs better or more desperately than a hunted human. And for a while, all was well. We supplied a demand, for a suitable price, the Court enjoyed their Hunts, and everyone was happy. Well, apart from the slaves, of course, but no-one cares about slaves. That's the point. But one cold winter there was a desperate shortage of slaves, and prices went through the roof. So Livia and I took to abducting people off the streets. No-one who would be noticed or missed—only the weak and the stupid and the poor."

"Only they were missed," said Livia. "And someone made a fuss, there's always some busybody sticking their nose in where it isn't wanted, and the Legions got involved. And they caught us in the act."

"We'd made an awful lot of money," said Marcellus. "And we spent most of it on lawyers, but it didn't do any good. I gave what I considered a very spirited defence before the magistrates, but they wouldn't listen. I mean, it's not as if we ever abducted a Citizen . . ."

"It was an election year," Livia said bitterly. "And so they took everything from us and sold us into slavery. But thanks to you, we now have a chance for freedom, and revenge."

"Revenge," said Marcellus. "On all our many enemies." And they both laughed.

They turned abruptly away from us and bowed low to the god Herne. I thought it diplomatic to bow, too, and even Suzie had the sense to incline her head briefly. The monstrous creatures of Herne's Court were watching us avidly, and I really didn't like the way they looked at us. Livia noticed my interest, and took it upon herself to introduce various members of the Court. Her voice was openly mocking.

Hob In Chains was a huge and blocky humanish figure, a good ten feet tall with huge slabs of muscle and a boar's head. Great curling tusks protruded from his mouth, and his deep-set eyes were fierce and red and mad. Long iron chains fell about his naked malformed body from an iron collar round his thick neck. Man had tried to chain him up long ago, but it hadn't taken. His hands and forearms looked as though they'd been dipped in blood, so fresh it still dripped and steamed on the air. Half a dozen little men with pig's heads squatted on their haunches about his cloven feet, grunting and squealing as they vied for position. They looked at Suzie and me with hungry, impatient eyes, and thick strings of slaver fell from their mouths. Some of them still wore rags and tatters, from the time when they used to be human, before Hob In Chains bent them to his will.

Tomias Squarefoot was quite clearly a Neanderthal. Barely five feet tall, he was nearly as wide, with a squat, hulking body and a face that was neither human nor ape. He had no chin, and his mouth was a wide, lipless gash, but his eyes were strangely kind. He studied Suzie and me thoughtfully, scratching unselfconsciously at his hairy, naked body.

A dozen oversized wolves were pointed out to me as werewolves, and I saw no reason to doubt Livia. Their eyes held a human intelligence, alongside an inhuman appetite. There were liches, so recently risen from their graves that dark earth still clung to their filthy vestments. They had dead white flesh and burning eyes, and hands like claws.

There were ogres and bogles and goblins, and other worse creatures whose very names and natures had been lost to human history. Herne's Court—wild and fierce and deadly. And backing them up, pressing in close from every side, all the wild animals of the forest, gathered together in the only place where they could know a kind of truce. They glared at Suzie and me like a jury, with Herne the hanging judge. The god leaned suddenly forward on his bone Throne, and will-o'-the-wisps circled madly above his horned head like a living halo.

"Marcellus and Livia," said Herne, in a voice warm as summer sun, rough as a goat's bray. "It has been some time since you graced our Court with your mercenary presence. We had heard that you had fallen from grace, in that damned city."

"So we had, wild lord," Marcellus said smoothly. "But we have escaped those who would hold us slaves, and we come to you to restore our fortunes again. My wife and I bring you a gift—two travellers called John Taylor and Suzie Shooter. They think they are here to beg a boon from you."

"They're really not very bright," said Livia.

"Told you so," murmured Suzie. "Who do you want me to shoot first?"

"Hold off a while," I murmured back. "There's still a chance I can talk our way out of this."

"I can always use two more victims for my Hunt," Herne said lazily. "But it will take more than this to restore you to my goodwill."

"But the man is special," said Livia. "He is the son of that old witch Lilith."

And at that the whole monstrous Court rose up as one. Herne surged up out of his Throne, roaring like a great bear, but the savage sound was all but drowned out in the massed braying and howling of his Court. They swept forward, from all sides at once, with reaching hands and claws and fanged mouths, and the hatred in their raised voices beat on the air like a living thing. Suzie didn't even have time to bring her shotgun to bear on a single target before the creatures of the wild were all over her. They tore the shotgun out of her grasp and bore her to the ground, fighting and kicking all the way.

I didn't fare any better. Marcellus hit me expertly behind the ear with a leadweighted cosh even as his wife sold me out to Herne, and I was already on my knees and only half-conscious when the Court hit me from all sides. And for a long time there was only the impact of blows and kicks, and the pain of flesh torn by tooth and claw, and blood spilling thickly onto the dirty ground around me.

Eventually they tired of their sport, or Herne called them off, and the monstrous Court reluctantly drew back, resuming their previous positions around the perimeter of the clearing. They were panting and laughing, and all of them had some of my and Suzie's blood on them. We were hauled to our feet and held roughly in position before the Throne by the pig-headed men. Herne sat regally before us and regarded the damage his people had done with smiling satisfaction. There was blood on my face and in my mouth, and I hurt everywhere I could feel, but my head was already clearing. I'd been worked over by professionals, and this bunch of animals didn't even come close. Let me get my thoughts together, and I'd show this wood god a few tricks he'd never forget. I grinned savagely at Herne, ignoring the blood that spilled down my chin from split lips, and for a moment he looked uncertain. He had made a mistake in not letting his creatures kill me while they could; and I vowed I would make him and them regret such foolishness.

And then I looked across at Suzie, and forgot about everything but her. Her leathers were torn and bloody, and her head hung low. Only the pig-headed men kept her upright. Blood dripped steadily from her damaged face. They'd really done a job on her; because Suzie Shooter would never stop struggling as long as there was an ounce of fight left in her. And so she hung between the pig men like a bloody rag doll, and didn't answer me when I called her name. Marcellus and Livia laughed at me, and the Court laughed, too, in their various ways. I fought madly against the hands holding me; but there were too many of them, and my head hurt too much for me to concentrate enough to work my usual tricks. I couldn't even get my hands near my coat pockets.

They hit me some more, just because they could, and I tried not to cry out. But of course I did. After a while, I realised dully that they had stopped, and Herne was speaking to me. I raised my head and glared at him.

"Lilith's son," said Herne, in a thick gloating voice. "You have no idea how pleased we all are, to have you here. In our presence, in our power. There is no name more hated to us than that of Lilith, who created the city Nightside, in the name of absolute freedom, then banned us from it. Because we are wild, and like to break the things we play with. Because we would tear down the city, and stamp out the human civilisation she favours. There is the city and there is the wild, and only one can triumph. We have always known that. Lilith offered freedom for all, but only on her terms. And only we were wise enough to see the contradiction in that, so only we were banished. Lilith has made us the past, a thing to be passed by, to be superseded and forgotten, and we will have our revenge for that."

"This is all news to me," I said, as clearly as I could. "But then, Mother and I have never talked much. What do you want with me, Herne?"

"To hurt you, and thus by proxy hurt Lilith," said Herne. "You shall be the prey in our Wild Hunt, and we shall chase and harry you all through the wild woods, hurting and killing you by inches, driving you on till you can go no further. And while you grovel before us and beg for mercy, we will tear you apart. Only your head shall be left intact, that we might send it to your mother, as a sign of our regard for her."

"She won't know me," I said. "My death will mean nothing to her."

Herne laughed, and the monstrous creatures of his Court laughed with him.

"This is all about me," I said. "You don't need the woman for this. Let her go . . . and I promise you, I'll give you the best run you've ever seen."

"I think not," Herne said easily. "She is your woman, and so by hurting her we hurt you. So she runs first. And when you see the terrible things we have done to her, it will give you reason to run even faster."

"You know," said Suzie, lifting her beaten face, "I am getting really pissed off with everyone assuming I'm Taylor's woman."

Her elbow shot back into a pig man's stomach, and he fell backwards, squealing loudly. She broke free of the hands that held her and kicked a pig man square in the nuts, actually lifting him off the ground. He folded up and hit the ground without a sound. She grabbed another pig man by the head and twisted it all the way round till the neck snapped loudly. She threw the body aside, and headed for Herne on his Throne. The pig men swarmed around her, trying to drag her down by sheer force of numbers, but she was tall and proud and strong, and would not yield to them. Her burning gaze was fixed on Herne, and step by step she forced her way towards him. I struggled fiercely against the hands holding me, but I was never as strong as Suzie Shooter. And I'd never been as proud of her, as I watched her fight against such odds and refuse to fall. And then the giant Hob In Chains stepped forward, and one of his long iron chains snapped out to wrap itself around Suzie's throat. The cold links tightened cruelly, choking all the breath and strength right out of her, until finally she fell to her knees, and the pig men brought her under control again.

"We really should be leaving now, Lord Herne," said Marcellus, a little nervously. "We have brought you a great gift and beg only a single boon in gratitude."

"You find me in a giving mood," Herne said lazily. "What do you want?"

"Power," said Livia, her voice cold and flat and vicious. "Power to revenge ourselves upon our enemies, to spread fear and suffering against all those who brought us low. Make us into Beings of Power, Lord Herne, that we might join your Court, and prey on Man as you do."

"And is that the wish of both of you?" said Herne.

"It is," said Marcellus, his voice thick with anticipation. "Give us Power, that we might never be parted, and we shall see that all suffer as we have suffered."

"As you wish, so shall it be," said Herne, and the disdainful amusement in his voice really should have warned them. Certainly they sensed something, for all their stupid wide grins, and they moved protectively together. Herne smiled upon them. "You shall be a Power, together forever, my curse to unleash upon Man and his Nightside city."

He laughed, and again his whole monstrous Court laughed with him, a horrible hellish sound. Herne gestured abruptly, and Marcellus and Livia slammed together. They both cried out as their bodies pressed so tight their ribs cracked and broke. Their flesh stirred and became fluid, merging and mixing together. Their faces melted into each other. They were screaming by then, in a single awful voice. And all too soon there before the wood god stood a single joined creature, twice the size of a man, with protruding bones and too many joints, and a horrible mad gaze burning in its single set of eyes. The creature tried to speak with its single mouth, but shock had driven speech from it, for the moment, so it mewled and howled piteously. It fell forward onto all fours, unable to find the balance in its single form, shaking its malformed head again and again.

"Go forth, and be a plague in the Nightside city," said Herne. "All who suffer shall be drawn to you, and from their pain you will find the Power you crave. Hurt and horror and despair will make you strong, and the suffering you cause in turn shall be your vengeance on an unfeeling world. And by my gift, you shall never be parted again. That is what you wanted, after all."

He sat back on his Throne and gestured contemptuously, and the creatures of his Court drove the new-born Power out of the clearing. It scrabbled away on all fours, like an animal, howling and screeching like a mad thing, its long torment just begun. And of all of us there, only I knew that someday it would be called the Lamentation, the Saint of Suffering; and I would be the one to destroy it.

Time has a great fondness for circles.

Hob In Chains stepped forward suddenly, and all eyes went immediately to his great form. He jerked cruelly on his chain, and Suzie was pulled forward to kneel before Herne. All the fight had been beaten out of her, for the moment. Herne looked thoughtfully at the giant with the boar's head and nodded his permission to speak.

"We have this woman for the Hunt," said Hob In Chains. Its voice was grunts and squeals, only made clear to me by Old Father Time's magic, but still it was a harsh and ugly thing to hear; the sound of something that should never have learned to talk. "Let us give the son to Lilith. Trade him back to her. Who knows what she might grant us in return? To spare him torment and death."

There were barks and yells of agreement all around the Court, but most stayed silent, watching Herne for his response. And the wood god was already shaking his great shaggy head.

"Lilith is too proud to yield to anyone, even over her own flesh and blood. She would never give up an ounce of power, no matter what we threatened to do to her son. She'd probably kill him herself rather than have him used against her. No; all that is left to us is a chance to hurt her, by destroying something that belongs to her. To show our contempt for her city and her restraints. A chance to prove that whatever she can create, we can destroy, as we will one day tear down her damned city."

"I really wouldn't bank on her being that upset," I said, in my most reasonable voice. "I'm from the future. Many centuries from now. She doesn't even know I exist yet."

The Court stirred uneasily as they tried to make sense of that, and again they looked to Herne for guidance. They weren't really equipped for abstract thought. Herne rubbed slowly at his bearded chin.

"I hear the truth in your voice . . . but past or present or future, you are still her son. She will recognise that in you."

"All right," I said, thinking quickly on my feet. "How about this—

since I'm from the future, I know what's going to happen to you, Herne. I know your future and your fate; and you really need to know what's coming if you're to stand any chance of avoiding it."

Herne considered this, while his whole Court looked confusedly at each other, then he nodded to the pig men holding me, and they beat me savagely, driving me back down onto my knees, my arms wrapped around my head to protect it. Suzie cried out and tried to reach me, but the iron chain around her throat tightened again, until she had to stop, to breathe again. I retreated deep inside myself, away from the pain. Finally, the beating stopped, and I slowly raised my head to look at Herne. I tried to speak, but all I could do was drool fresh blood from my slack mouth. He laughed in my face.

"Nothing matters as much as the pain and horror you will suffer, at my hands and by my will. Revenge will be mine." He stood up from his Throne, and raised his hands above his horned head. "Let there be a Hunt! A Wild Hunt, of old standing and most ancient tradition!"

The whole Court roared and bayed their approval, stamping their feet and hooves and paws upon the ground, and raising their faces and snouts and muzzles to the full moon above the clearing. There was a new hunger and urgency on the air, hot and heady, pulsing like a giant heartbeat. The fever of the chase was in their blood and in their heads, and they could already taste the bloody slaughter that would end it. They looked at me with hot and happy eyes, and their musky stench was thick on the air.

"We shall start with the woman," said Herne, smiling almost fondly down on Suzie. "A lesser sport, of course, but still a sweet and savage run, to pique our appetite for the main event. Look your last upon your woman, Lilith's son. When you see her next, or what's left of her, you probably won't recognise her."

He laughed at me, savouring the thought of my horror and helplessness, and so did his Court. But I am John Taylor, and I am never helpless. I pushed the pain and weakness out of my head, thinking furiously. I couldn't let this happen. Couldn't let Suzie suffer and die on my behalf. I had sworn to bleed and suffer and die before I let that happen, and I meant every word of it.

"What's the matter, Herne?" I said loudly. "Haven't you got the guts for a real Hunt? Haven't you got the balls to go after Lilith's son, that you have to work up your courage by first hunting a woman?"

The laughter broke off abruptly. The whole Court looked at Herne. He strode forward, raising his hand to strike me, and I laughed right into his face. He paused, suddenly uncertain. I shouldn't have had any fight left in me. I should have been broken in body and spirit by now. But I was Lilith's son, after all . . . and for the first time Herne began to get a feeling for what that really meant. He looked round his Court, to see how they were taking this, and saw uncertainty building in their eyes, too. I had planted a seed in his mind and in theirs, that he was only proposing to hunt Suzie to put off the moment when he would have to raise his courage to hunt me. I'd challenged his pride and his daring, in front of everyone, and he knew he couldn't afford to seem weak in front of his people. In front of Lilith's son.

"Very well," he said finally, and he gestured to the pig men, to hold me on my knees so he could stick his face right into mine. I'd forgotten how short he was. "Forget the woman. She shall die here and now in front of you, and you shall come to envy her swift and easy death, as we drive you screaming and bleeding through the wild woods, ripping and tearing at your hide every foot of the way, drawing every last drop of blood and suffering and horror out of you, killing you by inches . . . until you can't run any more—and then we'll rip you open and eat your entrails as you watch."

"Hell with that," I said flatly. "If you kill her, I won't run. I'll just stand here and die, to spite you, and refuse you the pleasure of the Hunt. No. The deal is, you get me instead of her. You let her live, and I promise you a run like you've never seen before."

Herne scowled. "You think you can make a deal with me? You think you can enforce terms with Herne the Hunter?"

"Of course," I said. "I'm Lilith's son."

He laughed suddenly, and turned away from me to bark orders at his Court. Hob In Chains released his hold on Suzie, and the iron chain slithered back to him like a shining snake. There was much milling about and raised growling voices, as the various creatures argued over orders of precedence, and the proposed route of the Hunt, and other matters I was too tired and too hurting to follow. I concentrated all my strength and will into moving slowly across the clearing on my knees, to join Suzie. It seemed to take forever, but eventually we were kneeling side by side. We leaned against each other, shoulder to shoulder, holding each other up. The pig men watched us carefully, but no-one had given them orders to do anything else. So Suzie and I sat together for a while, comforting each other with our presence, our blood-streaked faces close together.

"Not one of your better ideas, this, Taylor," she said finally.

"I'd have to agree," I said, testing my teeth with the tip of my tongue, to see which ones were loose. "Don't worry. I'll get us out of this. I always do."

"I'm in better shape than I look," Suzie said quietly. "Werewolf blood, remember? My strength's already coming back. All I need is for these swine to take their eyes off me for a moment, and . . ."

"They won't," I said. "They've done this before. And what could you do, anyway? Attack Herne, with one of those daggers you keep in your boots? You wouldn't get within ten feet of him before his creatures dragged you down. You could run; but they'd catch you, and kill you. Eventually."

"I wouldn't run, without you," said Suzie.

"If I work this right, you won't have to run," I said. "I've got a plan."

She smiled, briefly. "You always do, John."

I closed my eyes for a while. I'd never felt so tired, so beaten down. "God, I feel bad, Suzie. I'm sorry I got you into this."

"Stop it, John." She sounded worried, for the first time. "You give up here, and we're both dead."

"I'm all right," I said, forcing my eyes open.

She looked me over, her cold face controlled as ever as she took in the extent of my injuries. "You've looked better, Taylor. I don't think I like the odds on this one. You're in no shape to run before the Wild Hunt. Don't think you'd even necessarily make it out of the clearing. You'd better let me do it. Once the werewolf factor really kicks in, I can outrun anything they send after me."

"No you couldn't," I said. "Anyone else, maybe, but not Herne and his Court. They live for the hunt. You have to let me do this, Suzie. Trust me. I know what I'm doing."

She looked at me for a long while, her face cold as always. "You don't have to do this, John. Not for me."

"Yes, I do," I said.

I couldn't tell her why. I couldn't tell her I was ready to die, to save her from the future I'd seen for her. I couldn't tell her I needed to do this, to prove to myself that I wasn't just the ruthless bastard Tommy Oblivion had named me. To prove I was something more than my mother's son. So I would run, and maybe die, to save her life and my soul.

And besides, I had a plan.

I looked round sharply, as I realised the clearing had suddenly gone quiet. Every animal and creature in the Court had frozen where they were, all the beasts and Beings watching intently as Herne the Hunter and the Neanderthal known as Tomias Squarefoot squared off against each other, glaring unflinchingly into each other's face, neither prepared to give an inch. There was a new tension in the clearing, a clash of wills, and seniority. Herne was scowling fiercely, Squarefoot as calm as ever, but there was an ancient dignity and steadfastness in the Neanderthal that the wood god, for all his power, couldn't quite match.

"I am the oldest here," said Tomias Squarefoot, in a voice slow and steady as a flowing river. "I was here before you, Herne. I walked this land, this forest, long before there was a wood god, or any of the Forces you have gathered around you. I was here before the Nightside. I alone remember when the forest was truly alive, and the trees still talked, with slow, heavy voices. I remember the spirits of stone and water and earth. I have seen all my people die, and vanish, and the rise of Man. You came after Man, wood god, though you prefer not to remember that. I am the oldest here, and I say you have forgotten the way of the Wild Hunt."

"You are old," Herne acknowledged. "But age does not always bestow wisdom. I lead here, not you. I have made the Wild Hunt a thing to be feared, and spoken of in hushed whispers all through the land. And you dare to challenge my directing of the Hunt?"

"You gave the Wild Hunt new strength and power by imposing a stricter structure," Squarefoot said calmly. "You made up the rules that govern it, for the greater pleasure of all who participate in it. You cannot break those rules now, just because your pride has been challenged. For if the master of the Wild Hunt will not follow his own rules, why should anyone else? And then, where would be the point in playing?"

There was a growling murmur of agreement all across the Court. Herne heard it but did not dare acknowledge it.

"What rules have I broken?" he said. "What customs do I flout? I say this Hunt will be run as always, and all rules and customs shall be followed."

"Then the prey must know where he runs, and why," said Squarefoot. "And the prize he may yet win, if he is strong and fast and true. For the prey that runs without thought or hope makes poor prey indeed."

Herne's scowl deepened. "If you're thinking of interfering in this Hunt . . ."

"Of course not," the Neanderthal said calmly. "That would be against the rules. It is your Hunt, Herne. So name the conditions, and the destination, and the prize to be won."

Something like amusement moved through the Court, as the creatures saw how clearly Herne had been herded into a corner, but the sound died quickly away as Herne glared about him. He turned brusquely away from Squarefoot to face Suzie and me. He gestured sharply, and the pig men hauled us up onto our feet. I still felt like hell, but the brief respite had put some strength back into my legs. My head still pounded, but my thoughts were clear again. And my hands were very near my coat pockets. I grinned nastily at Herne. He really should have killed me while he had the chance.

Herne smiled back at me.

"Here are the rules of the Wild Hunt, Lilith's son. You will run, and we will chase you. You will run through the wild wood, in whatever direction you choose, along whatever paths you may find; and if by some miracle you find your way out of the wood, and back to the city, all you have to do is cross the boundary into the city, and you will live, safe from all pursuit. And to add spice to the game, you don't run for your own life but for your woman's life as well. She will be held at the city boundary, under guard. Reach her, and she will be set free. You both will live. But if you fail to reach her, then she will die as slowly and horribly as you. Think about that as you run." His smile widened. "I should perhaps point out that no-one in living memory has ever made it through the wild woods, let alone back to the city."

"But I'm not just anyone," I said, holding his gaze with mine. "I'm John Taylor. Lilith's son. And I'm smarter and craftier and nastier than you'll ever be."

He turned his back on me and stalked away. Suzie looked at me thoughtfully.

"That's your great plan? You run, and if you die I die, too? You look like shit, Taylor. You're in no condition to run any race."

"You heard the bastard," I said. "I have to run. At least now, I have a chance to save both of us. And he doesn't know about my gift, my little tricks, or even the contents of my coat pockets. I've outsmarted brighter things than him and his whole damned Court before this. Don't give them any trouble, Suzie. Let them take you back to the city. Your chances are better there. And then if you get a chance to escape, take it."

"I don't like any of this," said Suzie. "I thought you said you couldn't afford to use your gift in this Time."

"Hell with that," I said. "I'll worry about the consequences of using my gift if and when I survive the Hunt."

"If you die," Suzie said slowly, "I will avenge you, John. I'll kill them all. I will burn down the wild wood and everything in it, in your name."

"I know," I said.

Herne called my name, and I looked around. All the monstrous creatures of his Court had formed into two long lines, facing each other. They grinned and slavered and stomped their feet, showing me their teeth and claws. Some of them had clubs. Herne gestured grandly from his Throne, flanked by Hob In Chains and Tomias Squarefoot.

"And so the Hunt begins. Run the gauntlet, John Taylor, Lilith's son. Pass between your enemies. They won't kill you, not now, but they will shed enough blood for you to leave a clear trail when you run. When you finally get out of the gauntlet, you'll be facing in the direction of the Nightside. Our gift to you, to get you started."

I shuddered, despite myself. They'd tear me up bad, long before I could reach the other end. So . . .

"Some gift," I said. "I'll find my own way."

And I turned my back on the waiting gauntlet and ran in the opposite direction, out of the moonlit clearing and into the darkness of the waiting wood. Behind me, I heard outraged yells and howls, and I grinned. When you're playing a game and the rules are stacked against you, change the rules. I've always been a great believer in lateral thinking.

I plunged through the gloom between the tall trees, leaving the light of the clearing behind me. I'd worry about directions later; for the time being, I simply needed to put some distance between me and my pursuers. I ran steadily, keeping a good pace, careful to preserve what strength and breath I had. For now I was coasting on adrenaline, but I knew that wouldn't last. I hurt all over, but my head was clear. Behind me, I could hear the Hunt starting up, hear the rage and bloodlust in their raised voices. I grinned. Get your opponent angry, and you've already won half the fight. I hoped they wouldn't take their anger out on Suzie . . . No. I pushed the thought aside. Suzie could take care of herself. I had to concentrate on my own problems.

And so I ran, knowing they could run faster but trusting to my wits and my gift and my sheer bloody-minded stubbornness to see me through. I'd beaten worse than this and rubbed their noses in it. The forest air was cool and bracing, and I sucked in great lungfuls of it as I ran. My legs felt strong. My arms hurt, so I folded them across my chest. There was enough light to see where I was going, and the trees were so tightly packed the Hunt wouldn't be able to come at me en masse. I could hear them, drawing closer already. I tried to remember how far it was, back to the city, but the journey in had been on horseback. No. I couldn't afford to think about that. I had to concentrate on the here and now.

I unfolded my arms and scrabbled in my coat pockets, coming up with a disposable flashlight. I turned it on, and light sprang out ahead of me, warm and yellow and comforting. And then I turned it off, because I didn't want to attract attention. My eyes were pretty well adjusted to the gloom. But it might come in handy later, and I was glad I had it. I put the flashlight away and let my fingers wander over other useful objects in my pockets. They really should have searched me thoroughly, but that was something men did, not animals. Or perhaps they didn't care, secure in their overwhelming numbers and savagery. Perhaps they didn't see me as any kind of threat. I grinned unpleasantly. I'd change that.

I slowed my pace, as my breath began to run short. I'd hoped my wind would last longer, but the beatings had really taken it out of me. I pushed on, ignoring the tightening pains in my sides. Huge trees loomed all around me, and I deliberately chose the narrowest ways, so that whatever came after me would have to do it single file. Break up the numbers, and you take away the advantage. Gnarled branches loomed out in front of me all the time, and I had to duck and weave to get past them. Thick roots bulged up out of the ground, always threatening to trip me, and they slowed me down, too. The tightly packed earth was hard and unyielding under my feet, and the impact of every step shuddered up through my legs.

A sudden cry went up behind me, harsh and strident in the night, and something heavy came crashing through the branches, not far behind me. The sounds grew louder, closer. Something had found my scent. Time to break the rules again, to use the advantages they didn't know I had. I fired up my gift. Let my Enemies find me; the Hunt would take care of whatever my Enemies might send after me. And Lilith, present or future . . . was a problem for another time.

It only took a moment for my gift to find me the direction of the city, and I changed course, immediately shutting down my gift again. It was too confusing, to See clearly in the wild wood. In the brief glimpse through my third eye, I had Seen ghosts and phantoms, running frantically along paths that were no longer there, and old vast Beings who had lived in the woods long and long ago, but had since moved on to other places, other worlds. I Saw things I didn't understand, and couldn't hope to, Forces and Powers still abroad in the night, ancient and awful, beyond human comprehension. I think some of them Saw me.

I ran on, slipping as quietly as I could between the great trees, curving around Herne's clearing and back towards the city. According to what I'd Seen with my gift, it was a long way off. I slowed to a jog, to preserve my breath. I grabbed moss and leaves from the trees I passed, and rubbed them over my coat and bare skin, to disguise my scent. I might be a city boy, but I'd been around. I knew a few tricks.

I could hear animals running on both sides of me now, running fast and freely. They weren't even panting hard, the bastards. I stopped abruptly, breathing through my nose to keep silent, and looked carefully around me. There were wolves, dodging in and out of the trees, grey fur shining in the sparse moonlight. Real wolves from their size rather than werewolves, but no less dangerous for that. They stumbled to a halt, as they realised I'd stopped running, and milled back and forth, before and around me. I crouched in the deepest shadows I could find. Grey snouts rose in the air, trying to catch my scent. I stayed very still. There wasn't a trace of wind on the chill night air. The wolves gathered on my left, muzzles to the ground, searching for tracks. I heard fresh sounds on my right and slowly turned my head. Half a dozen huge boars came snuffling loudly through the wood towards me, grunting and tossing their great heads, moonlight gleaming on their vicious curved tusks. So, enemies to my left and to my right. Perfect.

I ran straight forward, deliberately making as much noise as possible. The wolves and the boars came charging forward, each keen to get to me first. I waited till the very last moment, then I slammed to a halt and dived to the ground. And while I lay there with my arms over my head, the wolves and the boars slammed right into each other. Confused by an unexpected attack, they tore blindly at each other. Howls and roars and squeals of pain filled the night air, as wolves and boars forgot all about me in their outrage over being attacked. They savaged each other in a great squabbling mess, while I rose carefully to my feet and slipped quietly away through the shadows.

I didn't even see the bear coming. It suddenly loomed out of the gloom right ahead of me, a huge dark shape against the night, big as a tree. One great clawed paw came sweeping through the air towards me, moonlight gleaming on the vicious claws, and then it slapped me to one side, as casually as that. It was like being hit by a battering ram. I flew through the air and hit the ground hard, before rolling on to slam up against a tree-trunk. The impact knocked all the breath right out of me. My shoulder was on fire, and it felt like half my ribs were cracked, maybe broken. I pulled myself up and set my back against the tree-trunk, fighting to get some air back into my lungs. The bear was already coming for me, snuffling and growling. It lashed out again, and I only dodged it by throwing myself to one side. The vicious claws tore a great chunk out of the tree. I scrambled to my feet and slipped round the other side of the tree. The bear paused, confused because it couldn't see me any more, and I was off and running again. I could feel fresh blood flowing down my left arm from my clawed shoulder, and my whole side was screaming with pain.

The wolves were after me again. They came flying through the shafts of moonlight, grey as ghosts, eyes gleaming brightly. Too many to count, running smoothly as the wind. They streamed ahead of me, then cut in to block my way. I grabbed a sachet of pepper from my coat pocket, tore it open, and threw the whole lot in their faces. They went mad as fire filled their sensitive noses and eyes, and they fell back, yipping and yelping, snapping at the air and at each other, unable to concentrate on anything but the horrid pain in their heads. I ran straight through them. Some snapped and tore at me reflexively, and I cried out despite myself as new pains cut through me, then I was past them and running on, into the night. I gritted my teeth against the hurt, breathing heavily.

I had to force myself on now, to maintain a good pace. I couldn't stop to rest, or see to my wounds. I was leaving a clear blood trail. I could hear the Hunt, crying out in many voices behind me. My breath was coming raggedly, and my whole chest hurt. Damn, I was out of shape. I'd got too used to fighting instead of running for my life. I plunged on, through shadows and moonlight, crashing through branches and sometimes slamming into trees I didn't see in time, following the direction my gift had given me.

And behind came the Wild Hunt.

I ran through a clearing, and a whole crowd of elves watched me pass, incuriously. They were moving slowly in strange patterns, leaving long blue ectoplasmic trails behind them, creating an intricate glowing web. I didn't call out to them for help. Elves have never given a damn for anyone but themselves.

It seemed like the whole wood was alive with howls and cries now, as though every living thing in the night was awake and on my trail. Long-buried instincts made my blood run cold and raised the hackles on the back of my neck. Old, atavistic instincts, from Humanity's distant past, when to be Man was to be hunted. I grinned fiercely. Things had changed since then, and I would show them how much. I'd show them all. I ran on, fighting for breath, ignoring the pain—hate and desperation and stubborn doggedness keeping me going long after exhaustion should have driven me to my knees.

In the next clearing I came to, Hob In Chains was waiting for me, surrounded by his pig men. He stood proud and tall in the shimmering milky light, his great boar's head looking straight at me as I stumbled to a halt on the edge of the clearing. Hob's iron chains rattled noisily as he swung a huge hammer back and forth before him. The thick wooden shaft was easily four feet long, and the head was a solid slab of iron, matted and crusted with old dried blood and hairs. I probably would have had trouble even lifting the thing, but he swung it lazily back and forth as though it was nothing. The giant smiled at me around his huge tusks and grunted loudly, a deep, satisfied sound. The pig men crowded round his legs grunted and squealed along with him, like hogs waiting for the swill to be poured into their trough, held back only by their master's will. They all looked at me hungrily, with nothing in their eyes of the men they'd once been. Hob In Chains moved forward, and they scattered to let him pass. I stood my ground. He knew I wouldn't run. The rest of the Hunt were too close behind me. I had to get through the clearing.

Even so, I think he was a bit shocked when I strode forward, heading straight for him. He hefted his great hammer, grunting greedily as he waited for me to come within range. I grinned at him, which I think unsettled him even more. He was only used to prey that screamed and sobbed and begged for mercy. He decided not to wait, and stamped towards me, raising his great hammer above his head with both hands. The pig men fell back to give him room, squealing hysterically. And I used my oldest trick, the one that takes bullets out of guns, to take all the air out of their lungs. The pig men collapsed as one, hitting the ground like so many hairy sacks. Hob In Chains staggered backwards, dropping his hammer as though it had suddenly become too heavy for him. Then he dropped to his knees, his great boar's head gaping stupidly. I walked right past him and didn't even look back as I heard him crash to the ground.

But the clattering of his iron chains gave me a new idea, and I stopped and looked round. The chains would make good weapons, and I could use every advantage I could steal. I went back to kneel beside Hob In Chains and tugged at one of the long iron chains, but it was firmly fixed to the collar round his throat. They all were. I could have wept with frustration. I lurched to my feet and kicked Hob In Chains in the ribs.

And Hob In Chains rose up. He lurched unsteadily to his feet, snorting and grunting, shaking his boar's head as he sucked air back into his great lungs. I hit him in the gut with all my strength, but all I did was hurt my hand. He reached out for his hammer, and I kicked him in the balls, putting all my strength behind it. The air shot out of Hob In Chains' lungs for a second time, and his beady eyes squeezed shut as he sank back down onto his knees again, forgetting all about his hammer. And I was off and running again.

The Hunt was close behind me still. Creatures and beasts came darting in, now from one side, then from another, to bite and claw and tear at me. Not even trying to bring me down, not yet. Just doing their bit to hurt and harry me, and enjoy the Hunt. Some of them I dodged, some I struck out at, but all of them left their mark on me. I didn't even try not to cry out any more, simply concentrated on keeping moving. I was deathly tired, stumbling and staggering as much as running, blood soaking my tattered trench coat. Blood and sweat mixed as they ran down my face, leaving the taste of copper and salt in my mouth. My left arm hung almost uselessly at my side, clawed open from shoulder to wrist by something I didn't even see coming. There was laughter in the woods, all around me. I hurt so bad it flared up every time my foot hit the hard ground, but my head stayed clear. Anywhere else, so much pain and accumulated damage would have brought me to my knees long ago, but I wasn't only running for myself. I was running for Suzie.

The Wild Hunt swarmed all around me, taking it in turns to dart in and hurt me some more, just enough to spur me on. And at the head of his Hunt, riding his glorious moon stallion ahead and to my left, Herne the Hunter. Laughing as he watched his prey suffer. His horse was made of pure moonlight, a glorious luminous creature that carried Herne effortlessly on. A pack of werewolves followed in his wake, howling with unnervingly human voices.

I had no idea how long I'd been running. How far I'd come, or how far I still had left to go. It felt like I'd always been running, like one of those nightmares where you flee forever and never get anywhere. I was staggering along now, gasping for breath, fighting to keep putting one foot in front of the other. Every breath hurt, in my chest and in my sides and in my back. I couldn't even feel my feet or my hands any more. I no longer lashed out at the beasts that attacked me, saving my strength.

I had a plan.

Herne the Hunter finally steered his moon stallion right in front of me, blocking my path, so I had to stop. I crashed to a halt, breathing so hard I couldn't hear anything else. I could still see him laughing, though. Hear the rest of the Hunt closing in around me. Herne leaned over his mount's shoulder to address me, and I ached to wipe the smile off his face. Dark shadows filled the woods around me, milling restlessly, impatient for the kill, held back only by Herne's will. He leaned right over, pushing his face close to mine, so I would be sure to hear his words.

"You ran well, for a mortal. Led us a merry chase, to our great entertainment. But now it's over. The Hunt ends as it always has and always will, in the slow, horrid death of the prey. Be sure to scream loudly, so perhaps your woman will hear you and know something of the fate that awaits her, too."

"She's not my woman," I mumbled through slack bloody lips. "Suzie can take care of herself. And just maybe, she'll take care of you, too."

Herne laughed in my face. "Die now, Lilith's son, alone and in torment, and know that everything you've done and endured has been for nothing. Your woman will suffer and die, just like you. After we've had our fun with her."

He leaned right over to spit these last words directly into my face, and at last he was close enough for me to grab him with both bloody hands, and haul him right off his glowing moon stallion. Overbalanced, he toppled off easily, and I slammed him to the ground. I hit him once in the mouth, for my own satisfaction, then used the last of my strength to grab the moon stallion's enchanted bridle and pull myself up onto his back. The stallion reared up on its hind legs, pawing at the air and tossing its head, but I had the bridle in my hands, and when I pointed the stallion's head in the direction of the city, the creature had no choice but to carry me there. I drove it mercilessly on, faster and faster, and we sped through the wild wood like a dream of motion, swerving effortlessly between the trees, never slowing or stopping, while I hung on desperately with all that was left of my hoarded strength.

Behind me I could hear the cheated howls of the Wild Hunt, and Herne crying out in rage and shame, and I laughed breathlessly.

I urged the moon stallion on to even greater speeds as the Hunt pursued us, and we fled through the night, the pounding hooves hardly seeming to touch the ground. The whole of the Wild Hunt was on my trail, but they were a long way back. I slumped forward over the neck of the moon stallion, horribly tired, but my hands had closed around the controlling enchanted bridle in a grip that only death would loosen. I'd snatched a second chance from the very edge of defeat, and I was going home—to the city, and the Nightside, and Suzie Shooter.

The great trees flashed past me on either side, seemingly as insubstantial as a dream, come and gone impossibly fast. And still the Wild Hunt followed. Until suddenly the tall trees fell away behind me, and the moon stallion was racing across the open grasslands. I slowly raised my aching head and saw the lights of the city burning up ahead. I risked a look back over my shoulder. All the monstrous creatures of Herne's Court were pouring out of the forest, so caught up in the bloodlust of the chase that they would even leave the safety of the wild wood to come after me. I couldn't see Herne. Perhaps he was having trouble keeping up, on foot. I grinned, then I coughed, and fresh blood spilled down my chin. Damn. Not a good sign. My head was swimming madly, and I could barely feel the moon stallion beneath me. For the first time, I wondered if there was enough left in me to hang on until we reached the city. But in the end I did, because I had to. Suzie Shooter was waiting for me.

The moon stallion pounded on, flashing across the grasslands like a streak of light, the city and its lights growing steadily before me. And almost before I knew it, we had crossed the boundary into the city, into streets and buildings, stone and plaster, and the moon stallion crashed to a halt. It was of the wild wood and would go no further, bridle or no. For a long moment, I sat there. I'd made it. The thought repeated slowly in my head. I looked down at my hands, slick with my own blood, but still gripping the enchanted bridle so firmly the knuckles showed white. I forced my fingers open, released the bridle, then slid off the side of the stallion and fell to the ground. And the moon stallion turned immediately and raced back across the city boundary, across the grasslands and back to the wild wood, where it belonged. I sat up slowly and watched it go, bright and shining as a departing dawn. I sat there, my head nodding, my hands in my lap, broken and bloodied. The whole of the front of my trench coat was a ragged bloody mess, but I was too deathly tired to feel most of my hurts. I didn't seem to have the strength to do anything, and that worried me vaguely, but I had made it back to the city; and that was all that mattered. I watched impassively as Herne the Hunter came running across the grasslands. He seemed so much smaller, so much less, outside the forest. The rest of his monstrous Court came after him, but they seemed to be hanging back. I smiled slowly. Let them come. Let them all come. I'd beaten him. Suzie was safe now.

I was cold, so cold. I started to shiver and couldn't stop. I wondered if I was dying.

Footsteps approached behind me, but I didn't have enough strength left to turn and look. And then Suzie Shooter was kneeling beside me, free and unguarded. I tried to smile for her. She looked me over, and made a low, shocked sound.

"Oh God, John. What have they done to you?"

"It's not as bad as it looks," I said, or thought I said. More blood spilled down my chin as my lips split open again. It was only a small hurt after so many worse ones, but it was the last straw, and I started to cry. Just from shock and weariness. I'd given all I had to give, and there was nothing left. My whole body was shaking and shuddering now, from simple exhaustion. And Suzie took me in her arms and held me to her. And bad as I felt, I knew how much it took for her to be able to do that. She rocked me slowly, my head resting against her leather-clad shoulder, while she made soothing, hushing noises.

"It's all right, John. It's all over. I'm free, and you're going to be fine. Find you a sorcerer, get you fixed up good."

"I thought you were under guard here," I said, slowly and distinctly.

She snorted loudly. "Beat the shit out of them the moment I was safely back in the city. There's no-one left here to hurt us."

"I knew you could look after yourself," I said. "But I couldn't take the risk . . . of being wrong."

Suzie sniffed. "Bloody pig men. You wouldn't believe how many times they felt me up on the way here. Smelled really bad, too. Couldn't kill them fast enough. Maybe we'll have a barbecue, later?"

"Sounds good," I said. "I'm cold, Suzie. So cold."

She held me tighter, but I could barely feel it. "Hang on, John. Hang on."

"Journeys end . . ."

"In lovers' meeting?" said Suzie, her cheek against my forehead.

"Maybe," I said. "If only we'd had more time . . ."

"There will be time for many things . . ."

"No. I don't think so. I'm dying, Suzie. I wish . . ."

She said something, but it couldn't hear it over the roaring in my head. I could see the blood running out of me, but everything was disappearing into darkness as the world slipped slowly away from me. I was ready to die; if it meant the future I'd seen for Suzie, and the Nightside, might not happen after all.

"I saved you," I said.

"I knew you would," she said. "I knew they'd never catch you."

That wasn't what I meant, but it didn't matter.

Then I felt her whole body tense as she looked up sharply. I pushed the darkness back through a sheer effort of will and lifted my head to look. And there before us was Herne the Hunter, standing on the other side of the city boundary, his face dark with rage. His Court was spread out behind him, keeping well back. Herne actually danced with rage in front of me, driven half out of his mind at losing.

"You cheated!" he screamed at me, spittle flying on the air with the force of his words. "You didn't run the gauntlet! You used tricks and magics! You stole my lovely moon stallion! Cheat! Cheat!"

I grinned at him even though it hurt. "Told you I was smarter than you. All that matters is I won. I got here. You and your whole damned Court couldn't stop me. I beat you, Herne, so go away and pick on someone smaller than yourself."

"You didn't beat me! No-one beats me! You cheated!" Herne was almost crying by then with the strength of his emotions, and his Court stirred uneasily behind him. He shook a gnarled fist at me. "No-one wins unless I say they win! You're dead, you hear me? I'll drag you out of there and back into the woods, and then, and then . . . I'll do such terrible things to you!"

Tomias Squarefoot stepped forward, and Herne turned viciously to glare at him. The Neanderthal stood calmly before the wood god, and his voice was cold and unmoved. "You cannot pursue them any further, Herne. They are in the city now, and beyond our reach. By the rules of your own Hunt, they are safe from you."

"I am the god of the wild places! Of the storm and the lightning! I am the glory of the hunt and the wolf who runs and the antlers on the rutting stag! I am the power of the wild wood, and I will not be denied!"

"He ran well and bravely," said Squarefoot, and some of the Court actually grunted and growled in agreement behind him. "He won, Herne. Let it go."

"Never!"

"If you do this," Squarefoot said slowly, "you do it alone."

"Alone then!" spat Herne, turning his back on them all, and he wouldn't even look round when Tomias Squarefoot went back to join the Court, and they all headed back across the grasslands, to the wild wood, where they belonged. Herne leaned slowly forward, as though testing the strength of some unseen, unfelt barrier, his curling goat's horns trembling with anticipation. His eyes were fierce and staring, and more than a little mad.

Suzie put me carefully to one side and stood up to place herself between Herne and me. They'd taken her shotgun, so she drew the two long knives from her boot tops. She stood tall and proud, and it looked like it would take the whole damn world to bring her down. Herne regarded her craftily, his shaggy head cocked slightly to one side, like a bird.

"You can't stop me. I'm a god."

"You wouldn't be the first god I've killed," said Suzie Shooter. "And you're on my territory now."

It might have been a bluff, or knowing Suzie, maybe not, but either way it did me good to hear her say it with such scorn and confidence. And I discovered I was damned if I'd sit there and let her face the threat alone. I forced myself up onto one knee, then onto my feet. I moved unsteadily forward to stand beside Suzie. I was swaying, but I was up. If I was going out, I was going to do it on my feet.

"Lilith's son," Herne whispered. "Child of the city and hated civilisation. You would wipe away all the woods and all of the wild. I'll see you dead even if it damns me for all time."

He stepped forward, and Suzie and I braced ourselves to meet the fury of the wood god. And that was when a dark-haired man in a long flowing robe, carrying a long wooden staff, appeared out of nowhere to stand between us and Herne. Suzie actually jumped a little, and I had to grab her arm to steady myself. Herne held his ground, snarling uncertainly at the newcomer, who slammed his staff into the ground before Herne. It stood there, alone and upright, quivering slightly.

"I am the Lord of Thorns," said the newcomer. "Newly appointed Overseer of the Nightside. And you should not be here, Herne the Hunter."

"Appointed by who?" snapped Herne. "By that new god, the Christ? You have his smell on you. I was here before him, and I shall hold sway in the woods long after he has been forgotten."

"No," said the Lord of Thorns. "He has come, and nothing shall ever be the same again. I have been given power over all the Nightside, to see that agreements are enforced. You set up the rules of the Wild Hunt, and so are bound by them. You invested your own power in the Hunt, to make it the significant thing that it is, and so it has power over you. You cannot enter here."

"No! No! I will not be cheated out of my prey! I will have my revenge! I will feast on his heart, and yours!"

Herne grabbed at the Lord of Thorns' standing staff, to tear it out of the ground and perhaps use it as a weapon; but the moment he touched it, the ground shook, and bright light surged up, and the wood god cried out despairingly in pain and shock and horror. He fell writhing to the ground, curled up into a ball, and sobbed at the feet of the Lord of Thorns, who looked down on him sadly.

"You did this to yourself, Herne. You are of the city now, by your own act, cut off from the woods and the wild places, only a small fraction of what you once were, now and forever."

"I want to go home," said Herne, like a small child.

"You can't," said the Lord of Thorns. "You chose to come into the city, and now you belong here."

"But what am I to do?"

"Go forth and do penance. Until finally, perhaps, you can learn to make your peace with the civilisation that is coming."

Herne snarled up at the Lord of Thorns, with a touch of his old defiance, and then the broken god, smaller and much diminished, crept past the Lord of Thorns and disappeared into the streets of the city.

I was watching him go, when suddenly I found I was lying on the ground. I didn't remember falling. I was tired, and drifting, and everything seemed so very far away. I could hear Suzie calling my name, increasingly desperately, but I couldn't find the strength to answer her. She grabbed me by the shoulder to try and sit me up, but my body was so much dead weight, and I couldn't help her. I thought, *So this is dying. It doesn't seem so bad. Maybe I'll get some rest, at last.*

Then the Lord of Thorns knelt beside me. He had a kind, bearded face. He put his hand on my chest, and it was like my whole body got jump-started. Strength and vitality slammed through me like an electric charge, driving out the pain and weariness, and I sat bolt upright, crying out loud at the shock and joy of it. Suzie fell back on her haunches, squeaking loudly in surprise. I laughed suddenly, so glad to be alive. I scrambled up onto my feet, hauling Suzie up with me, and I hugged her to me. Her body started to tense up, so I let her go. Some miracles take longer to work out than others.

I checked myself over. My trench coat was a thing of rags and tatters, mostly held together by dried blood, but all my wounds were gone, healed, as though they had never been. I was whole again. I looked blankly at the Lord of Thorns, and he smiled and bowed slightly, like a stage magician acknowledging a clever trick.

"I am the Overseer, and it is my job and privilege to put things right, where a wrong has been committed. How do you feel?"

"Bloody marvellous! Like I could take on the whole damned world!" I looked down at my tattered coat. "I don't suppose . . ."

He shook his head firmly. "I'm the Overseer, not a tailor."

I turned and smiled at Suzie, and she smiled back. The scratches and bruises were gone from her face, though the scars remained. "You should smile more," I said. "It looks good on you."

"Nah," she said. "It's bad for my reputation."

We looked back at the Lord of Thorns, as he coughed meaningfully.

"It is my understanding that you seek to travel further back in Time, to the very creation of the Nightside itself. Is that correct?"

"Yes," I said. "How did . . ."

"I know what I need to know. Comes with the job. I am here to help, after all. That's what the Church of the Christ is supposed to be about. Helping, and caring, and teaching others to take responsibility for their own actions."

"Even in a place like this?" said Suzie.

"Especially in a place like this," said the Lord of Thorns.

He slammed his long wooden staff against the ground once more, and the whole world flew away from us, as we dropped back into Time's river, sweeping back into Yesterday.

ELEVEN

Angels, Demons, and Mommie Dearest

This time it didn't feel like falling through Time but more like being flung from a catapult. A rainbow exploded around us, punctuated by exploding galaxies and the cries of stars being born, while from all around came the screaming and howling of Things from Outside, crying *Let us in! Let us in!* in languages older than the worlds. Suzie Shooter and I finally dropped out of the chronoflow and back into Time, slamming back into the world like a bullet from a gun. Breathing harshly like new-born children, we looked around us. We'd materialised standing among the trees at the edge of a great forest, looking out over a huge open clearing. The clear night sky was full of everyday stars, and the full moon was no bigger than it should be. Wherever or whenever we were, the Nightside hadn't happened yet.

Yet the clearing lying vacant and open before us, so vast its far side was practically on the horizon, was clearly no natural thing. Its edge was too sharp, too distinct, cutting through some of the surrounding tree-trunks like a razor's edge, leaving half trees with their insides laid bare, oozing clear sap like blood. The clearing itself held only dark earth, bare and featureless. Its making had definitely been unnatural; raw magics were still sparking and spitting and crackling on the air, the last discharging remnants of a mighty Working. Someone had made acres of forest disappear in a moment, and I had a pretty good idea who.

The forest around and behind us was dark and foreboding, with massive trees reaching up to form an interlaced canopy, like the intricate ceiling of some natural cathedral of the night. The air was cool and still, and thick with the heavy scents of slow growth. I could almost feel the great green power of the dreaming wood, which had stood for thousands of years and never known the touch of Man, or his cutting tools. This was old Britain, ancient Britain, the dark womb from which we all sprang.

And suddenly I was back running between the trees again, with Herne and his Wild Hunt howling triumphantly at my back. Terrible memories of pain and horror surged through me, and I swayed on my feet. I had to put a hand out to the nearest tree and lean on it to steady myself, as my knees threatened to buckle under me. I was shuddering all over, and I could feel my heart slamming painfully fast in my chest. No-one had ever hurt me so deeply, terrorized me so completely, as Herne and his monstrous Court. I'd won, but he had left his mark on me. Maybe forever. I made myself breathe slowly and deeply, refusing to give in. One of my greatest strengths has always been my refusal to be beaten by anyone or anything, even myself. My head slowly came up, my face dripping with sweat, and Suzie Shooter stepped in close beside me and put a comforting hand on my shoulder. The sheer unexpectedness of this pushed everything else out of my head, but I was careful not to react or even turn around too quickly. I didn't want to frighten her off. I looked round slowly, and our eyes met. Her face was as cold and controlled as ever, but we both knew what a big effort this was for her. She managed a small smile, then, seeing that I was myself again, she took her hand away and looked out into the clearing. The gesture was come and gone, but of such small steps are miracles made.

"How far back have we come, this time?" said Suzie, in her usual calm voice. "When is this?"

"I don't know," I said, still looking at her rather than the clearing. "But it felt a hell of a lot further than a few hundred years. If I had to guess, I'd say thousands . . . thousands of years. I think we're back before there were any cities, any towns, any gatherings . . ."

Suzie scowled. "Iron Age?"

"Further back even than that. I think we've arrived in a time before Man even appeared, as we would recognise him. Listen."

We stood close together, listening. The huge and mighty forest was full of the sounds of life—of birds and animals and other things, crying out in the night. The sound of hunters and their prey, up in the air and down on the ground, sometimes crashing through the undergrowth, snorting and grunting. Slowly we turned and looked back, and as our eyes adjusted to the gloom, we could see things moving cautiously in the shadows, observing us from a safe distance. Suzie drew a flare from inside her leather jacket, lit it, and threw it some distance into the trees ahead of us. The sharp crimson light was briefly dazzling, and all around us we could hear the beasts of the forest retreating into the safety of the dark. But there were other sounds now, new movements. Suzie drew her shotgun from its holster on her back.

The light from the flare was already dying down, but I could just make out strange shapes moving on the very edge of the light, large and powerful things, drifting eerily between the trees. I could feel their presence more than see them. Their shapes were huge, alien, almost abstract; and yet still I knew they belonged in this place more than I did. They were Forces and Powers, old life in an old land, barely material as yet, life in its rawest forms.

"What the hell are they?" whispered Suzie. "I can barely make them out, as though they're only just there . . . Nothing that lives looks like that . . . It's as though they haven't decided what they are yet."

"They probably haven't," I said, just as quietly. I really didn't want to attract the attention of such wild, unfocussed Beings. "These are the first dreams and nightmares of the land, given shape and form. I think in time . . . these forms will eventually define themselves into elves and goblins and all the fantastic creatures of the wild wood. Some will become gods, like Herne. All this will come with the rise of Man, of course. I think maybe these things need the belief and imagination of Man to give them fixed shapes and natures. Man's fears and needs will distil these Beings and Powers into definite shapes; and soon they will forget they were ever anything else. And they will prey on Man and serve him, as he worships and destroys them . . ."

"All right, you're getting creepy now," said Suzie.

The last of the flare's light flickered and went out, and the old deep dark of the forest returned. I couldn't see or even sense the abstract Forces any more, and though I strained my ears, all I could hear was the natural course of bird and animal, going about their nightly business. Reluctantly, I turned and looked out at the clearing again. Suzie turned and looked, too, but she didn't put away her shotgun. Moonlight lit the vast clearing bright as day, but though the open space was still and quiet, there was a feeling of anticipation on the air, as though some curtain was about to rise on a brand-new show.

"Lilith did this," I said. "And from the feel of it, not long before we arrived. This is where she will create and place her Nightside. Not far from here is undoubtedly a river that will someday be called the Thames. And men will come here and build a city called London . . . I wonder what form Lilith's creation will take, before Man invades it and rebuilds it in his own image?"

"How many living things did Lilith destroy when she made this clearing?" said Suzie, unexpectedly. "How many animals, stamped out in a moment, how many ancient trees, blasted into nothing, to serve her purpose? I don't care much, but you can bet good money she cared even less."

"Yeah," I said. "That does sound like Mommie Dearest. She never cared who she hurt, to get her own way."

"Why didn't she create the Nightside immediately?" said Suzie, suspicious as always. "Why stop at the clearing? Is she waiting for something?"

I considered the point. "It could be . . . that she's waiting for an audience."

Suzie looked at me sharply. "For us?"

"Now that is a disturbing thought . . . No. How could she know we'd be here?"

Suzie shrugged. "She's your mother. She's Lilith. Who knows what she knows or how she knows it?" She scowled at me, as another thought struck her. "We only got here because the Lord of Thorns used his power to send us here. How are we supposed to get back to our own time, assuming we survive whatever appalling thing happens next?"

"Good question," I said. "Wish I had a good answer for you. Let's wait and see if we do survive, and worry about it then. We have more than enough to worry about as it is." Then it was my turn to look at her thoughtfully, as something new struck me. "Suzie . . . I think we need to talk. About us. Right now."

Suzie looked straight back at me, not giving me an inch. "We do?"

"Yes. The odds are that we're not going to survive whatever comes next. I've always known that. It's why I didn't want you along on this case. But, here we are, and things have changed between us. So, if we're ever going to say anything, anything that matters, we need to say it now. Because we may never get another chance."

"We're friends," said Suzie, in her cold, controlled voice. "Isn't that enough?"

"I don't know," I said. "Is it?"

"You've got closer to me . . . than anyone," Suzie said slowly. "I never thought I'd ever let anyone get that close. Never thought I'd want anyone to. You . . . matter to me, John. But, I still couldn't . . . be with you. In bed. Some scars go too deep, to ever heal."

"That isn't what we're talking about," I said gently. "What matters is you, and me. It's a miracle we've made it this far, really."

She considered me for a long moment, with her scarred face and her single cold blue eye and her unyielding mouth. I didn't think she even knew she was cradling her shotgun to her chest, like a child, or a lover. When she finally spoke, her voice was as cold as ever. "My new face doesn't bother you? I never cared about being pretty, but . . . I know what I must look like. The outside finally matches the inside."

"You said it yourself, Suzie," I said, as lightly as I could. "We monsters have to stick together."

I leaned forward, slowly and very carefully, and Suzie watched me like an animal of the wild, that might turn and run at any moment. When our faces were so close that I could feel her breath on my mouth, and she still hadn't moved, I kissed her gently on her scarred cheek. I kept my hands by my sides. The ridged scar tissue of her cheek was hard and unyielding. I pulled back, looked into her cold blue eye, then kissed her very gently on the mouth. Her lips barely moved under mine, but she didn't back away. And finally, slowly, she put her arms around me. She held me only lightly, as though she might pull away at any moment. I moved my mouth back from hers, pressed my cheek against her scarred face, and put my arms around her, just as lightly. She sighed, just a little. Her leather jacket creaked quietly under my arms. She held me for as long as she could stand it, then let go and stepped back. I let her go. I knew better than to try and go after her. I knew she still had her shotgun in one hand, even if she didn't. She looked at me with her cold eye and her cold expression, and nodded briefly.

"You know I love you, right?" I said.

"Oh sure," she said. "And I care for you, John. As much as I can."

And then we both looked round sharply. The whole forest had gone quiet, and there was a new feeling on the air. Just for a moment everything was so still I could hear the rasp of my own breathing, feel the beating of my heart. Suzie and I looked out into the clearing, our attention drawn to the open space like beasts in the wild sensing a coming storm. There was a sound. A sound on the air, but not of it, coming from everywhere and nowhere. It filled the whole world, filled my mind, and it was not a natural sound. It was the cry of something being born, of something dying, an emotion and an experience and an ecstasy beyond human knowledge or comprehension. The sound rose and rose, growing louder and more piercing and more inhuman, until Suzie and I had to clap our hands over our ears to try and keep it out, and still the sound rose and rose, louder and louder, until it became unbearable; and still it rose. Finally, mercifully, it rose beyond our ability to hear it, and Suzie and I were left shaking and shuddering, breathing harshly and shaking our heads as though trying to clear something out. I couldn't hear anything, even when Suzie spoke to me, and we both looked out into the clearing again. Something was going to happen. We could feel it. We could still feel the sound, feel it in our bones and in our souls.

And then Lilith was suddenly *there,* standing in front of the trees at the edge of the clearing, perhaps as little as twenty feet from where Suzie and I stood watching. The sound was gone. Lilith had made her entrance. She stood staring intently out at the clearing she'd made, her dark eyes fixed and unblinking. Suzie and I silently stepped further back into the dark of the forest, concealing ourselves in the deepest shadows. Just to see Lilith was to be scared of her. Of the power that burned in her, like all the stars in all the galaxies. She might have been created to be Adam's wife, but she'd come a long way since then.

She hadn't simply appeared. It was as though Lilith had stamped or imprinted herself directly onto reality, by sheer force of will. She was there now because she chose to be, and somehow she seemed *realer* than anything else in the material world. She looked . . . pretty much as I remembered her, from the last time I'd seen her. In Strangefellows bar, at the end of my last case. Just before everything went to hell.

She was too tall and almost supernaturally slender, the lines of her bare body so smooth they looked like they'd been streamlined, for greater efficiency. Her hair and her eyes and her lips were jet-black, and together with her pale, colourless skin, she looked very much like a black and white photograph. Her face was sharp and pointed, with a prominent bone structure and a hawk nose. Her dark mouth was thin-lipped and far too wide, and her eyes were full of a dark fire that could burn through anything. The expressions that came and went on her face were in no way human. She looked . . . wild, elemental, unfinished. She wore no clothes. She had no navel.

I remembered the man called Madman, who Saw the world and everything in it more clearly than most, saying that the Lilith we saw and experienced was only a limited projection into our reality of something much greater and more complex. We only saw what we could stand to see. He also said that the human Lilith was really just a glorified glove puppet that she manipulated from afar.

Lilith. Mother. Monster.

I said as much to Suzie, and she nodded. "It doesn't matter. If she's real, I can kill her."

We both kept our voices low, but I don't think even a thunderclap could have interrupted Lilith's concentration. Whatever she saw in the clearing wasn't there yet. She spoke a Word aloud, and it hit the air like a hammer. The sound of it filled the world, its echoes reaching out to touch everything. It was a word from no language I knew or could ever hope to understand, even with the assistance of Old Father Time's magic; it was an old word out of an old language, perhaps the basic language from which all others evolved. I could understand enough of its meaning to be glad I didn't understand any more.

Summoned by that terrible Word, the world opened up to birth monsters. Awful creatures came stomping and hopping and slithering out of the trees behind Lilith. They towered over her and oozed past her feet, huge and dreadful and utterly appalling, even by Nightside standards. In them was found every forbidden combination of animal and lizard and insect, vicious and ugly beyond belief. Bulging muscles swelled like cancers under suppurating flesh. Dark carapaced things scuttled on broken legs, with complicated mouth parts working furiously under too many eyes. Tall and spindly things lurched out of the trees on tripod legs, flailing long tentacles like barbed whips. And still they came, bursting up out of the dark earth of the clearing. Great white worms with rows of human arms and hands, rotting hulks large as whales, chattering heads with long toothy spines. Bat-winged shapes dropped out of the night with a predator's grace, and terrible shapes swept across the sky, blocking out the stars and darting across the face of the full moon.

The air was full of the stench of blood and offal and brimstone. And Lilith looked upon them all, and smiled.

I suddenly realised Suzie was training her shotgun on the group and preparing to open fire. I quickly pushed the barrels down, then actually had to wrestle with her to keep the barrels pointing at the ground. I knew better than to try and take the gun away from her. She finally stopped fighting and glared at me, breathing hard.

"Let me shoot them! They need shooting, on general principles!"

"I feel the same way," I said, glaring right back at her. "But we can't afford to be noticed yet. And I'm pretty sure most of those things would shrug off a shotgun blast anyway."

She nodded reluctantly, and I cautiously let go of the gun. "I loaded up with cursed and blessed ammunition," she said, a little sulkily.

"Even so. I know what those creatures are, Suzie. After being thrown out of Eden, Lilith went down into Hell and lay down with all the demons there, and in time gave birth to all the monsters that have plagued Mankind. Those things out there . . . are her children."

"How can you be so sure of that?" said Suzie.

"I feel it," I said. "I know it like I know my own name. Those things will become the Powers and Dominations of our time, and their many descendants will become vampires and werewolves and ghouls and all the other predators of the Nightside."

"I've got some really powerful grenades . . ."

"No, Suzie."

She sniffed, then glared out at the monstrous creatures rising and falling around Lilith. "So," she said finally. "Lilith's children. Your half-brothers and -sisters. They are the audience she was waiting for."

Lilith looked out across the writhing, pulsating crowd before her, and her wide smile was as cold and unreadable as the rest of her. She could have been thinking anything, anything at all. Finally, she gestured briefly, brutally, and the crowd split in two, falling back on both sides as Lilith frowned, concentrating, and spoke another Word. Even her monstrous children cringed back from the sound of it, and I could feel reality itself shake and shudder as Lilith enforced her awful will upon it. The whole of the dark forest stirred and groaned, a living thing in pain, then, all in one terrible moment, Lilith gave birth to the Nightside through a single effort of will and determination.

A great city suddenly filled the clearing from boundary to boundary, shining bright as the sun, massive and ornate, a singular creation of wonder and beauty. It was a vision of great sparkling towers and massive shimmering domes, delicate elemental walkways and insanely elegant palaces—a glorious ideal city, a thing of dreams made real in stone and wood, marble and metal. It was magnificent, like the cities we see in our minds when we dream of distant places. All its shapes were curved, smooth and rounded, almost organic, the buildings rising and falling like waves in an artificial sea, and none of them were in proportion to each other. The city Lilith had created was inhumanly beautiful, and flawed, just like her.

"That . . . is not at all what I expected," said Suzie. "It's stunning. A city of light, and splendour. How could something as marvellous as that become the corrupt city of our time?"

"Because that thing before us isn't a city," I said. "It's an ideal. No-one lives in it. No-one ever could. That's simply a construct, a sterile unchanging place, designed to be looked at and admired, not lived in; even if Lilith doesn't realise that yet. Most of it's out of proportion, none of it belongs together, and from the look of those towers they only stay up because Lilith believes they will. The streets probably don't go anywhere, and I doubt she's left any room for the practicalities of city life, like clear entrances and exits, sewers and throughways. No . . . this is a dead end, like a beautiful cemetery. Can't you feel the coldness of it? This is only Lilith's idea of a city, a fantasy impressed on reality. No wonder Mankind eventually knocks it all down and builds a new one."

"An ideal," Suzie said slowly. "Like the human body she's made for herself?"

"Good point," I said.

"But . . . what is this city based on?" said Suzie, scowling fiercely. "There aren't any human cities around yet to inspire her."

"Another good point. I didn't know you had it in you, Suzie. I suppose . . . this could be a material reflection of places she's known.

Heaven, Hell, Eden. A wordly version of a spiritual ideal. The ur-city, which only exists in our imaginations, a glimpse of a better place waiting . . . You know, we are getting into some pretty deep philosophical waters here, Suzie."

"Yeah," said Suzie. "You could drown in waters like these."

"Look at the stars," I said suddenly. "And the moon, shining down on the new Nightside. They're still the same, the ordinary unaffected night sky we saw before Lilith even arrived. Nothing up there's changed. And that's not the stars and moon we're used to seeing over our Nightside."

"So?" said Suzie.

"So, I don't think our Nightside is necessarily where and when we always assumed it was."

I would have gone further with that thought, but Lilith turned suddenly and addressed her assembled offspring. Her voice rose on the unnatural quiet, strong and hard and vibrant, and only partly human. Or feminine. She spoke in that old, ancient, language that predated Humanity. And I understood every word of it.

"Denied the comfort of Eden, I have made myself a new home, here in the material world. A place where everyone can be free from the tyrannical authority of Heaven or Hell. My gift to you all, and to those who will come after you."

The monsters cried out in various unpleasant voices, praising her, and bowing and fawning before her. I smiled slowly. They hadn't been listening. The city had never been intended for them alone. And the more I thought about what she said, the more things finally became clear to me.

"You're scowling again," said Suzie. "Now what?"

"Freedom from Heaven and Hell," I said slowly. "Freedom from reward or punishment, or the consequences of your own actions. If there is no Good or Evil, then actions have no meaning. If you no longer have to choose between Good and Evil, if nothing you do matters, then what meaning or purpose can your life have?"

"You've lost me," said Suzie. "I don't think that much about Good and Evil."

"I had noticed," I said. "But even you make a distinction between friend and enemy. Those you approve of and those you don't. You understand that what you do has consequences. Look, think it through. Why is virtue its own reward? Because if it weren't, it wouldn't be virtue. If you only did the right thing because you *knew* you'd get to Heaven, or avoided doing the wrong thing because you *knew* you'd end up in Hell, then Good and Evil wouldn't exist any more. You have to do the right thing because you believe it's the right thing, not because you'll be rewarded or punished for doing it. That's why there's never been any concrete proof of the true nature of Heaven or Hell, even in the Nightside. We were given free will, so we could choose between Good and Evil. You have to choose which one to embrace, for your own reasons, to give your life meaning and purpose. Otherwise, it would all be for nothing. Existence would be meaningless."

"That's why Lilith will destroy the Nightside in the future," said Suzie, nodding slowly almost despite herself. "Because Good and Evil and consequences have a way of creeping in, whenever people get together. She will destroy what the Nightside has become because that's the only way she can restore the purity of her original vision. By removing or destroying all the living things that corrupted her city by inhabiting it."

"Yeah," I said. "That sounds like Mother."

Suzie looked thoughtfully at Lilith, standing tall and proud before her awful children. "Creating the Nightside is supposed to have weakened her," Suzie said, meaningfully. "If I could get close enough to stick both barrels up her nostrils . . ."

"She doesn't look that weakened," I said firmly.

Abruptly Lilith walked forward into the glorious city she'd made, to show it off to her children. They slumped and slithered and crashed after her, filling the night with a celebration of their terrible voices. Suzie and I watched them go, and were glad to see the back of them. Just the sight of them hurt our eyes and made our stomachs churn. Human eyes were never meant to deal with such spiritual ugliness.

And that was when the two angels suddenly appeared before us.

It was obvious they came from Above and Below. They were suddenly standing there before us, two tall idealised humanoid figures with massive wings spreading out behind their backs. One was composed entirely of light, the other of darkness. We couldn't see their faces. There was no question but they were angels. I could feel it in my soul. Part of me wanted to kneel and bow my head to them, but I didn't. I'm John Taylor. Suzie already had her shotgun trained on them. She's never been much of a one for bowing either. I had to smile. The angels looked at each other. We weren't what they'd expected.

"As if things aren't complicated enough," I said, "now Heaven and Hell are getting directly involved. Wonderful."

"Bloody angels," growled Suzie. "Bullyboys from the afterlife. I ought to rip your pin-feathers out. What do you want?"

"We want you," said the angel of light. Its words rang in my head like silver bells.

"We want you to stop Lilith. We can help you," said the dark angel. Its words stank in my head like burning flesh.

"I am Gabriel."

"I am Baphomet."

"This is not how we really are," said Gabriel. "We found thesé images in your heads."

"Comfortable fictions," said Baphomet.

"Designed to make you comfortable with our presence."

"But not too comfortable. We are the will of Heaven and Hell made flesh, and we have been given jurisdiction in this matter."

"You will obey us," said Gabriel.

"Want to bet?" said Suzie.

"We don't do the 'o' word," I said.

The angels looked at each other. Things were clearly not going as expected. "This new city was never intended," said Gabriel. "The material world is not prepared to deal with such a thing. It will . . . unbalance matters. It cannot be allowed to flourish."

"Lilith must be stopped," said Baphomet. "We are here to help you stop her."

"Why?" I said. "I really would love to hear the official line on this."

"We cannot tell you," said Gabriel. "We do not know. We only ever know what we need to know, when we are unleashed upon the material world. It is not for us to make decisions or have opinions. We only enforce the will of Heaven and Hell."

"We are here to do what must be done," said Baphomet. "And we will see it done, no matter what it takes."

I'd seen this kind of limited thinking before, back during the angel war. Angels of either House were always much diminished by being made material. They were still unutterably powerful, and their very nature made them unwavering in their purpose, but you couldn't argue or reason with them. Even when conditions had clearly changed so much that their original purpose was no longer relevant. Angels were spiritual storm-troopers. If a city had to be destroyed, or the first-born of a generation destroyed, send in the angels. Of course, that was still to come.

"You want Lilith taken out, why don't you get on with it?" said Suzie.

"We cannot simply walk into her city and destroy her," said Gabriel. "Lilith has designed her creation so that simply by entering it, all emissaries of Heaven and Hell would be terribly weakened."

"And then she would destroy us," said Baphomet. "She hates all emissaries of authority, whether from Above or Below."

"We do not fear destruction," said Gabriel. "Only the failure of our mission. You can help us."

"You must help us."

Neither angel had much of a personality, as such. Presumably that would come later, after centuries of interaction with Humanity. For the moment, they were more like machines set in motion, programmed to carry out a distasteful but necessary task. It occurred to me that both the light and the dark angel had more in common than they would probably care to admit.

"If you can't enter the city without being destroyed, what use are you?" said Suzie, blunt as ever.

"We cannot stop Lilith," Gabriel said calmly. "But we can make it possible for you to stop her."

"How?" I said.

"You could not destroy her, even with our help," said Baphomet. "She was created to be uniquely powerful, and so she is. Even here, in the material world. But together we could weaken and diminish her, so much so that the harm she could do in the future would be much lessened."

"How?" I said.

"We understand that this is important to you," said Gabriel. "It is not necessary for us to know why."

"We can make you powerful," said Baphomet. "Powerful enough to deal with Lilith as she deserves to be dealt with."

"How?" I said.

"By possessing you," said Gabriel.

Suzie and I looked at the angels, then at each other, then we stepped back a little way to discuss the matter in private. Neither of us felt comfortable under the implacable gaze of their blank faces. And the unblinking light and the impenetrable darkness of their forms was wearing, on both the eyes and the soul. There was something about the angels that made you want to accept everything they said, unthinkingly. But because they couldn't lie didn't mean they were privy to the whole truth.

"We can't destroy Lilith," Suzie said reluctantly. "Whatever happens. Because if she dies here and now, you couldn't be born, John."

"The thought had occurred to me," I said. "But if we could seriously reduce her power, while she's still vulnerable . . . it might make it possible for us to deal with her, back in our own time. We know something happens to weaken her in the past, because soon enough her own creatures will band together to banish her from the Nightside. Maybe what we do here will make that possible."

"We're back to circular thinking again," said Suzie. "Hate Time travel. Makes my head hurt."

"But . . . if we can learn how to weaken her," I said, "maybe we can do it again, once we get back to our own time."

"If we get back to our own time." Suzie considered the matter for a while, then nodded reluctantly. "You mean, we could weaken her again, and stop her destroying the Nightside in the future. Okay. Sounds like a plan to me. Except that there is no way in hell that I'm going to let an angel or anyone else possess me. One body, one vote, no exceptions."

We went back to the angels. "Explain exactly what you mean by possession," I said. "And be really, really convincing that this is necessary."

"We will not be controlling you," said Gabriel. "We will merely inhabit your bodies to grant you our power."

"One of us, in each of you," said Baphomet. "Your human nature will carry our power into Lilith's city, and together we shall bring her down."

"You will enable us to carry out our mission. And afterwards, we shall leave your bodies, and return you to where you belong."

"How can we trust you to keep your word?" said Suzie.

"Why would we want to stay in a human body?" said Baphomet. "We are spirit. You are meat."

"To stay would be contrary to our orders," said Gabriel. "And in many ways, we are our orders."

I sighed heavily. "I know I'm going to regret this, but . . ."

"But?" said Suzie.

"You want to get home, don't you?"

She scowled. "You talk me into the damnedest things, Taylor."

It was my turn to look at her uncertainly. "Can you cope with this, Suzie? With having an angel . . . inside you?"

She shook her head. "You pick the strangest times to get sensitive. Relax, John. Even I can make a clear distinction between a spiritual and a physical invasion. I'll be fine. I think . . . I kind of like the idea of having an angel trapped within me, having to do what I tell it to do. I could dine out on that story for months, once we get back . . ."

"All right," I said to Gabriel and Baphomet. "You've got a deal. Baphomet; you take me."

Even then, I was determined to spare Suzie whatever pain and trauma I could. And I didn't entirely trust the idea of an angel from Hell inside Shotgun Suzie's body. Some marriages are definitely not made in Heaven.

"I would have taken you anyway," said the dark angel. "We are the most compatible."

I wasn't at all sure how to take that. Without any warning, both angels stepped forward and into us, like swimmers diving into deep water. Suzie and I both cried out, more in surprise than shock, and as quickly as that it was done. Baphomet was in my mind, like an idea out of nowhere, like a memory I'd forgotten, like an impulse from a place I normally kept heavily suppressed. And with the angel came power. It was like being plugged into the energy that runs the universe. I could see for miles, hear every sound in the night, and every movement of the air on my skin was like a caress. Suddenly I had other senses, too, and all the worlds within the world, and above and beyond it, unfolded all around me. I was drunk with knowledge, raging with power. I felt like I could tear the whole material world apart with my bare hands. That I could lay waste to any enemy, or dismiss them with a look. I knew that I could breathe life into dying suns, speed the planets in their orbits, dance the dance of life and death, redemption and damnation.

I was still me, but I was more than me. I laughed aloud, and so did Suzie. We looked at each other. We shone so very brightly, our flesh burning with an intense light, and massive wings spread out behind our backs. Our eyes were full of glory, and halos of fizzing static sparked above our heads. The world was ours, to do with as we wished.

Slowly, we remembered why we had done this thing and what we had to do. The slow, steady purpose of the angels beat within us, stronger than instinct, more certain than decision. Suzie and I turned as one and walked into the city Lilith had made. Once I was moving, I felt more like myself again. Action helped to focus me. Both Suzie and I blazed with a light that was brighter and more genuine than anything the city could produce, and the ground cracked and broke apart under the spiritual weight we carried. The tall towers and mighty buildings seemed somehow shabby under our light.

It didn't take long for our presence to be noticed. We were uninvited guests, the first the city had ever known. One by one Lilith's offspring came leaping and slithering and striding through the streets to face us. Some watched from alleyways, some flew overhead, calling out warnings, but eventually a crowd of them blocked our way, and we came to a halt. The monstrous creatures cried out in shock and anger, seeing the angels we carried within us. Their voices were harsh and brutal, when they could be understood at all, and they threatened us, laughed at us, demanded we surrender or leave. Like the baying of beasts in a new kind of jungle.

"Stand aside," I said, and my voice crashed in the air like thunder, like lightning.

"Stand aside," said Suzie, and the buildings shook and trembled all around us.

The creatures rushed us, attacking from every side with tooth and claw and barbed, ripping tentacle. They hated us, just for what we were. For our having dared to enter the place that Lilith had assured them was safe from outside interference. Huge and monstrous, fast and strong, they came at us, death and destruction made flesh, hate and spite and bitter evil given shape and form. They never stood a chance.

Suzie and I looked at them with the power of angels in our eyes, and some of the creatures melted away under the pressure of that gaze, not strong or certain enough to withstand our augmented will. The flesh slipped from their bones like mud and splashed on the ground. Others simply disappeared, banished from the material world by our overwhelming determination. But most stood their ground and fought. They cut at us with claws and barbs, and mouths snapped all around us, while spiked tentacles sought to enwrap or tear us apart. We took no hurt. We were above that. We grabbed them with our strong hands and tore them limb from limb. Our fists punched through the hardest flesh and shattered the thickest carapaces. We crushed skulls and punched in chests and ripped off arms and legs and tentacles. More creatures came running, from every direction at once, spilling and bursting out of every adjoining street and alley. They outnumbered us a hundred to one, a thousand to one, living nightmares and killing machines of unnatural flesh and blood, every shape and form that darkness could conceive.

But Suzie and I had angels within us, and we were strong, so strong.

The street beneath our feet broke apart as awful things burst up out of the earth beneath the city. They wrapped around our legs and tried to drag us down. Bat-winged things slammed down out of the night sky, to tear and rend or snatch us up and carry us away. Suzie and I fought them all, our fingers sinking deep into yielding flesh. We picked creatures up and threw them away, and they crashed into elegant walls and brought down tall buildings. We walked steadily forward, and nothing could stand against us. The dead piled up everywhere, and the wounded crawled away, cursing and weeping and calling out for their mother. Wherever we turned our gaze or our hands, monstrous forms broke or faded away, and some splashed like bloody mud in the streets. Finally, the survivors turned and ran, disappearing back into the centre of the city, back to the dark heart of the Nightside, where Lilith waited for us to come to her. Suzie and I walked through the dead and the dying, the dismembered creatures and the splintered carapaces, ignoring the wounded and the weeping. They were not why we were there.

But still we smiled upon our work, and knew it to be just and good. I like to think this was the angel's thoughts, my angel's satisfaction, but I'm still not sure. I wanted to kill these awful things, these monsters who shared the same mother as I. I didn't want to think I had anything in common with them, but I did, I did. Angel or no, I was as much a monster in what I did then.

We followed the retreating creatures, all the way into the heart of the Nightside, and there was Lilith, sitting on a pale Throne, waiting for us. Her surviving offspring crouched and huddled around the Throne, and at her pale feet. She didn't look at them. All the power of her dark gaze was fixed on Suzie, and on me. The buildings were very tall, impossibly heavy and impressive, and I couldn't tell of what substance they were made. They just were, drawn out of her mind and stamped onto reality by her will, in this place that was not a place, hidden within the real world like a parasite deep in a man's guts.

Lilith watched unwaveringly as Suzie and I stepped unhurriedly into the courtyard and approached her throne. A dozen kinds of blood and offal dripped from our hands. Lilith's gaze was steady, her dark mouth unmoved as her wounded offspring surged restlessly around her feet, crying out for vengeance. Suzie and I came to a halt a respectful distance before her, and Lilith gestured sharply with one long-fingered hand. The clamour about her fell silent. She gestured again, and the creatures slunk away, fading into the dark shadows of the surrounding streets and alleyways. Until there was only Lilith and Suzie, and me.

"I see angels in you," Lilith said calmly. Her words came clearly to me, perhaps because they were filtered through Baphomet. "You carry Heaven's and Hell's restraints within you. I should have known they'd find a way to sneak into my perfect paradise. All I wanted was a world to play in, one world for my very own. A fresh start, I thought, but no; we have to follow the old ways, even here. So, which of you is the snake and which the apple, I wonder? Though I've never seen that much difference, between Heaven and Hell. Both so certain, so limited, so . . . unimaginative. Just bullies, determined to make everyone else play their depressing little game.

"Still, it doesn't matter. You've come too late. I have made a new realm, separate from both of yours, and what I have done here can never be undone, except by me. And you have no power to force me to do anything any more. The very nature of this city limits and diminishes you, while I . . . have designed this body to be very powerful indeed."

I could feel Baphomet boiling and churning within me, enraged by her words, desperate to unleash its power and follow its programming. But I was still in charge and pushed it back. There were things I needed to ask, needed to know.

"Why are Heaven and Hell so concerned about this place?" I said, and my voice sounded very normal to me. "Why do they see your little city as such a danger?"

Lilith raised a perfect dark eyebrow. "That isn't the angel talking. You're . . . human, aren't you? I've seen your kind, in visions. What brings you here, so many years before your time?"

"Is it the concept of true free will they find so threatening?" I persisted. "Why are they so scared of a place where freedom is more than just a word?"

"Your thinking is very limited," said the angel Gabriel, through

Suzie's lips. Her mouth, its voice. "We do not care about Lilith or her city. It is the creatures and powers this freedom from responsibility will someday produce that are our concern. They will be more terrible and more powerful than the rightful inhabitants of this world were ever meant to have to face. Humanity must be protected from such threats if it is to have its fair chance. Unlike Lilith, we take the long view. She has only ever cared about the here and now."

"Here and now is certain," Lilith said calmly. "Everything else is guesswork."

"She must be destroyed," Baphomet said suddenly, forcing the words through my lips.

"That is not what was agreed," said Gabriel, through Suzie.

"Lilith is here and at our mercy," said Baphomet. "And we may never have a better chance."

"Our orders . . . are more important than any local agreement," said Gabriel. "We must destroy the outcast while we have the opportunity."

And just like that, the two angels changed our deal. Using all their strength and will, they pushed Suzie and me aside, forcing us into the back of our heads so they could take control of our bodies and complete their mission. They were supposed to stop her, not destroy her; but their nature would not let them miss the chance of disposing of such a notorious enemy of Heaven and Hell. Lilith didn't move. I could sense the weakness in her, her strength drained by how much of herself she'd had to put into creating her Nightside. I could have sat back and let the angels kill her. I could have watched her die, knowing it would ensure the Nightside's safety in the future, even if it meant my own death, through not being born. I could have. But in the end, I had to do something. Not only for me, but for her. I couldn't let her die because of something she hadn't done yet and might never do. Humanity had to have its chance, but so did she. Making decisions like this is what Humanity is for.

I surged forward in my head, taking Baphomet by surprise. I forced my hand out towards Suzie, and her hand came jerkily forward to grab mine. And together, inch by inch, we took back control of our bodies. The angels raged every step of the way, but there was nothing they could do. I smiled at Lilith, and spoke with my own voice again.

"I have to believe in hope," I said to her. "For you, and for me."

You cannot defy our authority, said a small voice in the back of my head. *You have no power without us.*

"I'm just exercising the free will I was given," I said. "And you two are more trouble than you're worth."

Defy us, and Heaven and Hell will be at your back and at your throat for the rest of your life.

"Get in the queue," I said. "You only possess us by our will, and by our consent. You broke the agreement. And this is the Nightside, where you have no authority at all. So, get out."

And like that, Suzie and I thrust Gabriel and Baphomet out of us. They shot up into the night sky, great wings flapping frantically, then they shot up like living fireworks, fleeing the city before it destroyed them. They couldn't risk being destroyed before they could report what had happened there, in that spiritual blind spot.

Losing the angel's power was like having the heart ripped out of me. It felt such a small thing, to be merely human again.

Suzie quietly let go of my hand. I nodded, understanding. And then we both looked at Lilith, still sitting in state on her pale Throne. She considered us, thoughtfully.

"So," she said finally. "Alone at last. I thought they'd never go. You are humans. Not quite what I was expecting."

"We're what humans will be," I said. "We're from the future."

"I thought you must be," said Lilith. "Without the angelic presence to mask it, you're dripping with Time. Thousands of years of it, I'd say. Why have you come such a long way to be here, speaking a language you shouldn't be able to understand, knowing things you shouldn't know?"

Suzie and I looked at each other, wondering how best to put this. There really wasn't any diplomatic way . . .

"I envy you your travel through Time," said Lilith. "That's one of the few things I can never enjoy. I had to imprint myself so very firmly on your reality, in order to exist here . . . and even I dare not risk undoing that. Tell me—what dread purpose brings you here, from so many years ahead, to murder my children and destroy my pretty city?"

"We came here to stop you from destroying the Nightside, in the far future," I said.

"The Nightside?" Lilith cocked her head on one side, like a bird, then smiled. "A suitable name. But why should I wish to destroy my realm after I've put so much of myself into its creation?"

"No-one seems too sure," I said. "Apparently it's tied in with me. I am, or will be, your son."

Lilith looked at me for a long moment, her face unreadable. "My son," she said finally. "Flesh of my flesh, born of my body? By a human father? Intriguing . . . You know, you really should have let those angels destroy me."

"What?" I said.

"I have put too much of myself into this place to be stopped or sidetracked now. By emissaries of the great tyrants of Heaven or Hell, or by some unexpected descendant from a future that may never happen. The

Nightside will be what I intend it to be, here, and in all the futures that may be. I will do what I will do, and I will not accept any authority or restriction over me. That is why I was made to leave Eden, after all. You may be my son, but really all you are is an unexpected and unwelcome complication."

"You have to listen to me!" I said, stepping forward.

"No, I don't," said Lilith.

She rose suddenly out of her Throne and surged forward inhumanly quickly to grab my face in both her hands. I cried out, in shock and pain and horror. Her touch was cold as knives, cold as death, and the endless cold within her sucked the living energy right out of me. I grabbed her wrists with both my hands, but my human strength was nothing next to hers. She smiled as she drained the life out of me, and into her. Smiled with those dark lips and those dark, dark eyes.

"I gave you life, and now I take it back," she said. "You will make me strong again, my son."

I could no longer feel anything but the cold, and the light was already fading out of my eyes, when Suzie Shooter was suddenly there. She stuck her shotgun right into Lilith's face and let her have both barrels. The shock of the blessed and cursed ammunition at such point-blank range drove Lilith backwards, jerking her hands off my face. I fell to my knees, and didn't even feel it as they slammed against the ground. Lilith cried out angrily, her face undamaged but blazing with rage. Suzie knelt beside me, her arm around my shoulders to stop me falling any further. She was saying something, but I couldn't hear her. Couldn't hear anything. I felt cold, distant, as though inch by inch I was slipping away from life. And all I could think was, *I'm sorry, Suzie . . . to have to do this to you again.*

She shook me roughly, then glared at Lilith. Some of my hearing came back, though I still couldn't feel Suzie's arm around me.

"How could you, you bitch! He's your son!"

"It was easy," said Lilith. "After all, I have so many children."

She beckoned with one pale, imperious hand, and from all sides her monsters came creeping forward again, crashing and slumping out of the streets and alleyways from which they'd been watching. There were lots of them, even after all those Suzie and I had killed, more than enough to deal with two foolish humans. I fought to keep my head up, watching helplessly as the monsters circled slowly around Suzie and me, laughing in their various terrible ways, forms hideous and powerful beyond hope or reason, monsters from the darkest pits of creation. Some of them called out, in awful voices I could still somehow understand, boasting of the terrible things they would do to Suzie and to me for the destruction of their kindred and because they could. They promised us torment and horror, and death so long in the coming we would beg for it before they finally chose to release us. They would hurt us and hurt us until we couldn't stand it any more; and then they'd show us what pain really was.

And I thought, *Not Suzie . . . I'll die first, before I let that happen . . .*

She drew a slender knife from the top of her boot, and made a long shallow cut along the inside of her left wrist. I gaped at her stupidly, and she slapped the cut wrist against my open lips. Her blood filled my mouth, and I swallowed automatically.

"Werewolf blood," said Suzie, her face close to mine, her voice sharp and insistent, cutting through the fog in my head. "To buy us some time. I can't save us, John, and there's no-one here to act as the cavalry, this time. Only you can save us. So I'll fight them, for as long as I can, to buy you time to come up with some last throw of the dice. A miracle would be good, if you've got one about you."

She put the knife away and stood up to face the crowding monsters. She held her shotgun with familiar ease and sneered at Lilith, back sitting on her Throne. Suzie Shooter, Shotgun Suzie, stood tall and defiant as the monsters surged forward, and I don't think I've ever seen a braver thing in my life.

And maybe it was the werewolf blood, or maybe it was her faith in me, but I stood up, too, and looked at Lilith. For the first time she looked surprised, and uncertain. She opened her mouth to say something, but I laughed in her face. And using the very last of my reserves of strength, I forced open my inner eye, my third eye, my private eye, my one and only magical legacy from Mommie Dearest; and I used my gift for finding things to detect the familial mystic link between me and Lilith. The very same link she'd used to draw my life out of me. And it was the easiest thing in the world to reach back through the link, seize her living energy, and haul it right out of her. She cried out in shock, convulsing on her Throne as the strength flowed out of her, and back into me.

The monsters stopped their advance at Lilith's horrified cry and looked around, confused. My back straightened and my legs grew strong again. My head cleared, and I laughed again; and something in that laugh made the monsters draw back even further. And still the power roared out of Lilith, and into me, for all her struggles. Suzie grinned at me, her single blue eye shining. Lilith cried out again, in rage and horror, and fell forward from her Throne, sprawling inelegantly on the ground before me. Her monstrous children were silent now, watching in shock at their powerful mother brought low. I smiled down at my helpless, thrashing mother, and when I spoke my voice was every bit as cold as hers.

"One day," I said to her, "all your precious monsters will get together and turn on you, banishing you from your own creation. When that happens, do remember that I made it possible, by weakening you here and now. They'll throw you out because, deep down, the only freedom you believe in is the freedom you dispense to others. You could never allow anyone else to be truly free, free of you, because then they might some day grow powerful enough to have authority over you . . . You'll lose everything, and all because you never could play nicely with others."

She looked up at me, with her eyes darker than the night. "I will see you again."

"Yes, Mother," I said. "You will. But not for thousands of years. In my time, on my territory. Still, here's a little something, to remember me by."

And I kicked her in the face. She fell backwards, and I turned my back on her. I looked at Suzie, and she grinned and pumped one fist in the air victoriously. I grinned back, and using the power I'd drained out of Lilith, I broke Time's hold on us, and we rocketed back through history, all the way back to the future—and the Nightside, where we belonged.

EPILOGUE

Back in Strangefellows, the oldest bar in the world.

She said, "So, what do we do now?"

I said "We put together an army of every Power and Being and major player in the whole damned Nightside, and turn them into an army I can throw at Lilith's throat. I'll use my gift to track down wherever she's hiding herself now, then . . . we do whatever we have to, to destroy her. Because that's all there is left, now."

"Even though she's your mother?"

"She was never my mother," I said. "Not in any way that mattered."

"Even with an army to back us up, we could still lay waste to most of the Nightside, fighting to bring her down."

"She'll do it anyway, if we don't do something," I said. "I've seen what will happen if we don't stop her, and anything would be better than that."

I didn't look at her scarred face. I didn't think of her half-dead, half-mad, come back through Time to kill me, with the awful Speaking Gun grafted where her right forearm used to be.

"What if the others don't want to get involved?"

"I'll make them want to."

"And end up just like your mother?"

I sighed, and looked away. "I'm tired, Suzie. I want . . . I need for all this to be over."

"It should be one hell of a battle." Shotgun Suzie tucked her thumbs under the bandoliers of bullets that crossed her chest. "I can't wait."

I smiled at her fondly. "I'll bet you even take that shotgun to bed with you, don't you?"

She looked at me with her cold, calm expression. "Someday, you just might find out. My love."

SHARPER THAN A
SERPENT'S TOOTH

London holds an awful secret close to her heart, like a serpent to her bosom. The Nightside. A dark and corrupt place, a city within a city, where the sun has never shone and never will. In the Nightside you can find gods and monsters and spirits from the vasty deep, if they don't find you first. Pleasure and horror are always on sale, marked down and only slightly shop-soiled. I was born in the Nightside, some thirty years ago, and someone's been trying to kill me ever since.

My name is John Taylor, and I operate as a private investigator. I don't do divorce work, I don't solve mysteries, and I wouldn't know a clue if I fell over one. I find things, no matter how well hidden, though mostly what I seem to find is trouble. My father drank himself to death after discovering my missing mother wasn't human. The Authorities, those grey faceless men who run things in the Nightside, inasmuch as anyone does, see me as a dangerous rogue element. Mostly they're right. My clients see me as their last hope, while others see me as a King in waiting; and there are those who would risk anything to kill me because of a prophecy that one day I will destroy the Nightside, and the rest of the world with it.

Finally, after a trip through Time into past incarnations of the Nightside, I have discovered the truth. The Nightside had been created by my missing mother to be the one place on Earth free from the influence of Heaven or Hell. The only truly free place. Her own allies thrust her out of this reality and into Limbo, because they feared her so much. Now she's back, and threatening to remake the Nightside in her own terrible image. My mother, Lilith. Adam's first wife, thrown out of Eden for refusing to accept any authority. She descended into Hell and lay down with demons, and gave birth to all the monsters that have ever plagued this world. Or so they say.

Lilith. Mommie Dearest.

All I have to do now is figure out how to stop her, without destroying the Nightside and the whole damned world in the process . . .

ONE

Somewhere in The Night

Strangefellows is said by many and considered by most to be the oldest bar in the world, and therefore has seen pretty much everything in its time. So when Suzie Shooter and I appeared suddenly out of nowhere, looking half-dead in blood-stained and tattered clothing, most of the bar's patrons didn't so much as raise an eyebrow, cosmopolitan bastards and general scumbags that they are. Suzie and I leaned heavily on the long, polished wooden bar and spent some time just getting our breath back. We'd been through a lot during our trip through the Past, including being possessed by angels to fight demons from the Pit, so I felt very strongly that we were entitled to a little time out. Alex Morrisey, *Strangefellows'* owner, bartender, and general miserable pain in the arse, stood behind the bar putting a lot of effort into cleaning a glass that didn't need cleaning, while he fixed us both with his familiar unwavering scowl.

"Why can't you walk through the door like normal people, Taylor?" he said finally. "You always have to make an entrance, don't you? And look at the state of you. Don't either of you dare drip blood over my nice new and very expensively cleaned floor. I haven't seen the natural colour of that floor in more years than I care to remember, and I'm trying to memorise it before it inevitably disappears again. I have got to get some new clientele. When I inherited this place I was promised a nice upmarket bar with a select and discreet group of regular drinkers."

"Alex," I said, "you couldn't drive this bar upmarket with an electric cattle prod and a branding iron. Now bring me many drinks, all in the same glass, and a bottle of the old mother's ruin for Suzie."

"Two," said Suzie Shooter. "And don't bother with a glass."

Alex looked at Suzie, and his expression changed abruptly. During our brief stop-off in Arthurian times, Suzie had lost the left side of her face. The flesh had been ripped and torn away; then seared together with fire. Her left eye was gone, the eyelid sealed shut. Suzie glared at Alex with her one remaining cold blue eye, daring him to say anything. Alex's face tried to show several things at once, then went blank. He gave Suzie his best professional bartender's polite nod and went to get us our drinks. Suzie had no time for pity or compassion, even from those she considered her friends. Perhaps especially from them.

But I knew there was more to it than that. Alex and I had seen that face before, on a future incarnation of Suzie, who'd travelled back through Time from a potential future to kill me, right here in this bar. I might have killed that Suzie. I wasn't sure. Alex came back with a large glass of wormwood brandy for me, and two bottles of gin for Suzie. He scowled disapprovingly as I gulped down the expensive liquor, and tried not to see Suzie sucking gin straight from the bottle like it was mother's milk.

"How long have we been gone?" I said finally.

Alex raised an eyebrow. "About five hours, since you and Tommy Oblivion left here with Eamonn Mitchell, that new client of yours."

"Ah," I said. "It's been a lot longer for us. Suzie and I have been Time travelling. Back into the various Pasts of the Nightside."

"I've got no sympathy for you," said Alex. "Don't you have enough problems in the here and now, without upsetting people in the Past? Who did you piss off this time? You look like you've both been through a meat grinder."

"That's nothing," said Suzie. "You should see the meat grinder."

She belched and farted, then went back to sucking on her bottle.

"I don't suppose you thought to bring me back a present?" said Alex.

"Of course not," I said. "I told you; we were in the Past, not the Present."

"You're so sharp you'll cut yourself one of these days," said Alex.

I persuaded Suzie to put down her gin bottle long enough to make use of the rechargeable clothing spell Alex always keeps at hand behind the counter. A few Words of Power followed by a couple of quick passes with an aboriginal pointing-bone, and our clothes were immediately clean and repaired. Our bodies remained battered and bloody and exhausted, but it was a start. The spell was standard equipment in all Nightside bars and hostelries, where the general joie de vivre could be very hard on the appearance. Suzie and I admired ourselves in the long mirror behind the bar.

I looked like myself again, if just a little more world-weary around the eyes. Tall, dark, and handsome in the right kind of light, wrapped in a long white trench coat. I like to think I look like someone you could trust, if not take home to meet the parents. Suzie Shooter, also known as Shotgun Suzie, and *Oh Christ it's her, run!* looked as cold and dangerous and downright scary as she always did. A tall blonde in her late twenties, but with a lot of mileage on the clock, standing stiff-backed and arrogant in black motorcycle leathers, lavishly adorned with steel chains and studs, a pump-action shotgun holstered on her back, and two bandoliers of bullets criss-crossing her substantial chest. Knee-length black leather boots with steel-capped toes completed the distressing picture. She had a strong-boned face, a mouth that rarely smiled, and a gaze older than the world. She'd shot me in the back once, but it was only a cry for attention.

(Alex was dressed all in black, as usual, even down to the designer shades and snazzy black beret perched on the back of his head to hide a spreading bald patch. He was in his late twenties but looked ten years older. Running a bar in the Nightside will do that to you.)

"So," said Suzie, returning to her gin bottle, "what do we do now, Taylor?"

"We put together an army," I said, "Of every Power and Being and major player in the whole damned Nightside, and turn them into a force I can throw at Lilith's throat. I'll use my gift to track down wherever she's hiding herself, and then . . . we do whatever we have to, to destroy her. Because that's all there is left, now."

"Even though she's your mother?"

"She was never my mother," I said. "Not in any way that mattered."

Suzie considered me thoughtfully. "Even with an army to back us up, we could still lay waste to most of the Nightside, fighting to bring her down."

"She'll destroy it anyway, if we don't do something. I've Seen what will happen if we don't stop her, and anything would be better than that."

I didn't look at her scarred face. I didn't think of her half-dead, half-mad, come back through Time to kill me, with the awful Speaking Gun grafted where her right forearm should have been.

"What if the others don't want to get involved?"

"I'll make them want to."

"And end up just like your mother?"

I sighed, and looked into my empty glass. "I'm tired, Suzie. I want . . . I need for this to be over."

"It should be one hell of a battle." Shotgun Suzie ran one thumb caressingly over her bandoliers of bullets. "I can't wait."

I smiled at her fondly. "I'll bet you even take that shotgun to bed with you, don't you?"

She looked at me with her cold, calm expression. "Someday, you just might find out. My love."

She blew me a kiss, then returned all her attention to her bottle of gin. Alex looked at me with a mixture of awe, horror, and utter astonishment, and seized the opportunity for a quiet chat while Suzie was preoccupied. He pulled me aside and lowered his voice to a whisper.

"Did I just hear right, John? *My love?* Am I to take it you and the psycho bounty hunter from Hell are now an item?"

"Looks like it," I said. "I'm as shocked and surprised as you are. Maybe I should have checked the wording in my Personals Ad more carefully."

"But . . . *Suzie?* I mean, ten out of ten for courage, yes, but . . . she's crazy!"

I had to smile. "You think anyone sane would hook up with me?"

Alex considered the matter. "Well, there is that, yes. Good point. But John . . . her face . . ."

"I know," I said quietly. "It happened in the Past. There was nothing I could do."

"John, she's one step closer to becoming the future Suzie who tried to kill you. Shouldn't we tell her about that?"

"I already know," said Suzie. I hadn't heard her approach, and from the way Alex jumped, he hadn't either. She was gracious enough not to smile. "I've known for some time. You can't keep secrets long in the Nightside, especially when they include bad news. You should know that, John. Don't worry about it. I never worry about the future. Mostly because I don't believe I'm going to live to see it. It's a very liberating attitude. Worry about the present me, John."

"Oh I do," I assured her. "I do."

I put my back against the bar and looked out over the place. Just another night, in the oldest bar in the world. Alex's muscle-bound bouncers, Betty and Lucy Coltrane, were throwing out a bunch of burly masked Mexican wrestlers, and making them cry like little girls in the process. Never mess with the Coltranes. Especially when they're wearing their ROLLERBALL HELLCAT MUD-WRESTLING CHAMPIONS T-shirts. Not far away, a cyborg with glowing golden eyes ordered another bottle of neat ethanol from Alex, in a strange buzzing voice. He'd dropped in from a possible future via a Timeslip, and was currently trying to mend his left leg with a pair of pliers and a sonic screwdriver someone had left behind in the bar. I was actually pleased to see him. It was good to know that other futures apart from the terrible devastated future I feared so much, were still possible.

Not far enough away, half a dozen flower fairies in drooping petal outfits were singing a raucous Victorian drinking song, buzzed up on pollen. Soon they'd start getting nasty, and go looking for a Water Baby to beat up. Coming down the metal stairs into the bar proper was Kid Psychoses, in his tatterdemalion rags, doing his rounds and peddling his appalling wares. The Kid sold brief interludes of mental illness, for people who wanted to go really out of their heads. He once told me he started out selling mental health, but there was no market for it in the Nightside. I could have told him that.

And the King and Queen of America were passing through, smiling and waving.

"So," said Alex, freshening my glass, "what was the Nightside like, in the Past?"

"Messy," said Suzie. "In every possible sense of the word."

"Kill anyone interesting?"

"You'd be surprised," I said. "But a gentleman doesn't kill and tell. Have you seen Tommy Oblivion recently?"

"Not since he left here with you earlier. Was I supposed to?"

Tommy Oblivion, the existential private eye, had gone back into the Past with Suzie and me, but we'd had a falling-out. He accused me of being cold and manipulative and more dangerous than the people I was trying to stop. I had to send him back to the Present. It was either that or kill him, and I'm trying to be one of the good guys, these days. But I had a feeling I might have missed the mark, just a bit. I could remember Tommy appearing in this bar quite suddenly, out of nowhere, some months back when I was working the Nightingale's Lament case. Back then, he'd threatened to hunt me down and kill me. I'd wondered why, but now I think I knew.

I sighed and shrugged mentally. Tommy Oblivion could take a number and get in line. There was never any shortage of people trying to kill me, in the Nightside. There was a loud creaking of heavy leathers as Suzie moved in beside me, her back to the bar, gin bottle in hand. It was already half-empty, and she had a cigarette in one corner of her mouth. Smoke curled up slowly past her sealed-shut eye.

"I'll find you a spell," I said. "To repair your face."

"I'm thinking of keeping it," Suzie said calmly. "It'll help my image as a desperate character and ruthless killer."

"Your image doesn't need any help."

"You always know the right things to say, Taylor. But I've never cared about being pretty. At least now my outside matches my inside."

"Suzie . . . I won't have you hurt, because of me."

She looked at me coldly. "You start getting protective, Taylor, and I will drop you like a hot elephant turd."

"Speaking of really big shits," said Alex, "Walker was in here a few hours ago, John. Looking for you."

I didn't like the sound of that. Walker, that perfect city gent in his smart city suit and bowler hat, represented the Authorities. His word was law in the Nightside, and peopled lived and died and worse at his whim. They say he once made a corpse sit up and answer his questions. He doesn't approve of me, but he's thrown some work my way from time to time, when he's needed a deniable and completely expendable agent. He was mad at me at the moment, but he'd get over it. Or he wouldn't, in which case one of us would almost certainly end up killing the other.

"He brought his people in here and had them search the place from top to bottom," said Alex, sounding distinctly aggrieved. "Hence my need for a thorough and very expensive cleanup crew, just before you dropped in."

"You let them search your bar?" I said.

Alex must have heard the surprise in my voice, because he had the grace to look a little ashamed. "Hey, he brought a *lot* of people with him, all right? Serious people with serious weaponry. Some of whom are still missing, presumed eaten. I warned them not to go down into the cellars."

I shook my head. Walker must be getting really desperate to lay hands on me if he was prepared to raid a bar protected by Merlin Satanspawn. Merlin had been buried in the cellars under the bar, after the fall of Camelot; but being dead doesn't necessarily keep you from being a major player in the Nightside. I wouldn't go down into those cellars with a gun at my back.

"I have to go take a piss," I announced. "I've been holding it in for over two thousand years, and my back teeth are floating."

"Thank you for sharing that with us," said Alex. "Try and keep some of it off the floor this time."

I headed for the toilets at the back of the bar. Without making a big thing of it, people moved slowly but deliberately out of my way. Partly because of my carefully maintained reputation, but mostly because bad things had a habit of happening to and around me, and wise people kept a safe distance. I pushed open the door with the stylised male genitals painted on it, and headed for the row of stalls. I've never been one for urinals. Far too easy to be ambushed. I took a quick glance around me, breathing through my mouth to avoid the worst of the smell, but it seemed I had the place to myself. The small, dimly lit stone chamber looked as disgusting as ever. I don't think Alex ever cleans the place; he just fumigates it now and again with a flamethrower. The bare stone walls dripped with condensation, and the floor was wet with a whole bunch of liquids that had nothing to do with condensation. The graffiti hadn't improved either. Someone had daubed the Yellow Sign on one wall, and beside it someone had painted *Gods do it in mysterious ways*. Next to the row of stalls, someone else had written *For a good time, knock on any door*.

I entered the first stall, and locked the door securely behind me. I then unzipped and attended to business, letting out a long sigh of relief. First rule of the private eye—always go when you can, because you never know when you might have to stand stakeout. On the wall above the toilet, someone had written *What are you looking up here for? Ashamed?* I smiled, shook off the last few drops and put it away, then stood very still. I hadn't heard or seen anything, but somehow I knew I wasn't alone in the stall any more. In the Nightside, you either develop survival instincts fast, or you don't develop past childhood. I started to reach for one of the little surprises I keep in my coat pockets for occasions like this, then stopped as something small and hard pressed into my back, directly above the kidney.

"There's something small and hard pressing into my back," I said. "And I'm really hoping it's a gun."

"Heh-heh-heh," said a soft breathy voice behind me. "I can always rely on you for a little quip, Mr. Taylor. Helps the business go down so much more smoothly. Yes, it is a gun, and quite a special gun, I'll have you know. An energy pistol from some cyborg's future that I acquired just for this occasion. Heh-heh. So don't even try your little trick of removing the bullets from my gun. Because it hasn't got any."

"Sneaky Pete," I said, grimacing. "Bounty hunter, sneak thief, and all-around scumbag. How did you get past that locked door?"

"I didn't, Mr. Taylor. I was already hiding in the next stall. Heh-heh. Sneaked over the partition while you were . . . occupied. Heh. You know no-one ever sees me coming, Mr. Taylor. I have trained with ninjas. I am a thing of mists and shadows."

"You're a sneaky little bastard," I said firmly. "And lower than a worm's tit. What do you want with me, Pete?"

"Why, you of course, Mr. Taylor. There is an awful lot of money being offered for your head, not necessarily attached to your body, and I mean to collect it. Oh yes. Now, we can either walk out of here together, nice and easy with not a word to your companions, to where I have transport waiting . . . or I can carry you out. Or at least, part of you. Heh-heh. Your choice, Mr. Taylor."

"You mind if I flush first?" I said.

"Always ready with a cheerful quip! I do so enjoy doing business with a fellow professional. Makes it all so much more civilised. Heh-heh. Be my guest, Mr. Taylor. But carefully, yes?"

I leaned forward slowly and flushed the toilet. And while Sneaky Pete's attention was fixed on what I was doing with my hands, I fired up the spell I normally use for taking bullets out of guns, took all of the water flushing through the toilet and dumped the lot of it in Sneaky Pete's lungs. The thing pressing into my back disappeared abruptly as he fell backwards, making horrible gurgling noises. I spun round, ready to grab the energy gun, but his hands were empty. There never had been a gun, just a finger poking me in the back. Sneaky Pete. He sat down on the floor abruptly, water spilling out of his mouth, scrabbling frantically with his empty hands. I considered him for a moment. Bounty hunter. Sneak thief. Peeping Tom and blackmailer. He might not have killed me himself, but he would have handed me over to be killed without a second thought . . . I sighed, placed my foot against his chest and pushed hard. Water gushed out of him, and after a series of really nasty choking noises, he started breathing again.

I let him live. I didn't like to think I was getting soft, but . . . maybe I needed to convince myself that I wasn't my mother's son.

I left the toilets and returned to the bar. I gave Alex Morrisey my best hard look. "I just had a run-in with Sneaky Pete in the toilet, and not in a good way. Is there perhaps something you haven't got around to telling me yet?"

"Ah," said Alex. "Yes, there's been a whole lot of bounty hunters in and out of here recently. Apparently the rich and very well connected families of the thirteen Reasonable Men you killed, for perfectly good reasons I'm sure, have got together and placed a truly impressive bounty on your head."

"How much?" said Suzie. I looked at her, and she shrugged. "Sorry. Force of habit."

I was about to say something sharp when fortunately my mobile phone rang. I answered it with my usual "What?"

"Taylor," said Walker, in his smooth and very civilised voice. "So glad you've returned safely from your little trip into the Past."

"Walker," I said. "Word does get around fast, doesn't it? I didn't think you knew my private number."

"I know everyone's number. Comes with the job."

"I am not going to come in and give myself up to you and the Authorities. I have important things to do."

"Oh, I think you will, Taylor."

There was something in his voice . . . "What have you done, Walker?"

"Only what you have forced me to do, to get your attention. I have reluctantly given the order for your delightful young secretary Cathy Barrett to be kidnapped. By now she will be in safe hands, being held somewhere very secure. Turn yourself in peacefully, and you have my word that she will be freed unharmed. But if you insist on making life difficult for me by continuing to defy me in this manner . . . Well, I'm afraid I can't answer for the young lady's continued well-being."

"You bastard."

"I only do what I have to, John. You know that."

"If anything happens to Cathy . . ."

"That's entirely up to you, isn't it? I regret to inform you that the people entrusted with this kidnapping bear you a considerable amount of ill will. The longer you take to come to a decision, the more likely it is they'll vent their spleen on her. And much as I might regret that . . . the situation is out of my hands. I have my orders, and my duty. Whatever happens . . ."

I hung up on him. He had nothing else to say worth listening to. He was only keeping the conversation going in the hope his people would be able to track my location through my phone. I explained the situation to Suzie and Alex.

"I can't turn myself in," I said. "I have to be free to operate if I'm going to stop Lilith. The whole Nightside's at risk, and maybe the world, too. But I won't, I can't, abandon Cathy."

"Of course not," said Suzie. "She's your secretary."

"Your friend," said Alex.

"My daughter," I said. "In every way that matters."

"Then we must go and get her," said Suzie. "We can't give in to threats like this. If people thought we could be pressured into doing things, they'd take advantage. So go on, Taylor. Do your thing."

I raised my gift, my single supernatural inheritance from my inhuman mother, and opened up my Sight. And through my third eye, my private eye, I looked out over the Nightside, searching for Cathy. I can find anyone, or anything, if I look hard enough. I don't like to use my gift too often, because when I do I blaze so brightly in the dark that I am easy to see. And then my Enemies send agents to kill me. But for the moment, I was too mad to care.

The Nightside spread out below me, naked to my Sight, and I looked down upon it like an angry god. Streets and squares and places within places, with people and things not at all people coming and going. Bars and clubs and more private establishments flashed past beneath my searching inner eye, houses and warehouses and lock-ups and dungeons, and no sign of Cathy anywhere. The Fae sparked briefly in the shadows, and the Awful Folk moved unhurriedly on their unguessable missions, invisible to the material world. I could feel Cathy's presence now, all alone somewhere in the night, but I couldn't seem to pin her down. I concentrated till my head ached, but finally I was forced to settle for a general location. Something or someone was blocking my gift, obscuring my Sight, and that was a new thing to me. I shut down my gift, and carefully re-established my mental shields. You can't have an open mind in the Nightside. You never know what might walk in.

"She's somewhere near the Necropolis," I said. "But I can't be more specific than that."

Suzie raised an eyebrow. "That's . . . unusual."

I nodded shortly. "Stands to reason Walker wouldn't chose just anybody to hide Cathy from me."

"But Walker knows about your gift," said Alex. "He must know you'll come looking for her. It has to be a trap."

"Of course it's a trap," I said. "But I've been walking in and out of traps all my life. So, first Suzie and I will rescue Cathy, after making it clear to her kidnappers that getting involved in my business was a really bad idea, then . . . I will go walking up and down in the Nightside, and raise an army big enough to give even Walker nightmares."

"One thing first," said Suzie.

"Yes?" I said.

"Do up your flies, Taylor."

TWO

And Dead Men Rise up Never

Getting out of *Strangefellows* wasn't going to be easy. Knowing Walker, it was a safe bet that all of the bar's known and suspected exits were being watched by his people, heavily armed with guns, bombs, and spells of mass destruction. It was what I would have done. I said as much to Alex Morrisey, and he scowled even more fiercely than usual.

"I know I'm going to regret this," he said heavily, "but there is one way out of this bar I can guarantee Walker doesn't know about. Because no-one does, except me. My family have run this place for generations, and given the weird shit and appalling trouble *Strangefellows* tends to attract, we've always appreciated the need for a swift, sudden, and surreptitious exit. So we've carefully maintained a centuries-old hidden exit, for use by us in the direst of emergencies, when it's all gone to Hell in a handcart. Understand me, Taylor—the only reason I'm prepared to reveal it to you now is because I don't want Walker's people crashing back in here looking for you, wrecking the place again. The quicker you're out of here, the sooner we can all breathe easily."

"Understood, Alex," I said. "This isn't about friendship. It's just business."

"Damn right," said Alex. He beckoned for Suzie and me to join him behind the bar. "I wouldn't want people to get the idea that I was going soft. That I could be taken advantage of."

"Perish the thought," I said.

"There is . . . one small drawback," said Alex.

"I knew it," Suzie said immediately. "I knew there had to be a catch. We don't have to go out through the sewers, do we? I'm really not in the mood to wrestle alligators again."

"Even worse," said Alex. "We have to go down into the cellars."

Suzie and I both stopped short and looked at each other. *Strangefellows'* cellars were infamous even in the Nightside; they were so dangerous and generally disturbing that most sane and sensible people wouldn't enter them voluntarily without the holy hand grenade of St. Antioch in one hand and a tactical nuke in the other. Merlin Satanspawn was buried in the cellars, and he really didn't care for visitors. Alex was the only one who went down there on a regular basis, and even he sometimes came back up pale and twitching.

"I've got a better idea," said Suzie. "Let's go out the front door and fight our way through Walker's people."

"He could have a whole army out there," I said.

"Somehow that doesn't bother me nearly as much as it did a few minutes ago," said Suzie. "I could handle an army."

"Well, yes, you probably could, in the right mood," I said. "But we can't rescue Cathy if Walker knows we're coming. We need to stay under the radar, keep him off-balance. Lead the way, Alex."

"Have I got time to go to confession first?" said Suzie.

"You leave that priest alone," I said firmly. "He still hasn't got over your last visit."

Alex produced an old-fashioned storm lantern from underneath the bar, lit the wick with a muttered Word, and then hauled open the trap-door set in the floor behind the bar. It came up easily, without the slightest creak from the old brass hinges, revealing smooth stone steps leading down into pitch-darkness. Suzie and I both leaned over and had a good look, but the light from the bar didn't penetrate past the first few steps. Suzie had her shotgun out and at the ready. Alex sniffed loudly.

"This is an ancient family secret I'm entrusting you with. Whatever you see down there, or think you see, it's private. And don't show me up in front of my ancestors, or I'll never live it down."

He led the way down the steps, holding the lantern out before him. Its pale amber light didn't travel far into the dark. Suzie and I followed him, sticking as close as possible. The steps continued down for rather longer than was comfortable, and the roar of voices from the bar was soon left behind. The air became increasingly close and clammy, and the surrounding darkness had a watchful feel.

"There's no electricity down here," said Alex, after a while. His voice sounded small and flat, without the faintest trace of an echo, even though I could all but feel a vast space opening up around us. "Something down here interferes with all the regular means of power supply."

"Don't you mean someone?" said Suzie.

"I try really hard not to think about things like that," said Alex.

The stone steps finally gave out onto a packed-dirt floor. The bare earth was hard and dry and utterly unyielding under my feet. A blue-white glow began to manifest around us, unconnected to the storm lantern or any other obvious source. It rapidly became clear we were standing at the beginnings of a great stone cavern, a vast open space with roughly worked bare stone walls and an uncomfortably low ceiling. I felt like crouching, even though there was plenty of headroom. And there before us, stretching out into the gloomy distance, hundreds of graves set in neat rows, low mounds of earth in the floor, with simple, unadorned headstones. There were no crosses anywhere.

"My ancestors," said Alex, in a soft, reflective, quietly bitter voice. "We all end up here, under the bar we give our lives to. Whether we want to or not. Merlin's indentured servants, bound to *Strangefellows* by his will, down all the many centuries. And yes, I know everyone else who dies in the Nightside is supposed to have their funerals handled by the Necropolis, by order of the Authorities, but Merlin's never given a damn for any authority other than his own. Besides, I think we all feel safer here, under his protection, than any earthly authority's. One day I'll be laid to rest here. No flowers by request, and if anyone tries to sing a hymn, you have my permission to defenestrate the bastard."

"How many graves are there?" I said.

"Not as many as you'd think," said Alex. He put his lantern down on the bottom step and glowered around him. "We all tend to be long-lived. If we don't get killed horribly somewhere along the way. Only useful thing we inherited from our appalling ancestor."

He started out across the cavern floor. Despite the limited lighting, he was still wearing his sunglasses. Style had never been a sometime thing with Alex Morrisey. Suzie and I followed, trying to look in all directions at once. We passed by great barrels of beer and casks of wine, and bottles of rare and vicious vintage, laid out respectfully in a wine rack that looked even older than its contents. There were no cobwebs, and not even a speck of dust anywhere. And somehow I just knew it wasn't because Alex was handy with a feather duster.

"It occurs to me," I said carefully, "that there's no sign anywhere of the people Walker insisted on sending down here. Not any bodies. Not even any bits of bodies."

"I know," said Alex. "Worrying, isn't it?"

We stopped again, to consider a grave set some distance away from the others. Just another low mound of earth, but with no headstone or marker. Instead, there was a massive silver crucifix, pressing down the length of the earth mound. The silver was pitted and corroded.

"Presumably put there in the hope it would hold him in his grave and keep him from straying," said Alex. "They should have known better. You couldn't keep Merlin Satanspawn down if you put St. Paul's Cathedral on top of his grave."

"You have to wonder exactly what's in there," I said. "After all these centuries."

"You wonder," said Suzie. "I like to sleep soundly at nights."

"Just bones?" I said. "No different from anyone else's?"

"No," said Alex. "I think, if you dragged away the crucifix and dug him up . . . he'd look exactly like he did the day he was buried. Untouched by time or the grave. And he'd open his eyes and smile at you, and tell you to cover him up again. He was the Devil's son after all, the Antichrist in person, even if he did refuse the honour to make his own path. You really think the world is finished with him yet? Or vice versa? No . . . the bastard's still hoping some poor damned fool with find his missing heart and return it to him. Then he'll rise out of that grave and go forth to do awful things in the Nightside . . . and no-one will be able to stop him."

"God, you're fun to be around, Alex," I said.

We moved on, giving the grave plenty of room. The blue-white light moved with us, cold and intense, and our shadows seemed far too big to be ours. The darkness and the silence pressed in around us. Finally, we came to a bare and undistinguished-looking door, set flush into the stone wall. A gleaming copper latch, inscribed with blocky Druidic symbols, held it shut. I reached out a hand to the latch, then snatched it quickly back again. Some inner voice was shouting loudly that it would be a very bad idea for anyone but Alex to touch it. He smiled at me tiredly.

"This door will open out onto anywhere you want, within a one-mile radius of the bar," he said. "Announce your destination out loud, and I'll send you on your way. But be really sure of where you want to go, because once you're through the door, that's it. It's a one-way door."

"Who put it here?" said Suzie.

"Who do you think?" said Alex.

"You mean this door's been here for fifteen hundred years?" I said.

Alex shrugged. "Maybe longer. This is the oldest bar in the world, after all. Now get the hell out of here. I've got customers waiting upstairs with my money burning a hole in their pockets."

"Thank you, Alex," I said. "You didn't have to do this."

"What the hell," said Alex. "You're family. In every way that matters."

We smiled briefly at each other, then looked away. We've never been very good at saying the things that matter.

"Where do we want to go to?" said Suzie, probably not even noticing the undercurrents. She'd never been very good at emotions, even hers. "You can bet Walker's people will be guarding all the approaches to the Necropolis."

"Not if we go directly there," I said.

"Not possible," Alex said immediately. "I told you, nothing over a mile radius."

I grinned. "I was thinking of paying the Doormouse a visit."

Suzie winced visibly. "Do we have to? I mean, he's so damned . . . cute. I don't do cute."

"Brace yourself," I said kindly. "It'll be over before you know it."

I announced our destination in a loud, clear voice, and Alex hit the latch and pulled the door open, revealing a typical Nightside street. People and other things bustled briskly back and forth, and the gaudy Technicolor neon pushed back the gloom of the cellar. I strode forward into the welcoming night, with Suzie right behind me, and Alex slammed the door shut.

To the crowds in the street, we must have seemed to appear suddenly out of nowhere, but that was nothing new in the Nightside, so no-one noticed, or if they did, no-one gave a damn. They were all intent on pursuing their own pleasures and damnations. The twilight daughters catcalled to prospective customers from the street corners, sticking out their breasts and batting kohl-stained eyes. Club barkers cried their wares to the more unsuspecting tourists, and the traffic on the road roared past without ever, ever stopping.

I hurried down the rain-slick pavement, noting without surprise that some people were already muttering my name and Suzie's into mobile phones. Must be a really good price on my head. And there was the Doormouse's shop, right ahead. It was set between a new establishment called the Bazaar of the Bizarre, and a music emporium that specialised in rare vinyl LPs from alternate dimensions. I paused despite myself to check out the latest specials in the window. There was a Rolling Stones album with Marianne Faithful as the lead singer, a Pink Floyd debut LP where they were fronted by Arthur Brown, and a live double album of Janis Joplin, from her gigs as an overweight, middle-aged lounge singer in Las Vegas. I wasn't tempted. Not at those prices.

The frosted-glass doors hissed open as I entered the Doormouse's excellent establishment. Then I had to go back out again and drag Suzie Shooter in. Inside, it was all very high-tech, with rows of computers and towering stacks of futuristic technology, most of which I couldn't even identify, let alone hope to understand. The Doormouse had very good contacts and an uncanny eye for a bargain. But what he did best . . . was doors. He came bustling forward to meet us, a cheerful six-foot-tall roughly humanoid mouse, with dark chocolate fur under a pristine white lab coat, complete with pocket protector. He had a long muzzle with twitching whiskers, but his kind eyes were entirely human. He lurched to a halt before us, clapped his paws together, and chattered pleasantly in a high-pitched but perfectly clear voice.

"Welcome, welcome, sir and lady, to my humble establishment! Am I correct in thinking I am in the presence of two of the Nightside's most noted celebrities? John Taylor and Shotgun Suzie, no less! My, my, what a day! I know, I know, you weren't expecting all this technology, were you? No-one ever does. You hear the name Doormouse, and immediately your thoughts go all rustic, but I, sir and lady, am a Town Mouse! And proud of it! Now, what can I do for you? I have doors for everyone, to everywhere, and all points between. And all at very reasonable prices! So, just state your travelling needs, and I shall rush to satisfy them! Why is she growling at me?"

"Don't mind her," I said. "She's being herself. Are you the only mouse in the Nightside? That is . . ."

"I quite grasp your meaning, sir. There were others, once, but they all moved away to a small town in the countryside. Wimps. I am the only one of my kind currently residing here."

"Good," said Suzie. "I was beginning to think I'd have to start putting bigger traps down."

"I need a door," I said, loudly. "One that will take us directly to the Necropolis. Is that going to be a problem?"

"Oh no, sir, not at all," said the Doormouse, edging just a little further away from Suzie. "I always keep a number of the more common destination doors in stock, ready for sale. Both inside and outside the Nightside. This way if you please, sir and . . . lady . . ."

He scurried away deeper into his shop, with Suzie and me in close pursuit, to a showroom full of doors standing upright on end, apparently entirely unsupported. Neat handwritten labels announced the destination they opened onto. *Shadows Fall, Hy Breasil, Hyperborea, Carcosa.* Together with a whole series of doors that would take you practically anywhere inside the Nightside. But it was two other doors that caught my attention, standing a little off to one side. They were labelled simply *Heaven* and *Hell.* They looked no different than any of the others— simple waxed and polished wood, each with a gleaming brass handle.

"Ah yes," said the Doormouse, easing chummily in beside me. "Everyone notices those."

"Can they really take you where it says they go?" I said.

"That is a matter of some debate," the Doormouse admitted, crinkling his muzzle. "The theory's sound, and the mathematics quite clear. Certainly no-one who's gone through has ever come back to complain . . ."

"Let us talk of other things," I said.

"Yes, let's," said the Doormouse.

He led us past other doors, some labelled in languages and ideographs even I couldn't identify. And I've been around. We finally came to a door labelled NECROPOLIS. The Doormouse patted it affectionately with one padded paw.

"I always keep this one charged up and at the ready for people who need to visit the Necropolis for a sad occasion. Much more dignified than fighting the traffic in a black Rolls Royce. This door will deliver you and the . . . lady, to right outside the main entrance."

"Not inside?" I said sharply.

"She's started growling again," said the Doormouse. "No, no, sir. Never inside! My doors lead only to exterior locations. If word got out that I was willing to provide access to the interiors of buildings, thus circumventing all usual security measures, you can be sure the Authorities would send Walker to shut me down. With prejudice. Now, sir, let us talk of the price."

We haggled for a while, and he drove a really hard bargain for a mouse. We finally settled for an only moderately painful extortionate sum, which I paid with gold from the traveller's pouch Old Father Time had given me, when I travelled back in Time. The pouch was seemingly bottomless, and I'm pretty sure Time meant for me to give it back to him when I returned, but I fully intended to hang on to it until it was wrestled from my grasp. The Doormouse opened the door with a flourish, and Suzie and I stepped through into another part of the Nightside.

The Necropolis looked just as I remembered it; big, dark and supernaturally ugly. I'd been here not long ago, with Dead Boy, to clean up an incursion by Primal demons. Which meant that technically speaking the Necropolis staff still owed me a favour. How much weight that had, when set against Walker's publicly stated disapproval, remained to be seen.

The Necropolis itself was a huge towering edifice of old brick and stone, with no windows anywhere and a long, gabled roof. The various owners had been adding exteriors to it for years, in a clashing variety of styles, and yet the building maintained a traditional aspect of gloom and depression. The one and only front door was a massive slab of solid steel, rimmed with silver, covered with deeply etched runes and sigils and a whole bunch of nasty words in dead languages. Two huge chimneys at the back pumped out thick black smoke from the on-site crematorium.

The Necropolis serves all the Nightside's funereal needs. Any religion, any ritual, any requests, no matter how odd or distressing. Cash up front and no questions asked. People paid serious money to ensure that their dearly departed could rest peacefully in their graves, undisturbed and unmolested by any of the many magicians, necromancers, and creatures of the night who might profess an unhealthy interest in the helpless dead. And, of course, to ensure that the dead stayed dead and didn't turn up unexpectedly to contest the will. In the Nightside, you learn to cover all the bases. I considered the ugly, sprawling building before me. Cathy was being held there somewhere, very much against her will, and if she'd been harmed in any way, someone was going to pay for it in blood and horror.

"Enough travelling," said Suzie Shooter. "I feel the need to kill someone."

"Questions first," I said. "But if anyone doesn't feel like talking, feel free to encourage them in violent and distressing ways."

"You know how to show a girl a good time, Taylor."

"Except, your secretary isn't in there," said a calm, quiet and very familiar voice.

We both looked round sharply and there he was, Razor Eddie, the Punk God of the Straight Razor, standing unnaturally still in the pool of light from a nearby street-lamp. Even though he very definitely hadn't been there a moment before. Razor Eddie, a painfully thin presence wrapped up in an oversized grey coat held together by accumulated filth and grime. His hollowed face was deathly pale and streaked with grime, dominated by fever-bright eyes and a smile that had absolutely no humour in it. We walked over to him, and the smell hit us. Razor Eddie lived on the streets, slept in doorways, and existed on hand-outs, and he always smelled bad enough to make a sewer rat's eyes water. I half expected the street-lights to start wilting.

"All right," said Suzie. "How did you know we'd be here, Eddie?"

"I'm a god," said Razor Eddie, in his quiet ghostly voice. "I always know what I need to know. Which is how I know exactly where your secretary is being held, John."

I regarded him thoughtfully. Eddie and I were friends, sort of, but given the kind of pressure Walker was capable of bringing to bear . . . Eddie nodded slightly, following my thoughts.

"Cautious as ever, John, and quite right, too. But I'm here to help."

"Why?" I said bluntly.

"Because Walker was foolish enough to try and order me to do his dirty work for him. Like I give a damn what the Authorities want. I go where I will, and do what I must, and no-one gets to stand in my way. No-one tells me what to do. So, your secretary isn't being held inside the Necropolis building, but rather in their private graveyard. Which is so big they keep it in a private dimension that they sub-let."

"Who from?" said Suzie.

"Best not to ask," said Razor Eddie.

I nodded. It made sense. I'd heard that the Necropolis's extensive private graveyard was kept in a pocket dimension, for security reasons, protected by really heavy-duty magics. Getting in wouldn't be easy.

"You can't just crash into the Necropolis and intimidate the staff into giving you access," said Eddie.

"Want to bet?" said Suzie.

"They know you're here," Eddie said patiently. "And they're already on the phone to Walker, screaming for reinforcements. By the time you've smashed your way through that building's defences, you'll be hip deep in Walker's people. And your only real hope for rescuing Cathy is a surprise attack. Fortunately, I can offer an alternative way in."

His right hand, thin and grey, came out of his pocket, thin and grey, holding a pearl-handled straight razor. He flipped the blade open, and the steel shone supernaturally bright. I could feel Suzie tensing beside me, but she had enough sense not to go for any of her weapons. Eddie flashed her a meaningless smile, turned away, and cut savagely at the empty air. The whole night seemed to shudder as the air split apart, widening and opening up like a wound in the world. And through the opening Razor Eddie had made, I could see another world, another dimension. It was a darker night than ours, and bitter cold air rushed out into our world. I shuddered, and so did Suzie, but I don't think it was from the cold. Razor Eddie, unaffected, stared calmly through the gap he'd made.

"I didn't know you could do that," I said.

"I went back to the Street of the Gods," said Eddie, putting away his razor. "Got an upgrade. Did you know, John, there's a new church there, worshipping your image. Unauthorised, I take it? Good. I took care of it for you. Knew you'd want me to. Follow me."

Poor bastards, I thought, as the Punk God of the Straight Razor stepped through the wide opening, and Suzie and I followed him through, into another world.

The terrible cold hit me like a fist and cut me like a knife, burning in my lungs as I struggled with the thin air. Suzie blew harshly on her cupped hands, flexing her fingers so they'd be free and ready if she had to kill someone in a hurry. Before us, the graveyard seemed to stretch away forever. Row upon row and rank upon rank of massed graves, for as far as the eye could see in any direction, from horizon to horizon. A world of nothing but graves. The Necropolis's private cemetery lay silently under an entirely different kind of night from the Nightside. It was darker, with an almost palpable gloom, apart from a glowing pearlescent ground mist that curled around our ankles and swirled slowly over the rows of tombstones. There was no moon in the jet-black sky, only vivid streaks of multi-coloured stars, bright and gaudy as a whore's jewels.

"We're not in the Nightside any more," said Eddie. "This is a whole different kind of place. Dark and dangerous and dead. I like it."

"You would," said Suzie. "Damn, but it's cold. I mean, serious cold. I don't think anything human could survive here for long."

"Cathy's here, somewhere," I said. "Whoever has her had better be taking really good care of her. Or I will make them scream before they die."

"Hard-core, John," said Suzie. "And not really you. Leave the rough stuff to me. I'm more experienced." She looked around her and sniffed loudly to show how unimpressed she was. "The Necropolis could have chosen a more cheerful resting place for the Nightside dead."

"Perhaps all the alternatives were worse," I said. "Or more expensive."

"We didn't come here to admire the scenery," said Razor Eddie.

"Damn right," said Suzie. "Find me someone I can shoot."

I looked around. There was only the dark, and the graves and the mist. Nothing moved, not a breath of wind anywhere, and the place was utterly silent. The only sounds in the cemetery were those we made ourselves. Razor Eddie's rasping breathing, the creaking of Suzie's leathers.

"I don't see anyone," I said.

Eddie shrugged slightly. "Nothing lives here. That's the point. Even the flowers left on the graves are plastic."

There were headstones of all shapes and sizes, catafalques and mausoleums, statues of weeping angels and penitent cherubs and crouching gargoyles. All kinds of religious symbols, large and small, simple and complex, and a few even I didn't recognise. All the objects of death, and not one of life.

"I thought there might be at least a few mourners," said Suzie.

"Not many come here to visit," said Eddie. "I mean, would you? Now follow me and walk carefully. There are concealed traps here, for the uninvited and the unwary."

Suzie brightened up a bit. "You mean some of those stone gargoyles might come to life? I could use some target practice."

"Possibly," said Razor Eddie. "But mostly I was thinking about bear traps and land mines. The Necropolis takes security very seriously. Stick to the gravel path, and we should be safe enough."

"I never get to go anywhere nice," I said, wistfully.

I fired up my gift, hoping that since I was closer to Cathy, it would at least be able to provide me with a direction. My Sight was limited, in this new dimension. There was no hidden world here, no secret lives for me to See; just the dead, lying at peace in their graves and mausoleums, like so many silent strangers at the feast. And yet there was a feeling . . . of being watched, by unseen eyes. I tried to focus in on Cathy, but a strangely familiar shadow still hid her exact position from me. At least I had a direction.

I set off down the gravel path, with Suzie Shooter and Razor Eddie on either side of me. Suzie had her shotgun in her hands, alert for any opportunity to show off what she did best. Eddie strolled along, his hands in his pockets, his unblinking eyes missing nothing, nothing at all. The sound of our feet crunching the gravel was uncomfortably loud, announcing our coming. I watched the shadows between the stone mausoleums, ready for any sudden attack from behind the larger tombstones; but I wasn't at all ready for what lay in wait for us around an abrupt corner.

They were sitting at a picnic around a pristine white cloth, laid out on a long earth barrow. There was a food hamper, with plates of cucumber sandwiches and sausage rolls and nibbles on sticks, and a bottle of quite decent champagne chilling in an ice bucket. And smiling calmly back at us—Tommy Oblivion, the existential detective, and Sandra Chance, the consulting necromancer. Tommy's usual New Romantic silks were mostly concealed under a heavy fur coat, but he still managed a certain dated style. He smiled easily at us, showing off a broad, toothy grin in his long, horsey face, and toasted me with a brimming glass of bubbly. Sandra just glared coldly, pale of face and red of hair, wearing nothing but apparently random splashes of dark crimson liquid latex from chin to toe. She looked like a vampire after a really messy meal, and not by accident. Sandra went out of her way to make an impression on people. Supposedly, the liquid latex also contained holy water and other useful protections. The tattoo on her back could make angels vomit and demons hyperventilate. Interestingly enough, she'd had all of the steel piercings in her face and body removed, recently enough that some of the holes were still closing. A simple leather belt, carrying a series of tanned pouches holding the tools of her unpleasant trade, surrounded her waist. She didn't feel the cold because she thrived in graveyards. Sandra Chance loved the dead—and sometimes even more, if that was what it took to get them to talk.

We'd worked together on a few cases, successfully, if not entirely

happily. Sandra only cared about getting results, and to hell with whoever got caught in the cross-fire. I liked to think that wasn't true of me,
any more.

"Hello, old thing," said Tommy Oblivion. "So glad you could join us.
And you've brought company! How sweet. Do sit down and have a little
something with us, and a splash of champers. I think it's terribly important we all remain civilised in situations like this, don't you?"

"Want me to shoot him?" said Suzie.

"I'm thinking about it," I said. "Hello, Tommy. I should have known
it was you, with your existential gift, hiding Cathy. Still sticking with the
effete image, I see."

He flapped his long, bony fingers in an affable sort of way. "Stay with
what works, that's what I say."

"How's your brother?"

"Still dead. But he says he's starting to get used to it. And he's a better private eye now that he ever was while he was alive."

"I think that's enough civilities," I said. "Tell me where Cathy is, or
I'll have Suzie shoot you somewhere really unfortunate."

"Any violence and you'll never see her again," said Sandra. Her voice
was deep and vibrant and bitter as cyanide. "You'll never find Cathy Barrett without our help."

"Where is she?" I said, and my voice was colder than the night.
Tommy and Sandra sat up a little straighter.

"She's sleeping peacefully," said Sandra. "In one of these graves. I
put a spell on her, then Tommy and I opened up a grave, put her in it, and
covered her over again. She's quite safe, for the time being. All you have
to do is turn yourself in to Walker, and Tommy and I will dig her up and
return her safely to the Nightside. Of course, the longer she stays underground, the more difficult it will be to wake her from the spell . . ."

"Of course," I said. "You're never happy with a spell unless it's got a
sting in the tail." I looked at Tommy. "Why are you doing this? Sandra I
can understand. I've never known her to balk at anything if the price was
right. But you . . . what happened to those principles you used to trumpet
so loudly? Cathy's the only innocent in this whole business."

His cheeks flushed a little, but he held my gaze steadily. "Needs must
when the devil drives, old sport. You're just too dangerous to be allowed
to run loose any more. I saw what you did with Merlin and Nimue, remember? You don't care about anyone or anything, except getting your
own way."

"No," said Razor Eddie. "That's not true."

We all glanced at him, a little startled. He was so quiet and still it was
easy to forget he was there.

"You have to be stopped," said Tommy, a little more loudly than was necessary. "You're cold and ruthless and . . ."

"You got back from the Past months ago," I said, talking right over him. "Why didn't you do something before this? Why wait till now?"

"I was keeping my head down, out of sight, while I thought things through," said Tommy. He was trying hard not to sound defensive. "I put a lot of thought into how best to stop you. It took me a while to admit I couldn't hope to do it alone. So I came up with this plan, and went to Walker with it, and he put me together with Sandra. Not at all a nice plan, I agree, but you brought it on yourself. Fight fire with fire, and all that. You might say . . . this was my last test for you, John. One last chance to see what you're really made of, to see if you care for anyone other than yourself. Prove me wrong about you. Prove to me and to Walker that you're not the evil we think you are by turning yourself in. And I give you my word that Cathy will be released, entirely unharmed."

"I can't," I said, trying hard to make him hear the need and urgency and honesty in my voice. "My mother Lilith is back, and she's worse than I'll ever be. I'm the only one who can stop her from destroying the Nightside."

"Such arrogance," said Sandra. "We'll stop her, after we've dealt with you."

"I could blow your head right off your shoulders," Suzie Shooter said casually.

"You could try," said Sandra Chance. The two women smiled at each other easily. Sandra leaned forward to put down her champagne glass, and Suzie moved her shotgun slightly to keep her covered. "I am a necromancer," said Sandra. "And this is my place of power. With this much death to draw on, even the Punk God of the Straight Razor can't hope to stand against me. Your presence here was not expected or required, little god. This is nothing to do with you."

"Yes it is," said Eddie. "I know what you found in the future, John. I know who you found. I've always known."

I looked at him sharply. I saw him die, in the Timeslip future. I helped him to die. But I never told anyone.

He shrugged easily. "I'm a god, remember?"

"This doesn't have to end in violence," Tommy said urgently, sensing the undercurrents. "You know I'm an honourable man, John."

"You might be," I said. "But Sandra works for Walker. And Walker . . . has his own very personal take on honour, when it comes to the Nightside. He'd sacrifice any number of innocents to preserve the Nightside for the Authorities."

"He was supposed to be here," said Tommy, frowning slightly. "To reassure you of his good intentions. But unfortunately he was called away. It seems something really unpleasant is happening on the Street of the Gods."

We all looked at Razor Eddie, who met our gaze a little reproachfully. "Nothing to do with me," he said.

"Hell with this," said Sandra Chance, rising to her feet in one smooth feline movement. "It's time to take care of business."

"No!" said Tommy, scrambling untidily to his feet. "He has to be given a chance to surrender! You agreed!"

"I lied," said Sandra. "His existence offends me. He killed the Lamentation."

"Ah yes," I said. "Your . . . what was the term, exactly, I wonder? You never did have much taste in lovers, Sandra. The Lamentation was just a nasty little Power with delusions of godhood, and the world smells better now that it's gone."

"It was the Saint of Suffering, and it served a purpose!" Sandra said loudly. "It weeded out the weak and punished the foolish, and I was proud to serve it!"

"Exactly what was your relationship with the Lamentation?" said Tommy Oblivion. His voice was thoughtful and not at all threatening, as his gift manifested subtly on the still air. Tommy could be very persuasive when he chose to be. I don't know whether Sandra could feel what was happening, but she answered anyway, her cold green eyes locked on mine.

"I used to investigate insurance fraud," she said. "And a cluster of unexplained suicides brought me to the Church of the Lamentation. We talked, and we . . . connected. I don't think it had ever met anyone like me, with my fetish for death."

"Kindred spirits, who found each other in Hell," I said softly. "What did you do for the Lamentation, Sandra? What deal did you make with your devil?"

"Your devil, my god," said Sandra Chance. "I became its Judas Goat, leading the suffering to their Saint, and it taught me the ways of the necromancer. It gave me what I'd always wanted. To lie down with death and rise up wreathed in power."

"Of course," said Tommy, "such knowledge usually drives people insane. But you were functionally crazy to begin with."

"Takes one to know one," said Sandra. "Now shut up, Tommy, or I'll do something amusing to you. You're only here on sufferance."

"It was my plan!"

"No," said Sandra. "This was always Walker's plan."

"And you never gave a damn, for all the poor bastards you delivered to your nasty lover?" I said. "To die in despair, then linger in horror, bound even after death to the service of the Lamentation?"

"They were weak," said Sandra. "They gave up. I never broke under the strain, never gave up. I save my help for those who deserve it."

"Of course you didn't care," said Suzie Shooter. "You're even more heartless than I am. I'm going to enjoy killing you."

"Enough talk," said Sandra. "It's time to dance the dance of life and death, little people. I shall raise all those who lie here because of you—John Taylor, Shotgun Suzie, Razor Eddie. All your victims gathered together in one place, with hate and vengeance burning in their cold, cold hearts. And they will drag you down into the cold wet earth and hold you there in their bony arms until finally . . . you stop screaming. Don't say I never did anything for you."

She raised her arms high in the stance of summoning, and chanted ancient Words of Power. Energies crackled fiercely around her extended fingers . . . and nothing happened. The energies dissipated harmlessly on the freezing air, unable to come together. Sandra stood there awkwardly for a long moment, then slowly lowered her arms and looked about her, confused.

"The Necropolis graveyard is protected by seriously heavy-duty magics," said Eddie, in his calm, ghostly voice. "I thought everyone knew that."

"But the magics were supposed to have been suppressed!" said Sandra. "Walker promised me!"

"That wasn't the deal!" said Tommy. "I wasn't told about any of this!"

"You didn't need to know."

There was a pleasant chiming sound, a brief shimmering on the air, and there was Walker, standing before us in his neat city suit and old-school tie. He smiled vaguely about him. "This . . . is a recording. I'm afraid I can't be here with you, on the grounds it might prove injurious to my health. By now you should have realised that the magics of this place have not been shut down, as promised, Sandra Chance. My apologies for the deception; but it was necessary. You see, this isn't just a trap for John Taylor; it's a trap for all of you. Taylor, Shooter, Oblivion, and Chance. I'm afraid you've all become far more trouble than you're worth. And I need to be free to concentrate on the Really Bad Thing that all my best precogs insist is coming. So the decision has been made to dispense with all of you. I have at least extracted a promise from the Authorities that after you've all killed each other, or the cemetery has killed you, your bodies will be buried here, free of charge. It's the least I could do. Good-bye,

John. I am sorry it had to come to this. I protected you for as long as I could . . . but I've always known my duty."

The image of Walker raised his bowler hat in our general direction, then snapped off. There was a long moment of silence.

"We are so screwed," said Suzie.

I looked at Eddie. "He didn't know you'd be here. You're our wild card in this situation."

"It's what I do best," said Eddie.

"Walker, you supercilious son of a bitch!" said Sandra Chance, actually stamping one bare foot in her outrage.

"I wouldn't argue with that," I said. "Ladies and gentlemen, it would appear we have all been declared redundant. Might I suggest it would be in all our best interests to work together, putting aside old quarrels until we're all safely out of here?"

"Agreed," said Sandra, two bright red spots burning on her pale cheeks. "But Walker is mine to kill."

"First things first," I said. "Where is Cathy?"

"Oh, we put her in the mausoleum right behind us," said Tommy. "Sleeping peacefully. You didn't really think I'd stand for her being buried alive, did you? What kind of a person do you think I am?"

"I ought to shoot you both right now, on general principles," said Suzie.

"Later," I said firmly.

The mausoleum was a huge stone Victorian edifice, with all the usual Gothic trimmings, plus a whole bunch of decidedly portly cherubs in mourning. The Victorians could get really sentimental about death. Tommy heaved open the door, and when I looked in there was Cathy, lying curled up on the bare stone floor like a sleeping child. She was wearing something fashionable, under a thick fur coat someone had wrapped around her like a blanket. She was actually snoring slightly. Tommy edged nervously past me, leaned over Cathy, and muttered a few Words under his breath. Cathy came awake immediately and sat up, yawning and knuckling at her sleepy eyes. I moved forward into the mausoleum, and Cathy jumped up and ran forward into my arms. I held her very tightly.

"I knew you'd come and find me," she said, into my shoulder.

"Of course," I said. "How would I ever run my office without you?"

She finally let go, and I did, too. We went out of the mausoleum and into the night, where Tommy Oblivion and Sandra Chance were standing stiffly a little to one side. Cathy stepped briskly forward, got a good hold on Sandra's breasts with both hands, then head-butted her in the face. Sandra fell backwards onto her bare arse, blood spurting from her broken nose. Tommy opened his mouth, either to object or explain, and Cathy kicked him square in the nuts. He went down on his knees, tears streaming past his squeezed-shut eyes, with both hands wedged between his thighs. Perhaps to reassure himself that his testicles were actually still attached.

"Messing with the wrong secretary," said Cathy.

"Nicely done," I said, and Cathy grinned at me.

"You are a bad influence on the child," Suzie said solemnly.

Sometime later we all assembled around the earth barrow. Tommy moved around slowly and carefully, packing up the picnic things, while Sandra stood with her back to all of us, sniffing gingerly through the nose she'd reset herself. Suzie glared suspiciously about her, shotgun at the ready. She was convinced Walker wouldn't have abandoned us here unless he knew there was Something in the cemetery strong and nasty enough to see us all off. She had a point. I turned to Razor Eddie.

"Walker didn't know you'd be here. And I'm reasonably sure he doesn't know about your new ability to cut doors into dimensions with that nasty little blade of yours. Take us home, Eddie, so we can express our extreme displeasure to him in person."

He nodded slightly, and the pearl-handled straight razor gleamed viciously in the starlight as he cut at the air before him, in a movement so fast none of us could follow it. We all braced ourselves, but nothing happened. Eddie frowned and tried again, still to no effect. He slowly lowered his blade and considered the air before him.

"Ah," he said finally.

"Ah?" I said. "What do you mean, *ah*? Is there something wrong with your razor, Eddie?"

"No, there's something wrong with the dimensional barriers."

"I don't like the sound of that, Eddie."

"I'm not too keen on it myself. Someone has strengthened the dimensional barriers, from the outside. No prizes for guessing who."

Cathy hugged my arm tightly. "How does he know things like that?"

"I find it better not to ask," I said. "Eddie, I . . . Eddie, why are you frowning? I really don't like it when you frown."

"Something's . . . changed," he said, his voice stark and flat. He looked around him, and we all did the same. The night seemed no different, cold and still and quiet, the graves unmoving and undisturbed under the gaudy starlight. But Eddie was right. Something had changed. We could all feel it, like the tension that precedes the breaking storm.

"You achieved something, with that spell of yours," Eddie said to Sandra. "It's still trying to work, undischarged in the cemetery atmosphere. It's not enough to affect the dead, but . . ."

"What do you mean, 'but'?" I said. "You can't stop there!"

"She's disturbed Something," said Razor Eddie. "It's been asleep a long time, but now it's waking . . . and it's waking angry."

We moved closer together, staring about us and straining our ears against the silence. The atmosphere in the graveyard was changing. There was a sense of potential on the air, of something about to happen, in this place where nothing was ever supposed to happen. Suzie turned her shotgun this way and that, searching in vain for a target.

"What am I looking for, Eddie?" she said calmly. "What lives in this dimension?"

"I told you. Nothing lives here. That's the point."

"Could the dead be rising up after all?" said Tommy.

"It's not the dead," Sandra said immediately. "I'd know if it was that."

"It's coming," whispered Razor Eddie.

The ground rose sharply beneath our feet, toppling us this way and that. Headstones collapsed or lurched to one side, and the great mausoleums trembled. My first thought was an earthquake, but all around us the graveyard earth was rising and falling, lifting like an ocean swell. We all scrambled onto our feet again, finding things to cling to for support.

"There were rumours," said Sandra Chance, "of a Caretaker, set to guard the graves."

"I never heard of any Caretaker," said Razor Eddie.

"Yes, well, just because you're a god doesn't mean you know everything," said Sandra.

And that was when the graveyard dirt burst up into the air from between the rows of graves, great fountains of dark wet earth shooting up, high into the chilly air. It rained down all around us, forming itself into rough shapes. Dark, earthy human shapes, with rough arms and legs, and blunt heads with no faces. Golems fashioned out of graveyard dirt. They started towards us, slow and clumsy with the power of earth, closing in on us from every direction at once. The ground grew still again, save for the heavy thudding of legs with no feet.

Suzie opened up with her pump-action shotgun. She hit everything she aimed at, blowing ragged chunks of earth out of the heavy lumbering figures, but it didn't slow them down. Not even when she blew their heads off. Sandra chanted Words of Power and stabbed at the advancing earth golems with an aboriginal pointing-bone, and none of it did any good at all. Razor Eddie darted forward, moving supernaturally quickly. Several of the earth figures just fell apart, sliced through again and again. But for every golem that fell, a dozen more rose out of the graveyard earth and headed our way with silent, implacable intent.

I heard muttering beside me. Tommy Oblivion was using his gift to try to convince himself he was somewhere else, but it seemed Walker's dimensional barriers were too strong even for him. Cathy pulled a Kandarian punch dagger from the top of her knee-length boot, and moved to watch my back. She knew her limitations. Sandra was reduced to throwing things from her belt pouches at the approaching golems. None of them did any good.

"I'll have Walker's balls for this!" she screamed.

"Join the queue," I said.

I took out my Club Membership Card. Alex Morrisey gave it to me some time back, when he was in an unusually expansive mood. When properly activated, the magic stored in the Card could transport you right into *Strangefellows*, from wherever you happened to be at the time. I had perhaps used it more often than Alex had intended, because he was always nagging at me to return it, and yet somehow I kept forgetting on purpose to do so. But once again, the magic in the Card was no match for whatever Walker had done to the dimensional barriers. I turned to Suzie.

"Do you have any grenades?"

"Silly question," she said. "You think I'd go out half-dressed?"

"Spread some confusion," I said. "I need some time to concentrate, to raise my gift."

"You got it," said Suzie. "Blessed or cursed grenades, do you think?"

"I'd try both."

"Excellent notion."

She started lobbing grenades in all directions, and everyone else ducked and put their hands over their ears. The explosions dug great craters out of the ground, and bits of golem, coffin wood, and even body parts rained down all around us. Stone fragments from headstones and mausoleums flew on the air like shrapnel. The golems were shredded and rent, flattened and torn apart. And still more rose, forming themselves out of the torn earth.

I closed my eyes and studied the cemetery through my third eye, my private eye. Without Tommy's gift interfering, I could See clearly again. And it only took me a moment to find the source of the consciousness animating the earth golems. It was a diffused, widely spread thing, scattered throughout the whole of the cemetery, and beyond. This was the great secret of the Necropolis graveyard. The last line of defence for the helpless dead. This whole world, the earth and the soil of it, was alive and aware, and set to guard. The Caretaker. A living world, to protect a world's dead.

The Caretaker decided the golems weren't working, or perhaps it sensed my probings into its nature. All the earth in the cemetery rose before us, in a great tidal wave, and thundered forward like a horizontal avalanche. Enough earth to pulverise and drown and bury us all. There was nowhere to run, nowhere to hide, no way to defend ourselves. But I had finally found the weak spot in Walker's plan.

He'd strengthened the spells containing the cemetery dimension, made very sure that nothing could get out. But it had never occurred to him to stop anything from getting in . . . I reached out with my gift, and found a place in the Nightside where it was raining really heavily. And then all I had to do was bring the rain to me and let it pour down. The driving rain hit the tidal wave of earth and washed it away. Thick mud swirled around our feet, but its strength and power were gone. The rain kept hammering down, and the Caretaker couldn't get its earth to hang together long enough to form anything. And while the Caretaker was preoccupied with that, I reached out with my gift again and located the weakest spot in the dimensional barriers containing us. I showed Eddie where it was, and he cut it open with one stroke of his godly razor.

We all ran through the opening, while Eddie strained to keep it open. Then we were all back in the Nightside, and the opening slammed shut behind us. We stood together, soaking wet and smeared with mud, breathing hard. I looked around me. I'd been half-expecting a crowd of Walker's people, set to stand and watch in case we found a way out, but there was no-one. Either Walker hadn't expected any of us to get out . . . or his people were needed somewhere else. Sandra said he'd been called away, to deal with trouble on the Street of the Gods . . . Could Lilith be making her move at last?

Sandra stomped wetly towards me, and I raised an eyebrow. "Relax, Taylor," she said curtly. "You saved my life, and I always pay my debts. Walker has to be shown the error of his ways. I can help. Of course, once that's over . . ."

Cathy fixed Sandra with a thoughtful eye, and the consulting necromancer winced despite herself. Cathy smiled sweetly. "Leave my boss alone, bitch."

"Play nicely, children," I said. "We have to go to the Street of the Gods. I think the shit is finally hitting the fan. Tommy, escort Cathy back to *Strangefellows*, and stay there with her. And don't argue. Neither of you has the firepower for what we're going to be facing. Lock and load, people; we have a Biblical myth to take down."

THREE

Playtime's Over, Children

I wasn't there at the time, but the survivors told me what happened.

It was just another day on the Street of the Gods. That magical, mercurial, and entirely separate place where you can worship whatever you want, or whatever wants you. There are Beings and Powers and Forces, things unknown and things unknowable, and it's all strictly buyer beware. Religion is big business in the Nightside, and on the Street of the Gods you can find something to fit anyone's taste, no matter how bizarre or extreme. Of course, the most popular faiths have the biggest churches and the most magnificent temples, and the best positions on the Street, while everyone else fights it out in a Darwinian struggle for cash, congregations, and more commanding positions. Some gods are very old, some are very rich, and some don't even last long enough to pass around the collection plate.

Gods come and go, faiths rise and fall, but the Street of the Gods goes on forever.

Gargoyles crouched high up on cathedral walls, studying the worshippers below with sardonic eyes, chatting and gossiping and passing round a thick hand-rolled. Strange forms walked openly up and down the Street, going about their unguessable business. Wisps and phantoms floated here and there, troubled by every passing breeze—old gods worn so thin they weren't even memories any more. There were paper lanterns and human candles, burning braziers and bright gaudy neon. Living lightning bolts chased each other up and down the Street. Rival gangs chanted dogma at each other from the safety of their church vestries, and here and there mad-eyed zealots practised curses and damnations on hated enemies. Some of the more fashionable gods strolled up and down the Street in their most dazzling aspects, out and about to see and be seen. And Harlequin danced, in his stark chequered outfit and black domino mask, spinning and pirouetting as he always had, for as long as anyone could remember, on and on, dance without end. Under candlelight, corpselight, and flashing neon, Harlequin danced.

It had to be said—the Street of the Gods had known better days. Just recently, Razor Eddie had lost his temper in the Street and done something extremely distressing, as a result of which some gods had been observed running out of the Street screaming and crying their eyes out. Walker's people were still coaxing them out of bars and gutters and cardboard boxes. On the Street, people were clearing up the wreckage and taking estimates for rebuilding. Churches were surrounded by scaffolding, or held together by glowing bands of pure faith, while those beyond saving were bulldozed flat by remote-controlled juggernauts. The barkers were out in force, drumming up new business, and there were more tourists about than ever. (They do so love a disaster, especially when it's somewhere picturesque.) Some worshippers were still wandering around in a daze, wondering whether their deities would ever return.

Just another day on the Street of the Gods, then—until dead angels began dropping out of the night sky. They fell gracelessly and landed hard, with broken wings and stupid, startled faces, like birds who have flown into the windows of high-rise buildings. They lay on the ground, not moving, creatures of light and darkness, like a child's discarded toys. Everyone regarded the dead angels with awe and some timidity. And then they looked up, the worshippers and the worshipped, to see a greater dark miracle in the starry night sky.

A moonbeam extended lazily down into the Street of the Gods, shimmering silver starstuff, splendid and coldly beautiful, just like the great and awful personage who sailed slowly down it like an ethereal moving stairway, smiling and waving to the crowds below. Lilith had been planning her return for some time, and she did so love to make an entrance.

Inhumanly tall, perfectly formed, and supernaturally feminine, with a skin so pale it was the very antithesis of colour, and hair and eyes and lips blacker than the night, she looked like some screen goddess from the days of silent film. Her face was sharp and pointed, with a prominent bone structure and a hawk nose. Her mouth was thin-lipped and far too wide, and her eyes held a fire that could burn through anything. She was not pretty, but she was beautiful almost beyond bearing. She was naked, but there was nothing vulnerable about her.

Her presence filled the air, like the roar of massed cannon announcing the start of war, or a choir singing obscenities in a cathedral, like the first scream of being born or the last scream of the dying. No-one could look away. And many a lesser god or goddess knelt and bowed, recognising the real thing when they saw it, come at last to the Street of the Gods. There was a halo round Lilith's head, though it was more a presence than a light. Lilith could be very traditional, when she chose. She stepped down off the moonbeam into the Street of the Gods, and smiled about her.

"Hello, everyone," she said, in a voice rich and sweet as poisoned honey. "I'm Lilith, and I'm back. Did you miss me?"

She walked openly in glory through the night, and everyone fell back before her. The great and small alike bowed their heads, unable to meet her gaze. The ground shook and cracked apart beneath the thunder of her tread. Even the biggest and most ornate cathedral seemed suddenly shabby, next to her. She kicked dead angels out of her way with a perfect pale foot, not even looking down, and her dark mouth made a small moue of annoyance.

"Such simple, stupid things," she said. "Neither Heaven nor Hell can stand against me here, in the place I made to be free of both."

Some tourists made the mistake of pressing forward, with their cameras and camcorders. Lilith just looked at them, and they died screaming, with nothing left to mark their presence save agonised shadows, blasted into the brickwork of the buildings behind them.

Lilith stopped abruptly and looked about her, then called in a commanding voice for all the gods to leave their churches and present themselves before her. She called for them by name and by nature, in a language no-one spoke any more. A language so old it couldn't even be recognised as words, only sounds, concepts from an ur-language so ancient as to be beyond civilised comprehension.

And out of the churches and temples and dark hidden places they came, the Beings and Power and Forces who had called themselves gods for so long. Out came Bloody Blades and Soror Marium, the Carrion in Tears and the Devil's Bride, Molly Widdershins, Abomination Inc, the Incarnate and the Engineer. And more and more, the human and the humanoid and the abhuman, the monsters and the magical, the scared and the profane. And some who hadn't left the dark and secret places under their churches for centuries, unseen by generations of their worshippers, who, having finally seen the awful things they'd prayed to for so long, would never do so again. And last of all, Harlequin stopped dancing and came forward to kneel before Lilith.

"My masters and my mistresses," he said, in a calm, cold, and utterly hopeless voice. "The revels now are ended."

The watching crowd grew loudly agitated, crying out in awe and shock and wonder at the unexpected sights before them. They argued amongst themselves as to what it all meant, and zealots struck out at those nearest with fists and harsh words. No-one likes to admit they may have backed a losing horse. The quicker-thinking in the crowd were already kneeling and crying out praises to Lilith. The prophesiers of doom, those persistent grey creatures with their hand-made signs saying THE END IS NIGH seemed most put out. They hadn't seen this coming. Lilith smiled at them.

"You are all redundant now. I am the End you have been waiting for."

More shadows, blasted into crumbling brickwork, more fading echoes of startled screams.

Lilith looked unhurriedly about her, considering the various divine forms gathered before her, in all their shapes and incarnations, and they all flinched a little under that thoughtful gaze, even if they didn't remember why. She made them feel nervous, unworthy, on some deep and primal level. As though she knew something they had tried very hard to forget, or, if never known, had somehow always suspected.

"I am Lilith," she said finally. "First wife to Adam, thrown out of Eden for refusing to acknowledge any authority but mine own. I descended into Hell and lay down with demons, and gave birth to monsters. All my marvellous children—the first to be invited to dwell in my Nightside. You are all my children, or descendants of my children. You are not gods, and never were. It takes more than worship to make you divine. I made you to be splendid and free, but you have grown small and limited down the many years, seduced by worship and acclaim, allowed yourselves to be shaped and enslaved by the imaginations of humanity. Well, playtime is over now, children. I am back, in the place I made for us, and it's time to go to work. I've been away too long, and there is much to be put right.

"I have been here for some time, watching and learning. I walked among you, and you knew me not. You've been playing at being gods for so long you've forgotten you were ever anything else. But you owe your existence and loyalty to me. Your lives are mine, to do with as I please."

The Beings and Forces and Powers looked at each other, stirring uneasily. It was all happening so fast. One minute they were being worshipped as divine, and the next . . . Some of them were beginning to remember. Some shook their heads in hopeless denial, even as tears ran down their faces. Some didn't take at all kindly to being reminded of their true origins and obligations, and shouted defiance. And quite a large number were distinctly resentful at finding out they weren't gods at all and never had been. The watching worshippers retreated to what they hoped was a safe distance, and let the gods argue it out amongst themselves. The argument was getting quite noisy, if not actually raucous, when Lilith silenced them all with a single sharp gesture.

"You," she said, pointing to a single figure at the front of the pack. "I don't know you. You're not one of mine. What are you?"

The Engineer stared calmly back at her, while everyone else edged away from him. He was squat and broad and only vaguely humanoid, with blue steel shapes piercing blue flesh, and long strips of bare muscle tissue held together with bolts and springs. Steam hissed from his naked joints, his eyes glowed like coals, and if you got close enough you could hear his heart ticking. He was surrounded and protected by a group of gangling metal constructions, of intricate design and baroque sensibilities, though whether they were the engineer's worshippers or his creations was unclear.

"I am a Transient Being," said the Engineer, in a voice like metal scraping against metal. "A physical incarnation of an abstract idea. I am immortal because I am a concept, not because I have your unnatural blood in my ancestry. The world has become so much more complex since your time, Lilith. All of this . . . is none of my business. So I'll leave you to get on with it."

He turned and walked sideways from the world, disappearing down a direction most of those present couldn't even comprehend, let alone identify, and in a moment he was gone. The steel-and-brass constructions he left behind collapsed emptily, so much scrap metal littering the ground. Lilith stood silent for a moment, nonplussed. That hadn't been in the script. Emboldened by the Engineer's defiance, some of the Beings stepped forward to confront Lilith.

"We heard you were banished," drawled the Splendid, leaving a shimmering trail behind him as he moved. "Forced out of the world you made, by those you trusted and empowered."

"Thrust into Limbo," said La Belle Dame du Rocher, in her watery voice. "Until some damned fool let you out, let you back into the Nightside to trouble us again with bad dreams of our beginnings."

"Some say you've been here for years," said Molly Widdershins, showing her stained and blocky teeth in something that was only nominally a smile. "So where have you been hiding, all this time?"

"Not hiding," said Lilith, and the chill in her voice made them all fall back a pace. "I've been . . . preparing. So much to do, and so many to do it to. And then, of course, I had to produce a new child, and see to his education. He is mine, body and soul, even if he doesn't realise it yet. My dearest darling John Taylor."

The name rumbled through the crowd, from worshippers and worshipped alike, and not in a good way. Many shifted uneasily, and aspects flickered on and off in the crowd like heat lightning. The Splendid opened his perfect mouth to protest further, and Lilith reached out and touched him lightly on the forehead. He cried out in shock and horror as his life energy was ripped right out of him, to feed Lilith's endless hunger. She sucked him dry in a moment, watching calmly as he crumpled and shrivelled up before her, all his power nothing more to her than a drop in her ocean. The Splendid blinked out and was gone, as though he had never been. Lilith smiled about her.

"Just a little illustration of my mood, so everyone knows where they stand. I may be your mother, but I won't abide over-familiarity. Now, where are those who banded together to betray me, so very long ago? To banish me from my own creation? Step forward, that I might look upon your faces once again."

There was a long, uncomfortable pause, then the Devil's Bride stepped forward reluctantly, the conjoined twin in the hump on her back peering over her shoulder. "They're all gone, mistress," said the little twin, in a sweet seductive voice. "Long and long ago. They killed each other, or were brought down, or grew irrelevant to the modern world and just faded away. There's only one left that we know of. Its original name is lost to us. We call it the Carrion in Tears, and it is quite insane."

She darted back into the safety of the crowd, while others pushed forward the Carrion in Tears, a huge body of rotting flesh, red and black and purple, with jagged ends of bones protruding from suppurating flesh. Forever decaying, never dying, quite mad. It snapped at the world with broken teeth, dull grey in muddy scarlet flesh, and its cloudy eyes were fixed and staring.

"It incorporates dead things into itself," volunteered Molly Widdershins. "They keep it going. Make it strong."

"And this . . . has followers?" said Lilith.

"Of a kind," said Molly.

"Proof, if proof were needed, that some people will worship absolutely anything," said Lilith. "As long as it has the stink of immortality about it."

Some of the Carrion in Tears' worshippers were thrust forward through the crowd, to face Lilith. They dressed in soiled rags and torn plastic, with grime artfully smeared across their faces. The oldest among them raised his head proudly and stood defiantly before Lilith.

"We worship it because it shows us the truth. The real world is filth and rot, pollution and corruption. Our god shows us the dirty truth behind the pretty face. When all else is fallen into ruin, our god will remain, and we will be with him."

"No you won't," said Lilith. "You offend me even more than he does." And she killed them all, with a glance.

The Carrion in Tears didn't notice. It was too busy digesting a dead angel it had noticed lying by its foot. Inch by inch, the dead angel was sucked into the Being's corrupt flesh and absorbed. The smell was awful, and even other Beings looked away. The Carrion in Tears straightened up abruptly, as the last lingering traces of the angel's divine energies surged through it, and shocked the slumbering mind awake. It cried out, a thick choking sound of horrid awareness, and fixed Lilith with its staring eyes.

"You! This is all your fault! See what has become of me! Look at what driving you out did to me!"

"I see it," Lilith said calmly. "Fair punishment, I'd have said, for a traitor and a fool."

"It was necessary," said the Carrion in Tears, but it sounded tired, as though repeating an old, worn-out argument. "And now you're back, and it was all for nothing. I told them, but they wouldn't listen . . . Kill me if you want. I don't care. I was beautiful once, and adored . . . I don't recognise this Nightside. You won't either. It's all changed. It's moved on and left us behind."

"Killing you would be a mercy, in your current state," said Lilith. "But what the hell. Don't say I never did anything for you."

She absorbed all its living energies in a moment, then made a moue of distaste with her night-dark mouth as the Carrion in Tears vanished into her. "Nasty," she said to the silent crowd. "But I promised myself that I'd kill all of my old enemies who survived, and I always keep my word. Now, step forward, my children. The original productions of my young and lusty flesh."

She called for them by their original names, and again there was a long pause. Finally, a mere handful of Beings made their way to the front of the crowd to face their long-forgotten mother. First was the Harlequin, who knelt before her in his chequered finery and bowed his masked head to her.

"I am here, mother dear, though much-changed by time and circumstance. I allowed myself to be shaped by fashion and fad, but still I survive, and still I dance. I would like to think that you could still see something in me that you would recognise."

"I change, too, when I must," said the Incarnate, bowing elegantly to Lilith. He was young and pretty, dressed in an immaculate white suit of impeccable cut, his noble face attractively androgynous under a white panama hat. "The details change, but I go on, worshipped and adored. At present I am a pop sensation, singing for my supper, and teenage girls worship my image on their bedroom walls. I am the Thin White Prince, and they love my music and they love me. Don't you, my little doves?"

A pack of fierce young girls surrounded him, dressed just like him, their overly made-up faces sullen and aggressive. You could see in their faces that he was more than life itself to them, and they would die for him in a moment. Some actually spat and hissed at Lilith, sensing a threat to their beloved idol. The oldest of them couldn't have been more than fifteen.

"I know," said the Thin White Prince. "But one takes one's adoration where one can find it."

And finally, there was Bloody Blades. He crouched uncertainly before Lilith, snorting and quivering, held in place by ancient instinct. He was huge and hairy, with hooves and horns and terrible clawed hands. He stank of sweat and musk and uncontrolled appetites. He glowered at Lilith with stupid, crafty eyes, attracted by her femininity but cowed by the sheer power he sensed in her.

"There's not much left of Bloody Bones," said Harlequin. "He's been reduced to a purely animal nature, a god of wild actions and transgression without conscience. There are always men and women ready to worship the beast within. There are those who say he did this to himself, quite deliberately, to free his needs and appetites from the tyranny of reason."

"How very depressing," said Lilith. "From all the thousands who spilled from my fecund loins, only three remain? And all of you so much less than I made you to be."

She killed them all, contemptuously, sucking in their life energies, then murdered all of the Incarnate's child followers with a casual wave of her hand, just to be thorough. Her power beat on the air like a storm that sweeps all before it, and the assembled crowd quailed under her cold gaze.

"It's time," said Lilith, and all those present shuddered at the power in her voice. "Time for you to choose which side you're on. I'm back, ready to remake the Nightside in my own image, to restore it to what I originally intended it to be. It was never meant to be this . . . small, shabby thing. I will make the Nightside glorious again, and you with it. Unless you choose to stand against me, in which case no-one will even remember your names."

Beings and Forces and Powers glanced at each other uneasily, and there was much muttered conversation. The main gist of it was that they liked things the way they were. They liked being gods, being worshipped and feared and adored. They liked being rich and famous and revered. (And if these were all very human things for a god to value, no-one said so.) Give all this up, to see their world and their very selves remade according to Lilith's whim? Unthinkable. And yet . . . she was Lilith. No-one doubted that. Greater than the Nightside and destroyer of those who only thought themselves to be gods. In the name of survival, it might be wise to go along . . . for a while . . . and hope some opportunity might arise where they could rid themselves again of this unwanted matriarch.

And so the argument went this way and that, while Lilith waited patiently, amusing herself by killing people at random if they didn't look respectful enough. And in the end, it was left to one of the more modern manifestations, Abomination Inc, to step forward and speak first.

Ever since the law decided that corporations were, technically speaking, both persons and immortal, it was inevitable that one would grow large and powerful enough to be worshipped as a god. Abomination Inc manifested itself through a crowd of faceless worker drones, all dressed exactly the same. Grey men in grey suits, they spoke in chorus.

"We are a god of this time. It suits us, and we are suited to it. Why should we give up all that we are, and that we intend to be? We have no reason to believe that you have our best interests at heart."

Next up were the Little Sisters of the Immaculate Chain-saw. Terrifying figures in stark black and white, these nuns were dogmatists first and foremost, and modern dogmatists at that. They cursed and abused Lilith in rich, vibrant voices and defied her with awful threats.

Others stepped forward, representing the modern religions of a modern world, but already other voices were rising in the crowd to shout them down. Older voices, remembering old ways, and lesser voices seeing hope in a changed future. And so, just like that, the god war started. Beings and Forces and Powers went head to head, aspects clashing like mighty engines in the night, while strange energies boiled on the still air. And as above, so below, with whole armies of the faithful going for each other's throats. Hot and vicious murder ran up and down the Street of the Gods, sucking everyone in, and bodies piled up as blood flowed thickly in the gutters.

Lilith rose gracefully into the starry sky, looking down upon what she had brought about, and laughed aloud to see such slaughter done in her name. She encouraged those of her children who followed her to kill their brothers and sisters who didn't, and encouraged their followers to fight and riot and delight in the death of their enemies. She wanted them to get a taste for it. There would be much more of this, when they went out into the Nightside. But for now, murdering their fellows would help to bind the survivors more closely to her.

She walked in glory down the Street of the Gods, treading the air high above the conflict that surged back and forth, while lesser beings raged beneath her. Wherever she passed, churches and temples and cathedrals juddered and shook themselves to pieces, and were swallowed up by the ground breaking apart beneath them. Lilith was sending them all to Hell, by the direct route. Gods and followers caught within these sanctuaries, too scared to come out and face Lilith, died screaming.

"There shall be no other gods but me," said Lilith, her voice rising effortlessly above the roars and screams and howls of the violence below. "All who live in the Nightside shall worship only me. This is my place, and I am all you need to know."

And that was when Walker showed up. He came strolling casually down the Street of the Gods, in his smart city suit, and everything slowed to a halt as word of his progress went ahead of him. People and Beings stopped fighting, backing away from each other and from him. They withdrew to the sidewalks and watched silently as he passed by, not even acknowledging their presence. Beings and Forces and Powers stopped doing distressing things to each other and stood still, waiting to see what would happen. A slow sullen silence fell across the bloody Street, and the god war stopped. All of this, simply because Walker had come to the Street of the Gods.

He brought no backup with him, no bodyguards, specialised operatives, or armed forces. His presence was enough to calm and intimidate all those around him. Gods and their followers looked sheepishly at the destruction they'd wrought, like children caught in the act of doing something naughty. Because this was Walker, the Voice of the Authorities, whose word was law. The single most implacable force in the Nightside. He finally came to a halt, looking up at Lilith standing on the air. They considered each other for a while, then Walker smiled and tipped his bowler hat to her. Walker had style. Lilith dropped elegantly down to stand on the bloody Street before him, and if he was aware of her nakedness or the sexuality that burned in her like a furnace, he gave no sign of it. He looked around at the scattered bodies, the burning churches, then at the watching gods and their followers, none of whom could meet his gaze.

"That's quite enough of that," he said crisply, not looking at anyone in particular, though everyone just knew he was talking to them. "Never seen such a mess. You will stop this nonsense immediately and start clearing up. You wouldn't want me to get upset, would you?"

Some of the gods and their congregations were already backing away, muttering excuses and apologies, and in some cases actually trying to hide behind each other. They all knew the names and legends of those poor unfortunates who'd upset Walker in the past, and the terrible things that had happened to them. But all that stopped as Lilith addressed Walker in a loud and carrying voice that had not the slightest trace of fear or unease in it. If anything, she seemed . . . amused.

"Dear Henry, so good to see you again. You've come such a long way, since we last met."

Walker raised an elegant eyebrow. "You have the advantage of me, madam. I seem to recognise the voice, but . . ."

"Oh Henry, have you forgotten your dear little Fennella Davis so soon?" said Lilith, and Walker actually caught his breath, as though he'd been hit.

"So . . ." he said finally. "Lilith. This is what you really look like."

Lilith laughed, shaking her head a little coquettishly. "This . . . is as much of me as human senses can stand. You must remember that the whole Eden thing is just a parable. Really, this body is something I use to walk around in, in your limited world. Once I have refashioned the Nightside into something more suited to my needs and nature, I will bring all of myself here, and I will be glorious indeed."

"What are you?" said Walker. "I mean, what are you, really?"

"I am of the first creation," said Lilith. "I am what came first, long before this world was. I am also Charles Taylor's wife and John Taylor's mother. I am what three foolish boys summoned into the world, unknowingly. Oh dear Henry, am I everything you thought I'd be?"

"Stand where you are," said Walker, and his words thundered on the air. He was using the Voice the Authorities had given him, that could not be denied by the living or the dead. *"Surrender yourself to me, Lilith, and do no more harm."*

Lilith laughed at him, and the Voice's power shattered on the air like cheap glass. "Don't be silly, Henry. Your Voice was only ever designed to work on the things of this world, and I am so much more than that. Run away, dear Henry, and hide until I come for you. I have a special reward in mind for you. You will worship me, and love me, and I will make you immortal in some more pleasing shape, so that you can sing my praises for all eternity. Won't that be fun?"

"I'd rather die," said Walker.

Lilith slapped him aside contemptuously, and her slender pale arm hit him like a battering ram. His bones broke under the force of the blow, and blood flew on the air as he flew backwards, crashing into the wall of a half-buried church. He fell to the ground like a broken doll, and the church wall collapsed on top of him. The gods and their worshippers watched the rubble settle, then watched some more, but Walker, who could have called down armies from both Church and State with but a word, did not emerge.

The god war was over. Everyone had seen the Authorities' Voice crushed and broken in a moment, his power brushed aside like an annoying insect, and that was enough for them. They knelt and bowed their heads to Lilith, then joined up behind her as she led her army in triumph down the Street of the Gods and out into the Nightside.

Not long after that, I finally turned up, with Shotgun Suzie, Razor Eddie, and Sandra Chance. The Street was a mess, with ruined buildings to every side, unattended fires sending up thick black smoke that stank of incense, and the dead and the dying lying ignored. The survivors and the walking wounded stumbled this way and that, deep in shock, only left behind because they were too damaged to be of use. It said something for Razor Eddie's reputation that broken, dazed, and defeated as they were, many of them took one look at Eddie and started running. Rather more unsettlingly, a whole lot more took one look at me and came forward to kneel before me, praising me as Lilith's son and calling on me for mercy and deliverance.

"All right," said Suzie, curling her upper lip. "This is seriously freaking me out."

"You're not alone," I said. "You! Let go of my leg, right now."

"No-one ever kneels to me," said Suzie. "You there! Yes, you, stop shaking and tell us what the hell happened here."

It took a while, but we finally got the story out of them. Lilith had made her triumphant return to the Nightside, and I'd missed it. The shivering wrecks before us made it very clear that Mommie Dearest was looking for me. And not necessarily in a good way. It seemed she had some special purpose in mind for her only begotten child.

"Tough," I said. "I don't happen to feel like obliging her. At least, not yet. When we finally do meet, I want it to be on my terms, on my home ground."

By now, word of my arrival had spread up and down the Street of the Gods, and a mob of ragged people formed around us, half out of their minds with fear and anger, crying out *Blasphemer!* and *Drag him down!* and *Take him to Lilith!* Suzie and Eddie and Sandra moved in close beside me, but the mob didn't even see them. There were hundreds of them now, with more coming, faces twisted with hate and loathing, reaching out for me with clawed hands. They surged forward from all sides, and before I could say anything, Suzie opened up with her pump-action shotgun, blowing great holes in the advancing ranks. They kept coming. Razor Eddie cut a bloody path through them, moving too fast for the human eye to follow. Then Sandra Chance raised the bodies of the fallen dead to attack the living, and that was too much for the mob. The crowd broke apart and quickly dispersed, scattering in all directions, leaving the dead and dying behind. I couldn't feel angry at them. None of this was their fault, really. It was just that my mother made such a powerful impression on people. Suzie lowered her shotgun and reloaded. Eddie reappeared at my side, his razor dripping blood. Sandra let the dead lie down again. A shivering acolyte in an Aztec feathered headdress approached her timidly.

"If you can raise the dead, could you perhaps . . . ?"

"Sorry, no," said Sandra Chance. "Raising dead gods is beyond me. Besides, if he stays dead, he probably wasn't much of a god to begin with, was he?"

The acolyte burst into tears, and we left him sitting there on the shattered steps of what had once been his temple.

"Ms. Tact," said Suzie, to Sandra.

"You'd know," said Sandra.

"Where's Walker?" said Eddie. "I don't see a body anywhere, and you know what they say in the Nightside—if you don't see a body, they're almost certainly not dead."

"I think I can help you there," said a sad-eyed priest. "You'll find him over there, under what's left of my church."

We thanked him and approached the remains of what might once have been a pretty impressive edifice. Half of it was still on fire, burning sullenly in the still night air. In the end, we had to dig through a pile of rubble, hauling it away brick by brick, to uncover Walker. His suit was tattered and torn and soaked with blood, but he still opened his eyes the moment I leaned over him. He even managed a small smile.

"John," he said faintly. "Late, as usual. I've been having a few words with your mother."

"So I see," I said. "You can't get on with anyone, can you?"

We dug him out, and sat him up with his back against a wall. He never made a sound the whole time. Suzie checked him over with brisk efficiency. Suzie knows a lot about wounds, from both ends. Eventually she stood back and nodded to me.

"He's damaged, but he'll live."

"Oh good," said Walker. "For a while there, I was almost worried."

"You should be," said Sandra Chance. "You trapped us all in the cemetery dimension and left us there to die. We had an agreement, and you broke it. No-one does that to me and lives."

"You can't kill him now," I said.

"Why not?" said Sandra, turning the full force of her cold, angry gaze upon me. I looked back at her steadily.

"Because he was my father's friend. Because I don't kill in cold blood. And because I have a use for him."

"Practical as ever, John," said Walker.

Sandra frowned. "This plan. Will he like it?"

"Almost definitely not."

"Then I'll wait," said Sandra Chance.

I crouched down before Walker so I could look right into his face. "She's back," I said. "Lilith. My mother. Back to tear down the Nightside and replace it with something that will have no room in it for Humanity.

And if I try to stop her, just maybe she'll bring down the whole world. I can't do this alone, Walker. I need your help."

He smiled briefly. "We're finally on the same wavelength. Pity it took such dire straits to bring us together."

"Don't kid yourself," I said. "All we have in common is a mutual enemy."

"Yes. Someone who's worse than either of us."

"You should know," I said. "You brought her here, through the Babalon Working. You, and the Collector, and my father."

"Ah," said Walker. "So you worked it out, finally. I was beginning to think you were a bit slow. You'll have all the support I can raise from the Authorities, but it'll take more than an army of warm bodies and everyday magics to stop Lilith."

"I have a few old friends and allies in mind," I said. "And a plan I can practically guarantee no-one's going to like." I turned to Suzie. "Take Sandra and Eddie and get Walker back to *Strangefellows*. Alex can fix him up, but make sure he doesn't try to put it on my tab. Then you wait there, till I get back."

"Hell with that," Suzie said immediately. "Wherever you're going, you'll need me to watch your back."

"Not this time," I said gently. "I need you with the others. You're the only one I can trust. And besides . . . I don't want you to see some of the things I might have to do."

She smiled briefly. "You pick the damnedest times to worry about my feelings, John."

"Somebody has to," I said.

FOUR

Not Fade Away

How do you take down an army of ex-gods? Well, when the living can't help you, start with the dead. I left the Street of the Gods by one of the less-travelled exits and made my way through the crowded streets of the Nightside, heading for Uptown, where they keep all the really weird clubs. I was looking for Dead Boy, and I didn't have a lot of time. Given the sheer size and scope of the Nightside, it would take even Lilith and her army quite a while to make any real impression, but the news would start to spread soon enough. Bad news always does.

The night air was crisp and clear, the pavements were slick from a recent rain, and the scene was jumping, like always. There might be rumours of riot and mayhem and imminent apocalypse, but that was simply business as usual in the Nightside. Especially at weekends. And yet . . . I sensed a growing jittery feeling among people I passed, a sense of nervous anticipation, even if no-one seemed too sure about what. I fought down an urge to hurry, not wanting to attract attention to myself. I had time. Even with Walker taken out of the picture, the Authorities would still be able to throw whole armies into Lilith's path, armed with guns and blades and magics and all the usual nasty surprises. They'd slow her down. For a while.

People around me kept glancing up at the night sky, as though half-expecting the stars to have changed position, or the oversized full moon to have turned bloodred. Something new and dangerous had come into the Nightside, and they could all sense it, like cattle approaching a slaughterhouse. Everyone seemed sharper and almost spookily alert, and the intensity of the night moved up another notch.

Striding back and forth outside the ever-welcoming doors of disreputable clubs, the barkers hawked their wares with a new urgency, while on every street corner the come-ons from the scarlet lips of the twilight daughters was a little bit more aggressive. Tides of people surged this way and that, the casual stroll giving way to the determined march, as though the punters were afraid that what they were looking for might not be there when they got there. A new Special Edition of the Nightside's only daily paper, the *Night Times*, was just hitting the streets, and people crowded round the news vendors, almost snatching the papers out of their hands, then chattering animatedly over the heavy black headlines. I had no doubt that Lilith had made the front page, and probably most of the other pages, too. I needed to get my plan up and running before everything started falling apart. And for that, I needed Dead Boy.

It wasn't hard to find the lap-dancing club where he was working as a bouncer. Bit of a come-down, for the Nightside's most eminent vigilante, dark avenger, and first line of defence against the legions of the dead, but presumably there were fringe benefits. I stopped before the club and studied it carefully from what I hoped was a safe distance. The flashing neon sign over the gaping door spelled out the club's name, NOT FADE AWAY, in colours so bright and garish they practically stabbed into my eyes. To either side were neon figures of dancing girls, jiggling eternally from one uncomfortable-looking position to another, back and forth, back and forth. A grubby window held photographs of the glamorous girls one could hope to find inside the club, though experience led me to believe the girls actually on display would look nothing like the photos.

The barker lounging by the door inhabited a brightly coloured check coat, with a revolving bow tie and a grin so fixed it bordered on the unnatural. He'd started out life as a ventriloquist's dummy, and never really got over it. Seeing my interest he fixed me with his brightly shining eyes and launched into his spiel.

"They're dead, they're naked, and they dance!"

I fixed him with my best cold stare. "Do I look like a tourist?"

He sneered and moved away from the door, waving me in. I passed him by with as much dignity as was possible under the circumstances. Inside the lap-dancing club, someone tried to take my coat, and I punched him out. Start as you mean to go on . . . The transition from chilly night to sweltering lounge was abrupt, and I stopped inside the main area to get my bearings. The management kept the lights down to a comforting gloom, partly to give the punters a sense of privacy, but mostly so you wouldn't get too good a look at the rest of the clientele. The air was thick with all kinds of smoke, and rank with the stink of sweat and desire and desperation. There were ratty-looking tables and chairs for the scattered audience, and cheap plywood booths at the back for more private encounters. The customers were mostly men, mostly human, their eyes fixed hungrily on the four separate spotlighted stages where the dancers swayed back and forth to the over-amplified music.

There were girls, up on the stages and in and among the audience, showing off what they'd got and what they could do, all of them naked, all of them dead. The spirits of departed women, condemned to wander the Earth for this reason or that, lap-dancing for the living. Some seemed completely real and solid, while others were only wisps of smoke or mist, tinted all of the colours of the rainbow by the coloured gels rotating in front of the stage lights. Most of the girls drifted from one state to the other and back again, as they stamped and spun and shook their breasts, pumping their hips and curling around the steel poles on the stages, all the time favouring the nearest customers with wide smiles that meant nothing, nothing at all. Ghostly girls, the dancing dead—the ultimate look but don't touch.

There was a tacky-looking bar set to one side, and leaning up against it, the legendary Dead Boy himself. Technically speaking, he wasn't old enough to be in a club like this. Dead Boy was seventeen, and had been for some thirty years, ever since he was murdered—clubbed down in the street for his credit cards and mobile phone. He came back from the dead, after making a deal with someone he still preferred not to name, and took a terrible vengeance on his killers, only to find that his deal made it impossible for him to go to his rest afterwards. And so he walks the Nightside, forever young, forever damned, his spirit possessing his own dead body, doing good deeds in the hope that eventually he'll accumulate enough goodwill in Heaven to break the terms of the deal he made.

He was tall and adolescent thin, wrapped in a dark purple greatcoat, over black leather trousers and tall calfskin boots. He wore a black rose on one lapel and a large floppy black hat perched on the back of his head. His coat hung open, revealing a corpse-pale torso held together with stitches and staples and duct tape. He doesn't feel pain any more, but he can still take damage. If I looked closely I could see the bullet hole in his forehead that he'd filled in with builder's putty.

His long white face had a weary, debauched look, with burning fever-bright eyes and a pouting sulky mouth with no colour in it. He had experimented with makeup, but mostly he just couldn't be bothered. Long dark hair fell to his shoulders in oiled ringlets. He looked calm, casual, even bored. He was drinking whiskey straight from the bottle and eating Neapolitan ice cream straight from the tub. He nodded easily as I came over to join him.

"Hello, Taylor," he said indistinctly, around a mouthful of ice cream. "Pardon my indulgence, but when you're dead you have to take your pleasures where you can find them. I'd offer you a drink, but I've only got the one bottle. And don't order anything from the bar—their prices are appalling, and the drinks are worse."

I nodded. I already knew that. I'd been here once before, working a case, and had allowed myself to be persuaded to order what passed for champagne. It tasted like cherry cola. Nothing was what it seemed, here. Even the waitress had an Adam's apple.

"So you're the bouncer?" I said, leaning easily back against the bar beside him.

"I run security here," he corrected me. "I keep an eye on things. Most of the punters take one look at me, and know better than to start anything."

"I thought you had a steady gig, body-guarding that singer, Rossignol?"

He shrugged. "She's off touring Europe. And I . . . prefer not to leave the Nightside. This job's just temporary, until I can scare something else up. Even the dead have to earn a living. Hence the girls here."

I nodded. The Nightside accumulates more than its fair share of ghosts and revenants, one way and another, and they all have to go somewhere.

"Where do the girls go, when they're not working?" I asked.

Dead Boy gave me a pitying look. "They're *always* working. That's the point. It's not like they ever get tired . . ."

"What do the girls get out of this? The money can't be that good."

"It isn't. But a clever girl can make a lot from tips, and the management guarantees to keep the girls safe from necromancers, plus all the other unsavoury types who use the energies of the departed to fuel their magics. And of course all the girls hope to hook an appreciative customer, turn him into a regular, and milk him for all he's worth."

I looked out over the widely spread audience. "Anyone interesting in tonight?"

"A few names, a few faces, no-one you'd know and no-one worth noting. Though we do have several diminutive professors, who claim they're here researching modern slang. They loved it when I told them this club was licensed to dispense *spirits* . . ."

I smiled dutifully. Dead Boy shrugged and took a good slug from his bottle. It was nearly empty.

I watched the ghost girls dance. Putting off the moment when I'd have to tell Dead Boy why I was there. They were currently spinning and gyrating to an old Duran Duran number, "Girls on Film," and being ghosts they were all supernaturally beautiful, impossible lithe, and utterly glamorous. They danced with implacable grace, stamping their bare feet and jiggling their oversized breasts, rising from the stages to slide and sweep through the smoky air. Those in and among the audience drifted around and sometimes even through the customers, giving them a thrill they wouldn't find anywhere else. And why not? The steel poles were the only truly solid things on those stages.

"Don't get tempted," said Dead Boy, putting down his empty bottle and scraped-clean ice cream tub. "It's all just a glamour. You wouldn't want to see what they really look like when they drop their illusions between sets. Unfortunately, being dead I always see them as they really are, which takes a lot of the fun out of this job."

One girl swayed deliciously down from her stage, seemingly completely solid, until she extended one finger to a chosen customer, and he breathed it in, inhaling it like cigar smoke. The girl's hand unravelled, disappearing into his mouth and nostrils, until he couldn't take any more, and let it all back out again in coughs and snorts. The girl giggled as her hand reassembled. Up on one of the stages, a girl suddenly caught fire but kept dancing, unconsumed.

"An old flame of mine," Dead Boy said solemnly.

There are quite a few clubs in Uptown that cater to the various forms of death fetish, from mummification to premature burial, and some places that would freak out even hard-core Goths; clubs like *Peaceful Repose*, where you can try out being dead for a while to see what it feels like. Or the brothel where you can pay to have sex with female vampires, ghouls, and zombies. There are always those who like their meat cold, with the taste of formaldehyde on their lips . . .

I said as much to Dead Boy, who only showed any interest when I got to the brothel. He actually got out a notebook and pencil for the address.

"Trust me," I said firmly. "You really don't want to go there. You'll end up with worms."

And then one of the ghost dancers caught my attention, as she beckoned coyly to a customer and led him, half-walking and half-swaying, across the gloomy club to one of the private booths at the rear. The customer was tall and skinny, with a furtive air about him. The two of them disappeared into a booth and shut the door firmly behind them. I turned to Dead Boy.

"All right, what's the point of that? I mean, if she's not solid enough to touch . . ."

"Love always finds a way," said Dead Boy. "Instead of an exchange of fluids, an exchange of energies. All purely consensual, of course. The ghost girl absorbs a little of the customer's life energy, which I'm told feels very nice, and she becomes a little more solid, so she can . . . take care of him. A benefit to both sides. The more life energies a girl collects, the more solid and real she can become. Theoretically, she could even become alive again . . . Sometimes the girls go too far and drain the cus-

tomer dry. Then we end up with a really pissed off customer ghost haunting the place and acting up dead cranky. Management keeps an exorcism
service on speed dial for just such occurrences . . ."

The door to the private booth opened, and the customer came out
again. He hadn't been in there long. And when he'd gone in he'd been
skinny as a whip, but now he was noticeably overweight, with an extensive bulging belly. Dead Boy cursed briefly and pushed himself away
from the bar.

"What is it?" I said.

"The bastard's a soul thief," Dead Boy said curtly. "He's *inhaled* the
ghost girl, every last smoky bit of her, and now he's containing her inside
himself, hoping to smuggle her out. Let's go."

We headed purposefully across the floor, and the punters hurried to
get out of our way. The fat man saw Dead Boy coming, pulled an intricate glass charm out of his pocket, and threw it on the floor. The glass
shattered, releasing the pre-prepared spell, and Dead Boy stopped as
though he'd run into an invisible wall, his colourless face twisted in a
pained grimace.

"It's an antipossession spell," he grunted. "Trying to force me out of
my body. Stop the bastard, John. Don't let him get away with the girl."

I hurried forward to block the fat man's way. He stopped, studied me
cautiously, and reached into his pocket again. I fired up my gift just long
enough to locate the spell he was using to contain the ghost within him
and ripped it away. I shut down my gift as the fat man convulsed, staggering back and forth as his imposing stomach bulged and rippled like a
sheet in the wind. I got behind him, grabbed him in a bear hug, and
squeezed with all my strength. Thick streams of smoke came pouring out
of his mouth and nostrils, quickly forming into the ghost girl. The
bulging stomach flattened under my grip, and the ghost girl stood fuming
before us. She solidified one leg just long enough to kick the soul thief
really hard in the nuts, then she stalked away. I let go of the soul thief,
and he collapsed to the floor, looking very much as though he wished he
was dead.

I left him there and went back to Dead Boy, who was looking much
better.

"Cheap piece of rubbish spell," he said cheerfully. "Almost an insult,
expecting something like that to take me out. My soul was put back by an
expert. Leave the soul thief to me, John. I'll arrange for something suitably humiliating and nasty to happen to him."

We strolled back to the bar, where the barmaid had a fresh bottle of
whiskey waiting for Dead Boy. He reached for it, then hesitated, and gave
me a long, considering look.

"You didn't come here just to inquire after my nonexistent health, Taylor. What do you want with me?"

"I need your help. My mother is finally back, and the shit is hitting the fan in no uncertain manner."

"Why is it people only ever come to me when they want something?" Dead Boy said wistfully. "And usually only after everything's already gone to Hell and worse?"

"I think you just answered your own question," I said. "That's what you get, for being such a great back-stop."

"Give me the details," said Dead Boy.

I gave him the edited version, but even so he winced several times, and by the end he was shaking his head firmly.

"No. No way. I do not get involved with Old Testament forces. They are too hard-core, even for me."

"I need your help."

"Tough."

"You have to help me, Dead Boy."

"No I bloody don't. I don't have to do anything I don't want to. Being dead is very liberating that way."

"My mother is leading an army of Beings from the Street of the Gods. She has to be stopped."

"Good luck with that, John. Do send me a postcard as to how you got on. I'll be in the Arctic. Hiding under a polar bear."

"I have a plan . . ."

"You always do! The answer's still no. I do not go up against gods. I know my limitations."

I fixed him with my best cold stare. "If you're not with us, you're against us. Against me."

"You'd really threaten an old friend, John?"

"If you were really a friend, I wouldn't have to threaten you."

"Dammit, John," he said quietly. "Don't do this to me. I can't afford to have my body destroyed, and lose my grip on this world. Not with what's waiting for me . . ."

"If Lilith isn't stopped, the Hell she'll make of the Nightside will be just as bad."

"You're a real piece of work, Taylor, you know that? All right, I'm in. But I know I'm going to regret this."

"That's the spirit," I said.

"You're not even safe being dead, these days," Dead Boy said mournfully.

FIVE

Down in Dingley Dell

"So," said Dead Boy, "you've definitely got a plan?"

"Oh yes."

"But you're not going to tell me what it is?"

"It would only upset you."

"Can you at least tell me where we're going?"

"If you like, but . . ."

"I won't like that either?"

"Probably not."

"If I wasn't already dead, I think I'd probably be very depressed."

I had to laugh. It felt good to have something to laugh about. We were walking through one of the less salubrious areas of the Nightside, where the neon signs fell away like uninvited guests at the feast, and even working street-lamps were few and far between. We had come to Rotten Row, and the people who lived there liked it dark. We'd been walking for a while, and even though Dead Boy couldn't get tired, he could get bored, and downright cranky about it. He'd wanted to use his famous futuristic car, the gleaming silver sensation that drove itself out of a Timeslip from some possible future, and adopted Dead Boy as its driver. But I had to work on the assumption that Lilith had agents everywhere now, and they'd be bound to recognise such a distinctive car. And they might well have orders to attack it on sight, just in case Dead Boy was giving his old friend a lift. Nothing like having a Biblical myth for a mother to make you really paranoid. I wasn't ready for a direct confrontation with Lilith's people. Not yet. So Dead Boy and I walked together through increasingly dark and dingy back streets, in search of that great Victorian Adventurer, Julien Advent.

I'd already phoned the main offices of the *Night Times*, and the deputy editor had reluctantly confirmed that Julien wasn't there. He might be the paper's editor and owner now, but Julien still remembered the days when he'd been the Nightside's leading investigative journalist. So every now and again he'd disappear for a few days on a personal assignment, without telling anyone where he was going. No-one could say anything because he always came back with one hell of a story. Julien did like to keep his hand in, and assure himself he was still an Adventurer at heart.

The deputy editor actually asked me if I knew where Julien was, because the whole paper was going crazy without him, trying to cover the huge story breaking on the Street of the Gods. Did I happen to know anything about what happened on the Street of the Gods? I admitted that I might know a thing or two, but that I would only talk to Julien. The deputy editor tried threats, insults, and bursting into tears before finally giving up on me, and admitting that while Julien had turned off his mobile phone and pager, so he couldn't be traced, he had been heard asking questions about some of the nastier sweatshops still operating in the Nightside.

And so Dead Boy and I had walked to the extremely low-rent district that was Rotten Row. There were fewer and fewer people around, and those on view had a distinctly furtive air about them. There were the homeless and beggars, ragged men in ragged clothes, with outstretched grimy hands and ripped paper cups for small change. There were things that stayed in the shadows so you couldn't get a good look at them— possessed animals with glowing eyes and cancerous faces, and half-breed demons offering to sell you their bodies or blood or urine. Plus any number of hard-faced working girls with dead eyes, rent boys with scarlet lips, and speed freaks in alleyways ready to sell you any drug you had ever heard of. And darker things still, offering darker services.

Rotten Row, where dreams go to die, hope is a curse, and death is sometimes the kindest thing that can happen to you.

Long rows of dilapidated tenement buildings crouched sullenly on either side of a rubbish-strewn street. Half the street-lamps had been smashed, and sulphurous steam drifted up out of rusted metal grilles in the pavement. The tenement walls were stained black with soot and pollution and accumulated grime. Graffiti in a dozen languages, not all of them human, sometimes daubed in dried blood. Windows boarded up or covered over with brittle paper. Doors with hidden protections that would only open to the right muttered words. And inside every dark and overcrowded room in those ancient tenements, sweatshop businesses where really low-paid piece work was performed by people who couldn't find work anywhere else. Or had good reason to stay hidden, off the books. The sweatshop owners took advantage of these desperate people, in return for "protecting" them. The sad part was that there was never any shortage of desperate people, ready and willing to be "protected." The Nightside can be very dark, when it chooses.

Grim-faced enforcers sauntered casually out of alleyways and side streets to make their presence known to us. Dressed up as dandified gangsters, they wore guns and knives openly, and a few even had ideograms tattooed on their faces, marking them as low-rank combat magicians. Some had dogs with them, on reinforced steel chains. Seriously big dogs, with bad attitudes. Dead Boy and I strolled openly down the middle of the street, letting the enforcers get a good look at us. The dogs were the first to realise. They got one whiff of Dead Boy, and backed away whining and cringing. Their owners took one look at me and started backing away themselves. The enforcers huddled together in tight little groups, muttering urgently, then pushed one of their number forward to meet us.

He affected a nonchalant swagger that fooled no-one, least of all him, and finally came to a halt a more-than-respectable distance away. Dead Boy and I stopped and considered him thoughtfully. He was wearing a smart pin-striped suit, white spats, and a grey fedora. He had twin pearl-handled revolvers on his hips, and a pencil moustache on his scarred face. He gave us each a hard look, which he might have pulled off if he hadn't been sweating so profusely.

And on a cold night, too.

"You here to cause trouble?" he said, in a voice so deep he must have had a third testicle tucked away somewhere.

"Almost certainly," I said.

"Right, lads!" said the enforcer, glancing back over his shoulder to address the rest of the street. "Pick up your feet, we are out of here. This is Dead Boy *and* John bloody Taylor, and we are not being paid nearly enough to take on the likes of them. Everybody round to Greasy Joan's café, where we will wait out whatever appalling things are about to happen."

"You've heard of us," said Dead Boy, sounding just a little disappointed.

"Too bloody right, squire. I signed on for security work and a little light brutality. Nothing was ever said about having to face living legends and death on two legs."

Behind him, the rest of the enforcers were rapidly melting away and disappearing into the distance at something only a little less than a dead run. I looked thoughtfully at the man standing before us, and his left eye developed a distinct twitch.

"You seem to have a lot of influence over your fellow thugs," I said. "Who are you, exactly?"

"Union representative, squire. I look out for my boys, make sure they've all got health insurance, and I'd really like to run away after them, if that's all right with you."

I'd barely finished nodding before he'd turned and hurried away. There's a lot to be said for a good, or more properly bad, reputation. One young enforcer was still standing in the middle of the street, looking a bit bewildered. He yelled after his union rep, who didn't even look back.

"Hell with this shit," snarled the young punk, sounding actually outraged. "We're supposed to be hard men! Spreading fear with a glance and crushing all opposition! We don't turn and run when a couple of serious faces turn up!"

"He's young," said a voice from the shadows of a very dark alley. "Doesn't know anything. Please don't kill him. His mother would give me hell."

The young enforcer went for the gun on his hip, but Dead Boy was already moving. Being dead, his body wasn't limited to normal human reaction times. He darted forward impossibly quickly, closing the distance between himself and the young enforcer in a moment. The punk actually got off two shots, and Dead Boy dodged both of them. He crashed into the young enforcer, ripped the gun out of his hand, and head-butted him in the face. He then examined the gun while the young man crumpled to the floor, before finally throwing it aside.

"I take it there won't be any more opposition?" I said, to the general surroundings.

"Not from us," said the voice from the shadows. "You do whatever you feel like doing, sir."

"Thank you," I said. "We will."

I gathered up Dead Boy, and we continued down the street. There wasn't a single soul to be seen anywhere, but I had no doubt we were still being surreptitiously observed. I raised my gift, opening up the inner eye in my mind, my private eye, to locate exactly where Julien Advent was hiding himself in all this hostile territory. I kept my Sight narrowed down to just the task at hand. I really didn't want to See the kind of dark forces that moved unseen in a place like Rotten Row. I was also concerned that I'd recently been using my gift too much. My Enemies were always looking, to send their horror troops after me. I found Julien almost immediately, observing a firm called Dingley Dell from a place of concealment in a tenement building only a little further down the street. I shut down my gift, checked that all my mental barriers and safeguards were securely in place, and told Dead Boy what I'd learned.

"You are seriously spooky sometimes, you know that, John?" he said. "The way you *know* things. Still, I wouldn't worry too much about these Enemies of yours. They probably won't be able to locate you at all, what with Lilith and her pals on the rampage, jamming the mental aether."

We walked on a while in silence. *"Jamming the mental aether?"* I said finally. "What the hell does that mean?"

"I don't know," said Dead Boy. "But you have to admit, it sounded really good there for a moment. Now then, Dingley Dell . . . Sounds almost unbearably twee. Probably make lace doilies, or something . . ."

We came to a halt before the right building and studied the small cards tacked to the doorframe, beside the row of buzzers. The cards looked decidedly temporary, as though they had a tendency to change on a regular basis. The current occupiers of the three-storey building were Alf's Button Emporium, Matchstick Girls, Miss Snavely's Fashion House, Shrike Shoes, the Stuffed Fish Company, and Dingley Dell.

"Top floor," Dead Boy said disgustedly. "Why do they always have to be on the top floor? And how are we supposed to get all the way up there, past all the other businesses, without anyone noticing us?"

"Firstly, it's only three floors we're talking about," I said. "Undoubtedly because this entire shit heap would have collapsed if anyone had added a fourth floor. And secondly, while I doubt very much that a dump like this has a fire escape, you can bet good money that there's a concealed exit round the back so company executives can make a swift departure unobserved if their creditors turn up unexpectedly. So, round the back."

We made our way down a narrow side alley almost choked with garbage and general filth, and a couple of sleeping forms who didn't even stir when we stepped over them. I found the back door without having to raise my gift again because it was exactly where I would have put it. (Having had occasion to dodge a few creditors myself, in my time.) Dead Boy checked the door out for magical alarms and booby-traps, which didn't take long. He only had to look at them, and they malfunctioned.

"My being dead and alive at the same time confuses them," he said happily.

"It's always confused me," I agreed.

Dead Boy went to smash the door in, but I restrained him. There could still be purely mechanical alarms in place that we hadn't spotted, and I didn't want to risk attracting attention and perhaps blowing Julien Advent's stakeout. So I raised my gift for a moment, located the right spot on the door, directly above the lock, and hit it once with the heel of my hand. The lock disengaged, and the door swung open. Dead Boy averted his gaze so he wouldn't have to see me looking smug, and we entered the tenement, quietly closing the door behind us.

There was hardly any light, and the place stank of poverty and misery and blocked drains. Every expense had been spared in the construction of this building, and everything about it screamed *fire trap*. We moved quietly down the gloomy corridor, alert for any sign that we'd been noticed, but the whole building seemed silent as a tomb. The stairway was so narrow we had to go up in single file, so I let Dead Boy go first, on the grounds that he could take a lot more damage than I. There were any number of magical alarms and booby-traps, but they all blew up in silent puffs of fluorescent smoke, rather than try to deal with Dead Boy's presence. On the second-floor landing a monstrous face formed itself abruptly out of the cracks in the plaster wall, looked at us, mouthed the words *Oh bugger*, and disappeared again.

The next stairway was wide enough for us to walk side by side. I was starting to relax when a wooden step sank just a little too far under Dead Boy's weight, followed by a slight but definite click, and I threw myself flat. A metal shaft shot out of a concealed hole in the wall, passed right over me, and speared Dead Boy through the left arm. He looked down at the spike transfixing his arm, sighed heavily, and carefully pulled his arm free. I got to my feet again, and we studied the metal spike.

"Why did this work when the others didn't?" said Dead Boy.

"Purely mechanical," I said. "Least there's no harm done."

"No harm? This is my good coat! Look at these two holes in the sleeve. Going to cost a small fortune to put those right. I've got this little fellow in Greek Street who does all my repairs (you'd be surprised how many outfits I go through), but they're never the same afterwards. He calls it invisible mending, but I can always see it . . ."

"Do you think you could perhaps lower your voice a tad?" I said, quietly but urgently. "We are supposed to be sneaking in, remember?"

He sniffed sulkily a few times, and we continued up the rickety stairway to the third floor, and along the shadowy passage at the top of the building. Every room we passed was a different business, sub-let presumably, and we caught glimpses of shabby people slaving away, working silently in appalling conditions for nothing remotely like minimum wage. Whole families packed so tightly round rough wooden tables there was hardly any room to move. Fathers and mothers and children, all working intently in dim light in rooms with windows that wouldn't open, making goods for pennies that would sell for pounds to their betters. None of them ever said anything, bent quietly over their work. The overseers might not be visible, but that didn't mean they weren't there. Troublemakers didn't tend to last long, in sweatshops.

I'd never seen such blatant misery before. Capitalism, red in tooth and claw. It was one thing to know that such things still went on and another to see it with your own eyes. I felt like tearing the building down with my bare hands . . . but the sweatshop workers wouldn't thank me for it. They needed the work, needed the lousy money and the protection that went with it, from whoever was looking for them . . . And I couldn't risk blowing Julien Advent's stakeout and getting him angry at me. I was going to need Julien.

Dead Boy really didn't like sneaking around. It wasn't his style. "When am I going to get to hit someone?" he kept asking.

"You'll get your chance," I said. "God, you're like a big kid. You'll be asking if we're nearly there, next."

We finally came to a closed door with a card tacked to it, saying *Dingley Dell*. I tried the door handle, slowly and very carefully, but it was locked. Dead Boy raised a boot to kick it in, and I pulled him away, shaking my head firmly. I listened, one ear pressed against the wood of the door, but I couldn't hear anything. I straightened up, wincing as my back creaked, and looked around. And there at the end of the corridor was a spiral stairway, leading even higher. I led the way up the curving steps, Dead Boy pressing close behind like an impatient dog, and we ended up in a disused gallery, looking down onto the open room that was Dingley Dell. And there, at the end of the gallery, was the Timeslipped Victorian Adventurer himself, Julien Advent.

He was actually wearing his old opera cloak, the heavy dark material blending him smoothly into the gallery shadows. Dead Boy and I padded forward as silently as we could, but he still heard us coming. He spun round, ready to fight, and only relaxed a little as he recognised us. He gestured sharply for us to crouch beside him. He was tall, and still lithely muscular despite his years, with jet-black hair and eyes, and a face handsome as any movie star's; only slightly undermined by his unswervingly serious gaze and grim smile.

Julien Advent was a hero, the real deal, and it showed. We'd worked together, on occasion. Sometimes he approved of me, and sometimes he didn't. It made for an interesting relationship.

"What the hell are you two doing here?" he said, his voice little more than a murmur. "I put a lot of effort into getting silently into place here, and remaining unobserved, and now you two clowns . . . How do you know you haven't tripped off every alarm in the place?"

"Because I saw them all," said Dead Boy. "There's not much you can hide from the dead."

I looked at the two ragged holes in his coat sleeve, and sniffed. "You don't half fancy yourself sometimes."

Julien shook his head despairingly, then we all looked down into the open room of Dingley Dell, while Julien filled us in as to what was happening, in a voice I had to strain to hear.

It seemed Dingley Dell was a sweatshop for manufacturing magical items. Wishing rings, cloaks of invisibility, talking mirrors, magic swords, and so on. The usual. I always wondered where they came from . . . Gathered around a long trestle table were dozens of small shivering forms like undernourished children, with big eyes and pointed ears. Wee faeries no bigger than two-year-olds, with bitter faces and crumpled wings, all of them looking half-starved and beaten down. They would pick up some everyday object with their tiny hands and stare at it with fierce concentration until the sweat ran down their pointed faces. They were pouring their own natural magic into the items, making them magical through sheer force of will. As the faeries gave up some of their magic, they became visibly duller and less special. Dying by inches.

Every single one of them was held in place by heavy leg irons, and chains led from the irons to steel rings embedded in the bare floor-boards.

The faeries were refugees from a war in some other dimension, said Julien, fleeing and hiding from something awful: the Hordes of the Adversary. They were desperate not to be found, by anyone. Looking more closely, I could see they all had old scars, and more recent cuts and bruises. They wore rough clothing made from old sacking, with slits cut in the back for their crumpled wings to poke through. Now and again, in a brief look or a movement, I could see a glimpse of how wild and beautiful and charming they had once been.

And even as we watched, one small winged figure gave up the last of its magic and just faded away to nothing. His clothing slowly collapsed in on itself, and the empty leg iron clanked dully against the floor.

I couldn't remember when I'd last been so angry. It burned within me, knotting my stomach and making it hard for me to breathe. "This is sick!" I said fiercely. I actually glared at Julien Advent. "Why are you just sitting here, watching? Why haven't you done something before this?"

"Because I've been considering how best to deal with *that*," said Julien. "That is their overseer—the Beadle."

Dead Boy and I were already looking where he pointed. Emerging from an adjoining kitchen was a huge, hulking figure. He was easily eight feet tall—his head brushing against the ceiling—and his shoulders were broader and more muscular than any human's had a right to be. He was a construct, a patchwork figure of stitched-together human pieces. His only clothing was a collection of broad leather straps, perhaps to help hold him together, or maybe just to give him a feeling of security. He carried a large empty sack in one hand and a roast chicken in the other. He took a great bite out of the chicken breast, and waved the greasy carcass at the faeries, tauntingly.

Two feral children prowled beside him, one to each side, their naked bodies caked in old dried blood and filth. A boy and a girl, they were only ten or eleven years old, but still big enough to scare and intimidate the wee faeries.

"That is one big Beadle," said Dead Boy.

"Quite," said Julien. "I could probably take him, but I didn't want to start something I wasn't sure I could finish. For the sake of the faeries."

The Beadle approached the table, and the faeries all tensed visibly. Some started crying, quietly, hopelessly.

"Now then, have Santa's little helpers been busy, making nice little presents, like they were told to?" said the Beadle, in a harsh, growling voice. "Ho-ho-ho! I see another of you has escaped . . . but not to worry, my little cherubs; there's always fresh meat to replace the old."

He grabbed a handful of the completed magical items piled up in the middle of the table, and started stuffing them carelessly into his sack. One of the faeries wept a little too loudly, and the Beadle turned on it savagely.

"You! What are you snivelling for, you little work-shy?"

"Please sir," said the faerie, in a small, chiming voice. "I'm thirsty, sir."

The Beadle cuffed the faerie lightly across the back of the head, but it was still hard enough to slam the small face onto the table.

"No water for anyone until you've *all* made your quotas! And no food till the end of your shift. You know the rules." He broke off abruptly to examine a glowing dagger he'd just picked up. He sniffed dismissively and broke the blade in two with his bare hands, throwing the no-longer-glowing pieces aside. "Useless! Spoiled! All because *someone* wasn't concentrating! Don't think you can pass off inferior work on me! You all need to buck yourselves up, because the next one of you that doesn't mea-sure up . . . gets fed to my little pets here!"

The feral children grunted and snarled, stamping their bare feet on the bare floor and making playful little darts at the nearest faeries, who cried out and cringed away as far as their leg irons and chains would let them. The feral children laughed soundlessly, like dogs.

"That's it," said Julien Advent, in a calm, quiet and very dangerous voice. "I have seen enough."

He dropped gracefully down from the high gallery, his open cloak spreading out like the dark wings of an avenging angel. He landed lightly before the astonished Beadle, who reared back. The feral children re-treated, snarling. Dead Boy jumped down and landed heavily, the floor-boards cracking under the impact. He smiled easily at the Beadle, who threw aside his bag and his roast chicken so he could close his great hands into massive fists. I climbed down from the gallery, taking it one foot hold at a time. I knew my limitations. Julien Advent advanced on the scowling Beadle, and the giant construct actually backed away from the much smaller man, driven back by the incandescent rage in Julien's voice and eyes.

"I thought I'd left the evil of sweatshops behind me, in Victoria's reign. To see such cruelty still thriving in this modern age is an affront to all honourable men. To persecute such innocents, such helpless creatures, in the name of profit is an abomination! It stops now!"

The Beadle stopped backing away, and sneered down at Julien, his deep set eyes suddenly crafty as well as cruel. "I know you, Adamant. Crusading editor, bleeding heart, gentleman adventurer. Moves in all the best circles. But if I were to tell you the names of those who own this little business, and others just like them, I daresay you'd know them. Probably members in good standing of your precious gentlemen's clubs. They know the truth of the Nightside—that at the end of the day it's all about wealth and power. And what you can get away with."

"I'll deal with them, too, in time," said Julien.

"But you're here now," said the Beadle. "Far away from home, in my territory. And no-one plays by gentlemen's rules here. I am authorised to deal with any and all intruders in whatever way I see fit. So . . . let's see what I can get away with . . ."

He spoke a Word of Power, and the two feral children suddenly changed. Thick fur sprouted out of their bare skins, and their bones creaked loudly as they lengthened. Muzzles full of sharp teeth thrust out of their dirty faces, and in moments the two children were two wolves. The Beadle laughed and urged his pets forward. The faeries cried out hopelessly, cringing away from the slavering wolves, tugging piteously at the steel chains that held them in place. The wolves stalked slowly forward, and Dead Boy went to meet them, drawing two long silver daggers from the tops of his calfskin boots.

"No," I said sharply. "Don't kill them. I think they're as much victims here as the faeries."

Dead Boy glanced back at Julien, then shrugged and stepped back again. He didn't put the silver knives away. I confronted the two wolves, hoping I was right in my assumption. The Beadle had brought about their change with a Word of Power, which suggested the boy and girl weren't natural werewolves, that the change had been enforced upon them. So I fired up my gift and found the spell that controlled the change. Then it was the easiest thing in the world for me to rip the spell away, and just like that two wolves shrank back into two dazed children. Only a boy and a girl again, at last. They could feel they were free, and their feral instincts told them who was responsible. They charged towards me, and I made myself stand my ground. The boy and the girl pressed affectionately against my legs, nuzzling me with their heads and faces, pathetically grateful. The Beadle shouted orders at them, trying his Word again, and they turned and snarled defiantly back at him. I patted them comfortingly on their matted heads, and they settled down again.

Dead Boy and Julien Advent and I turned our full attention to the Beadle. He eyed the only door, but could tell it was too far away. He flexed his great muscles, showing off his size and strength. His fists were bigger than our heads. He sneered at us.

"This changes nothing! You're not big enough to bring me down. Not even together. I will eat your flesh, and crack your bones for the marrow, then I'll stick your severed heads on the railings outside, to show everyone what happens when you mess with the Beadle. And don't think your magics will help you against me. The owners made me proof against all magical attacks."

"Good thing I'm not magic then," said Dead Boy. "Just dead."

He went to meet the Beadle, daggers in hand, and the Beadle turned to run. He'd barely made two steps before Dead Boy was upon him, plunging both his daggers deep into the Beadle's kidneys. The giant cried out horribly and fell to his knees. And Dead Boy cut the Beadle up into his respective original pieces, undoing the work that had first put the huge construct together. The Beadle kicked and screamed for a long time. John and I watched in silence, while the two feral children grinned and stamped their feet approvingly, and the wee winged faeries clapped their tiny hands together in joy and relief.

Dead Boy went about his business as methodically as any butcher, until nothing was left of the Beadle but blood and gore and piles of separated pieces, some of them still twitching. When it was over, and the Beadle's eyes had stopped rolling in his severed head, Julien took the ring of keys from the discarded leather belt and set about freeing the faeries from their leg irons. I helped as best I could. The faeries thanked us tearfully, in voices like the singing of birds. The iron shackles had burned the faeries' skin where they had touched, and even after they were freed the faeries stayed on their wooden benches, huddling together for comfort. One of them looked at Julien and raised an uncertain tiny hand.

"Please, sir, we're hungry."

"No problem!" Dead Boy said cheerfully. He gathered up an armful of body parts and assorted offal, and marched off into the adjoining kitchen. "I know a great recipe for chunky soup!"

Julien looked at me. "Is he serious?"

"Almost certainly," I said. "Fortunately, I've already eaten."

We moved a little away, so we could talk privately. The faeries and the two feral children looked at each other, equally uncertain, but finally the boy moved towards them, one step at a time, and crouched before the nearest faerie. The boy put forward his head to be petted, and after a long moment the faerie reached out a small hand and gently tousled the matted hair. The boy grinned happily, just like a dog, and the girl padded forward to join him. I allowed myself a small breath of relief and gave my full attention to Julien.

"What are we going to do with them?" I said quietly. "All right, we rescued them. Great. But they've still got to live. They can't go back to their own dimension, but they don't have anywhere else to go. And there are things out there in the Nightside that would eat them alive."

"Well," Julien said thoughtfully, "they've got a really good business going here, so why shouldn't they take it over and run it for themselves? Someone has to make all the magic artifacts . . . They could make a comfortable living for themselves. I'm pretty sure the boy and the girl could be retrained as bodyguards. And I'll underwrite the business to begin with and provide the faeries with someone suitable to act as a front, so no-one will know about them."

"That's very kind of you," I said, and I meant it, "but what about all the other sweatshops in this building? What about all the other people slaving away for pennies, in buildings just like this all over the Nightside?"

Julien met my gaze steadily. "I know. There are hundreds of places as bad as this, if not thousands. But one of the first things you learn in the Nightside is that you can't save everyone. You just . . . do what you can, save whom you can, and try to be content with that."

"And what about this business's original owners?" I said. "Won't they kick up a stink about being frozen out of their own business?"

"Not after the piece I'm going to write for the *Times*," said Julien. "I'll change some of the details to protect the faeries, but it will still be fine, loud, incendiary stuff. The owners won't want to be identified with the stink I'm going to generate. May I mention you and Dead Boy by name in my story?"

"I don't mind," Dead Boy said cheerfully, from the kitchen. Something was cooking, and it smelled really good.

"If you think it'll help," I said.

Julien Advent considered me for a long moment. "Maybe I won't mention you, John."

"I quite understand," I said. "Lot of people feel that way about me."

"Why did you come here looking for me?" said Julien.

"Ah," I said. "Now, you're probably not going to like this, Julien, but . . ."

SIX

Guardian Angel

When you're about to do something really risky, or really dumb, or both, it's nearly always a good idea to do it in company. That way, at least you've got someone to hide behind when it all starts going horribly wrong. So, while the freed faeries gathered happily around a huge cauldron brimming over with chunky soup, and the feral boy and girl gnawed meat off oversized bones and cracked them open to get at the marrow, I took Julien Advent to one side, for a quiet word.

"I need to talk with you and Dead Boy, somewhere private."

"Does this concern your cunning plan, the one I'm really not going to like?"

"Got it in one."

"I know just the place."

It turned out that Julien had stumbled across the Beadle's private living quarters while he was exploring the building. He led Dead Boy and me back up onto the gallery, to a concealed door at its end, and through that into a loft conversion. The bare-raftered room turned out to be a lot bigger on the inside than it appeared on the outside, but that's a common spell in the Nightside, where living space is at a premium. The Beadle's living quarters were all hanging drapes and throw cushions, in assorted eye-dazzling colours, along with fresh flowers in tall vases, Andy Warhol prints on the walls, and delicate little china statuettes of wide-eyed kittens.

Dead Boy headed immediately for the rack of wine bottles at the far end of the room, sampled several of them in an experimental sort of way, before finally settling for a thick blue liquor that seethed heavily against the containing glass. Personally, I wouldn't have used it for cleaning combs. Dead Boy took a long drink straight from the bottle, shuddered slightly, then grinned widely.

"It takes a lot to affect you, when you're dead," he said cheerfully. "But this stuff's got a kick like one hundred and twenty per cent embalming fluid."

I wrestled the bottle away from him and put it to one side. "Trust me," I said. "You really don't want to do what I've got in mind while you're drunk."

"I hate it already," said Dead Boy.

We arranged ourselves as comfortably as we could on the embroidered throw cushions, and I explained slowly and carefully just what it was I had in mind. First, I described in some detail the devastated future Nightside I'd seen in the Timeslip. The ruined buildings and the terrible silence, in which the only things moving were swarming mutated insects. Humanity was gone, and all the world was dead and cold. A future that was my fault, somehow. Julien and Dead Boy listened intently, drinking in the details. They'd heard rumours of what I'd seen, most of the Nightside had, but I'd never told anyone the whole story. And even now, I kept a few things to myself. They didn't need to know about the Razor Eddie I found there, the last living man in the world. They didn't need to know I killed him, with his own razor, as a mercy.

Of course, when I finished my story they had to argue with me. They were far too sophisticated to believe in a single, unavoidable future. In Fate, or Destiny.

"There are any number of potential time-lines, possible futures," said Julien, a little condescendingly. "None of them more certain than any other."

"Right," said Dead Boy. "My own car comes from an alternate future that clearly has nothing to do with the one you described."

"Once, that might have been true," I said. "But our future, the future our timeline is heading towards, is getting more certain all the time. I've . . . seen things. Signs, portents, details coming true despite everything I could do to avoid them. According to Old Father Time, the number of possibilities for our timeline is narrowing down, steadily decreasing to only one inevitable future."

"Because of your mother," said Julien.

"Yes," I said. "Because of Lilith. She's such a powerful Being that her mere presence here is enough to overturn the whole apple-cart and rewrite the rules of reality itself."

I let them consider that for a while, then pressed on. They had to understand the background of my thinking, in order to appreciate what I intended to do.

"I have become increasingly convinced," I said slowly, "that the War I'm supposed to start with Lilith and her followers could be the very thing that will bring about the destruction of the Nightside. That we'll tear the world apart, fighting over it. So I've decided I can't go any further, in good conscience, without better information. And the only people who can offer me that . . . are my Enemies. The people who've been sending their agents to kill me for as long as I can remember."

Julien leaned forward eagerly. "You finally found out who they are?"

"Yes," I said. "They're the last surviving major players of the devastated future, hiding out in the final stages of the War, sometime before my visit in the Timeslip. The few remaining heroes and villains, desperately sending their agents back into the Past, to kill me before I do . . . whatever it is I do, to damn everyone."

Julien and Dead Boy looked at me, silenced by shock, by the staggering implications of what I'd just said.

"Who . . . ?" said Julien.

"Familiar names, familiar faces," I said. "You'd know them."

(I didn't tell Julien Advent that he would become one of my Enemies, in that terrible future. Or that he would die trying to kill me, and his dead body would be made over into one of the awful agents they sent back after me. He didn't need to know that.)

"Why have you never told me any of this before?" Julien said, finally.

"Because you would have told everyone," I said. "That's what you do. And I wasn't ready to trust . . . everyone."

"This is sounding more and more like a closed circle," said Dead Boy. "How can you . . . talk with your Enemies?"

"By travelling forward through Time into their future," I said steadily. "And confronting them. Because they're the only ones who *know* what happened, to bring about their future. They can tell me . . . what I mustn't do."

What can I do? I'd asked the future Razor Eddie, moments before I killed him. *What can I do to prevent this happening?*

Kill yourself, he said.

"But . . . they're your Enemies!" said Dead Boy. "They'll kill you on sight!"

"Then I'll have to be very persuasive," I said. "And talk really quickly."

"And if they kill you anyway?" said Julien.

"Well, that might solve the problem," I said. "But trust me, this is not a suicide run. I have every intention of coming back alive, with the information I need to put Lilith back in her box and avoid the end of the world."

"It's a good thing I'm already dead," said Dead Boy, "or I think I'd be very worried about this."

"Travel through Time takes a hell of a lot of power," said Julien, frowning heavily. "There's not many who can do it. Or would do it for you, John. I suppose I could talk to Old Father Time, on your behalf. Put in a good word for you."

"Oh, I think he's got a very good word for me," I said. "He's already arranged one trip through Time for me, and after the way that turned out, I don't think he'll be doing that again, anytime soon." Julien looked at me sharply, scenting a story, and I shook my head. "Trust me on this, Julien, you really don't want to know."

"All right," said Dead Boy, "if Old Father Time is out of the picture, who does that leave?"

"I've been thinking about that," I said. "The Collector is supposed to have a whole bunch of really weird Time travel mechanisms; but he's still mad at me. For a whole bunch of reasons."

Dead Boy sniffed loudly. "The Collector's mad at everyone. And vice versa. I wouldn't piss down his throat if his heart was on fire."

"Then there's the Chronovore," I said loudly. "Who eats up all the little lost moments of your life, the ones that you can never account for. But he works strictly for cash these days. Serious cash. There's always the Travelling Doctor, but you can never rely on him being around when you need him."

"That's everyone I know of," said Julien. "Who else is left?"

"This is where it all starts getting a bit risky," I said carefully. "I think I know someone On High who might owe me a favour. So . . . I plan to summon an angel down from Heaven."

I don't think I've ever seen two such appalled faces in my life. Dead Boy's eyes actually bulged in their sockets, and Julien Advent's face went as pale as Dead Boy's. They both tried to say something, but couldn't get the words out for spluttering.

"It's really not all that different from calling up a demon," I said quickly, trying hard to sound confident. "The principle is the same, only in reverse. That's why I needed both of you, for my plan to work. Dead Boy, to help me send my message beyond the planes of the living, and Julien, to help me contact the Courts of the Holy. You have a singular nature, Dead Boy, being both dead and alive at the same time, and I can use that ambiguity to punch my way through a lot of the usual barriers. Julien, you created a drug to split apart the best and worst elements in man. You embraced the best elements, of course, and became a hero, a pure soul. Or at least, as close to one as I'm going to find in the Nightside. Your purity of spirit will help my message to get to where it needs to go. Theoretically."

"And that's it?" said Dead Boy, when he finally got his voice back.

"That's your marvellous plan? You were right, I don't like it. In fact, I think I would go so far as to say I hate it! *Have you lost your mind, John?* I can't even count all the ways this could go horribly wrong. You and Julien could get killed, I could . . . well, I'm not entirely sure what could happen to me, but I am ready to bet good money that it would be really, really bad! I think I'm going to have one of my turns . . . Look, you can't just go banging on Saint Peter's Gates and demand he send down an angel to talk to you! We're all going to end up as pillars of salt, I know it . . ."

"For once I find myself in complete agreement with Dead Boy," said Julien, glaring at me sternly. "If we summon an angel, and please note the emphasis I am placing on the word *if*, what we'll get will be the real thing. A messenger of God, complete in all its power and glory. Not the weakened, limited things that are normally all that can manifest in the Nightside. And you of all people should remember how much damage and loss of life those weakened presences brought about during the angel war last year. They're still rebuilding parts of the city. If we call down the real thing, what's to stop it wiping us all out on a whim?"

"First," I said, "the angel will be contained within a protective circle, just like a demon. Second, your presence and Dead Boy's will add to the protections considerably. That's why I waited to connect with you two, before I tried anything. It is . . . possible, for things to go wrong, yes. Summonings are a bit like fishing—you can never be sure whether you'll hook a sprat or a killer shark. The last time I tried this . . ."

"Hold everything," said Julien. "You actually tried this before?"

"Once, when I was a lot younger," I said defensively. "When I was really desperate for information about who and what my missing mother was. I thought, if anybody would know . . ."

"What happened?" said Dead Boy.

"Well," I said, "you know that really big crater, where the Hotel Splendide used to be?"

"That was you?" said Julien. "It's still radioactive!"

"I really don't want to talk about it," I said, with great dignity.

"Give me back my bottle," said Dead Boy. "There is no way in Hell I'm doing this sober."

"I have yet to be convinced we should do it at all," said Julien. "In fact, I'm still rather hoping this is all some terrible dream I'm going to wake up from soon."

"God, you're a pair of wimps! Everything's going to be all right." I leaned forward, doing my best to project certainty and trustworthiness. "I'm going after a specific angel this time, and I'm sure having you two along will make all the difference."

"Don't worry," Dead Boy said to Julien. "It's not that bad, being dead. It's actually quite restful, sometimes."

Julien helped me clear away the throw cushions and the rugs to reveal the bare floor-boards beneath, while Dead Boy went downstairs, and came back with a bucket full of the Beadle's blood. He handed it over sulkily, muttering something about how he'd been saving that blood, to make blood pudding and stock later. I ignored him and had Julien prick his thumb and add a few drops of his own blood to the bucket, to purify it. (Working on the principle that some trace of the drug that brought out his best elements was still in his system.) I then used the blood to draw a really big restraining circle, surrounded by every protective symbol I knew. It took a long time and used up most of the bucket of blood.

"I don't even recognise some of the languages you're using," said Julien.

"Think yourself lucky," said Dead Boy, and I had to agree.

Finally, it was done. It looked pretty impressive, even if it did smell really rank. The three of us sat down together, inside a second smaller protective circle, holding hands; and that was it. No chanting, incense, dead chickens, or waving your hands around. In the end, most magic is really primarily a matter of will and intent. The signs I'd so carefully daubed were the spell's address, along with a few extra things to get the recipient's attention, and a few safeguards so the recipient couldn't simply wipe us all out for interrupting them at a particularly inconvenient moment. You'd be surprised how many demons screen their calls these days. Everything else was down to me, Julien Advent, and Dead Boy, and our combined will and determination.

"Something's happening," said Dead Boy, after a while. "I can feel energies forming all around us. I can See . . . I can See avenues opening up, levels of reality unfolding like the petals of a flower, more levels, more and more . . . I can See further than I ever could before . . . and I don't like it. It scares me. It's too big . . ."

"Look away," I said sharply. "Shut down your Sight and reinforce your mental barriers. Concentrate on the summoning."

"I can feel something," said Julien.

"Don't," I said.

Dead Boy and Julien both had their eyes squeezed shut now, beads of sweat standing out on their strained faces. I kept my eyes open. One of us had to, and I was more used to Seeing the unseen realms. I still kept my mental barriers firmly in place. There were things none of us could afford to see, if we wished to remain in the mortal world. The glory of the shimmering plains is not for mortals. By now we could all feel Something approaching, from a direction we all instinctively recognised but couldn't identify. It felt like *above*, in all senses of the word. Something was coming into our world, Something impossibly large and powerful, downloading itself into a mortal frame that wouldn't blow all the fuses in our merely human minds.

Brilliant light exploded within the main circle, and we all cried out and turned our heads away as an angel manifested; a blazing light far too fierce to look at directly. We could only catch brief glimpses of it, out of the corners of our watering eyes. It was vaguely human in shape, pure light, pure energy, pure magic, with just an impression of wide wings. Simply being close to it made me feel small and insignificant, simple and undeveloped, like a chalk drawing next to the Mona Lisa. The angel regarded us, and its attention embraced us all, like a judgement only barely tempered with mercy and compassion.

"Hi," I made myself say. "Glad you could drop in. Is that you, Pretty Poison?"

I don't use that name any more, said a Voice like thunder in my head. All three of us groaned out loud, as the angel's words filled our minds. *I have my old name back now. Thanks, in part, to you, John Taylor. I know what you want. We know everything. It's part of the job description. And yes, I will help you, just this once. Because of what you did, for me and my beloved. But understand this, John Taylor; although I can send you into the future, getting back again will be your own problem.*

"Can you help us against Lilith and her followers?" said Julien Advent. He was actually able to look at the angel for more than a few seconds at a time. Maybe he really did have a pure soul, after all. "You must know what she's done, what she plans to do."

Yes. We know. But all of Heaven and all of Hell are forbidden to intervene directly in the Nightside. Some of the lesser ranks from Above and Below volunteered to try to intercede, and were destroyed for their trouble. Lilith designed the Nightside specifically to diminish all spiritual messengers who entered it. So all future interventions have been forbidden, in the place where all the decisions that matter are made. In the Courts of the Holy. It's up to the Nightside to save itself, if it can. I am bending the rules to help you, John Taylor, and I will not do so again. Good luck. And don't call this number again.

I knew a hint when I heard it. She was telling me to get on with it, before Someone else called her back. So I raised my gift and focused my Sight on all the various time-lines radiating out from this place, this moment, this decision. I could only see the most immediate timetracks, but even so the sheer number of images almost overwhelmed me. I narrowed my regard still further, searching through the time-lines for the single path that led to my Enemies. Near futures flashed on and off all around me. I saw my friends die, fighting Lilith and her people. I saw different versions of myself, and them, and we all died fighting Lilith, over and over again. I saw my friends support Lilith, while I led a coalition of those who had once been my foes against her, and we all died again. I saw myself, wearing an expression I didn't recognise, sitting at my mother's feet as she contemplated a mountain of skulls and smiled, while monsters danced in the flickering light of burning buildings.

Other versions of the future pressed in from all sides—other, stranger, alien Nightsides. I saw inhuman structures that might have been buildings, with unnatural lights burning in them, while impossible forms lurched and mewled through the shifting streets. I saw huge cavernous shapes, rounded structures with an organic sheen, great insects crawling all over them. I even glimpsed a version of the carnivorous jungle I'd visited briefly in the Past, with its trees made of meat and lianas like hanging intestines, where hissing roses rioted in the ruins of long-abandoned cities. I fought hard to focus my gift, forcing aside all the irrelevant futures, until I found what I was looking for: the dark and devastated future that was home to my Enemies.

And once I was locked on to that terrible place, the angel tore me loose from the Present, and sent me rocketing forward through Time. The world speeded up around me, Time flashing by impossibly fast. Days became months became years, piling up behind me. I saw the Nightside fall, its great buildings crashing down, crumbling like sand castles in the path of an oncoming tide. I saw the great oversized moon in the night sky explode, its pieces raining down like fiery meteors. And I saw the stars start to go out, one by one by one.

There were Voices all around me, growling and muttering and howling, outside of Time. Strange Presences, all speaking at once in no human tongue, yet still I could understand the gist of it. Slowly they became aware of me, then the Voices began to cajole, to warn, and to threaten. I think they were frightened of me. I refused to listen, making myself concentrate only on my destination, until finally Time slammed to a halt again, and I was spilled out into the dark future I'd visited before. The dead end of the Nightside, and maybe all of history.

And all of it my fault.

SEVEN

The Night, So Dark

It was even worse than I remembered. A night dark as despair, cold as a lover's rejection, silent as the grave. Everywhere I looked, there were buildings fallen into ruin and rubble, whole areas stamped flat or burned down. As though a mighty storm had passed through the Nightside, levelling everything it touched. Only this storm had a name. I looked up into the night sky, and there was no moon and only a sprinkling of scattered stars. The end of the world, the end of life, the end of hope. And all because of me.

It was bitter cold, the harsh air burning in my lungs, so cold it even numbed my thoughts. All around me for as far as I could see, there were only the stumps and shells of what had once been proud, tall buildings. Shattered brickwork, cracked and broken stone stained from the smoke of old fires, windows with no glass and empty doorways like gaping mouths or wounds. The streets held only abandoned, crushed and burned-out cars, along with piled-up rubbish and refuse. And shadows, shadows everywhere. I'd never known the Nightside so dark, without its bright neon, its gaudy glare of bustle and commerce. What light there was had a deep purple hue, as though the night itself was bruised.

And yet I wasn't alone. I could hear something, vague sounds off in the distance. Something large, crashing through an empty street. I thrust my hands deep into my coat pockets, hunched my shoulders against the cold, and went to investigate. That's what I do. Curiosity killed the cat, but satisfaction brought it back. I made my way cautiously through the dark streets, stepped around and over all kinds of debris. I peered into the trashed vehicles I passed, but there was never anyone in them. Thick dust puffed up around my feet with every step, only to fall straight back again. There wasn't even a puff of wind. The cold air was still, lifeless. The sounds grew louder as I drew nearer. They were coming from more than one direction. I remembered the giant, mutated insects from my last visit and moved more slowly, more quietly. Until finally I came to the edge of a great open square, and when I saw what walked there, I shrank back into the darkest, deepest shadow I could find, holding my breath so as not to give away even the slightest sign of my presence.

It lurched across the open square, its weight cracking the ground with every step, huge and bulging like a living cancer growth, all red-and-purple striations, with rows of swollen eyes and mouths dripping pus. It stalked unsteadily forward on tall stilt legs that might have been leg-bones, once upon a time. It stopped abruptly as something else entered the square from the other side. Something tall and vague, made up of shifting unnatural lights. It surged forward in sudden spurts and jerks, spitting and sparking vivid energies, discharging lightning bolts at everything metal it passed. The two monsters howled and squalled at each other, terrible sounds, like two great Beasts disputing territory.

The hideous racket called others. They burst out of side streets and the shells of broken buildings, huge monstrosities that could never have survived and prospered in a sane and rational world. They snapped and snarled at each other, stamping and coiling and rearing up jagged heads full of teeth. Something big and brutal with too many clawed arms circled warily around something with a long scarred carapace that leaked slime. It waved long, serrated claws in the air, while something else like a massive squashed over-ripe fruit, big as a bus, humped its way across the square, leaving a trail of steaming acid that ate into the bare stone ground.

All their movements were sudden, erratic, disturbing. Their raised cries were awful, actually painful to the human ear. They struck at each other, or at nothing, or charged each other head-on, like rutting stags. They did not move or act like sane things. You only had to watch them to know that their minds had gone bad, their spirits broken by this terrible place, this end of all things. They looked as though they were sick inside, everything gone to rot and corruption, dying by inches.

I knew what they were. What they had to be. These hideous, distorted things were all that was left of Lilith's children, the last of the Powers and Beings she'd recruited from the Street of the Gods to follow her. Stripped of their might and glory, mutated and driven mad. I backed slowly away from the square, away from them, away from the world I'd made. But one of them found me anyway.

At first, I thought it was just another deep shadow, cast against the unusually high wall of a jagged building, but then it moved, lurching out into the street to block my way. It rose before me like a massive black slug, big as a building, wide as a lobby, made up of living darkness. It didn't gleam or glisten, and it had no discernable details; what light there was seemed to just fall away into it like a bottomless pit. It had no eyes, but it saw me. It knew I was there, and it hated me. I could feel its hatred, like a pressure on the air. Hatred without cause, or character, or even consciousness.

I took a cautious step backwards, and it came after me. I stopped immediately, and it stopped, too. Something else slowly manifested on the air, besides the hatred. It was hungry. I turned and ran, side-stepping and lunging across the piled-up rubbish in the street, and behind me came the Beast. I ran carelessly, taking crazy risks with my footing, not caring where I was going. I chose the narrowest streets and darted down side alleys, but it came relentlessly after me, crashing through the sides of crumbling buildings, never slowing or diverting from its path. Its bulk smashed through the material world like it was made of paper, while falling masonry bounced harmlessly off its dark hide. Dust rose in thick clouds, and I coughed harshly as I ran. I was faster, more manoeuvrable, but it was inexorable. And finally, it cornered me.

I chose the wrong turning and ended up in a side street blocked by piled-up cars. Too tall to climb and no way past. There was a door to one side. I grabbed at the brass handle and it came away in my hand, jerked right out of the rotten wood. I kicked at the door, and it absorbed my foot like spongy fungus. I pulled my foot free and turned around, and there was the great black slug, blocking the street, towering over me. I leaned forward, gasping for breath, coughing out the dust in my lungs. I had nothing on me that could deal with such a monster, no tricks or magics or last-minute escapes. I started to raise my gift, hoping it could find me a way out, then the black slug lurched forward, and my concentration shattered.

Up close, it stank of brine, of the sea. Of something that should have remained hidden at the bottom of the deepest ocean. It hung over me, impossibly huge, then it stopped, as though . . . considering me. I could have reached out and touched it, but I could no more have made myself do that than plunge my bare hand into a vat of acid. And then, slowly, a reflection formed on the flat black surface of the Beast, facing me, coming into focus like an old photo, or an old memory. An image of me. The Beast remembered me. Slow ripples spread across the black surface, increasing in speed and urgency, and it lurched backwards, returning the way it had come, until finally it disappeared back into the night.

It knew me. And it was terrified of me.

I sat down on some rubble and concentrated on getting my breathing back under control. I could feel my heart hammering like a pile-driver, and my hands were shaking. It was times like this that I wished I smoked.

Eventually my composure returned, and I looked around me. I had no idea where I was. All the landmarks were gone, beaten down into mess and ruin. Everywhere looked the same. Civilisation had come and gone, and only monsters stalked old London's streets. I shuddered suddenly. It was very cold, here at the end of the world. But I still had work to do. No rest for the wicked. I got to my feet again, beat my numbed hands together, and raised my gift. There was nothing to See. The unseen world was as dead and gone as everything else. But when I concentrated, it only took me a moment to find the lair of my Enemies. Their light was feeble and flickering, but still it shone like a beacon in this darkest of nights. I shut down my gift and set off in the direction it had shown me. It wasn't far.

I kept well away from the Beasts. Or maybe they were keeping away from me. Either way, nothing crossed my path till I came to my Enemies' hideout. Again, it looked just as I remembered it. A cracked, crumbling house in a rotted tenement, with nothing obviously different about it. No light showed at any of the shuttered windows, but I could feel light and life inside, hidden, barricaded against the monsters of the night. I advanced slowly, carefully, using just enough of my gift to See the concealed protections and magical booby-traps covering all possible approaches to the house. Most were of the *Don't see me, nothing here, move along* kind, but surprisingly they were all keyed to abhuman energies. None of them would activate even if I walked right through them. Perhaps they no longer had any reason to expect human visitors. Or maybe they just needed to be able to get back inside at a moment's notice. The outer door wasn't even locked.

I let myself in and moved silently through the gloom and tension of the broken-down house. My eyes had adjusted to the gloom of the end of the world, but it was still hard to see anything inside. I trailed the fingertips of one hand along the nearest wall, to keep my bearings, and the plaster crumbled into dust under my touch. I strained my ears against the quiet, and finally I caught the first faint traces of sound, from the end of the corridor before me. I padded forward and came to a door camouflaged in the wall. It wasn't locked either. I slipped through the door, and for the first time there was light, real light. I stopped to let my eyes adjust. Butter yellow light leaked round the edges of another door, in the wall ahead. The light looked warm and comforting. It looked like life. I eased over to the door. It was a little ajar. I pushed it open a few more inches, and looked through. And there were my Enemies, just as I'd seen them before, in my vision.

They had a great haunch of unidentifiable meat cooking over an open fire, turning slowly on a rough metal spit. They were all crouched around it, utterly intent, not even aware of my presence. Such familiar names and faces. Jessica Sorrow, Larry Oblivion, Count Video, King of Skin, Annie Abattoir. All of them major players and even Powers in their time, now fallen far from what they had once been. They were huddled together, as much for companionship and comfort as against the cold that seeped through even into the hidden room. All of them small ragged figures, with fear and hopelessness written deep in their bony, malnourished faces.

Jessica Sorrow, no longer the terrible Unbeliever, looked almost unbearably human and vulnerable as she sat cross-legged before the fire, as close to the flames as she could get without burning herself. She hugged an ancient teddy bear in her skinny arms, holding it close to her shrunken chest. She wore a battered black leather jacket and leggings, that looked a lot like the ones Suzie always wore.

Next to her sat Larry Oblivion, the dead detective. Betrayed and murdered by the only woman he ever really loved, brought back as a zombie, surviving now even when he would probably rather not, because he couldn't die again. His dead pale flesh showed through the tatters of what had probably once been a very expensive suit. Unlike the others, he didn't look tired, or defeated. He just looked angry.

Count Video was a mess. He wore nothing but a collection of leather straps, and his skin was wrinkled and loose in places, from where it had been stitched back on after the angel war. Heavy black staples held him together, in places. Silicon nodules and sorcerous circuitry projected from puckered skin, soldered into place long ago to form the necrotech that powered his binary magics. Plasma lights sputtered on and off around his wasted body, and a halo of intermittent energies cast an unhealthy light on his twitching face.

King of Skin was just a man here, stripped of his once-terrible glamour. In my time he could have killed with a word or enslaved with a look, but not here, not now. He was all skin and bone, his gaze distant and unfocused. Objects of power hung about him on tangled silver chains, half-hidden under a thick fur coat with patches torn away. He rocked back and forth on his haunches, perhaps lost in memories of better times, because memory was all he had left.

And finally, Annie Abattoir; assassin and seductress, secret agent and confidence trickster, praised and feared and damned in a dozen countries. She wore what was left of a long crimson evening gown, the low-cut back showing off the mystic symbols carved deep into the flesh between her shoulder blades. She'd always been very hard to kill, though many had tried, often with good reason. Though she was six-foot-two and still mostly muscle, her face held little of its old striking charm. She looked . . . diminished. Beaten down.

I finally announced my presence with a polite cough, and they all spun round, scrambling to their feet, ready to fight. Their eyes widened, and a few jaws dropped as they recognised me, then King of Skin cried out like a hurt child and scurried away to crouch in a corner, terrified and trembling. Count Video's face convulsed with rage, and new energies crackled around him as his necrotech sparked into life.

"Don't!" I said quickly. "I'm protected! And I mean seriously protected, by major magics. Anything strong enough to break through my defences would almost certainly attract the attention of the Beasts outside. And I don't think any of us want that, right?"

Annie Abattoir looked uncertain, a glowing dagger in each hand, but after a tense moment Larry Oblivion stepped forward and put a hand on her arm and Count Video's, and they both reluctantly nodded and stepped back. Larry Oblivion studied me coldly.

"I don't see any protections . . ."

I grinned. "Of course not. That's how good they are."

I was bluffing, but they had no way of knowing that. And they didn't dare risk being discovered.

"John Taylor," Larry said slowly. "How is it that you are here? Did you bring yourself back from the dead, too?"

"Time travel," I said briskly. "For me, Lilith has only just happened. The War hasn't started yet. I'm here looking for answers, and advice."

"Let me kill him," said Count Video. "He has to die. For what he did, he has to die!"

"Yes," said Larry. "But not now. Not here."

Annie made the Count sit down by the fire again. King of Skin was still shivering in his corner, in a spreading pool of urine, crying childish tears. It hurt me to see him that way. I'd never liked him, but I always respected him. Annie Abattoir and Jessica Sorrow stood before me, on either side of Larry Oblivion. They looked at me like I was a ghost, some horrid spectre at the feast, some ancient evil from their worst nightmares. And maybe I was.

"My brother Tommy fought on your side," Larry said finally. "In the great War against Lilith. He trusted you, even though he had good reason not to. And when they struck him down you just stood there, and watched him die, and did nothing to help."

I spread my hands helplessly. "You're judging me over something I haven't even done yet. And may never do . . . That's why I'm here. I need you to tell me what I have to do to prevent all this happening." They stared back at me, unconvinced. I took a step forward. When dealing with Enemies, it's all about confidence, or at least the appearance of it. I gestured at the great haunch of meat burning over the fire. It smelled really bad. "You seem to be preparing dinner. Do you mind if I join you?

There's nothing like struggling to avoid the Apocalypse to give you an appetite. What are we having?"

Larry snorted, amused despite himself. "That . . . is one of Lilith's children. Pretty much all there is left to eat, these days. Apart from the bodies. There are still a lot of dead people left over from the War, but we haven't been reduced to cannibalism. Not yet. Oh yes, they're still lying around, decades after the War. Nothing decays any more, you see. Except the buildings. All kinds of strange energies were released during the final days of your struggle with your mother. And now all the natural processes are . . . out of order. Existence follows new rules now. Sometimes we don't feel the need to eat or drink for days or even weeks at a time. And we don't sleep. Bad dreams can take on a life of their own, these days."

"It's hard to keep track of time any more," said Jessica, in a voice like a shell-shocked child's. "There's no way of measuring it, you see. There are no days, the night never ends, and watches don't work even though there's nothing wrong with them. Perhaps you and Lilith broke Time, during the War . . ." She cocked her head to one side, like a bird, still fixing me with her direct, unblinking gaze. "How did you know where to find us?"

"My gift," I said. "And a little help from an angel."

Her mouth twitched briefly. "You always did move in exalted circles, John."

"Heaven and Hell have abandoned us," Annie Abattoir said harshly. "Nothing left to fight over, any more. Do you know who we are? Why we stay together? Why we still struggle to survive, in this worst of all possible worlds?"

"Yes," I said. My mouth was suddenly dry. "You're my Enemies. You've been trying to kill me ever since I was born, striking back through Time, to kill me before I do . . . whatever it is I do that brings about the destruction of the Nightside."

"And the world," Larry said flatly. "Don't think this is just London. There's nothing else."

"We had to do it," said Jessica. "It was . . ."

"Oh please!" I said. "Don't you dare say *It was nothing personal!* You and your Harrowing have hounded me all my life! I've never been able to feel safe, feel secure, because I could never know when your bloody assassins would appear suddenly out of nowhere, killing everyone in their path for a chance to get at me! You made my life a living Hell!"

"You made the world a living Hell," said Count Video. "Everything we've done is justified by what you did."

"I haven't done anything yet!"

"But you will, John," said Jessica. "You will."

I made myself control my temper. I was here for their help. And there was still one question I hadn't asked. Something I had to know.

"Where's Suzie?" I said. "Where's my Shotgun Suzie?"

Larry looked a little surprised. "You expected her to be here?"

"She tried to kill me," I said. The words hurt, but I forced them out. "She told me she was one of you. That's why I came here, through Time, for information. The future isn't set in stone. This doesn't have to happen. Tell me what you know. The things only you know."

"She volunteered, to be made into one of our assassins," said Larry. "You do know she volunteered, to be made over into . . . what we made her?"

"Yes," I said. "She told me. We never did believe in keeping secrets from each other."

Jessica hugged her teddy bear tightly, resting her chin on its battered head. "She never came back. We assumed you killed her, like all our other agents. What did happen to her, John?"

"Merlin ripped off her arm," I said steadily. "The one with the Speaking Gun attached to it. Then she disappeared. She was still alive, the last time I saw her. I had hoped . . . she'd made it back here."

"No," said Annie. "We haven't seen her. We have to assume she's lost to us. Another death on your conscience, Lilith's son."

"He has no conscience," said Count Video. "He's not human. Not really. Why should he have human feelings?"

"I was human enough to get past your defences," I said.

"Then we'll have to tighten them up," said Larry.

I looked at Jessica. "I see you still have your teddy."

"Yes," she said. "You found him for me. I remember. He brought me back to life, and sanity."

"I'm glad I could help," I said.

She shook her head slowly. "I'm not. This world would be so much easier to bear if I was still crazy. Still safely mad."

"Ah well," I said. "No good deed goes unpunished."

"Especially in the Nightside," she said.

And we both managed a small smile, just between the two of us.

"So," I said, looking around me, "this is the end of the world, and it's all my fault. Now tell me why. Tell me what happened."

"You started it" said Larry Oblivion. "When you came back to the Nightside after five years away. That wasn't supposed to happen. We went to a lot of trouble to orchestrate the events that drove you out—working behind the scenes, always through agents who never knew whom they were serving. It took a lot of our strength and power, but since we'd had so little success in trying to kill you . . . we were ready to try anything else. You were supposed to be so traumatised by events that you would flee to London, and the normal world, and never return. We were so sure we'd succeeded, at last. But nothing changed here, and when Annie investigated why, she got a vision of you returning anyway. So we used the creature that pretended to be a house on Blaiston Street, and set a trap for you. If you were going to come back to the Nightside, we wanted it to be on our terms."

"But if it hadn't been for the house, I never would have come back," I said.

"Maybe," said Jessica. "Meddling with Time is an uncertain business. Sometimes I think the whole universe runs on irony. By interfering, we created a rod for our own backs and the seed of our own destruction. Doesn't it make you want to spit?"

"And once you returned, events proceeded with predictable inevitability," said Annie Abattoir. "By insisting on searching for the truth about your mother, though everyone warned you against it, you set in place the chain of events that led to the War between your forces and hers. The two of you destroyed the Nightside by fighting over it, like two dogs with a single bone, because neither of you would allow the other to control it. Between you, you sucked all the life out of the world, draining it dry to power greater and greater magics, for your precious War."

"You squandered your own people," said Larry. "Throwing them into the fray, again and again. Nothing mattered to either of you, except winning. And so the War went on, until you both ran out of people to throw at each other, and there was no-one left but you and Lilith."

"You killed each other," said Count Video, still staring into the fire. "Using the Speaking Gun. But by then it was far too late. The damage had been done."

"That's why we retrieved the Gun and bonded it to Suzie," said Jessica. "Even though the process nearly destroyed us. Because it was the only weapon we were sure would destroy you. She screamed like the damned when we fitted it to her, but she never once flinched away. Poor Suzie. Brave Suzie."

And then all our heads whipped round, and we fell silent, as we heard something impossibly huge and heavy dragging itself by, outside. We all stood very still, listening. Even King of Skin stopped whimpering in his corner. The whole house shook with each dragging movement, then the sounds moved on, fading away into the night. We all slowly relaxed. No wonder my Enemies were so diminished. To have to live like this, all the time, never free from fear, never knowing when they might be discovered and killed . . . Not unlike the life they made for me, really. But it was hard

for me to feel any real sense of revenge, or satisfaction. No-one should
have to live like this.

"All that remains of Humanity now," said Jessica, "is small groups
like us. Those who survived the War by hiding, like frightened mice in
their holes. We're still hiding, hanging on, surviving, doing what we can.
Hoping against hope . . . for a miracle. But we haven't heard anything
from the other groups for months now, and when we call out, no-one answers. So perhaps . . . we're all that's left. The last Redoubt of Humanity,
pinning all our hopes on the death of one man."

"Who would have thought it would come down to the likes of us, to
be Humanity's last hope," said King of Skin sadly, from his corner.

We all looked at him, waiting, but he had nothing else to say. He still
wouldn't look at me. But at least he'd stopped crying.

"Outside, all that lives now are the last few remnants of Lilith's children," said Larry Oblivion. "Mutated and monstrous, and quite mad.
Roaming the ruins, killing everything they find, including each other. I
sometimes wonder if they even know the War is over. They won't last
much longer. The energies loosed during the War, by you and your
mother, are still abroad in the night, changing everything, mutating every
thing. Soon enough they'll all be gone . . . and so will we, and what's left
of the world will belong to the insects."

"But now I'm here," I said forcefully. "And we've talked, and that
changes everything."

"Does it?" said Jessica.

"Yes," I said. "I have to believe that. And so do you. It's our only
hope. Humanity's only hope. Use your power. Send me back into the Past,
back to the time I came from. And I promise you I'll find a way to stop
Lilith that doesn't involve raising an army. There won't be any War, to
cause all this."

"You want us to trust you?" said Count Video. "Trust the man who
damned us all?"

"Why should we believe in you?" said Larry. "Why should we trust in
you, John Taylor, Lilith's son?"

"Because your brother Tommy did," I said. "Even though he had
good reason not to."

Count Video rose abruptly to his feet, turning to face me. "We could
kill you," he said. "Now you're here, finally, in our grasp. We could kill
you, even if it meant all our deaths. It might be worth it, to know you were
dead. And then maybe we could all rest peacefully."

"Do you want revenge, or do you want to stop the War?" I said. "If I
die, here and now, who's going to stop Lilith? You must know she plans to

remake the Nightside in her own image, kill everyone who stands against her, and remake Humanity into something more pliable, to serve her all her days. I think I'd rather be dead, than that. I'm the only chance you've got of stopping Lilith. Of stopping this. If I can find a way to bring her down, without fighting a War . . . that has to be more important than revenge. Doesn't it?"

In the end, they only argued for about ten minutes before reluctantly agreeing. Annie Abattoir opened a vein in her arm, and used the blood to draw a pentacle on the floor, while the others worked together to raise what power remained to them. Jessica Sorrow used her teddy bear as a focus for the right place and time. Count Video swept his hands back and forth, leaving sparkling energy traces on the air, weaving description theory and binary magics, while his necrotech sparked and sputtered on his wrinkled flesh. King of Skin stood tall and proud, doing what he was born to do, evoking powerful magics with ancient Words of Power. And Larry Oblivion took it all in, his undead body the conduit for the terrible energies they were raising, absorbing all the punishment so the others could concentrate on the Working.

Annie Abattoir gestured sharply with her bloody arm, and I stepped inside the pentacle. She closed the pattern with a final flourish, and the spell ignited. The crimson lines of the pentacle blazed with power, and the world outside it began to grow dim and insubstantial to me.

And then King of Skin lifted his head, his eyes huge. "They're here!" he cried. "They followed Taylor here! They broke through our defences, and we were so preoccupied with Taylor we didn't even notice! *They're here!*"

Monsters came crashing through all the walls at once. Huge brutish forms with eager eyes and dripping mouths. Long claws and taloned hands ripped through stone and brick and plaster, while something dark and leathery smashed a hole through the ceiling. The floor jarred upwards and split apart, as a great eye looked up through the widening chasm. My Enemies ignored them all, concentrating on the Working that would send me back through Time. A barbed tentacle shot down from the ceiling and wrapped itself around Count Video. Blood spurted from his mouth as his ribs collapsed, but he still fought to pronounce the last few Words of Power. A bone spike transfixed Annie Abattoir, gutting her, but still she stood and would not fall.

I faded away, falling back through Time, and that was the last I saw of them. Had the Beasts really followed me to their hiding place? Had I brought their deaths about, after all?

No. I could still save them. Save everyone. I would find a way. That was what I did.

EIGHT

While I Was Away

I came back to fire and screams, and the thunder of buildings falling. The street was full of rubble and overturned vehicles, and there were bodies everywhere. A shop-front blew out in a soundless explosion, glass fragments flying on the air like shrapnel. I hunkered down, arms over my head, and stared quickly about me. There was fighting going on all around, mad-eyed mobs attacking each other with spells and weapons and anything that came to hand. Fires burned to every side, consuming the few buildings still standing. The air was thick with smoke, and heavy with the stench of burned flesh and spilled blood. I'd come back to a war zone.

For the first time that I could remember, all traffic on the road had stopped. The way was blocked with blazing wrecks, crashed vehicles, and piled-up cars. Some of them had bodies in them, while others leaked blood and similar fluids. A lightning bolt slammed down only a few feet away from me, buckling the pavement, and I headed for the nearest cover. I scurried over to the broken hulk of an overturned ambulance and crouched down beside it, pressing hard against its blood-smeared side. I could just make out its dying whispers, fluttering on the edges of my mind, as the vehicle's animating spirit dissipated. *I've been good . . . I've been good . . . I'm scared. . . .* The ambulance coughed once, then was silent. All around me, the fighting raged back and forth.

I sighed heavily. Some days you can't turn your back for even a moment, without everything going to hell.

It would seem Lilith had started the War without me. I peered around me, trying to make out landmarks or details through the thick drifting smoke, while various combatants ran back and forth, screaming garbled war cries. After a while, I realised I was back in Uptown, in the heart of Clubland. Or at least, what was left of it. Half of it was already demolished, and there was a firestorm raging at the end of the street. Several of the buildings were burning hotter and brighter than any earthly flames should. Dark figures came and went in the smoke, and only some of them were human. Winged shapes soared by overhead, flapping huge membraneous wings, and none of them were angels.

Some people were trying to help. Staff from the various clubs sprayed the roaring flames with fire extinguishers that probably hadn't been tested in years. Magics sparked and flared on the grimy air, and a water elemental burst up out of several manholes to drench those buildings closest to it. A group of Christian Commandos chanted a blessing over a fire hose, and used the high-pressure holy water as a weapon against the more sorcerous blazes. Stone golems strode unflinchingly into burning buildings past saving, and pulled them down, using the weight of the rubble to smother the flames. Sometimes the golems came out again, and sometimes they didn't. All around me, famous clubs with old and honoured names were already gone, reduced to cinders and blackened frames.

A large group of naked men and women, armed with axes and knives and machetes, their ungainly bodies daubed with blood and woad and ashes, came stalking down the ruined street like they owned it. They struck out at everyone they passed, and carried severed heads on poles, all the while howling praises to their god Lugh, and the glories of destruction. They all had mad, happy eyes and broad smiles. Yet many of them were still wearing wristwatches, which was a bit of a give-away that they weren't quite as primitive as they were affecting. *Well,* I thought, *I've got to start somewhere.*

I rose from behind the dead ambulance and strode forward to confront the mob. They stumbled to a ragged halt, almost falling over each other. I got the impression it had been some time since anyone had done anything but take one look at them and run away screaming. Their leader fixed me with his best mad stare, and started screaming something nasty about blasphemers, and I walked right up to him and kicked him square in the balls. I put a lot of strength and all my displeasure at what had happened into that kick, and it actually lifted him a few inches into the air before dropping him to his knees. His eyes got very big, and though his mouth was working, not a sound came out of it. He looked like he'd be pretty busy for some time, trying to get some or indeed any air back into his lungs, so I turned my attention to the crowd before me. They looked at their fallen leader, then back at me, and some actually started to shuffle their feet guiltily.

"I am John Taylor," I announced loudly, giving them my best disturbing smile. The people at the front of the mob immediately tried to press backwards, away from me, but the ones behind them were having none of it. There was a certain amount of undignified scuffling. I raised my voice again. "Whatever you've been doing, it stops, right here and now. I have work for you."

"And what if we don't feel like working for you?" said a voice from somewhere at the back of the crowd. "You can't kick us all in the balls."

"Right," said someone else. "We can take him! He's only one man!"

I had to smile. I love it when they say things like that. "You may have heard about this little trick I do," I said. "Where I take the bullets out of guns."

Some of the mob began to stand a little straighter. Axes and machetes and knives were brandished.

"Guns?" said a woman, who would definitely have looked a lot better with her clothes on. "We don't need no stinking guns!"

I could feel my smile broadening. "I've been working on a new variation," I said.

I snapped my fingers, and all the fillings disappeared from their teeth. Along with all crowns, caps, bridges, and veneers. There were a great many howls of muted pain, an awful lot of clapping of hands to mouths, and suddenly everyone in the mob looked a whole lot less crazy and entirely willing to listen to whatever I had to say.

"Any more words of dissent," I said, "and I will show you another variation, that involves your lungs and a whole bunch of buckets."

Somewhat garbled voices hastened to assure me that they were all ready and willing to assist me in anything I might want done. So I set them to defending those people who were trying to fight the fires.

I left them to it and set off down the street, stepping carefully around and over the cracked and raised pavement. The air was painfully hot on my face from all the fires, and the smoky air was thick with floating cinders. Fighting was still going on, in fits and starts, but no-one bothered me. I stopped as I came to a club I recognised, the lap-dancing joint Not Fade Away. The ghost girls were out in force, using their smoky bodies to smother any flames that threatened their club's already scorched façade. The barker kept them moving, his tired and strained voice still rising easily over the general din. He nodded brusquely in my direction as I went over to join him.

"Club's closed, for redecoration," he growled out of the corner of his mouth. "We will reopen. Look for our ads."

"How long is it since I was last here?" I asked him.

"About a week, squire. Just before all this unpleasantness started. Now unless you've got something useful to contribute, be a nice gentleman and bog off. The ladies and I are busy."

I used my gift to find somewhere it was raining heavily, and brought the rain to where it was needed. It slammed down, a torrential downpour the whole length of the street, drowning all the fires and washing the smoke right out of the air. People shouted and cheered, and the ghost girls danced joyously in the street as the rain fell straight through them. I tipped a wink to the barker and continued down the street. I shouldn't have used my gift so blatantly. Lilith would be bound to detect it, and know I was back. But I needed to do something, and I've always had a weakness for the grand gesture.

Next, I needed to find out what had happened while I was away. It appeared my Enemies' return spell hadn't been as accurate as I'd hoped.

I eventually found the establishment I was looking for—*Simulacra Corner*. A discreet little joint, specialising in the sale of magic mirrors, crystal balls, scrying pools, and other less-well-advertised means of spying on your neighbour from a distance. Simulacra Corner dealt in everything from confidential connections to industrial espionage, and everything in between. The sign over the front door said FOR ALL YOUR VOYEURISTIC NEEDS. Tucked away down a side street that wasn't always there, none of the recent excitement had even touched it. As I approached the rough wooden door, an approximation of a face raised itself out of the wood. The blank eyes glared at me, and the brass letter box formed itself into a sneering mouth.

"Go away," it said, in a harsh, growling voice. "We are closed. As in, not open. Call back later. Or not. See if I care."

I've never cared for snotty simulacra. "You'll open for me," I said. "I'm John Taylor."

"Good for you. Love the trench coat. We're still not open. And you probably couldn't afford anything here even if we were."

"Let me in," I said pleasantly. "Or I'll piss through your letterbox."

The face scowled, then sniffed mournfully. "Yes, that sounds like John Taylor. I hate this job. When everyone knows you're not real, you get no respect."

The face sank back into the wood, disappearing detail by detail, and the door swung slowly open before me. I stepped inside, and the door immediately slammed shut behind me. An invisible bell tinkled, announcing a customer. The shop's interior was wonderfully calm and quiet, after the noise and chaos of the street, and the air smelled sweetly of sandalwood and beeswax. The entrance lobby was empty, apart from a few comfortable chairs and a coffee table half-buried under out-of-date magazines. The shop's owner came bustling forward to greet me, a small furtive type, badly dressed and overweight, and smiling a little bit too widely. He was already rubbing his hands together, and I stuck my hands into my coat pockets so I wouldn't have to shake hands. I just knew his would be cold and clammy. He looked like the kind of guy who always assures you the first hit is free.

"Mr. Taylor, Mr. Taylor, so good of you to grace my humble establishment with your presence! Sorry we didn't let you in straightaway, Mr. Taylor, but it's chaos out there! Absolute chaos, oh my word yes! Can't be too careful . . . Don't those fools realise what they're doing? Property values will be depressed for years after this!"

"I need to make use of some of your items," I said, declining to enter a conversation I knew wasn't going to go anywhere useful. "I need to catch up on what's been happening in the Nightside, while I was away."

"Well, I don't know about that, Mr. Taylor . . . you don't actually have a line of credit with us, and in the current circumstances . . ."

"Charge it to Walker," I said.

The shop's owner brightened immediately. "Oh, Mr. Walker! Yes, yes, one of my most valued customers. You're sure you have his . . . well, of course you do! Of course! No-one ever takes Mr. Walker's name in vain, eh? Eh? I'll just put it all on his bill . . ."

He bustled away, and I followed him through an inconspicuous door into a hall of mirrors. They hung in uneven rows on the two walls, with no obvious means of support. They were long and tall, round and wide, in silver frames and in gold, and one by one they opened themselves to me, to show me visions of the recent past.

I saw Lilith burst out of the Street of the Gods, at the head of an army of her monstrous children and maddened followers. I watched as she commanded them to kill every living thing who wouldn't bow down and worship her and swear eternal loyalty to her cause. I heard her order them to destroy every building and structure in her path. *Burn it all down,* she said. *I won't be needing it.* And I wouldn't let myself look away as the mirrors showed me bloody slaughter, ancient buildings crumbling, flames rising into the night sky, death and destruction on an almost inconceivable scale. The bodies piled up as people ran screaming through the wreckage of their lives.

I saw Walker, working desperately to organise resistance from the safe haven of Strangefellows bar. Hidden and protected, for the moment, by Merlin Satanspawn's defences. Someone had healed Walker of the injuries he'd taken on the Street of the Gods, but his face was gaunt with stress and fatigue, and there were heavy dark shadows under his eyes. For the first time in all the time I'd known him, he didn't look confident. I watched and listened as he tried again and again to contact the Authorities, to summon the armed forces that had always backed him up in the past. But no-one ever answered him. He was on his own.

I ordered the mirror before me to concentrate on a specific time and place: on what Walker was doing the day before I arrived back in the Nightside. The mirror narrowed its focus and showed me.

Walker sat at a table pushed right up against the long bar in Strangefellows, poring over reports brought to him by a series of runners, deathly tired men and women only kept going by duty and honour and the pills Walker passed out by the handful. Walker looked in really bad shape; but still he studied his reports and gave orders in a calm, unhurried voice, and his agents went straight back out into the night again, to do what was needed.

The bar had the look of a place under siege. It was dark and overcrowded, with people sitting slumped at tables or on the floor, nursing their drinks and their hurts and their remaining strength. A healer was running a rough-and-ready clinic in one corner, doing meatball sorcery on the worst wounds to get people on their feet, so they could be sent out again. The floor was stained with blood and other fluids. People were coming and going all the time, and most of them had that driven, damned, defeated look in their faces. A few were sleeping fitfully on pushed-together mattresses, twitching and crying out miserably in their sleep.

An unseen band was playing the old Punk classic "He Fucked Me with a Chain-saw and It Felt Like a Kiss." Which was worrying. Alex only ever plays Punk when he's in a really bad mood, and then wise men check their change carefully and avoid the bar snacks. Alex was behind the bar, as usual, making Molotov cocktails out of his reserve stock and complaining loudly about having to use some of his better vintages. He comforted himself by adding a splash of holy water to every bottle, to give the mixture that little extra bite. Alex had a particularly unpleasant sense of humour when he put his mind to it.

Betty and Lucy Coltrane stood poised in the centre of the bar, their bulging muscles distended, each of them holding a really vicious-looking shillelagh, carved out of blackthorn root and covered in deeply etched runes. Now and again some poor damned fool would force his way past Merlin's defences and teleport blindly into the bar, hoping to impress Lilith with feats of daring, and each and every time Lucy and Betty Coltrane would pound the living shit out of him, with extreme prejudice.

I didn't see what they did with the bodies afterwards, and I wasn't sure I wanted to know.

Walker got up from his table, stretched slowly and painfully, and leaned wearily against the bar. Alex sniffed loudly.

"Taking a break again, your high-and-mightyness? More Benzedrine with your champagne, perhaps, you heathen?"

"Not just now, thank you, Alex. Still no chance of Merlin's manifesting, I suppose?"

Alex shrugged. "I can't feel his presence, though I have no doubt he's keeping a watchful eye on things. Either he's biding his time, or he's keeping his head well down till it's all safely over. Trust me, when he finally does decide to Do Something, you'll almost certainly wish he hadn't. Merlin has always favoured a scorched-earth policy when it comes to dealing with problems."

"I like him already," said Walker, and Alex sniffed loudly again.

At the end of the outside alley that led to the bar's front door, Shotgun Suzie was standing guard. A tidal wave of Lilith's more fanatical followers came sweeping down the narrow alley towards her, and she met them with guns, grenades, and incendiaries. Explosions filled the alley with painful light and sound, throwing bodies this way and that, while shrapnel from fragmentation grenades cut through the packed ranks like a scythe. Suzie fired her shotgun again and again, blowing ragged holes in the surging mob of zealots before her, and the dead piled up into a bloody barricade that her enemies had to drag away or climb over to get at her.

The alleyway was narrow enough that only a dozen or so could come at her at one time, and none of them ever got close enough to touch her. She fired her shotgun over and over, constantly reloading from the bandoliers crossing her chest, until the gun got hot enough to burn her hands. And then she pulled on leather gloves and kept on firing until she ran out of ammunition. Blood sprayed across the alley walls, and gore ran thickly in the gutters. The screams of the wounded and the dying went ignored by both sides. And still Lilith's followers pressed forward, and still Shotgun Suzie stood her ground.

She tossed the last of her incendiaries into the thickest part of the mob, and a terrible flickering light filled the alleyway as men burned like candles. They thrashed back and forth, spreading the flames, and Suzie seized the moment to snatch up a Colonial Marines smart gun that had fallen through a Timeslip from a particularly militaristic future. She opened up with the smart gun, and thousands of rounds a minute slammed into the mob. The carnage moved up another notch as she swept the heavy muzzle back and forth, and the mob's front ranks disappeared in a bloody haze of exploding heads and bellies. There was a pause as the piled-up dead sealed off the alleyway completely, and Lilith's surviving followers had an earnest discussion over what to do next. Suzie grinned and lit herself a nasty black cigar. In the end Lilith's followers were more afraid of failing her than they were of dying, so they sent runners back to request more powerful weapons, pulled the barricade apart, and pressed forward again.

They kept coming, and Suzie kept killing them. Facing impossible odds, knowing they were bound to drag her down eventually, Suzie was still grinning broadly. I didn't think I'd ever seen her look happier.

Reluctantly, I switched to another mirror. I'd worn the other one out, and I had to see how Walker's agents were doing out on the streets against Lilith's far greater forces. The first one the mirror found was Dead Boy. He was striding carelessly down a half-demolished street, his long purple greatcoat flapping in the gusting wind, his dark floppy hat crammed down over his curly hair, while an armed crowd charged right at him. Dead Boy laughed in their faces, and didn't even bother to increase his pace. He took a deep sniff of the black carnation in his buttonhole, tossed back a handful of the nasty little pills that an Obeah woman made up specially for him, drank the last of the whiskey in his bottle, and tossed it aside. His corpse-pale face was full of a dreadful anticipation.

"Come on, you bastards! Show me what you've got! Give me your best shot. I can take it!"

The mob hit him like a hammer, flailing arms wielding knives and clubs and even broken glass, but he stood his ground, and almost immediately the crowd broke around him like a wave hitting a solid outcropping of rock. Dead Boy struck about him with his pale fists, and there was a vicious strength in his dead arms. He moved impossibly quickly, thrusting himself forward into the face of his attackers, and those he hit fell and did not rise again. The raging mob struck him and cut at him, and hit him with everything that came to hand, doing their best to drag him down by sheer force of numbers; but still he stood and would not fall. His dead body soaked up appalling punishment, but he felt none of it. He just kept going, forcing his way into the heart of the mob, going to slaughter as to a feast, laughing aloud as he crushed skulls and stove in chests and tore limbs from their sockets. He was dead, and his strength was no longer bound by the limitations of living flesh. Blood made his face a crimson mask, and none of it was his.

In the end the mob simply split apart around him, streaming past in search of easier prey. He was only one man, and he couldn't stop a crowd. Dead Boy cried out angrily after them, and struck out at those who passed, but the mob quickly learned to give him a wide berth, and soon enough they had all moved on and left him behind. Dead Boy stood alone on a burning street, surrounded by the dead and the dying. He shouted after the departing mob, demanding they come back and fight, but none of them were zealot enough or stupid enough to listen. Dead Boy shrugged, cleaned his face with a dirty handkerchief, then sat down on the nearest pile of bodies and opened his tattered purple greatcoat, to check the extent of the damage he'd suffered.

There were bullet holes, of course, but he'd dig the slugs out later. He liked to collect the more obscure brands. There were cuts, with pale edges but no blood, and puncture wounds that were nothing more than puckered holes in his unfeeling flesh. He'd stitch them up later. Or superglue them, if he was short of time. There were some wider tears, exposing pale pink and grey meat, and he scowled at one especially wide rip down his left side, big and deep enough to expose half his rib cage. Some of the ribs were clearly broken. He sniffed and pulled a roll of black duct tape from his coat pocket. He wrapped it round and round his torso, to hold himself together until he could perform more detailed repairs.

"Thank God for duct tape. Maybe I should invest in one of those industrial staplers . . ." He shrugged easily and tore off a length of the tape with his teeth. He smoothed the tape flat, then held up one hand and glared at it. "Shit, I can't have lost another finger . . ."

He was still searching through the rubble and the bodies for his missing finger when his head came up sharply. His senses might have been dulled, but his instincts had never been sharper. One of Lilith's children was heading down the street towards him. Dead Boy stood up and pushed his floppy hat onto the back of his head to get a better look.

Lord Pestilence was a stringy grey figure in a tattered grey robe, his face so gaunt it was little more than brittle leather over a grinning skull. Thick pus oozed from his empty eye-sockets and dripped from his mirthless smile. His bare hands were covered in weeping pustules. He rode a primitive hobby-horse fashioned from human bones, and wherever he went he spread disease. All around him people fell back choking and bleeding, dying slowly and horribly from a hundred different plagues. Lord Pestilence rode his hobby-horse down the middle of the road, and didn't care whether he struck down enemy or ally; it was enough that he was free at last from his prison under the Street of the Gods, free once again to spread sickness in the world and glory in the suffering he caused.

Dead Boy saw him coming, and was the only one to stand his ground, when everyone else did the sensible thing and fled. Lord Pestilence headed straight for him, giggling like a happy child, and Dead Boy considered the old god thoughtfully. Lord Pestilence lashed out with typhoid, cholera, polio, AIDS, Ebola, and green monkey fever, and everyone for half a mile around fell twitching and choking to the ground; but not Dead Boy. He just stood his ground, waiting, his pale face impassive. Enraged, Lord Pestilence urged his bony hobby-horse on, throwing increasingly obscure diseases and maladies at the single figure that stood so contemptuously in his path. Until finally the old god made the mistake of coming within arm's reach of Dead Boy, who lashed out with a move too fast for living eyes to follow. He clubbed Lord Pestilence right off his hobbyhorse and sent the old god crashing to the ground. He lay there a moment, crying out at the unthinkable indignity, and Dead Boy stamped on his chest. Old bone cracked and splintered under the force of the blow, and Lord Pestilence unleashed all his awful power in one terrible blow at the grim figure standing over him.

A hundred thousand diseases issued from the old god, every fever and blight and growth that had ever vexed mankind, and none of them could touch Dead Boy. Diseases were for the living. Thwarted, the magic recoiled and turned back upon its sender. Lord Pestilence screamed and howled horribly as the diseases took hold in him, all at once, eating him alive. Cursed to know at last all the pain and horror he'd spent lifetimes imposing on others. His leathery skin cracked and bubbled, and finally ran away like watery mud. He fell apart, bit by bit, crying out like an animal now as the diseases turned his insides to soup, and his bones cracked apart into shards and splinters, and finally dust. In the end, there was nothing left of that old god Lord Pestilence but a grinning misshapen skull. Dead Boy stamped it into pieces, just to be sure.

"It's not easy being dead," he said solemnly. "But sometimes it does have its advantages."

I moved to another mirror, and ordered it to show me Larry Oblivion. The dead detective, the post-mortem private eye. I'd heard a lot about him, most of it uncanny or unsettling, but I'd never met him in my own time. Only in the future, as one of my Enemies. And now there he was in the mirror before me, and looking very different. He looked . . . so much more alive. He strode purposefully down a smoke-streaked street, looking fine and sharp and so stylish with his Gucci suit, his manicured hands and his razor-cut hair. He had the look of a man who always travelled first class, and didn't have a care in the world. Except for being some kind of zombie. I never did get the full story about that.

A crowd of minor godlings with animal heads and inhuman appetites broke off from raping and feasting on the running people, and spread out to block his path. Blood dripped thickly from their clawed hands and furry mouths. And Larry Oblivion disappeared. Vanished into thin air, gone in the blink of an eye. I didn't know he could do that. Neither did the godlings, apparently, as they heaved themselves about, this way and that, stamping their hoofed feet on the ground. They weren't used to being cheated of their prey.

Blood flew abruptly on the air, gushing from a severed throat, and one of the godlings crashed to the ground, kicking spasmodically as its life-blood flowed away. More and more of the godlings cried out as they were attacked by something none of them could see, striking impossibly quickly, killing them with contemptuous ease. One by one they fell, old gods brought down by a more recent power. The dead detective, Larry Oblivion.

At first I thought he must be using some kind of invisibility, but the mirror said otherwise. It would have been able to see through that. So I got the mirror to slow the image right down, and sure enough there was Larry Oblivion, moving too quickly for the eye to follow. He was here, there, and everywhere, come and gone in a moment, appearing out of nowhere to strike down an unsuspecting godling with a shimmering silver blade and already disappearing before his victim hit the ground. He flickered on and off, only present for such small fractions of time that even the mirror had trouble keeping up with him. *I'm getting such a headache,* it complained, but I drove it ruthlessly on. I needed to know what was happening.

In the end all the godlings were dead, and Larry Oblivion appeared out of nowhere next to the bodies, looking as immaculate and stylish as ever, with not one hair out of place. He'd moved so quickly there wasn't even a single drop of blood on his Gucci suit. But he was holding a Faerie wand. I smiled, satisfied. A lot of things about the mysterious Larry Oblivion and his impossible exploits made sense now. He'd been using the wand to bring Time to a halt, while he kept moving. Very useful little toy, that. Of course no-one ever suspected, because wands were so pass_, these days. Everyone had just assumed he had a gift like mine, or his brother Tommy's.

And then Larry looked up sharply from adjusting his silk tie, as something far worse than a pack of minor godlings came crashing down the street towards him with murder on its mind. It was thirty feet tall if it was an inch, a giant mechanical apparatus stamping down the street on giant multijointed steel legs. It was all bits and pieces pressed into use and held together by unknown forces, all kinds of metal revolving around glowing sources of power. Everything about it shouted brute force. It was roughly humanoid, with mismatched arms and legs and a bulging brass head with two huge eyes that glowed red as hellfire. It had a long jagged slit for a mouth, its rising and falling edges sharper than any teeth.

It swung down the street with long ungainly steps, swaying from side to side, stamping the living and the dead to pulp under its heavy steel feet. Its long arms ended in fists as big as wrecking balls, and it struck out casually at every building it passed, smashing through stone and brick with equal ease. The ground shook with its every step. I had no idea what it was, god or construct or some mechanical ideal run by an animating spirit. The Spirit of Crap Robots Past, perhaps.

Certainly Larry Oblivion didn't look at all impressed by the huge clunky thing as it tramped and crashed its way down the street towards him. Everyone else hurried to get out of its path, at least partly because it didn't look too steady on its flat steel feet, but Larry just shot his immaculate white cuffs, brushed an invisible fleck of dust from one shoulder, and stood his ground. He waited until the huge construct was practically on top of him, then he gestured almost negligently with his wand, and disappeared. The massive contraption reared back, roaring like a deep bass steam whistle, swivelling its great brass head back and forth in search of its elusive prey.

A blur of motion surrounded the metal thing, swift glimpses of something appearing and disappearing too fast to be tracked, then bits of the construct began flying off in all directions. It took Larry Oblivion less than five minutes to dismantle the metal construct and reduce it to its component parts. Larry reappeared next to the detached brass head and kicked it down the street like an oversized football. I'm pretty sure people would have cheered, if there'd been anybody left to witness it.

Larry checked his suit carefully for signs of stress, then continued down the street.

The next mirror showed me King of Skin, slouching down a wide thoroughfare in all his sleazy glory, looking proud and potent and confident. His eyes were bright with a terrible aspect as he sallied forth, undoing probabilities and spreading nightmares through the power of his awful glamour. Even through the distance of the mirror, I still couldn't stand to look at King of Skin directly. These were his glory days, and he was still a Power to be reckoned with. Even following his progress out of the corner of my eye was almost too much to bear. Look at him for too long and I started to see . . . unbearable things. When King of Skin walked abroad, wrapped in his glamour, everyone saw what they feared most, and his power reworked probability to make those nightmares real, and solid. No man can stand to face his own nightmares, made flesh and blood. Hideous things manifested around King of Skin as he slouched along, the dreadful King with his dreadful Court.

He went where he would in the besieged city, surrounded by awful shapes, rich with terrible significance for those who saw them, like the monsters we see in the dark bedrooms of our childhood. They reared and roared and swaggered in the night, attacking everything within reach, broken free at last from the restraints of unreality. King of Skin went where he pleased, and all the Powers and Forces and Beings of Lilith's court ran screaming from him. King of Skin smiled and sniggered and continued on his way.

Until someone dropped a building on him, from a safe distance. He disappeared under a mountain of rubble, and although I watched the mirror for a long time, I didn't see him again.

Although I knew I would, in a certain, terrible future.

By now I'd exhausted all the mirrors. The scenes they showed me became hazy and blurred, and some couldn't even muster the strength to show me my own reflection. I tried the crystal balls, but their range was very limited, and half of them had gone opaque from the traumas of what they'd witnessed. Reluctantly, I moved on to the scrying pools. They weren't much to look at, just a selection of simple stone grottos in an underlit room, each holding pools of clear water. I knelt beside the first pool, pricked my thumb with a prepared dagger, and let three big fat drops of blood fall into the water. Scrying is old magic, with old prices and penalties. The clear water swallowed up my blood without taking on the faintest tinge of red, but the ripples kept spreading and spreading, until finally the pool focused in on what I wanted to see, and then the ripples cleared to show me an image almost painfully bright and clear.

Razor Eddie, the Punk God of the Straight Razor, walked through what was left of the Street of the Gods, and if he was at all affected by the destruction around him, the burned-out churches and demolished temples, it didn't show in his sharp, pinched face. A thin intense presence wrapped in a filthy old greatcoat, he strolled unconcerned past the bodies of dead gods and didn't give a damn.

A crowd of spiked and pierced zealots looked up from desecrating a sacred grove as Razor Eddie approached, and they swaggered out into the Street to block his way, laughing and calling out suggestively to him. They didn't know who he was, the fools. When he showed no fear of them, or any intention of doing something amusing, like running or begging for his life, the zealots grew sullen and angry, and sharp objects appeared in their hands. They were vultures, feeding on the carrion left behind by Lilith's crusade, hyped up on adrenaline and bloodlust and religious fervour.

They went to meet Razor Eddie with torture and horror and murder on their minds, laughing and squealing with delight, and the Punk God of the Straight Razor walked right through them. When he came out the other side they were all dead, nothing left of them but a great pile of severed heads. None of them had any eyes. I don't know how he did it. No-one does. Eddie might be an agent of the good these days, but even the good looks the other way sometimes. Razor Eddie is a mystery as well as a god, and he likes it that way.

He looked round interestedly at a sudden loud clattering sound, and a huge creature something like a millipede came writhing and coiling up out of the ruins of an ancient temple. It was impossibly huge and seemingly without end, its vast shiny bulk propelled along by thousands of stubby little legs. Hundreds of yards of it came hammering along the Street towards Razor Eddie, easily a dozen feet wide and made up of curving segments of shimmering carborundum, gleaming dull red in the light of a hundred simmering fires. It darted forward impossibly quickly, its bulging head covered with rows of compound eyes, its complicated mouth parts clacking expectantly. It could sense the power in Razor Eddie, and it was hungry. I don't know what it was. Some old nameless god from out of the depths, perhaps, no longer worshipped by anything but the worms of the earth.

Razor Eddie went forward to meet it, frowning slightly as though considering an unfamiliar problem. His pearl-handled straight razor was in his hand, shining bright as the sun. The creature reared up, its blunt head rising high above the surrounding buildings, then it slammed down again and snatched up Razor Eddie in its pincered mouth. Razor Eddie struggled briefly, his arms pinned helplessly to his sides, and the giant millipede swallowed him whole. He was there one moment, and gone the next. The millipede tossed back its carapaced head, and a series of slow ripples passed down the bulging throat as it gulped Razor Eddie down. The great head nodded a few times, as though satisfied, then it continued on its way down the Street of the Gods.

Only to pause, just a few yards later. Its head swayed uncertainly back and forth, its mouth parts clacking loudly, then it screamed like a steam geyser as its belly exploded outwards. The gleaming segments cracked and splintered and blew apart as Razor Eddie cut his way out from the inside. The huge millipede curled and writhed and slammed back and forth, demolishing buildings all around it, smashing stone and concrete and pounding the rubble to dust in its agonies, but still it couldn't escape from the awful, remorseless thing that was killing it. In the end, Razor Eddie strolled unhurriedly away from the wreckage of the dead god, ignoring the last spastic twitches of the cracked and broken body. He was smiling slightly, as though considering even more disturbing things he intended to do to his fellow gods.

Another pool, another three drops of bloods, another vision. Those of Walker's agents not strong enough to take on Lilith's offspring, or enter maddened mobs single-handed, had banded together to take on smaller targets, doing what they could to make a difference. Sandra Chance, the consulting necromancer, stabbed about her with her aboriginal pointing-bone, and wherever she pointed it, people crashed convulsing to the ground and did not rise again. When she'd exhausted the bone's power she tossed handfuls of carefully pre-prepared graveyard dirt from the pouches hanging at her waist into the air, and all around her Lilith's zealots fell choking, as though buried alive.

Annie Abattoir watched Sandra's back. A huge muscular presence and a head taller than most, she stalked the night in her best opera gown, tearing people limb from limb, biting out their throats and cramming the flesh into her ravenous mouth. Her crimson smile dripped blood and gore.

The Nightside's very own transvestite super-hero, Ms. Fate, the man who dressed as a super-heroine to fight crime, finally came into her own. She stamped and pirouetted through crowds of maddened zealots, felling them with vicious kicks and blows as she moved gracefully from one martial art to another. No-one could stand against her, and no-one could touch her. Now and again she'd throw handfuls of razor-edged shuriken where they would do the most good. She might not have been making a whole lot of difference in the great scheme of things, but at long last Ms. Fate was the dark avenger of the night he'd always wanted to be.

The three fighters roamed far and wide, combining their efforts to break up mobs, save those under threat, and do what they could for the wounded and the lost. Walker sent more of his agents to back them up, when he could spare them, but there were never enough to do more than slow Lilith's advance into the Nightside. Scene followed scene in the pool's clear water as Lilith's growing army marched in triumph through burning streets and devastated districts. Everywhere Lilith went, people flocked to join her growing army—either because they fell under the spell of her powerful personality, or because they were desperate to be on the winning side . . . or just because they were afraid Lilith's people would kill them if they didn't.

She walked up and down in the Nightside, and buildings exploded where she looked. Fires burned at her word, and the street cracked apart where she walked. Bodies piled up because there was no-one left to take them away, and people ran screaming or sat huddled in the doorways of burned-out homes, driven out of their minds by shock and suffering. The mad and the desolate staggered whimpering through streets they no longer recognised, retreating endlessly before Lilith's advancing forces. Walker's people did their best to guide Lilith away from those areas where she could do the most damage, by goading her with hit-and-run tactics, falling back just slowly enough that she would be sure to follow them.

Still the Nightside was a big place, much larger than its official boundaries suggested, and there was a limit to how much death and destruction even Lilith and her forces could bring about. Walker's people set up road-blocks, barricaded narrow passageways, and set up distractions, trying to herd Lilith into areas they'd already evacuated. Lilith didn't seem to care where she went, as long as she got to kill or destroy everything she saw. She knew sooner or later she'd reach the people and places that really mattered. She was in no hurry. For the moment, she was just playing, indulging herself. If she had an overall plan, Walker couldn't see it.

And neither could I.

I watched as Walker discussed his most recent stratagems with Alex Morrisey. They sat together round a small table, talking quietly in a quieter, darker *Strangefellows*. It wasn't crowded any more. Anyone who could was out fighting in the streets. People lay on bloody mattresses, quietly dying. Betty and Lucy Coltrane sat slumped in a corner, leaning on each other for support, their faces slack and exhausted. There was blood all over them, not all of it from their victims. Alex and Walker didn't look much better. Their faces were drawn and gaunt, older than their years. There was no music playing in the bar, and from outside I could hear the baying of monsters and the screams of their prey. *Strangefellows* didn't look like a bar any more; it looked like somewhere people went to wait to die.

"Tell me you've got a plan, Walker," said Alex, too tired even to scowl properly. He took off his sunglasses to rub at his tired eyes, and I was actually shocked. It was like seeing him naked. He looked like he'd been hit so many times he was broken inside. "Tell me you've got a really good plan, Walker. Even if you haven't."

"Oh, I have a plan," Walker said calmly. His voice tried hard to sound confident, but his face was too tired to cooperate. "You might remember a certain creature from Outside that pretended to be a house on Blaiston Street. It called people to it, then consumed them. After Taylor destroyed it, I had my people collect scrapings of the alien cell tissues and preserve them for analysis. As a result of what they discovered in their labs, I was eventually able to grow a new house, in a setting of my own choice. I had it lobotomized, of course, so it would only eat what I chose to feed it. Never know when you'll need a secret weapon to use against your enemies."

Alex looked at Walker. "Enemies? Like John Taylor, perhaps?"

"Of course," said Walker.

"Do you think he'll ever come back?" said Alex.

"Of course," said Walker. "The murderer always returns to the scene of his crime, and the dog to his vomit. Anyway, my plan is to lure Lilith inside the alien house and see what happens. I doubt very much it will be able to consume her completely, but it might be able to leach off a considerable amount of her power. Make her easier to deal with."

"You'll need to bait your trap," said Alex, peering listlessly at the almost empty glass before him. "She's bound to suspect something. What have we got, that she wants badly enough to walk into certain ambush for?"

"Me," said Walker.

The scene faded out, as the pool's waters went opaque. I fed it more blood, but it didn't want to know. It was tired and scared, and it didn't want to see any more. But I did. So I raised my gift and thrust it into the pool. The two magics combined, and the scrying pool screamed pitifully in my mind as I made it show me what happened next. I had no time for kindness. I'd almost caught up with what had happened while I was gone, and time was running out. The pool's waters shook and trembled, but finally showed me what Walker did next.

I saw Lilith parade through a burned-out business district, at the head of an army so large I couldn't see its full extent. I saw Walker step calmly out of an alleyway at the end of the street to confront her. Lilith stopped abruptly, and all the monsters and zealots jammed up behind her. A slow sullen hush fell across the empty street, broken only by the sounds of distant screams and the low crackle of guttering fires. Walker stood perfectly poised before Lilith, in his smart suit and bowler hat, as though he'd just stepped out of a tea room or a politician's office, to discuss the time of day with an old acquaintance. He'd pushed the tiredness away from him by an effort of will, and looked just like the Walker of old. He smiled easily at Lilith, and tipped his bowler to her.

"Walker," said Lilith, in a voice just like poisoned wine. "My dear Henry. You do get around, don't you? I thought you might take the hint from our last little encounter that I have nothing more to say to you. But you always were a stubborn soul, weren't you? I have to say, you heal remarkably quickly, for a human."

Walker shrugged easily. "Needs must, when the Devil drives. I'm here to take you in, Lilith. Surrender now, and no-one need get hurt."

Lilith laughed girlishly, and actually clapped her hands together before her. "Dear Henry, you were always able to surprise me. What makes you think you can take me in?"

Walker reached inside his jacket and pulled out a gun. It was a bright shining silver, with coloured lights flashing all over it. Walker handled it casually, but his eyes were very cold. "Don't make me have to use this, Lilith."

"Now you're just boring me, Henry."

"Really? Try this."

Walker raised the gun and shot Lilith in the face. The paint capsule hit her right between the eyes. Paint exploded all over her shocked face, a thick evil-smelling purple slime liberally spiked with Alex's holy water. Lilith actually fell back a pace, spitting and sputtering and clawing frantically at her face with both hands. Walker chuckled nastily, turned, and ran. White-hot with rage, Lilith chased after him. I have to give it to Walker; I'd never seen him move so fast in his life. He was already down the street and round the corner before Lilith was even up to speed. I don't think she was used to having to exert herself physically. Walker ran, and Lilith followed, and her somewhat confused army brought up the rear.

Walker paused outside the front door of a house that looked no different from all the others around it, then he darted inside, leaving the door that wasn't a door standing open. Lilith charged through the opening a few moments later, and it slammed shut after her. The army stumbled to a halt outside. One of the leaders tried the door, but it wouldn't open. One of Lilith's children pushed forward, placed an oversized hand on the door and pushed, then cried out in shock and pain as the door tried to eat his hand. The front ranks of the army looked at each other, and decided to stay where they were until Lilith emerged from the house to give them orders.

The scene in the scrying pool changed to show me a rear view of the house that wasn't a house, as Walker came running full pelt out the back door. He ran through the overgrown garden to the back gate, then leaned on it for a while, breathing heavily. He looked back at the house, shuddered once, and immediately regained his composure. The back wall of the house seemed to heave, and swell, twisting black veins standing out suddenly in sharp relief in the fake brickwork. First the wall, then the whole structure of the house began to shake and shudder. Black and purple splotches of rot and decay appeared, and the two windows ran away like pus. Holes like ragged wounds opened up all over the sloping roof, and the back door slumped, running away in streams of liquid foulness.

The house hadn't stood a chance against Lilith. She'd barely been in it a few moments, and already it was dead and rotting.

Maybe he shouldn't have lobotomized it, after all.

"Damn," said Walker, quite succinctly. He produced a Strangefellows Membership Card from his pocket, pressed his thumb against the embossed surface, said the activating Word, and was gone, teleported back to the relative safety of the bar. I shut off the scene in the pool. I didn't want to see Lilith's rage when she emerged from the trap Walker had set for her. I was actually a little jealous that Alex had given Walker one of his Cards. They were supposed to be reserved for close friends and allies. I was also just a bit concerned about what Walker might do with the Card, in the future. I really didn't like the idea of his being able to just drop in at the bar, whenever he felt like it.

Of course, that assumed any of us had a future . . .

The scrying pool was sobbing quietly to itself, but I made it show me one last vision—what Lilith did next.

Raging mad at being mocked and outmanoeuvred by Walker, Lilith transported herself and all her great army straight to the Necropolis. The main building was barricaded, boarded up, and rendered positively indistinct behind a dozen layers of magical defences, but Lilith ignored them. She tore the air apart with her bare hands, breaking all the barriers set between this world and that of the Necropolis's private cemetery. Nothing was hidden from her, and nothing was safe. The final barrier screamed as it went down, and the cobbled street in this world split from end to end. Through the ragged tear Lilith had made in reality, the grim and grey world of the Necropolis graveyard could clearly be seen. Long streamers of fog drifted out. Lilith gestured sharply for her followers to stay put and stalked forward into the private cemetery.

The vision followed her. The graveyard looked just as cold and depressing as I remembered it, with row upon row of graves and tombstones stretching away to the distant horizon. Lilith looked around her and sniffed contemptuously. The Caretaker reared its earthy head to observe her, took one look, and sank back into the ground again, diving for deep cover. It wanted nothing to do with her. It knew when it was outmatched.

Lilith walked among the graves, glaring about her, and finally stopped and stamped her bare foot impatiently. When she spoke, her voice cracked like a whip on the still and silent air.

"You can all stop lying around, right now! I want every single one of you up and out of those graves, and standing here before me! Why should you lie quietly, when there is work you could be doing for me? Up, now! And the Devil help anyone who dares to keep me waiting!"

She snapped her colourless fingers, and immediately every grave and mausoleum gave up its occupant. They stood in endless rows, in the good suits and gowns they'd been buried in, looking around them in a confused sort of way. Even I was shocked, and not a little impressed. There were major spells defending the private graveyard, but to a Power like Lilith, Life and Death were very similar states.

It had to be said, the returned from the dead didn't look at all happy about their new condition. They'd paid good money in advance, precisely to avoid being disturbed from their rest like this. But they still had enough sense not to argue with Lilith. Even those who had been major players in their day knew better than to cross the ancient and terrible Power standing before them.

"These are your orders," she said crisply. "I want all of you out of here, and back in the Nightside. Snip, snap, no dawdling. Once back in your home territory, you are to kill every living thing you see and destroy everything in your path. No exceptions. Any questions?"

One man raised his hand. Lilith snapped her fingers again, and the re-animated man exploded into a thousand twitching pieces.

"Any more questions?" said Lilith. "I just love answering questions."

There were no more questions. Some of the returned even stuck their hands deep into their pockets so there wouldn't be any unfortunate misunderstandings. Lilith smiled coldly and led her new army back into the Nightside. The newly revived dead didn't object, being ready to do whatever was required of them, as long as they could go back to the comfort of their graves afterwards. Anything for a little quiet resting in peace. Still, some of them did feel the need to discuss their new condition, in guarded whispers and mutters.

"She said kill everyone," said one voice. "Does that mean we're supposed to eat their brains?"

"No, I think that's only in the movies, darling."

"Oh. I think I'd quite like to try eating some brains, actually."

"Now that's just gross," said a third voice.

"Do we have to eat them raw, sweetie; or are we allowed to add condiments?"

"I think it's probably a matter of personal taste, dear."

The ranks of the returned dead streamed through the streets of the Nightside, falling upon every living thing they encountered. Some of them with more enthusiasm than others, but all of them bound to Lilith's will. They couldn't be hurt or stopped, and their sheer numbers overwhelmed any and all defences. A hell of a lot of people had died in the Nightside, down the centuries. Walker sent a small army, under Sandra Chance, of his best people to try and contain the returned dead, but they couldn't be everywhere at once.

Many people were distressed to find themselves fighting off deceased friends and relatives, now intent on killing those who had once been closest to them. There were tears and screams, sometimes on both sides, but the reanimated dead did what they had to, and so, eventually, did the living. The risen dead were burned, blasted, and dismembered, but still they pressed forward. Walker's barricades were soon overrun, and the defenders forced to run for their lives. Walker was forced to order a general retreat, just so he could control it. He ordered the demolition of whole areas, to seal off the better defended sections from those already fallen. There was fighting everywhere now, and fires wide as city blocks raged fiercely, unconfined.

There were those who still had the guts to fight. The Demonz street gang, minor demons who claimed to be political refugees from Hell, poured up out of their nightclub the Pit to defend their territory. Eight feet tall, with curling horns on their brows and cloven hoofs, scarlet as sin and twice as nasty. The reanimated dead stopped in their tracks. They knew real demons when they saw them. Lilith just laughed at the Demonz, said *Children shouldn't stray so far from home,* snapped her pale fingers, and sent all the Demonz back to Hell again.

After that, she went to Time Tower Square, deserted but almost untouched by the chaos all around. Lilith struck a mocking pose before the blocky stone structure that was the Tower, and called loudly for Old Father Time to come out and face her. She had work for him. Minutes passed, and Lilith snarled and stamped her feet as she realised Old Father Time wasn't coming out. She ordered her offspring to tear the Tower apart, and drag Old Father Time from the ruins to face her displeasure. But, as I knew to my cost, the Tower was seriously defended. The first few Beings to touch the Tower with bad intent just disappeared, blown out of existence like the flame of a candle. Other, greater Powers advanced on the Tower. A terrible stone Eye opened in the wall facing them, and the Powers froze in the glare of that awful regard. The life seeped out of them, and left behind only a handful of ugly stone statues, in awkward poses. The great stone Eye slowly closed again.

Lilith cried out a single angry Word, and the whole stone structure blew apart, until there was nothing left of the Time Tower save a pile of smoking rubble. Lilith glared at what she'd achieved, shaking with effort and reaction, while her army watched carefully to see what would happen next. In the end, it was clear that Old Father Time was either dead or trapped. Either way, he wouldn't be coming out to obey Lilith's wishes, so she spat and cursed, turned on her heel and led her army on to other ventures.

And that brought me up to date. The scrying pool had gone cloudy with shock and trauma, and I left it sobbing quietly to itself. The shop's owner trailed behind me as I left his emporium, complaining bitterly and wringing his hands over what I'd done to his best merchandise. I told him again to send the bill to Walker.

Outside the shop, it was relatively quiet. The fires had run out of things to burn, and the survivors were keeping their heads down and quietly licking their wounds. I walked slowly through deserted streets, and no-one bothered me. Just as well. I had some thinking to do. Why had Lilith been so determined to control Old Father Time? Could there be something about Time travel, or perhaps Time itself, that would be a danger to Lilith's plans? I smiled mirthlessly. It beat the hell out of me. I needed advice and information, which meant . . . I needed to talk to Walker.

I pulled my Strangefellows Membership Card from my pocket, activated it, and called for Walker. After making me wait a little while, to keep me respectful, Walker's face looked out of the Card at me. He looked calm and poised and completely confident. He might have got away with it, if he hadn't also looked like hell.

"Taylor!" he said brightly. "Back at last, after your extended vacation? I should have known you'd turn up for the main event. I didn't know these Cards could be used for communication."

So Alex didn't tell you everything, I thought, a little smugly. "I'm back," I said. "We need to talk."

"Couldn't agree more, old chap," said Walker. "I need to know everything you know."

"We don't have that much time," I said. I never could resist a good cheap shot. "Right now, we need to talk to the Authorities. Get their resources behind us. They need to hear what I have to tell them. I need you to set up a meeting."

"I've been trying to contact them ever since this whole mess started," said Walker, just a little tartly. "No-one's returning my calls."

"Call them again," I said. "Drop my name, and set up a meet. We need to do this in person. They'll talk to Lilith's son."

"Yes," said Walker. "Yes, they just might. Very well, I'll arrange a face-to-face, at the Londinium Club."

"Of course," I said. "Where else?"

NINE

Thrown to the Wolves

I found an undead Harley Davidson lurking in an alleyway, and persuaded it to give me a lift to the Londinium Club, in return for squeezing the essential juices out of several nearby corpses into the undead machine's fuel tank. I swear other people don't have days like this. The motorcycle carried me smoothly through the Nightside, weaving in and out of crashed and overturned vehicles littering the abandoned road. The air rushing into my face was hot and dry, thick with drifting smoke and ashes. It stank of burned meat. Even above the roar of the bike, I could still hear distant screams. Riding through the deserted streets, lit by the intermittent glow of burning buildings rather than the sleazy flush of hot neon, reminded me uncomfortably of the devastated future Nightside that was coming. A future coming true in front of my eyes, despite everything I did to try and stop it.

You're trying to steer again, said the Harley. *Don't. I know what I'm doing.*

"Then I envy you," I said. "Really. You have no idea."

That's right; condescend to me, just because I'm undead. You wait until the mystical Vampire Lords of the Twenty-seventh Dimension descend in their crimson flying saucers to make me Grand High Overlord of the Nightside . . . Oh. Damn. I said that out loud, didn't I? Sorry. I've not been taking my medication, lately.

"It's all right," I said. "We've all got a lot on our minds at the moment."

The Harley mournfully sang Meatloaf's "Bat out of Hell" as we cruised through the deserted streets. There were hardly any people around now. They were either hiding, or evacuated, or dead. There were bodies everywhere, and sometimes only parts of bodies. I saw piledup severed heads, and dozens of severed hands laid out in strange patterns. Something had strung a web of knotted human entrails between a series of lamp-posts. I didn't raise my Sight. I didn't want to understand. I didn't want to see all the new ghosts.

The motorcycle dropped me off outside the Londinium Club, then disappeared into the night at speed. It thought there was still somewhere safe to go, and I didn't have the heart to disillusion it. I wasn't blessed with the same delusion. I knew better. Walker was already waiting for me, of course. He stood at the foot of the Club's steps, looking sadly down at the dead body of the Doorman. The Londinium's most faithful servant lay sprawled across the steps, before the entrance he'd guarded for so many centuries. Something had ripped the Doorman's head off and impaled it on the spiked railings. The expression on the face was more surprised than anything.

"He was supposed to be immortal," observed Walker. "I didn't think anything could kill him."

"Now that Lilith's back, all bets are off," I said. "It is a pity."

Walker gave me a hard look. "You know very well you couldn't stand the man, Taylor."

"I gave him a rose once," I said.

Walker sniffed, unconvinced, and led the way up the steps to what was left of the Londinium. The oldest Gentleman's Club in the Nightside had seen better days. The magnificent façade was cracked and holed, smoke-blackened and fire-damaged. It looked like the outer wall of a city that had finally fallen to its besiegers. The huge single door had been burst inwards, forced off its hinges. The great slab of ancient wood lay toppled on the floor of the lobby, torn and gouged with deep claw marks. The once-elegant lobby had been thoroughly trashed and befouled. The statues had been shattered and the paintings defaced. The delicately veined marble pillars were cracked and broken, and the unknown Michelangelo painting that covered the entire ceiling was now half-hidden behind smoke stains and sprayed arterial blood.

Bodies littered the wide floor, left to lie where they had fallen. Many were mutilated, or half-eaten. Most of them looked to have been unarmed. Important men and servants lay together, probably killed fighting back-to-back, equal at last in death.

"Something got here before us," I said, because I had to say something. "You think any of the bastards are still around?"

"No," said Walker, kneeling beside one of the bodies. "The flesh is cold, the blood-stains are dry. Whatever happened here, we missed it." He looked at the dead man's face for a long moment, frowning slightly.

"Did you know him?" I asked.

"I knew all of them," he said, rising to his feet again. "Some were very good, some were very bad, and none of them deserved to die like this."

He stalked across the lobby, his back very straight, stepping carefully round the scattered bodies. I followed him, my shoulders tense with the anticipation of unseen watching eyes. Someone had gone to a lot of trouble to trash the Nightside's most visible symbol of power and authority. Walker finally came to a halt facing the right-hand wall, and solemnly considered a part of it that looked no different from any other part. I stood beside him, looking hard for any sign of a concealed door or panel, but I couldn't see anything. And I'm usually really good at spotting things like that. Walker fished in his waistcoat pocket for a long moment, but when he finally brought his hand out, it was empty. He held the empty hand up before me, the fingers pinched together as though holding something.

"This," he said, "is a key that isn't a key, that will open a door that isn't a door, to a room that isn't always there."

I considered his empty hand. "Either the strain is finally getting to you, or you're being cryptic again. This secret room . . . it's not by any chance going to try to eat me, is it?"

He smiled briefly. "It's a real key. But invisible. Feel it."

He put something I couldn't see into my hand. It felt cold and metallic. "Okay," I said. "That's creepy. If the door is as invisible as the key, how are we going to find it?"

"Because it isn't invisible to me," Walker said airily, taking the key back again. "I serve the Authorities, so I get to see everything I need to see."

"Show-off," I said, and he smiled briefly again.

He thrust the key only he could see into the lock only he could see, and part of the wall before us disappeared. I was staring so hard by now that my eyes were beginning to hurt. Walker strolled into the newly revealed room before us with just a hint of smugness, and I sighed and followed him in. It figured that the Authorities would have their very own special room to hold their meetings in, exclusive even from other members of the Nightside's most exclusive Gentleman's Club.

"The Authorities don't agree to meet with just anyone," Walker murmured. "You should feel honoured."

"Oh, I do," I said. "Really. You have no idea."

Walker actually winced. "Somehow, I know this isn't going to go well."

The wall reappeared behind us, sealing us in, and the room abruptly snapped into focus. It was protected by very powerful magics. I could feel them, crawling on my skin like living static. The room itself was something of a cliché, the very essence of a private room in a Gentleman's

Club. Oversized but no doubt extremely comfortable chairs, rich furnishings, and splendid decorations. Far more splendid, indeed, than the expensively tanned, personally trained but still sloppy, overdressed men sitting slumped in their big chairs, with their big drinks and their big cigars. I took my time looking them over, the ten powerful men who ran the Nightside, inasmuch as anyone did. You wouldn't know their names. You've never seen their faces in the glossies. These men were above that. They all had the same casual arrogance of people used to getting what they wanted when they wanted it. Somehow, I just knew we weren't going to get along.

Walker introduced me to the Authorities, then moved aside to stand leaning against the William Morris wallpaper, his arms folded, as though to indicate he'd done all that could reasonably be expected of him. Maybe he simply wanted to be out of the line of fire, for when everything inevitably went wrong. And though he must have had many questions of his own for his absentee masters, he seemed content to leave the lead to me. For the moment, at least.

"So," I said finally, "you're the grey men, the businessmen, the faceless men who only ever operate behind the scenes. Somehow, I always thought you'd be . . . bigger. Talk to me, Authorities. Tell me what I need to know. While there's still time."

"I am Harper, and I speak for us all," said the man nearest me. His face was far too old for his jet-black hair, and his waistcoat strained over a bulging stomach. It was covered with cigar ash that he couldn't be bothered to brush away. Presumably he had someone to do that for him, in his own world. He stared coldly at me with piggy, deep-set eyes. "Our ancestors made their fortunes operating in the Nightside of Roman times, during their occupation. Our families have spent generations building on those fortunes. We own all the businesses here, at one remove or another. There's nothing that happens that we don't take our cut. The Nightside belongs to us."

"Not for much longer," I said. "If Lilith has her way. This isn't just a corporate take-over she'd proposing, she plans to kill us all. Or hasn't that penetrated your thick skulls yet?"

My voice must have got a little sharp, because that was when the Authorities' bodyguards decided to make themselves known to me. They manifested abruptly, one on each side of the room, and I studied them warily. Two basically humanoid forms, large and overpowering, one made of pure light, one of pure darkness. It would be hard to say which was more unpleasant to the eye. They were presences rather than physical forms, and I could feel power radiating off them. It was like standing in front of a furnace when someone unexpectedly opened the door.

"They used to be angels," said Harper, with more than a hint of smugness. "From Above, and Below. Now they work for us."

"How are the mighty fallen," I said, just to be saying something. Never let the other side know when you've been seriously impressed. "I suppose that's why they don't have wings any more. Or halos."

"You cannot conceive how much we have lost," said the figure of light, its voice like cracking ice floes.

"But we have also gained much," said the figure of darkness, in a voice like a burning orphanage. "We are here because we developed . . . appetites. Tastes for things that can only be found in the material world. Our new masters . . . indulge us."

"We take our comforts here," said the light. "To our eternal shame."

"To our endless satisfaction," said the dark.

"But why serve the Authorities?" I said. "Even as diminished as you are, you must know they're not worthy of you."

"We have to serve someone," said the light.

"It's in our nature," said the dark.

"Enough," said Harper, and immediately both figures fell silent. Harper glared at me, and I glared right back. He raised his voice a little, to convince both of us who was really in charge here. "Normally, we run the Nightside from outside. We live in London proper, in the sane world. We're only here now because Walker summoned us with your name. What do you want with us, John Taylor?"

"Answers, to start with," I said, meeting his gaze unflinchingly. "Why haven't you sent your armies to support Walker? Don't you know how bad things are here?"

"We know," said Harper. "But what help could we send that could hope to stand against Lilith and her followers? We're not in the business of throwing good lives away after bad."

Walker stirred for the first time. "Bad? Those were my people!"

Harper didn't even look at him. "Not now, Walker. I'm talking."

"If not now, then when?" said Walker, and his voice was colder than I'd ever heard it before. "How many years have I and my people served you here, protecting your interests in the Nightside? Is this how you reward us—by throwing us to the wolves?"

Harper finally looked at him, but only to smile condescendingly. "You mustn't take it personally, Walker. It's just business."

"You look nervous," I said suddenly. "All of you. Uncomfortable. Sweating. You don't like being here, do you?"

"As you said, the Nightside has become a dangerous place." Harper took a long draw on his cigar. "Before Walker contacted us with your

name, we had been preparing to seal off the Nightside, closing every entrance and exit until all this . . . unpleasantness has run its course."

"You're abandoning us?" I said.

"Why not? You're only a business interest. A cash cow, from which
we squeeze every penny we can. We are aware of the powerful men and
women who come to your little freak show, to indulge in the pleasures
and excitements they can't find anywhere else, but we . . . We have only
ever cared about the profit they made us. For us, the Nightside is simply a
commodity, that we exploit. Correct, Walker?"

"Don't look at me," said Walker, surprisingly. "I see things differently, these days."

I looked at him for a moment. There was something in his voice . . .
but that would have to wait. I turned back to Harper.

"If the Nightside falls to Lilith, then so does the rest of the world. You
can't hope to contain a Power like her. She will break out, then there'll be
nowhere far enough or safe enough for you to hide."

"So we have come to believe," said Harper, reluctantly. He glared at
his cigar, as though it had failed him in some way, and stubbed it out in an
ashtray with quick, angry movements. "So, it seems we have no choice
but to make a deal with Lilith. Very well. We can do that. We're good at
making deals. It's what we do, after all. That is why we agreed to meet
with you here, John Taylor. Lilith's son. You will be our agent, our representative, in these negotiations. Talk to your mother and promise her . . .
whatever it takes, to reach an accommodation. We have already revealed
our presence to her and summoned her here to talk with us."

Walker stood up straight, pushing himself away from the wall he'd
been leaning on. "What? Why didn't you consult me first? Do you know
what you've done, you bloody fools . . ."

"Not now, Walker!" Harper didn't even look at him. He was still doing his best to intimidate me with an imperious stare. "We are rich beyond the nightmares of avarice, Taylor. We can afford to be flexible, if we
have to. Better to share the wealth of the Nightside with your mother than
risk seeing it destroyed. It's just a matter of finding out what she
wants . . . We're all reasonable people, after all. I'm sure we can come to
an understanding with Lilith, with your help."

"Lilith isn't reasonable," I said. "She isn't even people. You have no
idea what you're dealing with. She isn't interested in money, or even in
power, as you understand it. She just wants to wipe the whole slate clean
and start again. And replace Humanity with something more suited to her
needs."

One whole wall of the private room suddenly disappeared, ripped
away by an outside force. We all looked round, startled, to discover that

the room now looked directly out onto the Nightside. Nothing stood between us and the dark, the blazing buildings, and the streets filled with smoke and screams. And there before us stood Lilith, naked and magnificent, with all her monstrous Court ranked behind her. The Authorities rose to their feet, stumbling and awkward, staring with wide horrified eyes.

The two former angels surged forward, to stand between the Authorities and Lilith, their power shimmering on the air around them like a heat haze. Lilith smiled at them and said *Go home*, and the light and dark figures both disappeared in a moment, banished from the material planes by the sheer force of her will. I had a good idea where she'd sent them, and I doubted either of them could expect much of a welcome back.

"So," said Lilith, stepping gracefully forward into the private room, her voice light and teasing, "tou're the Authorities. The Secret Masters of the Nightside, the Big Men . . . We meet at last. Only, I have to say, you don't look very big to me. You look much more like little boys, way out of their depth. Come to me. Come to Mommie . . ."

Her presence ignited, filling the whole room, vast and overwhelming. I had to look away, retreating behind my strongest mental shields. While the ten most powerful men in the Nightside, and therefore the world, fell to their knees and went to Lilith on all fours, like swine before a goddess. Walker started forward. I grabbed him by the arm and hustled him towards the invisible door. He found the key and opened the door, his hand steady even though his face was torn with conflicting emotions. I looked back, briefly.

Lilith laughed, to see the high-and-mighty Authorities cringe and fawn at her colourless feet. "Why, you're so cute! I could eat you up . . . but I think you'd probably make me sick. Fortunately, my children have far more robust appetites . . ."

She laughed again, as her horrid offspring surged forward. I pushed Walker through the door, following him into the relative safety of the Club's lobby. As the door swung slowly shut behind us, I looked back one last time. And saw Lilith's monstrous children fall upon the screaming Authorities and tear at them hungrily, like wolves let into the fold.

TEN

A Chance for Revenge

I ended up having to drag Walker back through the lobby and out onto the steps of the Londinium Club. His eyes weren't tracking properly, and he was mumbling to himself. Once we were safely outside, I glanced quickly around to be sure we were alone, then sat down on the steps to get my composure back. With the invisible door shut again, Lilith shouldn't be able to come after us. For a while, anyway. Walker sat down suddenly next to me, all his usual poise and confidence gone. I suppose it's not an easy thing, to see the lords and masters you've followed all your life revealed as cowards and scumbags, then turned into monster food. The night seemed relatively quiet, and no-one came by to bother us. I looked at Walker. A pain in my arse for most of my life, I'd often wanted to see him brought down, but not like this. He was staring out into the night as though he'd never seen it before.

"The Authorities are dead," he said abruptly. "What do I do now?"

"Be your own man," I said. "You can still give the orders that need giving, kick the arses that need kicking. Get things done. Someone's got to lead the resistance. Who's got more experience than you? You're needed, Walker; now more than ever."

Walker turned his head slowly to look at me. "You're Lilith's son," he said finally. "You're the King in waiting. You're the legendary John Taylor, who always snatches victory from the jaws of defeat. Maybe you should be in charge."

"No," I said. "I've never wanted that. I have enough trouble being responsible for myself, never mind anyone else. And I've got other things to do. Don't ask what. It would only upset you. You've always been The Man, Walker. So suck it up and solider on."

He smiled briefly. "You sound very like your father sometimes,

John." He stood up, and just like that all his old poise and confidence were back again. "I suppose someone's got to turn you rabble into a disciplined fighting force. So, I'm going back to Strangefellows. Where will you go?"

"In search of some heavy-duty backup," I said, getting to my feet. "We need more big guns on our side."

"And if there aren't any?"

I grinned at him. "Then I'll improvise. Suddenly and violently and all over the place."

He nodded. "It's what you do best."

He took out his Membership Card, activated it, and stepped through into the relative safety of *Strangefellows* bar. The Card disappeared with a soft sucking sound and a brief flurry of sparks, and I was left standing alone on the steps of the Londinium Club. I pushed my hands deep into the pockets of my trench coat, and looked out into the night. All the buildings around me were wrecked or burned out. Bodies everywhere. Screams in the distance, strange lights flaring on the horizon. The Nightside was going down for the third time, and I was running out of ideas. There had to be someone else, some Power or major player who still owed me a favour, or could be fooled into thinking they did . . . but I couldn't think who. I couldn't do this on my own. I needed someone powerful enough, or tricky enough, to stop this War in its tracks before it got out of hand. Before it led to the terrible future that was becoming more real, more inevitable, by the minute. Unfortunately there was only one name left on my list, the one I'd been trying so hard not to think of. Because he scared the crap out of me.

The Lord of Thorns. The Overseer of the Nightside, appointed directly by God to keep an eye on things.

Mostly, he didn't intervene personally. He was the last judge of all disputes, the Nightside's court of last resort, the one you only went to when everything else had failed and you were tired of living anyway. I'd been half-expecting him to turn up and start smiting everything in sight for some time now. Since he hadn't, it looked like I was going to have to give him his wake-up call. Lucky old me. The Lord of Thorns lived in the World Beneath, the miles and miles of caverns, catacombs, and stone galleries that lay deep below the Nightside. The place where you went, when the Nightside wasn't dark enough for you. The Lord of Thorns slept his sleep of centuries in a crystal cave in the deepest, darkest part of the World Beneath, and God help anyone who disturbed him unnecessarily.

I had only met him once, and that was more than enough. *I am the stone that breaks all hearts,* he said. *I am the nails that bound the Christ to his cross. I am the necessary suffering that makes us all stronger . . .* God's power flowed through him, the power over life and death and everything between. He could save or damn you with a word or a glance, and his every decision was binding. I was pretty sure he didn't approve of people like me, even though he'd been friendly enough, in a distant sort of way, at our last meeting.

Why hadn't he come forth to confront Lilith?

I wasn't at all keen on descending into the World Beneath, to talk to him. It was a foul and dangerous place, and a hell of a long way to travel, besides. Especially if he had already surfaced somewhere, to show Lilith the error of her ways . . . I pushed the thought back and forth for a while, but I was only putting off what I knew I had to do, so in the end I just sighed heavily, took the risk, and raised my gift. Wherever the Lord of Thorns was, in or under the Nightside, my gift would find him.

My inner eye, my third eye, opened wide and soared up into the night sky, my Sight spreading out for miles in every direction, till the whole of the Nightside lay sprawled below me like a twisted and convoluted map. Whole areas were burning, out of control, while monsters roamed the streets and panicked mobs ran this way and that. I forced my Sight to focus in on the one individual soul I was searching for, and my mind's eye plummeted down, narrowing in on a single speck of light in the dark. I'd found the Lord of Thorns. Just as I'd thought, he had left the World Beneath for the surface; but much to my surprise, the most powerful man in the Nightside was currently hiding out in St. Jude's, the only real church in the Nightside.

I quickly shut down my Sight, and dropped back into my head. I took a few moments to make sure all my mental barriers were safely in place again. I really didn't want Lilith to know where I was till I was ready to face her. I considered what to do next. St. Jude's wasn't anywhere near the Street of the Gods, because it was the real deal. An ancient place of worship, almost as old as the Nightside itself, older by far than the Christianity that had given it its present name. (St. Jude is the patron Saint of lost causes, in case you were wondering.) It was the one place in all the world where you could go to speak with your Maker and be sure of getting a reply. Which is why most people didn't go there. Unless they absolutely had to.

St. Jude's was located way over on the other side of the Nightside, a long way from anywhere, and separated from me by miles and miles of very dangerous territory. Walking was not an option. I wished I'd told the Harley to stick around. I took my Membership Card out of my pocket, fired it up, and called for Alex Morrisey in a loud and demanding voice. There was a pause, just to keep me from getting above myself, then his face appeared, glowering out of the Card at me.

"Taylor! About time you turned up again. If only so you can pay your bar bill before the world ends. And what have you done to Walker? He showed up here a few minutes ago looking like someone had put the fear of God into him. I don't think I've ever seen him so pissed off at the world. He's currently charging round my bar yelling orders at everyone like Captain Kirk on crack, and organising everyone within an inch of their lives."

"Probably just a midlife crisis," I said. "Put Tommy Oblivion on, would you, Alex? I need to ask him something."

Alex sniffed loudly, just to remind me he was no-one's servant, and his face disappeared from my Card, which then played me a tinny Muzak version of the Prodigy's "Firestarter" while I was on hold. Tommy's face finally peered out of the Card at me, frowning suspiciously.

"What do you want, Taylor?"

"You," I said.

And I reached into the Membership Card, grabbed him by the front of his ruffled shirt, and dragged him through the Card to where I was. The Card expanded hastily to let him through, but even so it was a tight squeeze for a moment. Tommy sat down suddenly on the Club steps as his head spun from the sudden transfer, and the Card shrank back to normal size and shut itself off, possibly in protest at such rough handling. I put it away, and helped Tommy to his feet.

"Son of a bitch!" he said.

"Yes," I said. "That just about sums me up."

He glared at me. "I didn't know you could do that with a Card."

"Most people can't," I said. "But I'm special."

Tommy sniffed. "I suppose that's one way of putting it." He brushed himself down here and there, repairing his appearance as best he could, then looked at the headless Doorman, lying on the steps beside him. He moved fastidiously a little further away from the blood. "Been busy, I see."

"For once, not my fault." I filled him in on what had been happening, or at least as much of it as I thought he could cope with, and explained my need to get to St. Jude's in a hurry. He really wasn't keen on the idea, but I can be very persuasive when I have to be. Not to mention downright threatening. I only had to mention a certain video that had come into my hands, featuring him and a very athletic exotic dancer, who happened to be married to someone exceedingly scary, and suddenly he was only too willing to help me out. (I didn't actually have the video. I'd just heard of it and run a bluff. The guilty flee . . .)

Tommy Oblivion's gift manifested subtly on the air around us, and everything became uncertain. Tommy was an existentialist, and his gift allowed him to express his uncertainty about the world in a real and very physical way. The more he thought about a thing, the more possibilities he could see, and he fixed on the reality he preferred and made it solid. By concentrating hard enough, Tommy was able to convince the world that not only were we not where it thought we were, but actually we were somewhere else entirely.

And so, in the blink of an eye we left the Londinium Club behind us and materialised outside the Church of St. Jude. A dodo wandered past, hooting mournfully, a flock of passenger pigeons flapped by overhead, and an ostrich with two heads looked confusedly at itself, but they were only a few odd possibilities generated by Tommy's gift. He concentrated on shutting his gift down, while I looked around us. Everything but the church had been razed to the ground, for as far as the eye could see. It stood alone, an old squat stone structure in the middle of a wasteland. A wide-open plain of ash and dust, where thick curls of glowing ground fog surged this way and that under the urging of a fitful wind. It was very dark, with just the blue-white glare of the oversized moon shining off the church walls. In the distance, fires leapt up briefly, screams rang out, but it was all very far away. The War had come and gone here, and left nothing behind but the church.

"I'm trying very hard to be existential about this," Tommy said finally, "But this really is a god-awful place. I'd like to say something like . . . from the ashes of the old shall arise a brave new Nightside . . . but my heart isn't in it."

"If a new Nightside does arise, I doubt it would be anything you or I would recognise, or would want to," I said. "Not if Lilith has her way."

"God, you're depressing to be around, Taylor. My brother's more cheerful than you, and he's dead. Who are we here to see, anyway?"

"The Lord of Thorns."

"Right," said Tommy. "I am leaving now. Good-bye. Write if you get work. I am out of here . . ."

"Tommy . . ."

"No! No way in Hell! There is absolutely nothing you can say or do or threaten me with that would persuade me to have anything to do with Him! I would rather eat my own head! The Lord of Thorns is the only person who actually scares me more than Lilith! She only wants to kill me; he wants to judge me!"

"You could leave," I said. "But it's a really long walk to anywhere civilised. All on your own, in the dark. And if you try to teleport back using your gift . . . I'll just have the Lord of Thorns drag you back again."

"You know the Lord of Thorns?"

"I know everyone," I said airily.

Tommy kicked at the dusty ground. "Bully," he muttered, not looking at me.

"You're my ride home, Tommy," I said, not unkindly. "You don't have to come into the church with me, if you don't want to. You can guard the door."

"It'll all end in tears," said Tommy.

I tried the church's only door, and it opened easily at my touch. I left Tommy sulking outside, and went in. The bare stone walls were grey and featureless, with only a series of narrow slits for windows. Short stubby candles that never went out burned in old lead wall holders, casting a cold judgemental light. Two rows of blocky wooden pews, without a cushion in sight. The altar was just a great slab of stone, covered with a cloth of spotless white samite. A single silver cross hung on the wall over the altar. And that was it. You didn't come to St. Jude's for frills and fancies.

This was a place where prayers were answered, and if you didn't like the answers you got, that was your problem.

A single ragged figure sat slumped on the cold stone floor, leaning against the altar, embracing it with desperate arms. It was the Lord of Thorns. He looked like he'd been crying. He also looked like he'd been dragged through Hell backwards. Instead of the grand Old Testament Prophet I remembered, he looked like one of the homeless, like a refugee. The Overseer of the Nightside had been reduced to a man in torn and bloodied robes. His long grey hair and beard had been half-burned away. He didn't look up as I walked down the aisle towards him, but he flinched at the sound of my footsteps, like a dog that's been kicked once too often. I knelt before him, took his chin in my hand, and made him look at me. He trembled at my touch.

"What are you doing here?" I said. I didn't mean for it to come out as harshly as it did, but that's St. Jude's for you.

"It's all gone," he said, in a distant, empty voice. "So I'm hiding. Hiding out, in the one place where even Lilith's power can't touch me. I believe that. I have to believe that. It's all I've got left."

I let go of his chin, and made an effort to soften my voice. "What happened?"

His eyes came up to meet mine, and a Vision appeared in my mind's eye, showing me Lilith's descent into the World Beneath. She came in force, with all her monstrous Court, smashing through ancient defences and protections as though they weren't even there, and set her people to destroying everything and everyone. As above, so below. Just because she could. She wiped out the Eaters of the Dead, the Solitudes in their cells, the Subterraneans in their sprawling city of catacombs. A warning went out ahead of her, echoing from gallery to gallery, and some came out to fight and some dug themselves in deeper; but none of it did any good. Lilith and her terrible offspring pushed relentlessly on, destroying whole nests of vampires and ghouls and Elder Spawn, and even the worms of the earth in their deep deep tunnels.

The Lord of Thorns came forth from his crystal cave, wrapped in power and a cold, awful anger, to set his faith and authority against Lilith. For he was the Voice of God, and she was but a name out of the past. He had his staff of power, its wood taken from a tree grown from a sliver of the original Tree of Life itself, brought to Britain long and long ago by Joseph of Arimathea. The Lord of Thorns stood in Lilith's way, and she slapped him aside contemptuously. She took his staff and it shattered into pieces in her grasp. She walked on, leaving him lying helpless in the dirt, and not even the least of her offspring would deign to touch him. The killing continued, and there was nothing he could do to stop it. He made himself watch, as a penance. And when it was all over, the Lord of Thorns made his way up from the World Beneath and came to St. Jude's. To hide.

"You have to understand," he said, as the Vision faded from my mind. "When Lilith appeared, I thought I'd finally discovered my true purpose, my reason for being in the Nightside. That this was my destiny—to stop Lilith when no-one else could. But I was wrong. I was nothing, next to her. After so many years of judging others, I was judged . . . and found unworthy."

"But . . . you're one of the greatest Powers in the Nightside!"

"Not compared to her. I forgot . . . in the end I'm just a man, blessed with God's power. And my faith . . . was nothing compared to her certainty."

"All right," I said. "We need backup. Can we use St. Jude's to call for Heavenly help? For direct divine intervention?"

"What do you think I've been doing?" said the Lord of Thorns. "The Nightside was expressly designed from its first conception so that neither Heaven nor Hell could intervene directly. And it was decided long ago in the Courts of the Holy that this Great Experiment would be allowed to continue, to see where it would lead. I was placed here to Oversee the Experiment, to keep it on track. But now that the Nightside's creator has returned, it seems my time and my purpose are at an end. There will be no outside help. The Nightside must save itself. If it can."

"There is a resistance," I said. "Come with me. You can be a part of it."

But the Lord of Thorns just sat where he was, shaking his grey head. "No. I am not who I thought I was. So I will stay here and pray for guidance."

I tried to argue with him, but I don't think he really heard me. Lilith broke him when she broke his staff. So I left what was once the most feared man in the Nightside, sitting mumbling to himself, in the one place he still felt safe.

*   *   *

I went outside and found myself facing a crowd of hard-faced and heavily armed individuals. Their expressions lit up at the sight of me, and not in a good way. At their head stood Sandra Chance, resplendent in her thick crimson swirls of liquid latex and not much else. Though the old-fashioned pistol holstered on her bare hip was a new addition. She grinned at me, very unpleasantly. I looked at Tommy Oblivion, who was standing very very still, with his back pressed against the wall of the church.

"Sorry, old sport," he said miserably. "Didn't even hear them coming. Just popped out of nowhere."

"Have you at least asked them what they want?" I said.

"Oh, I'm pretty sure they want to speak to you, John. In fact, they were most insistent on it being a surprise."

"It's all right, Tommy," I said, trying to hide the fact that internally I was hyperventilating. "I know who they are. They're bounty hunters. How did you find me here, Sandra?"

"I can get answers from the dead, remember?" She was still smiling, not at all pleasantly. "And there are a lot of dead up and about just at the moment. The dead know many things that are hidden from the living. They have . . . an overview. And I can get them to tell me anything."

"Yes," I said. "And I know how. It's one thing to love the dead, but you take it far too literally. You coffin chaser, you."

"Am I understanding this correctly?" said Tommy. "You mean she actually . . ."

"Oh yes," I said.

"Now that's just tacky. I can't believe I shared a picnic with her."

"Shut up, Tommy," said Sandra, not taking her eyes off me.

"In case you hadn't noticed, there is a War going on," I said. "This really isn't the time . . ."

"There's always a war going on somewhere in the Nightside," said Sandra. "You should know—you've started your fair share of them. My associates and I have decided that we don't care. We want the reward on your head. It's a really big reward; one of the biggest bounties ever posted in the Nightside. The very well connected families of the thirteen Reasonable Men you slaughtered want you dead, John, and they don't care how much it costs them. There's enough money on the table to buy all of us a way out of the Nightside and into some distant dimension where even Lilith can't reach. And still leave enough cold cash for all of us to live like royalty, in our new home. So, revenge, escape, and all our dreams come true. In return for your head, preferably no longer connected to your body. See how neatly it all works out?"

"I thought you said you owed me," I said carefully. "For saving your life in the Necropolis graveyard?"

"Whatever small debt I may have owed you, I more than paid it off being a good soldier for Walker and defending the Nightside during your absence. I want you dead, John. I can't even breathe easily while you're still among the living. You murdered my sweet Saint of Suffering, my beloved Lamentation. You have to pay for that. I put together this little band of bounty hunters, some of the very best in the business, just so I could be sure you wouldn't dodge your death this time. Try your little bag of tricks against professionals, Taylor, and see where it gets you."

She had a point. I considered the dozen or so bounty hunters fanned out in a wide semicircle before me, covering all the possible escape routes. Most were vaguely familiar faces, and three of them were actually famous, almost in a class with Suzie Shooter herself. At least she wasn't here. Then I really would have been in trouble. The tall scarecrow figure in Sally Army cast-offs was Dominic Flipside, a short-range teleporter. Frighteningly quick and sneaky, you never knew from which direction he'd come at you next. Whispering Ivy was a rogue anima from Wales, made up entirely from flowers and thorns, an ever-shifting montage of natural forms in the vague shape of a woman. When she moved, it sounded like the whispering of owls. And Cold Harald, dressed as always in the starkest black and white, with a mind like a calculating machine. He always worked the odds, his logic unclouded by any trace of emotion or humanity. He held a machine pistol in each hand and looked like he knew how to use them. Any one of these three would have worried me, but all of them together . . . and Sandra Chance . . . I thought about running back into the church and screaming for sanctuary, but I knew I'd never make the second step.

"Don't even think about the church," said Sandra. "Or we'll shoot your friend."

Tommy looked at her, hurt. "After we worked together, such a short time ago? Have you no shame? You wound me, madam."

"If you don't shut up, I'll wound you somewhere really painful," said Sandra. "It's up to you, Taylor. Surrender, and we'll make it quick. You can go out with some dignity, at least. Make us work for your head, and we'll all take turns expressing our displeasure on your helpless body."

"Come and take it," I said. "If you can."

"I was hoping you'd say that," said Sandra Chance. "Remember, people, do what you like to the body but don't damage the head. Our patrons won't pay up unless the face is unquestionably his. I think they want to take turns pissing on it. Otherwise, anything goes."

Tommy Oblivion stepped forwards. He'd always been a lot braver than people gave him credit for. His gift manifested very subtly on the air, making his words seem the very epitome of reasonableness and good sense.

"Come," he said warmly, his arms reaching out to embrace everyone. "Let us reason together . . ."

"Let's not," said Cold Harald, in his flat, clipped voice, and he shot Tommy half a dozen times in the stomach. Tommy staggered back under the impact, slamming up against the church wall, then slid slowly down it until he was sitting on the ground. The whole bottom half of his ruffled shirt was slick with blood.

"Oh dear," he said quietly. "Oh dear." He bit his lip against the pain, and I could see him trying to concentrate, trying to raise his gift, so he could find a possibility where the bullets hadn't hit him. But his face was already white and beaded with sweat, his breathing hurried and shallow. I could feel his gift sparking on and off, but pain and stress were getting in the way of his concentration.

I couldn't expect any help from him. I was on my own.

I palmed an incendiary from out of my sleeve and tossed it into the midst of the advancing bounty hunters. Fire and smoke exploded noisily, and two of the bounty hunters fell broken and bleeding to the ground. The rest scattered. Dominic Flipside giggled, a long knife suddenly in each hand, then he disappeared, air rushing in to fill the space where he'd been. I felt as much as heard him reappear almost immediately behind me, and spun round, one arm raised. He cut me open from wrist to elbow, and disappeared again. Blood soaked the length of my coat sleeve.

Cold Harald stepped forward, raising both machine pistols to target me. Dominic Flipside was already gone. I fired up my gift, used it to find where he'd reappear, and stepped forward to meet Cold Harald. He hesitated, expecting some trick, some magic. Dominic Flipside appeared behind me, and lunged silently forward with his long knife. I stepped aside at the last moment, and Dominic plunged on to stab Cold Harald through the heart. His fingers tightened on the triggers of his machine pistols, and blew a dozen holes through Dominic Flipside. Both of them were dead before they hit the ground.

There was a rustling of plants, and the murmuring of dreaming owls, as Whispering Ivy stretched out a hand made of petals and thorns. She sprouted fierce tendrils of barbed greenery, her shifting shape rising up and towering over me, then she stopped abruptly. There was the sound of crackling flames, the smell of smoke. She looked back, turning her flowery head impossibly far round. While she was fixed on me, Tommy had crawled around behind her and set fire to her with his monogrammed gold lighter. Whispering Ivy shrieked as the flames shot up incredibly fast, consuming her construct body, and she ran off across the open ashy plain, howling shrilly, a shrinking flickering light in the gloom.

I looked at the remaining bounty hunters. They were all frozen in place, horrified at how quickly I'd taken out their star players. They all looked at Sandra Chance, to see what she would do. To her credit, she'd already thrown off any surprise or shock she might have felt, and had drawn the old-fashioned pistol from its holster. It was an ugly, mean gun, built with function in mind, not aesthetics. The metal was blue-black, the barrel unfashionably long. It looked like what it was—a killing tool.

"This is an enchanted pistol," Sandra Chance said steadily. "It never misses. It belonged originally to the famed Western duellist, Dead Eye Dick, renowned hero of dime novels and at least one song. I dug up his grave and broke open his coffin to get this gun. I had to break his fingers to make him let go of it. I'd been saving it for a special occasion. You should feel honoured, John."

"People keep telling me that," I said.

She pulled the trigger while I was still speaking, and shot me three times in the chest. It was like being kicked by a horse, an impact so great it knocked all the breath out of my lungs and sent me stumbling backwards. The pain was remarkably focused; I could feel each separate bullet hole. There was a roaring in my head, and I still couldn't breathe. I bent forward over the pain, as though bowing to my killer, to the inevitable, and then, suddenly, I could breathe again. I sucked in a great lungful of air, and it had never tasted so good. My head cleared, and the pains faded away to nothing. I straightened up slowly, not quite trusting what I was feeling, and pulled open my bullet-holed trench coat to look underneath. There were three more holes in my shirt, but only a little blood. I put my fingers through the holes in my shirt, and found only unbroken skin. I felt great. I looked at Sandra Chance, and she stared blankly back at me, open-mouthed.

"Honest," I said. "I'm just as surprised as you are. But I think I know what's happened. I once put werewolf blood into Suzie Shooter, to save her from a mortal wound. And later she put her blood into me, for the same reason. So it seems I have acquired a werewolf's healing abilities. The blood's probably too diluted to do anything else to me, but . . ."

"It's not fair," said Sandra. "You bastard, Taylor! You always have a way out."

I had a feeling silver bullets might still get the job done, but I didn't think I'd mention that to Sandra. I turned to the other bounty hunters, who were still as statues, watching with gaping mouths, and gave them my best nasty smile. Five seconds later all I could see was their backs, heading for the nearest horizon. They knew when they were outclassed. I turned back to Sandra Chance, and she shot me in the head. The impact whipped my head round, and for a moment it seemed like all the bells in the world were ringing inside my skull. I then felt the weirdest sensation, as the bullet crept slowly back out of my brain, the hole healing behind it, until it popped out my forehead and dropped to the ground. The bone healed with only the faintest of cracking sounds, and that was that.

I smiled at Sandra. "Ouch," I said, just to be sporting.

She stamped her foot. "Don't you ever play by the rules?"

"Not if I can help it," I said.

We stood and looked at each other for a long moment. Sandra lowered her gun but didn't put it away. I knew she was considering the possibilities of a bullet to a soft target, like an eye or my groin.

"We don't have to do this," I said. "All this kill or be killed bullshit. I don't want to kill you, Sandra. There's been enough death in the Nightside."

"I have to kill you, John," said Sandra, almost tiredly. "You murdered the only thing I ever loved."

"The Lamentation isn't actually dead," I said. "I only returned to its original human components."

"They weren't the Lamentation," said Sandra. "They weren't what I loved. So I killed them. And now I have to kill you."

"I never understood what you saw in it," I said carefully. "Even allowing for your well-known death fetish, and your preference for . . . cold meat. You must know the Lamentation didn't love you. It couldn't, by its nature."

"I knew that! Of course I knew that! It was enough . . . that I loved it. The only creature something like me could ever love. It made me happy. I'd never been happy before. I'll kill you for taking that away from me."

"I won't kill you, Sandra," I said. "And you can't kill me. Forget this shit. We've got a War to fight."

"I don't care," she said. "Let it all burn. Let them all die. That's the world I live in anyway. I'll find you, and I'll kill you, John. There's always a way. Wherever you go, I'll be there in the shadows, hunting you. And one day I'll step out of a door or an alleyway and kill you dead, when you're least expecting it. I'll watch you choke on your own blood and laugh in your face as you die."

"No you won't," said Suzie Shooter.

We both spun round, startled, and the roar of the shotgun was like thunder. Sandra Chance took both barrels in the chest, at close range. The blast tore half her upper torso away, and she was dead long before she hit the ground. Suzie nodded calmly, lowered the double-barrelled shotgun, and reloaded it from her bandoliers, and only then looked at me.

"Blessed and cursed ammo. If one barrel doesn't get you, the other will. Hello, John."

"Thank you, Suzie," I said. There was nothing else I could say. She wouldn't have understood. "How did you know to find me here?"

Suzie nodded at Sandra's sprawled body. "She was dumb enough to approach me when she was putting her little army together. She thought the sheer size of the bounty would sway me. I won't say I wasn't tempted, but I like to think I've moved beyond that, where you're concerned. So I came here. I thought you might need some backup."

"I had the situation under control," I said. "You didn't have to kill her."

"Yes I did," said Suzie. "You heard her. She'd never give up. That's why you'll always need me around, John. To do the necessary things you're too soft to do."

"That's not why I keep you around," I said.

"I know," said Suzie Shooter. "My love."

She extended a leather-gloved hand to me, and I held it lightly in mine, for a moment.

"Excuse me for butting in on such a tender scene," said Tommy Oblivion, "But I do happen to by dying here. I would appreciate a helping hand."

He was lying on his side on the ground, both hands at his stomach, as though trying to hold it together. Suzie knelt beside him, pushed his hands aside, and checked the extent of the damage with experienced eyes.

"Gut shot. Nasty. If the bullets don't kill him, infection will. We need to get him out of here, John."

"I can't use my gift," said Tommy. His voice was clear enough, but his eyes were vague. "Can't concentrate through the pain. But I absolutely refuse to die in such a drab and depressing location as this."

"Don't worry," I said. "I'll take us back to Strangefellows through my Membership Card, and Alex will fix you up. You can put it on my tab."

"Oh good," said Tommy. "For a minute there, I was almost worried."

I took out my Membership Card, activated it, then almost dropped the bloody thing as Lilith's face looked out of the Card at me.

"Hello, John," she said. "My sweet boy. My own dear flesh and blood. I haven't forgotten you. I'll come for you soon, then you'll be mine, body and soul, forever and ever and ever."

I shut down the Card, and her face disappeared. I was breathing hard, as though I'd just been hit. Suzie and Tommy were looking at me, and I realised they hadn't heard a thing.

"Bad news," I said. "We're going to have to do this the hard way."

ELEVEN

Truth and Consequences

I stripped off my trench coat and gingerly inspected my injured arm. Dominic Flipside really had sliced it open from wrist to elbow, and blood was coursing down my arm. It hurt a lot more once I saw how bad it was. It also showed absolutely no signs of healing on its own. Suzie bandaged my arm with practised skill, brisk efficiency, and a bedside manner that bordered on distressing. She kept her gloves on the whole time. I would have liked to make a lot of noise, or at least indulged in some impassioned cursing, but somehow I couldn't when Tommy Oblivion's wounds were so much worse, and he wasn't making a sound. Suzie tied off both ends of my bandaged arm, and I flexed it carefully.

"You'll need stitches later," said Suzie.

"That's right, cheer me up." I glanced at Dominic's body. "Trust a sneak assassin like him to use a blade with a silver edge. It's lucky you were carrying bandages, Suzie."

"Lucky, hell. I always carry a full med kit. Tools of the trade, when you're in the bounty-hunting business. Even though the powers that be won't let me claim them as a business expense, the bastards."

I put my trench coat back on. The slit sleeve flapped loosely around my injured arm. "I suppose," I said thoughtfully, "they won't let you claim because the med kit could be used by you, or your victims."

"Don't be silly, John, You know I always bring them in dead. Less paperwork that way."

We looked over at Tommy Oblivion, who was still sitting with his back propped against the wall of St. Jude's. Suzie had pushed his guts back into place, then wrapped his stomach with half a mile of bandages, but they were already soaked through with fresh blood. Tommy's face was grey and beaded with sweat. His eyes were wide and staring, and his mouth trembled. There was no way in Hell he was going to be able to concentrate hard enough or long enough to heal himself.

"We have to get him back to Strangefellows," Suzie said quietly. "And fast."

"I can't use my Membership Card, or his," I said, just as quietly. "Lilith has found a way to hack into it. She's closing in on me, Suzie, and I can't afford to be found."

Suzie looked out over the wasteland of ash and dust. Strange lights flared briefly on the horizon. "We're a long way from the bar, John. A long way from anywhere civilised. Tommy won't make it if we have to travel through the war zones on foot. Hell, I'm not even that sure we'll make it. Things are bad out there . . . How about if we go into St. Jude's, and pray for a miracle?"

"How about you go in?" I said. "Tommy and I will watch. From a safe distance. St. Jude's has a famously zero-tolerance policy when it comes to sinners."

"Could you two please keep the noise down?" Tommy said hoarsely. "I'm dying here, and I have a headache."

"He's delirious," said Suzie.

"I wish," said Tommy.

Suzie leaned in close to me, her mouth right next to my ear. "It might be kinder to kill him here, John. Rather than let him die by inches, dragging him through the war zones. His screaming would be bound to attract attention. I could do it. I'd be very humane. He wouldn't feel a thing."

"No," I said. "I won't let him down. I won't let him die. He saved my life. He crawled twenty feet in the dirt with half a dozen bullets in his gut to set fire to that rogue anima. Bravest thing I've ever seen. I wasn't the hero he wanted me to be, on our trip into the Past. But he was a hero for me."

I remembered Larry Oblivion's words, from the pitiful last redoubt of my Enemies in the future; *He trusted you, even though he had good reason not to. And when they struck him down you just stood there, and watched him die, and did nothing to help.*

I looked at Suzie. "How did you get here?"

"Razor Eddie cut a door in the air with his razor, opening up a breach between there and here. All I had to do was step through."

"I didn't know Eddie could do that," said Tommy.

"He's had an upgrade," I said.

"Now that is scary," said Tommy.

Suzie fixed me with her cold, unwavering gaze. "You want to save him, there's only one thing left. Use your gift, John. *Find* us a way back to the bar."

"Using my gift is like using the Card," I said reluctantly. "It's another way for Lilith to find me. If I keep pushing my luck, it's bound to run out. But . . . right now, I'd have to say Tommy's chances are much worse than mine. So."

I fired up my gift, concentrating as hard as I knew how on finding a way out of this mess. Not for me, but for my friends. Because they both came through for me, when I needed them. I pushed hard, gritting my teeth until my jaw ached. Sweat rolled down my face. I could feel some chance, some possibility, close at hand. Something we'd all overlooked. I concentrated till my head ached, a vicious pounding beat of pain, forcing my inner eye, my private eye, to focus in on what I needed. And finally my Sight showed me a door, or at least the essence of a door, hanging before me. It was the opening Razor Eddie had made, with his godly will and his awful straight razor. The door had closed behind Suzie when Eddie stopped thinking about it, but the rift he'd made was still there, if only potentially. I felt my lips pull back in a death's-head grin that was as much a snarl as anything else. I was back in the game again. I sensed Suzie moving in to stand very close to me, comforting me with her presence, but I couldn't see or hear her.

I hit the potential door with every bit of willpower I had, all my muscles locked solid from the strain, my stomach clenching so painfully I almost cried out; and slowly, inch by inch and moment by moment, the door grew more real and more definite. Sweat was pouring off me now, my whole body aching from the tension, and my head felt like it would fly apart at any moment. Blood poured from my nose and ears, and even oozed up from under my eyelids. I was doing myself some serious damage, pushing my gift harder than I ever had before. My breathing came harsh and rapid, my heart hammered in my chest, and my vision narrowed till all I could see was the door, as real to me as I was, because I made it so. I couldn't feel my hands. Couldn't feel my wounded arm. A terrible chill spread through me. I fell to my knees, and didn't even feel the impact. I could sense Suzie kneeling beside me, yelling my name, but even that was faint and far away.

The door swung open, and I cried out, a harsh rasping cry of victory. The door hung on the air before us, an opening, a window through space itself. I shut down my gift, and the door remained. I'd broken it to my will. Sight and sound and sensation returned in a rush. Suzie was kneeling beside me, shaking my shoulder with her gloved hand and yelling right into my ear. I slowly turned my head and grinned at her, blood spilling out over my lips, and said something indistinct. She saw I was back and stopped shouting. She produced a surprisingly clean handkerchief from inside her leather jacket and wiped the blood and sweat and tears from my face. When I was ready, she helped me up onto my feet again.

Through the gap in the air I could see right into Strangefellows. Walker and Alex Morrisey were looking back through the gap, their faces slack with almost comic expressions of surprise. I waved cheerfully at them, and they both recovered quickly. Suzie started to help me towards the door.

"No," I made myself say. "Tommy first. I'll heal. He won't."

She nodded and let go of me. I swayed a little, but stayed upright. Suzie picked Tommy up in her arms as though he was a child, and carried him towards the door. He cried out once at the sudden new pain, but that was it. Tough little guy, for an effete existentialist. Suzie took him through the opening into the bar, then came back for me. I walked through the door under my own steam, but it was a near thing. I'd pushed myself too hard this time, and I had a strong feeling I'd have to pay for it, later. I might have werewolf blood in me, but God alone knew how diluted it was, having passed through Belle and Suzie on its way to me. Suzie stuck close to my side, ready to catch me if I fell.

Is there a better definition of love?

We came home to Strangefellows, and I felt the door close very firmly behind me. Alex already had Tommy Oblivion laid out on a table-top, while Betty and Lucy Coltrane hurried to get Alex the repair spells he needed. Tommy's breathing didn't sound at all good. I started to go to him, but I was suddenly hot and cold at the same time, and the bar swayed around me. Suzie lowered me onto a chair, and I collapsed gratefully. I checked myself out as best I could. I didn't seem to be bleeding from anywhere any more, and feeling was flooding back into all parts of my body. It hurt like hell. Suzie snapped her fingers imperiously for some clean water and a cloth, and set about cleaning the last of the mess off my face. The cool water felt good on my skin, and my head settled down again.

Razor Eddie stood before me, an intense grey presence in his filthy overcoat, regarding me thoughtfully with his fever-bright eyes. He was holding a bottle of Perrier water. Flies buzzed around him, and up close the smell was really bad.

"You reopened a door I made," he said finally, in his quiet, ghostly voice. "I didn't know you could do that. I didn't think anyone could do that."

"Yeah, well," I said, as casually as I could, "nothing like having your mother around to inspire you to new heights."

Walker brought me a glass of wormwood brandy. I'd actually have preferred a nice ice-cold Coke, but I appreciated the thought. I nodded my thanks to him, and he nodded back. Which was about as demonstrative as we were ever likely to get. It did seem we were becoming closer, whether we liked it or not. Suzie stopped dabbing at my face with her damp cloth, inspected her work critically, then nodded and tossed the bloody cloth aside. She sat down on the edge of a table facing me, and concentrated on cleaning her double-barrelled shotgun.

At another table, not too far away, Tommy Oblivion thrashed about while Alex did necessary, painful things to him. Betty and Lucy Coltrane held Tommy down, using all their considerable strength, while Tommy used the kind of language you didn't expect to hear from effete existentialists. Alex's remedies tended to be swift, brutal, but effective. He chanted something alliterative in Old Saxon, while pouring a thick blue gunk into Tommy's exposed guts, while Dead Boy peered over his shoulder, watching interestedly.

"I could lend you some duct tape, if you like," he said. "I've always found duct tape very useful."

"Get the hell away from my patient, you heathen," said Alex, not looking up from what he was doing. "Or I'll use this superglue to seal your mouth up."

"Superglue?" gasped Tommy. "You're putting me back together with superglue? I demand a second opinion!"

"All right, you're a noisy bugger, too," said Alex. "Now shut the hell up and let me concentrate. Superglue was good enough for the grunts in Vietnam. It's not like you needed all that lower intestine anyway . . . There. That's it. Give the glue a few minutes to bond with the spells, then you can sit up. I've got the bullets here. Do you want to keep them for souvenirs?"

Tommy told Alex exactly where he could stick the bullets, and everyone managed some kind of smile. I looked around me, studying the small crowd gathered in the bar. My only remaining allies in the struggle to stop Lilith. It really was a very small crowd. I looked at Walker, who shrugged. He'd got his equilibrium back, but he still looked very tired.

"All my other agents are either out in the field, doing what they can, or they're missing, presumed dead. What you see . . . is all that's left."

There was Alex Morrisey, cleaning his bloody hands on a grubby bar cloth, all in black as usual, in perpetual mourning for the way his life might have gone, if only he hadn't been Alex Morrisey. He glowered at me, and said something about the mess I'd made of his place, but I could tell his heart wasn't really in it. Tommy Oblivion was already sitting up on his table-top, ruefully inspecting the tattered and bloodied remains of his ruffled shirt. He nodded almost cheerfully to me and gave me a thumbs-up. Betty and Lucy Coltrane had chosen chairs from where they could keep a watchful overview of the bar, ready to deal with any and all intruders. They looked muscular as ever, but there were deep black smudges of fatigue under their eyes.

Dead Boy struck a casual pose in his flapping purple greatcoat, while Ms. Fate struck an heroic pose in his leather superhero outfit, mask, and cape. Standing proudly at his side was my teenage secretary, Cathy Barrett, in an oversized black leather jacket covered in badges. I stopped and looked at her closely.

"Cathy . . . why are you wearing a black domino mask?"

"Ms. Fate made me his sidekick!" Cathy said cheerfully. "I thought I'd call myself Deathfang the Avenger, or maybe . . ."

I shut my eyes, just for a moment. Teenagers . . .

Razor Eddie was standing a little off to one side, as he always did. Eddie wasn't a people person. Julien Advent was nursing a glass of champagne and smoking a long black cheroot. As always, he was every inch the elegant Victorian, but his opera cloak was torn and tattered and even burned through in places. Of us all he looked the most like a real hero, tall and brave and unbending. Because he was. Larry Oblivion, in a soiled and battered Gucci suit, stood supportively beside his brother, and nodded briefly when my gaze landed on him.

"You saved my brother's life," he said. "Thank you."

"You're welcome," I said.

I hadn't let Tommy die. The thought warmed me. I'd finally broken one clear link between my present and the devastated future, and it felt good, so good. And then I felt guilty, for caring more about that than for saving the man who'd risked his life to save mine. I do try to be a good man; but my life gets so damned complicated, sometimes . . .

"We're all glad you're back, Taylor," said Walker, a little tartly. "But you'd better have some really good ideas, because we're all out. We're losing, John."

Outside the bar, I could hear the roar of unchecked fires and the rumble of explosions, running feet, human screams, and the cries of monsters loose in the streets. Merlin's shields were apparently still holding, but the War was edging closer. It occurred to me that this might be the last safe haven left in the Nightside. I remembered my Enemies, huddled together in their last refuge, and shuddered despite myself.

"What is there left for us to do?" said Walker. "We've tried open confrontation, manning the barricades, hit-and-run tactics, and guerrilla warfare, and none of it has ever done more than slow down Lilith's advance. Now there's just us . . . We're all good, in our own ways, but she's Lilith. Even her children were worshipped as gods for centuries. Lilith represents a kind of Power that's almost beyond our comprehension. And her army of followers is growing all the time. I like to think most of them have been terrorised into joining, and would cut and run if given a chance, but . . ."

Everyone looked at me, and the silence stretched, because I had nothing to say. I had no plans, no schemes, no last trick up my sleeve.

"Can't you use your gift, to find out what Lilith will do next?" said Cathy. It was hard for me to look at her. She still had faith in me. "Couldn't your gift find us a way to defeat her?"

I shook my head slowly. "I know you're trying to help, Cathy, but my gift doesn't work like that. And every time I raise my gift now, it's like running up a flag to tell Lilith exactly where I am."

"But you're always finding new things you can do with your gift," said Cathy.

"Specific questions lead me to specific answers," I said tiredly. "The vaguer the question, the harder it is to get any kind of answer that makes sense."

"Where did you get this gift, anyway?" said Ms. Fate, in his rough, smoky voice. "I would have loved to have a gift to help me. I had to create myself through hard work and long training."

"I won my gift in a poker game," said Tommy Oblivion, unexpectedly.

"It's true, he did," said his brother Larry. "And he was bluffing, with a pair of threes. I couldn't believe it."

"My gift was a legacy, inherited from my inhuman mother," I said. "My only legacy."

"Now that's interesting," said Julien Advent. "Why that gift, in particular, and no other? I mean, when your mother is an ancient Power and a Biblical myth, I think you could reasonably expect to inherit at least half of that power, simply through the operations of chance. If all you got was one specific gift, it's because that's what your mother intended. She wasn't prepared to risk your becoming powerful enough to challenge her, but she wanted you to have this gift for finding things. Why?"

An earthquake shook the bar. Tables rattled and chairs shimmied across the heaving floor. The walls creaked, and the long wooden bar groaned out loud. Everyone clung to each other, to keep from falling. Bottles toppled and crashed behind the bar, and the lights swung crazily. My first thought was that Lilith had found us at last, and was smashing her way through Merlin's defences, but as quickly as it started the disturbance faded away, and everything grew still again. We were all standing, prepared to defend ourselves in our various ways.

"The cellars!" Alex said abruptly. "I can hear something moving, down in the cellars!"

We all fell silent, listening. Nothing good could come from the cellars under Strangefellows. Finally, we heard faint but definite footsteps, coming up the stairs under the bar. Slow, measured, inexorable footsteps. And then the trap-door behind the bar flew open with a crash, and that ancient sorcerer, Merlin, came up into the bar. Merlin of Camelot, the Devil's only begotten son, risen up in his own dead body with the dirt still on him from where he'd burst up out of his own grave. I'd known that giant crucifix wouldn't hold him down if he wanted out.

Merlin strolled out from behind the bar, taking his time, enjoying the shock and apprehension in all our faces. Alex stared, open-mouthed. He'd never seen his ancestor before, because up till now Merlin had always manifested through him. This was the real deal, Merlin's dead body up and about again, raised from its long rest through an effort of supernatural will.

Merlin Satanspawn. A man born out of Hell who became a warrior for Heaven. And scared the crap out of both sides.

His face was long and heavy-boned, unrepentantly ugly, and two flames leapt in the empty sockets where his eyes should have been. (*He has his father's eyes,* they said . . .) His long grey hair and beard were stiff and packed with old clay. His skin was taut and cracked and stained with grave-moss, but still he looked in pretty good shape for someone who'd been dead and buried for fifteen hundred years. He wore the magician's robe they'd buried him in, a long scarlet gown with golden trimming round the collar. I remembered that robe. He'd been wearing it when I killed him, back in the Past. The robe hung open to reveal a bare chest covered in Druidic tattoos, interrupted by a great gaping hole, from where I'd torn the living heart out of his chest with my bare hands. For what seemed like good reasons at the time. As far as I knew, he didn't know I'd taken it.

Merlin came striding through the bar, and the tables and chairs drew back to get out of his way. His dead body made low, creaking sounds with every movement, and gravedirt fell off him. He wasn't breathing. He ignored Razor Eddie, standing ready with his straight razor shining impossibly bright in his filthy hand. He ignored Suzie Shooter, with her double-barrelled shotgun following his every movement. He ignored Dead Boy and Julien Advent and all the others. He came straight for me, his dead lips drawn back in a mirthless smile that showed brown teeth and grey leathery tongue.

He stopped right before me, and actually bowed slightly. "Here we are at last," he said, in a voice like everyone's favourite uncle. "Two sons of distinguished parents, who only ever wanted to be left alone to work out their own destinies. I was born to be the Antichrist, but I declined the honour and went my own way. And much good it did me. We've always had a lot in common, you and I, John Taylor."

"What brings you up here, sorcerer?" I asked. I kept my voice calm and easy through an effort of will. (First rule of operating in the Nightside—never let them see they've got you scared or they'll walk all over you.) "What brings you up out of your grave, after all these centuries?"

"To tell you things you need to know," he said, still smiling his unnerving smile. "I know why your mother bestowed only the one gift upon you, when she could have made you one of the greatest Powers in the Nightside. I am old and wise and I know many things I'm not supposed to. Being dead didn't stop me listening, and learning. Lilith gave you that one gift and no other because she intended to make use of you and it, on her return. Your gift will find for her the one thing that will make possible her control of the whole Nightside.

"I would have thought you'd have worked that out by now. If she could remake the Nightside by will alone, she would have done it by now, don't you think? But her creation has grown and changed so very much during the long centuries of her absence, become something far greater and more intransigent than she ever intended . . . Why else would a Power like Lilith need an army to subdue the Nightside?"

"Why haven't you manifested before?" Walker said sharply. "We could have used your help. Why wait till now, when it's almost too late?"

"I'm here now because you finally asked the right question," said Merlin, still looking only at me. He pulled up a chair and sat down before me, and his manner made it seem like a throne. His presence dominated the room, pulling all eyes to him. "Now I'm up and about again, Lilith will know I'm back. She'll know where to come, to find me. She has to face me, because I'm her only real rival. She'll never feel safe until she's seen me utterly destroyed and cast down."

"Can you stop her?" said Julien Advent.

Merlin ignored him, his fiery gaze fixed on me. "The protections I have set in place around this bar won't keep her out forever. She'll be here, very soon now. And if she finds me in my present condition, she'll strike me down with a look and a word and laugh while she does it. And then she'll take you over, John, make you her puppet, and use your gift as though it were her own. Just as she's planned from the very beginning."

I considered him for a long moment, letting the silence build. "But now you're here, to save the day. Because you have a plan, too, don't you, Merlin?"

He nodded. "Yes. I have a plan."

"Of course you do. You're Merlin Satanspawn, and you always have a plan."

"Don't drag my father into this," said Merlin. "You know very well

we never got on. Now, John Taylor, I need you to use your gift for me. I
need you to find my missing heart and bring it here to me. I will place it
back in my breast, and then . . . Ah then, I will show you wonders and
miracles beyond your wildest dreams! I will live again, my body made
new and vital, and all my old power will return! I shall be the greatest magician of this Age, and walk out of this bar, free at last . . . to teach Lilith
the error of her ways."

There was a long pause. I looked around, and it was clear that no-one
except Merlin thought this was a good idea.

"You might win against Lilith," I said finally. "Or you might not.
But even if you did . . . who's to say you might not prove as great a
threat as she?"

Everyone looked at me, then at Merlin. He rose slowly up out of his
chair, his dead body creaking and groaning, and I stood my ground, facing him unflinchingly.

"I could make you find my heart," said Merlin.

"No you couldn't," I said.

We stared at each other, both of us very still. I looked into the flames
that were his eyes, and I'd never felt colder in my life. And in the end,
Merlin looked away first. He sat down heavily on his chair. I sat down
quickly, too, so no-one would see how badly my legs were shaking. There
were impressed murmurs all around me, but I just nodded stiffly. I was the
only one there who knew for sure that I'd been bluffing.

"I've had enough of this," I said harshly. "Enough of guesses and
warnings and prophecies of doom. It's time to get to the heart of the matter, time to find out the truth, once and for all. You were right all along,
Cathy. The only way to find out what I need to know, is to use my gift. So,
gift, *Why did Lilith give you to me?*"

I was ready for another fight, another concentrated effort of will that
would half kill me, but in the end it was as easy as taking a deep breath.
As though my gift had been waiting all my life for me to ask of it the one
question that really mattered. My shadow stood up before me, separating
itself, taking on form and substance until it looked exactly like me, right
down to the white trench coat with the flapping sleeve. Exactly like me, in
every detail—except my doppleganger's eyes were full of darkness. It
leaned against a table and folded its arms across its chest, smiling mock-
ingly at me.

"Took you long enough," it said. Its voice was smooth, assured, and
only just short of openly taunting. "Well, here I am, John. Your gift per-
sonified, ready to answer all your questions."

"All right," I said. My mouth was very dry. "How do you work? How is it you're always able to find the things that are hidden from everyone else?"

"Easy. I tap directly into reality itself. I see everything that is, all at once. I'm really so much more than you ever allowed me to be, John."

"Damn," Tommy said quietly. "That is . . . really spooky."

"Why did Lilith give you to me?" I said.

"Because she intends to use you to find the Speaking Gun. The most powerful weapon in the world. It was originally created to kill angels and demons, but it can do so much more than that. Lilith will use the Speaking Gun to remake the Nightside in her own image. Return it to what she originally intended it to be, before Humanity infested and perverted it from its true purpose and nature. She was responsible for the Gun's creation, long and long ago. Adam gave of his rib and his flesh to make Eve, and after Lilith came back up from Hell, having lain down with demons and given birth to monsters, she also gave of her rib and her flesh, to make the Speaking Gun. With the help of Abraxus Artificers."

"Yeah," Suzie said suddenly. "That was engraved on the stock of the Speaking Gun; *Abraxus Artificers, the old firm, solving problems since the beginning.* I've always been very good at remembering things, where weapons are involved."

"Very good," said my double. "Now shut up and listen, and you might learn something. Abraxus Artificers were the descendants of Cain, the first murderer. How else do you think they could fashion such marvellous weapons of destruction?" My double paused. "You do all realise that I'm talking in parables, representing a far more complicated reality? Good. I shall continue. The Speaking Gun was designed to speak backwards the echoes of the original Word of Creation, which resonates on in everything, giving each separate thing its own true secret name. By speaking this secret name backwards, the Speaking Gun can thus unmake or uncreate anything. But the Speaking Gun could be used, by someone with enough power, someone who gave of their own flesh to make it, to *respeak* those secret names, and thus change their essential nature. Lilith will use the Speaking Gun to respeak the Nightside, making it over into whatever she wants it to be. Personally, I can't wait to see what she's going to do . . ."

"That's enough," I said, and shut down my gift. It didn't fight me, just collapsed back into darkness, and my shadow was nothing more than my shadow. I wondered if I'd ever look at it in the same way again. Or ever really trust my gift, knowing that it lived within me like a parasite.

"So," Walker said finally, "who has the Speaking Gun? My people lost track of it some time back."

"I last saw it here, in this bar, with the future Suzie Shooter," said Alex, glancing apologetically at Suzie. "Before Merlin banished both of them."

"Don't look at me," said Merlin. He sounded a lot smaller, since I'd stared him down. "I only sent them away. They could be anywhere now. Or anywhen."

"The last time I saw it, in the Present, Eddie had it," I said. I looked at him. We all looked at him, and he nodded slowly. "You were using it to kill angels from Above and Below, in the angel war," I said, being careful to sound not at all challenging or confrontational. "What did you do with it, Eddie?"

"I gave it away," said Razor Eddie, quite calmly. "To Old Father Time. The only Being I knew powerful enough to control it and not be corrupted by it."

"I thought all you cared about was smiting the bad guys?" said Suzie.

"No," said Razor Eddie. "I wanted to do penance. There's a difference. All the time I had the Speaking Gun, I could feel it working on me, trying to seduce me with its endless hunger for death and destruction. But I have been there, and done that. I am something else now."

"According to my agents' last reports, Lilith has destroyed the Time Tower," Walker said heavily. "Reduced it to nothing but rubble. Old Father Time is dead, and the Speaking Gun buried under the rubble with him."

"No," I said, feeling hope rise anew within me. "Time's domain isn't actually in the Nightside. The Tower was just how people got to speak to him. There is another way to reach him. . . . So, who's up for one last suicidal charge for glory? Don't all speak at once."

TWELVE

Last Train to Shadows Fall

I explained what I had in mind. Everyone looked at me. And somehow I knew they weren't too keen.

"You're crazy!" said Larry Oblivion.

"And if you think we're going along with you, you're crazy, too!" said Dead Boy.

"Hold everything," said Walker, holding up his hand, and it was a measure of the man that everyone else fell silent, like children when the teacher speaks. "Let me be sure I've grasped all the details of this cunning plan of yours, John. You want us to go out onto the streets full of madmen and monsters and run interference for you, at the risk of all our lives, so you can get safely to the nearest Underground station and catch a train to take you safely out of the Nightside? Is that it? Have I grasped all the nuances correctly?"

"I love it when you get all sarcastic, Walker," I said. "But actually, you're pretty much right. Look, Old Father Time resides in Shadows Fall, that small town in the back of beyond that's an elephants' graveyard for the supernatural. He only commutes into the Nightside to work. When Lilith destroyed the Time Tower, all she did was cut off his access to the Nightside. He's still safe in Shadows Fall, with the Speaking Gun. If I can get safely to the Underground, I can take a train straight to him. And just maybe I can persuade him to give me the Speaking Gun, to use against Lilith."

"Or, you could just run out on us," said Larry, fixing me with his cold unblinking gaze. "Even Lilith would think twice about going after you, if you were hiding out in Shadows Fall."

"He may be dead, but he has a point," said Walker. "You've never been the most trustworthy soul, Taylor. Why should we risk our lives to save your selfish skin?"

"Oh ye of little faith," I said. "We need the Gun, and I'm the only one he might give it to. Do you have any means of communicating with Shadows Fall, Walker? Any way we can talk to Time, and save me the journey?"

"No," Walker admitted reluctantly. "All outgoing communications have been jammed. Scientific and supernatural. We're completely cut off from the rest of the world."

"Then I have to go in person, don't I?" I said. "Is there anyone else here who thinks Old Father Time might surrender the most powerful weapon in the world to them? No, I didn't think so."

"Why should he give it to you?" said Julien Advent. From him, it was a fair question.

"Because I'm Lilith's son. Because he knows I'm the only one who can stop her now."

"I say!" Tommy Oblivion said suddenly, and we all jumped a little. "I've just had a brilliant idea! Taylor, why don't you get Old Father Time to send you back into the Past again, to before all this started, so you can warn yourself about what's coming?"

"I can't," I said patiently, "because I didn't."

Tommy frowned, his lower lip pouting out sullenly. "I can't help feeling there should be more to the argument than that." He pulled a notepad out of his pocket and started jotting down equations and Venn diagrams, muttering about divergent timetracks, opposing probabilities, experiment's intent, and whether or not someone's pizza had anchovies on it, so we left him to get on with it. In my experience, Time travel just complicated things even more.

"The Speaking Gun is what matters," I said forcefully. "It's the only weapon we can be sure will work on Lilith, because it's made out of her flesh and bone. I can use it to speak her name in reverse, and uncreate her."

"Or perhaps to respeak her?" said Walker. "Remake her into some more acceptable form? She is your mother, after all."

"No," I said. "As long as she lives, she'll always be a threat. For everything she's done, and for everything she intends to do, she has to die. She was never my mother. Not in any way that mattered."

Alex produced a rather grubby and much-folded map of the local Underground system out from behind the bar, along with half a dozen cards from local taxi firms, a stuffed cat and a dead beetle or two, and after a certain amount of argument and calculation (because the streets around

Strangefellows aren't always there when you need them), we finally de-cided the nearest Underground station entrance had to be Cheyne Walk. Within walking distance from the bar, under normal circumstances, which these weren't, but still . . . it was reachable.

"I don't like this," said Ms. Fate. "It's a war zone out there."

We all stopped and listened to the chaos raging outside the bar. Even be-hind the shuttered windows and the locked doors, even behind Merlin's an-cient defences, we could still hear screams and howls, the rage of fires and the rumble of collapsing buildings. Raw hatred ran loose in the streets, and it was hard to tell what sounds were human and which weren't, any more.

"So," I said, trying hard to sound confident, "who's coming with me?"

"I am," said Suzie Shooter. "But you knew that already."

"Yes," I said. "My love."

"I may puke," said Alex.

"I can't go with you," said Walker. "I have responsibilities, to my people. Many of them are still out there, fighting. Someone has to stay here, to organise the resistance. In case you don't come back. I will do my best to keep Lilith distracted while you make your run to Shadows Fall."

"I'll go with you, old thing," said Tommy Oblivion, throwing his notebook aside. "I feel fine again. Honest! And I owe you more than I can ever repay. I was so wrong about you."

"If you're going, then I'm going, too," his brother Larry said imme-diately. "You'll need someone to watch your back. You always do."

"You're not coming, and that's final!" snapped Tommy. "I don't care if you are dead, one of us has to survive this mess, to look after Mother."

Larry subsided, muttering under his breath. Razor Eddie drank the last of his designer water, tossed the bottle carelessly over his shoulder, and nodded to me.

"I'll go. I've always wanted to see Shadows Fall."

"I'm not going, and you can't make me!" said Alex Morrisey. "I've got a bar to run. And no, you can't have the Coltranes either. I need them, to protect the place."

Alex couldn't leave Strangefellows. The bar's geas held him there. We all knew that, but he had a reputation to keep up.

"I cannot go to Shadows Fall," said Merlin. "And no, I'm not going to tell you why. I'll just say . . . you'd think such a proud, ancient, and leg-endary town would have more of a sense of humour about . . . certain things. I'll stay here and keep Lilith's attention focused on me. I'm pretty sure I can set up a glamour, to fool her into thinking Taylor's still here with me. For a while, anyway . . ."

I looked at Julien Advent. "I really could use your help on this one, Julien . . ."

But he was already shaking his head. "I'm sorry, John. It's my responsibility to protect the Nightside, not risk my life on such a long shot. I'll help Walker run the resistance. I have contacts and associates and Beings who owe me favours, that even he doesn't know about."

"I wouldn't put money on that," said Walker. "But thanks, Julien. I could use someone level-headed around here."

"Who's he looking at?" Alex said loudly. "I don't know what he's talking about. Like to see him run a dive like this. I can feel one of my funny turns coming on."

In his own way, he was trying to cheer us up. I looked at Cathy before she could say anything.

"No," I said, "you can't come with me. You'd have to kill or be killed out there, and I won't have that on my conscience."

She nodded jerkily. Her eyes were full of tears she refused to shed. "You come back safe," she said. "Or I'll never forgive you."

"I'll keep an eye on her," said Ms. Fate. "She's stronger than you know."

"You keep her safe," I said. "Or I'll come back from my death to haunt your Bat-cave."

"You probably would, too," said Ms. Fate. "I wish I could go with you, but I know my limitations. Good luck, Taylor."

And that left Dead Boy. He scowled, shook his head, and finally shrugged. "Oh hell, why not? I could use a little excitement. Where did I put that duct tape . . . ?"

"I could use my gift to transport you right to the station entrance," Tommy said suddenly.

"No, you couldn't," I said. "Lilith will be looking for that. If she even guesses I'm heading for Shadows Fall, she'll stop me."

And that was that. People finished their drinks, said their good-byes, and set about preparing themselves for what was to come. Shotgun Suzie took me to one side, and looked at me solemnly. She put a leather-gloved hand on my chest and let it rest there, like a butterfly on a wall.

"I wanted us to have a moment together," she said, in her cold calm voice. "Because . . . things can always go wrong, and we might not get a chance to say a proper good-bye, later. We've been through so much together, and if this is it, well . . . I need to say something to you, John. You . . . matter to me. No-one's mattered to me for a long time. Not even me. Perhaps especially not me. But you . . . made me want to live again. So I could share my life with you. I care for you, John. I wanted you to know that."

"I knew that, Suzie . . ."

"Shut up and let me say this. It isn't easy. I love you, John Taylor, and I always will."

She made herself hug me. Her leather jacket creaked loudly as she put her arms around me, and her bandoliers of bullets pressed hard against my chest. She put her head forward, and deliberately pressed her unscarred cheek against mine. Flesh to flesh. I held her gently, as though she was brittle and might break. I could feel the effort involved, in what she was doing, of how much strength it took her to do a simple thing like this, and I was so proud of her I could hardly get my breath.

"If we do both make it out of this alive," she said, very quietly, her mouth right next to my ear, "I can't promise I'll ever be able to be a woman for you, John. But I will try."

"Suzie . . . it doesn't matter . . ."

"Yes it does! It matters to me. Do you love me, John?"

"Of course I love you, Suzie. Now and forever, and all the times between. I'd die for you, if I had to."

"I'd much rather you lived for me."

She let go of me and stood back. I let go of her immediately. I knew better than to push it. She looked at me, her face apparently entirely unmoved.

"I know about the future Suzie. I know what happened to her, here in this bar. You can't keep secrets in a dump like this. You mustn't worry about it, John. The future is what we make it."

"That's what worries me," I said.

And so, finally, I led my brave little band of heroes out of the bar. Shotgun Suzie, Razor Eddie, Tommy Oblivion, and Dead Boy. I eased open the door, slowly, silently, and one by one we crept out into the narrow cobble-stoned back alley. It smelled really bad. The piled-up bodies I'd expected from Suzie's defence were gone, and it was best not to wonder where, but the blood and gore remained, splashed up the alley walls and soaking the cobbled ground. The air was hot and heavy, thick with old smoke, and an overbearing sense of a world running down, of things coming to an end. There were screams and roars and howls, all the sounds of death and destruction, horror and fury. The Nightside might be going down for the last time, but it sure as hell wasn't going down quietly. I set off down the alley at a steady pace, ignoring the blood splashing under my shoes, trying hard to radiate confidence and a strong sense of purpose.

Suzie was right there at my side, shotgun at the ready, happy and smiling like a woman on her way to a really good party. Tommy and Eddie and Dead Boy moved along with us, and together we made our way to the end of the alley and looked cautiously out into the main street.

Fires blazed everywhere. Dead vehicles sprawled the length of the road, overturned and abandoned. A hearse had been broken apart from the inside out, and a taxi lay on its side with a wooden stake hammered through its engine block. Maddened crowds swept back and forth under a flickering twilight of burning buildings and half-smashed neon signs, attacking everything in sight. The noises they made didn't sound human any more. Reason had been blasted from their minds, by loss and horror and Lilith's will, leaving them only the most basic instincts and emotions. Men and women killed and ate each other, while monsters roamed freely, killing where they would and exhausting their various appetites on the fallen. Lilith was softening the Nightside up, before she went in for the kill. And because she enjoyed it.

"How the hell are we supposed to get to Cheyne Walk through *that*?" said Tommy.

"I'd suggest running," said Suzie.

"I'd also strongly suggest killing anything that isn't us," said Dead Boy.

"Works for me," said Razor Eddie. "But . . . loath as I am to be the voice of reason in this group, I really don't like the odds out there. Too many of them, too few of us. Enough hyenas will bring down even the strongest lions. If we have to fight for every step of the way, they'll drag us down long before we get anywhere near Cheyne Walk."

"We can't hit them head-on," I said. "In fact, we can't afford to be noticed at all. Lilith is bound to have people out there looking for me. Once she knows I've left Strangefellows and Merlin's protections, she'll come straight for me. So, Tommy, you're up."

"What?" said Tommy. "What?"

"Use your gift to hide us. Or at least hide our identities. Such a small use of your gift should slide past Lilith unnoticed."

"Yes," said Tommy, after a moment. "I think I could do that . . ."

He frowned, concentrating. It took him a while, to force his mind to deal with only one thing and ignore the madness and horror around him, but finally I could sense his gift firing up, as he imposed his existential will upon the world. Slowly and carefully, moment by moment, we became as uncertain as he thought we were, until the world couldn't decide whether we really were there or not, and even if we were, it couldn't make up its mind about who we were. I could feel Tommy's gift all around us, like a fog of possibilities. Everywhere I looked, it was like seeing through a heat haze, as though we were out of synch with our surroundings. I took that as a good sign and made myself concentrate on the only thing that really mattered—getting to Cheyne Walk Station.

I took a deep breath and led the way out onto the main street, walking openly, taking my time, doing nothing to attract attention. The others came with me, sticking close but not crowding. No-one even looked at us. Crazed mobs rioted up and down the street, and swept right past us without even slowing. I led the way down the street, through chaos and murder and foulness of all kinds, and no-one touched us. Sometimes they'd step out of our way, without even realising they were doing it. Suzie stayed at my side, the others spread out behind us. I tried to keep track of where they were without looking at them directly, but Tommy's gift made that difficult. It was hard to be sure of anything under the concentrated field of uncertainty he was generating. Terrible things happened, but none of them seemed real, or close, or threatening. Until a familiar face came running frantically out of a side alley.

Sister Morphine cared for the homeless and down-and-outs of Rats' Alley, trying to keep them fed and warm and alive, and save a few souls where she could. A good woman in a bad place, watching over those the world had abandoned. And now she came running out of the night, her nun's robes torn and tattered and soaked in her own blood. Her tear-stained face was dull with exhaustion and shock and the sight of too much horror. A mob was coming right behind her, screaming for her head. She burst out of the side alley and looked right at me. And even Tommy's gift was no match for her honest gaze.

"John! John Taylor! Help me! For God's sake, help me!"

The mob fell upon her and dragged her down, and she disappeared under a mass of flailing bodies. Knives flashed brightly in the night. She kept on screaming long after she should have stopped. And I let it happen, torn between the need to help her and the greater need to get to Cheyne Walk. I let a good woman die because I had somewhere more important to be. I walked on down the street, staring straight ahead, not even allowing myself to hurry in case that called attention to me. The screaming finally stopped, but I knew I'd be hearing it for the rest of my life. Suzie and the others stuck a little closer to me, but none of them said anything. They'd made the same choice I had. I could see the sign for the Cheyne Walk Underground Station up ahead, right at the end of the street. On a normal day, I could have walked it in a few minutes.

But the damage had already been done. Sister Morphine had called me by name, undermining Tommy's uncertainty. All around us, heads were slowly turning in our direction, not all of them human, not all of them sane. Perhaps that helped them see us, see me, more clearly. Someone pointed. Something said my name. The word flashed up and down the packed street, and men and monsters stopped the awful things they were doing to look for me. For Lilith's son.

"What do we do?" said Suzie.

"Run," I said.

And so we ran, pushing ourselves hard, ploughing through the crowds and slamming people out of our way if they didn't move fast enough. The press of bodies grew thicker as people came surging down the street towards us. My people formed a protective ring around me, without my asking. Suzie blasted a bloody hole in the crowd ahead, using both barrels, and bodies fell this way and that. Razor Eddie moved forward to take the lead while Suzie reloaded, gliding along like an angry ghost, his pearl-handled straight razor blazing fiercely in the twilight, as though it had come home. Eddie cut about him without even looking, and no-one could stand against him.

Suzie kept up a steady fire against anyone who even looked like getting too close, reloading on the run, though her bandoliers were almost empty now. She tossed the odd grenade or incendiary where she thought it'd do the most good, but from the unusually sparing way she was using them, I guessed she was running low on them, too. She was still grinning broadly, like she was having the best time, and maybe she was. Dead Boy hit anything that came within reach, while Tommy tried his best to wrap the last tatters of his gift around us, frowning fiercely with concentration as he ran. It must have been working. No-one seemed able to lay a hand on us.

We were all running full out, but the station entrance didn't seem to be getting any closer. My heart hammered in my chest, my lungs burned with the need for air, and my legs ached fiercely. It had been a long, hard day, and I was running on fumes now. It didn't seem fair that the world should require more effort from me, after everything I'd already done. I put my head down, and sweat dripped off the end of my nose. I concentrated on running. I could do this. I'd run harder, and longer, when Herne and his Wild Hunt chased me through the primordial forest of old Britain.

Mobs and monsters descended on us from all sides, from everywhere at once, driven by hate and bloodlust and the fear of Lilith's wrath if they let me escape. She knew I had to be stopped, before I stopped her. I ran hard, we all ran hard, sticking very close, striking out viciously at our many enemies, and Dead Boy was the first of us to fall. Hands from a faceless mob of howling savages caught hold of his flapping greatcoat and dragged him down by sheer weight and force of numbers. He was still lashing about him with his powerful dead hands as he fell, handing out death with every blow, but there were just so many of them.

We ran on, leaving him behind. We had no choice. I looked back anyway. The mob boiled around Dead Boy, stamping and kicking him and stabbing him with any number of weapons. I knew he wouldn't feel any of it, but that didn't make the sight any easier to bear. He was still struggling, the last time I saw him. I'm sure I heard him yell out to me, to keep going. I'm almost sure I heard him call out. I turned my head away, and kept running.

Razor Eddie fell back to cover our rear. Perhaps because there were more enemies behind than in front. Perhaps because even he was getting tired. Certainly even the most crazed individuals showed a marked reluctance to get too close to his infamous straight razor. He cut through the madness like a grim grey ghost, or a grim grey god, and no man and no monster came close to touching him. The street was full of people now, and things not at all like people, coming at us from every alley and side street, brandishing all kinds of weapons, yelling my name like a curse. Creatures loped through the crowds, or hovered above in the smoky night sky. I saw fangs and claws and membraneous wings, and shapes that made no sense at all, bursting out of the sides of crumbling buildings as though they weren't even there.

And then I swear I heard my mother's voice, abroad in the night, speaking Words of Power from a language so ancient it predated any human tongue or meaning. A trap-door opened up in the pavement right in front of Razor Eddie, a hole in our world, a door to somewhere else. Long tentacles with crocodile hide and suckers like barbed mouths shot up out of that other place and wrapped themselves around Razor Eddie. He cut viciously about him with his razor, but for every tentacle he severed a dozen more burst up through the trap-door. They finally whipped around both his arms, pinioning them to his sides, then they dragged him down into the hole, out of our world and into theirs. He never cried out, not once. The trap-door slammed shut, and Razor Eddie was gone.

I kept running. We all did. The Punk God of the Straight Razor could take care of himself. He'd find his way back. I believed that. I had to believe it.

The Cheyne Walk entrance was really close now. The crowds were thickening up before us, desperate to block our way. Suzie's shotgun fired again and again. The barrels were so hot that steam rose up from her leather gloves where she held the gun. Tommy was speaking gibberish, forcing his gift to manifest through sheer force of will. His face was very pale, his breathing laboured, his eyes dangerously wild. He wrapped the three of us in a cloud of uncertainty, and the mobs couldn't find us. And then a whole building collapsed as we ran past it, the smoke-blackened wall bowing suddenly outwards and slamming down like a hammer. Suzie and I forced out one last burst of speed, but Tommy was so focused on his gift he didn't realise what was happening until it was too late. The crumbling brickwork swept over him like a jagged tide, enveloping him in a moment, and we lost sight of him in a dark, billowing cloud of dust.

I stopped to look back, and through the settling dust I saw Tommy lying half-covered by rubble. He was hurt, but still conscious, still alive. Suzie was at my side, tugging my arm, calling my name. I looked at Tommy, and he looked right back at me. His gift was gone, and everyone knew exactly where we were. Voices were calling my name. Suzie pulled me away, and I turned my back on Tommy and started running again. The station entrance was right there. Tommy called out my name once, then I heard him scream as the mob found him.

I left Tommy Oblivion to die. I hadn't saved him after all. And all I could think was *What will I tell his brother?*

We came to the Cheyne Walk underground station entrance, and I started down the steps. It took me a moment to realise Suzie wasn't there with me. I looked round, and she'd taken up a position at the top of the steps, blocking the entrance. She glared at me.

"Go on, John. I've got your back."

"Suzie, no . . ."

"Someone's got to hold them off long enough for you to catch your train out of here. And I'm the only one left. Don't take too long, John. I'm seriously low on ammo and almost out of dirty tricks."

"I can't just leave you!"

"Yes you can. You must. Now get the hell out of here, John. And don't worry. I can look after myself, remember?"

She smiled once, then the mob came surging forward. She met them with both barrels and a handful of shrapnel grenades. I carried on down the steps into the Underground. She'd been right before, as usual. There hadn't been time for a proper good-bye.

Down in the tube station, it felt a lot later than three o'clock in the morning. The place stank of blood and sweat and desperation and far too many people. They sat huddled on the steps in filthy blood-stained clothes, rocking back and forth and hugging themselves tightly, as though that was the only thing holding them together. They didn't look at me as I squeezed my way past. Down in the tunnels they were packed even more tightly, refugees from the War above. The floors were filthy, wet and slick with every kind of waste. A recent attempt at graffiti on a tiled wall said *The End Is* but it finished abruptly in a splash of dried blood.

I forced my way through the increasingly packed tunnels and down the escalators, none of which were working. Half the lights were out, too, and the air was hot and close and clammy. People were shoulder to shoulder down on the platform, and I had to force my way through. No-one had enough strength left to object. The destination board on the wall opposite said STREET OF THE GODS, HACELDAMA, CARCOSA, SHADOWS FALL. I looked up and down the platform, hoping to spot someplace I could sit down and get my breath back, but there was nowhere. Only people, packed a lot closer than people can usually stand, their faces empty, their eyes dead. There was no energy left in them, no hope. They'd found a place to hide from the War, and the horror they sensed coming, and that was enough. Natives and tourists sat huddled together, equally traumatised, equally lost, giving each other what comfort they could. Every now and again, some especially loud roar or explosion would reverberate down through the tunnels from the street above, and everyone would flinch or shudder, and huddle just a little closer together.

There was a lot of dust in the air, and the taste of smoke, and I would have killed for a cool drink. All the food and drink machines had been smashed open and emptied, though I doubt their contents went far, among so many. A woman was talking tearfully on a courtesy phone, even though it was obvious there was no-one on the other end of the line. There were no quarrels or shoving matches anywhere, or even any raised voices. The people were all too tired or hurt or beaten down to cause any trouble. One area at the end of the platform had been set aside for the wounded and the dying, and a handful of assorted nurses and doctors did what they could, though they had damn all to work with. Blood and offal and other, worse things pooled on the floor, and the smell drifting down the platform was the stench of despair.

I asked people around me when the next train was due in. Most didn't answer. Some were so far gone they didn't even seem to understand the question. Finally, a man in a torn and scorched business suit, still clinging protectively to his briefcase, informed me that no-one had seen a train in ages. The general feeling was that all the trains had stopped running the moment the War began. I could understand that. The trains were frightened. (They might have started out as purely mechanical creations, but they'd evolved down the years, and now they were all quite definitely alive and sentient, in their own way.) They were probably hiding somewhere outside the Nightside, afraid to enter.

I powered up my gift, found the nearest train, and called it to me. I didn't have to worry about Lilith's finding me through my gift any more. By the time she got here, I planned to be long gone. Using my gift felt easier than ever before. Now that I knew the truth about it. As though . . . it had stopped fighting me. I called, and the train came, protesting loudly all the way. I shut down my gift, silencing the train's querulous mental voice.

It finally roared into the station, shaking the whole platform with its arrival, a long, shining, silver bullet, cold and featureless. The long steel carriages had no windows, and only the heavily reinforced doors stood out against the gleaming metal. But still there were scuffs and scrapes down the long, steel sides, and even a few deep gouge marks. People stirred and murmured, astonished. The trains were supposed to be untouchable, by long tradition. The first carriage slowed to a halt, and its door opened, right in front of me. I stepped inside. People on the platform surged after me, but I turned and glared at them, and something of my old legend stepped them in their tracks, just for a moment. Long enough for the door to hiss shut again. Fists hammered on the outside, while raised voices cursed and pleaded.

I ignored them all and sat down. They couldn't go where I was going. It felt good to sit down and take the weight off my feet. Rest my aching back against the leather seat. Tired, so tired . . . I let my head roll forward until my chin rested on my chest . . . but I couldn't let myself sleep. I had to stay alert. The train was already off and moving, leaving behind the angry and disappointed howls from the platform.

The air in the carriage was still and clear, almost refrigerator cool. I breathed deeply, savouring it. There were a few splashes of blood on the steel grille floor, and some scorch marks on the wall opposite, but hardly worth the noticing after what I'd been through. I relaxed further into the support of the dark leather seat, and raised my voice.

"You know who I am, train, so no arguments. Take me straight to Shadows Fall. No stops, no detours."

"Don't want to," said a quiet voice from concealed speakers. It sounded like a traumatised child. "It's not safe any more. Come with me, and hide in the sidings. We'll be safe there, in the dark."

"No-one's safe any more," I said, not unkindly. "I have to go to Shadows Fall."

"The badlands aren't secure, any more," said the train, sadly. "The places between destinations are all stirred up, by the War. Don't make me do this, John Taylor."

"I don't want to do it either," I said. "I'm scared, just like you. But if I can get to Shadows Fall, there's a chance I can stop all this."

"You promise?"

"I promise," I lied.

The train left the Nightside, gathering speed.

The badlands were very bad, now. In the places that lay between places the train was attacked over and over again, in defiance of all old pacts, customs and protections. At first it was only loud noises, and the occasional buffet as the train hit something on the tracks that shouldn't have been there, but then something hit the outside of the carriage I was travelling in, something big enough and heavy enough that the impact made a sizeable dent in the reinforced steel wall. I sat up straight, jerked out of the half doze I'd fallen into in spite of myself. Something hit the carriage again, and again; first from this side, then from that, and it even stomped about on the roof for a while, leaving deep dimples in the steel. The blows grew harder, and the indentations grew deeper, the steel forced inwards by the impact. I stood up, feeling my muscles creak, and moved to the aisle between the rows of seats, just in case.

The carriage wall on my left cracked open, splitting apart, a long, jagged rent stretching from floor to ceiling. For the first time I heard voices from outside, saying *Let us in! Let us in!* There was nothing human in those voices, nothing so small. They sounded like mountains crashing together, like old gods grown senile and vicious. The rent in the steel wall slowly widened, as something forced it open from outside. And through the rent, filling the gap from top to bottom, I saw a single huge monstrous eye, somehow keeping pace with the speeding train, staring in at me. And there was nothing in its fixed gaze but an awful, malicious madness.

I made myself walk towards the terrible eye, staring right back into that monstrous gaze, and when I was close enough I punched the eye as hard as I could. There was a scream like an insane steam whistle, and the eye was suddenly gone. Outside the rent in the wall there was only darkness, and an air so cold just a moment's exposure left hoarfrost on my face. There were no more voices, and no more pounding on the carriage walls.

The train kept going, and we left that place behind. The new silence had a weight all its own, as though it was but a precursor for something even worse. I didn't feel like sitting down, so I paced up and down the narrow aisle, peering out of the long rent now and again. A strange unearthly light streamed suddenly into the carriage as we entered another phase, another dimension. The light grew increasingly harsh and bright, until it burned my exposed skin where it touched, and I was forced to retreat from it. Thin shafts of the fierce light stabbed through unsuspected smaller rents in the walls and ceiling, and I was hard put to avoid them all.

From outside came sounds of a kind I couldn't place or recognise. They reminded me most of birds made of machinery, and the sound grated on my nerves like fingernails on the blackboard of my soul. The exterior atmosphere began seeping in through the jagged steel rent, driven by the greater pressure outside. It smelled like crushed nettles, thick and choking. It burned inside my mouth and nose, and I backed away from the crack in the wall, fighting an urge to vomit. I yelled for the train to go faster and curled up in a ball on the floor.

We left that place for somewhere else, and slowly the poison in the air diminished, left behind with the awful trip-hammer songs of mechanical birds. New air built up, flat and stale, from the carriage's reserves. I gulped it down anyway and slowly uncurled from my protective ball. My hands and face were still smarting from their brief exposure to the fierce light. I sank down onto the nearest seat, slumped and almost boneless. Too much was happening too quickly, even for me, with never a chance to rest. So tired . . . I think I'd have sold my soul for a good night's sleep.

Luckily, no-one was listening.

I looked up sharply as the quality of air in the carriage suddenly improved. Light from a bright summer's day came flooding in through the jagged rent in the wall, bringing with it new sweet air, rich in oxygen. It was hot and humid, thick with perfume, like the crushed petals of a thousand different flowers. The extra oxygen made me feel light-headed, and I grinned stupidly as I took in one deep breath after another. I got up and wandered over to the rent in the carriage wall, and that was when a hundred heavy vines with barbed thorns thrust their way into the carriage from outside. Decorated here and there with thick pulpy flowers like sucking mouths, they lashed around, thrashing and coiling with dreadful energy.

More and more of the vines forced their way in, twisting around each other, flailing back and forth in the confined space, taking up more and more of the carriage while I backed cautiously away. My feet made a scuffing sound on the grilled floor, and immediately every vine reached out in my direction. The flowered mouths screamed shrilly, a vile hungry sound. I cut at the nearest vine with the Kandarian sacrificial dagger Cathy gave me for my last birthday, and the slender blade sheared right through the vine, thorns and all. All the flowered mouths howled with rage and pain. The severed vine bled a clear oozing sap, and the stumpy end just kept coming after me. Half the carriage was full of the roiling, thrashing vines now, and more were forcing their way in, widening the steel rent in the process.

I slashed open one of the leather seats with my dagger, pulled out a handful of stuffing, and set fire to it with a basic elemental spell I normally only use for lighting friends' cigarettes. The stuffing flared up eagerly, yellow flames leaping high in the oxygen-rich air. I tossed the blazing mass into the midst of the crashing vines, and a dozen caught alight all at once. The pulpy flower mouths screamed in unison as the fire spread quickly through the vegetable mass. All the untouched vines whipped back out the rent, leaving the others to burn and die. The flowers howled like damned souls as they burned.

Thick black smoke filled the carriage. The vines and flowers were all dead, but they'd spread the fire to the carriage seats. The train screamed through its hidden speakers as flames took hold of the carriage. I yelled back at the train to keep going, then had to break off as a harsh coughing fit from the smoke took hold of me. I backed away from the growing inferno and crouched on the floor where the air was still clearest. Thick tears ran down my face from my smarting eyes. I couldn't see anything, but I could hear the roar of the fire drawing closer.

And then the whole carriage shook and shuddered as the train ground to a sudden halt. The carriage door cracked itself open, a few inches at a time, while I crawled towards it on my hands and knees. I forced the door open the last of the way with the last of my strength, and half fell out of the carriage, my lungs straining for air, my eyes blurred with tears. I could feel a hard floor underneath me, and I crawled forward, away from the smoke and fire. I heard the carriage door straining to close behind me, then the train sped off, heading for sanctuary. Its roar faded slowly away, along with its telepathic screams in my mind. Poor thing. Still, needs must when your mother drives. I lay there on the hard floor, shaking with reaction, waiting for my lungs and head to clear. Hoping I'd made it all the way to Shadows Fall.

I finally sat up and looked around me. I wasn't on any train platform. I got to my feet, a little unsteadily. The train had dropped me off at a huge, old-fashioned Hall, with towering wood-panelled walls and a raftered ceiling uncomfortably high overhead. The Hall stretched away to my left and to my right for as far as my smarting eyes could see, and it was wide enough to hold a football game in. The sheer size and scale of the Hall should have made it seem overpowering, but somehow it wasn't. If anything, it felt almost . . . cosy. Like coming home, after too long away from family and loved ones. The light was a cheerful golden glow, though there didn't seem to be any obvious source for it. And no shadows anywhere. No windows either, or doors, and no portraits or decorations on the walls. Only a single stone fireplace, right in front of me, with a banked and quietly crackling fire, as though it had been set just for me. It seemed to me that I could hear a great wind blowing, outside. Something about that sound made me shudder, though I couldn't say why.

I knew where it was. What it had to be. I'd done a lot of reading about Shadows Fall. Most people in the Nightside have, because Shadows Fall is the only place on this earth that's stranger, more glamorous and more dangerous than the Nightside. The place where legends go to die, when the world stops believing in them. Or perhaps when they stop believing in themselves . . . And since the world has believed in some pretty strange things in its time, and because not everything that comes to Shadows Fall is ready to lie down and die just yet, this little town in the back of beyond can be scarier than anything you'll find in the Nightside. We all read everything we can find about Shadows Fall. If only because we have a sneaking suspicion we might end up here someday.

I was in the Gallery of Bone, in All Hallows' Hall. The house at the heart of the world. The place where Time lives.

On the mantelpiece over the fireplace, there was a simple clock set in the stomach of a big black bakelite cat. As the clock ticked, the cat's red tongue went in and out, and its eyes went back and forth. It looked like something you'd win at a cheap carnival. Standing on either side of the cat were stylised silver figures of a lion and a unicorn. And on either side of them, a series of small carved figures that made me think of chess pieces, though they clearly weren't. I moved forward, for a closer look.

They were carved out of a clear, almost translucent wood, and I had no difficulty in recognising who the figures were. Razor Eddie, Dead Boy, Walker, Shotgun Suzie. I wondered if I kept looking . . . would I find one of me? I deliberately turned my back on the figures, and found that the centre of the floor was now taken up with a huge old-fashioned hourglass. It was easily a foot taller than I, and two feet in diameter, with sparkling clear glass supported by more of the strange translucent wood. Most of the sand had fallen through, from the upper glass to the lower, and something about that made me feel very sad.

I walked slowly round the massive hourglass, and met someone coming the other way, even though I was sure no-one else there when I started. I stopped short, and so did she, and we regarded each other suspiciously for a while. Tall and almost painfully slender, with long cords of muscle on her bare arms, she was a teenage punk, in battered black leathers adorned with studs and chains, over a grubby white T-shirt and faded blue jeans. Her hair was a spiky black Mohawk, shaved high at the sides, and her face was almost hidden behind lashings of black and white makeup. A safety pin pierced one ear, while a rusty razor blade dangled from the other. Her eyes were fierce, her black-lipped mouth a snarl. She glared at me, two large fists resting on her hips. She had HATE tattooed on both sets of knuckles.

"I'm Mad," she announced abruptly, in a deep harsh voice.

"Of course you are," I said, keeping my voice calm and soothing.

"It's short for Madeleine, you divot!" She brought up her right hand,

and suddenly there was a flick-blade in it, the blade snapping out with a nasty-sounding click. I think I was supposed to be impressed, but then, I knew Razor Eddie. And Shotgun Suzie. The punk girl snarled at me. "What are you smirking at? You think I won't use this? This is Time's house. I look after him, because, well . . . someone has to. Otherwise, he goes wandering . . . Look, we don't like unexpected, uninvited visitors, so you can just turn around and go straight back where you came from. Or there's going to be trouble."

"Actually, I'm afraid I'm stuck here," I said. "I came by train. From the Nightside."

She sniffed loudly. "That shit-hole? I wouldn't go there on a bet."

"Yes, well, a lot of people have been known to feel that way, but . . . I really do need to speak to Old Father Time."

"Well he doesn't need to see you, so piss off, before I decide to start cutting lumps off you."

I thought for a moment. "Is there anyone else I could talk to?"

"No! I'm Mad!"

"Yes, we've already established that . . . Is there perhaps someone who looks after you, makes sure you don't hurt yourself, that sort of thing?"

"Right! That's it! You're going back to the Nightside inside thirty-seven chutney jars!"

I think we were both about to do something unfortunate at that point, so it's just as well Old Father Time finally decided to make himself known. He appeared out of nowhere, looking exactly the way I remembered him from our last encounter in the Time Tower. A tall gaunt man in his late fifties, dressed to the height of Victorian fashion. Julien Advent would have loved it. Time wore a long black frock coat of a most severe cut, over severely tailored grey trousers, and, except for the gold watch chain stretched across his waistcoat, the only splash of colour in his outfit was the apricot cravat at his throat. He was handsome enough, in an old-fashioned way, with a determined chin held high, a steely smile, and old old eyes. A thinning mane of long white hair had been brushed back from a noble brow, and left to lie where it fell. An air of quiet authority hung about him like an old comfortable cloak, only slightly undermined by a certain vagueness in his gaze.

"It's all right, Madeleine," he said calmly. "I know who this is. I've been expecting him. Now go and find something useful to do, there's a dear, while I tell this gentleman things he almost certainly doesn't want to hear."

Madeleine sniffed loudly again, and made her flick knife disappear. "Well, that's something, I suppose. Are you sure you can trust him?"

"Absolutely not, but it's been that sort of a day for several centuries now."

Madeleine walked around the hourglass and disappeared, leaving Time and me alone in the great Hall. He smiled briefly as he looked down at himself.

"I really should change this image for something more appropriate. I am a Transient Being, after all . . . but so many of you seem to find this appearance comforting, these days. I think I know why, and the Travelling Doctor has a lot to answer for . . ."

"Quite," I said, because you have to say something, into pauses like that. "I'm sorry to intrude, but . . ."

"Yes, yes, my boy, I know. Lilith has come to the Nightside at last, and it's all falling apart at the seams. But unfortunately, I can't intervene. I can't help you. No-one can."

"Ah." Not what I wanted to hear. "I came here because . . ."

"Oh I know why you're here, John Taylor. I know what you want from me. I've got it right here. But you won't like it."

He gestured vaguely with his left hand, and there floating on the air between us was a small black case with a dull matte surface. The lid rose up on its own, revealing the Speaking Gun, lying nestled in bloodred velvet. It lay there quietly, for the moment, the ugliest gun ever made. Just looking at it made me feel as though a mad dog had just entered the Hall. The Gun had been fashioned from meat, from flesh and bone, with dark-veined gristle and shards of cartilage, all held together with strips of colourless skin. Living tissues, shaped into a killing tool. Thin slabs of bone made up the handle, held in place by tightly stretched skin with a hot sweaty look. The trigger was a long canine tooth. The red meat of the barrel gleamed wetly. I wondered just how much of my mother's body had gone into making this awful thing, this Speaking Gun. Up close, the ancient weapon smelled like an animal in heat. And I could hear it, breathing, in its case.

"I really don't care for the thought of such a powerful weapon, in the hands of the infamous John Taylor," Old Father Time said sharply. "Far too much temptation for any mortal. Let alone you. But . . . I'm going to give it to you anyway." He looked briefly at the huge hourglass. "Partly because time is running out for the Nightside. Partly because try as I might, I can't seem to find anyone else more fitting to give it to . . . But mostly because a future version of myself came back in time to tell me to give it to you, and I really wish I wouldn't do things like that to myself."

The lid of the case snapped shut, and the black box dropped unceremoniously into my hands. Time sighed heavily, shook his head, and snapped his fingers. And all at once, I was somewhere else.

THIRTEEN

Mother Love

I was back in the Nightside, in Time Tower Square, and my first thought was how quiet and peaceful everything was. I looked slowly around me, and no-one looked back. The mobs and monsters had all moved on, probably because there was nothing left in the Square to destroy, and no-one left to kill. The buildings were fire-blackened frameworks, collapsed inwards or outwards, cracked stone and broken bricks. There were bodies lying everywhere, men and women and others so damaged or torn apart it was impossible to tell who or what they might have been originally. They looked like so many broken toys someone had got tired of playing with. Nothing moved, anywhere. There weren't even any rats nosing among the bodies. Maybe they'd all been killed, too. Out beyond the Square, the War was still going on, in the distance. I could hear faint cries and roars and explosions, and now and again there'd be a sudden surge of light, pushing back the darkness. But the Square was still, and silent.

I couldn't help thinking of the devastated future Nightside I'd seen so many times. The dead lands, the broken world, and all because of me. A future that insisted on edging nearer, no matter how hard I worked to push it away, becoming more real, more imminent, detail by detail. Maybe some futures are inevitable, after all.

I slowly became aware of a soft, repetitive sound, and I looked round to see my mother, Lilith, sitting at her ease on the pile of rubble that was all she'd left of the Time Tower. In her large colourless hands she held a severed human head. Its face had been ripped away, leaving only a bloody mess, but that didn't seem to bother her. She was pulling out the teeth, one at a time and tossing them aside. And all the time her black mouth was moving silently, saying *He loves me, he loves me not* . . . She looked up abruptly and stared right into my eyes. She smiled brightly and rose to her feet, casually throwing the head to one side.

"John, darling! My most treasured son . . ."

"Don't move any closer," I said. "I'm armed. I have the Speaking Gun."

"Of course you have, sweetie. That's why I'm here."

She walked towards me. I held the black box up where she could see it, and she stopped just out of reach. She was calm, collected, utterly at her ease, and a slow anger burned within me. I gestured roughly at the bodies, at the wrecked buildings, at the War still going on in the distance.

"How could you do all this?"

She shrugged easily. "It's mine. I made it. I'll do what I want with it."

"Where are your children?" I said. "All your monstrous offspring? Where are your precious followers, your madmen and murderers?"

"Keeping themselves busy. I don't need them here. I thought it was time you and I had a nice little chat, in private."

I frowned, as something else occurred to me. "How did you know to find me here? Even I didn't know I was going to be here."

She nodded at the flat black case in my hands. "The Speaking Gun called to me. I always know where it is. It is flesh of my flesh, after all, and as such my child, every bit as much as you. It's your brother, John, in every way that matters. Thank you for bringing it back to me. I have a use for it. Just as I have a use for you."

I opened the black box, snatched out the Speaking Gun and pointed it at Lilith. She didn't flinch, or back away. I let the box fall to the ground as the Speaking Gun thrust its poisonous presence into my thoughts. It felt hot and sweaty in my hand, and burned like a fever in my mind, vicious and raging, like an attack dog tugging at its leash. It breathed wetly in my hand, wanting to be used. It needed to kill, to destroy, to tear down the whole world and everything that lived in it. The Speaking Gun hated, but it couldn't operate without someone else to pull its trigger, and it hated that most of all. Its filthy thoughts wormed through my mind, stoking the anger and outrage it found there . . . but I had felt its corrupting nature before, and I fought it back. I hadn't come this far to bow down to a spiteful machine.

And yet, even under its madness and its rage, I could feel the Speaking Gun yearning for my mother's touch. It wanted to go to her and nestle in her hand, and do terrible, awful things for her. I gripped the Gun so tightly my whole hand ached, and never once took my gaze off Lilith. She laughed soundlessly at me, and took a step forward. I aimed the Speaking Gun carefully, and pulled the trigger.

And nothing happened.

I tried again and again, but the long canine tooth that served as the

Speaking Gun's trigger wouldn't budge. I shook the Gun, and even hit it with my other hand, but it did no good. In my mind, I could hear it laughing.

"The Speaking Gun won't work on me, John," Lilith said calmly. "It will never operate against the wishes of its creator. Just a little safeguard I had built into it, back at the Beginning. It loves me, you know. It aches to serve me, and make me happy. Such a good son . . . Unlike you. Give me the Gun, John. It was never meant for you. And in my hands it will re-speak your most secret name and remake you into the respectful, obedient son I always intended you to be."

She held out her hand, and the Speaking Gun jerked in my grasp, as though desperate to go to the one who would let it do what it had always wanted to do.

I couldn't let her take the Gun. So I raised my gift, and forced it to find the one way in which the Speaking Gun could be destroyed. The answer was simple: by making it speak its own secret name backwards, and uncreate itself. My gift fought me, and the Gun fought me, but I had come a long way in the past few years, down a long hard road, perhaps to prepare me for moments like this. I bent all my will and all of my soul against the gift and the Gun, beating them down step by step and inch by inch, until finally the Speaking Gun choked out a single awful sound, then howled in despair as its very existence was reversed and undone. Uncreated.

My hand was suddenly empty, and I staggered and almost fell, wiped out by such a tremendous effort. I felt as though I'd just lifted a mountain with my bare hands, and turned it over on its side. Lilith grunted suddenly with surprise, and clapped one hand to her bare side. I studied her warily, but she just smiled back at me.

"Why thank you, John. For returning my flesh and bone to me. I'd forgotten how much I missed that rib till I had it back again. You always give your mother the best presents."

"The Speaking Gun is gone," I said. "You can't remake me without it, which means you can't remake the Nightside. So, it's over. Your precious scheme is dead in the water. Stand down your armies. This isn't your Nightside any more. You don't belong here. Just . . . go away, and leave us alone."

But she was already smiling and shaking her head. "You always did think too small, John. The Speaking Gun was never that important to me. It was just there to make things easier for you. It would have been a more . . . merciful method, that's all. Now I'll just have to do it the hard way. And don't you dare cry. You brought this on yourself. The Speaking Gun was never intended to be my main weapon against the Nightside, John. That was, and is, you. That is why I gave birth to you, after all."

"What?" I said. My mind was numb, from too many reverses. "I don't understand . . ."

"Of course you don't. I arranged for you to inherit one particular gift from me, John, so I could make use of it when the time was right. I will make you do what you were born to do. I will make you use your gift to find for me the perfect form of the Nightside, the original uncontaminated model that I always intended it to be, and when you've found that for me I will enforce that version on all the world."

"I won't do it," I said. I tried to look away from her, from her deep dark eyes, and couldn't. "I won't do that!"

"You don't have any choice, sweetie. I decided your fate before you were even born, working on you while you were still forming in my womb. All through the first few years of your childhood, I built a geas deep within your mind, so I'd be able to use it in this place, on this day. A geas to bend your will to mine. That's why you've never been able to re-member your early years with me. It became necessary for me to leave the dear bosom of my family before I was quite finished with you, but there's enough there to do the job. I can see it, squirming deep in your mind, wrapped around your soul."

"You do love the sound of your own voice, don't you?" I said. *Never let them see they've got you rattled . . .* "Why didn't my gift tell me any of this, when I questioned it earlier?"

"Because it's not your gift, it's mine. I gave it to you, to do my will." She pirouetted slowly, arms outstretched, mistress of all she surveyed, smiling like a cat with a small bird in its jaws. "Time to redecorate, I think. The old place has become terribly infested. I will spread my Night-side across all the Earth, freeing it from the influence of Heaven and Hell. I'll steal the world away from both those Tyrants, and make the Earth my playground, for all time. And everything that lives on it, including Hu-manity, that bothersome breed, will be swept aside and replaced with something more to my liking. Including you, my dearest boy. You'll be so much happier when I've remade you in my own true image. You will kneel at my feet and sing my praises through all eternity. Won't that be nice? A mother and her son, together, forever."

And I had just destroyed the Speaking Gun, the only weapon that might have stopped her.

Unless . . . the last time I went face-to-face with Lilith, long and long ago, back at the very creation of the Nightside, I'd found a way to hurt and weaken her. I grinned nastily, inside. I'm John Taylor. I always have one more trick up my sleeve. I fired up my gift, driving it ruthlessly with the last of my will, and used it to find the link between my mother and me.

The physical, mental, and magical connections between a mother and her only son. A trick I'd used before, to drain the life energy right out of her.

But when I reached out through the link, she was right there waiting for me. Her will slammed through the link, slapping me aside, monstrously strong and utterly overpowering. I cried out and fell to my knees as she drained the life energy out of me, despite everything I could do to stop her. She smiled down at me.

"You didn't really expect to catch me with the same trick twice, did you? Not when I've had so many years to think about this day, this moment, planning it all down to the very last detail . . . Poor boy. This isn't your story, John; it's mine. Time to start your makeover, I think. And then what fun we'll have, tearing down everything you ever believed in. Open wide and say aaah! John. It'll only hurt for a moment . . ."

FOURTEEN

The Things We Sacrifice, For Love

Time slowed, cranking down to a crawl. The hand Lilith was extending towards me ground to a halt, inches short of my face. Her voice became a long growl and then cut off abruptly as the Collector appeared out of nowhere, in an improbable device. Trust him to bring Time itself to a stop, just so he could make an entrance. The Collector, con man, thief, and snapper up of anything collectible that wasn't actually nailed down or guarded by enraged wolverines. An old acquaintance of mine, but not what you could call a friend. I don't think the Collector had friends any more. They got in the way of his collecting.

A portly middle-aged man with a florid face, the Collector was currently wearing a stylish dark blue blazer with white piping, and a large badge on his lapel bearing the number six. He was crouching inside a strange contraption that hovered uncomfortably close above my head. It looked like an overcomplicated climbing frame, made up of long quartz-and-crystal rods that sparked and shimmered against the night sky. The whole framework couldn't have been more than ten feet wide, but there was something more to it, as though it extended away in more than just the usual three dimensions. The air was thick with the smell of discharging ozone.

The Collector reached down out of his contraption and grabbed the collar of my trench coat. He hauled me up into the framework with him, and immediately I could move again. I grabbed at the nearest rods to steady myself, and they squirmed unpleasantly in my grasp as though they weren't fully there. I wasn't entirely sure whether I might have been dragged out of the frying pan and into the fire. The Collector has always been famous for not being on any side but his own. Below us, Lilith was slowly turning her head to look in our direction.

"Shit," said the Collector, "the field's collapsing. Brace yourself, Taylor, we are out of here!"

He wrapped both his plump hands around a control like a fragmented crystal flower, and the whole structure tilted sideways through space. Time Tower Square disappeared abruptly as we spun round and round, dimensions of space snapping in and out of focus. I tried closing my eyes, but it didn't help. I was sensing the movement on some basic spiritual level, and my stomach really hated it. I clung desperately to the crystal rods, which seemed to be deliberately trying to slip out of my grasp. I could still hear Lilith's voice, screaming *No* . . . in a howl that seemed to go on forever. The crystal contraption actually buckled under the force of her rage, and solid crystal rods cracked and shattered. The Collector fussed over his controls, swearing and blaspheming, and suddenly the whole device crashed to a halt, and I fell out of it into Strangefellows bar.

I sat there for a long moment, enjoying the solid support of a floor that stayed still, then I hauled myself painfully slowly to my feet. I don't know when I've ever felt so tired. I looked across at the Collector, who was walking round and round his crystal contraption and cursing loudly as bits fell off it. He actually chattered with rage and kicked spitefully at the pieces on the floor.

"Bloody thing! I'll never get another one like this! Not after the extra security they've installed since my last visit . . . This trip had better have been worth it, Henry!"

Walker strolled over to pat him soothingly on the shoulder. "Leave strategy to me, Mark. You know I've always been the devious one. You never did explain. What is this thing, exactly?"

"Well, originally it was a four-dimensional climbing frame for really gifted children in the thirtieth century. I acquired it when no-one was looking, and adapted it for interdimensional travel. Not as accurate as some of my other Time travel mechanisms, but just basically wired to sneak in and catch Lilith by surprise. And now look at it! I'd better get compensation for this, Henry."

"I'll see you're provided with the correct forms," Walker said briskly. "And how are we, Taylor?"

"We feel like shit," I said, collapsing into the nearest chair. "Why did you send that creep to rescue me?"

"Because you were obviously incapable of rescuing yourself, you ungrateful little turd!" snapped the Collector. "We watched you talking with Lilith through one of Merlin's visions, once he detected your reappearance, and a right balls up you were making of it. So Henry sent me in as the cavalry. And if you're wondering why someone of my good sense has joined this doomed resistance, reluctantly and very much against my better judgement, I can only put it down to emotional blackmail."

"I simply pointed out that if Lilith has her way with the Nightside, there will be nothing left to collect," said Walker.

"Bloody vandal!" said the Collector. "I haven't spent the best part of my life putting together the greatest collection of treasures and wonders in this or any other universe, just so the Great White Bitch can wipe it all out. Women never appreciate the true value of collectibles . . ."

"I knew you'd come, if I asked," said Walker. "What are old friends for?"

The Collector looked at him coldly. "Don't push it, Henry. We haven't been friends for over twenty years, and you know it. You've been doing your best to have me arrested, ever since that unfortunate incident over the dome of St. Paul's Cathedral. Hell, I haven't seen you in the flesh since Charles's funeral." He looked at me, then back at Walker. His voice softened, just a little. "You've got old, Henry. Respectable."

"You got fat."

I left them to their somewhat prickly reunion, forced myself up out of my chair, and stumbled over to the bar. Lilith had taken a lot out of me. Alex was in his usual place behind the bar and actually had a large wormwood brandy waiting for me. He'd put a little umbrella in it, just because he knew I hated them. He didn't want me to think he was getting soft. I threw the umbrella away, took a long drink, and nodded gratefully to him. He nodded back. We've never been very demonstrative.

"Did any of my people make it back here?" I said finally.

"Only me," said Suzie Shooter.

I turned around, and there she was. Shotgun Suzie, her black leathers almost falling apart from tears and slashes, and soaked with dried blood. Her bandoliers were empty of bullets, and all the grenades were gone from her belt. Even her shotgun was missing from its holster on her back. She half sat, half collapsed onto the bar stool beside me, and Alex put a bottle of gin in front of her. I was too tired to do more than smile at her, to show how glad I was to see her still alive, and she nodded in return.

"You should have seen the shape she was in, when she came back without you," said Alex. "Took three of my best repair spells to put her back together again. I put them on your tab, Taylor. Though given the way things are going, maybe you should settle up now, while there's still time."

"I broke my shotgun," said Suzie, ignoring Alex with the ease of long practice. "Had to use it as a club when I ran out of ammo. And I left my best stiletto in some bastard's eye. All my weapons are gone. I feel naked."

"How did you make it back here, through all those mobs?" I asked.

"A variety of blunt instruments and a whole lot of bad temper," said Suzie.

"Have you seen any of the others?"

"No," said Suzie, staring at her bottle of gin without touching it. "But Dead Boy was dead to begin with, and Razor Eddie's a god. I wouldn't be surprised to see either of them stroll back in here, eventually."

"But not Tommy Oblivion," I said.

"No. His brother Larry went out to look for him, as soon as he heard what happened. No-one's heard anything from him since."

"Julien Advent is out and about," said Alex. "Supposedly pulling Walker's remaining people together into an army, for one last desperate assault on Lilith's forces."

"No!" I said. I pushed myself away from the bar, and stalked over to confront Walker. He deliberately ignored me, continuing his talk with the Collector, so I grabbed him by the shoulder and hauled him around. I don't know which of us was more surprised. It had been a long time since anyone had dared treat Walker like that. "You can't fight Lilith's army with an army of your own," I said, as forcefully as I could. "You'll destroy the Nightside, fighting over it. Nobody wins. I've seen it."

"You're sure of this?" said Walker.

"Oh yes. I've talked to people in the future, people who lived through it. They were the only ones left. You'd know some of the names if I said them, but trust me on this, Walker, you really don't want to know. Believe me, you can't win this with an army."

"Then what do you suggest?" said Walker, and I swear his voice was just as calm and courteous and civilised as ever, even though I'd just kicked away his last hope. "What else can we do, except fight?"

"You have to do something," said Merlin, his voice just a harsh rasp. "And you'd better do it soon. My defences are under constant attack. I don't know how much longer I can maintain them."

I looked round. I'd actually overlooked the ancient sorcerer, sitting slumped and alone at a table in the corner. He looked very old and very tired, even for a fifteen-hundred-year-old corpse. His grey face was slack, the crimson flames barely stirring in his empty eye-sockets.

"Keeping Lilith out, holding her off, is taking everything I've got," Merlin said, not even looking at me. "It's draining me dry, Taylor. I need my heart. There's still time. Find my stolen heart for me, bring it here, and put it back in my chest, and I could be a Power again. I could bring myself back to life, wrap myself in glory, and go out to face Lilith head to head."

"I don't think so," I said. "You are Satan's only begotten son, born to be the Antichrist. I won't risk loosing that on the Nightside."

"That's right, blame me for my family background! You of all people should know that we aren't always our parent's children. Do you want me to beg, Taylor? Then I'll beg! Not for me, but for the Nightside. For all of us."

"I can't do it," I said. "I know where your heart is. And there's no way I can get it for you."

"Then we're all dead," said Merlin. "Dead and damned."

"Look, if he can't protect me, then I'm getting the hell out of here." said the Collector. "Come on, Henry, I only agreed to come here because you assured me this bar was safer than any of my bolt-holes. I only agreed to rescue Taylor because you said he was vital to our survival."

"Shut the hell up," I said, feeling the anger build within me. "You don't get to complain, Collector. Not when all of this is your fault anyway! You made possible the Babalon Working that brought Lilith back out of Limbo! You put my father together with my mother and made me possible!"

The Collector wouldn't meet my eyes. "I was misled," he said finally. "I thought I was doing the right thing."

"Leave Mark alone," said Walker, moving forward to stand beside the Collector. "We all thought we were doing the right thing, back then. Including your father. We never meant for any of this to happen. . . . You're looking at me strangely, John. What is it?"

"I've just had an idea," I said. I could feel my smile spreading into a broad grin, and suddenly I didn't feel tired any more. "I'm John Taylor, remember? I always have one more trick up my sleeve. And this one's a beauty! There is a way to stop Lilith that doesn't involve fighting. All we have to do is put together the three men who originally summoned Lilith through the Babalon Working, have them restart the spell, then reverse it, sending Lilith back into Limbo! The door you created with the Working is still open, isn't it?"

"Well, yes," said Walker. "We never got the chance to close it. By the time we realised the door hadn't shut itself, the three of us had separated, determined never to work together again. It wasn't as if the door mattered; it was only slightly ajar, undetectable except to the three of us. No-one else could use it. Lilith's entrance had attuned it to her, and her only."

"But the three of you working together could restart the magic," I said. "Push the door all the way open, force Lilith through it, into Limbo, then close the door after her! It would work! Wouldn't it?"

"Technically, yes," said the Collector, frowning. "Though one of us would have to go through the door with Lilith, to make sure she couldn't open it again from the other side, until we closed the doorway. And whoever went through . . . would be trapped with Lilith in Limbo, for all eternity. So you needn't look at me. I have far too much to live for. And I never got on with her anyway, even when she was only Charles's wife."

"You never did understand about duty," said Walker. "I'll do it."

"No," I said. "I'll go. You know it has to be me."

"No it doesn't!" said Suzie, almost savagely. "Why does it always have to be you, John? Haven't you done enough?"

"This is all, unfortunately, quite irrelevant," said Walker. "It's a good plan, John, but there's no way we can make it work. It took the three of us to establish the Babalon Working, and only the three of us could hope to restart it. And your father is dead, John."

"Not any more," I said. "Lilith raised the dead in the Necropolis graveyard, remember? Brought them all back to life and sent them out into the Nightside." I could see the light of understanding dawning in everyone's eyes. "He's out there, somewhere. My father. Charles Taylor. And who's better suited to find him than me?"

I forced my gift awake, and it showed me a vision of my returned father. He was doing research in the Prospero and Michael Scott Memorial Library, rooting through the ruins and collecting books from overturned stacks. He piled the books up on a desk, and searched desperately through each volume, looking for . . . something. I studied him for a while. He didn't look much older than I was. In fact, he looked a lot like me. I took hold of Walker's and the Collector's hands, so they could see him, too.

"Typical Charles," said the Collector, almost wistfully. "He never could abide taking orders from anyone. Including, it would seem, an ex-wife who brought him back from the dead. She should have known he'd go his own way."

"I don't think she knows about him," said Walker. "She's got other things on her mind, just now."

"What's he doing, burying himself in books when the world's coming to and end?" said the Collector.

"Doing what he always does," said Walker. "Research. He's looking for answers."

I looked back at Merlin. "Open a door for me, between here and there. I need to talk to my father."

The dead sorcerer scowled at me. "If I remove my concentration from the bar's defences, even for a moment, Lilith will know what's happening here."

"Let her," I said. "All that matters now is getting these three old friends back together. So they can put right their old wrong."

"God, you sound like your father sometimes," said the Collector. "He could be a right pain in the arse on occasion, too."

Merlin gestured angrily with an unsteady hand, and the Library vision became real as an opening appeared in space, linking the bar with the Library. My father was so immersed in his books he didn't even notice. I stepped carefully through the opening into the Library and coughed meaningfully. My father scrambled up out of his chair and backed away from me, holding a heavy paperweight like a weapon. I slowly raised my hands, to show they were empty.

"Take it easy," I said. "I'm not here to hurt you. I need your help."

Charles Taylor studied me suspiciously, then put the paperweight down on the desk. "You look familiar. Do I know you?"

It hit me harder than I'd expected, to hear my father's voice again after so many years. It made him real again, in a way just the sight of him hadn't. I lowered my hands, and suddenly I didn't know what to say. Too many things I wanted to tell him, needed to tell him, but I couldn't find the words.

"How did you find me here?" he said. "You don't have the look of one of Lilith's creatures. Though I'm sure I've seen you somewhere before . . . but it doesn't matter. I can't help you. You'll have to leave. I'm very busy."

"You know me," I said. "Though it's been a long time. I'm John. I'm your son, John."

"My God," he said, and he sat down suddenly on his chair, as though all the strength had gone out of his legs. "John . . . Look at you . . . All grown-up. You look . . . a lot like my father. Your grandfather. Of course, you never knew him . . ."

"You went away," I said. I tried to keep the anger out of my voice, but that only made it sound even colder. "Abandoned me to my Enemies, when I was just a child. You left me alone when I needed you the most. You drank yourself to death rather than raise me. Why?"

Charles sighed heavily. He looked at his books, as though for answers, and then he made himself look back at me. "You have to understand . . . I'd been betrayed so many times: by friends I thought I could trust, by the woman I believed loved me. Your mother . . . was my last chance. To be a man again, to be sane again. To do good work, work that mattered. She was my life, my hope, my dreams. I never loved anyone like I loved her. When Pew told me the truth, showed me the hard evidence . . . I almost killed him. I went looking for her, but she was already gone. Just as well. I don't know what I would have done . . . And you, John, you'd meant so much to me, and now I was afraid you were a lie, too. Because if I couldn't depend on my wife to be my wife, if she wasn't even human . . . how could I depend on you to be my son? I was afraid you'd turn out to be a monster, like your mother."

"No," I said. "I'm nothing like my mother."

He smiled, and it was like a hand crushing my heart. I remembered that smile, from long ago, though I'd forgotten it till that moment.

"I've been reading about you, son. Reports of your old cases, in the *Night Times*. Quite the adventures, I gather. Helping people who couldn't help themselves, solving mysteries, bringing down the bad guys . . . I also read some of the editorial pieces, by Julien Advent. The great Victorian Adventurer. He doesn't seem too sure whether he approves of you, but he approves of what you achieved, and that's good enough for me. You've made yourself the hero I always meant to be, but life got in the way . . ."

"It's not too late," I said. "There is a way you can stop Lilith. Come with me. Two old friends are waiting to greet you."

He got up from his chair and stood before me. We were exactly the same height. Two men of roughly the same age, but with far more than our share of experience.

"There is a way?" he said. "Really?"

"I believe so."

"Then let's do it." He put a hesitant hand on my shoulder. "I'm sorry I let you down, son. Sorry . . . I wasn't strong enough."

"Everyone else let you down," I said. "They all lied to you. Betrayed you. That stops now."

"I read everything they had on you here," said Charles Taylor. "You've done well, in my absence. I'm proud of you, son."

"That's all I ever wanted," I said.

I think he would have hugged me then, but I wasn't ready for that. I still had to be strong. I led the way back through the opening, into the bar, and he came through after me. Merlin immediately shut the opening down. My father looked around him.

"My God, it's Strangefellows! Is this dump still going? Damn, I had some times here . . ."

"Yes, you did," Walker said dryly. "Though I seem to recall I always ended up having to foot the bill. You were famous in those days for never having your wallet on you."

My father turned round and looked at Walker, then at the Collector. He frowned, clearly uncertain, and then his face broke into a broad grin, and all three of them laughed. It was an open, happy laugh, blowing away all the old hurts and quarrels, and the three men fell on each other, clapping shoulders and backs with loud happy words. It was odd to see Charles Taylor looking so much younger than his contemporaries, but there was no denying how naturally they fit together. As though they belonged together, and always had. Eventually they stood back and studied each other.

"It's good to have you back, Charles," said Walker. "You're looking good. Being dead clearly agreed with you."

"I've missed you, Charles," said the Collector. "I really have. No-one could hold their own in an argument like you. So; what was it like, being dead?"

"I really don't remember," said Charles. "Probably just as well. But look at you . . . both of you! Henry . . . what happened? You look so distinguished! And you always swore you'd rather die than be trapped in a suit and tie, like all the other city drones. Are you really part of the Establishment these days?"

"Hell," said the Collector. "He is the Establishment."

"And Mark . . . Ten out of ten for style, but when did you get so fat?"

"Now don't you start," said the Collector. "Do you like the blazer? I got it from this retired secret agent. I got his weird car, too, while he was looking for his blazer. You have got to see my collection, when all this is over. I've acquired more fabulous junk and Kitsch than any man living!"

"I always knew you had it in you, Mark," my father said solemnly, and all three of them laughed.

"This is a new thing," Merlin said quietly to me. "Unforeseen and unexpected. Who knows what might come of this?"

"You never foresaw what's happening here?" I said.

"I don't think anyone ever foresaw this, boy! So many disparate elements needed, so many unlikely happenstances, to bring these three together again, after so many years. And all because of you, John Taylor."

"So," I said. "We have a chance now?"

"Oh no," said Merlin, turning away. "We're all still going to die, or be destroyed, along with the rest of the Nightside."

"The Babalon Working," said Charles Taylor, and I immediately paid attention again. My father was frowning thoughtfully. "Our greatest achievement, and our greatest crime. Do we really dare start it up again?"

"Do we have time?" said Walker. "Back then, it took us days to get the ritual up and working properly, nearly destroying ourselves in the process. And we were a lot younger and stronger and better prepared, back then."

"We don't need to go through the whole ritual again," the Collector said confidently. "You never did listen when I explained the theory of it, Henry. The magic is still operating in infraspace, because we never shut it down. It's hanging there, suspended at the moment we were interrupted. That's why the door we opened is still ajar. All we have to do is make contact with the magic again."

"And that should be easy enough," said Charles. "We're the only three keys that fit that lock."

"On the other hand," said the Collector, "a lot could go wrong. It's always dangerous, picking up an interrupted magic. We could all be killed."

"Dying would be vastly more pleasant than what Lilith has in store for us," said Walker.

"True," said the Collector. "And I think . . . I'd like a chance to be the man I used to be, one last time. Let's do it."

In the end, there was no need for any chalk circles, no chanting or invoking of spirits; the three old friends simply closed their eyes and concentrated, and a powerful presence filled the whole bar, beating on the air. There was a feeling of something caught on the edge, struggling to be free, to be finished. And after more than thirty years the three old friends stepped effortlessly back into their old roles, meshing like the parts of a powerful engine that had forgotten just how much it could do. Raw magic sparked and flared on the air around them, and the Babalon Working was up and running again, as though they'd never been away.

But almost immediately another presence forced its way into the bar, slamming through Merlin's defences. A door appeared in a wall where there had never been a door before, a ragged hole in the brickwork like a mouth or a wound, and stretched out beyond it was a narrow corridor, impossibly long. It led off in a direction I couldn't identify, which had nothing to do with left and right, up and down, that my mind couldn't deal with or accept, except simply as Outside. And down that awful corridor, slowly but inexorably, a single figure came walking. It was too far off in that unacceptable distance to see clearly, but I knew who it was, who it had to be. Lilith knew what we were up to, and she was coming to stop us.

Merlin came forward to stand before the corridor, staring down it and blocking the way. He looked . . . smaller, diminished. He raised his dead grey hands, already spotted with decay, and traced vivid shapes on the air, living sigils that spat and shimmered with discharging energies. He forced old and potent Words out of his ruined mouth, summoning up ancient forces and terrible creatures with the authority of his terrible name, but nothing happened. The Princes of Hell were more afraid of Lilith than they were of him. Merlin tried to open up interspatial trapdoors under Lilith's feet, to drop her into some other, dangerous dimension, that she'd have to fight her way back from . . . but Lilith just walked right over them, as though they weren't there. And perhaps for her, they weren't. She was Lilith, imprinted on the material world by an effort of her own will, and he was only a dead sorcerer. Step by step she drew nearer, smiling her awful smile, despite everything Merlin could do to stop her, or even slow her down. And, finally, she stepped out into the bar, and the corridor disappeared behind her, the wall just a wall again.

"Hello, Merlin," she said. "What a fuss you made. Anyone would think you weren't glad to see me. And after I went out of my way to find a nice present to bring you." She held up her left hand, and showed him a dark necrotic mass of muscle tissue. He knew what it was immediately, and made a sound as though he'd been hit. Lilith laughed prettily. "Yes, it's your long-lost heart, little sorcerer. That's what I've been doing all these years, since I had to give up being a wife and a mother. I knew I had to find your heart before you did, because you were the only one who might have stood a chance against me. If only you'd been whole. Merlin Satanspawn, born to be the Antichrist, but you didn't have the nerve. By the way, I spoke with your father recently, and he's still really mad at you."

"Give me my heart," said Merlin.

"It was very well hidden," said Lilith. "You wouldn't believe when and where I finally found it."

"What do you want from me?" said Merlin.

"That's more like it," said Lilith, smiling on Merlin like a teacher with a slow pupil. "You can have your heart back, Merlin. All you have to do is bow down to me, kneel at my feet, and vow on your unholy name to worship me all your days."

Merlin laughed abruptly, a flat ugly sound, and Lilith reacted as though he'd spat in her face. "Kneel to you?" said Merlin, and his voice was full of amused contempt. "I only ever knelt to one person. And you're not fit to polish his armour."

Lilith's left hand convulsed, crushing the decaying heart into crimson-and-purple pulp. Merlin cried out once and collapsed, the magic that had sustained him for centuries torn away in a moment. He curled up in a ball on the floor, withering and falling in on himself as the flesh fell away from his old bones. The fires in his eyes went out. Lilith took a bite out of the crushed heart and chewed thoughtfully.

"Tasty," she said. "Now die, fool, and go to the place appointed for you. Your daddy's waiting."

Merlin twitched and shuddered for a few moments more, but finally lay still, little more than a desiccated mummy. But I would swear that just before the end, I heard him say *Arthur?* So maybe he escaped his fate, after all. I'd like to think so.

Lilith looked unhurriedly about the bar. While I was still thinking what to do to distract her, and keep her from realising what three old acquaintances of hers were up to, Alex produced a pump-action shotgun from behind the bar, and handed it over to Suzie.

"Do something with this, Suzie. Avenge my ancestor. He might have been a pain in the arse, but he was family. The magazine holds silver bullets rubbed with garlic, napalm incendiaries spiked with holy water, and buckshot made from the ground-up bones of saints. Something in that mix ought to upset her. I find it works very well for crowd control on nights when the trivia quiz gets out of hand."

"Why, Alex," said Suzie, training the shotgun on Lilith, "I'm seeing you in a whole new light."

She fired the shotgun at Lilith again and again, working the pump action incredibly fast, emptying the whole magazine. And Lilith just stood there and took it, entirely unaffected. Suzie lowered the gun, and Lilith shook a finger at her admonishingly. She turned away to look at the three men working their magic, so wrapped up in what they were doing they hadn't even noticed her arrival. Lilith studied them for a moment, her head cocked on one side.

"What are you doing, you naughty boys? Some last desperate spell, to wish me away? It feels . . . familiar." She broke off, her face suddenly blank. "Henry? And Mark, and . . . Charles. Well, well . . . Dear husband. I'd forgotten they buried you in the Necropolis graveyard. Stop this nonsense and look at me, Charles. And let me tell you what I have in mind for our special, gifted, ungrateful son."

"Tell me," I said. "If you dare."

I strode right up to her, radiating poise and confidence and arrogance. I had to hold her attention, buy some time for the three to get their Working under control again. I glared right into Lilith's face, and she smiled back at me.

"You shouldn't have come here," I said. "This is my ground, my territory, and I am so much more, here. You think you can compel me to do your will and find you the Nightside you want? Let's see you try. Mommie Dearest."

"How sharper than a serpent's tooth it is, to bear a stupid child," said Lilith. "You will do whatever I want you to do, John. You don't have a choice. I saw to that long ago. So let's start with something simple. Make your mother happy, John. Kill your father."

Her words went right to the geas she'd planted deep in my mind. And braced though I was, all my mental shields in place, I still shuddered and almost collapsed. Because her little time bomb was set *inside* my shields . . . But still I stood my ground, refusing to move, refusing even to look at my father. I could feel her will taking hold of my body, my mind, pressing down on me like an unbearable weight. My hands knotted into fists so tight they ached, and I wouldn't, wouldn't move. Except I already was, my head turning slowly to look at my father despite everything I could do to stop it, the geas burning in my thoughts like a gleeful traitor. And then, suddenly, I wasn't alone in my head any more. Suzie was there, and Alex, adding the strength of their will to mine, holding me where I was.

Well, said Suzie. *This is different. Stand your ground, John, the cavalry's just arrived.*

How? I said.

I do know a little magic, Alex said smugly. *I am Merlin's descendant, after all. How do you think I've been able to run this bloody place, all these years?*

Shut up and concentrate, said Suzie.

So the three of us stood together, and we fought Lilith with all the strength of wills hardened by long lives of loss and hardship and adversity, honed by a refusal to give in to forces that should have broken us. Three old friends, closer now than ever, who cared more for each other than they'd ever been able to say. We stamped down the geas in my mind, breaking its hold over me through a concentrated effort of will, and it died screaming. Lilith's will slammed against us openly, like an ocean storm battering a single rock, but we would not yield.

Even though it was killing us, by inches. We had to tap into our life energies to power the magic that held us together, and even our combined energies were nothing compared to the resources Lilith had to draw on. We felt our lives draining away, felt the darkness closing in around us, but not one of us wavered. Suzie and Alex could have withdrawn, saved themselves, but it never even occurred to them. I was so proud of them.

We couldn't hope to hold Lilith off for long. We knew that. We were buying time, for three old friends to work their magic and open the door into Limbo. We were holding Lilith's attention, so she wouldn't understand what was happening until it was too late. She could have stopped them easily if she hadn't been so determined to break my spirit. But still we three were dying, and we knew it, and we didn't care. We were friends together, doing something that mattered, something we believed in. Perhaps for the first time in our lives we had no doubt we were doing the right thing, and that was worth dying for.

And then, finally, the Babalon Working manifested, and it was glorious indeed. Its presence saturated the whole bar, soaking into everything, making us all unbearably vivid and significant. Strange energies sleeted in from unfamiliar dimensions, as a door left ajar for so long finally swung wide open. I couldn't see it, but its presence filled my mind, as though someone had pushed back the curtains to give me a glimpse of what lay behind the scenes of the world. Lilith howled with rage and horror as she finally realised what was happening, and tried to attack the three men responsible, but Suzie and Alex and I held her where she was with the last of our strength. Dying as we were, we held her there.

A great wind blew out of Limbo, through the open door, redolent of other realms, other places, then reversed itself, surging back in. It tugged at Lilith, and we let her go. Step by step, fighting it all the way, she was pulled towards the door. She stopped, right on the edge, and would go no further. Someone had to force her back through that door, and go with her into Limbo, to hold the door shut from the other side until the Babalon Working had been properly dismantled and shut down. And that had to be me. Because that was the only way I could be sure that never again would I ever threaten the safety of the Nightside. I swore an oath, to a dying future Razor Eddie, that I would rather die than see the Nightside destroyed because of me; and I meant every word.

But I never got the chance. My father broke away from his friends, grabbed his ex-wife by the shoulders, and sent the two of them hurtling through the open door into Limbo. The door swung shut; and, in the very last moment, my father looked back at me, and smiled.

"For you, John! For my son!"

Lilith's final scream was cut short as the door to Limbo slammed shut. Without the three to maintain it, the Babalon Working collapsed, and Walker and the Collector quickly shut it down, forever. And that was that. All was still and quiet, in *Strangefellows*. Walker and the Collector stood together exhausted, leaning on each other for support, looking older than their years. Suzie and Alex, no longer in my mind, came unsteadily forward to stand with me. I looked at the place where the door had been, and thought of my father and my mother, together again, for all eternity.

And the things we sacrifice, for love.

EPILOGUE

With Lilith gone, her army of followers soon broke up and turned on each other. They were quickly defeated and dispersed by Walker's people, commanded by Julien Advent. Lilith's surviving offspring, seeing which way the wind was blowing, quietly slunk back to the Street of the Gods. And as quickly and easily as that, the War for the Nightside was over.

With the Authorities dead and gone, Walker is in charge of the Nightside now. Inasmuch as anyone ever is. No-one's seen the Collector since that night in the bar. He disappeared when no-one was looking, along with what was left of Merlin's heart. Alex is back behind his bar. Suzie and I are talking about becoming partners, in a detective agency. And about other things, too. One step at a time.

Many old friends and enemies are still missing, presumed dead.

The Nightside goes on. The terrible future I first saw in the Timeslip is now only another timetrack, no more likely or inevitable than any other glimpsed future. For the first time in a long time, the Nightside is free to make its own destiny.

And so am I.